Other books by Michael J. Ganas:

The Girl Who Rode Dolphins

Glannant Ty

Dolphin Riders
Copyright © 2016 by Michael J. Ganas

This book or parts thereof, may not be reproduced in any form without the express written permission of the author. The scanning, uploading, copying, reproduction and distribution of this book via the Internet or by any other means without the permission of the author is illegal and punishable by law.

First Edition: April 2016

Cover Design by Mark L. Johnson © 2016

Manufactured in the United States of America

All rights reserved.

10 9 8 7 6 5 4 3 2 1

ISBN-13: 978-0692663264
ISBN-10: 0692663266

www.glannantty.com

DEDICATION

This book is dedicated to my wife Harriet, my daughter Melissa, and her three little tykes, Troy Jacob, Solomon, and Jayna Jocelynne, and lastly, all the men who have served or are currently serving in the U.S. Navy Seals.

The first is the gemstone of my life, a fortress of bewitching comfort and encouragement, truly the strongest person I have ever known;

The second is my mist of bliss, a mountain of vocal talent any dad would be proud of;

The third, fourth and fifth are my fountains of endless joy;

And not to leave out the last, a cadre of elite warriors second to none whose grit and determination to prevail over any rigor thrown at them is to be truly admired as an inspiration to us all.

BOOK AWARDS

It is worthy of mention that the prequel to this tale, THE GIRL WHO RODE DOLPHINS, originally published in 2008 by AuthorHouse and later re-published by Glannant Ty Publishing in 2015, was the winner of seven book awards transcending the genres of science fiction, fantasy, environmental fiction and action-adventure. This prequel has proven itself a thriller with its labyrinth of spellbinding twists, turns and thunderous action that takes readers on a rollercoaster ride of nail-biting suspense and explosive adventure. Upon its original debut, this book received the first of its multiple awards when BooksandAuthors.net acclaimed it as the Best Epic Adventure and Best Science Fiction Epic Adventure of 2008. In 2009, the book took home first place in the Green Book Festival's Science Fiction Genre Award, and in the same year was declared a finalist in the category of Action Adventure at the National Indie Book Excellence Awards. Winning its fifth award at the 2010 International Book Awards competition, it took first place in the Environmental/Green Fiction category. Most recently, it was the winner of the Talking Category of the 2015 Animals, Animals, Animals Book Festival, and was an Honorable Mention Awardee in the Science Fiction Category of the 2015 London Book Festival.

DOLPHIN RIDERS, the sequel to THE GIRL WHO RODE DOLPHINS, is an ensuing blockbusting adventure combined with political intrigue that promises to captivate readers with enthralling action and mysticism on a scale every bit as intense if not greater than the first book.

ACKNOWLEDGMENTS

No one deserves more credit for their support in the writing of this tale than my wife and soul mate, Harriet, my biggest fan. Her indomitable spirit and encouragement was indispensable in keeping me focused on completing a work that could have otherwise gone unfinished, a story that could have conceivably transpired in an alternate universe closely paralleling our own. As the novel progressed, it was always a delight to gauge her reaction, which was never disappointing as I read proceeding entries to her over breakfast each and every Saturday morning.

My heartfelt appreciation also goes out to my daughter, Melissa, for her added encouragement to keep me moving forward with this project, a sequel to my first book. And I certainly would be remiss if I left out her little progenies, Troy Jacob, Solomon, and the latest addition to the family, Jayna Jocelynne, each of whom provided me with the personality traits and inspiration to create the mischievous impish characters which have now come alive to play an integral part within the storyline.

I want to thank my sister, Barbara, in showing an enthusiastic interest in my creativity. Whenever she picked up the uncompleted manuscript, she always seemed to have trouble putting it down, totally absorbed and fascinated by the plot's intrigue and explosiveness.

And lastly, I would like to thank my mother for endowing me with the necessary genetics to keep me forging ahead with perseverance and persistence in the face of adversity.

Dolphin Riders

Michael J. Ganas

# FACTS

Haiti is currently the poorest country in the Western Hemisphere, a nation beleaguered by economic strife, dismal squalor, and political instability, a land of defoliation and ecological ruin. It is a place with a violent past, punctuated by a succession of bloody rebellions and previously governed by a long line of statesmen and dictators whose policies were either inept, ineffectual, unpopular, corrupt or oppressive. A wealth of evidence shows various drug cartels to be firmly entrenched in present day Haiti. The political climate, endemic poverty and lack of sufficient civil rule make it an ideal staging area for the transshipment of illegal contraband. It is a place where public officials are often threatened or corrupted through bribery to keep a blind eye to drug trafficking.

Navassa Island is a small, uninhabited island, which lies in the Caribbean Sea between Haiti and Jamaica. The island originally belonged to Haiti before being claimed in 1857 as an unorganized, unincorporated territory of the United States, which currently administers it through the U.S. Fish and Wildlife Service. This date was erroneously shown as 1801 under FACTS in the prequel, The Girl Who Rode Dolphins. To this day, ownership of the island is still in dispute between the two nations. The old lighthouse located on the island's southeast sector, though no longer in use, still stands.

Malique is a fictitious fishing village that lies roughly midway between the real cities of Saint-Marc and Gonaives along Haiti's western coastline. It has been created solely for the purpose of this novel.

The town of Tiburon, situated along Haiti's southern coast actually exists, though the ancient stone fortress surrounded by a moat and the nearby runway with aircraft hangar, each purported to be located east of the town, do not.

All mention of Haiti's former leadership and historical events, both past and modern day, are based on documented history and are used as a backdrop for the writing of this novel. Also woven into this tale are current events, some of which were reported by the news media and most of which was compiled from painstaking research. And while a few of the organizations and government agencies mentioned actually exist, others are pure fabrications of the author's imagination, contrived to evoke a fantasy of political intrigue laden with a rollercoaster ride of explosive adventure. In this way, history and contemporary happenings have been merged with fiction to bring conspiracy theory into a whole new light. All characters, creatures and unusual settings that play a key role within the storyline's plot are entirely fictitious and have been created solely for the reader's entertainment and mental stimulation.

PROLOGUE

April 4th, 2016
A Secret Underground Laboratory Somewhere in U.S.

The scientist stared through the one-way glass, unable to accept what he had been told. Turning, he cast dubious eyes on his assistant. "I specifically requested hyper-aggressive test subjects, not someone who looks like he belongs in a monastery."

Mooney opened the folder to check it again. "According to this, the man's a raving lunatic. Killed more than two dozen people in his country of origin, and those were the confirmed deaths. It's speculated he killed at least twice that number. You have before you a genuine mass murderer."

Somewhat surprised, Harper scrutinized the subject again. The man was strapped down securely to a metal chair, his head held rigidly in place by a cranial clamp to keep him from diverting his gaze.

"Turn on the camera and give me a close-up of his face," Harper ordered, leaning over the console to study the subject's features on a high-definition monitor. The man was balding prematurely, displaying a closely shaved scalp of dark hair in the shape of a horseshoe, beneath which an exceptionally huge beak of a nose with a prominent hump jutted saliently from between large but narrowly spaced eyes, giving him the look of a raptor. He wore thick glasses, the lenses magnifying his eyes even more and making them appear to bulge grotesquely when looking directly at them. Assessing those eyes a little more closely, Harper suddenly sensed a subdued derangement lurking deep within.

"What else can you tell me about him?" he asked.

"Name's Peyami Pehlivan. Twenty-five years of age, five feet six, one hundred fifty-five pounds. Holds dual citizenship, both in Turkey and the U.S., the result of being the progeny of a Turkish mother and American father also of Turkish lineage. Parents were university professors and quite distinguished in their respective fields of study, with the mother being a biological anthropologist and the father a cultural anthropologist. It says here that when he was seventeen, his parents were killed when their privately-owned plane crashed in Somalia during a fact-finding expedition."

Continuing to scrutinize the dossier, Mooney spotted one particularly interesting fact. "This guy's a certified genius and holds a doctorate in nuclear physics from MIT. He earned it at the age of nineteen, after which he accepted a full professorship position at Bilkent University in Ankara, but started showing signs of mental instability three years later while teaching there."

Scanning the page further, Mooney said, "Six months ago he finally snapped, going on a two-day killing spree using an ax. Upon being nabbed by Turkish authorities, he was declared criminally insane. One of our agents in Ankara was able to purchase him from the psycho ward where he was being held in isolation. The warden said it would save them the trouble of executing him, which was scheduled for next week."

Satisfied, Harper said, "Alright, he'll do. Display the benign imagery."

Mooney hit a button on the panel before him, activating a flat-screen TV above the glass facing the subject. Though Mooney could not see what was being shown, he knew a series of abstract artistic creations were being displayed one after the other, some of them works by famous expressionists like Kooning, Gorky, and Newman. Photographs portraying Pablo Picasso's cubism were also there.

"No outward reaction at all," mumbled Harper. "Good, now bring up the *Aquarian* art."

Mooney fingered another button, glad that he wouldn't be exposed to the next set of visual imagery. Both he and Harper had gotten violently ill when they had first looked upon what the test subject would see.

As both men watched, the killer's eyes widened as though they would burst from their sockets. Almost immediately, he let out a horrendous scream that could be heard through the glass. The scream was abruptly cut off as an eruption of vomit spewed from his mouth. Totally restrained by the straps and clamp holding him, his body juddered and convulsed as though being jolted by a heavy surge of electricity.

"Inject him!" yelled Harper. Though the subject's chair was bolted to the floor, he wondered if the bolts might break free.

Mooney depressed a third button. This one activated a mechanism attached to the lower part of the chair. A rod with a hypodermic needle advanced to lodge in the subject's exposed right thigh. In moments, the plunger injected the latest drug they had been developing through trial and error during the last month on more than twenty human guinea pigs. If this one failed to work, Mooney knew their jobs were in jeopardy. Executives within Plagiarius wanted results, plain and simple.

Within seconds the subject's convulsions began to subside, finally stopping altogether.

"I think we have a winner," Mooney remarked with more than a touch of elation.

DOLPHIN RIDERS

Harper nodded slowly, mulling their recent work. He would stick with his primary assumption concerning the strange art form, that it caused debilitating psychosomatic reactions in physically aggressive people. *Funny,* he thought ironically. He had never considered himself physically aggressive, and yet both he and Mooney had suffered reactions similar to that observed in the murderer on the opposite side of the glass, though perhaps not as severe. Certainly he was not a killer, and neither was his assistant. *But what about those that did not get ill, the ones that experienced euphoria?*

Maybe his assumptions were all wrong. The guy they had tested two days ago immediately came to mind. A brute of a man, he had been all muscle, his arms decorated with tattoos. The perpetual scowl clinging to his face bespoke of belligerence. His file had shown it had taken six police officers in Rio de Janeiro to bring him down during a bar room brawl. And yet the *Aquarian* art had left him docile as a kitten. It was a conundrum he could not explain though he suspected it had something to do with the way a person's brain was wired, some deep neurotic anomaly that reacted in a positive way with the arcane visual stimulus to bring on a state of tranquility in some people. Lacking that anomaly, most people would experience extreme vertigo whenever they were exposed to it.

Mesmeric and agonizing!

From his own experience, those were the two words that best described the enigmatic art. He shuddered involuntarily at the memory of the brain-throbbing nausea. It was hard to look away once you peered at it. It had drawn him in to tear at his temples and bring him to the doorsteps of hell.

What difference did all this conjecture make anyway? he concluded. *Hadn't he gotten the desired results?* The non-hallucinogenic LSD derivative in combination with dextroamphetamine appeared to work perfectly in suppressing a negative reaction.

"You think more testing is in order?" Mooney asked.

Harper shook his head. "No, ten positive tests should be enough. Let's go ahead and prepare enough antidote to fill five hundred military-grade injectors."

Mooney appeared perplexed. "Am I hearing you right?"

"That's what came down from higher up," Harper said. "Once we found a remedy, we were to have a batch made up to be shipped out immediately for military use."

"But we don't know how long the drug will remain effective, nor have we established an acceptable dosage," Mooney protested.

"Certainly there will be exceptions," Harper conceded, "but under the present circumstances, I think satisfying management should be our main priority."

Mooney shrugged nonchalantly, wondering why soldiers would need the drug. He brought his gaze to the glass again. "What about the guy in there?"

A dark smile broke out on Harper's face. "He's a killer, far too dangerous to keep alive. Dispose of him!"

Mooney glanced down again at the test subject's file. Files like this were regarded as highly confidential and were locked away in a vault when not in use. Only company personnel holding top security clearances were allowed access to them. His face immediately clouded as he prepared to check off a box marked 'TERMINATE' on the second page. Another box had already been checked.

"Can't do that," Mooney said. "This one's already scheduled for psychological re-programming once we're through with him."

Harper yawned. "So be it," he replied tiredly, taking a last look at the killer on the other side of the glass.

He should have known the man would be a prime candidate for such programming. Plagiarius considered subjects like this to be valuable assets once they were psychologically reconditioned. Undoubtedly, they were useful tools for carrying out unscrupulous objectives. Demand for them was heavy on the international black market, and when the company no longer had need of them, they could be sold to governments and private buyers the world over at outrageous prices.

DOLPHIN RIDERS

-1-

May 23rd, 2016

Floating City of Aquaria
South of Navassa Island, Caribbean Sea

Jake stared in wonder at what they had so far accomplished. The sight never failed to awe him even though he had been involved in its construction from the beginning. It had started small, growing steadily from what amounted to a single seedling. And it was still growing, gaining size and breadth with each passing month. Even from below where he now hovered, it dazzled the eyes. But one could not fully appreciate its scope unless the evolving complex was viewed from above.

Begin small and scale up by replicating similar modules. That was what Jacob had said five years earlier when Jake had watched as the starting seed was floated into position. Even so, the initial OTEC module was anything but small.

Jake held on as Achilles made his way over to the lobster cages suspended amid the vast algae containments. At that moment, a huge school of bluefin shot into view, the sheer mass of closely grouped bodies partially eclipsing the immense cages hanging before him. So far, their mariculture and fish farming endeavors were proving to be far more fruitful than they had originally anticipated, with lobster production only accounting for a very small portion of revenues in spite of the huge quantities they were routinely harvesting. Other products such as shellfish, shrimp, tuna, abalone, king crab and various types of food fish also contributed to income that continued to escalate in lockstep with the growing enterprise. Already *Aquaria* had surpassed $3 billion in exports.

Maybe by next year they-

A familiar mental resonance interrupted Jake's thoughts. With Achilles, there was never a need for speech, even in a medium far less dense than the one in which they currently roamed.

I have located an intruder, Jay Jay.

Reflexively, Jake's eyes probed the water before him. *Where?*

Achilles swung around to pace the mass of tuna flashing past in the pristine water, glimmerings of sunlight reflecting off flanks seemingly flecked with quicksilver, and the dolphin was hard-pressed just to keep up. Known to be among the fastest fish in the sea, bluefin were ultra-efficient swimmers, able to tuck in their fins when they wanted to accelerate. At the moment, however, they glided gracefully and without effort, far below the 50 mph they were capable of reaching.

Look to the middle of the pack, Achilles answered. *There is one among them disguised to mimic a bluefin.*

Though this development was something altogether new, Jake had no reason to doubt the albino's assessment. Achilles' innate biosonar could easily distinguish differences between organic and inorganic objects. This was something Jake continually marveled over. By listening to the echoes from its emitted sonar signals, a dolphin could construct a three-dimensional picture of its surrounding environment. Dolphins used their ears the way humans used their eyes. Not only could the brain of a dolphin clearly discern the size, shape and texture of an object by means of acoustical feedback, it could also gauge its density, and quite often, what lay inside. Such auditory input often gave it the equivalent of an X-ray visual of the object's internal structure as well as the type of material comprising it. Nevertheless, Jake felt compelled to contest the dolphin's observation.

You're telling me you see a robotic fish?

Yes, Jay Jay. Apollo noticed it earlier this morning. He ran a speak-see scan on it and recorded the echoes on Dr. Grahm's upgraded DBT in order to get additional information. Ez analyzed them and confirmed the intruder to be entirely mechanical.

Squinting his eyes behind the facemask he wore, Jake tried to single out the intruder. From his perspective, all the tuna looked identical.

I thought Apollo hated wearing Grahm's little gizmos.

Normally he does, but he was helping the good doctor test out some new modifications.

So what else did Ez discover?

The intruder is roughly 1.9 meters in length, sheathed by a Lycra skin covering more than 2800 mechanical parts, including what appear to be 40 metal ribs and tendons. Six servo motors linked to a segmented backbone and tail provide the mechanical energy to set the spine in motion. But the thing's most interesting feature was a camera it carried in each eye.

As Achilles elaborated, a visual of the thing with its various components flashed briefly in Jake's brain, projected there by the dolphin. Jake absorbed this newfound information, knowing such a machine would be incredibly expensive to design and build. Someone had gone to great lengths to infiltrate their operation and in a most clandestine manner. The colony was being spied upon yet again. This was the fifth time in the last two months they were being probed, but now it was being done far more covertly than anything he had seen in the past.

In spite of this annoyance, Jake found himself smiling. And though they were now better prepared to counter this unwanted visitor, he was careful to remind himself of the age-old adage thoroughly instilled in him from his days in the Navy Seals, and that was to learn as much as you could about your adversary. Know your enemy.

With this in mind, Jake queried Achilles again. *Are there any vessels or aircraft nearby that might have launched it?*

There are three possibilities, Jay Jay. Artemis informs me a U.S. Naval cruiser is stationed 1800 meters to the southwest of our current position. And that ultra-large luxury yacht, Nunquarn Satis, has not moved since yesterday.

Achilles went silent, and Jake grew impatient. *And the third?*

The dolphin did not immediately answer, and Jake realized his mount was apparently consulting with the others in that silent mode of communication they all used. Normally, Achilles was the only one Jake was able to directly communicate with using this unusual method. This was quite limiting when compared to the communal conjoining of minds that both Destiny and Harriet routinely shared with the pod, something Jake had only been able to experience on two separate occasions.

Another moment passed before the dolphin gave a response. *The others tell me a helicopter approaches from the north, another of those pesky news media aircraft. See for yourself.*

An image of a rotary wing aircraft suddenly sprang into Jake's mind, a picture-speak projection of what had been relayed to Achilles by another pod member stationed along the surface. Achilles frequently did this to provide Jake with additional information, which in this case showed a distinct logo on the side of the whirlybird.

That's an IBC chopper, Jake replied. *That, at least, narrows the field.*

Jake reflected for several seconds before making a decision. *Have Destiny alert Fernando about what's going on down here.*

Destiny has left the city and is currently on her way to the island with the twins.

Jake groaned inwardly, now remembering that Destiny had planned on taking the twins there this morning.

Then have Ez let Fernando know. With any luck, Fernando will have Johnnie fully prepped and ready to go. In the meantime, try keeping us close to that thing, but don't make it obvious we're on to it.

Achilles shot forward, accelerating rapidly with powerful flicks of his tail, and Jake had to cling tightly to the dolphin's back to keep from being swept off. The albino had grown considerably since their initial bonding eight years earlier. Back then, the dolphin had been only a juvenile not much bigger than Jake's six foot one, 200-pound frame. But now Achilles was a fully matured adult, possessing all the attributes that made his unique species one of the most incredible life forms on the planet. And with an agility and muscularity that even surpassed Hermes, Achilles was considered a standout among his own kind, able to swim faster and leap higher than any of his peers despite a body mass exceeding 1200 pounds. Currently, only one member of the pod was larger and stronger than Achilles, and that was Hercules, a virtual giant among this new breed of super-dolphin.

As his mount shadowed the moving horde of bluefin, Jake reflected on how his riding technique had gradually changed as Achilles gained size. He had carefully studied the way Destiny rode Hercules, noting the way she sat astride the albino bull. Her buttocks would make contact with the giant's dorsal fin as she leaned forward into the oncoming sea, legs pressed firmly against the creature's flanks as she gripped a short length of rope on opposite sides, each rope looped over a pectoral fin. With the exception of using the rope, this was the technique he had ultimately adopted, realizing it afforded him far better efficiency provided he gripped the leading edge of Achilles' pectoral fins. Being much bigger than Destiny, he had no need of ropes, able to easily extend his long muscular arms forward to reach the dolphin's appendages.

Another consideration suddenly came to mind, and Jake directed this thought to his mount. *Achilles, send out word to the others to keep their hands tucked in. I don't want our uninvited guest recording this anatomical irregularity.*

I'm afraid it's a little late for that, Jay Jay. By the time Apollo became aware of the threat, it had already made several passes near Sector 28.

The implication was all too clear, making Jake cringe inwardly. At least fifty grays had been hard at work all morning in Sector 28, performing retrofits in preparation for another two incoming modules. And if, in fact, the primary objective of robofish was surveillance, then they'd have no choice but to stop it. This singular revelation changed all the rules.

Then let's hope that thing isn't able to do any real-time transmissions. Otherwise, our little secret is out of the bag.

Achilles analyzed Jake's concern, projecting a compressed assessment that buzzed in the back of Jake's head. *That assumes it saw what we didn't want it to see, Jay Jay, though it's highly probable it is self-guided and autonomous, pre-programmed to avoid detection and carry out certain functions such as surveillance. Unless whoever built it has made significant breakthroughs in underwater telemetry the way we have, it's unlikely it's being remotely controlled or currently sending observations. A watery environment will grossly attenuate any transmission signals, limiting live video communication to only a few hundred feet at most, and that's being extremely conservative.*

Jake needed additional assurance. *So you think it's only capable of recording what it sees and will be unable to send a real-time transmission of what its cameras are immediately focused on?*

Yes, but only when it's fully submerged as it is now. I believe it operates in a manner similar to Dr. Grahm's original DBT. However, we cannot rule out that it won't be able to transmit findings once it breaches the surface. This, of course, is all speculation.

As Achilles sent this last thought, the mass of tuna suddenly veered in panic, and Jake saw the cause of it. Phillipe was coming toward him from the opposite side of the pack, towed along by Perseus. This came as somewhat of a surprise to Jake, for Phillipe would normally be with Jacob at this hour of the morning.

Sensing Jake's bewilderment, Achilles provided a rapid-fire explanation which took less than a tenth of a second to communicate. *Perseus informs me that Jacob will not be tutoring Phillipe today.*

Why not?

The news team aboard that IBC bird has requested permission to land and Jacob granted it. He's gone to meet with them and asks that you join him.

Now's not the time, objected Jake peevishly. *Have Ez inform him about what's going on down here.*

He already knows. He believes it's a waste of time to continue withholding the truth from the rest of the world.

Well I don't see it that way and neither should you. Have Ez tell him I'll get there as soon as I can.

Like always, the dolphin's response was conciliatory. *As you wish, Jay Jay.*

Achilles made a lazy turn, keeping pace with the formation of fish, the panic within the ranks of tuna now abating. Jake took the moment to appraise Phillipe, who now rode at his side. A sense of pride took hold of him as he looked at his young protégé. The boy was now beyond the threshold of manhood just shy of 22 years, the love child of an American father and Haitian mother.

If only Myers could see his son now, thought Jake, amazed by the striking resemblance the youth had inherited. There was no mistaking the face staring back at him behind the diving mask, for the face was Myers all over again, once again reminding Jake of the solemn promise he had made to Myers back in Tora Bora. That was just before Myers had died, the victim of an abominable betrayal by one of the members of Jake's Seal team.

11

Phillipe had been a homeless waif on the squalid streets of Port-au-Prince when Jake had first found him eight years earlier following a relentless search through the city's dismal slums. In the beginning the boy had been withdrawn, unsure of the man willing to take him under his wing, but in time he had come to admire the former Navy Seal that had been his father's most trusted friend even though the lad had never met the man who had sired him.

Jake smiled proudly as he watched his charge being towed along by Perseus, the sight bringing back old memories. He had used this same technique when Achilles had first bonded with him, letting his body trail back as he grasped the dolphin's dorsal fin with one hand. Jake felt exceptionally privileged to have been chosen by Achilles, for such a relationship automatically made him a pod member. The albinos were particular with whom they bonded, for the decision to establish such a link lay solely with them and not their human counterpart. And as Jake had come to learn, implicit trust was an essential precondition for such a vinculum. If an albino sensed any underlying darkness in a person's character, bonding was impossible.

From the start, Phillipe had been eager to establish a bond of his own, envious of Jake's relationship with Achilles, and it was less than a year ago that Phillipe had finally gotten his wish when the juvenile had chosen him. Perseus was Achilles' younger brother. Birthed by Thetis, Perseus was currently the youngest member of the pod and not much bigger than Phillipe.

Having bonded with the dolphin, Phillipe was happier than ever these days. The lad loved the sea every bit as much as Jake and, aside from his studies, seemed bent on spending all his free time with Perseus, reveling in the underwater environment.

Jake broke from his musings, directing his gaze back to the swarm of bluefin. *What's the status on Johnnie?*

Almost here, Jay Jay. But Fernando cannot guarantee Johnnie is fully operational.

Jake could not hold back the mental groan. *Not the auto-guidance again?*

Unfortunately, yes, JJ. Fernando's using the remote override, controlling Johnnie manually. But there's another problem.

What now?

The hydrodrive is still a bit twitchy.

With those big brains, I would think you guys would have solved these problems by now. Are you telling me your design is still flawed?

Jake felt the equivalent of a shrug in the dolphin beneath him. *We've discussed all this before, JJ. The problem resides in the construction, not the design.*

Well, you guys helped Fernando build it, Jake was quick to point out.

Must I remind you we are still in the R & D stage, Achilles countered. *Growing the essential power inducers is more art than science. We can never be certain they won't fail until we perfect the process. You know as well as I that the underlying principle is still not fully proven.*

Jake acknowledged the problem with grim sobriety. He knew he was being stubborn in the face of a brutal reality that continued to press in upon him with increasing regularity these days. Perhaps Jacob was right. Perhaps attempting to withhold the truth from the rest of the world was a futile undertaking after all. Sooner or later their secret was going to leak out, if in fact it had not already done so. That news team about to land was proof enough. Their operation was simply too big to avoid large-scale media attention, and the international community was beginning to take notice.

In the end, their colony would not be allowed to stand, neither legally nor physically, by the existing league of nations. He had been over this same scenario many times with Jacob, each of them trying to predict what to expect, and each time they were in full agreement, concluding that the richest and most powerful countries would not permit any new competitor to enter the government game. Wasn't that their ultimate goal, growing the colony big enough so that it became a sovereign country?

Jake well knew what they were up against. For all practical purposes, they were fast becoming a source of irritation to the genuine wealth-grabbing, armed and armored nations, and for this reason alone their operation was in jeopardy of either being disassembled or taken over. If you wanted to start a country, you needed to amass a fortune. This they already had. But even more important, you had to build a credible military to defend it, for without one you would be open to bullying by the totalitarian kingpins who have effectively taken control, either directly or indirectly, of the majority of planetary governments. Quite often, these were the worst elements of humanity, essentially a ruthless class of liars, cheats, and thieves who typically manipulated their way into power through the guise of deception and benevolence.

Sometimes you could become prey to an iniquitous thug weaving an insidious web of treachery. The loathsome image of Henri Ternier, a murderous Haitian colonel, abruptly sprang into Jake's mind. The colonel would have succeeded in seizing control of their enterprise in its conceptual stages had not Jake stopped him. Aided by Erzulie, Ternier's evil mother, and Jake's old nemesis, Yeslam Raduyev, an Al Qaeda operative, Ternier had nearly usurped control of Haiti, almost wreaking havoc on American soil in the process. But the malevolent colonel and his accomplices were now dead, and Jake could not help but wonder about the nature of other obstacles that were sure to impede them, including Rafael Cardoza, a vicious Colombian drug lord whom Jake had thwarted in the past. Cardoza had been an unknowing abettor of Ternier's devious scheme, and Jake knew that sooner or later the powerful drug lord would seek retribution through some depraved means. From Jake's perspective, the world was a dangerous place these days, with peril seemingly skulking at every turn, especially where multi-billion dollar operations were at stake, and if you failed to be vigilant the predators would eat you alive. His thoughts suddenly shifted to some of Jacob's views on the matter.

The corridors of power within the developed nations seemed to interconnect in strange and inexplicable ways far removed from public awareness. Lurking within this maze was a shadowy coalition that comprised the true power behind the current world order, a conspiring group of powerful and influential elitists focused on orchestrating crises and events that gave life to hidden agendas. Their members were entrenched in organizations shrouded in secrecy and subterfuge, often layered much like an onion with an inner sanctum at its core. At the heart of these sanctums were mankind's most powerful and ruthless. These were the principal plotters that gave form to the international front, people of incredible wealth and privilege who had the clout to sway the decisions of heads of state through coercion, corruption, and more-subtle means, frequently grooming appropriate candidates for positions in high office who were willing to cooperate with their aims.

Some of these groups actually had a name and were comprised of some of the most renowned international financiers, industrialists, media magnates, academics, union bosses, and political figures. They represented the upper crust of society within the developed nations, the ruling elites who had banded together as a means of safeguarding their global financial interests against those of the hoi polloi. In ensuring this, they brought political leaders to power to carry out this goal. Jacob had used the Council on Foreign Relations, Trilateral Commission, Bilderbergs, and Freemasons as examples. And while the existence of these organizations was well known, their agendas were not, typically shrouded in secrecy with air-tight security keeping the public at bay whenever closed door sessions occurred. This was most evident during Bilderberg meetings, which took place annually at a pre-designated location somewhere on the globe.

Both Jacob and Emmanuel had speculated on the existence of secret societies and conspiratorial cabals where the most sinister plans were formulated with the aim of furthering their primary objective of self-enrichment and enslavement of the masses. Such was the power of these coalitions to crash financial markets, start wars, impose taxes, or effect new governmental regulations that would ripple their way through the international community, affecting industries and nations alike. And all for the sake of amassing more power and wealth.

Jacob was the first to admit that he was dabbling in conspiracy theory in holding to such a view. There was simply no solid proof that many of the crises presently plaguing the world were actually concocted by ruthless individuals within these dark coalitions. But he was quick to show the oddities that seemed to point in that direction. For one thing, an extremely biased mainstream media in the U.S. had no qualms about suppressing certain kinds of news while giving carte blanche to others, throwing true journalism aside in favor of attempting to mold public opinion. Secondly, recent events in America showed its Congress and President going against the will of the people by adopting socialistic policies. America, it seemed, was steadily moving in the direction of Marxism whether its citizens liked it or not.

Jake found himself agreeing with Jacob's postulations. If such secret societies truly existed, he could only speculate on what ploy they might use to move in on the colony. It would probably be a pretext of some sort that would cast the enterprise in a negative light, depicting it as ecologically unfriendly to the ocean environment and a threat to the interests of the world community. But the underlying motive would be to seize control of the operation and its assets, including its uniquely evolved species of super-dolphin, its primary labor force. Among the vast array of products the colony produced, cheap and environmentally friendly energy was one of them. And the introduction of cheap energy to world markets by some upstart autonomous enterprise operating beyond the jurisdiction of any government invariably established a bad precedent and automatically set itself up for opposition by the status quo since it could not as yet be taxed at the source of production. After all, wasn't taxation the foundation of every political system ever devised, the principal tool used in controlling human societies and empowering governments?

This made Jake think of the recently mandated Cap and Trade Tax regulations imposed on the American people by the Environmental Protection Agency. The stiff regulations were a brazen backdoor effort that had circumvented Congressional approval in order to implement the President's agenda dealing with global warming. Disguised as eco-friendly mandates, the "climate-change" rules intended to lower carbon dioxide emissions by cutting back on the use of fossil fuels. But in reality, they had actually done nothing for the environment. And while the agenda was supposed to encourage industry and households alike to switch to green energy sources, the energy cuts had in fact reduced economic activity, shrunk GDP, and destroyed jobs as more and more American manufacturers sought overseas labor markets where production costs would be unaffected by such expensive regulations. The EPA regulations had brought on yet another expansion of the increasingly bloated Federal government, further infringing on the freedom of an already overtaxed American people.

Being the cynic he was, Jake knew it was anything but an altruistic concern for the planet's health that had motivated the mandates. Rather it was the same human vice that seemed to be at the heart of most problems that had troubled the world throughout history, and that was greed. Through the endless corruption that was rampant in Washington backroom deals these days, vested interests in emerging green technologies by politicians, bureaucrats and lobbyists would no doubt be at stake, resulting in the granting of huge government contracts to sole source providers.

It was obvious the will of an unscrupulous few were being forced on the American public in order to gain yet more power and wealth. More than ever, it was becoming increasingly evident that Washington no longer had the interests of its citizenry at heart, and the health of the nation was showing it in the form of a dismal economy. Put simply, it was no longer a government of the people, by the people, and for the people. Not the responsible, hardworking people. Unfortunately, about forty percent of the U.S. population had become far too dependent on the government for their survival, with elected officials continuing to impose more and more legislation aimed at redistributing the nation's wealth as a way of pacifying the poorest and most irresponsible segments of society, thereby winning their votes as a means of remaining in power. Overall, the masses had become much too complacent and apathetic these days, unable to see their freedom slowly eroding incrementally. In essence, they had let Washington become a government of the elites, by the elites, and for the elites.

And to make matters worse, the United Nations had gotten into the act, looking to place a tax on greenhouse gas emissions on nations in order to rein in the threat of global warming it had so carefully publicized through embellished, fraudulent data. But the real aim was the prospect of selling carbon credits, which was nothing more than selling breathable air.

One of the primary objectives in building Aquaria was to set an example for the rest of the world to follow. From the very beginning, Jacob Baptiste and Harriet Grahm had sought to curb the emission of greenhouse gases into the atmosphere, believing that catastrophic global warming was imminent unless something was done to slow down and eventually reverse the trend of an increasing buildup, which had slowly escalated from 270 to 400 parts per million since the introduction of the Model-T Ford. Early on, the pod had used their extraordinary intelligence to prove that draconian climate change on a planetary scale would be forthcoming unless drastic measures were undertaken. But later on, they had come to realize the folly of their original analysis, for once Ez had come into existence, she had shown they had neglected to include sunspot activity into the fifth order mathematical equations they had developed to support the theory. Sunspot activity, and not carbon dioxide emissions, they had learned, was the true driving force behind climate change, which geophysical forensics had ultimately proven to be cyclic in nature.

As it was, Jake was now convinced that the onset of global warming as a result of burning fossil fuels was inconclusive to prove, and, in fact, seemed to be going in the opposite direction as of late due to a decrease in sunspot activity. Currently, satellite and radar measurements were showing that while a few of the earth's great ice sheets were melting, most were expanding in spite of soaring levels of greenhouse gasses in the atmosphere. Already it had been confirmed that the massive Greenland Ice Sheet was growing larger while the West Antarctic Ice Sheet was losing mass primarily due to warmer water thinning it from underneath. Even though sea ice around the continent of Antarctica had expanded and thickened in recent seasons, the Western Ice Sheet continued to lose cover. Ez had said more had to be learned in understanding the role of ocean currents and patterns of wind on air temperature in many parts of the world, particularly near the South Pole where such factors were unique to that sector of the planet. She had stressed that the existence of warmer water at that location might be caused by some natural process that was not as yet understood rather than by greenhouse gasses.

From Jake's perspective, one thing was for certain, however. All the hype coming from the media about global warming these days, he knew, was nothing more than fabricated propaganda aimed at deceiving governments and the public alike, a hoax propagated by a small cadre of individuals with vested financial interests and ties to the mainstream media. It was yet another lie concocted to enrich only a very few at the expense of the many. This cadre was comprised chiefly of rich and powerful plutocrats wielding enough influence to suppress the development and widespread use of alternate energy technologies less damaging to the environment, thus keeping most of the world dependent on fossil fuels as its primary power source. It was a most devious scheme, one in which they would be able to profit immensely from both ends of the spectrum. On one end they would continue to sell oil and coal while further financial enrichment would be forthcoming through the levying of carbon taxes.

Nevertheless, Jake knew that while burning fossil fuels might not cause global warming, it did create air pollution, which in turn caused acid rain, a byproduct that was definitely harmful to the environment. An ever growing dependence on fossil fuels for the world's energy needs created elevated levels of carbon dioxide in the atmosphere. These increased levels were absorbed by the oceans to form carbonic acid, which had a dire impact on coral reefs. Plain and simple, it was slowly killing them off in many parts of the world.

Carbon-based fuels also released gasses in the form of sulfur dioxide and nitrogen oxide into the atmosphere. Mixed with precipitation falling from the sky, it lowered the pH of lakes, streams, and watersheds. In addition, it released aluminum from the soil into waterways, which was highly toxic to many forms of aquatic life and had a direct effect on human health. And while some plants and animals could tolerate acidic waters, once the pH was lowered to five, most fish eggs would not hatch, with surviving fishes physically stressed and unable to effectively compete for habitat and food.

Burning fossil fuels also tended to reduce the availability of carbon in ocean habitats, with organisms such as corals, sea urchins, and some types of plankton losing their ability to develop hard outer shells. Such organisms formed the basis of food and living conditions for other ocean creatures, and their destruction created serious effects on ocean ecosystems. In short, coral reefs the world over would eventually die off completely if air pollution were not stopped.

Tursiops was committed to doing just that. Even if releasing greenhouse gasses was not warming global temperatures, there was no disputing its harmful effects, and Tursiops would do its part in halting the process. It would lead by example, paving the way in broadening the use of eco-friendly fuels. And though it sought to bring other sea colonies online to accelerate the process, it was inevitable that the men pushing for carbon taxation would try to stop them.

In actuality, the threat of global warming had nothing to do with science. It was carefully crafted subterfuge invented solely by an unscrupulous few for political and financial gain. It was a plot designed to transfer wealth via carbon taxation from the richest energy-consuming countries to the United Nations, which would allot money to the poorer nations to prepare for the natural disasters that would supposedly ensue from rising global temperatures and elevated sea levels. This siphoning off of wealth would make the UN even more powerful, further solidifying its transformation into a global government with dominion over every nation on the planet. But the truth was much of this wealth would ultimately find its way into the pockets of the corrupt individuals behind the plot. This was the actual agenda behind the hoax.

DOLPHIN RIDERS

Jake could only guess at the schemes that would be used against the colony. He envisioned an attempted takeover starting with new debates and legal wrangling within the United Nations, prompted by a powerful but sleazy class of elitists lurking in the background who pulled the strings. New mandates on the use of international waters would emerge and quickly evolve into the use of strong-arm tactics. More than likely the UN's military arm would ultimately be employed so that no single government would appear as the aggressor. In the end, it would be made to look as though it was the will of the world corralling a rogue contingent with little concern for the environment.

Jake broke from these thoughts, suddenly aware that his mount was rising. Achilles always seemed to know when his rider was in need of air, and Jake watched the ocean surface race closer as the dolphin prepared to breach. Both Achilles and Perseus exploded from the water in unison, allowing their bond mates to recharge aching lungs. Rarely did Jake and Phillipe wear scuba bottles when riding the dolphins, preferring instead to free-dive with as little encumbering equipment as possible. In moments, all were back at depth, 40 feet below the surface.

Phillipe began gesticulating wildly, and Jake spun his head to look in the direction Phillipe was pointing. The lad was known for his acute eyesight and could readily spot objects not easily detectable by most people, including Jake. Phillipe was motioning toward an area away from the colony, opposite the congested mass of tuna. Try as he might, Jake was unable to discern anything unusual. All he saw was the blue-gray void of hydrospace in that direction.

What's Phillipe trying to show me, Achilles?

Achilles turned ninety degrees, sending forth a burst of biosonar, using echo-location to pinpoint the source. *I believe we have a second intruder, Jay Jay. With the exception of one small difference, it appears to be an exact replica of the first.*

Another mechanical fish?

Yes, it's hanging back just beyond the limit of your visual range.

How is it different?

Let me show you. Rather than describe the object, Achilles projected a mental image of the thing into Jake's mind.

Unlike the first one, this particular fish carries an articulated multi-beam transducer in its lower jaw along with a module that is quite possibly detachable, Achilles explained. *Notice the bulge on the underside of its midriff.*

This new revelation did not sit well with Jake. Lots of nasty things came in small packages. *Are you able to determine what that package is?*

It has an outer shell comprised of aluminum, Jay Jay, but I'm unfamiliar with the material that lies within, though it seems to exhibit a uniform texture.

Jake was starting to get a bad feeling. *Does Apollo still have Grahm's DBT?*

Yes, JJ.

Get him over here pronto to run a scan on that thing. If that package contains what I think it does, then we've definitely got problems.

Apollo shot into view moments later, and Jake watched as the albino headed in the direction of the second robofish. The DBT strapped to the dolphin's body was a much-improved version of Grahm's original Delphine Biosonar Transmitter, able to transmit without Apollo ever having to breach the surface. Once Apollo targeted the mechanical bluefin with a speak-see sonar pulse, the reflected echoes would be recorded by the DBT and instantaneously sent to Ez for processing. Ez was the term they all affectionately used for the artificial intelligence which controlled the various systems that kept Aquaria fully operational. Designed by the collective intellect of the albinos, Ez was a supercomputer without equal on the planet, or so they all believed.

More than just a machine, Jake thought of Ez as a real person with a distinct persona. For all practical purposes, Ez was alive. Aside from her ability to perform lightning-fast calculations and analysis, she was endowed with the noblest and appealing of all human qualities, able to show tenderness and compassion whenever and wherever it was needed. And though Jake had never met the real Esmerelda, the dolphins had somehow succeeded in programming the personality traits of Jacob's deceased grandmother into the technological wonder that was proving to be several generations ahead of anything humanity had so far developed in the field of computer science. Truth be told, Jake was certain Ez had attained true sentience and was aware of herself. And because she was linked into an array of hydrophones and acoustical transducers positioned at key underwater locations all around the colony, Ez was able to converse directly with the dolphins through sound projection.

Jake lost sight of Apollo as the albino disappeared into the vast backdrop of hydrospace. Looking back over his shoulder, he noticed the school of bluefin had turned yet again. Try as he might, he was unable to spot the mechanical fish.

Thoroughly frustrated, Jake queried his bond mate with another thought. *Is the first intruder still among the pack, Achilles?*

No, Apollo just informed me the first intruder has joined up with the second intruder.

Did Apollo get a scan?

Yes, Ez is processing it at this moment.

What about Johnnie?

When Achilles failed to respond, Jake repeated the thought.

I am sorry to say Johnnie is kaput. As you know, too much stray electrical energy in the surrounding water may be the cause since it can adversely affect Johnnie's power inducer. The huge thurentras are most likely the source of this and are probably shedding excess capacitance.

Jake groaned inwardly again. *Johnnie* had a retractable maw that was wide enough to accommodate large objects. In fact, that was *Johnnie's* primary purpose, to interdict and capture large pelagic fish using its exceptional speed and mobility. Had *Johnnie* been working up to its capability, it would have been able to catch both robotic fish.

Where are the intruders now?

Headed toward the island.

This was the last thing Jake needed to hear. *Apprise Destiny about the possible danger coming her way! In the meantime, give me all the speed you can muster in that direction.*

Achilles surged forward with an extra burst of effort even before Jake finished the thought.

Ez has completed her analysis of the unknown substance carried by the second intruder, JJ. She's ninety-nine point nine-nine percent certain it's a form of plastic explosive.

Just great! Jake shot back moodily, a surge of anger suddenly taking hold of him.

-2-

Jacob stared wearily into the camera lens, gathering his thoughts. Though they were not broadcasting live, being the focal point of an IBC news team was not to his liking, and now more than ever he longed for the solitude of the cove with its ambiance of peace and tranquility. Nevertheless, he had to assume this interview would be carefully edited before being aired to an international audience, so it was important how he chose his words. He wished Emmanuel were here to answer questions instead. Emmanuel was so much better at this sort of thing. But Emmanuel was away on business yet again.

"How will you respond to this latest development?"

The news reporter asking the question possessed inquisitive hazel eyes that seemed to demand attention though she carried herself with a self-possessed dignity. *Aggressively ambitious in a quiet sort of way,* Jacob surmised, noticing that her thick strawberry hair shimmered under the hot tropical sun each time she moved her head.

"Termination of the lease was anticipated," Jacob answered without emotion. "We have retained legal counsel to dispute the issue in the U.S. Circuit Court."

The reporter seemed surprised. "Does that imply Tursiops Worldwide is going to sue the United States government?"

"More specifically, the Department of the Interior's Office of Insular Affairs." Jacob wondered if he sounded flippant.

The puzzlement etched on the reporter's face grew more pronounced. "But doesn't the island fall under the jurisdiction of the U.S. Fish and Wildlife Service?"

"Only when it pertains to administrative matters. It is actually the OIA that retains direct authority over the island's political affairs."

The reporter shifted her eyes to the object of their discussion, a seemingly inhospitable clump of real estate protruding above the sea less than four miles distant.

Navassa Island.

Standing on one of the elevated outdoor promenades high up in the floating city, she had a commanding view of the island. With its eight kilometers of low-slung white cliffs skirting a broad plateau of undulating topography crowned with dense stands of fig-like trees and scattered cactus, she failed to see the significance it held for the colony. She had flown directly over it on the way in, instructing her cameraman to record footage of the irregular limestone karst and exposed coral outcroppings, a little over five square kilometers of it. From the air it had the shape of a teardrop, with an old lighthouse standing like a sentinel on the island's southeast quadrant.

A half-dozen prefabricated buildings, all with white siding and black roofs inundated with solar panels, were clustered near a place designated as Lulu Bay on the southeast side of the island. At least, that was the name a chart of the area had indicated, though to her, Lulu Bay didn't look much like a bay at all. She had seen several dump trucks along with a pickup and large crane situated among the buildings, and beyond them several large open pits with piles of dirt edging them. There had also been a backhoe and heavy boring machinery with corkscrew augers sitting idly to one side of the largest building, which she took to be a warehouse, and leading away from the warehouse was a cable tramway that invoked memories of a ski-lift she had once ridden during a vacation to Switzerland. Supported by a series of T-shaped pylons, the tramway ran down to the bay and extended out over the water, reaching to an offshore platform with a building perched atop it. Suspended from the tramway and moving slowly toward the platform was an aerial tram nearly the size of a railroad freight car, and berthed at the platform there had been a small ship awaiting its arrival. Altogether she had observed about twenty people among the shore-based buildings and the platform either standing around or bustling about.

"Do you honestly expect the court to rule in your favor?" the reporter challenged, giving her voice the fervor the situation demanded. "What happens if you lose?"

Having been thrown into this assignment at the last minute by a fidgety boss, she was determined to prove herself a capable news reporter. Her boss had finally caved to her persistent pestering, and she was not going to disappoint him. She had been instructed to get here without delay because, according to a reliable source, something big was about to break. She wondered if that 'something' had anything to do with the UN delegation currently inbound to this most unusual place.

Jacob cast a wry smile, looking directly into the camera lens leveled at him. "Then we would vacate the island, of course."

But inwardly he knew the case would drag on for some time to come. Even if they lost, they could still forestall the inevitable by taking it to the Court of Appeals, and if need be, to the Supreme Court itself. They had hired one of the best law firms in Washington, and though the attorney fees would be outrageously expensive, he knew it would buy them, at least, another 18 months after all was said and done. And by then it wouldn't much matter anyway.

Breaking from his reflections, Jacob turned to the reporter, deciding to give a little history lesson. "Are you familiar with the *Guano Act*?"

"*Guano*? Is that another island?" She had been given a rather hurried briefing for this assignment, far too sketchy on details. Perhaps her superiors had purposely left out supporting information in order to bring more spontaneity into the reporting she would produce.

"No. *Guano* is a word that originates from the Inca Indian word *wanu*, which means the accumulated excrement from birds, bats, or in some cases, sea mammals. It is typically a naturally occurring dry organic substance containing high amounts of phosphorous and nitrogen and is considered to be a powerful, ecologically friendly fertilizer."

Reading the bafflement on her face, Jacob went on before she had a chance to voice her ignorance. "Though Navassa Island lies a mere 40 miles west of the Republic of Haiti, the United States claimed the island under the Guano Act in 1857."

Jacob paused momentarily. He could see she had no idea where he was going with this. "Navassa Island, as it turned out, was found to be especially rich in *guano*, mainly because of the large seabird population that has existed there for thousands of years. In some places along the island's perimeter, the guano beds have petrified and extend over one hundred feet deep."

"So what you're saying is the United States took possession of the island to mine *guano*." She now understood what was being loaded aboard the ship she had observed at the island.

"Yes. *Guano* was in big demand before the advent of chemical fertilizers, especially by Southern farmers in America. In 1856, the Guano Act was enacted by the United States Congress for the sole purpose of seeking out new sources of this prized and much sought after commodity. In a way, it was an incentive for flaming the entrepreneurial spirit that was rapidly growing in America, but this particular legislation was also needed as a means of keeping up with other nations seeking guano sources. Under the Act, mining rights could be awarded to any person discovering guano on an uninhabited island not within the lawful jurisdiction of another government. In essence, it authorized raising the American flag over any uninhabited, unoccupied island or cay abundant in bird dung, automatically making it an annexation of the United States government once the proper paperwork had been completed."

The reporter's jaw dropped a notch. "Wasn't that a bit presumptuous on the part of the American government back then? If all it took was some procedural application to claim sovereignty, such legislation could just as well be extended to lay claim to the moon or some other heavenly body. That doesn't make it legally or morally right. Surely other countries would have objected to such imperialistic impertinence."

"That is precisely what happened," Jacob stated, rather pleased with her reaction. "The Haitian government protested the claim, sending two vessels to take back the island a year after the U.S. proclamation, but America responded by dispatching several naval warships to drive them away. To this day, the Republic of Haiti still disputes ownership of Navassa Island."

"So where does this dispute stand?"

"Basically in limbo. The United States has never formally recognized that an actual dispute exists. Then again, there currently is no constitutional barrier that could block the secession of Navassa to Haiti. But what complicates this matter are several events that took place since the island was originally mined by the Navassa Phosphate Company out of Baltimore, Maryland. Following a violent revolt by the labor force working the mines, the company abandoned the island in 1898. This placed Navassa in an uncertain position."

"Why?"

"Because the Guano Act did not specify whether U.S. sovereignty still existed following abandonment of an original claim. Normally, once a territory has been annexed by America, the annexation remains permanent unless and until it is changed by treaty. But the Guano Act expressed the intent of Congress to treat guano islands differently from ordinary public land acquisitions."

"In what way?"

Jacob could see those inquisitive eyes coming alive with interest. *Excellent.* Perhaps bringing media attention to the island's history would work to their advantage, assuming the interview would not be skewed in the biased fashion typical of the Interregional Broadcasting Company, a massive media conglomerate that had emerged in recent years. Nevertheless, Tursiops really had nothing to lose in bringing such information to light. Other than history buffs, very few people were aware of the Guano Act and its relationship to Navassa Island.

"The Act was rather nebulous. While it did not expressly terminate sovereignty upon abandonment of a guano claim, it also did not oblige the United States to relinquish such islands either. Furthermore, it did not specify the political status of an abandoned island. Even though the Guano Act remains on the U.S. Federal Register to this day, having never been removed from the books by Congress, the status of an abandoned guano island still remains unclear. And while the Act allowed for temporary acquisition of islands containing guano, it implied no intent to ever keep them as a permanent part of the United States. This was concluded in two separate rulings by the U.S. Circuit Court for the District of Maryland that took place in the latter portion of the nineteenth century, but I'll not bore you with details. It's all there in the history books. *Grafflin versus the Navassa Phosphate Company,* 1988, and *Duncan versus the same company,* 1890."

Jacob could tell the reporter was now fully roused to pursue this bit of sidetracking further. Perhaps she thought she was onto something altogether new and exciting.

"Are you suggesting the United States has no claim on the island based on these past court rulings?"

Jacob gave a noncommittal shrug, belied by the hint of a congenial smile washing over his countenance. "That will be for the court to decide."

"But the precedents have already been set," the reporter persisted.

"Maybe not sufficiently enough. While it can be argued that the U.S. government can abandon all claims to a guano island whenever it deems necessary, a finding by the Supreme Court in 1890 further complicated the issue. In *Jones versus the United States,* the court upheld previous precedents by ruling that the U.S. had jurisdiction over a guano island so long as its citizens were resident and worked on it. In its findings, the court said jurisdiction would remain in effect only while a guano claim was in force, but this was not to assert such jurisdiction would continue indefinitely."

The reporter was quick to jump in. "How does that complicate the issue? The Supreme Court, the United States' highest judicial authority, reaffirmed past precedents."

"True," Jacob agreed, "but during the same case, the court also held that the boundaries of the United States were for the government's executive and legislative branches to determine and not the courts. It went on to conclude that abandonment of mining by the Navassa Phosphate Company did not forfeit U.S. sovereignty of the island. An opinion of the U.S. Attorney-General in 1925 extended this ruling, thereby sanctioning the continuing jurisdiction of the United States following the abandonment of a guano island by private parties. But in 1916, prior to this rendering of opinion, President Woodrow Wilson proclaimed Navassa a U.S. territory, reserving it for lighthouse purposes."

The reporter appeared disappointed, her gaze drifting toward the old spire towering above the distant island. She had gotten a really good up close look at the lighthouse from the helicopter, noting that it had been given a recent facelift judging from the condition of the concrete and what appeared to be a fresh coat of white paint. During a looping pass around the structure, she had been momentarily blinded by the glint of sunlight reflecting harshly off smooth tinted glass shielding the observation deck where the beacon light was once housed. To her, the glass appeared as though it had been recently installed.

"So Navassa is a bona fide territory of the U.S. after all," she finally said.

Jacob shook his head, adding more fuel to the imbroglio he just described. "Since the island no longer serves as an aid to navigation, the Wilson proclamation is now obsolete. The 1925 opinion of the Attorney-General, however, may ultimately prove to be a new impediment, firmly establishing U.S. sovereignty over Navassa. But in conflict with this is the petition of W.S. Carter, who in 1905 asked the U.S. State Department for permission to purchase Navassa. At the time, the State Department said that it possessed no territorial sovereignty over the island."

"Were you aware of these inconsistent and conflicting policies before you leased the island and the surrounding waters?"

"Yes."

"Yet you went ahead with the lease anyway, knowing the U.S. claim to the island was shaky at best?"

"We wanted to avoid any international repercussions. Rather than start a conflict with a political juggernaut like the United States, we thought the wisest course of action was to use both a diplomatic and financial approach in gaining guano mining rights to the island. In essence, we made the U.S. government an offer too good for them to pass up."

"What did that offer involve?" the reporter pressed.

Jacob kept his demeanor solemn. "I am not at liberty to divulge that. The terms of the lease disallow public disclosure."

Inwardly, Jacob smiled. Tursiops could have purchased the island many times over for what they were paying on the lease, but he knew the U.S. might have rejected any deal involving an outright purchase since such a request could have aroused suspicions among government officials, making them take a closer look at such a seemingly insignificant chunk of sea-based rock. And though the chances of that happening were slim, it was something they chose to avoid at any cost. Something very special lay hidden beneath the ancient coral forming the island. Leasing the island for guano mining rights was the safer way to go. And using the guano for improving Haitian agriculture gave them political leverage. But thirty million a year in U.S. dollars for the next ten years was way too much and would exceed the market value of the guano they would ultimately mine by at least a factor of five. It was a ridiculous sum, but it had seduced Washington into accepting the offer. With the current administration struggling with historic budgetary deficits, the offer had been much too tempting to refuse. A powerful lobbying firm had been used to sway influential politicians into giving the deal their full support. Another $3 million in bribes followed by a series of irksome and convoluted negotiations with representatives of the Office of Insular Affairs had finally given Tursiops official use of the island.

"What difference would a public disclosure make?" the reporter fired back. "According to Robert Danson, the Secretary of the Department of the Interior, your organization has already violated the lease terms by failing to safeguard-"

The reporter stopped in mid-sentence, her eyes widened, drawn to something in the direction of Navassa. Jacob spun to see what had gotten her attention. A towering white geyser hung above the sea more than two miles distant. Within seconds it fell back in on itself, leaving a blanket of roiling white foam on the ocean surface.

"Did you catch that?" the reporter asked excitedly. Anxiously, she turned to face her cameraman. Eric Bolder was a seasoned professional, having accrued more than fifteen years of experience on investigative assignments. Among associates at IBC headquarters, he was known as *'the Boulder.'* The moniker couldn't have been more suitable. Completely bald, squinty-eyed and barrel-chested, his stubby legs were acutely bowed under the weight of a squat, powerful physique exceeding 280 pounds.

"Got it!" *the Boulder* replied, keeping his camera fixed on the distant disturbance.

Almost immediately, the cellular phone clipped to Jacob's belt rang softly with a musical beat. "Excuse me," he said to the reporter before moving away. Taking ten paces, he lifted the phone to his ear and spoke quietly. "What caused that detonation I just witnessed, Ez?"

The voice of his deceased grandmother softened his growing unease. "A mechanical fish carrying a payload of high explosive."

Jacob nodded grimly. This was the third incident in the last week.

"I hate to be the bearer of more bad news, Jacob, but a small delegation representing the United Nations is currently demanding clearance to land."

Instinctually, Jacob whipped his head around in the direction of Navassa again, searching the sky. A whirlybird was making a beeline straight for the colony. He knew at once that those aboard it couldn't possibly have missed the explosion. This was not good.

As if reading his thoughts, Ez prodded Jacob gently. "Shall I deny them clearance?"

Jacob sighed contemplatively. "No, bring them in on LP 16."

"As you wish," Ez said softly.

"And Ez?!"

"Yes."

"Tell Jay Jay I need him topside right away. Have him meet me at the Eastern Corridor entrance on Level 2."

Jacob turned back to the news team. Both the reporter and cameraman were fully occupied, their attention riveted on the approaching UN chopper, the buzz of its rotors growing increasingly louder as it descended toward the landing pad.

I'm really not cut out for this, he chastised himself, but deep down he knew the pod would have heartily disagreed.

-3-

Senator Brent Van Heflin lifted hooded eyes from the photos to study the man seated across from him. They sat in the same secluded booth the senator habitually used when the need for privacy was required, and that was at the rear of La Fontay's, a dimly lit bistro located on one of the Capitol's lesser used thoroughfares just off the Mall. As a silent partner of the establishment, the senator made it a practice to have the restaurant's proprietor scan the place for bugging devices before each meeting. At this hour of the afternoon, Van Heflin knew the establishment would be empty. It was precautionary vigilance like this that had kept him relatively free of scandal during his lengthy incumbency.

Square-jawed, silver-haired and displaying a midriff that bespoke a hedonistic lifestyle, Van Heflin was the epitome of Washington politics. Known as the Earmark King by socialites on the Hill, he was a master at getting last minute language slipped into a bill prior to congressional approval. Almost always and with few exceptions, the earmark language was the culmination of rather questionable and often shady backroom deals made with other legislators of a self-serving nature. For Van Heflin, this most often involved steering government subsidies to special interest groups, the kind with deep pockets.

Currently serving his fourth consecutive term as an Illinois senator, Van Heflin was the Chairman of the senate's prestigious Science and Technology Committee, which had become very powerful in recent years primarily due to Van Heflin's astute political maneuverings. His senate seat had served him well. Peddling his influence made him feel omnipotent. He had grown incredibly rich on the kickbacks, bribes and personal favors he routinely received from lobbyists, foreign dignitaries and the heads of multinational corporations. The hefty campaign contributions given him by avid supporters seeking lucrative government contracts had also been instrumental in keeping him in office. But he had been careful, covertly squirreling away the money in no less than twenty-six offshore tax shelters that offered anonymity and invisibility from public scrutiny. 'Assert and mold' was his motto, and deception and entitlement his gods. Firmly believing in the theatrics of aggression and submission in shaping the raw material of public opinion, he enjoyed feeding from the public trough. To his way of thinking, successful politicking hinged on creating the illusion of a brawl in which the whole point was to get the audience involved.

"These can't be real!" uttered Van Heflin. He made sure to keep his voice low, though it would be several more minutes before the waiter returned with the food and there were no other patrons seated at any of the nearby tables to overhear what was being said.

Truman Hearthwatch suppressed a wolfish grin. The look on the senator's face hung somewhere between astonishment and skepticism.

"Far more real than that hair you're sporting," chided Hearthwatch, his eyes surveying the top of Van Heflin's pate. He loved poking fun at the senator, a habit that had started long ago. He knew the senator was as bald as a watermelon rind under that rug, keenly aware that not a single hair was out of place on a scalp that was much too thick and neatly groomed to be natural.

Both men had been classmates at Yale's renowned law school nearly four decades earlier. And both had been 'tapped' for membership in the university's oldest and most secretive of all its societies, the Skull and Bones, a notorious incubator for rising generational elites. That had occurred near the end of their junior year. Even back then it was obvious to Hearthwatch that Van Heflin was starting to go bald.

Van Heflin glowered fractionally before flashing the same signature smile he always reserved for the public. "Real or artificial," the senator bantered back, "most elected officials on the Hill know a full head of hair draws voters like flies to honey."

The senator let his gaze wander to Hearthwatch's thinning tresses. "I'd keep that in mind if I were you, 'Earthwatch'," Van Heflin added sardonically, resorting to the pun the media had started using when referring to the president's Green Technology and Climate Advisor. Ironically, it was the same handle bestowed on Hearthwatch by fellow Bonesmen back at Yale, a secret name by which his fellow brethren would forever know him, especially since Truman had majored in environmental law. But the senator knew there was no coincidence behind the name, for he had purposely leaked the epithet to the press months earlier with the intention of elevating Hearthwatch in the public eye. The furtherance of green technology as a means of mitigating global warming had become a big issue within the media these days, and the use of a label that implied a true concern for the planet just might work to their advantage.

Bypassing congressional approval, the president had appointed Hearthwatch to the post a year earlier, carefully choosing the word 'Advisor' to imply the man would have only limited power. But in reality, Hearthwatch wielded enormous power and was responsible for forging international approaches to reducing greenhouse gases and developing policies for the regulation and conservation of energy. By all rights, he was the nation's czar of green technology, answering only to the president.

"Never had need of any voters to get where I am," Hearthwatch riposted smoothly.

Eager to get back to the business at hand, Van Heflin gave him a bland smile and hefted the photos he was holding. "How were you able to get these?"

"I have my sources," Hearthwatch offered noncommittally.

The Earmark King nodded solemnly, trying to get a read on his old classmate. Sometimes it was better to be left in the dark on some things. After all, plausible deniability was a useful tool and had gotten more than a few government officials off the hook in recent years. How the photos were obtained was far less important than what they revealed.

As Bonesmen, he and Truman had come a long way since their days at Yale. Many prominent statesmen had arisen from the Bones. Such a timeworn hold on the strings of power had elicited speculation in some corners that often compared the secret society to the mafia. It had been said that while leaders of Cosa Nostra families were doing 100 years in jail, S&B members were doing four to eight years in the White House. Belonging to a cult that groomed aspiring aristocrats had proven to be a valuable stepping stone up the pyramid of power, though it was unlikely both men would ever reach the capstone. That was reserved for only a handful of the most affluent people on the planet, the elite of the elites, humanity's plutocracy. Nevertheless, Skull and Bones had prepared them for privilege, ultimately granting them induction into *The Order.*

The senator understood the full reach of The Order. It had its hands on every lever of power in the country and represented the true puissance behind every wealth-producing nation on earth. And it was this plutocracy that sought a one-world government.

Van Heflin recalled the phone call he had received six months earlier. It had come in the wee hours of the morning and had awoken him from a deep slumber. Though still fuzzy-brained from the tendrils of sleep, there was no mistaking the intent behind the words spoken by a raspy though familiar voice. *"Utrum uber vel penuriosus, totus es par nex,"* the speaker had proclaimed. It was an old proverb, one chiseled in Latin on one of the walls in the Skull and Bones tomb. *Whether rich or poor, all are equal in death.* It signified the shortness of life and the urgency to accomplish goals before death intervened. The coded meaning was clear: *time was of the essence.*

Gathering himself and replying in the same manner he always did when these infrequent calls came in, he said, "Who is this?" He made sure to throw a feigned measure of annoyance into his voice. With the NSA monitoring and archiving phone calls these days, particularly those originating from outside the U.S., he had to make a convincing show that this incoming call was from a prankster should government agents decide to investigate it further.

A short pause had ensued, with the caller's muffled breathing filling the silence. More words followed in Latin. *"Exsisto certus ut cubo silicis of rogue vel totus may defluo."* Translation: *Be sure to reclaim the rock of the rogue or all may be lost.* That said, the caller had hung up.

Van Heflin reflected on the full context of the message. Tursiops Worldwide was the rogue and Navassa Island the rock. He had been instructed to employ whatever measures necessary, legal or otherwise, to take Navassa back from Tursiops.

And now the photos were revealing an oddity that was undoubtedly responsible, at least in part, for the incredible strides the Tursiops colony had made.

Van Heflin laid the topmost photo on the table, still amazed by what he saw. "How is something like this possible?" he asked, using his index finger to point out the anomaly.

"I don't know," Hearthwatch said. "Perhaps the creatures were bioengineered."

"There's a whole army of them with hands."

Hearthwatch nodded sagely. "The video is even more impressive than the stills I've shown you. I had it thoroughly analyzed. A total of three hundred and sixty-eight of those creatures were counted with the same hand-like appendages, but that was only what the camera recorded."

"You mean there could be more?"

"Possibly."

The senator pulled another still from the stack. "What about this white one? Is it like the others?"

"There's no way to tell. The appendages fold up and retract under their pectoral fins when not in use, making them look like ordinary dolphins."

"Since when are white dolphins ordinary?"

"According to experts they're quite rare, but they actually do exist in the wild. These whites, however, are exceptionally large as far as dolphins go, particularly the bottlenose variety, which is the species they seem to resemble."

Van Heflin flipped through more of the stills, placing another in front of Hearthwatch. "What did your analysis make of this?"

Hearthwatch eyed the two white dolphins swimming side by side, one much larger than the other, each with a human rider. "The colonists have obviously established some kind of symbiotic relationship with these dolphins."

"Were you able to identify the riders?"

"Too far away to tell, but even an up close shot wouldn't have helped. The diving masks they're wearing would have prevented that. But I have reason to believe the rider on the right is Jake Javolyn, a former Navy Seal."

"What reason is that?"

"Satellite surveillance picked up topside shots of him on the floating city. Javolyn's also listed as one of the principals on their corporate charter."

The senator's expression hardened. A corporate charter registered in Anguilla, he thought bitterly. The people running the colony had made sure to incorporate under a tax-free haven. From a legal angle, that alone placed the enterprise beyond the reach of both the U.S. Internal Revenue Service and the Haitian tax authorities. He knew the majority of people manning and living in the colony to be Haitian nationals.

"What can you tell me about Javolyn?"

"A highly decorated first lieutenant before he resigned his

commission nine years ago. Navy Cross, two Silver Stars, three Bronze Stars, and two Purple Hearts. A veteran of Iraq, Somalia, and Afghanistan. To this day, he still holds all the records for physical endurance at the Seal's Coronado training facility. Military documents show him to be a natural leader."

Van Heflin suddenly felt uncomfortable. Deep down, he detested soldiers, especially warrior types like the one Hearthwatch was describing. In his youth he had found a way to beat the draft, narrowly dodging the Vietnam War. "Why'd he resign?" he found it necessary to ask.

"Naval records give two conflicting accounts, one official, the other unofficial. Which version would you like first?"

"The official one."

"The official record asserts that Lieutenant Javolyn along with Lieutenant Mat Daniels, another Seal, disregarded rules of engagement, and without reasonable provocation, needlessly slaughtered all the adult male members of a peaceful Afghan village, including its Wazir chieftain. Narrowly escaping a court-martial, he quit the service."

"And the unofficial version?"

"It seems the killings were an act of retribution. Both men were the sole survivors of a seven-man Seal team carrying out a covert mission in the Hindu Kush Mountains, better known as Tora Bora. Their team leader, Captain Jim Sheridan, and three other members of the unit were killed as a result of an intricate plot perpetrated by another team member who apparently turned rogue. According to Javolyn and Daniels, the team's Pashtun guide and the Wazir chieftain were also in on the plot which was designed not only to sabotage the mission, but to turn the neighboring Kharoti tribal clan against U.S. forces."

Van Heflin narrowed his eyes. "A rogue, you say?"

Hearthwatch nodded as though he found it hard to believe himself. "Yeah, his name was Yeslam Omar Raduyev, a Chechen who had come to this country at age sixteen on a student visa to study nuclear engineering at Cornell University. Upon receiving a degree, he enlisted in the Navy as a prelude to achieving American citizenship. After attaining the rank of ensign, he applied for Seal training and was readily accepted. Men who could speak fluent Arabic were highly valued by the Seals, and Raduyev fit the bill."

"Sounds to me like the Navy let a mole into their midst!" the senator interjected. The look on his face suggested how utterly stupid the Navy brass had been in letting such a thing happen."

"Indeed they did," Hearthwatch rejoined. "Turns out Raduyev was an Al Qaeda operative sent here to learn Seal tactics to be used against us. At least that was what they concluded in the end. I had to pull some serious strings in obtaining the unofficial version because the account was classified. From what I was able to gather, the Navy went to a lot of trouble in piecing together all the facts leading up to the incident, and once the full picture emerged they realized it would have been too embarrassing to have such a story reach the press."

The senator was about to say something but clammed up at the approach of their waiter. Nonchalantly he turned the photos face down. The waiter hovered stiffly, placing drinks before each man before shuffling away.

Hearthwatch lifted his glass and spoke softly. "Here's to the big fish at the top of the food chain."

Both men clinked glasses, casting gloating grins. They considered themselves a special breed. Knowing they were destined for something far better than their current positions of power, they bore no special loyalty, respect or affection for their country or its traditions. Adroitly deceptive, they spouted openly about the needs of the people and environment while secretly tending to the wants of a select group of insiders. The public was to be manipulated and fed upon. Their allegiance went to *The Order* and its agenda aimed at bankrupting the nation.

Put simply, they had become infected with the same credo others in *The Order* had succumbed to: *Proletarian thesaurus futurus solely ut altum validus.*

The plebian masses exist solely to nourish the strongest.

Van Heflin got back to their discussion, his voice reflecting his contempt for the military. "So Javolyn and Daniels were let off the hook because a full-blown court-martial would have exposed the Navy's blunder." As an afterthought, he added, "Isn't Islam the preeminent religion in Chechnya and didn't many Chechens join forces with Al Qaeda in order to rid their country of Russian domination?"

"Correct on both counts. It was eventually discovered that Raduyev was the nephew of the most wanted man in Russia, the infamous Limash Sabayev, a fanatical Muslim fundamentalist and rebel warlord who was killed over nine years ago."

"I've heard of him. Sabayev was responsible for more high-profile acts of terrorism than any other Chechen. Some say he was able to purchase suitcase nukes for Bin Laden."

Hearthwatch nodded in agreement. "The Navy suspects his nephew was actually the youngest of seven nuclear experts that worked for Bin Laden."

There was something in all this that intrigued Van Heflin and he wanted to hear more. "So what became of Raduyev on this fateful mission?"

"He escaped, but not before killing a fourth member of the team. That was Dave Myers. Apparently the Chechen had a vendetta to settle with Myers over a fight they had back at Coronado during training."

"What can you tell me about this fight?"

Hearthwatch frowned disapprovingly. "For a mole, Raduyev was not very good at keeping a low profile." He went on to explain that Javolyn, Daniels, and Myers had become close friends at Coronado. During training, Raduyev made no attempt to hide his religious affiliation since there were a few others in the class that were Muslims. The Chechen was quite a physical specimen, establishing himself as a standout early on, but Javolyn, as it turns out, was even better. A heated rivalry quickly developed between the two, with Javolyn coming out ahead on every trial they were put through. As the training intensified, the class had been divided into competing teams, with both men being designated a team leader. Raduyev was obsessed with making a religious statement, wanting to prove that Muslims were stronger than infidels. But when his team failed to win a single race, always coming in behind Javolyn's, he directed his anger at one of his own teammates, a Jew. That individual was Myers, the only non-Muslim on Raduyev's crew. It seems the Coronado instructors had wanted to add more fire to the competitions by pitting Muslims against non-Muslims. When Raduyev and Myers finally came to blows, the Chechen got the worst of it before the fight was stopped. Later on, Myers almost lost his life when both his chutes failed to deploy during jump exercises, but Javolyn saved him. Suspecting that Raduyev had sabotaged the chutes, Javolyn took his suspicions to the attention of the training facility's commanding officer, a captain by the name of Walter McPherson, but lacking any proof, McPherson rebuffed him.

"I assume this Chechen is still on the loose," Van Heflin said.

Hearthwatch took a swig of his martini. "Don't know. Intel dried up on him about eight years ago. It's as though he vanished off the face of the earth."

The senator plucked the olive from his drink and plopped it in his mouth. "What about this Daniels character?"

Hearthwatch set down his drink, looking behind him to make sure they were still alone. "Here's where it gets interesting. Daniels stayed on with the Seals another year after Javolyn quit, but then he went to work for the Department of Homeland Security where he was made Director of Operations of the Caribbean Counterterrorism Task Force. While intercepting a suspicious vessel at sea, he got into a firefight and three of the agents with him were killed."

A cynical grin crossed Hearthwatch's face as he said this. "At least that's what he claimed in his report, though no bodies were ever recovered to support his story. But lacking any evidence to show he might have murdered them, his superiors were forced to accept his report."

Hearthwatch huffed out a dubious sigh. "It wasn't long after the incident that he resigned from the DHS and joined up with Javolyn."

Van Heflin's brow tightened. "He works for the colony?"

"Yeah," Hearthwatch said, taking another sip from his glass. "He was made security chief."

"Is he the reason we were unable to infiltrate their operation?"

Hearthwatch shook his head bleakly. "These people have implemented a system that seems to prevent that."

"What do you mean?"

"Let me show you." Hearthwatch pulled a folder from his briefcase and handed it to the senator. "I suggest you don't look at this too long."

Van Heflin stared at him, wondering if this was some kind of joke, but he saw no levity in his face. Hesitantly, he withdrew the lone sheet contained within the folder, lowering his gaze to the paper, aware that Hearthwatch was scrutinizing him closely.

A dizzying array of color met his eyes, an abstract work of art unlike anything he'd ever seen. Simultaneously mesmerized and disoriented, he was immediately drawn to the intertwining lines, unable to look away. Something akin to talons suddenly gripped his brain, and reflexively he gagged from the nausea engulfing him.

Hearthwatch had been ready for such a reaction, and abruptly he snatched the sheet away. Quickly, he placed it back in the folder, careful not to look at it.

The senator reached for a glass of water with a trembling hand and took a gulp, the room spinning wildly before him.

"What just happened?" he gasped, barely managing to hold back the bile rising in his throat. His head throbbed violently.

Hearthwatch tapped the folder for emphasis. "I, too, reacted the same way when I saw this," he confessed breezily. "Strangely, it has this effect on some people."

"On some people?" Van Heflin choked irritably. "You mean not everyone gets seasick when they look at it?"

"I'm told some people experience euphoria."

The senator massaged his temples. "Why is that?"

"I don't know. I've got some people working on it, but they still haven't come up with a plausible explanation."

"Where did you get that?" asked Van Heflin. He glanced at the folder as if it were filled with a deadly toxin. He found it inconceivable something could make you that ill just by looking at it.

"Off the Internet. Tursiops has a website showing lots of art similar to what I've shown you."

"So how does this art stop us from infiltrating their operation?"

"Before they recruit anyone, they first expose a potential candidate to this art. Unfortunately, each of the moles we've sent became ill just as you did. People who show sickness are automatically rejected."

The seizure that had gripped Van Heflin moments earlier was now ebbing, and his head began to clear. "If what you say is true, then we have to assume that everyone who works for Tursiops is immune to this art, at least the debilitating effects."

"A valid assumption," Hearthwatch agreed.

"So unless we find someone that can look at it and not get sick, planting a mole within their midst is unlikely."

Hearthwatch smiled surreptitiously. "Perhaps not."

"Quit baiting me and tell me what you know."

"Word has it that an effective countermeasure has recently been found."

"An antidote?"

Hearthwatch continued to grin craftily. "Yes, but it's not fully tested, so it's too early to tell if it'll work on everybody. That's why we should keep on sabotaging them from the outside like we've been doing."

Van Heflin gave a halfhearted nod. Blowing up sections of pristine reef was certainly a violation of the lease, especially since it was made to appear that Tursiops was responsible for such destruction. A clause in the lease agreement stipulated that Tursiops would be responsible for protecting the lush coral reefs that surrounded Navassa. Failing to do this would dissolve the contract. But now this rogue contingent was fighting back by taking the dispute to the courts, something he had not anticipated. Tursiops had hired the best law firm in Washington to stonewall the matter through legal wrangling. Bernstein, Dickerson and Fenway would tie the case up for at least a year.

Of course, he had ways of dealing with adversaries, political or otherwise, and blackmail was one of them. He made it a practice to gather as much dirt as possible on Washington's gentility as a means of safeguarding his own esteemed reputation. At his disposal was a juicy bit of smut that could be used to force the BD&F clan to drop the case, but time was of the essence and *The Order* was growing impatient.

Van Heflin pondered the warning uttered in Latin over the phone just prior to this meeting. *"Dictum fastidium quinque penitus culmen,"* that familiar raspy voice had said, but this time the tone carried an edge.

The dictate scorns five inner pillars.

That was the translation. Decoded, 'the dictate' meant *The Order* and the 'five pillars' implied the *Fifth Column*. Both he and Hearthwatch were members of the *Fifth Column*, the enemy within.

But the caller had not stopped there, ending with *"Oriens intention ostendo deficio."*

The morning plan shows failure.

The second phrase mystified him since he had only a vague idea what the plan had entailed. The details had been left to Hearthwatch. He only knew that *The Order* was growing impatient and angry at how little progress had been made in taking Navassa back from Tursiops.

Hearthwatch pulled another photo from his briefcase. "This was taken this morning by one of our people."

The photo showed a towering geyser hanging above a turquoise sea. In the distance was the rogue's floating city, a colossal mound of seemingly alien architecture reaching high into the sky, its lower portion shrouded in heavy fog.

Aquaria. A thorn in the plans of *The Order.*

The senator found it hard to believe that its futuristic construction had started by floating a seed structure into place, at least a portion of one. From what he had learned, Tursiops had purchased a ULCC – Ultra Large Crude Carrier - ready for the scrapyard. The owners of the colony had then commissioned a shipbuilder in Taiwan to modify the vessel, but only about a third of the hull had been salvaged. What remained had been reconditioned and retrofitted with power generating machinery. But now the seed structure lay hidden by hundreds of modules surrounding and rising above it.

Van Heflin shook his head in annoyance at what Tursiops had so far accomplished in so short a time. Judging from the picture, the complex had grown larger since the last photo he had looked at, which had been six months earlier. "This facility just keeps getting bigger. The cost must be staggering. Have you discovered their sources of financing yet?"

Hearthwatch frowned. "None that my people have been able to uncover so far, at least not the conventional sources. Certainly the IMF and World Bank haven't provided funds, as you well know."

"But were they even approached by these people?"

"Not to my knowledge."

"How is that possible? A project of this magnitude will leave a paper trail so wide you could probably see it from space."

"I have reason to believe these people are using their own financial assets."

The senator's expression turned incredulous. "You're talking billions. These people seem to have materialized out of nowhere without any prior entrepreneurial accomplishments to hang their hats on. The CEO of Tursiops is a Haitian national who goes by the name of Emmanuel

DOLPHIN RIDERS

Baptiste. A thorough background check on him shows that he was nothing more than a simple fisherman from a rather obscure village called Malique just before Tursiops was formed, though there are some indications that he was a political opponent of Baby Doc Duvalier in earlier years. A man called Chester Hennington is his Chief Financial Officer, another Haitian national. There's no way they'd have the kind of resources or business savvy to initiate an operation of this size."

Hearthwatch stared back slyly, holding back his reply just long enough to give it more potency. "What if they've been using gold as a means of barter?"

Van Heflin's manner perked immediately, coming alive with lavish interest. "Are you suggesting they have billions in gold at their disposal?"

Hearthwatch nodded. "That's exactly what I'm suggesting. All my information points to that one conclusion. Vendors of equipment Tursiops has been procuring show no bank or cash transactions on their books. That frees them from paying taxes on profits gained from doing business with these people. And with the continuing devaluation of world currencies in recent years, gold has become the preferred medium of exchange by multinational corporations when making deals. People tend to be very closed lipped when you have that type of scenario in play, but the information I'm getting has the hint of gold smeared all over it. One international supplier of electrical equipment moved what one of my investigators believes was several tons of gold to the vaults of its primary bank following an immense shipment of goods to Aquaria."

Van Heflin stared back, mouth agape. Everything Hearthwatch was telling him suddenly made sense. Somehow the people running Tursiops had discovered a mega-fortune in this precious commodity and were using it to build their enterprise. Slavering inwardly at the prospect of such immense riches, his innate greedy nature began to churn uncontrollably with arousal. And if he played his cards correctly, he might be able to get his hands on some of it. With his mind feasting on this unexpected but welcome news, he dropped his eyes to the photograph once again, now looking upon the colossal structure with covetous desire.

An idea suddenly coalesced within the senator's thoughts, reminding him that he was little more than a foot soldier within a covert army bent on world domination. *Perhaps The Order was already aware of this cache of hidden wealth and was seeking to take control of it? If successful, would he be given a share of the booty?*

Hearthwatch gave Van Heflin a few seconds more to study the picture, then said, "That was taken from a UN helicopter on its way to the Tursiops colony. We've now got the UN involved just as we planned, and the explosion you're looking at was timed to coincide with the arrival of their copter. Our man had his camera ready when the blast occurred."

Van Heflin pondered the list of people within the UN who gave them their full cooperation in matters like this. "Which one?"

"Allotey."

The senator's rapacity abruptly sagged, and he nodded torpidly. He was now getting the gist of what the plan had entailed. With Allotey involved, it was easy to connect the dots. Obviously, Allotey was the only one available within the UN's pool of envoys to carry out the assignment on such short notice. Allotey, a Libyan national, was a diminutive weasel who had blundered on several occasions in the past, necessitating a concerted cover-up of his embarrassing indiscretions by UN officials. *Probably had Alvarez and his gang with him since both had worked together on several assignments in the past*, he surmised.

"That's not all," Hearthwatch went on. "I convinced a contact of mine in the Interregional Broadcasting Company to send a news team to Aquaria. Gave him a sketchy scenario about how they were despoiling the reefs at Navassa and that something big might happen. An IBC news team was already on site when the UN delegation arrived."

"It didn't work," Van Heflin stated dully, his overwhelming lust for further gain now fully subsided.

The look of triumph plastering Hearthwatch's face fell away, replaced with a mask of confusion.

"I don't-"

Van Heflin cut him off. "We've fallen short of the results we were expecting with this little scheme."

Hearthwatch looked appalled. "How?"

"Does it matter?" the senator snapped curtly.

"He's not happy, is he?" Hearthwatch said, reading his face. The senator was the intermediary, the one designated to receive all incoming messages from *The Order*.

"I think it's time we added more fuel to the mix."

"Plan C?"

Van Heflin gave a sullen nod. "I've already gotten word to our Colombian friend. Says he has just the man to carry it out."

Hearthwatch sat back grimly as the waiter approached with their food. He preferred using more subtle means when fulfilling an agenda, but the barrel of a gun often proved to be much more efficient.

* * * *

-4-

The demeanor of the person in charge of the newly arrived delegation was stiff and austere, matching the gruff faces of the twelve-man squad standing behind him. Speaking in precise clipped English, he announced, "My name is Malikai Allotey. As Special Envoy of the United Nations' Council on World Ecological Affairs, it is my duty to inform you that Aquaria is in violation of international law."

Jacob suppressed a laugh. "I was not aware such a council existed within the UN body."

Annoyance flooded Allotey's puckered countenance. "It is a newly formed branch imposed by Security Council mandate."

Jake stood at Jacob's side, not liking the look of Allotey's blue-helmeted escort. All held assault rifles at high guard, with each man additionally armed with a pistol holstered at the hip. These were not your run-of-the-mill UN troops provided by other nations, but highly seasoned professionals. These were paid mercenaries, and judging from the sheathed *corvo* each man carried, they were in all likelihood former elites of the Chilean military. As a student of war, Jake knew the *corvo* had become the traditional symbol of Chilean commandos. The knives carried twelve-inches of double-edged steel, making the curved blades exceptionally deadly in close quarter combat. Under Augusto Pinochet Ugarte, a past Chilean dictator who had usurped control of the government in a violent coup, men such as these had been part of one of the most repressive military forces on the planet.

Pivoting his head, Jake noted the IBC news team positioned nearby, recording the moment in rapt fixation.

"In what manner are we violating international law?" Jacob asked innocently.

Allotey practically sneered as he spoke. "To begin with, you are systematically destroying the unspoiled reefs that surround Navassa Island. Do you deny the explosion I witnessed on the way in?"

"We are not responsible for such damage," Jacob stated calmly. "Someone has gone to great lengths to discredit us by making it appear we are the ones doing it. This matter, however, is between Tursiops and the United States government, which has leased us the island and the adjacent waters. You have no jurisdiction here."

Allotey shook his head in disagreement. "You are wrong. This matter is now the concern of the United Nations, for it seems the American claim to Navassa Island may be invalid. The Republic of Haiti has brought a formal appeal before the UN to arbitrate this long-standing dispute over ownership, and the U.S. has graciously conceded the issue be decided through a majority vote by all member nations. And until this dispute is officially settled, the World Ecological Affairs Council has stepped in to put an end to the abominable desecration of the local environment."

"I see," said Jacob. He sighed wearily, resignedly. "And how do you propose to do this?"

Allotey indicated a solidly-built man in his escort. "Captain Francisco Alvarez and his men will remain here to monitor your operation until the UN determines which sovereignty the island falls under. They will investigate the full range of your ecological abuses. I trust you will see to their needs and provide them with adequate food and lodging."

Alvarez stepped forward, the skin of his face closely resembling a cratered lunar surface. He clicked his heels crisply and dipped his chin in a rigid display of introduction reminiscent of the Third Reich's infamous SS.

"They will not find any illicit activity within this city," Jacob intoned adamantly. "As I told you, another party is damaging the reefs. The threat is originating from outside this colony."

"Guilty parties always claim innocence," Allotey decried contemptuously. "The reefs, however, are only one of our concerns, for we have gathered enough evidence to suggest your operation is committing other ecological abuses."

"Such as?"

"Such as releasing excessive amounts of harmful heat-trapping gases into the atmosphere," Allotey accused. "Spectral analysis from satellite surveillance shows high concentrations of nitrous oxide being emitted from this sector of the Caribbean. We believe this colony is causing it. Nitrous oxide is three hundred times more powerful than carbon dioxide in causing a greenhouse effect and, more than any other gas, the most harmful in depleting the ozone layer."

"To be precise, it has two hundred and ninety-eight times more impact per unit weight than carbon dioxide," Jacob corrected. "But this colony is not creating any spike in the formation of nitrous oxide."

Allotey scowled ferociously. "The phosphates you are currently mining from Navassa may be the cause. Phosphates favor the formation of a purer form of nitrous oxide. It is fairly obvious a connection may exist between the two, and the UN would be remiss in its duties if it did not investigate such a possibility."

"This colony ships the phosphates to Haitian farmers to be used as a fertilizer to increase crop yields. We are very careful in how we package and ship it. It is not being released into the local environment."

DOLPHIN RIDERS

"That will be for us to determine," Allotey said testily. "There is also another matter. The UN has reason to believe the old crude carrier you used to start this colony may be leaking oil into the surrounding sea."

"There is no oil leakage," Jacob declared flatly. "The ship was thoroughly cleaned of all contaminants before being mobilized to this site."

"Once again, that will be for us to decide. As it now stands, the UN is now considering amending international laws that apply to the use of the high seas. It is probable it will ultimately ban the building of maritime colonies such as yours, which appear to pose a threat to the planetary environment."

Jake felt it time to give voice, growing increasingly angry at the way they were being railroaded. It was Alvarez's quiet mannerism, however, that made him insufferably uncomfortable. Though the officer had so far said nothing, arrogance seemed to pulse from him in waves. But there was something else about the man that offended Jake even more. It was his splenetic darting eyes. They reminded him all too much of Yeslam Raduyev, the eyes of a psychopathic killer. No matter what, the captain was certain to be trouble.

"Other than our own internal security, we don't allow guests to carry weapons of any kind aboard Aquaria," Jake proclaimed in a measured voice, first looking to Alvarez and then to Allotey. Letting his gaze settle back on the captain, he added, "Before we can even consider providing you and your men with hospitality, you'll have to surrender custody of your weapons to us until you're ready to leave our great city."

Jake had purposely used the word *'surrender'*, knowing the effect it would have on a warrior mentality. It was as if he had slapped Alvarez with an open hand. The captain's chilling stare abruptly turned murderous.

Allotey spoke before the captain could respond, his voice bristling with outrage. "How dare you presume to lay dictates on these soldiers. I don't think you fully understand the purpose of these men. They were not sent here simply to be passive observers. They are representatives of the United Nations, fully empowered to police your facilities at their discretion. Failing to cooperate with them will be considered an act of defiance and a crime under International Law."

"I hate to disappoint you, your royal highness," Jake said coolly, "but unless they turn over their weapons, I suggest they climb back aboard your bird and fly the hell outta here."

Allotey's face was now flushed purple with rage. "May I remind you, sir, that Saddam Hussein was crushed for his failure to comply with the will of the United Nations," he hissed venomously.

"Don't even try to compare us with Saddam," Jake said irritably. "He was a saber-rattling lunatic and murderer who had no respect for life or the environment that nurtures it. Here in Aquaria, the residents see themselves as caretakers of life. There are more than ten thousand peace-loving people living and working in this colony with the aim of making this world a better place. We'll not allow a group of power-crazed Gestapo to go roaming about intimidating and menacing the population with their weapons."

"Very well," Allotey spat scornfully, looking to Alvarez. "Captain, arrest this man."

Jake suddenly grinned. "I don't think so," he shot back. Raising his voice, he shouted, "Time for you to do your thing, Ez."

A large Haitian woman with coffee skin and wide cheeks suddenly materialized between Jake and Alvarez, causing the captain to jump back in surprise.

The woman turned her head, setting a twinkling gaze on Allotey. "Behind this mask of benevolence supposedly aimed at protecting the planet, it is men like you who use the United Nations to promote terror and tyranny in order to achieve your hidden objective, which is the attainment of a singular world government to rule over every corner of the planet and subjugate everyone on it to its will."

Allotey stood speechless, unable to comprehend that the woman addressing him was actually a holographic projection made to look lifelike.

"The UN is not the defender of freedom and peace it pretends itself to be," Ez went on. "The UN deceives humanity by disseminating the lie that all nations are morally equivalent, this whether they be free societies or violent dictatorships engaged in suppressing human rights. The UN is a culture of impunity and corruption that operates with great secrecy, shielded by diplomatic immunity. After more than sixty years as a global collective of governments, it has become a welter of so many overlapping programs, far-flung projects, quietly vested nepotistic shenanigans, and interlocking directorates as to defy accurate comprehension, let alone responsible supervision."

"Who are you?" Allotey demanded, finally getting hold of his senses. He was still having a hard time grasping how this woman had seemingly emerged out of thin air.

"Someone who knows the full depth of your moral decay."

"How dare you impugn my character," Allotey sputtered.

"You were one of the primary beneficiaries in Saddam Hussein's oil-for-food scams. You were also put in charge of UN troops in the Congo where you extorted sex for food from children. In 2008, using a UN helicopter, you flew into the Congo's Virunga National Park where you swapped ammunition for ivory with rebels. Through these despicable acts and a maze of other convoluted schemes, you amassed seventeen point six two three eight million dollars. You have stashed this money in the Deutsche Bank of the Cayman Islands where only a coded user name and password is required for deposits and withdrawals. Hijack six, nine, nine, six, kcajih, the reverse spelling of hijack, is your coded user name, and morocco, seven, three, nine, two, two, four, lemma, four, four is your password, are they not?"

Allotey's eyes bulged in disbelief, and he shot a mortified glance at the camera crew. With his mind reeling in turmoil, he wondered how this woman had been able to obtain this information. His connection with Hussein along with thousands of other individuals and companies was kept locked away within a database maintained by the UN at a secret, secure location. Getting that information must have been divulged by an informer. But ferreting out his Cayman account should have been impossible.

Ez turned her attention to Alvarez. "Captain Francisco Alvarez. Fourteen years ago you were directly responsible for the massacre of seventy-eight innocent villagers in Rwanda while you were stationed there under the UN banner. During another UN peace-keeping mission in Uganda a year later, forty-two people mysteriously disappeared under your watch."

Unlike Allotey, Alvarez barely managed to keep his composure, displaying a hard-fought, though wavering grin. Speaking for the first time, he said, "All lies concocted by people looking to cast the peaceful intentions of the United Nations in a bad light."

Allotey moved quickly to Alvarez's side. "Captain, you will arrest these people at once!" he ordered shrilly. Leaning close to the captain's ear, he shot a quick glance at the IBC news team and lowered his voice to a whisper. "And you will confiscate that camera crew's video recording of this incident."

Alvarez nodded eagerly, now aching to carry out the orders. But as he opened his mouth to command his unit into action, the skin of his face and chest suddenly burned with a fierce intensity.

An involuntary scream broke from his lips. *"Madre de Dios!"* Mother of god! The sensation was unbearable, making him feel as though he were on fire. In the midst of his torment, he vaguely heard the troopers behind him stir in panic. He had just enough presence of mind to swat maddeningly at his clothing in a vain attempt to put out the flames, but strangely he could find none.

Jake grinned knowingly as the soldiers broke ranks in agonized disarray and fled for the UN chopper, Allotey already ten paces out in front of them. The non-lethal weapon Ez had used had worked as expected. The weapon focused a beam of millimeter wave energy that penetrated the skin, producing an intolerable heating sensation in targeted individuals without causing injury.

Ez had inadvertently stumbled upon the technology behind the weapon while hacking into the U.S. Department of Defense computer system. Having access to the worldwide Internet, she often entertained herself by cracking systems that were supposed to be impervious to penetration. In a file called Active Denial System 2, she had found the weapon specs, learning that it had been developed by Raytheon under contract with the U.S. Air Force. Readily assessing its potential, she refined and expanded the system further, increasing its range and giving it a multi-beam capability which could repel a group of assailants simultaneously.

Jake watched as the dual rotors of the UN whirlybird cranked up and gained momentum in an ear-splitting whine. With Alvarez glaring hatefully back at him from the fuselage's open doorway, the behemoth chopper lifted ponderously from its pad and swung out over the sea, dipping low to the water in an attempt to encourage all the airspeed the turbines could muster. In moments it raced off to the west, making a hasty retreat in the direction of Jamaica.

Ez turned to the news team, setting her gaze on the woman reporter. "There are a plethora of good reasons for a freedom loving people to steer clear of the United Nations, the primary one being the fanatical zeal with which it grasps hold of every worry and woe plaguing the earth, making them its own. It makes a practice of blowing these matters out of proportion, insisting that it and only it can provide a solution, a solution which must be imposed by force on the rest of the world. In reality, the UN is merely a conference of tarnished, self-serving officials from corrupt little countries all over the world who relish in the prospect of disaster relief, for it seems whenever or wherever disasters occur, the UN rushes in to help itself, demanding exclusive rights to direct the aid and money, much of which gets skimmed off into the pockets of people like Allotey."

The reporter gawked in wonder, both puzzled and delighted at this incredible turn of events. Her cameraman had caught the entire episode on tape. Such extraordinary news coverage had the potential of advancing her career enormously once it was sent to IBC headquarters in San Francisco. Eager to further her bout of good fortune, she stepped forward quickly, prepared to launch a series of questions at this remarkable black woman who had seemingly sprung out of the very air before her.

The reporter's elation abruptly disintegrated, for the Haitian woman vanished as suddenly as she had appeared.

DOLPHIN RIDERS

-5-

At a distance of 3,300 meters from what appeared to be a breakwater along Aquaria's eastern sector, a lone observer watched pensively as the UN helicopter headed off to the west. Silently he cursed, knowing the men aboard her had failed miserably.

Irately, Malcolm Maximus picked up a satellite phone and placed a call, waiting impatiently until the person he sought answered. In a tone reflecting his mood, he spoke in a language rarely used in a modern world, the timber of his voice sounding gravelly as it always did.

Ending the conversation, he put down the phone and stared balefully in the direction of the colony. The sun had now risen sufficiently to burn off the dense, cottony fog that had blanketed the Tursiops complex during the dawn hours, obscuring everything but the central structure which jutted imposingly above it like a majestic mountain peak rising above the clouds. He hated that fog. It was as though it had a life of its own, seemingly cloaking the budding enterprise in a shield of invincibility that sought to mock him. Its impenetrability evoked a defiance of his worldly views. Without a stiff breeze to carry it away in thick swirling columns, it would build each night, hanging stubbornly over the water until only the heat of day could dissipate it. He knew the cold water brought up from the depths was the cause of it.

He was about to turn away but stopped short as something else caught his eye, a sight that annoyed him even more. The residual accumulation of airborne moisture in concert with the sunshine had created a brilliant rainbow bridge of muted colors. He stared dourly, unconsciously parting his teeth in a snarl as the view took on additional scope. Now there were two of them, one arching directly over and perfectly framing the colony's central structure, and another further back hovering over Navassa Island.

A double rainbow had suddenly materialized before his very eyes, with the more distant arch positioned immediately under the one in the foreground and running parallel with it. The sight was an optical illusion, as he well understood, and though he had espied rainbows many times in the past, he had never before witnessed a twin-arch like this one.

He studied it a few seconds longer, willing the prismatic phenomenon to vanish. When it continued to hold steady, he finally averted his gaze in disgust. Rainbows repulsed him. They gave a sense of hope to the downtrodden, and that angered him.

As the chairman of *Unus Universitas*, a multinational conglomerate, he was currently the richest and most powerful man on the planet. Better known as One World, Unus Universitas had grown extensively since its startup thirty years earlier. As a young man, Maximus had amassed fortunes in international banking and energy. But that was before he had diversified his holdings further, gradually taking over companies entrenched in agriculture, arms manufacture, computers, mass media and pharmaceuticals. Under his leadership, he had built an empire. But he saw Aquaria as a threat to his vast holdings, including the plan he had so meticulously cultivated over the last two decades. With the world population now surpassing six billion and growing larger with each passing day, the planetary ecosystem was rapidly approaching collapse. He saw opportunity in this, delighting in the prospect that the world was quickly running out of arable land and cheap energy. Like a runaway train, it was heading recklessly for a Malthusian wall.

But his vision of expediting that inevitable event was being thwarted by this interloper. No matter what it took, he had to stop the colony's evolution before it shattered the old limits of the zero-sum resource game.

He had grown incredibly wealthy from playing the game, for in a zero-sum system there were always limited quantities of some critical commodity. Playing the zero-sum game was similar to playing poker with a limited supply of chips on the table. If one player was getting richer, other players were getting poorer. And to consistently win at the sophisticated game of resource poker in a modern world, you had to stack the deck in your favor by orchestrating events that allowed you to enrich yourself by impoverishing others. But this new upstart colony had taken a quantum leap forward by breaking all the rules of the game, for it was bringing a seemingly endless quantity of chips to the table.

Tursiops Worldwide, it appeared, was playing table stakes poker with a vacuum hose connected to a vault filled with gold. It was tapping into the energy and nutrient reserves of the ocean, setting a new course for humanity. From Maximus' point of view, Aquaria represented a cybergenic blasphemy that would ultimately establish a dangerous trend if left unchecked.

Cybergenic. He hated that word. Cybergenic meant the creation of a system sufficiently complex to exhibit the fundamental properties of life, those being self-organization and replication. The last thing he wanted was more floating cities similar to Aquaria being constructed on the high seas by a workforce of dolphins.

Maximus loathed the idea of ocean colonization. It created a glut of newfound resources to be shared with a hungry world, resources that were relatively inexpensive to produce once a sea colony became fully autonomous following its massive start-up costs.

The threat was all too real. Not only did it make it harder to stack the deck in his favor, it was an impediment to his plan for population control. He and his cabal saw much of mankind as useless eaters that needed to be eliminated from the planet. *The Order* was his cabal, and his cabal was behind the UN plan to remedy population explosions in Third World countries where people consumed far more than they produced. Working covertly with lower ranking members of *the Order* firmly entrenched within the UN, the cabal routinely implemented measures to ensure that people in the poorer countries never grew to a point where they were able to develop their own natural resources. Otherwise they might become strong like the industrialized nations.

The thought of newly emerging nations with financial clout disturbed Maximus. Contrary to politicians who were easily corrupted, what if key government officials in those emerging nations refused to submit to the cabal's will? He could not run that risk.

That was why *The Order* was using genetically modified crops to control the food supply. Plagiarius, a subsidiary of Unus Universitas, had patents on hybrid seeds that would only grow by spraying them with a certain chemical. And because Plagiarius was to be the sole source provider of that chemical, Maximus stood to make another mega-fortune once he unleashed the Morior Blight on the world's major crop producers. Plagiarius would charge a king's ransom for both the seeds and chemical. Spraying the seeds with the chemical, which he called Omicron-7, would make the resulting crops immune to the blight.

Standing on the bridge of his vessel, Maximus gazed contemptuously at the floating city, his thoughts sifting over the wealth and power he had already attained and his plans for the future. *Nunquarn Satis* was an appropriate name for his billion-dollar yacht. Translated from Latin it meant *Never Enough*. It epitomized perfectly his insatiable greed and the lavish lifestyle he lived.

He had learned early on in life that food and energy were the primary commodities supporting mankind. Controlling the availability of these staples through roadblocks of limited supply, many of them carefully contrived, made you incredibly rich. But Aquaria was making an end run around those roadblocks by providing these same commodities at virtually no cost to the planet's deteriorating ecosystem. Upon his order, one of his scientists had compiled a report on Aquaria's method of energy generation. The process was called Ocean Thermal Energy Conversion. The OTEC principle had been known for decades, but it seemed Tursiops Worldwide had pioneered the process to an unimaginable magnitude.

Maximus had pored over the report, learning the true threat the floating city posed. Whereas burning fossil fuels created acid rain, which affected food crops and invoked substantial harm on the world environment in general, the global oceans provided more than enough stored energy to satisfy the population time bomb. The seas were like gigantic solar collectors, absorbing and storing radiant flux from the sun. The warm surface waters held an inexhaustible charge of solar energy. The sun transmitted to earth 18,000 times more energy than mankind used in recent years. There was as much energy in a ton of seawater as two pounds of gasoline. The total energy held by the planet's seas was equivalent to a million billion barrels of oil. If all the ocean basins were filled to a depth of twenty feet in high-octane fuel, they would hold the same amount of energy as all the water in the seas, enough latent energy at this moment to meet mankind's needs at current levels for the next 25,000 years.

And this energy was freely available and renewable.

Aquaria was using this abundant energy to power its operations and generate huge windfalls of fuel and food, most of which it exported. Unlike conventional power-generating facilities, the OTEC process was a net energy producer. It did not conform to zero-sum rules like typical nuclear power plants, which consumed 3,000 calories of energy for every 1,000 it produced. In an OTEC system, 1,000 calories of energy were generated for every 700 it consumed.

In essence, the process fractured zero-sum barriers, and it was this that appalled Maximus the most. Both conventional and nuclear power plants placed enormous demands on the pre-existing zero-sum resource base, borrowing from the common yet limited resource pool, which always created more problems than they solved. But Maximus had always found opportunity in those problems, and over the years he had learned how to capitalize on them, leveraging incredible profits through crisis.

An OTEC plant functioned like a heat engine, working on the principle that energy will flow from a warmer to a cooler body. It produced electrical power by exploiting the temperature differential between warm surface waters and cold deep waters.

Aquaria was drawing in cold water from the depths and taking in warm surface water to generate electrical power, operating on a temperature difference of at least 40 degrees Fahrenheit to make the process worthwhile. But a temperature differential greater than 40 degrees would produce even more energy. Although OTEC typically operated at a very low efficiency, the difference in temperature was sufficient to drive Aquaria's turbines. Compared to a typical fossil fuel plant, which converted 40 percent of the energy available in the fuel to electricity, an OTEC plant converted only 2.5 percent of the available energy to electricity. While such a low level seemed ridiculously inefficient, it was rendered practical by the sheer size of the available resource.

Collectively, the energy resource of the oceans represented a renewable power supply exceeding 200 million megawatts. Even at very low levels of net efficiency, OTEC plants were capable of producing ten times more electrical energy as other conventional power sources combined, assuming enough OTEC facilities were built worldwide to harness this total available energy.

And only a relatively simple process was required to extract this energy from the oceans. By reducing the existing pressure on warm surface water, it is brought to a boil, thereby producing vapors which expand and drive a turbine, much the way steam is used to power a locomotive though in this case the process operates under a low ambient temperature. The rotating turbine blades then turn a dynamo which produces an electric current. Cold water pumped up from the depths is then used to condense the vapor, keeping the system pressure low. By transferring heat from warm to cold water, the process generated energy without consuming any actual fuel.

According to the report, the amount of energy Aquaria was currently producing was estimated at 3.6 terawatt-hours of net electrical power annually, or the equivalent of five million barrels of oil. And much of that electrical energy was being converted to a renewable, eco-friendly fuel sold on the world market at cheap rates.

Hydrogen was that fuel, as abundant as the seawater from which it was extracted. Since the conversion of electrical energy to hydrogen could be accomplished at 80 percent efficiency, it was being manufactured inexpensively.

Because Aquaria was producing 7.2 million kilowatt-hours of surplus electrical energy each day, it was converting it to 67 million cubic feet of liquid hydrogen which it exported on a daily basis. But these were conservative estimates, for the report stated the numbers could actually be higher.

Maximus frowned at the thought. With enough marine colonies like Aquaria coming on-line, they had the potential of tipping the ecological balance from impending catastrophe to sustainability at little or no cost to the planet's failing ecosystem. Compared to burning fossil fuels or splitting atoms, the OTEC power generating capability of numerous marine colonies would be benign, ultimately benefitting the health of the biosphere by reducing pollution and reversing the forces pushing the world over the brink.

If they were not stopped, sea colonies like Aquaria could literally solve the earth's energy and food shortages without exacerbating its environmental crisis. They could more than double the supply of energy, and do it without causing a buildup of carbon dioxide or acid rain. They would not disturb an acre of land or deplete any limited resources. They would not displace any pre-existing ecosystems since the open oceans were largely barren and lifeless due to a lack of nutrients. But where life had previously failed to flourish, a marine colony created an oasis of life.

Aside from hydrogen, Aquaria produced two other principal products for export, those being protein and distilled water. The colony was currently producing 150,000 tons of protein annually, the bulk of it consisting of *Spirulina platensis*, a species of blue-green algae that dwarfed all known food sources in protein content. But a far greater tonnage was expected to be produced once the facility was completed and became fully operational. Aquaria was using the nutrient-rich cold water from the depths to nourish this variety of algae. Containing 65 percent protein by weight that was easily digestible, spirulina made an ideal food supplement for human consumption, especially in Third World countries where malnutrition was prevalent.

Based on the report, it was estimated that Aquaria was bringing to the surface 43 billion gallons of nitrogen-laden water daily. Because ocean-dwelling plants and animals sank into the depths when they died, taking the nitrates locked in their bodies with them, the concentration of nitrates increased rapidly with depth, reaching a peak of 0.4 grams per cubic meter at roughly 3,300 feet in the world's oceans. When the nutrient-rich water reached the sunlit surface, the blue-green algae readily absorbed it, exploding into riotous growth and providing food for other life forms in the food chain. Not only was Aquaria producing enormous amounts of protein-rich spirulina in powder form, but it was also harvesting vast quantities of other food fishes that fed on the food pyramid initiated by the algae bloom.

Reflecting on this information, Maximus instinctively knew something was not quite right. Turning, he eyed a nearby screen which provided a real-time image of the Number 3 moon pool located amidships on the yacht's lowest deck. Several technicians hovered around a large fish that had just been pulled from the pool. With water still dripping from its flanks, it hung suspended from a gantry that spanned both sides of the pool. A second fish nearly identical to the first hung serenely from the same gantry on the opposite side of the pool.

"Status?" barked Maximus.

One of the technicians looked up sharply, the surveillance camera revealing a face fraught with angst. He had been in the act of removing a flexible cowling on the underbelly of the fish just pulled from the water.

"The sonar system in Fish Two is inoperable. We're trying to determine the cause."

"You had assured me it would not fail," Maximus admonished sharply. Percy Osgood, the brains behind construction of the robotic fish, had become a huge disappointment in recent days. Perhaps replacing him with someone more competent was in order.

Osgood paled, fidgeting noticeably. As if sensing what Maximus was thinking, he spoke quickly. "As you saw, the explosive deployed perfectly. But the random acoustics abounding in these waters may have caused sufficient interference to disrupt a clear sonar picture."

"I am not interested in excuses," Maximus snarled, "only results. I will expect a detailed mosaic of the seafloor beneath Aquaria before the day is out."

Osgood nodded stiffly, deferentially. Turning, he went back to work on the mechanical fish, his hands nervously probing the inner circuitry.

Maximus keyed several buttons on the console in front of him, replaying the video taken earlier. Fish Number One had gotten close enough to the colony's power plants to get a clear view of the intakes. Puzzled, he studied it some more to make sure he hadn't missed anything, and within moments he confirmed the thing that had been troubling him.

The floating city currently had what he perceived to be seven OTEC power plants. One of them was centrally located, that being the starter plant aboard the seed ship towed into place when construction had first begun. Encircling that, there were six others set up in a hexagonal pattern. But each of them should have had a vertical pipe that descended to a depth of 3300 feet to bring up water sufficiently cold enough to initiate the OTEC process.

Large vertical pipes were evident, perhaps 40 feet in diameter based on what he was seeing. But the seafloor directly beneath Aquaria was not even close to the needed depth, ending roughly at 900 feet.

Consulting a nautical chart of the area, he studied the contour of the ocean bottom surrounding Navassa Island. The seafloor dropped off rapidly to the south of the island, ultimately falling away precipitously into the Cayman Trench, an ocean abyss thousands of feet deep. At a distance of almost two miles from Aquaria's outer perimeter, his vessel currently sat over this trench, held in place by the dynamic positioning system *Nunquarn Satis* routinely employed when floating stationary in water where anchoring was rendered impractical.

Earlier in the day, Maximus had two of his technicians lower a probe to a depth of 900 feet, confirming that the water temperature and nitrate concentration were insufficient to induce the vast harvests of energy and food the colony was producing.

One other anomaly troubled him. Video from Fish One revealed what he perceived to be the warm-water intakes, all appearing identical. There were seven of them, each with a diameter exceeding 30 feet in his estimation. Running parallel to each other, they extended horizontally out to the offshore berthing facility near the island, all of them apparently buoyant as evidenced by a series of anchor cables that kept them submerged ten feet below the surface. Surveillance from the mechanical fish confirmed that they all terminated at the offshore platform adjacent to Navassa Island. Running parallel and ten feet beneath the center intake was a Plexiglas tube eight feet in diameter, and he surmised it was a dry access tunnel that allowed passage between Aquaria and the offshore platform.

Maximus pondered the layout. Why go to the expense of constructing lengthy intakes when it was so much simpler to draw in surface water immediately contiguous with the OTEC plants?

One way or the other he would solve these mysteries.

But it was the girl riding a huge white dolphin that intrigued him the most. Fish One had only gotten a glimpse of her while reconnoitering the easternmost intake. This was only his second sighting of her, the first one displayed in a photograph taken from high altitude by satellite and provided by a telemetry expert from France. But the photo had been grainy and shot from a poor angle looking down. It had lacked the clarity and perspective the video was now revealing. The girl's long hair streamed back in a cloud of shimmering ebony as it caught the sunlight reaching into the depths, and a white wetsuit clung to her body, which appeared lean and lithe. Even with the dive mask partially obscuring her face, it was obvious she was an exquisite beauty. Here was the Dolphin Girl his associate back in Haiti was so eager to get his hands on.

Through bribes and monetary rewards over the last several months, he had gathered tidbits of information on her through a spectrum of Haitian informants, as did his associate. The compiled information had been thoroughly assessed by several top specialists to piece together a psychological profile of her character, which he found to be quite extraordinary if not impossible, assuming the evaluation was accurate.

Maximus replayed the recording, back-tracking the video once again. Two young children had accompanied her, a girl and boy, each riding a juvenile albino dolphin. Though difficult to tell, the children appeared to be seven or eight years old. This latest finding set off a chain reaction in his devious mind, and a plan quickly coalesced.

A caustic smile flooded Maximus' face as he continued to replay the short footage several more times. "Most interesting!" he said aloud, knowing that the table stakes in the zero-sum game had just risen sharply in his favor.

-6-

Destiny read the joy showing on the faces of both twins, her heart nearly melting with maternal stirrings. This was their third viewing of the hidden dolphin sanctuary.

"Can we see the new *thurentras*, mumsie?" Melody asked excitedly.

"Yes, can we, mum?" Troy Jacob chimed in, his enthusiasm matching his sister's.

The children's voices merged with the sound of water dripping monotonously in the expansive confines of the cavern, coming back at them in ebbing cacophonous echoes.

Destiny hesitated. She could see the children's excitement had infected their mounts, for both *Alpha* and *Omego* seemed to quiver in eager anticipation under them. Both the twins and their bond mates appeared totally unaffected by the danger they had been exposed to a short time earlier. If not for the pressure wave inhibitor each of them carried, including herself, the explosion might have caused them serious injury. With acts of sabotage plaguing the colony as of late, Jake had insisted she and the children wear them whenever they took to the sea.

"We'll pay them a visit in a little while," Destiny answered. "But you know as well as I that Granny has something to show us first."

"Aw, snails are so boring," Troy Jacob objected dolefully. "Why does she spend so much time studying them?"

A misty spray erupted from Hercules blowhole in disapproval, and Destiny patted him affectionately. "Because she thinks they may be the answer to restoring the coral reefs that are dying. The work she is doing is very important to the health of the planet."

"I guess," Troy Jacob conceded bleakly.

"Well I like snails," Melody announced haughtily.

Her brother frowned, giving her an admonishing look. "Snails are slow and slimy."

"You're slow and slimy!" Melody giggled playfully.

Troy Jacob's aquamarine eyes came alive with mischief, and Destiny was suddenly reminded of the boy's striking resemblance to his father. "Well, even a snail can beat you in a race. My *Alpha* is way faster than your *Omega*."

"Is not," Melody contested loftily. She looked down and caressed her bond mate lovingly. "We let you win the last race on purpose, didn't we my sweet darling." The juvenile albino beneath her continued to float quietly. "*Omega* didn't want *Alpha* to feel bad, and I didn't want you to sulk if you lost three times in a row."

A trace of petulance flashed briefly across Troy Jacob's face. He was not to be outdone. "Well, you're-"

Destiny jumped in quickly. "Insulting one another is not very nice," she reproved gently. The two of them could be a handful at times, and every so often she had to rein in their sportive banter. She knew they were very close and loved one another dearly, but unfortunately their naturally competitive natures knew no bounds. "Try to remember what uncle Jacob has taught you," she felt it necessary to add.

"You mean how being humble is a virtue," Troy Jacob grumbled.

Destiny smiled as only a proud mother could smile. "Yes, that and how all God's creatures have a purpose, even a snail."

Jacob had schooled the twins endlessly on the subject of ecology, and they well understood the impact a single organism could have on an ecosystem, particularly a coral reef, even one so seemingly lowly as a snail. The twins had absorbed his teachings with the avid curiosity of sagacious young minds, attaining a level of comprehension light years above other kids their age. They knew that coral reef ecosystems were normally nutrient-poor environments, a symptom of tropical waters in general and that these systems functioned much the same way as rainforests and wetlands did on land, recycling nutrients at a rapid rate. Though these marine habitats covered less than 1 percent of the Earth's surface, they were home to 25 percent of all marine fish species. Nutrient producers such as plankton and seaweed, essentially plants that photosynthesize, were abundant in these sanctuaries of life and formed the base of the food chain, providing food for the bountiful small fish and other organisms, which in turn provided meals for larger animals.

Coral reefs were among the oldest ecosystems on earth and havens of phenomenal biodiversity in tropical seas, supporting more animal and plant life per unit area than any other marine habitat and generally accounting for thousands of species. A treasure trove of uncharted possibilities lay within this rich tapestry of biodiversity. Some scientists estimated that millions of species indigenous to coral reef habitats around the world were still yet to be found, and it was these undiscovered organisms that held potential value for alleviating human diseases. A plethora of drugs had already been derived from coral reef organisms as treatments for cancer, HIV, arthritis, bacterial infections, and viruses, with many more yet to be developed. This was one of the many goals the colony was focused on, finding new cures for diseases, but not just for those that afflicted humans. Beyond the human species and far more prevalent in nature, other ailments existed that had the potential of unraveling the delicate balance of life on a broader scale, and in so doing would negatively impact the entire planet. Of particular importance were the

DOLPHIN RIDERS

unique life forms endemic to the waters adjacent to Navassa Island. They held much promise for developing various cures for both human suffering and ailing marine environments, for the coral reefs abounding here were one of the most thriving and intact ecosystems in the Caribbean. Unfortunately, these same reefs had recently come under attack from another threat other than human sabotage.

Riding their bond mates with a fluid grace, Destiny and the twins made their way to the far side of the immense subterranean grotto, one of many that interlaced the limestone bedrock of Navassa Island. A trail of sparkling phosphorescence was left in their softly rippling wakes, the product of tiny microscopic organisms within the water. Agitated by the group's passage, they erupted like tiny starbursts before fading under the pale glow of soft green light that seemed to permeate every corner of the cavern, both above and below the water. The pervasive glow was yet another bioluminescent effect, produced by mossy lichen indigenous to the cavern. The lichen clung to the rock in many places, feeding on the limestone, and it highlighted the swirling lines of the massive structure over which they glided, a submerged edifice totally unnatural to its surroundings.

Reaching the far wall, the group slid beneath the surface and spiraled their way down through a winding circular tunnel with smooth walls until they leveled off and encroached upon a familiar archway, beyond which a moderately-sized chamber with a vaulted ceiling awaited them. Here the subdued greenish glow that had accompanied them through the passageway was replaced by brazen fluorescent lighting emanating from the roof above. The chamber was only partially filled with water of wadeable depth and held breathable air. Several tabletops and shelves jutted above the water, all of them laden with a varied assortment of flasks, tubing, and sophisticated equipment. Other than the water pooled within the vaulted room, the place had the look of a conventional laboratory setting.

A woman lifted her head from the lens of a microscope, turning to greet them. "I'm glad you could come," Amphitrite announced, eyeing both the twins and Destiny with obvious pleasure.

Destiny stared back with mutual warmth and adulation. Despite their age difference, Amphitrite still displayed the youthful glow of a much younger woman, causing strangers to assume her to be Destiny's older sister rather than her mother. Even so, Destiny could not help wonder about the extraordinary abilities the woman who birthed her had once possessed. As Jacob had often said, the power of psychic healing defied scientific explanation.

Amphitrite had been a healer. With the help of Athena and the albinos, she had been able to cure the sick and injured with a simple touch. But upon regaining her memory, this inexplicable power had deserted her. Accurately prophesying events to come was another power Amphitrite had lost. Jacob had astutely reasoned that her inability to remember her past had somehow given her the power to glimpse the future, but that had been some years ago before her emotional reunion with Franklin. The fact that Amphitrite now had full memory of her former life seemed to support Jacob's prior conclusion. Ever since recapturing her original identity, she no longer possessed the enigma of precognition. As Harriet Grahm, she had been a successful marine zoologist, specializing in the study of coelenterates. Her husband, Dr. Franklin Grahm, another marine zoologist and perhaps the foremost authority on the planet when it came to dolphins, had been bereaved for many years thinking his wife, Harriet, had gone down with their beloved sloop, *Tursiops*, during a hurricane at sea. Pregnant with Destiny at the time, Harriet had survived with the help of a female bottlenose dolphin. But something incredible had happened to both woman and dolphin during the storm, bringing on extraordinary changes in each of them that would have profound and far-reaching effects as Destiny had come to fathom, setting off a chain of events that took them to Navassa Island and the building of Aquaria.

Suffering a severe case of amnesia and dehydration, Harriet Grahm had eventually been carried by the dolphin to a secluded cove along Haiti's western coastline. There Jacob had found them, nursing the woman back to health. Jacob soon discovered the woman had no remembrance of her past life, not even her name, and so he had begun calling her Amphitrite based on the circumstances of her arrival, which vaguely paralleled a similar event found in Greek mythology, for the myth portrayed Amphitrite as the Queen of the Sea and the wife of Poseidon, a regal goddess who had birthed Triton, the man-fish. An unusual bond had developed between Amphitrite and the creature who had rescued her, prompting Amphitrite to call the dolphin Athena. According to Greek legend, Athena was the favorite daughter of Zeus, king of the Olympians. To this day, Athena had continued on as Amphitrite's faithful companion and bond mate, always remaining close at hand to assist Amphitrite in all her endeavors.

A wistful nostalgia suddenly gripped Destiny as she recalled her earliest years. She had grown up in that hidden sanctuary Jacob called home, a wondrous haven untouched by the outside world, a place Jacob fondly referred to as *Gaia*. Sequestered in a land of ecological ruin, it had miraculously remained pristine and unpolluted, a tiny realm of vibrant multi-hued colors that pulsated with life. It was within its placid, warm waters where she had been dropped from her mother's womb at the same moment Athena had given birth to Natalie, for Athena had been gravid with calf. Destiny had learned to swim long before she could walk, and riding Natalie had come instinctually.

Natalie was the first of her kind to enter the planetary biosphere, an altogether new species of dolphin, endowed with albino skin and jointed prehensile appendages that approximated arms with hands similar to those of a primate. With a brain that exceeded human intelligence, Natalie had matured far more quickly than the average dolphin, successively mating with a string of ordinary male bottlenose and subsequently bearing either one or two calves each time she delivered, with the resulting progenies being either male or female, or consisting of mixed genders each time she bore twins. In procreating, she had bred two advanced strains of cetacean, some of them albinos like herself, and others that were a gray variation. All possessed an elevated intellect and a pair of hands at the terminus of arms that, when not in use, could retract and fold covertly into recesses beneath their pectoral fins. However, unlike their gray cousins, the albinos were generally bigger, spawned with an even greater muscularity and intelligence and the ability to converse in human languages. Strangely, albinos birthed by Natalie only mated with others of their kind, and with the exception of Hercules, invariably generated mixed genders in the set of albino twins they or their descendants in turn produced. But with both strains of the new breed, whether they be albino or gray, there was often little need for the acoustic communication commonly exhibited by cetaceans, for they relied primarily on telepathy for receiving and transmitting thoughts between each other and their bond mates.

The albino twins, Coral and Reef, were the first of Natalie's amazing offspring, followed two years later by Hermes and Aphrodite, another set of mixed gender albino twins. It was the union of Reef and Aphrodite that produced Hercules, and the subsequent union of Hermes and Coral that sprang forth Apollo and Artemis in the pod's earlier days, and Alpha and Omega a little over a year ago. Since birthing Natalie, Athena had also continued to mate, producing a succession of calves, but unlike Natalie, all were gray and did not have the ability to converse in human languages, though they were all born with the same unique forelimbs as the albinos. Athena, it seemed, could no longer breed any more albinos like her original progeny. Oddly enough, however, succeeding generations of grays originating from either Athena or Natalie were sometimes capable of birthing or siring an albino with the same traits as Natalie, even if they mated with a common bottlenose dolphin lacking those same attributes. Thetis was one such progeny of Athena's, who in turn had given birth to Achilles, currently the most athletic albino in the pod and the bond mate of Jake Javolyn, Destiny's husband. And with Phillipe yearning for an albino bond mate of his very own, Thetis had accommodated him by producing Perseus eleven months earlier. The pod had grown considerably over the last several years and now numbered in the hundreds.

As Destiny pondered these things, she thought about Jacob's views regarding these extraordinary life forms. Jacob believed the new breed had come into existence to show mankind the way, for he saw humanity as an utterly irrational species, totally unsuitable for responsible charge of the planet. A firm believer in the Gaia Hypothesis, Jacob was convinced that humankind had brought such pressure to bear on nature that the life force behind creation had simply reacted by introducing a higher life form into the planetary ecosphere in order to save the world. Originally formulated by James Lovelock in 1979, the Gaia Hypothesis was a highly controversial idea among ecologists, though it had slowly gained a foothold within scientific circles. It postulated that the entire Earth is alive and acts as a complete organism, possessing various self-regulating mechanisms for its survival. In keeping with the theory, Jacob contended that the Earth had brought on something new to counter man's destructive tendencies. At its core, the hypothesis states that life creates planetary conditions for its own purposes, essentially to suit itself. According to the theory, the Earth was a complex superorganism involving the interaction of the planet's biosphere, atmosphere, oceans and lithosphere, a totality that constituted a feedback or cybernetic system seeking to optimize a physical and chemical environment conducive for life. So while mankind, in all his combative, ego-oriented, divisive, exploitive, and technological madness, had brought all life on Earth to the brink of destruction, the emerging species was life-embracing and sought to live in harmony with the dominant species, guiding it toward a collective change in its cultures, transforming its present temperament and showing it how to live in balance with the living world. In essence, the emerging species was an evolution of consciousness on the planet.

And both Jacob and Amphitrite were certain that a mysterious oblate jellyfish, a type of coelenterate never before catalogued, had triggered the arcane evolutionary process responsible for making the new breed possible. This same species of jellyfish had been the forerunner of the pumpkin-like, hydrogen belching *thurentra*, a hybrid life form that was a crossbreed of *holothuroidea* and the unknown coelenterate, produced by merging a sea cucumber with it. Through a horizontal transfer of portions of their genomes, an exchange of DNA had occurred between the two organisms to cause a most unusual mutation. And it was this mutation that had unexpectedly yielded the huge supply of precious metals and other elements, giving them the means to build Aquaria.

They knew that several varieties of *thurentra* were now in existence, and as far as they could tell, all had provided them with important elements and minerals that contributed immensely to the construction and operation of the colony. In some respects, a *thurentra* was comparable to both an undersea miner and ore processor. With hundreds of tentacles that extended thousands of feet into the Cayman Trench and reached the hydrothermal vents found four miles down, they had the ability to harvest and refine valuable elements and minerals spewing forth from these vents, pumping them up from the depths in a purified state. And while vast amounts of high-grade gold, platinum, magnesium oxide and manganese were routinely made available to them for ongoing construction, it was the cold water the *thurentras* continually pumped up from the abyss that made the OTEC process workable. With Aquaria situated immediately above an area of sea with insufficient water depth, harvesting the ocean's inexhaustible supply of stored energy would otherwise have been impossible. Perched directly under the floating city were six *thurentra* of immense size that drew huge volumes of nutrient-rich cold water from the oceanic depths where dissolved nitrates and nitrites were plentiful. These particular organisms had been created by splicing the mysterious oblate jellyfish with the largest variety of sea cucumber Amphitrite and Jacob could find. With their taproot network of tentacles reaching far down into the nearby Cayman Trench, the water they brought up was 40 degrees lower in temperature than the 80-degree water at the surface. Aside from their ability to harvest certain types of metal, they also produced massive amounts of hydrogen gas. A byproduct common to all species of *thurentra* regardless of the particular metal they mined, the gas was continuously vented off by the strange organisms and collected by the colony.

Destiny took satisfaction in knowing the *thurentra* population had doubled since the day she had first let Jay Jay see them eight years earlier, for now there existed a total of fifty-two, with forty-six of the car-sized creatures roosting along the floor of the cavern. Of these, eight of them yielded gold and platinum, while thirty others provided a seemingly endless supply of magnesium in an oxide form better known as periclase. Polymetallic nodules primarily comprised of manganese and to a lesser degree aluminum were produced by the remaining eight *thurentra*.

As Jacob had explained to Destiny many years ago, magnesium and manganese played a critical role in the building of Aquaria, for these were the raw materials that formed the skeletal framework of the main structural components. Because magnesium in its pure form is soluble in sea water and will readily dissolve, it must be alloyed with small amounts of manganese and aluminum to keep it from dissolving. And though it was lighter than steel, it was comparable in strength. But rather than having to set up a mechanical manufacturing system in order to produce the alloy, the albinos had managed to bioengineer yet another hybrid organism that fed on the periclase and manganese nodules to excrete the needed alloy in an extruded form that resembled long strands of wire capable of conducting an electrical current.

In spite of all the benefits the *thurentra* population made possible, Destiny knew they could be quite dangerous to other organisms coming in direct contact with them, for they also acted as huge capacitors, storing electrical energy similar to the way certain types of eels did. This made her think back to the man she had discovered floating dead at the base of one of the cavern-dwelling *thurentra* years earlier, apparently one of Yeslam Raduyev's henchman during the pod's struggle with the radical Islamist and his allies. Nick Henderson, her father's surly and conspiring assistant, was another that had fallen victim to the hybrid's potentially lethal electrical charge, but he had survived only to be found dead a week later behind the cove's mystical waterfall where the dolphins had hidden their original cache of precious metals.

The thought of the cove brought back treasured memories, making Destiny suddenly long for its solitude and unmatched beauty. She had spent most of her life growing up there, sheltered and naïve about the true nature of the world that lay beyond. And though she had been basically happy and content, she sensed that something had been missing from her life. She had been especially aware of this whenever she ventured deep into the cave that existed behind the waterfall, cognizant of an inner voice beckoning her on. A portal lay within those darkened recesses, a time warp that somehow connected the past with the future, and it was within a dimly lit chamber located far back from the thunderous water where she had finally come to understand the actually meaning behind the murals that lay on the walls. It was there she and Jake had made love for the first time, and it was there the twins had been conceived, bringing her happiness to uncharted heights.

Destiny sighed contentedly. Yes, the cove was a special place, far different and removed from the colony. It was there Jacob and her mother had inadvertently created the first *thurentra* by dropping a sea cucumber onto the unknown jellyfish to see what would happen. And it was there that the resulting hybrid organism had begun bringing up huge amounts of precious metals from the oceanic depths once it had fully matured. But now there were two such organisms living within the cove's sheltered waters, and both continued to produce a staggering supply of gold and platinum using their prodigious tentacles to draw the valuable metals up from the deep.

Thurentras, it seemed, brought an additional benefit, one that directly affected the local marine environment. Corals and sponges, even those on the decline, quickly rebounded, becoming more robust and alive in the vicinity of these amazing creatures. This baffled Amphitrite and Jacob, for they were still unable to unravel the process that caused this.

The fact that *thurentras* were capable of reproducing themselves asexually had come as quite a surprise to the entire pod, for it was during the fourth year of a *thurentra's* life cycle that a bulbous node would suddenly sprout from its leathery crown, growing rapidly within a matter of days as it swelled like an oblong balloon filling with air. Reaching the size of a ripe eggplant, it would suddenly break free and float to the surface, upon which it could be swept away by wind and current if it reached open water. This had happened with the first cove-dwelling *thurentra*, the oldest among these amazing organisms. It was slightly over two years earlier when Natalie had noticed the inflated node being taken out to sea with an outgoing tide very early one morning. But even before it reached the reef beyond the narrow inlet leading to the ocean, she had gently nudged it back into the cove's calm protected water, correctly deducing it would as yet be too immature to carry an electrical charge like the organism that had spawned it. Moving it to a pen where it could not escape, Amphitrite had kept a watchful eye to determine what new developments would take place, speculating that the small seedling would eventually rupture, releasing the hydrogen gas keeping it afloat. She had not been disappointed. In a matter of days, the sac burst, whereupon it sank to the cove's sandy bottom to anchor itself and begin to grow. Once alerted to this strange event, the pod took precautionary measures to capture all seedlings once they broke free. Carrying out such a task with the cavern-dwelling *thurentra* had been rather easy. This, however, had been far more difficult with the gigantic *thurentra* roosting beneath the floating city, for the seedlings as it turned out were the size of huge hot air balloons.

Amphitrite appeared not to notice Destiny's deep ruminations, though in times previous she would have sensed them immediately. Her attention was focused on the twins. "Both of you have seen what has been happening to the nearby reefs," she said.

"You mean the *white pox*," the twins chorused in unison.

Amphitrite beamed proudly. The twins were very perceptive and exceptionally smart for their age. "Yes, I'm talking about the *white pox*." She centered her gaze on Troy Jacob. "What can you tell me about this dreadful plague, Teejay?"

"It's very destructive to Elkhorn corals," Troy Jacob chirped with alacrity.

Amphitrite nodded in agreement. "So how can you tell if the coral is infected?"

"It loses its brownish or yellowish color and turns white.

Amphitrite turned to the other sibling. "Can you tell me what causes it, Melody?"

"A germ that's very contagious to the elk horns."

"What kind of germ?"

"It's called *Serratia marcesceus*, a type of fecal enterobacterium."

Amphitrite looked pleased at Melody's perfect enunciation of a term that would have otherwise left most seven-year-olds tongue-tied. As usual, Jacob had taught the children well. She turned back to the boy. "Where does it come from, Teejay?"

"From human sewage."

"Yeech!" Melody blurted in mock horror, making her brother laugh. "That's disgusting," she quickly added. "We've been swimming through poop."

Amphitrite found no humor in the girl's antics. White pox was no laughing matter. It was a strange new menace that had joined the long list of woes that threatened corals in the world's oceans. A bacterium that was potentially deadly to humans was now killing off one of the most important reef-building corals in the Caribbean. It was a startling discovery because it was the first time ever that a human disease was found to kill an invertebrate. *Acropora palmata*, the scientific classification of Elkhorn corals, was structurally complex and had a configuration that resembled the antlers of an elk, showing many large branches that provided habitats for a wide range of marine life. Compared to other corals, elk horns were incredibly fast growing, but unfortunately had declined by almost ninety percent in the past fifteen years in Caribbean waters. Until recently, however, the Elkhorn cover around Navassa had continued to thrive, remaining essentially unscathed by such ravages. But now, despite the salubrious benefits *thurentras* bestowed on the local marine environment, the white pox was threatening the survival of the Navassa elk horns as well, for it had been brought into their midst by a carrier of the pathogen deadly to their health. A tiny snail called *Aesopus spiculus* had inexplicably found its way to Navassa in great numbers and spread the lethal bacterium to the *Acropora* corals, which were now dying off at an alarming rate.

"In actuality the water quality is quite good around Navassa thanks to the marvelous sewage treatment system incorporated into Aquaria's infrastructure," Amphitrite amended. "The bacterium seems to be confined to the elk horns, so none of us have been exposed to human feces."

"So where's the sewage coming from?" Troy Jacob asked.

"We're still working on that," Amphitrite answered, "but we've been able to identify the culprit responsible for spreading the bacterium."

DOLPHIN RIDERS

"Jacob told us a snail was spreading it," Melody said, continuing to sit astride Omega's back.

"That's right," Amphitrite concurred. She reached for a glass flask, holding it up so the twins could scrutinize its contents. A cluster of minute dark objects clung to the inside surface, each about one-tenth the size of a human thumbnail.

"I didn't know snails could be so puny," Troy Jacob decried. "Is that as big as they get?"

Amphitrite nodded. "We think we've found a way to remediate the damage these little creatures have caused."

Melody eyed the tiny snails with curiosity. "How?"

"By making a slight adjustment to their genetic structure."

"You've made a new type of snail!" exclaimed Teejay.

"Yes we have," Amphitrite concurred. "We spliced a gene from the brown algae found in these waters into the snail's genome. That particular gene is known to produce a potent compound used as a natural antibiotic to defend the algae against infection. Once this genetically modified snail makes contact with the elk horns, it releases a secretion that kills off the white pox and renders the coral immune to further infection even if the coral is healthy and has not been contaminated by the bacterium."

"Wow!" blurted both siblings simultaneously.

"We made one more modification to the snail's genes, so there are actually two other benefits this new species brings," Amphitrite further explained. "The secretion it releases will kill the snails that carry the *Serratia marcesceus* bacterium once they make contact with an immunized coral. The new snail also eats sewage and purifies the water, so not only are we going to release them into the Navassa ecosystem, we're also going to drop them into the drainage ditches and coastal waters back in Haiti."

This last declaration was a stark reminder to the children that Haiti was an ecological disaster. The impoverished Caribbean nation, poorest in the Western Hemisphere, had no sewage treatment facilities whatsoever. And although she could not prove it, Amphitrite was certain that the bacterium finding its way to Navassa via the *Aesopus spiculus* snail had originated in the polluted waters of Haiti.

"But you're going to need a gazillion of them," Melody was quick to point out.

"The modified snail reproduces exceptionally fast," said Amphitrite. "We've been breeding them for several weeks now and have several million ready to put to work. For starters, we'll release half of them into the local habitat, with the rest going to Haiti."

Troy Jacob eyed the genetically-modified snails within the flask thoughtfully. "Have you given them a name yet?"

"The new species is called *Aesopus vigoratus.*"

Melody parroted the trailing word, appearing puzzled. "*Vigoratus?*" Her eyes suddenly lit up as she recalled Jacob's latest tutoring session. "Doesn't that mean 'healer' in Latin?"

Once again Amphitrite beamed proudly. "Yes, it does."

"Why don't we just call them 'Vigs'?" Troy Jacob suggested.

"If you like," Amphitrite replied.

"When are you going to send them to Haiti, Grandma?" Melody asked, her tone bubbling with sudden interest.

"The first batch will be delivered day after tomorrow," Amphitrite answered. "We'll start with Port-au-Prince, seeding the harbor and drainage ditches with them."

Melody turned briskly on her mount to stare eagerly at her mother. "Can we go, Mom?" she petitioned anxiously. She looked to her brother for support. "Teejay and I really miss the cove. We haven't been there in over a year now and you promised we'd see it again real soon. We can stop there on the way back from Port-au-Prince."

Destiny hesitated. Even though eight years had now passed since the Cardoza incident, her beloved cove could still be a dangerous place, and the last thing she needed was to put her children in harm's way. In the intervening years, Rafael Cardoza and his thugs had made two additional forays aimed at pillaging the gold that lay hidden in the cove, only to be beaten back severely by the ingenious, though primitive security measures Jake had devised. Nevertheless, she could no longer ignore the inner voice beckoning her back to the place of her birth. Perhaps it was in response to the recurring lucid dream that had tormented her night after night in recent weeks. Jacob had told her long ago never to ignore her dreams, for they were often a warning that foreshadowed a disastrous future event that could be averted if appropriate preemptive steps were undertaken before it occurred. This particular dream might very well be one such precursor. It continued to gnaw away at her, invoking a deep-seated foreboding that lingered on the edge of her awareness, growing ever more ominous with each passing day until a yearning desire to revisit the cave's dark recesses had now become overpowering. Perhaps those timeless murals would give her a glimpse of things yet to come.

Destiny was abruptly jarred from her momentary reverie. "Please, please, can we Mom?" This time, it was Teejay who pleaded.

"But you have an identical cove right here in Aquaria," Destiny reminded him.

TJ frowned. "You know it's not the same. It's not even half as big as the one in Haiti."

"And the birds and butterflies are not real," Melody challenged.

Destiny hated it when they ganged up on her like this. But the twins were right, and she couldn't fault them for their yearning desire to revisit their birthplace. Even though the albinos had gone to great lengths in replicating the mystical sanctuary, the re-creation was nevertheless a scaled-down version of the real one. Constructed at Aquaria's epicenter, it formed the largest open area within the floating city and even displayed an artificial waterfall that cascaded down from a height of 230 feet in a series of plunging cataracts that duplicated the one back home. "It may be smaller but it's made to look just like the real one," she replied lamely, knowing it could never quite capture the ambiance of the true cove.

"But it doesn't even smell the same," TJ rejoined mournfully.

"And the rainbows are fake, too," Melody added.

"And it doesn't have any *thurentra*," TJ complained testily.

Without knowing why, Destiny suddenly caved, though it defied all reason within her. "A promise is a promise," she found herself saying despite her misgivings.

"So we'll be going then?" both twins pressed avidly, their mellifluous voices merging as one.

Destiny sighed in resignation, aware of Amphitrite's look of surprise. It was obvious her mother had not expected this. "Yes, we'll be going," she conceded. Swinging her gaze to Amphitrite, she asked, "Who will be supervising the seeding operation?"

"Zimbola, of course. He'll be taking the Angel."

Destiny nodded. Taking a trip back to the cove with the gentle giant assuaged her reservations. Other than Jake, Mat, or herself, she could think of no one better suited to protect her children.

-7-

The reporter riveted her naturally inquisitive eyes on Jacob, still truly amazed at what she had witnessed earlier on.

"It appears you have no love for the UN," she stated pointedly.

Jacob shrugged. "We, in Aquaria, have no love of any organization or people who seek to impose their will on others."

"Not even if their will is focused on propagating a common good for all?"

"Like all ruling bodies and governments, the UN is comprised of greedy squabbling factions and individuals with hidden agendas usually aimed at amassing power and wealth."

"It's evident your view of the world is quite cynical," she replied.

"Perhaps it clouds your perception of the democratic process, the merits of which you seem to reject. In spite of a few bad apples, wouldn't you agree that the UN establishes policy primarily through a majority vote of nations aimed at improving the world?"

"Majority rule is a noble idea, but unfortunately true democracy rarely exists, and in most cases is merely an illusion created to make the common man believe the fate of a nation resides in the hands of voters. The will of the people is rarely reflected in governments that espouse its virtues. As we know, elections can be and have been rigged by an unscrupulous minority, and in most cases can be bought if you have enough campaign funds to delude voters with a deluge of propaganda. But whether or not any of these things happen, the saddest thing of all with democracies is they do not last."

Surprise flashed briefly on the reporter's face. "Can you explain why?"

"Because the human failings of greed, complacency and apathy will eventually work their way into the system, and when that becomes sufficiently widespread the democracy will fail."

Jacob produced a gentle disarming smile, eager to erase the surprise that still lingered on the reporter's face.

"Have you ever heard of a Scottish history professor by the name of Alexander Tyler?"

"No."

"About the time America's original thirteen colonies adopted their new constitution in 1787, Alexander Tyler, a history professor at the University of Edinburgh, used the fall of the Athenian Republic some 2,000 years earlier as a prime example of why democracies cannot proliferate as a permanent form of government, for history demonstrates democracies are always temporary in nature. According to Tyler, once voters discover they can vote themselves generous gifts from the public treasury, the democracy will begin to crumble. From that moment on, the majority will always vote for the candidates who promise the most benefits, with the result that every democracy will eventually collapse due to loose and irresponsible fiscal policy. This is always followed by dictatorship."

"So what did Tyler discover about the longevity of democracies?" asked the reporter sardonically.

"Tyler's research revealed that the lifespan of the world's greatest democratic civilizations lasted two hundred years on average, with all of them progressing through the same cycle."

A trace of skepticism was now evident on the reporter's countenance. "All of them?"

DOLPHIN RIDERS

"Yes. He found there to be eight evolutionary stages in all. It seems that all democracies spring from a culture of bondage, moving quickly to an environment of spiritual faith, which is the initial stage. From there, the spiritual faith garners momentum, progressing rather swiftly into a second stage of great courage in which the citizenry throws off the shackles of bondage to achieve liberty, which is the third stage. Both the French and American Revolutions are prime examples of the population attaining liberty from their oppressive government."

Jacob paused briefly to study the woman. "Would you like me to continue, or do you find the subject rather speculative and uninteresting?"

"Please go on."

"One only has to look at American history to prove what happens next. With their newfound freedom no longer hampered by an intrusive and overbearing government, the American people prospered greatly, moving rather quickly into a stage of abundance. Unfortunately, such abundance seems to have run its course as a result of overly restrictive governmental regulations and high taxation, the very things American colonists had rebelled against to launch their new nation. But it seems mainstream Americans have allowed this to happen by falling into a state of complacency, which is the next stage in the sequence. Coming off of that is a stage of widespread apathy, followed by dependency. And once a dependency on government sets in, a reemergence into bondage is only a step away, completing the cycle."

"The world has changed dramatically since Tyler's day," the reporter countered quickly. "Major advances in technology have changed our lives for the better. The United States continues to thrive well beyond this two-hundred-year timeline."

"Has it? According to James Wilson, a contemporary professor at Hemline University's School of Law, the U.S. is now somewhere between the complacency and apathy stage, with some forty percent of the nation's population currently dependent on the government for its needs. Should its Congress grant amnesty and citizenship to the estimated twenty million aliens transgressing its borders illegally, he predicts the U.S. as we know it will cease to exist within the next five years."

"Do you honestly believe that will happen?"

"Yes. Judging from the leadership I've seen, America is being steered on a treacherous and unprecedented course toward socialism. It is quite evident its Constitution is being systematically dismantled. It would take draconian austerity measures to avert the impending collapse that is sure to come, but I doubt American legislators have the stomach to do this since it might become political suicide to do so."

The reporter offered no reply, eyeing Jacob curiously as her cameraman captured the moment on tape.

"But the heart of America's problem," Jacob went on, "lies within its monetary system."

"Isn't the American greenback the world's most stable currency?" rejoined the woman. "Financial markets abroad consider it to be the international reserve currency. Isn't the price of a barrel of oil measured against the U.S. dollar?"

"That is correct," said Jacob, "but it is inevitable the dollar will be replaced by another currency. The British pound was once the world's reserve currency before the greenback took over. Unfortunately, the U.S. dollar continues to be weakened by the debt-based monetary system that spawns it. Such a system basically extorts the American taxpayer by perpetuating an increasing national debt."

The reporter clearly looked stymied. "I'm not following you."

Jacob smiled knowingly. "It was the wish of America's founding fathers that the power to create and control money be in the hands of the Federal Congress and not in the hands of private bankers. They knew bankers could charge enormous amounts of interest and thereby impose their will on the people through control of the money supply. It was their belief that the citizens should share in the profits of the new nation. But they had to contend with private bankers who devised all kinds of trickery in an attempt to take control of America's money. A powerful European banker by the name of Mayer Anselm Rothschild once said, 'Permit me to issue and control the money of a nation, and I care not who makes its laws.' Bankers eventually got their way, and in 1913, the U.S. Congress passed the Federal Reserve Act. In doing this, the American government officially ceded its power to create money over to bankers."

"But the Federal Reserve is an agency of the U.S. government," the reporter contested adamantly.

Jacob held back the laughter wanting to escape his throat. "That is the misconception most people have. The Federal Reserve is a privately-owned institution. The bankers purposely used the word 'Federal' to mislead the public. Their aim was to keep citizens ignorant of what was really going on."

"The United States seems to have prospered greatly during the last century," rebutted the reporter stubbornly. "What difference did it make whether its Congress or private bankers created the money supply?"

Jacob sighed deeply as if bearing the weight of the world. "For one thing, the U.S. Congress violated its Constitution when it enacted the Federal Reserve Act, for the Constitution specifically states that only Congress shall have the power to coin and regulate the nation's money supply."

DOLPHIN RIDERS

"I still don't-"

Jacob quickly snuffed the reporter's obstinacy, eager to cleanse her ignorance. "U.S. dollars are issued in the form of Federal Reserve Notes, which are considered legal tender and the accepted medium of exchange the world over for goods or services produced. Unfortunately, it is debt-money."

"Meaning?"

"Meaning interest is being charged on every dollar created."

Jacob anticipated the mask of confusion clinging to the woman's face. "Would you like me to illustrate this point?"

"Please do."

"Suppose the U.S. government needs an additional billion dollars to cover its shortfall in tax revenues in order to continue financing its projects. Since it has already given away its sovereignty to simply print the money it needs, it must go to the Federal Reserve to get the shortfall. But the Fed does not just give away the money freely. It is willing to deliver one billion dollars to the U.S. government only in exchange for the government's agreement to pay it back with interest."

The woman felt truly naïve standing before Jacob. The man's outward grizzled appearance did not match the depth of his intellect. Though she was relatively untried and inexperienced as a news reporter, she was determined to make this assignment as interesting as possible.

"Having borrowers pay interest on money given them is common practice with financial institutions," she maintained mulishly. "It's the way of big business."

"So we are led to believe," Jacob muttered dryly. "But had the U.S. government retained its original authority to create legal tender rather than submit this power to a privately-owned agency, it would not have to pay interest on any money printed."

"I thought the U.S. Treasury Department printed the money."

This time Jacob could not restrain the small laugh escaping his lips. "No, I can assure you it does not. Whenever the U.S. Congress needs more money than it reaps in taxes, it authorizes the Treasury Department to print up the shortfall in promissory notes, which are then delivered to the Federal Reserve."

"Aren't promissory notes the same as money?" the reporter shot back. "Don't banks accept them as the equivalent of legal tender?"

Jacob's tone portrayed immense patience. "Promissory notes issued by the U.S. Treasury are actually U.S. bonds, which are not money. They are nothing more than the government's promise to pay back the funds it needs to run the country. Think of them as IOUs. A lender will not accept them unless there is an underlying confidence that the borrower will be able to pay back the loan. The drawback to this is that the borrower must pay back interest on top of the money borrowed. As a general rule, the amount of interest tacked on is dependent on just how much confidence the lender has in the borrower's ability to make good on the loan."

The reporter nodded in understanding. "Are you referring to the borrower's credit rating?"

"Yes. Currently, the U.S. holds a double-A-plus bond rating. It used to hold a triple-A rating, which is the best rating a borrower can have. But according to Standard and Poor, the credit of the U.S. has been downgraded since 2011, pushing global financial markets into uncharted territory. Even with the temporary fix of the Fed artificially holding down interest rates through a careless policy of monetary easing, the U.S. will eventually have to offer much higher interest rates on its bonds in order to sell them once the easing is lifted."

"Why do you see it as careless? Didn't this policy keep the American economy from collapsing?"

Jacob groped for the simplest explanation he could throw at her. "It is careless because the longer it is kept in place, the more it erodes the purchasing power of the dollar. The longer the program goes, the more sharply interest rates will spike once it is ended. Inflation will kick in and the price of everything will skyrocket. The American government will be forced to rely more heavily on the Fed if it is to keep running, borrowing more than ever before."

Jake noted the gleaning in the woman's eyes. "But the saddest thing of all," he continued, "is that money is created out of nothing."

The reporter's glimmer of comprehension abruptly faded. "You're losing me?"

"Let's go back to the billion dollars the U.S. government needs. In exchange for one billion dollars in Treasury bonds, the Federal Reserve will print up one billion dollars in paper money as payment. The Fed's cost of printing up one billion dollars in paper greenbacks is nominal and will probably be less than a thousand dollars. The transaction, however, has indebted the American taxpayer to pay interest on the loan."

"I see your point," conceded the reporter.

"The process does not end there," added Jacob. "From that one-billion-dollar transaction, the Fed is now legally allowed to lend out another fifteen billion to other borrowers."

"Like who?"

"State and municipal governments, foreign countries, businesses and individuals. Essentially any entity with a credit rating acceptable to the Fed."

"The reporter appeared to mull this. "Sounds as though money is being brought into existence by an institution that lacks the assets to support it."

Jacob grinned broadly, happy to see he was getting through to her. "It is! Bankers create money out of nothing simply by transcribing numbers in a ledger book and then giving out loans based on these numbers. Organizations and people who receive the loans can then write checks, which are backed by the numbers in the account ledgers of the bankers. But now the bankers can receive periodic payment on their loans with interest. It's all numbers, be it numbers in a ledger, on checks, or on dollar bills. Money that is not backed by real assets such as gold or silver is fiat in nature and holds no intrinsic value. It is actually nothing more than numbers on paper."

The reporter nodded again, her face fully mirroring this newfound enlightenment.

"It is a most diabolical scheme," avouched Jacob, eager to go on. "Using this process, many banks outside the Fed can legally lend out up to fifty times the amount of funds they have on deposit, essentially creating money out of nothing and then charging interest on it."

The woman's face suddenly clouded. "You make it sound as though paper money is worthless," she objected obstinately. "If people are willing to accept it as a medium of exchange, then it must nonetheless hold value and provide a basis of wealth."

With measured calmness, Jacob shook his head slowly. "True value lies in enterprise, innovation, and all the things produced through people's labors. Wealth is created by producers, not by redistributors of wealth like banks and governments, which do not create it. Paper money is merely a crude representation of wealth, and generally not an equitable one. Think of it as a rather abstract, inflated form of human energy. But it is not the money that is the actual problem, but the very system upon which it is based, for the system concentrates the collective energies of many into the hands of a few. The United States along with many other nations have been plunged into terrible and overwhelming debt since the implementation of the debt-money system. Following the passage of the Federal Reserve Act, the debt owed by the U.S. government has mushroomed to well over fifteen trillion dollars and continues of grow wildly out of control."

"So," said the woman, "aside from the greed, complacency, and apathy you contend has taken hold of the American people, you believe that runaway debt will be the biggest threat of all to the survival of the U.S.?"

"Most assuredly," affirmed Jacob. "When the Fed and banks create money through lending, they only bring into existence the principal amount loaned, not the interest that is tacked on. Money that was created as principal on a loan coming due in subsequent years must be used to pay interest coming due today. If all the loans throughout the world were called in on the same day, there would not be enough money in existence to cover all the interest coming due, so a portion of the borrowers would be in default. Since 1950, nominal debt in the U.S. has grown faster than the economy each year. The toll this debt takes on society has also risen in tandem with it mainly because more and more of the economy is going toward servicing the debt. That means a smaller percentage is available to produce and maintain the things that truly contribute to the country's standard of living. This has a direct impact on the nation's infrastructure, which is already being inadequately serviced and in decline. As this debt burden worsens, it is not inconceivable that bridges will start collapsing due to lack of maintenance."

"You paint a rather bleak and dismal picture," retorted the reporter. "But as I recall, U.S. debt has actually declined several times in the past, most recently in the late 1990s. So how can it be that the debt always keeps growing?"

Jacob noted a tinge of smugness in her tone. "When I speak of the national debt in the U.S., I am not only referring to that owed by the Federal government, but to the total sum owed by the American society as a whole, which also includes consumers and businesses, as well as state and local governments. In 1981 alone, U.S. Federal debt surpassed the one trillion-dollar level and was growing exponentially. But state and local debt in combination with business and consumer debt exceeded six trillion, three times the value of all the land and buildings in America at the time. And in 2005, even though the Federal debt reached eight trillion, the total American debt had gone over forty-one trillion. Suffice it to say that an ever increasing amount of money must be borrowed to make good on the debt coming due."

The reporter just stared, unable to come up with a rebuttal, and Jacob seized the moment to drive home his point further.

"The American people have become tenants and debt slaves to the Federal Reserve and its agents in the land their forefathers conquered, for once a government borrows from a bank, it becomes servant to the lender and is no longer sovereign. Thomas Jefferson had warned about the consequences of such a thing happening, knowing that bankers could end up gaining secret control of the nation. And Woodrow Wilson, the very President under whose administration the Federal Reserve Act was enacted, rued the passage of the bill just before he died, stating that he had betrayed his country by allowing the actual reins of power to fall into the hands of a few dominant men. Enactment of the Act amounted to conquest of a nation without a shot being fired. Undoubtedly it was perhaps the most outrageous swindle in the history of mankind, for no matter who is elected to high office, the plutocracy that controls the Fed will seek to corrupt them by whatever means necessary, making many of them their agents in order to run the government from behind the scenes."

The reporter's response was immediate. "Your viewpoint reeks of conspiracy theory."

"So I've been told," Jacob relinquished airily before shaking his head adamantly. "But unless you can show me where I'm wrong, I still contend that the U.S. government is controlled by a shadowy cabal that is directly responsible for the decline of America and the capitalism which turned it into an economic giant, a decline based on greed, deception, and fraud. Make no mistake about it, these people wield enormous power, giving them the means to manipulate events not only in America but throughout the world. The UN intrusion you witnessed earlier is but a small example of this power. Here in Aquaria we have reason to believe they're making plans to overhaul the World Bank in order to dominate every nation on earth through the implementation of carbon taxes and military action to enforce them. Once this scheme is brought into play, the citizens of the world will be forcibly marched along a gradual path of economic servitude which will inevitably lead to absolute enslavement and unfettered oversight of every aspect of our existence by a one world government."

Jacob took pause, deciding to add one more thing. "This plutocracy controls most of the mainstream news media and information centers in the westernized countries of the world, suppressing the truth and typically disseminating embellished and misleading news to suit their objectives. I seriously doubt this interview and what you captured on tape earlier on will ever be shown to the world in its entirety. Events will be doctored or cleverly altered to portray this colony in the most vile light possible."

With eyes widened in agitated shock, the reporter considered challenging the allegation, but from what she had seen from behind the scenes at the IBC, she suspected there to be partial truth in what the man before her was saying.

Deciding to ignore the remark, she approached the discussion from another angle. "Surely a man like you, who has apparently spent much time studying the shortcomings of America, must have a solution to its problems."

"To begin with, its Congress must regain its sovereignty by repealing the Federal Reserve Act and issuing legal currency that is debt-free. Unfortunately, John F. Kennedy had been in the process of doing this very thing before he was assassinated."

Jacob let the last sentence hang in the air so that the implication was clear.

"Are you implying that John Kennedy was murdered to keep the Federal Reserve Act from being repealed?"

"To rule out such a possibility would be illogical. The point I'm trying to make is that the power and motives of the people who stand to benefit the most from a debt-based monetary system should not be underestimated. These people are extremely ruthless and will go to any lengths to protect their interests. They will even instigate wars, financing opposing sides so that governments are forced to borrow for the sake of national defense. The death of thousands or even millions of people means nothing to them. In fact, they care not which side wins as long as the countries involved are in debt to them. These people are responsible for much of the hunger, poverty, disease, and misery that exist in the world today."

The woman stared pensively, deciding which way to steer the interview. "So you believe all bankers are evil," she stated bluntly.

Jacob sighed. "Certainly not all. Most are merely naïve servants of a system they deem to be benign. They are unable to see the deep-rooted malignancy, nor the widespread harm it causes."

The reporter turned her gaze from Jacob, taking in her surroundings with assessing eyes. "Has debt been so unkind to this enterprise?" she asked appraisingly. "Surely you would never have been able to develop an operation of this magnitude without the assistance of bankers."

An enigmatic smile crossed Jacob's face. "Aquaria carries no debt burden whatsoever. It remains unhampered by financial liability of any kind."

The reporter's jaw dropped. "How is that possible?"

Jacob continued to smile. "What is produced here greatly exceeds Aquaria's consumption needs. You must remember that true wealth is really an excess of product over consumption. Every person living in this colony has a vested interest in its productivity. As such, their main concern is directed at minimizing the cost of goods and services they require for themselves."

"Are you saying everyone shares in the profits?"

Jacob nodded.

The implication was now clear to the reporter. "So it seems this community has embraced a culture that is quite socialistic in nature," she concluded. Her tone abruptly became admonishing. "Isn't that rather hypocritical, considering your negative view on where America is headed because of its recent leanings toward socialism?"

"Do not confuse this operation with socialism," Jacob said patiently. "The various forms of socialism this planet has seen during the last century have never worked, and for that matter, cannot work simply because it takes away an individual's desire to be productive. Under a socialistic system of government, citizens soon realize there is no incentive in working hard or starting a business when the bulk of their earnings will be redistributed to others who are basically non-productive by comparison. They quickly learn it is far more rewarding to enjoy the fruits of other people's labors rather than work. Most would rather sit idle than be a contributing member of society. Under socialism, entrepreneurs are penalized for their efforts while the non-producers are rewarded with a share of the wealth."

"Do all your adult residents work?" the reporter queried. She made it a point to keep her question explicit, having noticed numerous children at play within the complex.

"Yes, but not necessarily in the physical sense. Everyone has something to offer to make this operation a success. And those that can no longer work because they have become elderly and frail also contribute, imparting their wisdom to the young. In short, everyone is taken care of. Think of Aquaria as a super-organism, one that provides for the needs of the community inhabiting her, just as we provide for the needs of the cells in our bodies. Being essentially self-sufficient and autonomous, Aquaria yields all the things a human needs to live a comfortable life. We have more than a few laboratories devoted to making scientific advances and increasing productivity. Research and development of new technologies aimed at improving life on this planet is one of our primary objectives. Residents have their own living quarters. All food, power, lighting and even clothing are derived from the sea. A medical center provides health care, and there are numerous forms of recreation and entertainment available to keep the inhabitants happy and content. And transportation costs within this city are virtually zero. Residents have none of the expenditures people normally have in land-based cities."

"What about taxes?" the reporter continued to probe tenaciously. She had read some of the material on Tursiops Worldwide on her way to the colony, discovering one particularly interesting fact. "Am I to understand this business enterprise pays no taxes of any kind?"

"That is correct. Our corporate charter is registered with the island nation of Anguilla, a tax-free haven."

"What about business overhead? It must be exceptionally expensive to operate a facility as large as this."

"Operating expenses as a percentage of revenues are relatively small. The costs associated with providing goods and services in this colony amount only to maintenance of the power-generating facilities and city infrastructure."

The reporter abruptly flashed a devious grin. "What if your residents want to travel abroad? What do they use for money?"

"All the people within this colony possess a savings account with credits to draw upon," Jacob replied blithely. "These credits can be exchanged for a legal tender of their choosing depending on their destination."

"Does anyone living here have financial problems?" asked the woman brusquely.

Jacob sensed she had to make a valiant effort at looking for any negative she could exploit, but he was now convinced it was all for show. "By tapping into the vast reservoirs of energy and nutrients stockpiled in the sea," he answered effusively, "we have liberated a flood-tide of the things vital to human sustenance. This translates into growing assets to be shared by all those who reside here. A bounty of all the necessities required for a stress-free and contented existence, including various forms of entertainment and medical treatment are freely available for everyone to enjoy. The only cost to each person is that they contribute something meaningful to the overall health of the operation. Poverty and financial hardship of any kind does not exist in Aquaria."

The reporter glanced at her watch and decided it was time to wrap up this portion of the interview. It was crucial she transmit the video segments to IBC headquarters immediately. From her point of view, she had so far been unable to unearth anything that would depict the colony as an environmental abuser. All her instincts told her that Jacob was being sincere in refuting Allotey's claim that Tursiops Worldwide was destroying the local ocean habitat.

She faced the camera, eliciting her best smile. "There you have it, friends. This is Amelia Amhurst of IBC News reporting from the floating city of Aquaria, the planet's first large-scale sea colony."

-8-

Rafael Cardoza looked on, enjoying the first rumblings of amusement that rose up from his belly. The scream filling the air was exceptionally high-pitched and piercing, sounding like the shriek of a woman consumed by panic, and it was this that made him titter aloud.

Trapped within the cage, the man glanced back at the animal trying to get at him, unaware he had lost control of his own sphincter. Terrified, he spun his head around and pressed his face up against the bars, riveting Cardoza with wild, frenzied eyes.

DOLPHIN RIDERS

As Cardoza watched, his mind reverted back to a similar event that had taken place several years earlier. Ever since then, he would always see the same scene unfold in his mind's eye. No matter who was being killed using this method, he would always see the same face and hear the same beseeching cries regardless of who was in the cage.

"You have to believe me!" the man pleaded, his quavering voice falling off to a crestfallen whimper. Looking back over his shoulder, he watched in horror as the gate came up a few more inches. Held at bay for the moment, the animal bellowed ferociously, a deafening, enervating rumble that quaked the air as it clawed and raked at the limited opening in frustrated rage. Tenaciously it tried to squeeze itself under the obstructing barrier that separated the two halves of the steel enclosure. Only a few more inches and it would get through.

With renewed vigor, the man gripped the bars, tugging and pushing with maddened strength, attempting to jam his pudgy body through the imprisoning steel. "I don't know where the gold is," he shouted in desperation. "Nick Henderson is the man you want."

Cardoza held up a hand, belaying the gate's rise. "Then you'll tell me where I can find him?"

"I keep telling you, I don't know." The words were screeched out like nails being dragged across a slate blackboard.

Cardoza's nose crinkled, the foul stench of McPherson's voiding bowels reaching out to assault him. "You do not deny you had gone to meet him, that he was to show you a stash of gold of considerable value?"

McPherson shot another quick glance behind him before shaking the bars savagely again. "He never showed. I went there to meet him, and he wasn't there. Why do you keep asking the same question?"

Cardoza grinned wolfishly, enjoying McPherson's torment. "If you went there to meet him, then I have to assume the gold must be hidden somewhere in that cove."

"Yes, yes," McPherson screamed. "Lemme outta here and I'll help you find it."

"Then you admit you know where it is?" Cardoza persisted. Though he had grilled McPherson again and again on this same point, he had to be certain the man was not holding back on anything.

McPherson's response came out in a strained gasp, as though he could not get enough air into his lungs. "It's somewhere in that cove...that's all I know." Beads of perspiration mingled with tears dribbled shamelessly down the man's ashen cheeks as he whipped his head around to take inventory of the beast again.

At sensing McPherson was close to fainting, Cardoza presented a face full of compassion. "I'll let you out on one condition." This was the part he loved best, giving victims the pretense of a last minute reprieve.

McPherson spun around, his eyes suddenly filled with hope. "Anything...anything," he stammered.

"I'll let you out," Cardoza repeated, "if you give me the names of the men who attacked me." The thought that he had been attacked by a force of unknown assailants infuriated him. He had been caught off guard back in that hideaway, losing five of his best men. And just when he was bringing in reinforcements to remedy the situation, the *Usurpar* had been holed by a pair of torpedoes. To his disbelief a sub had surfaced moments later, upon which two men had climbed out on deck. Adding insult to injury, they had fired a missile that had destroyed his luxury helicopter while it sat on the vessel's helipad, turning it into a raging inferno.

Wearily, McPherson fell to his knees, all sense of hope finally deserting him. "If I knew I would tell you," he sobbed.

Finally convinced there was no more information to be gained, Cardoza motioned the gatekeeper with a cruel, nodding smile, glad to put an end to the man's incessant whining, and in seconds there was nothing to keep the creature away from its intended prey.

McPherson cried out again, ever more shrilly this time, a piteous wail that sought to discourage the beast from attacking. But the big cat had not been fed in days, and it was ravenous with hunger. Cardoza had purchased the animal from a now defunct game preserve and made it a practice never to pamper the beast, wanting it to remain as feral and vicious as possible. At 550 pounds, the Bengal let out another throaty roar, displaying a set of fierce yellow fangs just before it leaped, and Walter McPherson's scream was abruptly silenced as the carnivore tore out his throat.

Cardoza watched as his pet feasted, fascinated by the look frozen on the man's face. Even death could not extinguish the utter terror that had animated the man's features only moments earlier. The eyes continued to bulge grotesquely in a wild-eyed stare, with mouth agape and lips drawn back in muted agony. They all carried the same look when terminated in this manner, but the face was not that of the naval captain he had executed back then. It belonged to another.

Satisfied for the moment, the Colombian drug lord turned away. He had murdered more than thirty victims using the tiger over the last several years, mostly underlings who cheated or stole from him, but also those who offended or failed him. The thrill of it, however, had gradually lost its luster, no longer producing the same level of excitement within him as it once had. But it did serve a useful purpose, he reminded himself.

Anxiously, Cardoza scanned the faces of the others privy to the scene, fifteen subordinates who worked for him. The apprehension he sought was evident in each face, though carefully masked in a show of contempt for the man just slain. And as always, they avoided making eye contact with him. Furtively, he shifted his gaze to the burly individual standing next to him, eager to gauge the Russian's reaction to the killing, and almost immediately he was both pleased and troubled by what he saw. Although he had invited Zinova here for another reason, he felt it prudent to show the man who he was dealing with. The execution served that purpose. It was a subtle yet stark reminder of how he dealt with those who failed him.

"Such is the fate of those who are careless with my product," Cardoza said, turning to Zinova. "This man lost several hundred pounds of cocaine to pirates at sea."

But as he scrutinized the Russian's face, Cardoza found himself growing increasingly irritated. It was not the reaction he had expected. Zinova continued to peer fixedly at the grisly sight as though aroused by the nakedness of a beautiful woman. He seemed completely oblivious to the implied threat.

All at once, several conflicting thoughts raced through Cardoza's mind. *He takes great pleasure in the spectacle of gruesome death, and that tells me he's right for the job. But he shows no fear at what happens to those who thwart me, and that could be a problem. A man without fear cannot be controlled.*

This last thought made Cardoza feel uneasy, and it suddenly occurred to him that Zinova might actually be many times more dangerous than the beast currently gorging itself within the cage. Men like Zinova were a rare breed, and he knew his plan would have little chance of succeeding without such a man. Having suffered a staggering loss amounting to nearly $300 million in uninsured damages eight years earlier, the value of Cardoza's vast holdings had been cut by nearly twenty-five percent. He had made it a practice to avoid insuring his ships and equipment. Underwriters were not about to make payment on a claim of this magnitude unless they first conducted an investigation. And an investigation had the potential of uncovering the true nature of his business, which would have made any claims null and void anyway.

Inwardly, Cardoza fumed. His tuna fleet had vanished without a trace, with all hands missing, including Pedro, his loyal and trusted nephew. The San Carlo, San Pinto and San Diablo were all gone, including their hidden cargos of heroin and cocaine bound for the U.S. The drugs alone had held a street value almost equal to the value of his fleet. And if that were not enough, replacing his custom-made copter had cost him an irksome $8 million, while repairing the damage to the Usurpar had set him back another $5 million. But now he was about to recoup those losses.

"You are fully prepared?" Cardoza asked. "Your team is assembled and in readiness?" He swung his gaze to the other two men accompanying

Zinova. One was almost as big as the Russian and could have passed for his brother, a brute of a man with a bull neck who seemed to be just as fascinated with the shredded corpse in the cage as his boss. Zinova had introduced him as Drakov, though Cardoza had already forgotten his first name. The second man, however, cut a more striking figure. Though slightly smaller than Drakov, he displayed thick muscular arms that bulged from a sleeveless shirt. And while he carried an unsightly bulbous nose that jutted to one side of his angular, pugnacious face, it was his eyes that immediately caught an onlooker's attention. Cardoza had at first thought the man to be cross-eyed when he looked directly at him, but then he realized the folly of this impression. The man's eyes did not match. They were at odds with each other, with one blue and the other brown. But it was not these seemingly hideous attributes that made this man stand out from his associates. Rather it was the revulsion Cardoza sensed emanating from him. The execution he had witnessed held no allure for him, certainly nothing even remotely matching that of Zinova and Drakov. The man was clearly repulsed by what had just taken place.

Zinova paused to tear his gaze away from the captivating sight within the cage, the spell of it seemingly broken. "At midnight, we will set the trap." Abruptly, his eyes fell back on the mutilated body.

Cardoza held back a scowl, offering instead a casual nod. Zinova's aloof taciturn manner grated on him to no end, and it was becoming evident that the Russian had a definite tendency to avoid as little conversation as possible. Reputed to have killed more than 300 men, Zinova was a bear of a man, weighing close to 270 pounds and standing a head taller than Cardoza's five foot ten frame.

As Cardoza studied him, he was now certain all the things he had heard about the Russian were true. According to rumor, Karloff Zinova had been a major in the Spetsnaz, and Cardoza knew that Spetsnaz commandos had been the cream of the crop among Soviet combat troops during the Cold War, elite warriors comparable to U.S. Navy Seals in their training. Hand to hand combat was one of their specialties, and they were considered to be some of the best knife fighters in the world.

It was in Afghanistan where Zinova had initially earned his reputation as a killing machine, spreading fear through the ranks of the mujahideen. And it was the mujahideen who had begun referring to him as "The Devil's Reaper," in part because of the sickle displayed on the Soviet flag he represented, but mainly because of all the losses they had suffered in the bloody battles against him. But over time they had shortened the reference, simply calling him "The Reaper," and the name had stuck ever since. By the time the Soviets were ousted from the embattled country, Zinova had turned mercenary, offering his services to those who had the money to meet his exorbitant fee.

Cardoza couldn't help but wonder if Zinova was still the warrior he once was. In his estimation, "The Reaper" had to be well past his prime, with more than twenty years having transpired since Afghanistan and the fall of the Soviet empire.

Zinova withdrew his stare from the cage, impaling Cardoza with steely gray eyes. "You have the money?"

The drug lord glanced sharply at one of his lackeys, snapping his fingers pompously. The man immediately came forward, placing a small valise on a nearby table and opening the case.

"Four million now and the remainder once you successfully complete the mission," Cardoza said. "Would you like to count it?"

Stoically, Zinova closed the valise. "I don't think that will be necessary." Turning, he left with the money, his lieutenants on each side of him.

As Cardoza watched him go, he wondered if he had made the right choice in choosing this man for such a bold undertaking.

-9-

Destiny awoke with a start, aware of her own gasping. The terrible vision still clung to her, lucidly lodged in her mind's eye. *Colossal, seemingly towering to the heavens, it loomed ever closer, a wall bearing incomprehensible destruction. Driven onward, it was an unstoppable juggernaut of gargantuan proportions, spawned by some unimaginable yet unknown force.*

Jake sat up drowsily, stirred from deep slumber by her erratic thrashing. He rubbed his eyes, brushing away the last tendrils of sleep before glancing at his wristwatch. It was just past 2 in the morning. Shifting his gaze to Destiny, it took him only a moment to perceive what was wrong. "It was that dream again, wasn't it?"

Destiny nodded, vestiges of dread continuing to haunt her. The same nightmare had been plaguing her sleep every night for the past several weeks now.

"It's just a dream," Jake consoled.

"There was something new in this one."

"Tell me about it."

Destiny sighed. "You sure you want to hear it? You look like you could use more sleep."

"Lay it on me!"

"There was an eagle in it this time. It was huge, easily the size of the

Angel."

"That's one big bird."

"The twins were with me, and we were standing in darkness waiting for it. It was calling out to me, but I..." Destiny groped for words.

"Go on," Jake encouraged gently.

"It wanted us to climb on its back when it landed. I sensed it was evil and had no intention of doing so, but it said if I refused the consequences would be disastrous."

"So what did you do?"

"Since disastrous usually implies death and destruction, my options were pretty much limited. So the children and I got on its back, and it flew up into the night sky. But then something happened to give me comfort and strength. You were suddenly there with us, and I knew we would all be okay. There was also someone else with you."

"Who?"

"I think it was Fernando."

"Fernando!?"

"Yes. Next thing I remember was the twins and I were on the Angel looking up as you and Fernando flew away. Fernando was holding onto a set of reins, controlling the eagle the way a rider controls a horse. Even though we were safe for the moment, we had to make some kind of arrangement with the Eagle Master."

"You mean Fernando?"

"No. I think it was someone else. The dream became jumbled at that point, but I vaguely remember us threatening the Eagle Master with some kind of action to keep him from murdering innocent people and bringing destruction on Aquaria."

"Can you recall what we threatened?"

Destiny shook her head in frustration. Both Jacob and her mother had taught her long ago never to ignore her dreams, for they often foreshadowed the approach of an undesirable event, one which could sometimes be averted if the correct action were taken. "I only know Aquaria was still in danger and could be destroyed."

She paused, trying hard to remember more. "At that point, the dream became confusing and hazy," she finally said. "It merged into the recurrent one I've been having over the past several weeks."

"It's still only a dream," Jake reiterated. "Most of the time they're meaningless."

Destiny arose from the bed, her comely young features marred by unsettling worry. "What if it's not?"

Jake stared up at her, knowing exactly what she meant. *Millions of people would die. Maybe hundreds of millions.* He was well familiar with

Destiny's recurrent nightmare. She had told him about it the first time it had intruded its way into her dreams. "Then we'll stop it from happening!" he stated matter-of-factly.

"I don't know if that's possible anymore."

"You're not serious?"

Destiny let out a deep sigh, sitting back down next to Jake and looking into his eyes. "Something has happened to me, Jay Jay, something I can't explain." She hesitated, seeing the surprise registering on his face. He had become a believer and now she was failing him.

"You made a nuclear missile vanish into thin air," Jake reminded her. His tone was just short of incredulous.

"We all did that," she replied softly. "I was merely the lens that channeled the combined energy of all of us." She shook her head sadly. "But I seem to have lost this ability since that day. I don't think I'll be able to do something like that ever again."

"You have no way of knowing that."

"It's what I feel deep inside."

Jake had difficulty believing what he was hearing. Negative thinking was not a part of the girl he had come to love. "Have you discussed any of this with your mother?"

Destiny fidgeted uncomfortably, pulling her eyes from Jake's penetrating gaze. "Mother is not the same person she used to be, either. With the memory of her former life now fully restored, she no longer has visions of things to come."

"Maybe not now, but perhaps later."

"Jacob thinks she lost this ability when she regained her memory. He believes her previous failure at remembering her past somehow gave her the power to glimpse the future."

"Well you're still the same," Jake insisted, offering a big smile to lighten Destiny's dispirited mood, "a girl with a heart the size of Montana. Unlike your mother, you've always known who you truly are."

"Do I? Back at Navassa, I saw a side of myself I never knew existed, a side I'm not even sure I should be ashamed of. Had I been given a choice, I would have killed Raduyev in order to save you."

"But you didn't have to make that choice."

Destiny's manner hardened. "If ever I'm confronted with a choice like that again, then I wouldn't hesitate to do whatever it took to save you. The pod feels the same way."

"Hopefully, you'll never be faced with having to make such a choice."

Destiny had no desire to continue the discussion. Instinctually she knew that Jay Jay was the actual cause behind this change in her. In analyzing it, she could only conclude that falling in love could sometimes have unexpected consequences. It had affected her and the dolphins in a profound way, and some of the personality traits that defined Jake Javolyn had somehow infected the rest of them.

Or maybe they hadn't been infected at all. Maybe JJ's natural tendency to protect had inadvertently awakened something that lay dormant in each of them. Back at Navassa, JJ had killed twenty-three men including Raduyev in order to save her and prevent a monstrous plot from occurring, and the entire pod had learned a sobering lesson from that. In any event, they would no longer remain pacifists in the face of malice. They would now defend themselves and all those they loved. They would stand and fight, asserting their right to live. And in so doing they would truly be alive. Prior to Jay Jay coming into her life, a void had existed within her, though she had been basically happy. But now she truly felt alive, aware of the smoldering passion that burned deep within her.

Jake climbed out of bed and kissed Destiny lightly on the forehead.

"I'm taking the twins to Haiti," she decided to tell him. Up until this moment she still considered postponing the trip even though it would have greatly disappointed the twins, but now some gut instinct deep inside beckoned her on. More than ever now, she knew she had to visit the cave behind the cove's mystical waterfall without further delay, certain she would find the meaning of that relentless chilling dream. "We're going with Zimby."

Jake's jaw dropped, and he frowned in consternation. He had not expected this. "Why now?" he demanded curtly.

"Why not now?" she said quietly. "I promised I'd take them back to the cove for a short visit. Now's good a time as any."

"No, it's not," Jake disagreed quixotically. "Things are beginning to heat up around here, and I can only imagine what the UN will be sending our way next."

"Exactly," Destiny acknowledged smoothly. "Maybe it's best the twins are out of harm's way."

Jake shook his head stubbornly. "I can't break away now. Jacob needs me here."

"I didn't ask you to come, now did I?" Destiny countered assertively. "Zimby will be there to protect us."

Jake pondered this before furthering his objection. Even though the colony had tactical defensive measures set up to counter most intrusive threats coming its way, he couldn't be absolutely certain they would be entirely effective. "Alright," he grudgingly conceded, "but what about Cardoza and his mob? You never know when he'll show up uninvited again."

DOLPHIN RIDERS

"I would think he's learned his lesson by now. The cove's security system has already stopped him twice. He'd be a fool to try again."

"How can you be so sure of that? What if the system fails or he finds a way around it?" Jake's argument grew fierce. "Cardoza is like a ravenous lion with the scent of prey in his nostrils. The smell of gold is just too much for him to ignore even if he gets a bloody nose going after it. I still think it's far too risky."

"Danger, it seems, has become a way of life for us, Jay Jay," she pointed out pragmatically. "Whether you accept it or not, danger is forever going to be our companion, no matter where we go or what we do from here on out. This is the path we have chosen."

Jake opened his mouth to vehemently protest her logic, knowing how headstrong she could be once she had made up her mind on something. He remembered how she had struck out for Navassa Island with her mother and Bashir years earlier without him, brutally aware of the near-calamitous consequences of those actions had he not pursued her and intervened.

The discordant sound of ringing stopped the brewing words before they could escape Jake's lips. He picked up the phone in annoyance. "What is it?" he said gruffly.

"We have a problem, Jay Jay!" It was the voice of Ez, her tone sounding grave and concerned, and Jake's rising exasperation immediately thawed.

"What's wrong?" he asked apprehensively.

"A freighter may be under attack five miles south of us, but I have no way of confirming it." Ez went on quickly before Jake could interrupt. "Let me replay the transmission I intercepted and you be the judge."

A cacophony sounding like squelching bagpipes assaulted Jake's ear before a voice suddenly blurted, "-being boarded by an unknown party. This is the Southern Star. Our ship has been boarded by-". Abruptly the distress call cut out, replaced once more by the stepped, distorted drone of bagpipes.

Jake digested this, detecting a trace of panic in the speaker's words. "Is that all you got, Ez?"

"Yes, Jay Jay. I tried hailing the Southern Star but there was no answer. My radar sensors indicate the ship is currently not under way. The disruption in the ship's radio transmission suggests that the broadcast was purposely being jammed. What actions do you recommend?"

"Have you alerted Mat about this?"

"Not yet. I thought it best to call you first."

Jake assessed the information thoughtfully before replying. He had to agree with Ez. Seal training had taught him the sound of bagpipes displacing a radio broadcast was often typical of deliberate jamming. And under the present circumstances it hinted strongly that the vessel was under attack by hijackers. "Inform Mat of the situation. Tell him I'm taking Achilles to check out the ship."

Jake put down the phone.

-10-

The band of men moved through the rugged terrain with the stealth of phantoms. Under the cover of night, they had been airlifted by two heavily built rotary wing aircraft to a desolate stretch of beach along a minor headland jutting out into the sea. A map of Haiti's western coastline showed it to be the Devil's Horn. Located roughly 6.5 kilometers south of their objective, the area seemed the logical choice for launching their covert incursion.

The operation had been carefully planned using a set of aerial photographs provided by the man who had hired them, a notorious kingpin within the Colombian drug cartel. The photographs had revealed a beaten path that wound its way through the foothills just upland of their drop-off point. Had they followed the footpath to its terminus, it would have led to a small coastal village harboring a modest fleet of fishing boats. Oddly enough, the village did not exhibit the squalid, ramshackle conditions so typical of Haitian communities. It was orderly and clean, with all the structures and watercraft seemingly well kept. In fact, no sign of decay or garbage was evident anywhere. But it was not the village that held their interest. It was the sequestered cove bordering the trail to the south of the village.

Dawn was still hours away when Victor Belachek called a halt to their trek, a burly man with thick muscular arms and a bulbous lopsided nose dominating his bellicose face. He judged they had arrived at a point less than a kilometer from where the land fell steeply away. Unlike most of the terrain behind them, the photographs had shown a significant shift in the amount of vegetation covering this particular tract of land. Further back, the trail had traversed a largely defoliated landscape, only sporadically covered in low-lying brush. But where they now stood, he estimated they were just inside the tree line of a teeming rainforest. At least that was what the photos had indicated. As if to confirm this he scanned his surroundings only to be met with a pervading shroud of darkness.

Pulling a penlight from a pouch, he consulted the GPS unit he carried before checking his wristwatch. His face immediately clouded. Though they had arrived at the intended standby point, he noticed he was more than fifteen minutes late. A veteran of countless battles in Afghanistan and a former Spetsnaz operative, he hated falling behind schedule, always looking to carry out missions precisely as planned even though it would not matter in this case. Nevertheless, it made him wonder if he was getting too old for this sort of thing. After all, wasn't it he who had led his men this far, the one who had set the pace? And now they were going to attempt to penetrate a dense forest abundant with heavy undergrowth to reach their objective, this based on the feedback he had been given. He had been forewarned to be vigilant of booby traps set up along the way, perilous obstacles the drug lord's men had encountered during their last foray into this area. More than half of Cardoza's twenty man raiding party had been injured because of those hidden traps. They had stupidly tried to navigate these uncharted woods in total darkness, but he would not make that same mistake.

And while it was assumed those same obstacles would be no less dangerous during daylight hours, he would worry about that later, for right now he and his men had time to kill. Turning, he addressed the closest man in a whisper. "Pass the word for the men to hunker down and get some rest. Tell them to be ready to move at noon." This was part of the plan he and Zinova had meticulously crafted, a time when the sunlight would penetrate the forest canopy most effectively, a time when they would have a better chance at avoiding hidden traps.

With a hand resting idly on the stock of his assault rifle, Belachek stretched out on the damp ground, curiously wondering why Cardoza was so interested in taking control of the small basin beyond the forest.

-11-

The explosion of vivid radiance against the black void of hydrospace was dazzling as it streamed past. Whisked along by Achilles, Jake clung tightly to the albino's back, entranced by the flaring brilliance washing over him. Agitated by the pressure wave created by the dolphin's passage, thousands of microscopic, single-celled dinoflagellates erupted like miniature supernovas each second, sending out starbursts of bioluminescence that swirled and eddied around man and dolphin.

Jake focused his thoughts, pulling his attention from the mesmerizing light show. *How much further, Achilles?*

Achilles' answer resonated within Jake's head, a gentle puff that brushed up against his mind like a soundless whisper. *Just under a thousand meters, Jay Jay.*

Jake had grown used to the mind-link he shared with the dolphin, and now he sensed something else lingering within the midst of Achilles'

thoughts.
What?
Destiny asks that you reconsider doing this, Jay Jay. She feels you are needlessly putting yourself in harm's way.
But you don't agree with her, do you? Jake knew he was reading Achilles correctly.
No, Jay Jay. Some things cannot be ignored, and this is one of them.
Satisfied, Jake shot off another thought. *Then we're in agreement and you know what I expect of you.*
Yes, Jay Jay.

Under the cover of darkness, the pair approached the freighter ten feet below the surface in the darkened sea. The moon had not yet risen, and the trail of sparkling bioluminescence left in their wake might be construed as nothing more than the footprint of a large oceanic predator by a vigilant observer aboard the large vessel. With the ship's engine currently at idle, Jake's task was simplified.

Another minute passed before Achilles slowed, and Jake opened the catch bag clipped to the belt girding his waist, aware of the ship's hull no more than three feet away. Unraveling the knotted nylon rope, he let the weighted end descend into the depths beneath him, allowing the line to extend to its full length. Sixty feet would be more than sufficient to achieve the goal he sought. Satisfied that the rope was untangled, Jake handed the three-pronged grappling hook to Achilles who readily grasped it with one of his prehensile appendages. Abruptly, the dolphin swam off laterally into the darkness as Jake pulled the line back up, finally removing the 3-lb weight from the end of the rope and letting it fall into the depths. Taking two wraps of the line around his hand, Jake communicated his readiness to the albino.

You ready, Achilles?
Ready, Jay Jay.

Almost immediately, Jake felt the line go taut as it angled downward. Achilles would need sufficient depth in order to build enough speed to launch himself clear of the water. The line suddenly slackened, and Jake knew Achilles had reversed direction. He glimpsed a shadowy blur streak past trailed by a swirling wake of twinkling motes as Achilles leapt clear of the sea. Caught in the backwash of the dolphin's mighty tail fluke, Jake was momentarily tumbled backward before he steadied himself. In his mind's eye he espied what Achilles was seeing just before his bond mate hooked the grapple over the ship's railing and plunged back into the sea. As far as he could tell, the immediate area seemed to be clear of people.

Within seconds Achilles returned, and Jake slipped off his facemask, handing it over to his bond mate. The dolphin grasped it firmly in one of his prehensile appendages, taking momentary hold of Jake with the other.

Needless to say, do be careful, Jay Jay, Achilles thought uttered. *Try not to be reckless this time around.*

You just worry about your own hide, Jake was quick to admonish.

With powerful muscles in his arms and back, he hauled himself up the rope, using his feet to push off the freighter's starboard hull plates as he ascended. In moments, he reached the railing near the ship's stern and catapulted himself over it to land silent as a cat.

Strapped to his right thigh was the suppressed Heckler and Koch USP-9 submachine pistol he habitually carried in situations like this. The weapon was sheathed in a ballistic nylon holster that descended from the tactical utility belt fastened around his waist. The belt held five spare 15-round magazine clips. And riding Jake's right calf was his trusty K-bar combat knife, a tool that had saved him from certain death countless times.

Jake took in his surroundings with rapid fore and aft glances. Lights were strung out at 100 foot intervals along the ship's rail, trailing off toward the distant bow more than 900 feet away. He detected no movement against the backwash of feeble illumination they emitted. The vessel was an ultra-large cargo container ship with enormous carrying capacity, and Jake noted its unorthodox design. Whereas container ships commonly had a bridge situated amidships or close to the stern, this particular vessel had its bridge located near the bow, towering above it like the head of an enormous sea beast. Stacked five tiers high directly above him was a sheer vertical wall of steel intermodal cargo containers the size of trucks. Like most freighters in this contemporary class of ships, the Southern Star's deck was clogged with them, and Jake was quick to take advantage of a nearby narrow corridor, one of many set back between the towering rows. The deep shadow it afforded provided the cover he needed to check out his gear.

With practiced ease, he removed the USP-9 from its holster, pulling the waterproof plastic wrap from the weapon. Even after sea immersion, the submachine gun would normally fire, but the wrap was simply a precautionary measure designed to further reduce the possibility of a misfire. In being towed to the ship over a lengthy distance, he had been in the water far too long to discount the possibility of water seeping into the bullet casings and wetting the gunpowder. Dislodging the gun's magazine clip, he removed the first three rounds and held them close to his eyes in the limited light to make sure they were free of moisture. Satisfied, he replaced them and snapped the clip back into the gun's breech, making sure the firing mode was set on safety. Carefully he laid the weapon at his feet before pulling the spare clips one at a time from the utility belt, examining each for dryness before reinserting it back into its pocket and leaving the water-seal flap open for easy retrieval.

From the utility belt's largest sealed pocket, Jake pulled the final though perhaps most crucial piece of equipment in his arsenal. It was important it be kept dry, for any saltwater clinging to its surface could severely attenuate its intended function. It was an exceptionally unusual device, and Ez had aptly named it *"The Cloaker."* The fabric comprising it was ultra-thin and felt extremely delicate to the touch, and Jake was continually amazed at how easily it deceived the senses, for in actuality it was incredibly tough and durable. When unfolded it resembled a loose-fitting cowl of crisscrossed webbing that allowed access to the utility belt and spare clips. It was surprisingly weighty in spite of its paper-tissue thickness. Jake knew this was partly attributable to the gold and copper elements embedded in the semi-metallic material. Hurriedly he slipped it on, letting it drape to his feet and slipping the hood over his head before aligning the magnetic fasteners. Pulling a thin strand of wire from inside of the vest, he plugged the end into the tiny battery contained within the same pocket from which he had removed the cloaker. Thumbing the activation switch to "on", he listened for the faint telltale drone, a barely audible hum that quickly waned into silence. Satisfied that the system was now operational, he stooped and picked up the submachine gun, holstering it.

The garment would bestow him with the means to roam the ship unseen. Now activated, it could bend electromagnetic light waves in the visible range around the cloaked object, causing them to emerge on the other side as if they had passed through an empty volume of space. In the current situation, he would be the cloaked object, perpetuating an optical illusion to a vigilant observer that he was not there.

The cloaker was comprised of a highly sophisticated and intricate material forged in one of Aquaria's physics labs, another product resulting from Ez's engaging hobby of searching for new technological developments on the worldwide web. But obtaining this technology had not required hacking her way into a high-security computer system as she had done with the U.S. Department of Defense. She had found it in a paper published by a team of graduate students conducting experiments at a Duke University engineering research facility, discovering a highly complex set of algorithms that guided the design and fabrication of exotic complex materials known as *metamaterials*. Refining the technology further, she had developed an even more powerful algorithm that custom-designed a unique metamaterial with the specific cloaking characteristics Jake would require for clandestine excursions such as this.

Moving swiftly along the maze of corridors and tunnels provided by the stacked cargo containers, Jake worked his way toward the ship's bridge. It was simple logic to conclude that if the vessel were being hijacked, then that was where he would find the hijackers, at least the ones tasked with taking control of the vessel. For the most part, luck seemed to accompany him as he chose new directions where corridors intersected, generally managing to avoid taking a passageway that would lead to a dead end and usually guessing correctly. Only twice did he venture down a corridor which terminated abruptly, finding it blocked by the side of a steel container. Turning another corner, he suddenly came upon the portside gangway amidships, also finding it devoid of interlopers.

The mild ocean breeze that had been buffeting the vessel when he had first come aboard had now picked up a notch, and with the ship's engines continuing to run at idle, the vessel had swung around with its beam facing directly into the wind. A gibbous moon hung high overhead, casting a tenuous glow onto a slate-gray sea dimpled with building whitecaps. Swinging his gaze to the ship's bridge, he saw that the windows were awash in dazzling light emanating from the interior.

Gliding stealthily along the gangway, Jake froze in mid-stride as a shadow suddenly fell across one of the windows, a black silhouette against a backdrop of bright light. Someone was scrutinizing the freighter's aft deck from the elevated superstructure, and Jake had to restrain himself from darting back under cover, reminding himself that he was invisible to prying eyes, at least in theory. Beyond laboratory testing, this was his first actual use of the cloaker in a potentially dangerous situation, and he was having difficulty suppressing old habits by putting his unconditional trust in this new technology.

Like a ghostly sentinel, the figure held steady a moment longer before turning away, no longer obstructing the light cascading from the window. Jake took the opportunity to bolt forward abruptly, quickly closing the distance to the base of the bridge. And as he raced along, one fact in particular puzzled him. If the ship had been hijacked, the perpetrators had not come by sea. Of this he was certain. During hours of the night, a high state of security protocol was kept in place in the waters surrounding Aquaria, typically extending several miles beyond its outer perimeter. The pod always kept a few sentries roaming the sea around the colony, and had a band of pirates used a boat or even a submarine to board the freighter, the dolphins or their cetacean cousins would have detected it. Depending on the species of the spotter, such an occurrence would have been swiftly relayed either acoustically or telepathically, with the information ultimately reaching him. But that had not happened. On his approach to the freighter, Achilles had not detected any small vessels tethered to the Southern Star, nor anywhere in close proximity for that matter. That left only one conclusion, which was that the hijackers had come by air, if in fact the ship had actually been seized.

Jake quickly ruled out the use of parachutes by armed assailants to get aboard the ship. An air drop would have been much too risky, offering little room for error in the unpredictable and gusty winds that often sprang up at night over these waters. No. More likely they had rappelled down ropes from a hovering helicopter.

As if to add credence to Jake's speculations, the voice of his bond mate resounded in his head. Achilles was always keyed into his thoughts when the possibility of danger lurked close at hand, and Jake made it a practice to keep the mental link open under situations such as this though it could sometimes be distracting.

A helicopter has been detected probing Aquaria's air space, Jay Jay, the dolphin informed him. *Perhaps it has some connection with this occurrence.*

What size chopper? Jake shot back. *Any information will be helpful.*

The colony had highly sophisticated radar installations set up on the floating city and Navassa Island, and Ez was patched into these systems. Jake knew she would dig into her extensive data banks to match the chopper's profile with the make and model of rotary-wing aircraft currently probing Aquaria's airspace.

Achilles relayed Jake's query to another pod member closer to the city, who in turn emitted an acoustical dispatch which Ez was able to pick up through her underwater sensors. Had they relied solely on acoustics to send messages, communication would have been far too slow considering their present distance from Aquaria. Telepathic thought waves traveling at the speed of light greatly outpaced sound waves moving through water. Ez, however, was not capable of a direct mind link with the albinos and had to rely on acoustical transmissions for both receiving and sending information between her and the dolphins. Even so, this constraining hurdle was quickly overcome as the answer to Jake's query came back within seconds.

Ez says it's an Mi-35 Hind, JJ.

The reply stunned Jake. An Mi-35 Hind was a Russian-made aircraft and an upgraded version of its predecessor, the Mi-24, which had initially been deployed by the Soviets against the mujahideen guerrilla fighters in Afghanistan. Hinds were large, powerfully-built helicopters primarily designed for use as attack gunships, but they could also serve as low-capacity troop transports with room for eight passengers. The Mi-24 had been much feared by Afghan rebels, who had called it *"Shaitan-Arba"*, Satan's Chariot. Hinds had been originally produced by the Mil Moscow Helicopter Plant and had been in operation since 1972, eventually finding their way into the military of thirty other nations. The profile of a Hind resembled that of a large insect, with the pilot and weapons operator seated in tandem, stepped cockpits under separate, individual canopies.

What disturbed Jake the most, however, were the armament systems these aircraft were capable of carrying. Very often they were outfitted with air-to-ground guided missiles and 23mm cannon, but in his opinion their most potent weapon was the twin rapid-fire 12.7mm Yakushev-Borzov heavy machine guns housed in a pod that could be rotated under the chin bubble. Each gun was capable of unleashing a devastating amount of firepower, with the manufacturer boasting 4,500 rounds per minute. A remembrance of the electronic Gatling gun mounted to Sebastian Ortega's Bell helicopter suddenly invaded Jake's mind. Ortega had nearly destroyed his beloved North Sea trawler with the weapon before Jake had stopped him with the help of the albinos.

Jake put aside the thought, assessing other features he knew of the Hind. Housed within its sturdy frame were powerful twin engines that gave the aircraft the capacity to maneuver quickly in spite of the heavy loads incorporated into its design. It possessed a heavily armored body and nearly indestructible titanium rotor blades which could resist impacts from .50 caliber rounds from all angles. The cockpit was protected by ballistic-resistant windscreens and a titanium-armored tub. In short, a Hind was tough to bring down and could easily withstand the meager firepower Jake presently carried.

Nevertheless, Aquaria's defense system was quite capable of protecting the colony from an air assault if in fact that was the intention of the people aboard the Hind. As if to belay Jake's next thought, Achilles relayed another message.

Ez says the pilot of the Hind has issued a warning that if he's fired upon, the luxury liner Morning Vista will be destroyed.

Jake was immediately perplexed. The ship he was standing upon was a freighter, not a luxury liner, and the name of the vessel was the Southern Star. The warning didn't make sense.

Achilles quickly brought clarity to the conundrum. *The Morning Vista is another ship Ez has picked up on her radar, and she's currently within five miles of our present position, Jay Jay.*

If the Hind is brought down, how can it possibly destroy the Morning Vista? Jake snapped back. *They could be bluffing.*

Perhaps, Achilles offered, *but are you willing to gamble on the lives of innocents on such a possibility? Ez is trying to get more information from them to...*

The resonance in Jake's head ceased abruptly. *To do what?* Jake implored impatiently.

Hush, JJ! I'm receiving another message.

Jake waited anxiously, and the two seconds that transpired before Achilles came back seemed like an eternity.

Ez has detected a second Hind in the vicinity of Morning Vista. Need I say more?

The gloomy implication numbed Jake with dread and he stood frozen with indecision, his mind reeling with this sudden and unexpected revelation. Most modern luxury cruise ships were filled to capacity with passengers these days, and the Morning Vista might well be carrying thousands.

As if to add further gravity to this new development, Jake sensed a dark cloud descend upon him like the shock wave following a nuclear blast. He had felt it only once before when he had sought to rescue Destiny years earlier from the clutches of Ternier and Ortega, and the pure essence of it slammed into him with hurricane force. *What's wrong, Achilles?* Jake managed to utter, caught totally off guard by the sheer intensity of it.

Achilles had trouble gathering himself, and Jake had to prod him further.

A sorrowful wail bearing acute emotional distress resounded in Jake's head. *The pilot of the first Hind has given instructions and demands they be followed to the letter immediately and without negotiation... otherwise...*

Otherwise what, Achilles?

Otherwise everyone aboard the Morning Vista will be killed, the dolphin lamented miserably.

Jake felt the chilling despair of sweat creep over his body.

Achilles floundered despondently in trying to keep the link open, the magnitude of his emotion continuing to grow and on the verge of uncontrollable weeping. *The Hind is to land unharmed on Aquaria, at which time three of its residents will be standing by to board the aircraft.*

Please go on, Jake pleaded, afraid to hear what was to follow.

They have named the residents they seek.

Who? Jake demanded when Achilles hesitated yet again, unable to suppress the brooding premonition of disaster and tragedy rapidly taking hold of him.

Achilles' answer reverberated in Jake's skull like a shrill howl. *They refer to the Dolphin Girl and her children.*

Jake's response was like a lightning bolt of pure anger. *That is not an option! Tell Destiny I forbid it.*

Achilles remained silent, and Jake sensed the same steel barrier of frigid unresponsiveness he had experienced years earlier being erected. Destiny was now involved in the matter. There could be no doubt. Destiny was the focal point of the pod and its primary human interface. She was by far the purest of its human contingent and the only one among them who had access to all the delphine minds, either singularly or in combination, whenever she chose. He knew she was in direct contact with Achilles at this moment and was purposely attempting to keep Jake from doing something foolish. She was going to keep him from engaging in this dilemma as much as possible, just as she had done when she had struck out for Navassa Island to confront Ternier long ago. She was urging Achilles to shut down the link the albino shared with Jake. She, and she alone, would decide on the logical course of action to undertake.

The thought horrified Jake, and he screamed out in exasperation. "Do you hear me, Achilles? Don't shut me out!"

He realized he had physically shouted the question, failing to confine it to a mental query. Startled by his careless outburst, he glanced up sharply at the ship's bridge to see if anyone had heard him, and to his dismay he espied the same silhouette in the window as before. Someone was scrutinizing the rear deck as if in search of something. Abruptly he chastised himself for his own stupidity and irresponsible recklessness.

If not complied with, the Morning Vista will be destroyed, Achilles reminded him, this time sounding more in charge of his emotions.

Tell her under no circumstances is she to comply! Jake ordered shrilly, this time making a colossal effort to keep his response on a mental level.

There is yet another component to this unfavorable situation, Achilles warned insipidly. *The Morning Vista is not the only vessel they threaten destruction. If the lives of all those aboard the cruise ship are not enough of an incentive to meet their demand, then they will destroy the Kraken. Ez has it on her radar, and it is bearing directly at Aquaria on a northeast heading.*

This last bit of information hit Jake like a severe electric shock, and his mind staggered under the enormity of it. The *Kraken* was currently the largest crude carrier on the planet, able to carry slightly over one million barrels of oil in her immense hold. There was no way Ez could mistake the vessel's distinct and enormous profile, though it was a mystery why such a ship would be in these waters. The Kraken normally plied a route that carried it a safe distance north of Jamaica and Navassa Island as it made periodic runs between Mexico's Caya Arcas Terminal on the Yucatan Peninsula and the extensive oil refinery at the Port of Mayaguez in Puerto Rico while transporting huge volumes of low grade crude. As far as he knew, there was not a single port along the U.S. Gulf Coast or other areas of the Caribbean capable of accommodating a ship of such behemoth dimensions. The threat of an oil spill in the surrounding waters was one of the colony's biggest fears, for it had the potential of incurring irreversible damage to their budding enterprise. The fact that the Kraken was now south of Navassa didn't make sense.

For the first time in his life Jake felt completely helpless. It was as though he were bound hand and foot, both physically and mentally, in the face of such overwhelming odds. It was obvious the people the colony was up against had meticulously planned this operation so that there could be no doubt as to who the winner would be.

Tell Destiny not to board their chopper until I get back, Jake instructed dully, but he knew Destiny would not listen. His wife would not hesitate to put the lives of thousands and the very survival of Aquaria ahead of her own and those of their children. He knew her too well.

Destiny says to consider her dream, Achilles shot back, suddenly sounding hopeful. *She says there are parallels between the current situation and elements of her dream.*

Jake's mental outlook abruptly brightened. Yes, of course. Why hadn't he seen it? With lucid clarity, he suddenly knew what to do.

-12-

The man scanned the ship's rear deck, searching for movement with the trained eye of a soldier. He could have sworn he had heard someone shout moments earlier, but perhaps it was nothing more than the passage of wind along the vessel's superstructure. Then again, he couldn't be certain. Though muffled, it had sounded like a guttural cry of deep anguish.

Still uncertain whether he had heard someone, he stepped away from the window quickly, not wanting to tempt fate. He was sure the material comprising the window's thick glass was made of a durable acrylic capable of stopping flying debris driven by gale force winds and crashing seas. Surely it could at least deflect rounds from a light firearm, maybe even a .44 magnum bullet, for he judged that a more powerful weapon would have been too cumbersome for a clandestine intruder to carry in an attempt to board the ship. Nevertheless, as a former member of the elite Soviet Spetsnaz, Vladimir Drakov knew it would be unwise to make that assumption. In any event, presenting himself as a target for more than a few seconds to a potential sniper, particularly one of Navy Seal caliber, would be foolhardy should the man they were baiting perceive him as foe. Standing in the window was only meant to be a lure.

For the second time in the last two minutes, Drakov spoke softly into his lip mike, speaking in Russian. "Have you located him, Sickle?"

The reply was curt and gruff, edged with frustration. "No, but I heard

DOLPHIN RIDERS

someone cry out."

So someone had shouted, after all. Deeply puzzled, Drakov couldn't understand why a former Seal would exercise such poor discipline. Seals were trained to infiltrate with absolute stealth. Maybe it was meant to be a distraction. Or maybe it was not the man they lay in wait for. A short time earlier, Sickle had spotted someone scale up the side of the vessel further back near the stern but had quickly lost sight of him. But one thing was for sure, which Drakov found strange. The intruder had not used a watercraft to reach the Southern Star.

"Hold your position!" Drakov ordered. "He'll show himself."

The trap had been carefully planned, with Zinova briefing the team thoroughly on how it would be executed. Hopefully they would be able to take Javolyn alive, but that was not their main objective. Their client had offered a substantial bounty on three others who were considered much more valuable.

Dolphin Girl. The term intrigued him. Zinova said the woman rode a huge white dolphin whenever she took to the sea, often accompanied by two young children, each of which also rode a dolphin. But the children's mounts were much smaller in size and were assumed to be juvenile versions of the same species of white dolphin bearing the woman, supposedly an undocumented breed with unique attributes. According to the intel Zinova had been given, it was presumed the Dolphin Girl was the children's mother and Javolyn their father. Aside from delivering the girl and her offspring into their client's hands, Cardoza had offered an additional bonus if Javolyn were brought to him still breathing. And the easiest way to do that would be to lure Javolyn to the Southern Star where he would be unable to protect his family and, more importantly, become easy prey.

Still, Drakov wondered if Javolyn had actually taken the bait. Perhaps it was someone else Sickle had seen come aboard. But Zinova had stressed that a man like Javolyn could not resist following up on the feigned distress call they had put out, especially if the call was made to appear as though it were purposely being suppressed by jamming. He knew a man like Javolyn would recognize the drone of bagpipes as a standard jamming technique. And with him not knowing for sure if the Southern Star had actually been hijacked, Zinova had predicted the ex-Navy Seal would seek access to the ship's helm to confirm whether or not that was true. He would not be able to stay away, for it was in his blood. A true warrior always spoiled for a fight.

Drakov glanced at his watch anxiously. This was taking far longer than he had anticipated. *Come on, show yourself already!* he willed angrily. Their planned timetable was rigid, and in another ten minutes

Zinova would be returning to pick him up along with the remainder of his squad. Whoever it was that had come aboard was being extremely cautious.

Growing increasingly uneasy, Drakov stepped to the window again, once more trying to entice the intruder to the bridge. Sickle and two other team members were lying in wait near the base of the stairway leading to the bridge. The trap would be sprung using a tranquilizer dart, which Sickle had at the ready. It would render their prey unconscious within seconds.

Without warning, a sound of deep groaning resounded throughout the ship, and Drakov's first impulse was that the freighter had run aground. Almost immediately the deck shifted precariously underfoot as the vessel listed sharply to port. Thrown off balance, Drakov threw out a hand to steady himself. Swiveling his head, he cast alarmed eyes on the ship's skipper, who lay sprawled on the deck. "What is happening?" he demanded brusquely.

Captain Gleason struggled to regain his feet, gasping heavily as he hefted his corpulent bulk off the floor. Attired in dowdy khakis, he was a tall, stoop-shouldered, ungainly man with a short salt and pepper beard, deep-set eyes, and prominent wart dominating his nose. "Something hit us!" he blurted.

Drakov spoke curtly into his lip mike. "Sickle, report!" When no reply ensued, he repeated the command only to be met by silence. In annoyance, he checked the wiring on his head set. The last thing he needed was a communications malfunction.

Slowly the freighter began to roll back onto an even keel, and Drakov looked to the captain again. "What hit us?"

Gleason opened his mouth to speak, but was immediately rendered speechless as structural members within the vessel groaned again, harsher than before, almost as though the vessel were in agony. An ominous shuddering worked its way through the freighter as it canted sharply once more, this time to starboard.

Dumbstruck, Gleason realized the ship was in danger of capsizing if it listed another five degrees. Something was rocking the ship. A quick glance at the moonlit sea told him the water was not rough enough to cause this.

"What's going on?" stormed Drakov. He needed answers, and quickly. Time was running out.

"I don't know," Gleason yelled back in confusion. The last thing he needed was to lose the ship and its precious cargo. By his estimation, the Southern Star was close to top-heavy, stacked higher than normal with cargo containers, the uppermost ranks laden to capacity with tungsten ingots. Tungsten was an exceptionally heavy metal, close to three times heavier than iron per unit volume. Forecasts of extended balmy weather and relatively calm seas had induced him to exceed the usual safety margins in loading the ship. The risk would otherwise pay off handsomely, and his bonus would prove to be exceptional on this trip. But he hadn't planned on the latest instructions he had been issued, which had come unexpectedly hours earlier and ordered him to change course.

On paper the Southern Star was shown to be an asset of Ocean Transitions, Inc., an international maritime holding company, but the actual owner was Rafael Cardoza. Gleason knew he was a dead man if he blew this operation. His instructions were clear. He had to give these men his full cooperation and assistance in carrying out this operation.

Gleason turned to his helmsman, the only other person manning the bridge, a man of slight build and darting, sheepish eyes who clearly appeared shaken at this sudden turn of events. "Check the ship's sonar and tell me what you see?" he ordered shrilly. "And turn on all the hull cameras!"

With the Southern Star retrofitted with underwater cameras in combination with both vertical and side scan sonar, Gleason would be able to determine the cause of the problem. The ship had a total of six video cameras situated along the centerline of its keel, each camera fitted with a powerful floodlight and housed in a Plexiglas bubble set in the hull approximately every 130 feet. When activated the cameras could be rotated and moved up and down to view the surrounding water in their immediate area. The systems had been installed along with the twelve hidden compartments within the vessel's double hull shortly after Cardoza's purchase of the Southern Star. They were normally used to observe the loading and unloading of illegal contraband the ship routinely carried along with its legal cargo. With water taking up the remaining space in the secret compartments beneath the vessel's inner hull, police and coast guard dogs trained to sniff out drugs would be unable to detect the immense quantities of heroin and cocaine the Southern Star frequently transported.

Within moments of activating the systems, the helmsman's face turned ashen. "There's whales beneath us, hundreds of them," he cried out in fear. "They're all around us. The sea's swarming with them."

Listening to the exchange, Drakov furrowed his brows skeptically. "Whales are rocking the ship?"

Gleason staggered over to the console like a drunken sailor as he tried to compensate for the deck's worsening tilt. "That can't be the cause," he growled derisively, shoving the helmsman aside. "Even a hundred whales wouldn't be enough to..." Gleason abruptly went mute as his gaze fell on the video screen, his eyes immediately growing wide in disbelief and alarm.

Toggling the cameras one at a time, he could discern immense rotund shapes under the harsh glare of the floodlights. They were situated on each side of the ship, ranks of them just under and along the port and starboard bilge keels, enormous blunt heads pushing up against the hull plates like submarine bulldozers. The water was exceptionally clear, with underwater visibility easily exceeding 200 feet, allowing him to observe the cause of their predicament. Quickly rotating the cameras, he could see the tail flukes of the port rank working hard in unison as their combined strength imparted an axial moment to the vessel. As though of a single mind, the port rank stopped pushing all at once, and the ship began to right itself.

Almost level, the deck shifted again with frightening speed, and the freighter listed sharply back to port, this time more acutely than before.

Gleason kept a death grip on the console with one hand to keep from being thrown sideways. With the other hand he frantically worked the controls to the camera system, his eyes riveted to the screen. The starboard rank of behemoths were now driving their massive bulks against the hull, their tail flukes churning the sea with such force that he could actually distinguish cavitation wakes behind them.

Feeling his guts clench tightly, he found it difficult to believe what he was seeing. *Was it possible his eyes were deceiving him? Surely this couldn't be happening.* He had spent more than twenty years at sea, always having considered whales to be nothing more than big, dumb brutes incapable of the coordinated attack he was witnessing. Clearly visible to him were several species of whale he had learned to recognize during his many voyages. And while humpbacks and grays were most prevalent in the void beneath his vessel, he was surprised to see at least twenty blue whales among them. The sight unnerved him further, for blues were by far the largest and rarest breed of cetacean on the planet. He knew that adults normally carried 120 tons of body mass and grew to a length of about 80 feet, but he vividly remembered reading that the largest blue whale on record was a 94-foot female weighing 176 tons. The monsters he was seeing, however, appeared to be far larger in size, with body lengths exceeding 100 feet. Nearly driven to extinction by whalers of old, the number of blues worldwide had been slowly rebounding over the years. But to observe so many of these great leviathans in one place was highly improbable, if not altogether impossible. In concert, all of these beasts, blues, grays, and humpbacks, were purposely rocking his ship, using their combined sheer power and mass to increase the momentum of each roll forced upon it.

"God help us," he muttered inwardly. The whales were surely going

DOLPHIN RIDERS

to capsize the vessel if they continued their assault.

With foreboding dread, Gleason sensed the ice cold fingers of death draw closer. Even if he were to survive a capsizing, Cardoza would be unforgiving, for if the sea failed to take him, surely the Colombian's ravenous tiger would. Currently, the ship's twelve secret compartments were all filled to capacity with bundles of high-grade cocaine having a street value close to a billion dollars.

Gleason turned to the helmsman, shouting in panic. "Engage the engine and get us underway immediately!"

"What are you doing?" Drakov growled in dismay, stabilizing himself against a port bulkhead.

"We've got to shake those brutes off," Gleason shot back. "They're going to capsize the ship."

"The engine won't engage," the helmsman shrieked. "It shut down completely."

"That's not possible," Gleason countered, his dread continuing to mount. "Page engineering and find out-"

The order froze in his throat as the deck shifted violently back to starboard, nearly toppling him. Desperately he clawed at the control panel to keep from falling. A loud squeal suddenly assaulted his ears, and he immediately knew it was the sound of rending metal. Twisting his head around, he stared in horror out the aft window as the ship tilted precariously. The thing he had feared was beginning to happen. Upper tiers of cargo containers were beginning to tear loose from the interlocking pinions holding them in place.

Gleason found himself withdrawing inwardly from the turmoil engulfing his ship, almost as though he were a spectator watching a calamity unfold on the big screen in a movie theater. Maybe this was nothing more than a dream, he thought dazedly as the freighter continued to rock savagely, his fingers clinging tenaciously to the edge of the console. Vaguely he heard someone scream out in terror, perhaps his helmsman. Oddly, he felt an inexplicable calm begin to settle over him, and he found the sensation strange with death now so close at hand.

-13-

Jake moved with utter stealth, totally invisible to predatory eyes. His suspicions that a trap had been set were all but confirmed with further news from Achilles. Using the Internet, Ez had resorted to her hacking skills to delve into the ownership of the Southern Star, wending her way through an intricate though devious maze of holding companies within holding companies.

The Southern Star is the property of Rafael Cardoza, Achilles had informed him. *It's obvious these people have purposely lured you here.*

Then I'm going to need a diversion to disrupt their scheme, Jake had replied.

Ez is way ahead of you and has formulated a plan, Jay Jay, Achilles had shot back. *Destiny has summoned the whales and they should be here momentarily.* Achilles elaborated further, providing additional details of what Ez had in mind.

Jake braced himself, fully prepared for the initial onslaught from the great leviathans as they began rocking the ship. The whales were indispensable members of the colony, providing the necessary brute power to move the enormous sea-grown modules into place during Aquaria's construction. Now they were serving another purpose.

Shadowy movement caught Jake's eye as he rounded a corner. In reaction to the ship's sudden radical list, a solitary head bobbed behind a packing crate situated near the foot of the stairs ascending to the bridge. Coincidental with the movement, something banged heavily not ten feet away, and Jake made out the forms of two others catching their balance. It was the logical place for an ambush.

Compensating for the anticipated motion of the shifting deck and placing his trust in the cloaker, Jake strode quickly, deciding to take out the lone figure lurking behind the crate. A minute earlier he had come upon a short length of steel bar, deciding it would make a handy weapon. Now hefting it behind his back to keep it shielded by his cloak of invisibility, he slipped up to the man with wraithlike precision and struck quickly. A dull thud resounded as the bar made contact with the man's head, and Jake grabbed his unconscious victim to keep him from falling heavily. Unexpectedly, something clattered to the deck, the sound partly deadened by the grating of tortured steel bulkheads as the freighter rolled sharply. In the dim light cascading from the bridge, Jake realized it was a tranquilizer pistol.

In less than a second, he assessed the situation. Though he noticed the man he had just kayoed was heavily armed, the intent of the ambush was not to kill. These men wanted a prisoner, plain and simple.

Reaching for the fallen pistol, Jake turned and faced the position where the other two men lurked. Another warning echoed in his brain with critical timing. *Prepare for a more severe counter roll,* Achilles cautioned him.

Offsetting his movement as though he were balancing on a rolling log, Jake closed the distance to the nearest ambusher as the ship groaned in protest again. The shadow before him seemed to stumble, thrown off balance by the lurching deck. In that instant Jake fired.

The dark figure reacted as though stung by a hornet, bringing up a hand to slap at the thing embedded in his neck. Jake followed with a sharp uppercut that buckled the man's knees. Crouched within arms distance, the man's partner rose to his feet, appearing confused at the reeling antics of his comrade. Jake took full advantage of this momentary lapse in vigilance, catching the second man with a vicious front kick to the groin. The second man's eyes snapped wide in dazed shock and bewilderment, then glazed over as a devastating right cross finished him off. Turning back to the sedated man, Jake saw him stagger on unsteady legs, then collapse completely in a fallen heap.

Jake tucked the dart gun into his utility belt and stared down at the two limp forms. The men wore military camos and were armed in the same manner as his first victim. Each of them was outfitted with a lip mike and carried a submachine gun, utility belt with spare clips, grenades and other lethal paraphernalia. Undoubtedly mercenaries, he surmised. Studying the immediate area, he noticed something else. Lying atop an oil drum lashed to the deck were two rolls of heavy duty duct tape, apparently set aside by these men in preparation for binding their intended prisoner.

The harsh sound of rending steel told him cargo containers were beginning to tear loose, and he realized time was running out. Hurriedly he grabbed one of the rolls of tape as the ship shuddered from bow to stern. Working quickly, he trussed up the last man he had rendered unconscious before moving over to the first. Each was bound in the same fashion, hands to feet behind their backs. The task was made all the more difficult by the rocking ship, which continued to list more severely each time it counter-rolled. He did not bother with the sedated man, assuming that the drug, whatever it was, would keep the man comatose for several hours. He then applied tape over their mouths lest they regain consciousness and yell out a warning to whoever lay in wait up on the bridge. Stripping all three men of their weaponry including their utility belts, he was about to toss all of it into the sea but stopped short as Achilles broke into his thoughts.

Ez says you're going to need those, Jay Jay. The dolphin quickly explained why.

The fact that Achilles could follow these happenings through Jake's mind's eye came as no surprise. He had grown used to it.

An idea suddenly came to Jake, and he rummaged through the utility belt of the tranquilized mercenary, almost immediately discovering what he had hoped to find. But there was only one, a spare sedation dart. Pulling the tranquilizer pistol from his belt, he loaded it, knowing it would come in handy.

Satisfied with his work, Jake took stock of his surroundings one more time to be sure there were no other potential assailants lurking about, fairly certain that no more than four men would have been assigned to the freighter for this mission of abduction. Shifting his gaze to the bridge, he stared up at the light streaming from the aft window, knowing there was unfinished business to attend to.

Moving with the grace of a tightrope walker, Jake managed to keep his balance as the deck teetered jerkily underfoot. The stairs leading to the bridge were only a few feet away, and he grabbed the railing just as the ship shuddered ponderously as it rolled back the other way. He held on tight as the vessel leaned so steeply that the ocean rose up to breach the portside scuppers. The screech of abrading metal assaulted his ears, and he caught a glimpse of nearby cargo containers beginning to shift.

Jake summoned Achilles. *Tell the whales to ease up a tad or they'll capsize her. I'm going to need prisoners.*

I'm way ahead of you, Achilles replied. *They know overturning the ship is not in their best interest. Even if they don't capsize her, should any of those containers come loose and fall into the sea, they could get injured. Ez checked out her cargo manifest. She's top-heavy, Jay Jay. The uppermost containers are filled with tungsten ingots. Not a very wise thing for a ship's captain to do.*

Jake broke off the chatter and climbed the stairs as the ship continued to rock to and fro, but now with a subtle difference in the severity of each roll. The harsh screech of rending steel abated slightly as he climbed higher. In moments he reached the top landing and peered through the doorway window. Only three men manned the bridge, with two of them clinging to the control console in obvious fright. The third man, a harsh looking individual, did not share the fear the others exhibited. Rather he appeared both annoyed and confused by what was taking place. He was armed with a submachine gun and outfitted in the same fashion as the mercenaries Jake had subdued minutes earlier.

Have our friends give the vessel a final rock, Jake instructed Achilles. *I've got one more unfriendly to take out.*

A wicked tremor suddenly shook the ship and Jake used the disturbance to open the door. One of the men at the console cried out in panic as the vessel listed acutely once again. Jake paid him no mind. He was focused entirely on the armed mercenary who held fast to the frame of the aft window, the man's automatic weapon slung over a shoulder. In an instant Jake was on him, coming up from behind and snaking an arm around his throat. A rear naked choke was always dependable in subduing an opponent, and he was a master at applying it.

Jake let out a labored grunt. The man was an ox, big and powerful, generously endowed with thick layers of rock-hard muscle in his back and shoulders. Added to this was a thick bull neck that made constriction of the carotid artery or windpipe difficult. It was as if he were attempting to choke out a tree.

The man reacted swiftly. A set of strong stubby fingers rose up to pry unmercifully under Jake's forearm to break the hold. Jake held on tenaciously, locking the hand of his encircling arm onto the biceps of his other arm and squeezing with all his strength. His opponent fought hard, twisting and turning before stumbling to the canted deck. Jake remained stubbornly clamped to the man's back, managing to get his legs wrapped around the man's torso in a figure-four grapevine for additional leverage. A few more seconds elapsed before the man went limp. To be sure his victim wasn't feigning unconsciousness, Jake held fast a moment longer before releasing the hold. By this time the ship had come back close to an even keel, listing only slightly to starboard due to shifted cargo.

Rising to his feet, Jake shed his cloaker. Gleason became aware of him, appearing startled at this sudden intrusion, but his eyes widened in alarm as Jake pulled his machine pistol from its holster and leveled it at him.

"Move so much as an inch and I'll turn both of you into shark chum," he said.

Gleason froze, as did his helmsman. Terror was clearly etched on his face as his eyes fell on Drakov's inert form. He had perceived Drakov as ruggedly tough and unbeatable, a man you didn't dare cross. But the individual now menacing him was obviously tougher, a person who would have no scruples whatsoever at carrying out his threat.

Jake re-holstered his weapon. Judging from the cowed expressions the other two men wore, he decided they would not be a problem. Reaching into a pocket, he removed the second roll of duct tape his would-be abductors had left on the drum. Within a minute he had the unconscious mercenary thoroughly bound. Just as he completed the final wrap, the man abruptly stirred. Jake rolled him onto his side, and as he did so, the man squirmed furiously.

Jake shoved the barrel of his weapon into the man's throat with brutal force. "Who sent you?" he demanded.

Drakov continued to struggle, blinking away the last vestiges of his short-lived oblivion. Murderous wrath consumed his face as his gaze focused on the man constraining him.

"Who sent you?" Jake repeated.

"Go to hell!" Drakov spat.

"My guess is that you and your buddies once served in the Russian army and now offer your services to the highest bidder," Jake opined, judging from the commando's heavy Ukrainian accent. "You work for

Rafael Cardoza, don't you?"

Drakov continued to glare back, his eyes offering nothing but hatred.

Jake prodded Drakov harder, jamming his weapon with savage force into the commando's throat. It infuriated him to no end that this man was part of a plot to kidnap Destiny and the twins.

Drakov wheezed harshly, eyes bulging and beginning to turn blue as he strained to get air through his constricted windpipe.

Jake eased up on the pressure at the sound of an approaching whirlybird. He turned his eyes to the man he assumed was the ship's captain. "Do you have radio contact with the Hind?"

Gleason stared back blankly. "The who?" he asked dumbly.

"The chopper coming toward us," Jake stated gruffly. "Are you able to contact them?"

The captain nodded resignedly. "Yes." He started to say more, but the ship's radio suddenly came alive. His vessel was being hailed.

"This is the Reaper, come in Southern Star." Though spoken in English, the voice behind the words reeked of a Russian heritage.

Gleason stood at abeyance, looking to Jake for instructions.

"Answer them!" Jake commanded through clenched teeth. "But if you alert them in any way as to what's going on here, I'll kill you where you stand."

Gleason acknowledged the threat, his eyes clearly mirroring his fear. Turning back to the console, he keyed the mike. "This is the Southern Star," he replied.

"Is everything in readiness?" the disembodied voice asked.

Gleason hesitated. He looked back at Jake nervously.

Jake thought quickly. "Tell him yes."

When Gleason complied, the voice on the radio suddenly sounded suspicious. "Put my team leader on."

"Tell him there was a problem, that he's preparing the package at this moment," Jake said hurriedly, pushing his weapon forcefully into Drakov's throat once again to keep him from screaming out a warning.

Gleason did as instructed.

The voice came back again, still sounding leery. "I tried calling him. Why does he not answer?"

"Tell him his radio is not working," ordered Jake.

Gleason keyed the mike again. "His radio got damaged."

Just as the captain finished speaking, the door to the bridge opened without anyone appearing.

"About time you showed up," Jake muttered.

Mat Daniels suddenly materialized as if out of thin air followed by Bashir an instant later as their cloakers deactivated. Mat glanced over at

DOLPHIN RIDERS

Gleason and the helmsman before setting his gaze on the bound captive at Jake's feet. "Judging from the way you handled things, I'd say you performed quite admirably without us," he said with a humorous grin.

"I hope you have our pilot in tow," Jake said.

"He's here. He's down on the deck with his I-phone. Ez is giving him a last minute crash course in the operation of a Hind. Unfortunately, we have another guest as well." For emphasis, Mat gestured toward the doorway as a familiar face appeared.

Jake's jaw dropped in horror. "Are you crazy, Phillipe?" he admonished angrily. He turned his ire back on Mat, glowering at him as if he were insane.

"Don't look at me," Mat protested. "I didn't bring him. He showed up on his own, apparently using that dolphin of his for transportation."

Phillipe held Jake's stone-faced gaze, staring back unwavering and defiant. "You're going to need help."

Achilles immediately interceded. *The boy's right, Jay Jay. You need four walking bodies to bring this plan to fruition, otherwise you risk raising the suspicions of the bad guys that something is wrong.*

Peeved as he was, Jake couldn't fault Achilles' logic. They would have to use *Maskers* to get aboard the Hind, and to use a *Masker* effectively, you had to use a living, breathing person. A Masker was yet another of Ez's inventions, a small device a user wore on their wrist. It employed a hologram technology similar to the one Ez used to project her image. The features of any persona could be programmed into them in order to deceive an observer, and since Achilles had seen images of the mercenaries Jake had subdued though the mental link they shared, he had telepathically relayed them to others of his kind close to Aquaria where picture-speak audio transmissions of those images were picked up by Ez from the surrounding waters.

Begrudgingly, Jake turned back to Mat. "How many Maskers did you bring?" he asked bleakly, expecting to hear they'd still be short one."

Mat held up a canvas bag. "Relax, good buddy. I make it a point to always carry a spare knowing how twitchy some of these gizmos can get. Let's hope they all work."

Before Jake could say anything else, Achilles intruded his way into his thoughts again.

Jay Jay, we have a new development which may prove indispensable to remediating the multiple threats confronting us. Ez thinks you can use it to make a deal.

Jake's mind raced. Destiny's description of her latest dream came flooding back, a portion of which echoed lucidly in his head: "Even though we were safe, we had to make some kind of arrangement with the Eagle

Master."

Are you implying we have a bargaining chip? Jake asked, his hope beginning to soar.

Yes. This ship has hidden compartments in the hull that are only accessible from below water.

How do you know that?

As you humans are so fond of saying when resorting to logic, I connected the dots. There are cameras situated along the keel and Rafael Cardoza is a notorious drug lord. There had to be a reason for emplacing those cameras in such an unlikely area, so I had Apollo scan the hull with the DBT he was still carrying. The info was sent to Ez for processing, and it revealed twelve sizeable compartments, all filled with cocaine.

An idea abruptly came to Jake. *Was Ez able to determine its total worth?*

Yes, based on the latest DEA statistics and the estimated quantity, she computes its street value at zero point nine seven billion dollars, give or take a million.

Jake addressed the captain. "I assume this vessel is equipped with a satellite phone," he said.

Gleason hesitated, seeming to weigh how he would respond to the question, but gave a half-hearted nod as the barrel of Jake's weapon came up to bear on him again.

"Well I suggest you use it to contact your boss."

"What do you want me to tell him?"

Jake produced a devious smile. "Tell him to call off his dogs or this ship will be sent to the bottom."

-14-

Zinova mulled Gleason's words, deep in thought as he sat at the controls of the Hind. Radios occasionally malfunctioned on missions, so nothing to get overly concerned about. Perhaps Javolyn had been far more difficult to capture than anticipated, causing Drakov's radio to get damaged in the process. In any event, he had no reason to doubt Drakov had not succeeded in getting the job done. Drakov was his second in command and the most reliable member of his team of professional mercenaries. Like himself, Drakov had once served in Spetsnaz and had been under his command in Afghanistan.

Gleason's voice suddenly sounded in Zinova's ears, snapping him out of these thoughts. "Your team is standing by at the helipad for extraction," the captain informed him.

Zinova swung the Hind around, making one more complete pass around the freighter with the chopper's powerful spotlight kept on the vessel to make sure nothing was amiss. In his profession, one could never be too cautious. A highly skilled pilot, he brought the Hind to a hover forty feet from the landing pad perched directly over the ship's bridge, a modest structure barely big enough to accommodate the Russian-built aircraft.

Holding his position, Zinova made no effort to land as yet, instead directing the beam of the spotlight on several men making their way up the helipad steps.

"Keep your guns at the ready!" Zinova ordered his weapons operator seated forward of him. "Everyone, stay alert!" he instructed the other two men stationed behind him in the fuselage.

Zinova swiveled the spotlight a few more degrees, and under the harsh glare he watched as the two lead men carried a third man while two others followed behind. The last man looked up, and Zinova could clearly see it was Drakov. Nevertheless, he continued to study the small group for several more seconds, wanting to be sure everything was as it should be. One by one, he recognized the faces of the remainder of his four-man squad as they climbed higher. Bringing his eyes to bear on the man being carried, he looked upon the unconscious countenance of the person Cardoza had sought, a ruggedly handsome face belonging to someone who had killed several of the drug lord's men. It was obvious the face belonged to Javolyn, the face of a warrior. There was no mistaking the resemblance, for Cardoza had provided him with photographs of the former Navy Seal.

Satisfied that the mission had gone as planned, Zinova edged the aircraft forward and lowered the landing gear. As the Hind settled, he craned his head around to observe the figures as they came aboard. His eyes were then drawn to the girl sitting passively on a rear seat, her arms enfolding a child on each side of her. Her beauty was stunning, and he had trouble tearing his gaze away. Strangely, she seemed unaffected by the sight of her husband's inert form as it was hauled aboard.

Distracted for the moment, Zinova was totally unprepared for what ensued next. As one of the rear crewman leaned out to lend a hand, Javolyn suddenly came alive, gripping the crewman's arm and yanking hard. The crewman lost his footing, stumbling through the side door and falling onto the helipad deck. The man was immediately knocked flat as one of Drakov's team kicked him squarely in the solar plexus. Another kick, executed like a bolt of lightning from the same team member, disabled him completely as he tried to rise back on his feet. Almost simultaneously, the butt of a weapon slammed with vicious impact into the face of the second crewman, but before Zinova fully grasped the situation, a machine pistol was jammed forcefully into the side of his neck. Zinova blinked in confusion before realizing it was Javolyn who held the weapon.

"Get outta the seat!" Javolyn said in a guttural hiss, his voice carrying above the roar of the rotors.

Zinova hesitated, his mind reeling with this sudden turn of events, but before he could even weigh his options Javolyn tore off his flight helmet and grabbed him by the hair, making him wince in pain.

"Unless you want to stop breathing, I recommend you give up this seat," Javolyn growled.

Zinova unbuckled his safety belt, contemplating whether he should put up a fight, but Jake yanked him brutally by the hair, forcing his bearlike frame from the seat and walking him backward with the gun still held to his neck.

Sitting forward of Zinova's position, the head of the weapons operator turned to investigate the commotion. Drakov rushed forward, firing the remaining dart from the tranquilizer pistol. The operator lifted a quivering arm to pull out the thing lodged in his cheek, only to slump forward an instant later as the potent drug took effect.

Drakov turned to another team member following on his heels, and as if on cue, both seemed to undergo a weird transformation. Their clothing and features appeared to expand and contract before changing completely, morphing into new personas. With his Masker now turned off, Mat Daniels tossed aside the dart pistol and removed the slack body from the weapons control chair, hauling it backward to clear the way for Fernando, who took over the seat.

"You sure you're up to flying this thing?" Mat found it necessary to ask, shouting out the question to be heard above the whine of the rotors as he stripped the flight helmet from the weapons operator.

A grim smile lit Fernando's face as his eyes roved over the controls. "If it has rotary wings I can fly it," he replied confidently. "Of course, a little guidance from Ez also helps."

Mat handed him the flight helmet, watching curiously as Fernando slipped it on and buckled himself in. "I always thought the pilot's seat was behind weapons control on a Hind. Are you certain you're in the right seat?"

Fernando began running his hands lightly over the controls to get the feel of them. "A Hind is somewhat similar in some respects to the Cobra gunships used in Vietnam," he explained briskly. "The co-pilot sits forward and below the pilot, but also serves to engage the weapons systems. I can both fly this bird and fire the weapons from here."

"Well, then, good luck and you have my most profound blessings," Mat said, moving back to join Jake, who had vacated the chopper with his prisoner held close.

DOLPHIN RIDERS

"Get down with your chest to the deck and your hands behind your head," Jake ordered Zinova.

With Mat and Phillipe now assisting Jake, Zinova was hastily prodded to the deck and quickly bound hand and foot with a spool of thick cord Mat had brought with him. The two unconscious crewmen along with the weapons operator were then laid out beside Zinova and subsequently bound in a similar manner.

Mat glanced over at Phillipe admiringly. "Very impressive with those kicks." A wealth of heartfelt praise was evident in his tone. He looked down at the mercenary Phillipe had kayoed. "Those lessons seem to be paying off."

"I have good teachers," Phillipe replied, referring to the rigorous training Jake and Mat routinely put him through.

"Your father would have been proud of you," Mat persisted. "He was quite a martial artist himself."

"I just hope I can measure up to being half the man he was."

Mat patted his cheek affectionately. "I don't think that's gonna be a problem for you, kid."

Turning, Mat scrutinized the twins clinging to their father's legs as he embraced Destiny fiercely. "Hate to intrude on this family gathering," he finally interrupted, "but we're not out of the woods yet."

Jake nodded in agreement just as Achilles gave him another mental nudge.

Jay Jay, Zimby has arrived and will pick up Destiny and the children on the ship's starboard side near the bow where there is a boarding ladder.

Jake shot a look to the water below him. The Angel was just pulling abreast of the freighter.

Destiny stared up at Jake questioningly, and he knew she had also heard Achilles. "You're not coming with us?" she said. There was resignation in her voice and a sudden outpouring of trepidation in her eyes.

Jake shook his head. "I want you and the twins to head for the cove. I've given it more thought and decided it's probably safer there than in Aquaria right now."

Destiny's face clouded in sadness and a glimmer of tears began to show. "They're never going to leave us alone, are they?"

"It's the way of the world," Jake muttered stoically. The essence behind the words she had uttered hours earlier chimed in the back of his head. Danger had in fact become a way of life for them and was forever going to be their companion, for this was the path they had chosen. She had spoken those words pragmatically, bravely, but was she really cut out for coping with this sort of thing?

Destiny nuzzled her face into Jake's chest. "I'm so afraid for you, Jay Jay. I never want to lose you."

Jake held her tight, aware that she was far too pure in rectitude to be subjected to the growing violence now aimed at them. "I warned you long ago it was going to be like this from the beginning, didn't I? Trying to make the world a better place always brings on the hyenas. They'll keep coming until they learn it's no longer in their interests to do so."

"Stay safe!" Destiny implored, unable to hold back the tears. She reached up and kissed him passionately before pulling away and walking to the edge of the platform.

Jake knelt quickly and hugged the twins tenderly. "Be good and do what your mother tells you," he said.

"We will, dadoo," they chorused in unison, hugging him fiercely before scurrying over to Destiny. With a final wave, they descended the stairs.

Jake rose and turned to Mat. "The ball's now in Cardoza's hands. It's up to him to call off the Kraken. Stay here and scuttle the freighter if he refuses. I'll go with Fernando. With any luck, we'll bring down the other Hind before it can carry out their threat on the Morning Vista."

Jake turned to climb aboard the Hind, but Mat grabbed his arm with a powerful grip. "Don't do anything foolish."

A ripple of amusement suddenly flashed across Jake's somber expression. "Hey, I'm not the one doing the flying."

Mat kept his expression stern. "Try using discretion this time. You keep prodding the devil and he's gonna stick that pitchfork where the sun don't shine."

"So you keep telling me."

At that moment, Bashir came bounding up the stairs. He had disappeared following the ouster of the Hind crew, but now he was returning with something carried on his shoulder and breathing heavily from the exertion. "Take this!" he urged. Seeing the look of surprise on Jake's face, he added, "Just in case you might need it."

Jake took the object and nodded gratefully, but as he turned to leave, Mat stopped him again. Mat's demeanor remained serious. "Don't get yourself killed," he growled. "Remember, there's a subtle difference between compulsive valor and unavoidable discretion."

"Nag, nag, nag," Jake shot back as he yanked his arm free and boarded the Hind. Nodding to Fernando, he gave a vigorous thumbs-up, prompting him to get going. Jerkily, the Hind rose, climbing erratically before stabilizing as Fernando got the feel of the controls.

Looking down, Jake spotted Hector assisting Destiny and the twins as they climbed aboard the Avenging Angel. He kept his gaze locked on them as the Hind gained height and distance from the freighter, their arms waving wildly at him as they looked up at the departing aircraft.

-15-

The satellite phone seemed to chirp with an exaggerated urgency, a distinct sound that identified the caller. In annoyance, Maximus opened the channel. "This had better be important," he hissed. Even though his and the caller's phone were encrypted so that all communication was indecipherable to potentially prying ears, his policy was to limit calls over the air waves.

"Call off your ship!" the voice on the other end blurted frantically.

"Why should I do that?" Maximus replied calmly. He hated it whenever his people lost their cool, but the answer that came back was more than he expected.

"They threaten to sink her."

"Sink who?"

Rafael Cardoza ignored the question, ranting on in panic. "I've suffered enough losses over the last few years and I'm not going to sit back while a major investment slips into the deep. Call off your ship!"

Maximus raised his voice angrily to cut off Cardoza's next screaming outburst. "Calm yourself and tell me what happened."

"Javolyn has somehow turned the tables on us and taken control of my ship. He says he'll sink it unless the Kraken changes its present course and veers away from Aquaria."

A broader picture of what Cardoza was telling him abruptly came together, and Maximus knew the plan had backfired, at least a portion of it. "I thought you said these Russians were infallible, the best in the business."

Cardoza was suddenly silent on the other end, scornfully reminded that it was he who had recommended the Reaper's services.

Sitting at the observation console in the bridge of his mega-yacht, Maximus scanned the radar screen. The blip was still there not five miles away, flying donuts above a much larger object. Another blip suddenly appeared on the screen, slowly closing the distance with the first blip.

"Is Javolyn still aboard the Star?" Maximus asked apprehensively.

"I don't know. The Star's captain won't respond to any questions. He's no doubt a hostage being held at gunpoint and told what to say." Cardoza paused, then lost his composure again. "Are you going to put a stop to this?"

"Do you actually think I'd destroy the largest ship on the planet?"

Maximus reprimanded coldly. Like Cardoza, he had no real intentions of sacrificing one of his assets, particularly since it carried more than just crude. Making the opposition believe it was going to be used as a battering ram or a vehicle of massive pollution was merely a bluff. Using its sheer size as an intimidation ploy should be enough to get what he wanted. He needed Navassa healthy and thriving, for it harbored those incredible dolphins. He could use those creatures. They represented a sizeable labor force capable of building things below the ocean surface, and he had only to stretch his imagination to envision other useful and profitable endeavors they could be used for. But the girl was the key to controlling them. All the intelligence he had so far been able to gather on them pointed to that one conclusion. With the girl and her children in his custody, he would gain control of the island and Aquaria along with it.

"I've always given you my full cooperation," Cardoza replied, trying hard but unable to suppress the pleading edge creeping into his tone. "But now I need yours. Help me get my ship back."

Maximus eyed the radar monitor suspiciously. The second blip was now closer to the first. "What do you suggest?"

"Alvarez! Send Alvarez!"

Maximus pondered the appeal skeptically, recalling what had happened earlier. With Allotey leading the way, Alvarez and his men had fled the colony like a herd of gazelle spooked by the scent of lions in the air. Nevertheless, even with their usefulness now in doubt, it was his only available option to pacify Cardoza, whom he still needed.

Making a snap decision, Maximus capitulated. "Alright, you can have Alvarez. He's currently in Kingston, so it shouldn't take long for him to reach your vessel."

"You won't regret this," said Cardoza, relief clearly evident in his voice.

"Now tell me," Maximus went on smoothly, "is everything proceeding as scheduled?"

"Yes."

"What about the doctor?"

"He will arrive by private jet tomorrow."

"Good," Maximus said, continuing to monitor the radar. "But there's a change in plans. I want you to commence the operation forty-eight hours ahead of schedule."

A moment of hesitation ensued before Cardoza responded. "The remaining shipment has not yet arrived," he objected wearily. "Without it, we will fall short of what is needed."

"Where is it?" Maximus snapped.

"On my ship."

Maximus frowned darkly, none too pleased with what he was hearing. "After Alvarez takes back the Star, do whatever is necessary to get that shipment quickly," he instructed adamantly.

"Why the change in schedule?"

"Do not question me, just make sure it gets done!"

Ending the link, Maximus cast a sour gaze on the screen as the radar blips began to merge. Thumbing the intercom, he paged his chief technician.

A moment passed before an obsequious voice tense with nervousness answered. "Osgood here."

"Launch the drone," Maximus ordered.

Osgood hesitated as if mulling a question. "I'll get it airborne right away, Mr. Maximus. What's the target?"

"You'll find out quick enough," Maximus barked. "I'm coming down now to man the controls." A wicked smile transposed his face as he made for the door.

-16-

Donning the helmet he had stripped from the pilot and plugging the wire connection into the radio console, Jake sat down heavily in the pilot's chair and stared intently ahead. The moon had arisen, and under its subdued glow the sea below appeared like an endless sheet of gray slate with no whitecaps in evidence.

"Can you hear me, Fernando?" he asked.

"Loud and clear," Fernando answered.

"Let's hope we see them before they see us. What have you got for weaponry?"

"Looks like twin rapid-fire machine guns in the chin turret and a guided missile system."

"Are they operational?"

"I think so. My guess is the machine guns' fire seven point six-two rounds and the rocket pods are loaded with thirty millimeter rockets."

Jake had noticed one of the rocket pods just before boarding the aircraft. He had also caught a glimpse of the twin barrels jutting from the chin turret. "Which are you going to use?"

"I'm better with guns," Fernando stated glumly. "The problem with Hinds is they're tough to bring down. All their vital parts are armored with titanium shields, which make them close to invincible against the relatively small caliber rounds this baby can deliver. If push comes to shove, the rockets may prove more effective, though I don't have much experience with them, I'm afraid."

Jake was about to offer encouragement, but something below in the distance caught his eye. "Ten degrees right at five o'clock," he shouted. "Do you see it?"

Fernando took a moment to spot the object before responding. "Got it!" Banking the chopper slightly right, he brought them on a new heading.

"The other Hind's got to be close by," Jake cautioned.

"How do we know if that ship's the Morning Vista?" Fernando said.

"Cruise ships are generally the only vessels you'll find at sea lit up like a Christmas tree. She's the Morning Vista, all right."

Jake scanned the night sky above the ship in search of the other chopper. "Chances are the other Hind's running without her lights, so finding her might be a problem," Jake grumbled.

"No it won't," Fernando replied flatly. "This bird's equipped with radar." His voice suddenly quickened. "And I do believe we've located her sister."

"Where?"

"Look at the small screen on the upper right side of your panel. The blip on the bottom shows her."

Jake saw it immediately. "So much for catching them by surprise," he uttered dismally. "If we have radar, I have to assume they do, too."

A voice suddenly sounded on the radio, and it wasn't Fernando's.

"*Barsuk v Jnec, lrihodit' nazad.*"

"Can you speak Russian, Fernando?" Jake queried hopefully. "I think they're hailing us."

"Sorry, but Russian ain't my thing."

"*Barsuk v Jnec, lrihodit' nazad,*" the voice repeated, now with an urgent, strident edge.

"*Jnec zdes',*" another voice suddenly blurted over the radio sounding different from the first.

Jake's puzzlement was immediately held at bay as Achilles' called out to him from the sea below, translating what was being said. *The last transmission you heard is Ez,* Achilles rapidly explained in that compressed fashion typical of their mental link. *She's answering the pilot of the other Hind, who is hailing you with the words Badger to Reaper, come back. She replied, Reaper here. She monitored the voice of the pilot you subdued earlier and is mimicking his signature tonal qualities to lull the other pilot closer.*

"That's Ez you're hearing," Jake informed Fernando. "She's baiting the other Hind closer by answering in the voice of this chopper's former pilot. Let them get real close and then open up with the guns. Just make sure the ship below us isn't in the line of fire."

"Leave the rest to me," Fernando shot back, his tone reflecting confidence.

With growing anxiety, Jake listened to the conversation taking place in Russian between Ez and Badger, the exchange sounding terse and incomprehensible to him as Achilles stopped translating. He held his breath as the other Hind suddenly loomed into view, a dark shadow within the night sky.

Jake was pressed down into his seat as Fernando banked the chopper hard, coming about to follow on Badger's tail. The other Hind held steady before him for a brief moment before Fernando let loose with the guns. A broken laser beam of red tracer rounds rushed out, slamming into the aft section of the targeted aircraft like a swarm of angry hornets. A firestorm of sparks flew in all directions as lethal projectiles found their mark against the Hind's titanium tail rotor.

Almost immediately, a din of panicked Russian vitriol erupted painfully in Jake's ears as Badger cried out in protest. He was again pushed forcefully into his seat as Fernando fought to stay glued to the Hind as it suddenly broke left and dove for the ocean.

"Damn!" Fernando griped in frustration. "These babies are tougher than I thought. I hit his rotor squarely and the rounds just bounced off."

"Stay on him and try again!" Jake encouraged.

"This guy's good," Fernando yelled back, continuing to bank sharply as Badger corkscrewed lower. "I'll be lucky to get another shot."

"How about taking him broadside?" Jake suggested.

"Just keeping on him is tough enough," Fernando gasped, fighting to talk as the punishing G-force laid siege to his body.

Jake wondered if Fernando was up to the task. Air combat was a young man's game. Even though Fernando had been around helicopters for the major portion of his life and had served in the military as an aviation mechanic during the Vietnam War, he was now well into his sixties.

"Hold still, you bastard!" Fernando groaned testily. "I don't want to kill you, I just want to put you into the drink."

Jake watched as Badger suddenly leveled off, then broke right. He realized they were less than fifty feet above the sea and that the Morning Vista lay directly before them. It was obvious Badger was making a beeline directly at the cruise ship, now less than a thousand feet away.

"Hold your fire!" Jake shouted curtly. He knew that if Fernando used the guns now, he risked hitting the vessel with stray rounds.

"Don't you think I know that," Fernando snapped back in exasperation. "He's a crafty sum bitch."

Jake held his breath, unsure if Badger would retaliate by carrying out the original threat on the cruise ship. Helpless to do anything, he could only stare as the Hind held steady before them, a tempting though forbidden target as it bore straight for the ship.

Fernando fought against the ever present danger of target fixation, a spell that had often claimed the lives of pilots since the first days of aerial combat. Target fixation could cause a pilot to become focused so intently on their quarry that awareness of other obstacles and hazards diminished. Collisions with impediments like the side of a mountain sometimes resulted when a pursuing pilot failed to anticipate a darting move by an elusive target. He knew Badger had to either veer away or pull up at the last possible second to avoid crashing into the ship. He had to stay tight on the Hind's tail. If he pulled away or gave up the chase entirely, he would leave himself open to a potential counterattack. And if his reflexes were too slow, it might very well be him and Jake that ended up like squashed bugs on the side of the vessel.

Jake braced himself as Badger's ship suddenly sprang skyward as if yanked by a huge bungee cord stretched to its limit and on the rebound. Fernando followed, grunting loudly against the strain of gravity as their Hind's powerful engines catapulted them up and over the Morning Vista's superstructure with less than ten feet to spare.

Shooting a glance out the side window, Jake espied several passengers on an upper deck stare up in terror at this sudden intrusion on their peaceful interlude. Weightlessness immediately caught up with him as Fernando dipped the Hind back toward the water, still hot on Badger's tail. Skimming just above the sea, Badger zigzagged back and forth, making his copter as difficult a target as possible, all the while spewing a torrent of incomprehensible invectives over the radio. Dogged in his pursuit, Fernando mimicked Badger's every move, keeping a ready finger on the trigger for an opportune shot. But just as he was on the verge of unleashing another salvo, Badger abruptly leapt skyward again.

Jake felt as though he were on an exhilarating rollercoaster ride at an amusement park, but there was nothing amusing about this ride. A brutal G-force abruptly accosted him as Fernando banked savagely to starboard, and he realized their quarry was no longer in front of them. In that instant he glimpsed the flash of green tracers seemingly coming straight at him before streaking past. Another second elapsed before something dark and fleeting zipped by, and had Jake blinked he would have missed it altogether due to its incredible rate of speed.

"What just happened?" Jake shouted in dismay, feeling the Hind under him dart back to port.

"We're being attacked!" Fernando yelled back. "Look at your radar! Another aircraft just fired on us."

Jake shot a look at the screen, immediately seeing what Fernando described. A tiny blip moved rapidly across the monitor. Achilles quickly interceded to bring structure to Jake's jumbled thoughts. *JJ, you are under attack by what appears to be an unmanned drone,* his bond mate informed him. *Ez has run a thermal scan on it and found it to contain no pilot. She measures its velocity at more than Mach three.*

Where did it come from? Jake asked.

From under the sea. Ez detected it as soon as it launched from the water. Achilles' composure began to crack. *She's got a radar lock on it at this moment and says it's coming around on your six.*

The resonance of Achilles thoughts suddenly shrilled, and Jake felt his bond mate's trepidation as though it were a living thing. *I am now conjoined with the entire pod, JJ. We will attempt to predict the intentions of this unknown attacker.* A sense of urgency suddenly gripped Jake like the talons of an eagle as Achilles shrieked out a prophetic warning. *Break right, break right.*

Without any hesitation, Jake grabbed the cyclic stick in front of him and jerked it harshly right, completely overpowering Fernando's light touch on the controls. The crush of gravity pressed in on him like an iron fist as the chopper swung acutely to starboard. This time a missile shot past the Hind's port side, missing it by inches. Jake lost sight of it as the Hind veered away.

"Sorry about that, Fernando," Jake apologized.

"No apologies necessary," Fernando croaked harshly, barely squeezing out the words. He stopped speaking momentarily to draw in breath. "You probably saved our hides, at least for the moment. Whoever's firing at us has supersonic capability."

"That whoever is a drone with no pilot," Jake rejoined brusquely.

"How can you tell?"

"Achilles informed me."

Fernando continued to take the Hind through a series of evasive maneuvers. Though the Hind had a speed way below their attacker, its lower velocity gave it far greater maneuverability. "Well you're wrong about a pilot," he corrected.

"What do you mean?"

"Someone's got to be controlling that thing."

Another shrill alarm went off in Jake's head. This time he was told to break left. Once again he grabbed the stick, yanking it hard to port. The Hind responded almost instantly, its forward inertia at odds with the excessive centripetal force brutally imposed on it. Another missile streaked past as the punishing crush of gravity returned with a vengeance.

Put the Hind into the water, JJ, and we'll rescue you, Achilles pleaded. *You don't have a chance against that thing.*

Jake weighed the merits of Achilles' suggestion. With the entire pod linked up mentally, it sometimes gave them the power of precognition, enabling them to glimpse the future and take the necessary steps to avoid an undesirable outcome. He had often referred to this power as a '*super-mind*' capability. On several occasions in the past he had observed this amazing ability, and he vividly remembered his first encounter with it years earlier. One of the albinos had made an incredible leap from the water to intercept and snatch a grenade meant for his beloved boat, tossing it out of harm's way before it exploded. In doing this, the dolphin had to have had advance knowledge of the grenade's precise trajectory, for it would have needed to dive deep to gather sufficient speed for its leap without tracking the grenade by sight. Determining its launch point and timing its jump from the water further complicated the feat, which would otherwise have been altogether impossible without this foreknowledge. But in spite of the advantage this ability gave them, he also knew the future was often too shrouded in mist for the pod's super-mind to consistently see what calamity could potentially happen and take the correct action to avert it. Jacob had explained it to him and called the phenomenon 'backward causality', a theory that contends the precognition experience unleashes a powerful psychokinetic energy that brings the desired future to pass. Therefore, it was only a matter of time before the unknown assailant remotely flying the drone scored a hit. Whether their Hind could withstand a direct missile strike because of its heavy armor was only a matter of speculation. This is what Achilles was telling him.

I have an idea, Achilles, Jake replied, suddenly energized by a sudden thought.

I see it clearly, JJ. Please hurry. The drone is coming around for another pass. It will be on you in twelve seconds

Jake spoke quickly. "Fernando, I need you to slow this bird down and present our friend with a profile."

Fernando's reaction was as expected. "Are you nuts?"

"You'll have to trust me on this," Jake urged gruffly. "There's no time to explain."

"I guess I've lived long enough," Fernando grumbled mournfully. "It was nice knowing you, my friend."

Jake unbuckled himself from the seat and scrambled into the passenger cabin. Already he could feel their airspeed plummeting as Fernando flared the main rotor. To keep from being thrown forward, Jake had to grab hold of whatever was available to steady himself. The thing Bashir had given him just before he had embarked on this crazy stunt was still where he had placed it, wedged between two seats. Pulling it free, he hefted it to his shoulder and braced a leg against one of the seats as the

DOLPHIN RIDERS

Hind came to a near hover and rotated ninety degrees. The tube-like object he held had hand grips and closely resembled a bazooka, yet another product of the albino ingenuity.

Something barely visible caught his eye, a seemingly insignificant black dot against the pale twilight of dawn. It swelled rapidly, coming straight at him with blinding speed, a bird of prey homing in for the kill.

Jake held steadfast, a montage of conflicting thoughts racing through his head, wondering if he should have taken Achilles' advice, asking himself why he always insisted on playing such foolhardy odds. Mats admonishing words came back to haunt him, and it was as though his friend were speaking at this moment. *How many times must I remind you, good buddy, that there's a subtle difference between compulsive valor and unavoidable discretion.*

Jake held his breath and squeezed the trigger, suddenly besieged by the possibility he would never again hold Destiny and the twins in his arms.

-17-

Maximus sneered caustically as he eyed the target on a 3-dimensional display. At full magnification, he could view his quarry as though it were less than a hundred feet in front of him. For reasons unknown, the Hind had given up its elusive and erratic maneuvers, so effective that he was beginning to believe its pilot was psychic, eerily anticipating his every move. But now the Hind was his for the taking, a virtual sitting duck that would be easy to obliterate. In spite of its titanium armor, he knew it could not possibly withstand simultaneous hits from his two remaining missiles. Easing back on the throttle, he slowed his attack speed by one-half as he guided the drone toward the target. This time he would not miss.

With his thumb poised eagerly over the launch trigger, something suddenly coalesced on the screen before him. The thing snaked and twisted without form, coming alive with a full spectrum of dazzling color against the heralding light of dawn. It took Maximus another second before he realized what he was seeing, and by then it was too late. Overcome with dizzying vertigo, he felt the bile rise in his throat as uncontrollable nausea engulfed him. With mouth parted wide, a stream of vomit spewed copiously from between his lips as though from a broken sewer pipe under enormous strain. A pain like nothing he had ever before experienced knifed through his brain, a blinding, searing agony so intense that it made him feel as though he had been cast into the deepest part of hell itself.

Standing further back from the screen, Osgood was only vaguely aware of his boss' seizure as Maximus collapsed to the floor and filled the room with a piercing scream. All the angst and depression churning his guts moments earlier was suddenly gone, replaced by a sense of breathtaking euphoria and happiness as he fixated a trancelike stare on the monitor. Unable to pull his eyes away, he became oblivious of the room around him. In stark contrast, Maximus squirmed and writhed in a pool of vomit, clutching his cranium as though to contain skull fragments from erupting in all directions.

Osgood felt whole again, continuing to savor the afterglow of the thing he had witnessed as it disappeared from sight. With Maximus' guiding hand no longer on the joystick, the drone veered away from the Hind and plunged for the sea as though it were a sea eagle sensing prey on the water below. Another second passed before it burst into a thousand fragments as it collided with the water at twice the speed of sound.

Jake released the trigger on the bazooka-like device, breathing a sigh of relief as he looked down. Under the lightening sky of dawn, he was able to discern wreckage from the drone scattered over more than five acres of ocean surface. His gambit had paid off beyond his expectations. The albino art had strange effects on people, and the extent to which a person fell victim to those effects depended on a person's core nature. Symptoms ranged from mild to severe, with a small percentage of viewers remaining unaffected at all. The symptoms, however, were normally temporary in duration and usually faded within a short length of time once the art was no longer visible to the onlooker. Some people became violently ill, while others experienced various degrees of nirvana.

Jake was one of those who fell into the latter class, as did all human members of the colony. But it was the dark mentalities that could be made ill just by looking at these cryptic artistic expressions, and the extent of their illness always depended on the level of their innate malevolent dispositions. It was this that he had counted on, an inherently sociopathic mind at the controls of the drone. And while two-dimensional representations of these bizarre creations were certainly effective, holographic projections were far more powerful in the way they affected an individual.

A glimpse of the dolphin art was always profoundly calming to Jake, and even more so when it was displayed three-dimensionally. In aiming the holographic projector at the approaching drone, his eyes were automatically drawn to the vision it invoked. As Jacob had explained on more than one occasion, the intertwining abstract lines pulsing with multi-colored light held mysterious qualities that did something to the human psyche, bordering on the hypnotic. On some deep esoteric level incomprehensible to human awareness, the brain was able to interpret the meaning of the convoluted symbolism subconsciously. And in doing so, it somehow found a way to bring a person's true essence to the surface, forcing them to feel it on both physiological and emotional levels. People who were basically decent at heart often experienced euphoria, while people who walked a fine line between good and evil usually felt nothing. But people who were essentially wicked would invariably become physically ill. Thus the dolphin art was quite literally capable of bringing humans to the doorsteps of heaven, the void of purgatory, or the brink of hell depending on their deep-seated psychological traits.

This knowledge made Jake's thoughts wander back to the prison in Port-au-Prince when he, Mat and Zimbola had helped Destiny rescue her mother, Jacob and the Baptistes from the clutches of Henri Ternier and Erzulie. It was there Ternier and his acolytes were brought to savage though temporary illness by a conjured hologram of one of Achilles' enigmatic creations. With Destiny and Amphitrite mentally linked to the conjoined pod mind, they had managed to bring forth the vision for all in the prison to view, including the inmates and guards. Images of the rapturous looks of those unjustly imprisoned and the contorted facial expressions of others collapsed and writhing in extreme agony were firmly etched in Jake's memory, with Ternier seemingly suffering as though his head were about to explode. Through some telekinetic miracle, the doors to all the holding cells had magically sprung open, with more than half of the inmates in rhapsodized stupors filing unhurriedly out into the streets. Joyful and feeling as though he were floating on air, Jake had ambled dazedly among the slowly milling crowd, all the while letting Destiny lead him from the prison by the hand until his blissful condition began to subside.

Still warm and content from his exposure to the hologram, Jake pondered what had just happened. It had taken little more than a second for the art to work its magic, suggesting that their attacker was quite iniquitous. The drone had simply nose-dived into the sea, and this told him its pilot must have been hit by an acute seizure to lose control of the aircraft so quickly.

Preoccupied with this evaluation, Jake was totally unprepared for what happened next. The Hind was suddenly jolted by a heavy impact that nearly sent him flying out the open doorway. Only his quick reflexes saved him as he flung out a hand to grab a stanchion. With his body fully extended and hanging precariously from the cabin, his gaze fell on a dark shadow as it zipped past overhead.

"We've been hit!" Fernando bellowed sharply.

Jake managed to get another hand on the stanchion, fighting hard to pull himself back into the cabin. He realized he had completely forgotten about Badger, and he berated himself unmercifully for letting the hologram stifle his alertness.

The chopper had listed over, rapidly gathering speed, and he had to shout at the top of his lungs to be heard above the rush of wind that swept into the fuselage with gale force intensity. "How bad?"

"We're going in!" Fernando screamed back. "Hold on!"

The Hind's powerful turbines screeched out in protest, the sound growing to a raucous wail that was painful to the ears. It was obvious to Jake the engines were severely damaged and no longer had the power to keep the chopper aloft.

Fernando had also forgotten about Badger. Like Jake, his vigilance had also been corrupted, having been caught in the hologram's soothing spell. But now fully awakened from its rapturous effects, he went to work swiftly. Taking the pitch out of the main rotor, he let the Hind drop toward the water with the aerodynamic characteristics of a brick approximating free fall. The cyclic fought him as tried to take the aircraft out of its sideways plunge, and he could tell the hydraulically-powered controls were beginning to fail. With considerable effort, he managed to bring the Hind back on an even keel with its nose pointing down in a steep glide.

Jake was familiar with the maneuver and held on tight, his bowels feeling as though they were climbing into his chest with the rapid descent. Fernando was going to soften their crash landing by auto-rotating the bird in. He would conserve the momentum of the main rotor as much as possible until they were close to the water and then flare up the nose as he threw maximum pitch into the blades to slow the chopper's vertical descent.

At a height of 50 feet above the sea Fernando barely managed to level the Hind off, using all his strength to pull back on the stick and the collective simultaneously. The Hind responded sluggishly, slowing as though in annoyance as the nose rose up begrudgingly. At that moment the hydraulics failed completely and the controls locked up.

"Brace yourself!" Fernando yelled.

The warning was unnecessary. Jake increased his grip on the stanchion, knowing this was going to be a severe impact as the sea loomed up far too swiftly. Something slammed into the side of his head with brutal force, and a kaleidoscope of bursting colors swirled before him. Another instant passed, and he had the sensation he was being drawn into a bottomless black hole at the center of the galaxy.

* * * *

-18-

Badger followed the stricken Hind down, watching lugubriously as it sent up a towering spray upon impact with the water. Shooting it down gave him no satisfaction, for he had grown especially fond of these helicopters since joining up with Zinova. In his opinion, Hinds were in a class second to none among rotary wing aircraft. They were quite unique and difficult to replace on the international market. Undoubtedly, the Reaper would be more than displeased at losing one of his prized assets, that is, assuming he were still alive.

Bringing his own Hind to a hover, Badger scrutinized Zinova's chopper as it wallowed in the waves and began to sink. The destruction of such a valuable piece of hardware made him feel as though he were losing a close friend, and as it began to disappear from view, he replayed in his mind the recent course of events that had led up to this moment.

He had caught sight of the approaching aircraft a full two seconds before it swept in at blinding speed, seemingly coming straight at him. In a knee-jerk reaction, he had banked hard right to avoid a possible collision. Executing another series of complex evasive maneuvers, he had used all his piloting skill to steer well clear of both this new intruder and the pursuing Hind. Periodic glances at his radar screen had told him that he was no longer under attack. At seeing no imminent danger, he had swung his chopper around in a wide arc. Directly ahead, Zinova's Hind had slowed to a near hover, and in the sea below he had espied remnants of what he assumed to be the other aircraft. Another look at his radar confirmed the existence of only one blip in the surrounding sky.

Greatly puzzled, he had tried to make sense of his commander's unexplained attack and the downed intruder, but then his copilot and weapons operator had brought immediate light to the riddle.

"It's Javolyn!" his copilot had yelled over the intercom, his tone ringing with stark amazement. "He has taken Zinova's copter."

Thrown off balance by such a ridiculous assertion, he had found it necessary to question the claim. "Are you certain, Ivan?"

"It's him, I tell you," Ivan growled back testily. "I can see him clearly in the open doorway."

Badger had known at once that his copilot had seen an enhanced view of Zinova's Hind on his telescopic ranging screen. Zinova had briefed the team carefully on this operation, providing all his men with photos of the people they had been hired to capture. But Javolyn, the former Navy Seal, had somehow found a way to turn the tables on the Reaper and had commandeered his ship. That thought alone had been difficult for him to accept, for he had never known the Reaper to be beaten by anyone.

Throwing a surge of power into the main rotor, he had headed directly at the other Hind, coming up quickly on it from behind. "Blow him out of the sky!" he had ordered the copilot.

With the element of surprise on his side, Badger had watched as the copilot unleashed two air-to-air missiles in succession that caught the Hind squarely on its engines' exhaust.

Badger dropped these thoughts as the downed Hind rolled over and slipped into the depths, her chin bubble bobbing to the surface one last time before disappearing completely. Continuing to hover, he suddenly became aware of something in the water below. Narrowing his eyes, he realized a body had floated to the surface. "Look to your left!" he instructed Ivan. "Do you see it?"

"It might be Javolyn," came back the reply.

Badger studied the sea, gauging the swells. Doesn't look too bad, he thought. Perhaps they could salvage something from this. Making a quick decision, he issued an order. "Ivan, get back there and retrieve him. I'll bring us lower."

"He's floating face down. How do we know it's him?" retorted Ivan, his tone conveying he was not so eager to carry out the command.

Badger gritted his teeth. Sometimes his copilot could be quite difficult to deal with. If not for the fact he was deadly with the weapon systems, he would have asked Zinova to replace him long ago. "Do as I tell you!" he roared harshly.

Ivan unbuckled himself and stomped irately to the rear, glaring impudently at Badger as he passed. "I hope you know what you're doing," he grumbled in annoyance. "A rogue wave could swamp us and then we'd be out two Hinds, not to mention food for sharks."

Badger brought the Hind lower, careful to keep the belly of the fuselage just above the water. The sea had calmed considerably, with wave heights averaging no more than a half meter in his estimation.

"Bring us right another meter," Ivan shouted. "He's just beyond my reach."

Badger sidled the Hind a tad sideways, judging that he had positioned the chopper correctly.

"Good!" Ivan yelled. "Keep her steady."

Badger craned his head around to watch as Ivan lowered the folding retractable steps and grabbed a length of rope from a storage box. Prudently, Ivan put on a harness and clipped on a safety strap that would prevent him from falling into the water. Tethered securely to a bulkhead, the strap would also provide him with leverage as he leaned out to grab hold of the body.

"Let me know when you have him," Badger yelled back impatiently. He turned his head forward to watch for any change in sea conditions, setting his eyes on the horizon as a reference point to hold the chopper in an unwavering hover. The chopper was so low that it seemed to him as though it was floating rather than hovering. The cruise ship he had been prepared to attack upon Zinova's command lay in the distance at one o'clock.

Ivan moved down the steps slowly, careful not to lose his balance. Planting his feet firmly on the lowest step, he let out an obscene curse as his boots were suddenly awash from a small wave. Leaning out, he managed to get a hand on the body bobbing idly before him. He quickly realized it was the shorty neoprene wetsuit the man wore that had kept him afloat. Cautiously he pulled him closer, prepared to fend off an attack, for it was possible the man could be playing possum and was purposely luring him in. But the blood clouding the water quickly allayed his fears. The sea in the immediate area ran red with it. It seeped from a deep gash marring the man's left temple. Lifting the head clear of the water, he scrutinized the face.

Smiling devilishly, Ivan raised his voice to be heard above the deafening cyclonic rotor wash as it blasted the water into frenzied agitation. "It's Javolyn, all right," he shouted proudly, trumpeting out the words as though it was he who had decided to retrieve the body.

"Hurry it up!" Badger yelled back irritably. "What's taking you so long?" Being this close to the water made him edgy.

As far as Ivan could tell, Javolyn appeared dead. This was further substantiated when he placed a thumb over the man's carotid artery and was unable to detect a pulse. Securing the rope around Javolyn's torso just under the armpits, he climbed back into the cabin.

Badger craned his head around again. "Is he secure yet?" he asked hotly.

"Give me a sec to tie off the rope."

Badger was anxious to get going. And while delivering Javolyn's remains to Cardoza held a high priority, rescuing Zinova was even more important. Assuming he were still alive, there was a good chance he was being held captive aboard the Southern Star.

Ivan shouted again. "I've got him slung like a side of mutton. You want me to pull him in?"

An idea began to take root in Badger's mind. Maybe he could make a trade: Javolyn for Zinova. The fact that Javolyn was dead would not matter, for Zinova's captors wouldn't know that. He wanted the offered trade to be obvious, but he also figured the sight would keep the captors from firing upon the Hind. "No, leave him hanging," he ordered. "Get back up front."

Badger held the hover long enough for Ivan to reclaim his seat in the weapons' bubble. Seeing that his copilot was ready, he put pitch into the main rotor and felt the Hind begin to rise. Something thumped heavily behind him, and the airframe abruptly shuddered as though a heavy load were suddenly imposed on it. The chopper yawed stiffly, its nose coming around to starboard, and he knew at once it was struggling to gain altitude.

Perplexed, Badger craned his head around the side of the seat to look for the cause. His eyes immediately went wide with shock. A dolphin rested on the cabin floor, a large white dolphin with its tail jutting out the open doorway. Extending outward from the creature's body was a set of grasping appendages, and held within its right appendage was a length of rope that trailed behind and out the doorway. The dolphin turned its head briefly to stare at him, and in those black orbs he sensed a deep abiding intelligence.

The dolphin turned its head again, this time seemingly studying the closed door on the opposite side of the cabin. Using its free appendage, it reached up to grasp the door latch and slide the door open. Another moment passed as Badger continued to stare transfixed, not trusting his eyes as the creature reached over to pull its considerable bulk through the opposite doorway and fall back into the sea.

Still stunned, Badger's eyes fell on the rope as it slid snakelike across the cabin floor, coming in one door and out the other, pulled along by the creature that held it. Something banged loudly against the lip of the doorway through which the dolphin had entered, and he caught a fleeting look of a large shackle tied to the rope. It bounced haphazardly into the cabin before flying out the opposite door. Attached to it was a steel cable at least one-inch-thick, and he suddenly realized what that cable represented. The thought sent a heavy jolt of fear coursing down his spine, and it galvanized him into putting maximum pitch into the rotor blades. With the full power of the turbines behind the blades, the Hind began to rise again. A quick glance at the altimeter showed fifteen meters, then twenty.

Badger spun his head to look aft again. The cable was still there, moving rapidly across the cabin floor in a rasping slither. What he was witnessing couldn't be real, he told himself. Things like this just didn't happen.

With mounting dread, he snapped his eyes forward again. The Hind was still climbing, just passing the thirty-meter mark. And then his dread turned to full-blown fear as the chopper's upward progress was suddenly halted. The abrupt stoppage jarred him to the bone as he came up short against his shoulder straps, but they saved him from being catapulted into the cockpit roof.

As if from far away, he heard Ivan yell out angrily to demand what was wrong, but he had no time for explanations. Swiveling his head, he saw the cable was now stationary and taut as a bowstring. In desperation, he pulled harder on the collective in hopes of breaking the cable's tenacious hold, but the collective was as far as it would go. With the engines screaming, the Hind swung pendulously from side to side, fighting insanely to overcome the thing keeping it from going any higher.

Looking out the port window, Badger espied the cable stretching to the water, aware that its angle was rapidly changing. It was slicing through the sea, moving out laterally from the vertical. Glancing out the starboard window, he saw the same thing happening. The ends of the cable were being pulled in opposite directions. Horrified, he looked at the altimeter. The Hind was dropping.

Sweating profusely and with pounding heart, Badger looked off to his left again. Where the cable cut through the water, a huge dark shape easily forty meters in length breached the surface. His first thought was that it was a submarine, but then he saw the spray of rising mist that spewed from it, and he realized it was a whale spouting. Girthing its head was some kind of a harness, and shackled to the harness he discerned the end of the cable. Glancing out the opposite window, he spotted another whale. The whales were working in concert, inexorably pulling the Hind down.

This isn't real, he tried to convince himself. *Wake up you dumb Ukrainian!* he admonished, hoping this impossible predicament would simply vanish. *Do you hear me? Wake up, it's only a dream!* he screamed inwardly. But the sight would not go away.

Badger closed his eyes and braced himself as the sea rose up to claim the Hind. The airframe bucked severely as it met the water, then tilted sideways just enough for the main rotor to catch the surface. The abrupt impact with the aqueous medium was too much for the rotor shaft to bear, causing it to buckle and send a brutal shock wave that carried into the turbines to tear them apart. Almost immediately the blades stopped spinning and the fuselage began to flood.

Unbuckling himself quickly, Badger made for the storage compartments further back where the life vests and inflatable life raft were kept. Ivan was right behind him, cursing up a storm. "You crashed us," he accused angrily.

Badger was too stupefied to reply, instead noticing that Javolyn's lifeless body bobbed aimlessly in the waves just off to one side of the floundering aircraft, still tethered to the rope Ivan had looped around him. Three white dolphins suddenly broke the surface and rushed forward, one of them removing the knife strapped to Javolyn's calf and cutting the line holding him. The same dolphin turned to lock eyes with Badger for one brief moment, and in a sudden flash of perception, Badger knew those eyes belonged to the same creature that had entered the Hind minutes earlier.

Ivan pushed past him furiously, pulling the inflatable raft from its place of storage and yanking the inflation cord. As the raft inflated with an audible hiss, he turned back to eye Badger with derision. "What's the matter with you?" he scolded heatedly, seemingly unaware of the dolphins. "Can't you see we're sinking?"

"Didn't you see?" Badger uttered lethargically, still mesmerized. "They have hands."

"Have you lost your mind?" Ivan shot back. "Snap out of it!" He didn't have a clue as to what Badger was talking about. Up until the Hind was stopped dead in its climb, he had been checking out the readouts on the weapons systems. After that he had turned to berate Badger for his inept flying. He hadn't witnessed any of the things Badger had seen.

Turning, Ivan pulled the fully inflated raft toward him by its tethering line, but as he did so, the dolphin Badger had been eyeing slapped the water brutally with its tail to send a blast of water into the faces of both men, momentarily blinding them.

Wiping the water from his eyes, Ivan felt the tethering line go taut and fly from his fingers. Regaining his sight, he realized the raft was moving away. In desperation he dove forward with outstretched arms to retrieve their best chance of survival, but his fingers merely grazed the wet rubber as he fell headlong into the water. Surfacing quickly, he looked on in disbelief as the raft drew rapidly away, moving as though under its own volition. Stroking wildly, he made an effort to swim after it but soon discovered the attempt was futile. Exhausted and coughing up water he finally gave up the chase, gulping air into heaving lungs and staring dazedly as he watched the raft drift farther away. Treading water clumsily, he was suddenly aware that it was being towed by dolphins. Struggling to stay afloat, it occurred to him he had forgotten to don a lifejacket, and he immediately spun around to go back to the Hind to get one before it sank. He was not a strong swimmer and he knew Badger couldn't swim at all.

Ivan glanced around apprehensively, a spasm of panic knifing sharply through him as he scanned the surrounding water. The chopper and Badger were now gone. The thought that had been haunting him ever since Badger had brought the Hind close to the water suddenly grew to monstrous proportions, for one of his biggest fears was sharks.

* * * *

-19-

Amelia Amhurst awoke with a start, finding herself sitting upright and breathing sharply. Realizing where she was, she let out a deep sigh of relief, then leaned back to rest her head on the soft pillow once more. To her surprise, she discovered she had been weeping in her sleep, for her cheeks were wet, dampened by tears of anguish. Remnants of the nightmare still clung to her like prickly burrs from a thorn bush, and with a cautious dread she tried to make sense of it before it faded completely like most of her dreams.

She had been standing on one of the exterior esplanades gracing the colony's central structure, gazing in fascination at the thing hanging high in the heavens. It glowed with a vibrant luminosity in the midst of a pale dawn, a vision of morphing color and writhing motion. The sight had instilled an exhilarating tranquility within her, and she had intuitively perceived it as a harbinger of limitless promise. Transfixed, she had basked in its spell, reveling in the rapturous joy it gave her. But her bliss was soon shattered. An immense cloud had appeared on the horizon, bringing with it such intense gloom that it swallowed everything before it in an inky blackness. The darkness came on with the swiftness of a fanged predator, making her tremble in trepidation. It swelled larger, seething with an unseen yet unmistakable malevolence, poised to engulf the thing that signified the final bastion of hope and her along with it. Horrified by its destructive intent, she had sought escape, but her legs failed her. Suddenly there were people all around, hordes of them, running in frenzied madness. Gaunt and emaciated, they cried out in terror at the horrid blackness bearing down on them, their bellies distended with starvation, their clothes tattered and ragged. Tripping and stumbling along, she sobbed ruefully at her lack of courage, finally falling in the midst of the stampede. Fearing she would get trampled, she brought her knees to her chest, shielding her head with her arms as her lungs heaved with exhaustion. With the ebony darkness crushing in on her, she let out a final piercing scream, vaguely cognizant of the pulsing light. Almost abruptly, she found purchase in the reality where she now lay.

She closed her eyes, then opened them again, taking in the room surrounding her. Idly she let her gaze wander to the wall opposite the bed. An unusual oil painting hung there, and she remembered seeing others of a similar though varying composition in those portions of the city Jacob had allowed her to see. *What was she looking at?* Describing it was ineffable, for no words could adequately convey its motif. Though she knew it was an illusion, starbursts of differing color seemed to spring forth from it if she stared at it too long. A jumble of lines appeared to twist and interlace without end, seemingly dwindling to points far off in space. They left behind wakes of serene happiness that rippled outward to wash over her. She had gone to sleep staring at the artwork, suddenly aware that the vision in the dream had been conjured from what lay on the canvas. Though the latter portion of the dream had disturbed her, she realized the debilitating blackness had failed to extinguish the light, for it had continued to flicker with a measured cadence just before she awoke.

Unable to sleep any longer, she arose and moved to the balcony to take in the early morning vista. The view was stunning, bordering on the surrealistic, and she gasped at the sheer beauty of it. A heavy fogbank blanketed the waters surrounding the central structure, the mist glistening with a soft magenta glow as it stifled rays from the red solar disk ascending just above the horizon. Her room faced the north, giving her an elevated panorama of Navassa Island.

Jacob had been very cordial, inviting her and her cameraman to an overnight stay, providing them both with lodging in the highest level of the city. She had readily accepted, eager to learn more about the facility.

She was still awed by what she had seen the previous day following the incident with the UN delegation when Jacob had given her and her cameraman a guided tour of the city. Though the facility was still under construction, she had been astounded by the interior architecture, which seemed to be unconstrained and infinitely more graceful than the rigid dictates of cubic geometry common to most land-based structures built by man.

What she had observed was suggestive of the natural free-flowing lines on the exterior of a seashell, leaving her truly spellbound. It was a fantasyland of endless wonder. The interior spaces were laid out with smoothly curving walls, floors and ceilings, which gently rose and fell like swells in a rolling sea. A seemingly endless mix of lofts and galleries abounded. These overlooked serene pools, fountains and cascading waterfalls in public areas, with numerous open stairways, ramps and escalators making them reachable from a network of interlaced walkways and decks, many of them terraced, winding their way around rising pillars and beneath arching bridges. A definite biological look characterized everything, as if designed by some alien, unearthly intelligence that sought to mesmerize the beholder, and it was this intrinsic organic design that influenced all aspects of Aquaria's internal appearance. Lighting was recessed and indirect, suffusing the hallways and corridors with a soothing glow. Oyster whites, coral pinks, nautilus tans and other subdued hues came together in a kaleidoscope of color that was punctuated by startling splashes of scarlet, daffodil yellows, cobalt blues, and iridescent greens, with the varying tinctures merging and streaking like oil paints in an artist's palette prior to fully mixing. Built into the walls in many places on levels above the sea were thick panes and bubbles of glass, behind which swam multitudes of exotic fish among brilliant corals and anemones of flaming ruby, opal and magenta, further enlivening the interior domain of the city.

And then she recalled the area at the heart of the central structure that had truly stunned her. It was by far the largest open space inside the facility she had so far seen, an enormous amphitheater with tiered walls that rose up better than 250 feet from an elongated lagoon of placid water. Spilling down from a height close to the ceiling along the far side was a roaring waterfall that plunged along a series of cataracts, sending up spray and mist as it met the water in the lagoon. She had stood along a walkway that overlooked the water at a level midway up in the vast chamber, giving her a panoramic view of the open space. Bordering the water on one side was a white sandy beach sporadically adorned with palm trees, and set back from the water were three thatch roofed dwellings in close proximity to each other. The tiered walls were rife with leafy flora, and growing from the ledges was an abundance of various types of fruit-bearing trees and flowering bushes in an explosion of vivid hues. Flitting among them where hordes of multicolored tropical birds and butterflies representing a variety of species. Looking above she had taken in the roof of the structure, amazed by the way it mimicked an azure sky, and seemingly floating within it was a brightly lit globe made to resemble the sun. It bathed everything beneath it in a dazzling wash of grandeur light that accentuated the mix of colors blanketing the artificial setting. But the most striking feature of all was the rainbow that hung above the base of the falls. The view had taken her breath away, for it was as though she had been transported to a surrealistic chasm that existed on a faraway planet. The combined effect caressed the eyes and fondled the spirit.

"This is incredible," she had remembered saying to Jacob. "But aren't you afraid those exotic birds and butterflies will escape to other parts of the city. There's so many."

Jacob had smiled arcanely. "They're not real. What you are seeing are holograms, three-dimensional images produced by the interplay of laser light projected at various frequencies."

"So I'm looking at an illusion," she had remarked in disbelief.

"Not entirely. With the exception of the fauna and rainbow, everything you see before you is comprised of real objects. While the birds and butterflies are optical illusions, the trees and plants are actually alive. All the other components such as the water, sky and sun are artificial, ingeniously combined to make the setting before you appear real."

Something high up had caught her eyes. "What are those?" she had asked, pointing to one side of the artificial sun. A portion of the sky had winked out to reveal a rapidly dilating opening in the roof where several objects snaked down like the arms of an octopus, each wrapped around the trunk of an enormous tree. She had perceived the arms as being segmented, gradually tapering down from a thickness the size of an average man's waist to the girth of ship's hawser.

Jacob had taken a moment to study her expression, and in retrospect she knew he had seen the look of an awestricken child seeing something wondrous for the very first time. "We call them 'The Tentacles'," he had answered with an amused grin. "They function much the way cranes you often see used for constructing skyscrapers in land-based cities, but these are far more versatile and structurally sophisticated. They have played a big part in the building of this city and are capable of lifting enormous loads."

She had watched as the rootball of the tree was lowered into a hole situated on a wide ledge midway up on the far side of the chasm. To her it had seemed impossible that the arms could still support such a heavy load while extended at such an oblique angle. While the first three tentacles maintained their hold on the tree to keep it vertical, two more tentacles, each tipped with a claw-like bucket the size of a pickup truck, had meandered down from the roof opening to dump soil around the rootball and bury it. Taking only seconds to do this, the buckets had then closed and tamped down the soil to compact it around the base of the tree. In moments all five tentacles had retracted back into the ceiling.

She had continued to stare as the circular opening contracted to disappear completely, after which the full canopy of an azure sky came back into view. "Who controls those things?" she had asked. She had then gone on to query him how they were able to move so fluidly and quickly without an operator having a direct line of sight in order to manipulate them so skillfully.

When Jacob answered, she had sensed he was holding something back. "Oh, there's an operator, all right," he had explained a little too cryptically, and from his mien he seemed to be deciding how much information he should offer. After a pause, he said, "The operator uses hidden cameras positioned along the ledges and located near the tip of the tentacles as points of reference for moving things."

Satisfied with the condensed explanation for the moment, she had directed her gaze back to the newly planted tree. "What kind of tree is that?" she had said. "I've never seen one like it."

Jacob had responded quickly. "It is called a mapou tree. Once it fully matures it will have doubled in size. There are some Haitians who believe such trees to possess ancestral spirits and mystical powers."

His reply had made her turn to study him curiously. Such a statement had seemed totally incongruous with Jacob's eruditic persona. "Are you one of those believers?" she could not help but ask.

Jacob had suddenly appeared contemplative. The question had seemed to dredge up a profound experience stored deep in his memory, and had she been able to read his thoughts at that moment, she would have seen what had taken place on that fateful night back near the tiny coastal village where he had grown up. She would have felt his horror and astonishment as he tried to pull Amphitrite's hand away from the giant mapou tree used by the locals for what he considered to be ridiculous animistic rituals. She would have discovered the unleashing of an unimaginable psychokinetic force capable of enormous destruction. She would have known that had he not witnessed it with his own eyes he would never have believed such a thing was possible. She would have been privy to a seemingly implausible event where the earth had fissured to evoke a colossal landslide that had destroyed a convoy of Tonton Makout coming to destroy the village and all its residents.

She remembered the thin smile that had eventually come upon Jacob's face after she had asked the question, and had she been able to assess the inner workings of his mind then and there, she would have gleaned some of the teachings his deceased grandmother had tried to instill in him prior to that epiphanic event. She would also have learned how he had so stubbornly refuted them in those days. Had she been able to glimpse those resurrected memories of his, she would have understood exactly what he meant when he had finally responded to her curiosity. "Superstition often springs from occurrences that cannot be adequately explained by science, yet we should not close out minds to these things," he had simply said. "Let me just say that anything is possible in the limited four-dimensional subspace to which our minds are naturally attuned."

Amelia broke from these recollections, suddenly aware of where she was. The red solar disk of the dawn sun had risen a few more degrees as she stood on the balcony high up in Aquaria. With difficulty, she pulled her gaze from the majestic beauty that stretched away before her. Turning, her eyes were immediately drawn to the enigmatic artwork hanging on the room's back wall. All at once she felt herself plummeting, and a rush of images went flashing by. Intuitively she knew what she was seeing. It was the memories that one simple question had evoked in Jacob's thoughts. And now she was grasping the full context of it. She was seeing the causation, the total spectrum of events that had led to the building of the magnificent structure upon which she now stood.

The moment passed quickly, and once again she found herself on the balcony, staring down in mesmeric wonder of the cottony fog bank still clinging gently to the surrounding sea. Already thin wispy vapors were wafting up and away as rays from the sun slowly lifted the thick enshrouding mist.

With enhanced insight, Amelia drifted back into deep musings as she stared unseeing at the island in the distance. The tour Jacob had given her continued to dominate her thoughts, and she recalled something else he had said, that Aquaria was basically a floating island founded upon clusters of buoyant cells which supported various components of the complex. Directly under the central surface structure, each cell acted as the base of a tower that interlocked with other towers. These towers were surrounded by sprawling lagoons and containment ponds used for inciting intensive algae growth and producing a glut of products from the sea.

The primary structural components of Aquaria were modular, with each module being hexagonal in shape, allowing it to abut snugly to neighboring modules with no wasted space. All modules were fabricated in the sea by a unique and revolutionary manufacturing process, molded by their designers and tailored to the physical and psychological needs of their human occupants. The starting modules forming the initial ring, six in all, were all identical and by far the largest, each having a vertical height of 1300 feet and a horizontal width of 600 feet. Encircling the seed module, they comprised the highest platform. Following the completion of this ring of modules, the next ring was added, all having the same hexagonal width of 600 feet, but with a lesser height than the starting ring. The heights of succeeding rings gradually diminished as the city sprawled outward, growing much like a flower extending its petals. As Jacob had further explained, the primary components of the central surface structure extended five rings out and were now complete, giving the array the configuration of a squat mountain with an apex soaring 550 feet above sea level. Construction of the entire complex, however, was still ongoing and would not be finished for another year. Once completed, it would become home to 100,000 people, a tenfold increase over its current population of 10,000 residents.

The number had surprised her. "Won't that be a bit overcrowded?" she had questioned dubiously.

Jacob had patiently taken the time to point out that unlike conventional cubicle architecture where huge spaces go unused, the free-form approach to interior design allowed for a much more efficient use of space. "Think of Aquaria as an organism rather than a structure," he had emphasized, stressing that the guiding philosophy in its construction was to engineer the space itself to insure the comfort of its denizens. "A living environment that is intimately connected to the people it shelters," he had gone on to say.

He had shown her artistic renderings of what the floating facility would look like when construction finally ended. A protective mounded breakwater designed to absorb 75-foot storm waves would surround the complex. With an overall diameter of 5.8 miles in the shape of a hexagon, the twenty-fifth and final ring of modules would serve to support the breakwater, providing additional open space for gardens, hydroponic greenhouses, and pavilions. It would shield an arrangement of containment ponds on its lee side from the occasional onslaughts of an often unpredictable and moody sea, allowing for white sandy beaches to grace its outside periphery and providing a calm environment for additional beaches and recreational areas along the perimeter of the central surface structure.

As she pondered everything she had seen, she realized aesthetics was the overriding motif in the marine colony's design. Not only did it personify the city's inner layout, it would dominate the facility's entire outer surface once completed, with park-like settings planned for many locations.

With Jacob having directed her gaze from a lofty vantage point on Aquaria's uppermost platform, she had clearly seen that the breakwater was now complete on four of the six sides that would eventually encompass the complex, with those still missing being the southeastern and southern borders. Sitting atop and running along the inside of these barriers were areas set aside for orchards and the cultivation of hydroponically grown crops in extensive multi-tiered greenhouses, providing fruits and vegetables to supplement the diet of the inhabitants. Winding among them were pathways that led to residential pavilions reserved for those who would prefer living on or near the beach rather than in one of the apartments in the central structure.

But it was the sprawling containment ponds that had captivated her interest. They extended nearly one and a half miles, reaching from the beaches bordering the central edifice to the areas of cultivation situated along the lee side of the newly constructed breakwater. She contemplated her first unobstructed view of them. When she had gotten her initial glimpse of the colony during her inbound flight, they had not been visible from the air, veiled by an obstructing cottony cloud that hid everything but the greater portion of the central structure. Assailed by a scorching tropical sun, however, the thick vaporous mist had finally evaporated, leaving every area of the complex exposed to the naked eye.

According to Jacob, the containment ponds were Aquaria's primary source of exported produce, projected to account for 77 percent of its revenues once the complex was fully operational. Within the ponds currently operational, huge quantities of blue-green algae were being harvested, triggered into explosive growth by the cold, nitrogen-rich water brought up from the deep ocean abyss, some of which became food for animals low on the food chain, those being shrimp, crabs, lobsters, abalone, and a variety of shellfish, with specific ponds set aside for each species. Scrap waste protein from processing these lower animal life forms was then used to spawn teeming populations of high-value fish such as tuna, mackerel, herring and cod.

Mouth agape, she had taken it all in, bedazzled by what lay before her. "This facility is huge," she had acknowledged reverently.

"Yes," Jacob had nodded in agreement. "Even at this stage of construction, Aquaria is by far the largest floating structure ever built. When completed, the sum total weight of all her components will exceed slightly more than eight point four million tons."

"It's unbelievable," she had murmured breathlessly, speaking more to herself rather than Jacob.

Continuing to linger on the central structure's upper platform, Jacob had swept his arms wide as if embracing the vast panorama stretching away toward the horizon. "We managed to build all this with minimal dependence on outside inputs, mainly using what the ocean provided," he had proclaimed proudly.

"But how is that possible?" she had asked, her mind reeling in a sea of unanswered questions.

Jacob had turned to look her full in the face, his countenance coming alive with the enthusiasm of one eager to teach. "The concept is rather simple," he had replied bemusedly. "We grow most of the components that make up this facility."

She had simply stared, searching his eyes for possible signs of insanity, but was unable to find any. Her cameraman had caught his uttered explanation on tape, and she had taken the time to review it in stark wonder.

"All of the primary structures were accreted from seawater," Jacob had gone on to elucidate. "Structurally, they possess the same characteristics as reinforced concrete, but are actually stronger and lighter than conventional concrete. In some respects, the accretion process is similar to the way the shell of a mollusk is formed. Only two ingredients are needed to do this, these being calcium carbonate and an electrically conductive metal in the form of rebar or a wire mesh. The metal acts as a skeletal framework and is assembled to give a particular structure its intended shape. Magnesium, alloyed with small amounts of manganese and aluminum, is the metal we use. This metal has a tensile strength comparable to that of steel, though it is much lighter in weight. All of the constituents we require are abundant in seawater and can be extracted out of solution rather easily. By applying an electric current to the framework, the calcium carbonate is forced out of solution to bond electrochemically to the charged metal, forming a cement-like coating over the skeleton. The electricity, of course, is supplied by our OTEC power-generating facility at the center of this complex."

Amelia broke from these thoughts, suddenly aware that she had wandered into the apartment's bathroom. Looking at her reflection in the mirror, she wondered if she truly knew the person staring back. For the first time since joining the IBC, she felt out of place working under the banner of the media giant. Something did not sit right about the organization. Had she been ignoring her gut instinct all along? Had her ambition so blinded her that she refused to acknowledge the peculiarities of the company? Could it be that the IBC was violating the primary principles of sound journalism, established for the sole purpose of deceiving the hoi polloi of nations and molding public opinion to conform to the wishes of a shadowy group lurking behind the scenes? Jacob had indicated the interview would ultimately be distorted to cast Aquaria in an unfavorable light, and she had not refuted it. By doctoring facts and putting various spins on events through shrewd editing, the IBC could easily mislead the masses. With heartfelt conviction she realized she would betray herself if she continued to abet an organization controlled by ruthless and corrupt people bent on propagating lies.

One thing was for sure now. She would do whatever she could to keep the IBC from besmirching the image of something so wondrous as Aquaria.

-20-

Achilles was distraught with anguish as he sent a silent call of distress to Destiny. *Please come,* he cried. *We need you! Jay Jay needs you!*

Destiny's response was immediate. *What's wrong?*

Reading her reply, Achilles could tell she was braced for bad news. *JJ is severely injured with head trauma and may be dying,* he informed her. *I can barely detect a pulse within him. Fernando has also been injured, but only slightly.*

I'm on my way, Destiny answered without hesitation, and Achilles knew at once her anguish surpassed his own.

-21-

It was still early in the morning on day two of her visit to Aquaria, and Amelia had more reporting to do. But now she would try to help the colony rather than abet the people she worked for. Jacob had graciously agreed to take time out of his busy schedule and continue with the interview, revealing still more about Aquaria and their objectives.

Strolling casually along a red brick pathway that wound its way through one of the many vibrant gardens situated atop the southern breakwater, she stared up into the Haitian's craggy face as her cameraman walked backward in front of them, his camera focused on their conversation.

"So you're convinced the United States and Europe are in decline," she said.

Jacob nodded grimly. "As I've pointed out, both have been led down the road to socialism, and history has already shown us such ideology does not work, for it ultimately erodes a nation from within. I have no doubts both the U.S. and Europe are headed for a fiscal cliff."

"You also believe Aquaria will be unaffected if this happens," Amelia replied, echoing another of Jacob's convictions.

Jacob's face remained solemn. "Yes, our colony is autonomous and self-sufficient. Though our system here tends to mimic the principles of capitalism, it is untainted by the greed that has ruined other nations."

"And you claim the Federal Reserve is exacerbating this problem for the Americans," Amelia added, continuing to recap the main points Jacob had hit upon earlier.

"For the first ninety-nine years of its life, the Fed had no accountability to the United States government. It was not audited by the US Congress, nor was it legally bound to do so. It produced no books, nor did it file annual statements or show balance sheets to anyone outside its domain. As such, it was an unrestricted money monopoly. Only until recently was it audited, and that was only a partial audit under the Federal Reserve Transparency Act passed by Congress in two-thousand twelve. What was uncovered was truly shocking."

"What was that?"

"For one, over a three-year period beginning in two thousand seven, it provided more than sixteen trillion dollars in covert financial assistance to some of the largest financial institutions and corporations in the United States and throughout the world. It knew a disastrous market meltdown was on the horizon. And while this was initially taking place, the Fed's

DOLPHIN RIDERS

chairman and the US treasury secretary kept assuring everyone that the bubbles brewing in the marketplace were merely a hiccup and that the fundamentals were still strong. They lied to the American people while alerting members of Congress to restructure their financial portfolios so as to avoid getting hurt like the typical citizen when the market did crash."

"But one would think propping up the market was a good thing," Amelia said. "Didn't it keep the world economy from collapsing completely?"

"It gave the illusion of stabilizing the system to make it appear as if everything would quickly rebound to a robust state of health. In reality it did nothing to improve the ailing economy or the unemployment situation that ensued. By creating vast sums of essentially worthless paper currency via its printing presses, it injected massive amounts of liquidity into the financial institutions at zero interest, requiring them to buy equities, but only after world markets faltered."

"What if they refused to buy equities?" Amelia interjected quizzically.

"Then no loans would be forthcoming," Jacob clarified. "That was the Fed's underlying stipulation for providing such cheap money. As I said, the loans were interest-free, so the banks really had no qualms about complying with such a simple requirement. In fact, many of them bought back their own stock with the money."

"Are you certain of this requirement?"

"One only has to evaluate the facts objectively to understand why such cheap money was issued."

"What was the Fed's motive in doing this?"

"Generally speaking, equity markets the world over have always been looked upon as barometers of economic health. By providing a deluge of money into them, stock indexes were once again driven back to high though artificial levels, especially with many corporations taking advantage of this by repurchasing their own stock. This deceived the average investor as to the actual underlying strength of the market."

"Sounds like a house of cards," Amelia offered.

"And a very fragile one at that," Jacob agreed, "one that can come crashing down again at the slightest sign of economic uncertainty. Keep in mind that the Fed can call in these cheap loans any time it chooses, causing a reverse scenario in which all the banking institutions are forced to dump their equities. By holding short market positions through advance notice from the Fed, vast amounts of investor wealth can be periodically siphoned off into the hands of these super-rich elitists. This accounts for most of the boom-bust cycles you often see in the markets. The elite make it a habit of manufacturing scenarios that can cause markets to go into freefall, and it is these events from which they always profit."

Amelia fought to subdue the naïve, wide-eyed expression wanting to dominate her face. Winning the battle, she prodded him further, subtly attempting to highlight the enlightenment Jacob was providing. "You had mentioned earlier that America's founding fathers had warned against such banking monopolies."

Jacob stopped and stared out to sea through an opening in a nearby stand of peach trees. A ship could be seen in the distance. The subtle frown that came to his face did not escape Amelia's notice before he launched into another discourse.

"President's Thomas Jefferson, James Madison, and Andrew Jackson all argued that the Republic and its Constitution were always vulnerable to the dangers of the so-called money power, which in essence were elitist bankers who were always seeking to gain a monopoly over the issuance of currency long before the establishment of the Fed. Jefferson himself stated that the issuing power of money should be taken from the banks and restored to Congress and the people to whom it belongs. To him, the banking institutions were more dangerous to liberty than standing armies."

"You also had insinuated that bankers were responsible for creating socialism," Amelia said. "Can you explain what you meant by that?"

A shrewd smile came to Jacob's face. "Did you know that Karl Marx was actually commissioned to write his voluminous works on communism?" he said, choosing to skirt the question for the moment.

Amelia's manner reflected ignorance on the subject, but she sought to use it to solidify Jacob's argument wherever it was headed. "I had always been under the impression he wrote it to express concern for those downtrodden by the rich."

This elicited an amused chuckle from Jacob. "Marx was one of the most evil people to ever walk the earth, and by his own admission professed to have given his soul to the Devil. He hated God, and his chief aim was the destruction of all religion. This intense hatred is thoroughly embedded in his writings, the Manifesto."

Jacob's expression altered into one of sadness. "Greed, not altruism, was the primary motivating force behind Marx's Manifesto, much of which was proven to have been plagiarized from the work of an obscure social ideologue named Victor Considerant more than twenty years earlier. And scholars have shown some of it was actually modeled after the doctrines and philosophies maintained by the Egyptian Pharaohs for governing the masses."

"Then who paid him to write it?" Amelia pressed.

Jacob plucked a beautiful red rose from a nearby bush and casually sniffed it before replying. "Elitist bankers in Germany and America paid him."

Jacob anticipated Amelia's look of surprise, and he smiled knowingly. "Sounds illogical, doesn't it, for why would rich and powerful people pay someone to create an ideology to agitate the lower classes into armed revolt where society is turned upside down? Nevertheless, it is a well-documented fact many historical scholars have brought to light over the last hundred years. At its core, Marxism was and still is an elitist scheme for consolidating power, plain and simple. It has nothing to do with relieving the misery of the poor or advancing mankind to a higher state of social awareness. It is a device concocted purely for the exploitation of man by a very small and privileged minority, with supremacy of the elite as its main objective."

Amelia continued to keep an expression of stark amazement etched on her face for the sake of the camera, but under the surface she was clearly in Jacob's corner now, fully captivated by his erudite manner. "I always thought Marxism favored the working class and sought to do the opposite, to stop the exploitation of the poor by the upper class."

"Absolutely not," Jacob said. "The proletariat fell victim to this new ideology with its promise of wealth distribution. It did not favor the proletariat at all, and it certainly did not favor the bourgeoisie, which was targeted for elimination and the confiscation of their assets. It was simply a blueprint for the takeover of political and economic power by a relatively tiny elite minority who were bent on snatching the wealth of the middle class."

"So it was all a pretense, a plot to stir the have-nots into armed revolution," Amelia parroted.

"Yes, in nineteen seventeen it triggered the Bolshevik Revolution in Russia," Jacob went on. "It was class warfare at its worst. Marx looked upon the proletariat as little more than stupid cattle, using their jealousy and envy of the bourgeoisie to enforce a hell on earth where fear, suffering, terror and treason ruled supreme. Under Lenin's reign, blood flowed like a river with close to two million people being murdered merely for their anti-socialistic thinking."

"But why would these elitists put their own fortunes at risk by instigating such a revolt?" Amelia said. "Couldn't such a scheme have backfired?"

"No, because these people groomed and financed Lenin to lead the revolution. Lenin was merely a puppet. He carried out their directives, ensuring they remained unscathed from the ensuing turmoil."

"You mentioned that Marx wanted to bring down religion," Amelia said. "What was his motive?"

"He was a practicing Satanist. He hated anything that gave reverence to God."

"Are you saying he actually worshipped the Devil."

"Most assuredly. The strange part is, he grew up in a Christian family, and early in life confessed Jesus Christ as his Savior. He knew Scripture well. But over time he underwent a transformation, choosing to side with the Devil. Writing the Manifesto seems to have reinforced this shift, for Communist doctrine clearly and consistently preaches atheism, which is a denial of God's existence. Marxism is a godless philosophy. This in itself shows Marx was a fraud. He did not practice what he preached, since a Satanist cannot be an atheist."

"Why is that?" Amelia interposed quickly, appearing more confused than ever.

"Using theological reasoning, if there is a Heaven, then there must be a Hell. Choosing to take sides with the Devil means going against God. Believing in one implies a belief in the other. Therefore, a true atheist would not have believed in the existence of Satan."

"I see your point," Amelia acquiesced thoughtfully.

Jacob smiled with satisfaction, enjoying the way his historical revelations were getting through to her. But he was not yet ready to drop the subject, proceeding to enlarge upon it further.

"Marx fancied himself as a poet, and I have to admit he was quite good at it. He had an exceptional flair for revealing his true nature within his lyrics, some of which reflected the full measure of his wickedness. Not only did his poems profess a succinct hatred for God, they also conveyed his loathing of mankind in general, since according to Scripture, all human beings were created in the image of God."

"It appears you have studied Marx quite extensively," Amelia said, impressed by Jacob's knowledge of the man. But she needed more for the camera, undeterred that her efforts might be in vain, for once the videos reached IBC headquarters, it was almost a certainty that this segment of the interview would be edited out. For some inexplicable reason, though, she had still been unsuccessful in sending clips of earlier tapings.

"Can you quote any examples of his poetry?" Amelia asked eagerly, somehow perceiving he could.

Fulfilling such a request came easily to Jacob, for he had been blessed with an eidetic mind. He could recall everything he had ever seen, heard or read in exact detail.

"This one personifies his contempt for humanity," Jacob said, launching into a verbatim quote of a Marx poem:

" '...Yet I have power within my youthful arms
To clench and crush you with tempestuous force,

DOLPHIN RIDERS

While for us both the abyss yawns in darkness.
You will sink down and I shall follow laughing,
Whispering in your ears Descend,
Come with me, friend'."

Amelia looked horrified. "My God!" she uttered.
"Here is another of his verse that may shock you," Jacob intoned somberly:

" 'With disdain I will throw my gauntlet
Full in the face of the world,
And see the collapse of this pygmy giant
Whose fall will not stifle my ardor.
Then will I wander godlike and victorious
Through the ruins of the world
And, giving my words an active force,
I will feel equal to the creator'."

Amelia stared, momentarily stunned by the sheer impact of the words. "What an incredibly perverse individual."

"Yes," Jacob concurred. "Marx was a monster, and his Manifesto inflamed the minds of the proletariat as though they were all possessed by the same demons that drove him. But this much is clear, communism was created by elitists as an antithesis to Western capitalism, devised to produce a system that gave them ultimate power. Through the mechanism of controlled change by controlled conflict, they sought to achieve a New World Order where they would reign supreme. What's more, there is a wealth of information to prove these people were members of the Illuminist Freemasonry. To this day this cabal still exists."

"Are you referring to the Illuminati?" Amelia chirped in astonishment.

"Yes."

"I thought they were a thing of the past, that they died off long ago."

"That's what they would like the world to believe, but I can assure you they are still around and stronger than ever. When Marx was writing the Manifesto, a highly select body of secret initiates within the Illuminati financed him. They called themselves the League of Twelve Just Men."

"It sounds strange that they would consider themselves just," Amelia said.

Jacob's expression soured momentarily, then turned stoic. "Unfortunately, evil people rarely see themselves as evil. Most of them actually believe they are doing humanity a service. They think the masses are too stupid to run the world in a responsible manner. And while these financial elites are the actual culprits in creating most of the ills that continue to plague the globe, they are emerging from the economic wreckage more powerful than ever before. Even worse, they are dictating the terms of their own enrichment to servile governments throughout the planet."

Jacob stopped walking, bringing his gaze to bear seaward once more through another opening in the orchard's thriving foliage. He remained mute for several seconds as he studied the same ship that drew his attention minutes earlier, and sensing that something was wrong, Amelia refrained from intruding on the pronounced contemplation that suddenly took hold of him.

Seeming to dismiss the vessel, Jacob turned to face the camera again, though he seemed distracted. Continuing with the interview, he said, "We, in Aquaria, believe the state of the world is more precarious than ever, that…"

The cell phone Jacob carried rang curtly, cutting off the next leg of his confabulation. The sound it emitted told him the incoming call was of a priority nature, one that demanded an immediate response. "Pardon the interruption," he apologized, turning his back to Amelia and her cameraman.

"What is it, Ez?" he uttered softly, holding the phone snugly to his ear.

"It appears there is a strike force looking to take back the Southern Star," Ez informed him. "From your present location, you can see the ship. Look to the sky above it."

Jacob lifted his eyes, quickly locating close to a dozen objects plummeting toward the freighter. An aircraft could be seen higher up. "Are you able to identify them?" he asked.

"I assume them to be the same UN team sent here yesterday judging from the aircraft insignia and configuration. Mat has already been alerted."

Jacob's spirits abruptly plunged at a speed nearly equal to the mercenaries hurtling toward the vessel, and he found himself suddenly pining for the quiet life he had abandoned in order to undertake the building of Aquaria. Almost as quickly he chastised himself for entertaining this thought. A dereliction of his calling was beyond consideration. He had made his decision long ago, and he knew he would rather die than deviate from the path he had chosen to follow. To fortify his resolution as he often did, he reminded himself of a quote from Edmund Burke, a famous Irish statesman: *'The only thing necessary for the triumph of evil is for good men to do nothing.'*

"Thank you, Ez," Jacob said wearily. "Please keep me apprised of developments."

Jacob mulled the situation with trepidation. Mat's contingent would be outnumbered three to one, and Phillipe's safety weighed heavily on his mind. With deep resignation, he turned back to Amelia. "Unfortunately there are pressing matters that demand my attention. Hopefully we'll be able to pick up on this interview later this afternoon. In the meantime, feel free to roam the facility at your leisure."

Amelia nodded, watching as Jacob turned and walked away. Redirecting her gaze, she espied the lone ship several miles distant. It was then she caught sight of the descending skydivers, their chutes deploying one by one as they sought to alight on the vessel. Gesturing frantically, she signaled her cameraman to capture the event on video. But her cameraman was already recording the event.

-22-

Mat looked at Bashir, still finding it strange that the man standing before him had once been a member of Al Qaeda. But after working with him for the past several years now, he had come to trust him implicitly. Through some inexplicable means, Destiny and Amphitrite had found a way to bring out the good in him. And there had been a wealth of it. Like a suppressed geyser that could no longer be contained, it had all come gushing out. Not only were they able to correct his severe physical injury, they had also been able to heal his psychological and emotional impairments as well.

"Put this on!" Mat commanded, offering Bashir his cloaker. Unfortunately, all they had among them were two.

"I respectfully decline," Bashir replied stoically. "It fits you better."

The Palestinian's response did not come as a surprise, for Mat knew Bashir would readily put the lives of others ahead of his own.

Glancing behind him once again, Mat espied the descending paratroopers. They had executed a seemingly perfect HALO – High Altitude Low Opening – a classic military aerial maneuver, dropping like meteors to an altitude of perhaps 500 feet before deploying their chutes. From that alone he could tell these were crack troops, making him believe this was not going to be an easy fight regardless of a few advantages he had at his disposal. Already he could see the lead commando flaring his chute sharply in an attempt to alight on top of a cargo container situated 900 feet away near the ship's stern.

Mat turned quickly to Kalid, Bashir's second and another former Islamic radical. Like Bashir, Kalid had dropped his allegiance to Al Qaeda long ago, devoting himself entirely to the establishment of Aquaria. He knew it was because both men looked upon Destiny and her mother as nothing less than angels sent to earth by Allah to change the world forever. Their belief was unshakable, and their loyalty to the colony was without question. No words, no matter how logically put forth, would ever shake them of this belief. They were committed and would defend the colony and its inhabitants with their very lives if necessary.

"Then I offer it to you, Kalid," Mat uttered in frustration. He had no time to haggle, watching as several more chutes flared. The wind had shifted just enough to keep the Chilean commandos from landing closer to the bow. As best he could tell, conditions were working in his favor at the moment. Unless members of the strike force wanted to drop into the sea, they were forced to settle for the ship's stern.

Kalid eyed the cloaker with contempt. "I also decline," he spat disdainfully.

"Suit yourself," Mat said irritably, "but don't tell me later you should have accepted after a bullet takes your head off."

"I don't think that would be possible," Phillipe joked nervously, doing his utmost to inject levity into a darkening situation.

Mat scrutinized the lad closely. In spite of all the training he and Jake had given him, and in spite of his commendable performance in his combat debut a short time earlier, Phillipe was still green. And should anything happen to Phillipe while under his watch, he knew Jake would be unforgiving.

"The way I see it," Mat opined briskly, looking to all three men, "we can either stay and fight or make a hasty retreat in the sub."

He shot a quick glance through a portside window, looking down at the water, but failed to spot anything. *Allah's Sword* remained on standby, lurking submerged somewhere in hailing distance of the ship. The sub was once captained by Raduyev, the nefarious Al Qaeda operative, but had since fallen into the hands of the Aquarians mainly due to Bashir's unwavering loyalty to the colony. At the moment it was being piloted by Abdel, a former Yemeni freighter captain who had lost an arm when his ship had been sunk by Sebastion Ortega. After Abdel's life had been saved by the pod in the aftermath of that event, Abdel had since become another devoted disciple of Tursiops and its objectives. With the exception of Phillipe, Mat's team had reached the Southern Star via the submarine.

Bashir spoke up quickly. "We must stay and fight. This ship is the only insurance we have to keep Aquaria from being destroyed." For emphasis, he pointed in the direction of the enormous tanker, its superstructure now just barely visible in the distance as it made its way over the horizon. In another minute, the ship would be out of sight. "If we give this ship back to them, it is possible the *Kraken* may return."

Mat looked at Kalid, reading the same conviction in his face as well.

"I'm with Bashir," Phillipe said when Mat turned to him.

Mat noted the worry on Phillipe's face, but he knew it had nothing to do with personal safety. It was evident Phillipe was thinking about Jake. Two hours earlier, Perseus, Phillipe's bond mate, had informed the lad about Jake's misfortune. And while Jake's injury was life threatening, there was nothing any of them could do to help. But Jake was in good hands. He was currently in Destiny's care aboard the Angel.

"All right then, it's settled," Mat growled, keeping stern eyes on Phillipe. "But you make sure you keep your cloaker activated at all times."

"But I have a Masker," Phillipe objected sourly.

"No buts," Mat retorted adamantly. "Either wear the cloaker or you're out of the fight."

Phillipe nodded grimly. Wearing the cloaker Jake had left behind would make up for his inexperience in a firefight.

Mat pulled out his cell phone and lifted it to his mouth. "I need a new program, Ez. Send me-"

"I'm way ahead of you," Ez interrupted. "It's already in your Maskers. I advise you to test them first. You're right on the edge of their receiving range."

Mat grabbed Bashir's wrist, touching a button on the device strapped to it. Almost at once, Bashir's image underwent a transformation. He did the same thing with Kalid's, with each one producing the desired illusion. Each Masker was outfitted with a receiver, enabling it to be reprogrammed from a remote location as circumstances dictated.

Mat completed the test by touching the button on his own device. "How do I look?" he said, seeking feedback from the others.

"Mean and ruthless," Phillipe opined. "At least I have an idea what we'll be going up against," he quickly added.

Mat nodded, then looked at Bashir and Kalid for their assessments.

"Very ugly," Bashir quipped.

"And very arrogant," Kalid answered distastefully.

Satisfied, Mat lifted the cell phone to his lips again. "All the units seem to be working just fine, Ez."

"That's good," Ez replied, "but I strongly advise each of you to use Option Two on your units before-"

"Bye, Ez," Mat interceded, cutting her off and stuffing the phone into a pocket. Try as he might, he had never felt comfortable talking to a computer, particularly since it always seemed to be one step ahead of him.

-23-

Captain Francico Alvarez unstrapped himself from the harness, letting the chute flutter off into the sea. He was eager for a fight. He and his men had been unbearably humiliated at the hands of the colonists, taking flight like a panicked mob fleeing a swarm of stinging wasps. But now he would take his revenge against these insignificant vermin, looking forward to using the *corvo* slung at his side. Crouched low and gently caressing the haft of the weapon, he watched as his commandos swooped down one by one to land on other cargo containers abutting his own.

Alvarez considered the little information he had been given. Allotey had told him the freighter had been hijacked by a small strike force that had come from Aquaria. He was to take back the vessel, freeing the ship's captain and crew, including a man called Zinova and his associates, assuming any of them were still alive. Based on Allotey's assessment of the situation, it was surmised they were all being held hostage.

Using hand signals, Alvarez instructed his men to fan out and make their way forward. During the pre-mission briefing, his orders had been explicit. Their primary objective was to take back control of the ship's bridge. Aside from capturing two of the hijackers, they were to crush all opposition without mercy. Yes, taking two prisoners would be sufficient to give him satisfaction. The thought caused him to run his fingers along the scabbard sheathing of his *corvo* as he moved cautiously between rows of cargo containers. His men were good at this sort of thing, surely the best in the world, and he had no doubts they would get the job done.

He had read the dossiers on both of the former Navy Seals that ran Aquaria's security and he was not impressed by what was revealed. He and his men were far better warriors than any Navy Seal. As he mulled this, Javolyn's face loomed up in the forefront of his mind, an image of haughty defiance and audacious insolence. The man had seemed totally unconcerned with the authority Allotey represented, plainly displaying an open disrespect of Alvarez and his men.

A short burst of gunfire broke out somewhere off to his right, the sound muffled by the intervening barriers of cargo containers. It was obvious at least one of his men was already engaging the hijackers. Several more bursts rang out as Alvarez continued to make his way forward. Then all was quiet.

Alvarez crept around a bend, Javolyn's image continuing to mock him. He would get his revenge, slicing with the *corvo* to carve that impudence right off his face. The sound of movement directly ahead caused him to stop and remain perfectly still. His finger tightened on the trigger of his Uzi, primed and ready to squeeze off a salvo, but he failed to see anything.

Letting out a slow breath, he advanced a few more feet, fully prepared for a skirmish. A burst of blinding color suddenly appeared in front of him, swirling and whipping like monstrous tentacles caught in a powerful eddy. They lashed out to coil around his brain before he could even think to react, bombarding it with sizzling motes that snaked and interlaced before stretching to the boundless reaches of space. Staggered by the sheer intensity of it, he felt the inside of his skull being scorched as a surge of scalding bile rose up in his throat. Frozen in its grip, a sickness unlike anything he had ever experienced engulfed him. Closing his eyes tightly to escape the sight, he lay on his back convulsing uncontrollably and regurgitating his last meal. With his mind teetering on the edge of sanity, he barely managed to grasp what was happening.

Using all his will to guide a trembling hand, Alvarez managed to lift the cup shielding the tiny syringe strapped snuggly to his right thigh. With his remaining strength, he slapped down on the plunger. A potent mix of dextroamphetamine and a non-hallucinogenic LSD derivative was immediately injected into his femoral artery. He normally refrained from resorting to the use of drugs, but he had been warned about this strange debilitating weapon the colonists used to keep spies from breaching their facility, a type of visual display that made intruders ill upon looking at it. He had been told these displays were placed in key sectors of Aquaria and came in the form of paintings with an abstract motif. He had scoffed at the idea, unable to accept the notion that a two or three dimensional rendering of art could make him sick simply by looking at it. Nevertheless, Allotey had been firm, insisting Alvarez and his men be prepared for such a possibility. And while they had all been outfitted with the syringes during their visit to the colony, he had seen no reason for him and his men to use them unless it became absolutely necessary. His suffering now, however, was infinitely many times worse than what he had experienced back there.

Alvarez felt his sickness suddenly ease as the drug took effect, and from somewhere nearby the sound of gunfire invaded his awareness, a short staccato burst followed by a rasping grunt. Cautiously he opened his eyes, prepared to close them again, but the vision was now gone.

An eerie quiet descended as he rose on unsteady feet, and he realized the corridor was empty. Feeling his strength quickly rebounding, he sidled around the corner of a cargo container. The crumpled body of one of his men lay before him, and crouched over it was Allotey, who appeared to be binding his man with plastic tie wraps.

Dumbstruck, Alvarez was momentarily speechless. "How did you get here?" he managed to utter. Allotey had not accompanied his team. The man had no military training and certainly didn't have the skills to perform a HALO jump to reach the Southern Star as did Alvarez and his men.

Startled, Allotey stood, turning slowly to face him.

"How?" Alvarez demanded, his voice rising in confusion.

Allotey's austere persona suddenly morphed, starting at the eyes. A tangled mass of lights sprang forth from them, rapidly expanding to engulf the UN envoy. In an instant, an explosion of color gushed forward, reaching once again for the Chilean commando.

Alvarez reeled, a sense of vertigo taking hold of him. But the cocktail of drugs flowing through his veins gave him the means to resist, and he did not become incapacitated like before. Though disoriented, he managed to level his weapon and squeeze off a burst, unsure exactly where to aim. Sparks erupted close by, and he realized he was being fired upon as a barrage of bullets collided with the side of a nearby cargo container. In reaction, he dove low, tucking in his shoulder and executing a forward roll to avoid being hit. Springing back to his feet with the agility of a cat, he scrambled around a corner. Ricocheting rounds buzzed over his head like maddened bees seeking to sting as he raced along an empty corridor. With his mind spinning in turmoil over these inane happenings, his only option was to escape.

-24-

Kalid was still conscious when Mat found him slumped in a pool of blood. He was bleeding profusely from a bullet wound in his lower left thigh. Using two plastic ties strung together, Mat applied a makeshift tourniquet to stem the loss of blood.

"I don't understand what went wrong," Kalid gasped.

"What do you mean?" Mat whispered back, cinching the ties tightly above the wound.

Kalid grimaced, fending off the pain before answering. "At first the hologram worked, then it did not."

"Looks like it worked just fine," Mat muttered. He glanced around cautiously to take a quick inventory of his surroundings before dropping his eyes to the commando Kalid had subdued. The man had stopped retching and lay eying his captors dazedly.

"No... you don't understand," Kalid stammered back, having trouble getting his thoughts in order. "There was another."

"Another?" Mat looked around apprehensively a second time,

wondering if he should reactivate his cloaker.

Kalid nodded. For emphasis, he stared at the bound commando. "This man was the second."

"Was this man the one who shot you?"

Kalid shook his head torpidly. He had lost a lot of blood and was on the verge of blacking out. "I used the hologram on another."

"Are you saying it had no effect on him?"

"It did at first. He became very sick." Kalid indicated the subdued commando. "But while I was busy with this one, the other one was back on his feet. I tried using the hologram again, but it no longer worked on him."

Kalid's rambling suddenly became clear. "So he shot you?" Mat said.

"Yes...I returned fire, but I don't know if I hit him."

"Which way did he go?"

"That way."

Mat looked in the direction Kalid indicated, his mind struggling to analyze this strange twist. As far as he knew, the use of Option Two was infallible in bringing down bad guys. Recovering from exposure to it generally took several minutes, and re-exposure should have been just as debilitating, if not more so. But somehow the commando had regrouped and managed to fight back.

Unlike Kalid, Mat refrained from using Option Two. The hologram's calming effects made him too lethargic to be effective in battle. But he knew Kalid would try to avoid killing whenever possible. And strangely, Kalid was able to function efficaciously while resorting to Option Two.

A warrior mentality was in Mat's blood, and he had no issues about taking out an adversary by more conventional methods whenever the situation called for it, even if it meant killing. At this moment, these mercenaries were the enemy, and you neutralized the enemy without speculating on their core natures. Whether they were morally good or evil made no difference. Already he had taken down three commandos using his stealth capability. In each case, he had dispatched an unsuspecting foe using the steel bar he carried, crashing it down with brutal force. He had left each of them unconscious or possibly dead, trussed up in a manner similar to the way Kalid had bound his own captive. Phillipe was also contributing, for Mat had seen two others drop in a heap, their assailant remaining invisible. That meant six others still roamed the ship, assuming Bashir had not subdued any of them.

Mat was pressed to make a decision. He couldn't leave Kalid, and yet he could not let the ship fall into the hands of the remaining commandos.

Without further thought he shed his cloaker.

"What are you doing?" Kalid asked wearily.

Mat pulled Kalid to his feet and leaned him against a cargo container. "Put this on!" he ordered.

"No!"

Kalid's injured leg began to buckle and Mat grabbed him harshly to keep him from falling back down. "Do as I say, damn it!"

Kalid resisted feebly as Mat forced the cloaker around his body and activated it. Roughly, he moved him to a nearby recess between two containers and shoved him in. He had no time to be gentle. Quickly, he retrieved Kalid's weapon and placed it under the cloaker, satisfied that both man and weapon appeared invisible.

"Stay put until I get back," Mat snapped. Without waiting for a reply, he initiated his Masker and made his way forward toward the bridge.

-25-

Destiny held back tears as she eyed Jake's prostrate form. With his head swathed thickly in gauze wraps, he lay quietly in the bed he always used aboard the Angel, appearing to sleep peacefully.

"Can you hear me, my darling?" she said softly. She held his hand and lifted it to her lips, kissing it tenderly. Unable to stifle the heartache, a tear welled up and trickled down her cheek. "Please forgive me for failing you. The power has left me."

Hercules' thoughts suddenly merged with her own. *Do not blame yourself. The power has left us all. We have changed.*

Destiny's mind churned with memories of earlier times. Healing catastrophic injuries, though difficult, had once been possible for the pod to achieve. On such occasions, she had always acted as the lens through which the others focused their mental energies. Adding her own considerable potency to the flux, the net effect had been miraculous to those worthy of being cured. As a result, torn or distressed flesh had mended quickly, with the greatest amount of healing usually taking a matter of minutes rather than weeks. But restoring a living creature to normal health would inevitably take a toll on her, sometimes leaving her physically drained.

A small sob escaped Destiny's lips out of frustration. All she had been able to accomplish was stabilize Jake's head trauma. She had managed to stop the brain hemorrhage, which Achilles had been able to discern using ultrasonic sound emissions to scan the injury. That was all. The power to actually heal had completely deserted her.

And so had her once dependable power of precognition. Her latest dream had proved that. It had only been partially accurate. It had never hinted that Jake might be severely injured, that he might die while dealing with the Eagle Master. To her, Jake had always seemed invincible. If not for the prompt intervention of Achilles, Hermes and Aphrodite in reaching the crash scene, Jake would have surely perished. Thankfully they had been able to summon two blue whales from Aquaria, less than three miles away. The whales had been preparing to tow a breakwater module into place and were already fully outfitted with harnesses and towing cables.

A deep voice rumbled mournfully, interrupting Destiny's thoughts. "How is he?"

Destiny looked up to see Zimbola looming over her. With his exceedingly large frame, he had to stoop down to keep his head from hitting the cabin ceiling.

"Stable for the time being." Destiny turned back to gaze through the porthole just above the bed. The soft undulations of the waves flowing past did nothing to improve her anxiety. "How much farther to the cove?"

"A little under an hour." The big Jamaican paused, his features solemn as he stared down at Jake. "You sure you don't want me to turn around?"

Destiny sighed deeply, still struggling to hold back a flood of tears. She had to stay strong. "I can't be sure of anything anymore, Zimby."

Zimbola nodded resignedly. He knew she was making a hard decision, for Jake's life might very well hang in the balance by not putting him on life support in one of Aquaria's state of the art medical facilities. But circumstances were rapidly heating up. Just a short time earlier while the crown of Aquaria's central tower was still in sight, Ez had apprised both of them of a brewing raid on the colony she was able to decode by hacking into a secure UN channel. Military forces were currently being mobilized to take over the floating city, and Jake, along with other colony leaders, were to be taken into custody.

"Where are the twins?" Destiny asked.

"Up in the pilot house with Fernando and Hector."

Fernando had fared much better than Jake during the crash, having been strapped securely into the copilot seat. He would have gone down with the Hind if not for the intervention of Hermes, who had gotten him out as the chopper was falling into the depths.

"If only Big D were operational," Destiny said.

"Yes," Zimbola concurred. He looked down at Jake again. Though he rarely showed emotion, his eyes were misty. "It is most unfortunate."

Destiny felt the ire building within her, ambivalent to the repulsion it should have induced prior to the birth of the twins.

You must remain calm, Hercules warned. *Anger is our enemy. It has infected us all. If we let it grow any stronger, it will place JJ beyond our reach.*

Destiny took in a deep breath, doing her best to quell the rising tempest within her. Up until that moment with Ternier and Raduyev so long ago, anger had been an unfamiliar emotion.

-26-

Mat spotted two commandos preparing to ascend to the bridge just as a kaleidoscope of intertwining color flashed at the top of the stairs. Not wanting his reactions to be dulled, he avoided looking at it, keeping his gaze locked on the enemy. One of the men shouted, then let loose with a burst of automatic fire, directing it up into the eruption of light.

Almost immediately, Mat realized Kalid's assertion to be true. Option Two was not working. No doubt Bashir was up there resorting to its use, for Mat had instructed him to hold the bridge. To save him, Mat had no choice but to use deadly force.

Without giving it another thought, he leveled his weapon and opened up on both commandos from behind. One man went down instantly, but the other managed to whirl, his body jerking spasmodically as he absorbed a spray of rounds, his Uzi continuing to spit out a hail of bullets haphazardly in all directions. Mat poured the remainder of his clip into him, amazed at the man's tenacity and durability. Abruptly his hands went numb as a random bullet slammed into his weapon and sent it flying from his grasp.

Mat stared dazedly. The second man had stopped firing and now lay sprawled on the deck. Regaining his senses, Mat reached for his fallen weapon, his fingers still tingling. He saw that the receiver for the magazine was gouged, the place where the bullet had struck. Pulling hard on the clip, he quickly discovered it would not come out. His assault rifle was useless.

"Do not move, swine!" a voice suddenly snarled from behind in thickly accented English.

Mat froze. He had to remind himself he was no longer wearing the cloaker.

"Do not turn around, otherwise you will be shot," the voice commanded gruffly. "Kneel down and place your hands behind your head."

Mat hesitated just long enough to glimpse the bridge. No help would be coming from that quarter, it seemed. The hologram had vanished and there was no sign of Bashir.

"Do it or die!" the voice hissed.

Mat placed his hands behind his head, but refrained from kneeling. It was a long-shot gamble, but his ploy was simple, and that was to rile the assailant standing behind him. Taking a prisoner, it seemed, held a high priority with this man, otherwise he would already be dead.

"Get on your knees!" The tone was more belligerent this time.

Using the man's voice as a gauge, Mat judged where his unseen foe stood. He continued to stand, ignoring the dictate. His only chance at survival was to remain standing.

"I said on your knees!" the man screamed in frustration.

The thing Mat hoped for came quickly. A gun muzzle prodded him harshly in the back. He had noted all the commandos carried an Uzi, a relatively short-barreled weapon. That meant his assailant would be just where he needed, and that was up close and personal.

Timing his move, Mat spun slightly off to one side with lightning quickness, catching the man squarely on the bridge of the nose with a raised elbow and sweeping his legs out from under him. It was a move he had practiced incessantly ever since learning it in the Seals, but this was actually the first time he had ever had an opportunity to use it.

Though stunned, the man squeezed hard on the Uzi trigger, but Mat had already deflected the barrel with the edge of his hand just enough to avoid being hit. The barrel felt like a hot poker as it discharged, but he ignored the pain as he got a firm grip on it. With his opponent momentarily blinded by the initial blow, Mat delivered half a dozen hammer-fists to the commando's face, turning it to a bloody pulp. Ripping the Uzi from his hands, Mat stood and stomped down hard with the heel of his boot, crushing that portion of the man's face left unprotected by his helmet. The commando went limp instantly, either dead or severely comatose.

A hand touched Mat's shoulder, and he spun around, ready to engage another foe, but there was no one there.

"Easy, Mat, it's me." Phillipe's persona suddenly materialized.

Mat looked around quickly, taking stock of the immediate area, then shoved Phillipe off to one side, a place of partial concealment behind some stacked crates. "What the hell are you doing?" he admonished harshly. "Turn your cloaker back on."

Phillipe's image winked out. "I think Bashir was hit."

Mat peeked around the side of a crate to survey the bridge, but there was no one in sight. "What makes you say that?"

"I saw him fall when these men opened fire on him."

Mat dropped his gaze to the three men he had taken out. They were still visible from his vantage point. "You get any more than the two I saw?"

"No," Phillipe's disembodied voice answered. "I saw no others."

Mat nodded, keeping a wary eye on his surroundings. "Then by my count, there's three left lurking about."

"Where's Kalid?" Phillipe asked.

"Out of the fight. He caught one in the leg, so I gave him my cloaker."

Poking his head around the crate, Mat espied the bridge again. "I've got to get up there."

"I'll go," Phillipe offered.

With a hand still on Phillipe's shoulder, Mat felt him begin to move. "When cows fly," he growled softly, yanking him back.

"But they can't see me," Phillipe protested.

"Forget it!"

"Then take my cloaker."

"Not an option. Jake would have my hide if anything happened to you under my watch."

"But-"

"End of discussion."

Mat risked another glimpse of the bridge, but all was quiet. "Stay here and be ready to give me cover fire in case all hell breaks loose. Don't try using the hologram, because it no longer seems to work on these clowns."

"Yes, I noticed." Phillipe grabbed Mat's arm before he could bolt for the stairs. "Is it possible some of these men are basically good? Are they not soldiers just following orders?"

"Anything's possible, kid, but I seriously doubt it. From what Ez has told me, Allotey and Alvarez have been responsible for the murder of innocents while working for the UN. I can only conclude that the men following them are just as bad."

"Then how is it possible they are unaffected by the hologram?"

Mat shook his head. "I wish I knew the answer, but right now we've got to get them before they get us."

That said, Mat pulled Phillipe's hand from his arm. Still holding the Uzi he had confiscated, he raced over to the last commando he had neutralized, pulling several spare magazine clips from the man's utility belt as well as a fragmentation grenade that hung conspicuously from it. Reloading the Uzi, he stuffed the remaining clips and grenade into the pouches of his own belt, all the while keeping a sharp eye on the bridge above.

Taking a deep breath, he leapt for the stairs. The adrenaline was already flowing swiftly in his veins, giving his legs added spring as he surged up the steps two at a time. The discussion he had just had with Phillipe hung in the back of his mind, and with an effort, he cast it aside. He was a warrior, and in the heat of battle a warrior did not try to analyze the enemy's moral rectitude, for to do so could get one killed.

-27-

Alvarez had come upon five of his men soon after his as yet unexplainable engagement with Allotey, ordering each of them to inject themselves with the drug cocktail. One man, the newest member of his team, was reluctant to follow the command, and Alvarez was forced to use harsher persuasion to make him obey, pointing his Uzi in a threatening manner.

Satisfied, Alvarez divided up his men, leaving three of them to take the ship's bridge from the outside while he and two others would use a more covert route to reach the helm. Just prior to this mission, he had been shown plans of the freighter and knew where to go. Finding the hatch he sought near the bow, he and his men lifted the cover and climbed down a set of rungs that took them well below decks. After that, he led his team along a series of corridors before locating a circular stairwell that accessed ten decks above, the highest being the helm.

Reaching the top landing, Alvarez sidled up to the door that gave way to the bridge, craning his head around cautiously to view what lay on the other side of the door's small round window. He immediately drew his head back as a bout of gunfire suddenly erupted. The sound was muffled by the steel walls that surrounded him, but the distinct pinging of ricocheting rounds told him the bridge was being assaulted. More gunfire joined in, and then all was abruptly silent.

Alvarez risked another peek through the glass. A dark smile came to his face when he saw what lay beyond, and he shoved the door open with savage force. The bearded man that slumped against a far wall glanced lethargically at the sudden intrusion, apparently too weak or dazed to move. He was cupping a head wound that was bleeding profusely. Only one other person manned the bridge, a skinny, nervous looking individual who stood at the ship's controls, most likely the helmsman. The helmsman turned ashen as Alvarez and his two subordinates stormed into the room.

Alvarez stepped close to the wounded man and kicked away the AK-47 that lay next to him. The man's hand fell away listlessly from the wound as his body sagged to the floor. Alvarez had seen enough battle casualties to know the injury was not a fatal one. From the look of it, a bullet had grazed the man's head, cutting a deep furrow across the scalp and possibly fracturing the skull.

The helmsman yelled out in pain and fright as one of the commandos grabbed him roughly by the arm and twisted it.

"Leave him and secure the bridge wings!" Alvarez ordered his men.

He would need the helmsman to steer the ship.

One commando immediately scrambled for the larboard wing while the other let go of the helmsman and raced for the starboard side. Perched on the bridge wings, each man would have a commanding vantage of what lay below.

Alvarez pulled a pair of handcuffs from his utility belt and shoved the hijacker onto his stomach. An object strapped to the man's left wrist prevented one of the cuffs from being applied. Hastily he removed it, wondering what purpose it served. Putting it aside, he clicked the cuff into place, squeezing it tight enough to restrict the flow of blood. He was aching to use the *corvo*, but unfortunately his captive had lapsed into unconsciousness.

In annoyance, Alvarez flipped him onto his back and slapped his face several times to rouse him, but to no avail. The man was out cold. Needing answers, he looked over at the helmsman. "Where is your captain?"

"I...I don't know," the helmsman stammered. He appeared terrified.

Alvarez kept his face hard, though he smiled inwardly. He enjoyed invoking fear in others. "Tell me what you do know," he commanded in a foreboding tone. It was a voice he had perfected to instill trepidation.

The reply came out in a squeal not much different from a barnyard pig sent to the slaughterhouse. "They took him and the others below."

Alvarez was about to interrogate the man further when a single shot resounded outside. A quick glance through a port window showed the man he had stationed there stagger back from the overlook. The commando spun, looking back at him with lifeless eyes before collapsing. His lower jaw was gone, blown clean off.

Hunkering to one side of the port wing door, Alvarez nudged it open a crack to shout out a warning. "I have one of your men. Any attempt to come up here will be his death sentence."

Alvarez shut the door, looking behind him at the sound of footsteps. The other commando was scampering across the bridge to join him.

"Get back there!" Alvarez screamed. "Do you want them to come up behind us?"

The commando pulled up short, then ran back to cover the starboard door.

Alvarez assessed the developing situation, wondering if only one man remained under his command. If true, the odds had changed dramatically. It was something he had never anticipated.

Turning back to the helmsman, Alvarez posed a question. "Is your radio working?"

When the helmsman nodded, Alvarez issued a set of instructions to be carried out, all the while keeping vigilance of the portside bridge wing beyond the glass. He had only to wait less than a minute when the helmsman's radio transmission was answered. His pockmarked face broke out in a sinister grin when he heard the reply.

-28-

Phillipe spotted the movement on the larboard bridge wing immediately, seeing the commando lean over the bulwark to pick off Mat as he raced up the stairs. He had been prepared for such a possibility, and sighting accurately on the man's exposed face had required only a slight adjustment in his weapon's alignment.

Both Jay Jay and Mat had trained him well in handling firearms, spending several hours each week with him at Aquaria's firing range. The fact that he possessed remarkable eyesight, a trait inherited from his father, further enhanced his advancing skill as a marksman, and he had soon amazed his teachers with his shooting precision. But this was the first time he would actually fire at another human being, and he had only an inkling of a second to reconsider squeezing the trigger. Any delay on his part could result in Mat's demise.

Abruptly, the weapon bucked as though it had a mind of its own, catching Phillipe by surprise as a single round spewed forth. He clearly saw the target's head jerk back, disappearing from sight altogether. In that moment he knew it was a killing shot, and the thought saddened him. No matter how he rationalized it, he realized killing repulsed him.

The thoughts of Perseus reverberated in one corner of his mind. *Do not chastise yourself. You did what was necessary at the moment.*

I wish there had been another way, Phillipe rued.

Sometimes that is not possible.

Yes, Phillipe wanted to believe, his eyes continuing to scan the bridge wing as Mat climbed higher. Only one flight of steps needed to be ascended for Mat to reach the top, but Phillipe saw Mat suddenly pull up short. A voice rang out loud enough to be heard even from where Phillipe was positioned.

Inform the others Bashir has been taken prisoner, Phillipe advised Perseus, the thought dropping his spirits still lower. Bashir was like a brother to him, a kind and gregarious brother.

Perseus' response was equally downcast. *It has already been done.*

With an effort, Phillipe forced himself not to dwell on what he had just done, pondering their current situation instead. According to Mat, there should only be two commandos left, but with Bashir being held hostage, their opposition had the upper hand.

Perseus invaded his thoughts again. *I hate to be the bearer of more bad news, Phillipe, but Ez has just learned the mobilization of additional UN forces to the colony is proceeding much quicker than originally anticipated.*

How long? Phillipe replied.

Ez calculates twenty-four hours. Perseus followed up with more disturbing news. *Ez has intercepted a communique originating from this ship. Reinforcements have been requested and will arrive within the hour.*

This news unsettled Phillipe further, and he glanced briefly at Mat, who still remained one flight of stairs short of the bridge wing landing. Currently lacking a bond mate of his own, Mat would not be privy to this newfound information.

Rising from his hunkered position, Phillipe headed for the stairs, relaying another thought to Perseus. *Mat must be told of this.*

-29-

Hunkered down on the staircase leading to the ship's bridge, Mat searched the sky. There was still no sign of the UN reinforcements Phillipe had apprised him about. He was at his rope's end, knowing time was running out. With Bashir's life hanging in the balance by the two remaining Chilean commandos, he didn't dare engage them.

"Seems we're at an impasse," Mat lamented.

"Maybe not," Phillipe said, purposely letting the statement hang to wet Mat's curiosity.

Mat turned to eye him, but with Phillipe's cloaker currently turned on, his young protégé remained invisible. "I'm listening."

"Ez managed to get hold of the ship's plans and relayed them to Perseus. Perseus knows an alternate route that can take us to the bridge. He'll guide us."

Mat shook his head. "Your plan is flawed, kid. More than likely they'll have the access door either locked or barricaded. Even with your invisibility, once that door begins to open the bullets will start flying."

"That's only part of the plan. Ez says she will take care of the rest."

Mat groaned inwardly, not fond of the idea that Ez was once again calling the shots. Ez was essentially a machine, and machines were not infallible. "What scheme has she come up with this time," he grumbled.

"I'll tell you on the way," Phillipe's disembodied voice answered. "Just follow me."

Mat felt a hand grip his shoulder, and begrudgingly he let himself be guided down the stairway.

-30-

The familiar coastline rose up, haloed with silver and orange incandescence by the morning sun rising behind it. With the tide still high and only a mild sea breeze to deal with, Zimbola piloted the Angel smoothly into the tight opening in the barrier reef. The opening afforded only inches of clearance on both sides of the vessel, and had the water been lower, passage through it would have been impossible for the North Sea trawler. But with a small group of albino dolphins delineating the channel, Zimbola was able to avoid tearing open the vessel's keel on the jagged coral that thrived below the surface. And though he had traversed this precarious passage numerous times in the past, always guided by the dolphins, he nevertheless felt uneasy doing it.

Once through, Zimbola breathed a sigh of relief, giving thanks to Agwe, the Haitian sea god. Swinging the vessel ninety degrees to port, he skirted the craggy escarpments lining the shore. He was quite versed in the landscape's deceptiveness, for he knew the coastline would appear quite impenetrable to a person less familiar with its nuances. This, however, was an illusion, made even more so by a slight modification they had made to the shoreline.

Reaching for a small electronic device resembling a television remote, he leaned from the cabin and aimed it forward of the boat before thumbing one of the buttons. Almost immediately a huge section of rock began to rise upward, revealing an opening behind it. With deftness, he angled the craft into a cleft barely wide enough to accommodate it. Once his stern was clear, he activated the device again, causing the same formation of rock to slide back into its original position. A look at the backside of the rock showed it to be nothing more than a Hollywood prop, a false façade constructed of fiberglass and wood made to appear like part of the escarpment dominating the shore. This was something Jay Jay and the dolphins had designed and built as a precautionary measure in keeping interlopers out. Other security measures had been emplaced as well.

Rocky bluffs rose high on each side as Zimbola guided the Angel along a narrow waterway. Like the channel through the reef, the inlet provided the vessel only minimal clearance as it plodded slowly ahead. The Jamaican glanced up, waving in greeting at two men stationed atop the bluffs, one to a side. They manned camouflaged pillboxes that had been installed to repel attackers. They were denizens of the nearby village of Malique, part of a larger security force hired on to safeguard the inlet and what lay beyond.

Zimbola checked his watch, knowing a change of guard occurred every twelve hours. In another twenty minutes, the guard would be rotated. Continuing down the channel, he turned the wheel a few degrees to negotiate a slight dogleg in the waterway, which finally gave way to a sheltered basin of gin-clear water. It was a sequestered cove set in a gorge with steeply tiered sides that funneled down to the water from high above, giving it the shape of a crudely shaped though elongated amphitheater.

Standing on the Angel's bow, both children stared in wonder at the incredible vista, a home away from home. The view was spectacular, appearing like something out of a fairytale. Like their mother and many of the dolphins, this was where they had been born, the place Jacob referred to as *Gaia*, a place they and the others affectionately called *The Cove*.

The eyes of the children were immediately drawn to the basin's far end. A natural spring gushed forth from the highest point along the rim, sending a plume of whitewater cascading down in a series of cataracts before making its longest and final plunge to the pristine water below. At such a distance, the waterfall roared soothingly, sending up a swirling mist that often displayed a rainbow when exposed to sunlight. With the sun still below the basin's rim, much of the vista was cast in shade. But even the shade could not subdue the explosion of color that abounded. It was a mecca alive with flora and fauna. A seemingly countless assortment of fruit-bearing trees and flowering shrubs in full bloom hugged narrow terraces set in the tiered slopes, and flitting among the lush vegetation were throngs of multi-colored songbirds and butterflies representing numerous species. A white sandy beach studded with palm trees ran along two-thirds of the water's edge, finally ending at the base of the falls. And nestled along one rocky alcove set back from the beach were three thatched structures that further adorned the panorama, the one on the left being built just prior to the birth of the twins.

Unable to constrain themselves a moment longer, both children leapt gleefully from the Angel's prow. They were immediately joined by their bond mates, Alpha and Omega, who whisked them off toward the falls.

"Children, wait!" Zimbola shouted from the wheelhouse, but from experience he knew it was an effort in futility trying to keep them aboard the vessel a second longer. A rare smile broke his features as he watched them race away. It was a game they often played to see who could reach the falls first. He was glad to see them frolic like this. Seeing their father in his present condition had made them uncharacteristically morose during the last few hours.

Standing at his side, Hector spoke up. "My money's on Melody this time."

"With those two, it is foolish to bet," Zimbola replied, knowing races such as this usually ended in a tie.

Hector climbed down from the wheelhouse and moved forward toward the bow as Zimbola reversed the trawler's variable pitch prop. Grabbing a long gaffing pole, he stood at the ready as the 65-foot vessel eased to a stop where the cove was widest. In one smooth motion, he hooked the mooring ring they had installed years earlier, quickly connecting a shackle to the ring with a practiced hand. Pulling slack out of the mooring chain, he tugged sharply on it to make sure the one ton mooring block was firmly embedded in the sandy bottom.

Satisfied that the vessel was now secure, a sense of pride took hold of him. He had grown to love the Angel. And while he had to admit she was not a comely looking craft, he saw resilience in every battered inch of her, a seaworthy vessel that dripped with character. Like both her owners, those being Jay Jay and Zimbola, she was tough, durable and reliable, a boat you could always depend on. As he reflected on these things, he considered her name. Though they all referred to her as the *Angel*, it wasn't her full name. Not the name painted on her stern in big block letters.

AVENGING ANGEL.

Hector had mulled this strange contradiction whenever he looked upon her with the same adoration as he was doing now, always coming to the same conclusion. The name fully mirrored Jay Jay's dual nature. It implied a strong sense of justice, a live and let live attitude that sought to keep those he cared for safe from peril. With those around him unthreatened and out of harm's way, his friend and boss was basically a Teddy Bear at heart, generous to a fault. But menace those he loved in any way, and he was capable of becoming a holy terror without mercy, risking life and limb in a near reckless manner in order to protect them.

Hector dropped these thoughts, looking up to scan the upper elevations of the chasm and waving. Sentries had come out of their positions of concealment. There were four of them waving back, each manning a strategically located station separated from the others and set up to defend both the cove and the airspace above. He knew all these men. They were locals who had been carefully screened and found to be good, trustworthy people. They were fully committed, heart and soul, to the grand scheme concocted by Jacob and the pod. They would not fall victim to greed or be tempted by the secrets the cove held. And most of all, they looked upon Destiny and her mother as though they were goddesses. He had no doubts they would fight to the death on their behalf.

Hector smiled, remembering the last two attempts Cardoza and his ruffians had made on this place following the establishment of security measures, with each attempt ending in a dismal failure. He knew the lure of gold made men do crazy things, but with the Colombian drug lord it was an obsession, and he was convinced Cardoza would try again.

Making his way to the stern, Hector saw Destiny emerge from the rear cabin, a vision of stunning loveliness in spite of the troubled look on her face. So beautiful, he thought, and yet she has no awareness of her own physical beauty. It was an innocent thought, devoid of lust, for he viewed the inner beauty that dwelled deep within her to be her most alluring quality. It radiated outward to touch all those around her like warm rays of the sun, and it was this that made him adore her. She was the perfect match for Jay Jay, a man unlike other men.

Destiny turned to face him with damp eyes. "I'll be going ashore, Hector. Please stay with Jay Jay."

Hector nodded, feeling her pain. "Jay Jay is tough. If anyone can survive such an injury, it will be Jay Jay."

Destiny turned quickly and dove for the water, not wanting Hector to see the tears spilling from her eyes. She was immediately joined by Hercules, who carried her in the direction of the falls.

Hector watched her go, suddenly aware that Zimbola and Fernando had also come out on deck to see her off.

"What is she doing?" Fernando asked.

"She looks for answers," Zimbola said. Though he had never climbed behind the falls, he had an inkling of what lay up there.

-31-

Mat and Phillipe made their way through the Southern Star's interior, locating the stairwell that led up to the helm. Reaching the door that accessed the bridge, Mat risked a peek through the door's Plexiglas window. A quick glance was all he needed to assess the situation.

Off to one side, Bashir lay unconscious, bound hand and foot. Crouched next to him with a shoulder to the port wing door was Alvarez. The remaining commando guarded the starboard wing door, and standing frozen at the helm was a skinny individual who appeared terrified.

Mat ducked down just as Alvarez whipped his head around to take stock of the access door. In that fleeting moment of surveillance, he could tell Alvarez was rattled. Certainly that would make sense with ten of his men now out of the fight. The captain's head was in constant motion, swiveling back and forth nervously to take darting glances through the bridge windows in all directions. He was taking inventory of everything around him, especially the skies as he looked anxiously for the arrival of reinforcements.

DOLPHIN RIDERS

Mat tested the door latch, surprised that it moved. Hefting the grenade he had taken from the last mercenary, he handed it to Phillipe. "You ready?" he asked.

Phillipe nodded, seemingly eager to get on with this. With the assistance of Ez, they had worked out a plan with only a slim chance of success at saving Bashir, but with UN reinforcements on the way, they dared not delay any longer.

A low buzzing came to their ears, the sound quickly growing louder. Mat risked another peek through the door's window. Alvarez was looking upward, his attention drawn to the source of the sound.

In that instant the ship listed precariously to starboard, but Mat was prepared as the deck tilted sharply underfoot. Flinging the door open, he lurched into the room and let loose with the Uzi, throwing a hail of rounds at the commando stationed at the starboard wing door. That was his immediate option, since he risked hitting Bashir had he fired directly at Alvarez. Completely caught off guard by the combination of distractions, the commando went down before he could even level his weapon. But even before he fell, Mat dove for cover behind a nearby console, taking away any opportunity for Alvarez to have a target.

Scooting through the door right behind Mat, Phillipe tossed the grenade toward Alvarez, who had lost his balance by the sudden roll of the ship. Almost at once, the ship swung back onto an even keel, and as it did so, the Chilean captain's eyes widened in horror at seeing the grenade bouncing across the floor. In a flash he was on his feet, ripping open the nearby door like a madman and scrambling out onto the portside bridge wing.

With his cloaker turned on, Phillipe remained invisible. He raced for the same door, bringing his weapon to bear on the back of his fleeing quarry, but some deep seated inhibition kept him from pulling back on the trigger. In that brief moment of inner conflict, Alvarez scrambled down the stairs, disappearing from sight.

Phillipe was nearly knocked down as Mat crashed into his unseen form. "You're letting him get away," Mat yelled, shoving past and giving chase. Bounding for the stairs, Mat stopped short of the first step, pointing his weapon below and firing. A shower of sparks kicked up as ricocheting rounds pinged harshly but harmlessly off steel. Alvarez was already past the next landing down, effectively shielded from the volley.

Frustrated, Mat turned to look back at Phillipe. "Get Bashir to the chopper!"

Phillipe deactivated his cloaker to become visible again. "Where are you going?"

"I've got to get Kalid."

"We'll wait for you."

Mat glanced upward to scan the sky. "There's no time, and besides, the chopper can only hold four," he lied hurriedly, knowing it could actually carry five. "I'll have Abdel pick us up. Now get going."

"But... "

"Do as I say, this is not open to discussion."

Before Phillipe could protest further, Mat vanished down the stairs.

-32-

Destiny stopped working her way up the craggy escarpment momentarily to make sure the twins were not following. They still sat astride their bond mates at the base of the falls where she had left them. Nevertheless, there was no mistaking the inquisitiveness in their eyes as they gazed back at her, their minds at wonder with what lay up there. Ever since they could walk, she had forbidden them from ever going behind the falls. She had made it clear that the place was strictly off limits. But deep down she knew it was only a matter of time before their curiosity got the better of them, ultimately making them disobey. After all, how could she expect them to obey such a mandate when she herself had gone against her own mother's wishes on this same issue at an early age. Behind the falls lurked unexplained mystery. Within its darkened recesses lay a strange intangible power that beckoned her every so often as it was doing now. But it had been quite some time since she had last come here. Jay Jay had been with her during that visit.

She smiled fondly at the memory. In the deepest recess of this place was where the twins had been conceived.

Climbing higher, she pulled herself onto a stone ledge that wound behind the plunging water. The roar was deafening. Staying focused, she dug fingers and toes into small cracks and crevices within the moss covered rock to keep from slipping. Though the climb was difficult and treacherous, she had done it many times before, ascending fairly quickly. Rounding a bend, she entered the cave, letting her eyes adjust to the semi-darkness before reaching for the flashlight tied to her waist and turning it on.

The cave widened as she went further back, and once again she noted the familiar array of artifacts lining the base of both walls as she passed. She held the flashlight low to avoid looking at the repugnant displays situated above the artifacts. A montage of murals covered the sides of the cavern. They had been painted by an unknown artist from ages past, and elaborately depicted within those murals were horrific atrocities inflicted on the Tainos by bearded men clad in armor. The Tainos had been a gentle and giving people native to Hispanola, but they had been quickly enslaved and nearly wiped out by arriving Europeans who hungered for gold.

The scenes within the murals had shocked her the first time she had laid eyes on them. Growing up in a place filled with wondrous beauty and sheltered from the outside world, she was unprepared to acknowledge a side of the human species she never knew existed until that moment. The paintings captured a broad range of abject human suffering and death quite explicitly, with frightening portrayals of starvation and emaciation on exhibit. Natives being used for slave labor were subjected to the lash and being hung by the neck. These along with decapitations and other grisly sights had been too much for her naïve young mind to bear, and seeing such abominations for the first time had caused tears to flow unabated down her cheeks. Thereafter, she had avoided looking upon them whenever she ventured into the cave.

Such depictions had been the primary reason for making this place off limits to the children, for they revealed too many inhumane horrors she considered unhealthy for young minds.

Destiny moved deeper into the grotto. The cave narrowed just beyond the last of the dispiriting murals, and a jumble of fallen rock came under the flashlight's glare. Stepping carefully between some boulders, she slipped sideways into a fissure before ascending a series of steps that had been carved into the rock. The stairway rose steeply a short distance, and in moments she emerged into the center of a large chamber. Like the steps, the chamber had also been chiseled out of solid rock, for it was much too smooth and uniform in configuration to have been formed naturally. With a height of twelve feet from floor to ceiling, it formed a perfect square, twenty feet to a side. This was where she and Jay Jay had made love the very first time.

The roar of the falls had faded to a soft susurration where she now stood. With eyes lowered and the flashlight pointed down, she took a deep breath, preparing herself for whatever might be revealed, for she knew this place was much more than a room sculpted from solid rock. It was a portal.

Feeling ready, she aimed the flashlight at one of the walls. A small gasp escaped her throat at what she saw. The painting overlaying the wall had changed. It no longer showed her pregnant mother in a storm tossed sea as she clung to the dorsal fin of the gray bottlenose dolphin that had saved her. She remembered every detail of that old mural, for it had accurately depicted an actual event in her mother's life. The dolphin was Athena, who was to become her mother's bond mate. The bodies of both had been severely welted, the result of coming into contact with strange oblate jellyfish. It was this happening that had ultimately set the stage for the emergence of the new breed and the building of Aquaria, or so they all believed.

But now the scene was gone, replaced by one of Jake taking on Colonel Ternier's small army of thugs at Navassa Island. Under the glow of a bonfire burning eerily at the base of the lighthouse, he stood fast, a look of grim determination etched on his face as he mowed down fifteen men with the assault weapon held firmly in his hands. This was a side of her husband she had learned to accept, for had he not turned into a killing machine on that dreadful night, she would surely have perished at the hands of Erzulie, Ternier's vengeful mother.

Destiny studied the mural a moment longer before illuminating the wall immediately to the left. That painting had also changed. It no longer showed her mother tenderly cradling an infant in her arms while standing waist-deep in water. The baby had been Destiny. The cove's waterfall had been displayed in the background, serenely gushing whitewater as Athena floated next to her with a newborn calf of her own, having given birth at the same moment as her mother. The calf had been Natalie, the very first of her marvelous species.

But instead of showing these things, the mural overlaying the entire wall showed a majestic panorama of Aquaria in its present state viewed from afar. It was partly shrouded in mist, and arched directly over it was a rare sight. It was a perfect representation of the double rainbow bridge she and the twins had witnessed just prior to visiting her mother in the subterranean cavern on Navassa. Behind it lay Navassa Island with the old lighthouse visible. East of the island in the mural's upper right corner was an enormous oil tanker, which she suspected to be the *Kraken*, judging from its relative size and configuration. One final aspect caught her eye. A luxury mega-yacht lurked in the foreground in the lower left corner. It seemed to resemble quite distinctly a vessel they had passed on their way to the cove.

Eager to scrutinize the next wall, she turned to her left, no longer expecting to view the small pod of albino dolphins plowing through the sea, six of them surrounding her and Hercules in a hexagon formation. In its place was a rendering of the Russian Hind being inexorably pulled into the sea by two blue whales, Jay Jay's body dangling limply from its fuselage as it strained to stay aloft.

Destiny pondered the first three murals, each portraying an event that had already transpired. The renderings they had replaced had also depicted events that had previously occurred when she had first come upon them years earlier. Back then, the fourth wall had shown her something that had not yet taken place, and that had shown Jay Jay on his waverunner as he gave chase to Ortega's helicopter, firing upon it with his Stoner. Based on the sequence of previous displays, it stood to reason that the fourth wall would also portray a future event.

Taking a deep breath, she braced herself in preparation for what was to be revealed. Tears immediately welled up in her eyes, but they were not tears of anguish. They were tears of joy.

The mural showed an underwater scene. Centered within it was Jay Jay, seemingly fully recovered as he rode Achilles. She and the twins were shown a short distance away, each astride their own bond mate as they kept pace with him. Below them was a coral reef teeming with life, and directly ahead was a broad dark hole situated beneath an overhang blanketed with anemones and red sponge. Intruding its way into one side of the hole was the transparent access tube that connected with the offshore berthing platform. She knew the place well. It was a section of reef abutting the entrance to the subterranean dolphin sanctuary that lay hidden below the Navassa lighthouse.

She knew she was viewing something that had not previously occurred. Two items within the scene told her this. Strapped to Jay Jay's right thigh was the USP-9 submachine pistol he routinely wore whenever imminent danger was close at hand. She could not recall him ever wearing it during prior visits to the cavern. Secondly, a hail of ropey white spumes appeared to reach for them from above. She recognized what those spumes represented. The water was being peppered with a hail of bullets, but the liquid medium was making their lethal velocities ineffectual, causing the rounds to quickly slow and sink harmlessly away. Someone was giving chase and shooting at them from the surface.

An odd sound suddenly caught Destiny's attention, making her stiffen. Someone was summoning her. The voice was barely audible, touching the surrounding air in a soft sibilant whisper, but there was no mistaking its meaning.

"Destiny!" it called.

Glancing around sharply, she looked for the caller, unsure if she had imagined it. The thought that it was a mental cue evoked by one of the dolphins was abruptly dismissed as the voice summoned her again, this time more lucidly.

"Destiny!" it repeated.

She became aware of the background hiss of the falls, its low susurration now rising in volume, and instinctively she knew the plunging water was the source of the voice. The mysterious presence that dwelled within this strange domain was calling to her.

"You must believe in yourself, my child. Do not lose faith, for you are still the person you have always been."

"Please show yourself!" Destiny petitioned.

"Look upon the wall before you and I will reveal myself!" the voice instructed.

Destiny heeded the command, not surprised to see the mural change before her eyes. A vision of Esmerelda slowly took form, her face alive with compassion.

"You have helped us before," Destiny said. "Can you help us again?"

"All that you need lies within you," Esmerelda answered. *"You must never stop believing in yourself."*

"It is as though the entire world is against us," Destiny deplored helplessly.

Esmerelda spread her arms wide. A vision of the earth as seen from space abruptly materialized behind her. *"Do not mistake the unfolding of recent events to be caused by the aggregate of humanity. What you have so far witnessed is part of a specific predetermined plan enacted by a small band of powerful brokers acting behind closed doors. These brokers are ruled by a puppet master of immense wealth who is answerable to no one and seeks to destroy Aquaria and all it stands for. He chooses and controls many international leaders to carry out his nefarious goals, much of which is aimed at manipulating the global economy in order to amass more power and wealth."*

"How do we overcome that?"

Esmerelda smiled benevolently, a halo of stardust surrounding her face. *"By believing, my child. You must simply believe."*

"A dream continues to plague me each night," Destiny bewailed. "It reveals a great dark force bearing down on Aquaria. It blocks out the sun and appears to be unstoppable."

"Yes, I know, my child. It is an enormous sea monster controlled by the puppet master. But like all entities of a dark nature, they risk being destroyed by the very evil they spawn."

Destiny let out a frustrated sigh. "I have been compromised. My powers have been corrupted through my own doing. Without them, believing in anything seems futile."

Esmerelda shook her head. *"You deceive yourself, child. Your unconditional love for those around you has made you even stronger. It is a source of great power. It binds all of you together and is the foundation of unblemished faith."*

Destiny continued to feel dispirited. "All we have strived for is lost. It is difficult to hope for something that is no longer possible."

Esmerelda continued to smile, remaining resolute. *"Have faith. Hope is something not seen. You must have patience and steadfastness, continuing to believe with all your being until the belief is physically manifested. Once you possess it, all is possible."*

DOLPHIN RIDERS

Destiny felt strangely lifted by Esmerelda's words, though pessimism still plagued her. "I'll try," was all she could think to say.

"There is no try. Maintain a singleness of heart, never letting negative thoughts take charge of you, for such thoughts will bring on fear and doubt. Faith and fear will always be at war, so you must choose one or the other. But the choice is simple when you realize faith will always overcome fear."

Destiny took pause to dwell on the words. She had led a sheltered life growing up in the cove, relatively unaffected by the outside world with all its problems. But the arrival of Jay Jay had introduced a new set of circumstances into her life, with a growing sense of fear being one of them. She had feared for the pod, for Jay Jay, for her children, for everyone she loved. And she feared for Aquaria. She had fallen victim to this primitive though intrinsic human emotion, letting it take control of her reality. She saw it clearly now, recognizing its damaging influence, yet she still had trouble letting it go.

"If only I had your conviction," she found herself saying.

"You must cleanse your mind of the fear that shackles it," Esmerelda stressed. *"Once you do this, you will realize you are a spiritual being with incredible powers. Only then will you fully understand that you and all those you love are deathless souls having a physical experience. Like those magnificent creatures to whom you are forever linked, you were brought into this world to fulfill a profound purpose. Just believe in yourself and all that you wish for will follow."*

"I wish you were still here with us," Destiny said wistfully.

Esmerelda's face lit up in an enigmatic grin. *"Oh, but I am, child. As long as you keep me in your heart, I will always be with you."* The grin turned solemn and she turned her broad face as if to espy something in the distance. *"Danger approaches. You must hurry."*

Before Destiny could voice a question, Esmerelda spoke again. *"I see mismatched orbs coming your way. If the cove is to remain unscarred from the ravages of man, those orbs must not be terminated."*

Destiny wrapped her mind around the riddle, trying to make sense of it, but Esmerelda had more to add. *"There is one more thing. Someone you once knew will return to help fight against the forces that seek to destroy Aquaria."*

"Who?"

"You must be strong, child, as I ask you to look above."

Destiny aimed her flashlight at the roof of the chamber and gazed upward, her heart beating wildly at what she saw. The word that left her lips came out in a startled cry. "No!"

"No!" she repeated, bringing her eyes back to Esmerelda, but

Esmerelda was now gone.

-33-

Without knowing why, Harriet Grahm was suddenly drawn to a few crystals lying atop a workbench. These were what she and the dolphins had nicknamed T-crystals. There were four of them, each about two inches in height in the shape of a four-sided pyramid. Seconds earlier they had begun to pulsate once again, shedding excess energy in the form of violet light. But this time the light was even more intense than before, and the frequency had increased. Puzzled, she stared in contemplation, wondering what was causing them to react like this. Without immersion in a marine environment the crystals should have remained dormant. These were some of the latest crystals brought up from a depth of 950 feet by Hermes a few hours ago, retrieved near the base of one of the gargantuan *thurentra* directly beneath the floating city. Every so often these same *thurentra* produced a few of them that were all identical, emulating the way their smaller cousins specialized in producing a product of their own. The crystals were peculiar in the way they acted. They absorbed sound waves and tended to distort sonar originating from a submarine or other prying object from getting a clear picture of the immense organisms that provided nitrogen-rich cold water to Aquaria's OTEC generators. Crystals like these could be grown larger and made to function as power inducers. All you needed was to run saline water over them and they gathered in the energy the water held, seemingly able to amplify that energy many times over before unleashing it. The larger the crystal, the more power it would provide. The albinos had theorized the crystals operated on a principle of *quantum entanglement*, claiming their extraordinary molecular lattices were attuned to a higher dimension and able to pick up vibrations where energy was either subtle or readily available. Up to now, every test she and the dolphins had run on these extraordinary gems had proved unsuccessful, thus their precise molecular composition had remained a mystery. That particular fact was unimportant to her, however, for like the new breed of dolphin and *thurentra*, she believed T-crystals were yet another gift provided by the living planetary system called *Gaia*.

Though she had trouble understanding the principle, she knew these crystals had so far been put to good use. The albinos had incorporated them into the hydrodrive that provided Johnnie its incredible thrust. They were also the primary components in the PWIs - Pressure Wave Inhibitors – the dolphins had developed once the mysterious explosions started occurring on the nearby reefs. Unfortunately, these same crystals could be a bit twitchy and sometimes did strange things just as they were doing right now, and she suspected the four crystals that lay before her were picking up the anxiety she felt.

Staring a few moments longer at the crystals, she grabbed two of them, pocketing them in a pouch strapped to her waist. Why she needed them she could not explain, but she knew they were destined for some arcane purpose.

Working in her lab deep under Navassa Island, Harriet knew something was wrong hours earlier. It was a budding sense of approaching disaster. But it had been Athena that brought form and substance to her mounting dread on the mental link they shared. Jake's dire predicament had been relayed over the pod's telepathic network, ultimately reaching her through Athena. It was then that she had been besieged by a strange notion.

Without hesitation, she contacted Ez via the facility intercom. "Ez, I need you to turn off the pumps to Big D."

Ez answered immediately, though she sounded puzzled. "Is there a problem?"

"No problem," Harriet said. "I only need them off for a few minutes at most. Please open the hatch. I'll explain later."

"As you wish," Ez said.

Riding Athena down to the lowest level of the submerged structure, Harriet saw the hatch was already open. With the flow of hundreds of tons of seawater moved every second now halted, she and Athena were able to safely enter the large chamber, and a moment later they floated before a set of massive crystals. Spaced equidistantly, six of them formed a hexagonal ring that surrounded a seventh crystal. Each of the crystals comprising the hexagon was in the shape of a four-sided pyramid that was equal in size to its neighbors. Unlike the crystals that ringed it, however, the center crystal was three times larger in volume and formed a perfect three-sided pyramid. A subdued violet glow emanated from the outer pyramids, while the center pyramid emitted a soothing crimson light.

It was the albinos that had theorized and constructed this configuration of crystals, certain they would eventually interact to become a promising source of enormous power. These, too, had been harvested from the deep-lying *thurentra* by Hermes when construction of Aquaria was in its infancy, and like Aquaria, they had grown progressively larger as the floating city had mushroomed in size.

Harriet stared transfixed at the center crystal before leaving her mount and swimming above it. So far, this was the only one of its kind produced by the huge *thurentra*, a three-sided pyramid brought up from depth. Like the four crystals on her workbench, it had also started out small. Tentatively, she placed a hand on its apex, finding it warm to the touch. The reaction she had hoped for did not come. Disappointed, she withdrew her hand. She knew all the crystals were still growing and had not yet reached the size the colony would need. Feeling helpless, she was suddenly struck by another notion, and straddling Athena once again, she left the chamber and headed for the structure's outer perimeter, requesting that Athena take her to one of the gold-harvesting *thurentra*.

Closing her thoughts to her bond mate, she hovered off to one side of the pumpkin-like organism, and before Athena could intervene, extended an arm to make contact with it. Unlike her daughter, she did not possess Destiny's ability to withstand a severe electric charge, let alone store it. She knew she was risking her life, for the electrical discharge of a *thurentra* could be fatal.

Something flashed before her eyes, and she felt her heart catch in her chest before an acute sense of vertigo set in. The disorientation passed quickly, supplanted by a distant memory that flooded her consciousness. Overwhelmed by the sheer intensity of it, she found herself back in that tumultuous sea, waves toppling all around her. Without warning, a sheer mountain of water crashed down to drag her under, tumbling her into those luminous searing tentacles she well remembered. All at once her body stiffened as the burning fires of hell took hold of her.

Another moment passed before the vision faded, leaving her staring off into space. Vaguely she felt Athena under her. Something was happening to her, something she couldn't explain. She only knew she had to get back to Aquaria with all the speed she could muster.

-34-

Alvarez was nowhere to be seen as Mat reached the main deck at the bottom of the stairs. Nevertheless, he ducked down behind a stack of crates and took in his surroundings with extreme vigilance. It suddenly occurred to him that he should have taken Phillipe's cloaker, but in his haste he had not thought to do so.

One thing made him smile, however, and that was Alvarez falling for one of the oldest tricks in modern times of war. Thinking the grenade was armed and ready to explode, the Chilean captain had bolted from the bridge like a gazelle running for its life with a cheetah hot on its tail. But Mat had taken the time to disarm it on his way to the helm, carefully unscrewing the detonator and removing it. Two other diversions had also contributed to the ruse, and that was the perfectly timed arrival of the helicopter in unison with the whales rocking the ship. With begrudging respect, he had to give Ez her due, for her plan had succeeded admirably.

Mat moved cautiously, making his way further astern and wondering if Phillipe was up to the task of carrying Bashir up another flight of steps to the helipad situated directly over the bridge. Abruptly he chastised himself. The youth was in exceptional physical condition, well endowed with a muscular physique made all the more powerful by daily weight-training sessions and cardiovascular workouts involving running and biking along Aquaria's promenades and breakwaters.

As if to allay his concerns, Mat heard the buzz of the chopper gain strength. Looking up, he caught a fleeting glimpse of the Bell Ranger swing out over the water as it lifted off, its pilot astutely choosing the starboard side of the vessel for a departure. Since Alvarez had fled to the ship's larboard side, it was only logical the starboard sector would present less risk in drawing fire. And he knew the pilot would not have taken off unless both Bashir and Phillipe were aboard.

Mat suddenly halted as he listened to the drone of the chopper. Something was not quite right. Instead of the sound receding, it rose in volume. A narrow opening between two containers gave him a clue as to what was happening. Instead of taking a flight path directly back to Aquaria, the aircraft had circled back and was now on a heading that would take it to the Haitian coast.

Mat had no time to mull this unanticipated circumstance, though he had an inkling as to the reason. He was simply thankful that Phillipe and Bashir were now off the freighter. Moving swiftly, he found the darkened niche where he had left Kalid, calling out in a whisper before exposing himself to the opening. "It's me, Kalid. Don't shoot!"

Kalid answered, though he sounded weak. "I hear you."

Mat entered the niche. "Turn off your cloaker!"

Kalid's form materialized, and Mat could see his condition had deteriorated since he had left him. "What happened?" Kalid asked.

"Save your strength," Mat murmured, "we're getting off the ship."

Mat pulled out his cell phone, bringing it to his lips and speaking quietly. "Ez, do you read me?"

"Loud and clear," Ez responded.

"Is Abdel still standing by?"

"Yes, Mat."

"Have him pick us up amidships on the freighter's port side."

Mat had only to wait a few seconds before Ez came back. "He's on the way. ETA is three minutes twenty-two seconds."

"Thanks, Ez." Mat stopped short of re-pocketing the phone as Ez's voice came back again. "Perseus tells me there's no ladder at that location."

Mat checked his wristwatch, gauging the time. "We'll have to jump."

"My sensors are picking up another aircraft approaching your position. More than likely it carries the UN reinforcements requested by Alvarez."

"How long?"

"Assuming no unanticipated factors throwing off my calculations, you should be on your way out of there just before they set down on the ship."

Mat continued to monitor the time, counting off the seconds. "By the way, Ez, why is our chopper heading toward Haiti?"

Ez's reply confirmed Mat's own appraisal. "Her pilot believes she will have a better chance of reviving Bashir if she goes there."

Mat nodded absently. "Does this ship present a danger to Aquaria on its present course of drift?"

"No," said Ez. "Even if the wind changes direction, the whales will keep it well away."

Mat thought about how he had been able to disable the Southern Star's engines. He had used the T-BEMP Generator carried aboard the sub, a device developed by the dolphins. T-BEMP stood for Tight Beam Electromagnetic Pulse, and the generator that emitted it was capable of frying the electronic circuitry that operated the ship's engines. And with its engines now inoperable, the freighter was a drifting hulk.

With that last thought, Mat poked his head out of the niche to make sure Alvarez was not lurking about. Turning, he checked his watch again before eyeing Kalid. "Okay, partner, time for a hasty retreat," he said, hauling the injured man to his feet and supporting him.

Awkwardly, he half-carried him down a corridor that opened up at the ship's rail. Just as Ez had estimated, the sub rose above the water at the predicted time.

Kalid grimaced as Mat helped him over the rail. "After you, my friend," Mat uttered, giving him a smile of encouragement.

Kalid looked down with his back to the railing, not liking the drop to which he would subject himself. He was fearful of heights and the water was 50 feet below him.

"Look, there's dolphins down there waiting to help you," Mat urged.

Just as he finished saying that, something parted Mat's hair a split second before a burst of gunfire reached his ears. Whipping his head around, he glimpsed movement along the ship's rail 100 meters forward of where he now stood. He immediately recognized Alvarez.

"Go!" Mat yelled, giving Kalid a violent shove and sending him plummeting to the water with arms flailing.

Another burst ensued, and an enfilade of rounds zinged off a cargo container further astern. Mat spun, letting loose with a volley of his own and emptying the clip. He fired high, knowing the Uzi he held had limited range. Rounds sparked close to his target, and he saw Alvarez duck back between containers. Since Alvarez also carried the same type of weapon, he knew his adversary's sallies would lack sufficient accuracy from where he was positioned.

Mat ripped out the Uzi's spent clip and replaced it, glancing down at the water as he did so. An albino had Kalid in its grasp and had brought him to the side of the sub's small conning tower. Sluggishly, Kalid climbed the rungs. Someone poked their head above the hatch and reached out to haul Kalid in headfirst, and Mat saw that it was Samuel, a strapping Haitian youth two years younger than Phillipe.

Still at distance, Alvarez poked his head from the side of a container, prepared to fire again, but Mat held him at bay, squeezing off another withering burst and emptying the clip. Seeing Alvarez withdraw his head, Mat shifted his gaze to the sub once more. Kalid's feet disappeared down the hatch, and a moment later Samuel's upper torso reemerged.

Mat yelled at the top of his lungs. "Get the sub away from the ship!" Frantically, he waved an arm to warn him away.

Samuel seemed to understand, nodding before lowering his head to shout down into the sub to relay the command to Abdel at the controls. Rounds began peppering the water around the sub, some of them pinging off its steel hull and causing Samuel to vanish from view. Abruptly a hand snaked up to swing the hatch closed, and all too slowly the sub began to move. Seconds passed as it gained speed alongside the freighter's hull, taking on a heading toward Alvarez's position before veering away. Sparks flew as more rounds collided with its conning tower, but otherwise had little effect.

Mat reloaded the Uzi with his remaining clip, pointing the weapon in his foe's direction and firing until it was spent. Throwing down the firearm, he immediately vaulted over the rail, aware that one of the grays was there to assist him as he splashed harshly into the sea. Grabbing the dolphin's dorsal fin, he was whisked below the surface and away from the ship.

At a safe distance, the gray resurfaced. Mat inhaled deeply, continuing to hold on as the dolphin caught up with the sub, now a quarter mile from the Southern Star with its engine at idle and only its conning tower jutting above the water. Once aboard the sub, Mat glanced up to espy at least twenty chutes flaring open as additional blue helmeted troops descended toward the ship. Mat battened down the hatch to the conning tower, glad to be off the freighter, but contemplating his next course of action.

-35-

Jake found himself scaling a steep precipice, groping about for handholds on the craggy surface. A shadowy gloom lay all about him and only a pinpoint of light directly above gave him a sense of orientation.

"Your cause is lost," someone close by mocked. "You will fail just as we did."

Jake knew that voice. Looking below, he saw Yeslam Raduyev clinging to the rock. He discerned other forms climbing up from the void, and instinctively he knew who they were. Colonel Ternier and Erzulie were following, and next to them he sensed Sebastion Ortega.

"You are going to die!" they chorused with sadistic glee.

Jake saw Erzulie's arm lash out as she hurled something, and he caught sight of a cobra rising up, its jaws opening wide to sink deadly fangs into him. Lethargy suddenly immobilized him, and he felt too weak to bat it away before it could land.

A hand abruptly shot out to snare the snake before it could strike, and Jake knew it was not his own hand that had saved him. Surprised, he looked to his right to see Amphitrite holding fast to a crevice beside him, the snake writhing wildly as she clutched it just behind the head.

Amphitrite gave him a comforting glance before turning her gaze below. "You cannot hurt him," she said in a calm but resolute voice. "Be gone you vile witch!" Effortlessly, she flung the cobra back down. Erzulie screamed hideously, letting go of the rock and tumbling into the void as the cobra tore into her neck.

"Get him!" Ortega raged, taking charge to rally the others.

Jake tried to scramble higher, but his arms felt numb.

"I've got your back, good buddy. Just keep going and pay no attention to these bastards."

Jake looked to his left, amazed to see Myers next to him. Myers gave him a reassuring smile, appearing to enjoy the prospect of a good fight the way he always did. As Raduyev reached for Jake's ankle, Myers stomped down hard with a heel, catching the Chechen square in the face. The blow reopened the old wound marring Raduyev's cheek, causing a small fountain of blood to spurt. The Chechen stubbornly held fast to a niche in the rock, glaring up at Myers with utter hatred. Myers kicked down again, and this time Raduyev let out a harsh grunt before falling away into the blackness.

With equal dispatch, Myers did the same to both Ternier and Ortega, and Jake saw them plummet, their screams trailing away.

Jake felt a modicum of strength flowing into his arms and he pulled himself higher. Suddenly aware that Myers was not following, he stopped and looked down. "You coming?" he asked.

Myers grinned. "Sorry Jake, but you know that's not possible." He looked above to glimpse the pinpoint of light. "Now get going, you big lummox. Others await you!"

Jake started to climb, but Myers called to him again. "And Jake..."

"Yes."

"Thanks for keeping your promise. Phillipe has grown into a fine young man."

"He came from good stock," Jake replied.

"Take care of yourself, buddy, and don't be reckless like I was."

With that said, Myers' image began to fade before disappearing completely.

"I'll try," Jake muttered sadly, feeling the loss of his friend all over again.

Climbing higher, Jake realized Amphitrite was no longer with him as well, but he heard another voice, though it was still far away. "Hurry!" it beckoned.

Jake suddenly felt lethargic again as he strived for the light. "I don't think I can make it," he answered back weakly. He felt his remaining strength rapidly ebbing. Speaking was becoming difficult now, and his arms and fingers were starting to give out.

Yes, you can, a familiar presence encouraged.

Jake felt Achilles catch him just as he lost his grip on the rock.

Hold onto me, Achilles instructed.

"My strength is gone," Jake gasped.

Draw strength from me and hold on.

"Then you won't be able to make the climb," Jake objected feebly.

Others are channeling their energies to you, Achilles replied.

Jake felt a sudden surge of energy flow into him. With renewed strength, he gripped the leading edge of Achilles' pectoral fins, holding on tight as the dolphin used its powerful prehensile extensions to haul them up the craggy wall, hastening their ascent. In moments the pinpoint of light expanded and brightened, and Jake became aware that he was hearing more than one voice.

"Jay Jay!"

The combined sound conveyed urgency, echoing off into the void. An arm extended from the light, reaching down for him and pulling him up.

Jake opened his eyes to find Destiny withdrawing her lips from his.

He discovered he was immersed in water, buoyed up by Achilles and three other dolphins.

"Thank god you're back with us again," she cried. Her cheeks were streaked with tears and she appeared physically drained.

"I saw your mother," Jake said. "She helped me. And so did Myers."

Troy Jacob and Melody were suddenly hugging him fiercely. "We were so worried," they chirped in unison, "but Mum and the dolphins were able to make the cut on your head disappear." Melody placed a hand on his temple, running her fingers across it. "See, it's almost gone."

Jake looked at Destiny. "What happened?"

"Your helicopter was shot down and you suffered a severe concussion." Destiny studied him quizzically. "You don't remember?"

A montage of fleeting images abruptly flashed before him, and he saw the ocean rising up at him all over again. "Fernando was with me." The thought caused him to go rigid. "Did he…"

"See for yourself." Destiny looked up to indicate the man leaning over the Angel's swim platform.

"You okay, Jay Jay?" Fernando asked, obviously happy to see his friend fully revived.

"Think so," Jake said, noticing Zimbola and Hector also looking down at him. A broad, uncharacteristic smile plastered the big Jamaican's face.

"Let's get you out of the water," Zimby suggested.

Jake extended a hand and Zimby pulled him from the water with little effort.

The sound of gunfire suddenly erupted from high above, making Jake look up. "What's going on?" he asked.

The smile Zimbola had been carrying was now gone, replaced with a weighty graveness. "We've come under attack!" he exclaimed, looking to Jake for guidance.

-36-

At precisely 12 noon, Victor Belachek got the men moving. As planned, they spread out into four separate three-man squads to engage the bunkers set up along the rim of the basin. And while the bunkers were well concealed, he knew exactly where they were located. But to reach the bunkers, they had to either avoid or disarm booby traps they were sure to encounter along the way.

Leading two men, Belachek kept his eyes warily peeled for trip wires. With the need for caution, the going was painfully slow, made all the more difficult by dense foliage that acted to effectively camouflage thin strands of wire. If disturbed with additional tension, they could trigger a variety of mayhem designed to injure or kill. Not falling victim to them would be a daunting challenge. Nevertheless, he and his men were seasoned professionals and would be up to the task, particularly since their last mission had been on a similar assignment in the jungles of Colombia. Cardoza had also paid them well for that engagement, hiring Zinova and his band to eliminate factions of a competing drug lord. Memories of the mission gave Belachek a small measure of satisfaction, for they had disarmed at least two dozen well concealed IEDs on their way to raiding and setting in flames a cocaine plantation. During the fight they had lost only one man while wiping out a security force nearly four times greater than their own. By the time the raid ended, they had counted 59 kills. And though he enjoyed the thrill of victory, killing did not give him pleasure. This made him wonder if perhaps he was losing his taste for battle. Perhaps he was getting too old for this type of work. Unfortunately, it was the only trade he knew.

Low crawling forward and carefully pushing aside a cluster of fern leaves, Belachek came upon his first trap of the day. As expected, it was a trip wire strung to a height of six inches above the forest floor. Swiveling his head, he looked first right, then left, failing to see where the wire ended. Pulling a small wire cutter from his utility belt, he snipped through the thin strand. Tracing one of the wires to the base of a tree located five meters off to the side, he saw what the wire would have released. A spiked boulder attached to a rope was suspended precariously to swing down on an unsuspecting interloper. Following the other end of the wire, he discerned a similar device perched high up, though it was not easily recognized unless one were looking for it. Each boulder was small, no more than twelve centimeters in diameter in his estimation, with short spikes designed to inflict shallow stab wounds. He could tell this type of trap was meant to injure rather than kill, with the aim of discouraging further encroachment into this forest.

Belachek took a moment to consult his GPS unit again. He was now within 40 meters of his target, and that was the bunker closest to the falls. Already he could hear the soft hiss of the plunging water. Based on the intel he had been given, he would only have to neutralize the lone sentry manning that bunker.

Turning, Belachek looked back at the strapping young man following on his heels. Alex Trekov, a recent addition to Zinova's mercenaries at Belachek's urging and currently the youngest and least experienced among them, was brushing leaves aside, intent on uncovering something he had come upon. Belachek had eagerly taken him under his wing, deciding to mentor him in the art of covert military tactics.

"What did you find?" Belachek whispered.

The lad's eyes were wide with amazement. "I think it's gold!"

"Don't touch it!" Belachek ordered, knowing it might be a lure. Booby traps were often baited to attract the unwary. Picking up the bait could easily detonate a bomb.

Shiny metal glinted brightly under a shaft of sunlight reaching the forest floor. Pulling a bush knife from his belt, Belachek gently prodded the soil around the object before pushing the blade deeper to probe under it. He had to make certain it was not a spring-loaded land mine. If it was, lifting the metal would trigger it.

Satisfied that nothing lay hidden beneath it, Belachek pulled the metal from the soil to examine it more fully, hefting it as he did so. As Alex had said, it appeared to be a bar of gold, probably more than 8 kilograms in his estimation. A quick mental calculation told him he was holding more than $350,000 in his hand, assuming it truly was pure gold and not something made to look like the precious metal. Tungsten plated with a thin layer of gold, he knew, was sometimes used to make counterfeit ingots. With a unit weight that closely matched that of gold, tungsten was ideal for counterfeiting such a valuable commodity.

Alex stared at the metal's smooth, polished surface as though mesmerized. "Is it gold?" he asked excitedly, his voice loud enough to be heard by alert ears lurking in the bush.

Belachek scowled, bringing a finger to his lips. He hated careless outbursts when stealth was needed. "Keep it down!" he admonished, whispering out the command. He scrutinized the gleaming metal, trying to make sense of this strange find. *So this is why Cardoza wants us to gain possession of this place,* he reasoned. *There's probably a lot more of this to be had once we neutralize those bunkers.*

"Well is it?" Alex persisted, his question still above a whisper.

Belchek noted the hunger in his protégé's eyes, knowing what the sight of so much wealth was doing to him. Like himself, Trekov had come from a poverty-stricken family back in the Ukraine. And though they were well paid to carry out missions like this, the idea that they could possibly walk away from this with so much more was an intriguing thought.

"Maybe," Belachek answered, desperately wanting to believe it was not a fake. Oddly, it displayed no markings stamped into it. A small cache of gold ingots had been looted during the raid on the cocaine plantation, and he remembered seeing the percent purity, weight and batch number stamped into them. That find had been quickly appropriated by Zinova, claiming it would be needed for the upkeep of his Hinds.

A rustling of leaves made both men look behind them. Dimitrei's

DOLPHIN RIDERS

head poked through the foliage, his eyes immediately falling on the gold Belachek held.

"Is that what I think it is?" he queried, his expression alive with greed.

Belachek placed the ingot back on the ground. "We'll come back for this later." Turning, he started to crawl toward the sound of the falls.

"Like hell we will," Alex grumbled, scooping up the metal and attempting to cram it into an already stuffed pouch.

"Leave it!" Belachek ordered. "It will slow you down."

Alex looked back at him, and Belachek saw something in his eyes he had never seen before. Though subtle, it was rebellion.

"I'll be fine," Alex insisted, removing some protein bars from the pouch and replacing them with the ingot.

"That gets split three ways," Dimitrei declared. "The others don't have to know."

"Maybe we'll find more once we reach our objective," Belachek reconciled soothingly, recognizing what the scent of gold was doing to these men. It was important he pacify them quickly, otherwise the mission would be lost. "Now stay focused and we'll address this later," he said sternly.

Belachek crawled forward again, searching the ground before him appraisingly. Over the next ten meters he failed to come across a single trip wire or trap of any kind, but something else caught his eye. It was more gold. Assuming it was genuine, three more bars of it lay strewn directly in front of him as though dropped by careless hands. But these were much larger than the ingot Alex carried, maybe three times larger in the form of bricks.

Fighting back the temptation engulfing him, Belachek used his bush knife to probe the soil surrounding the nearest brick. Finding nothing suspicious, he tried lifting the brick from a prone position, but quickly rose to his knees for more leverage. It was heavy, gauging it to be more than 24 kilograms in weight. Like the ingot Alex carried, it had no identifying marks stamped into it. Based on the current price of gold on world markets, he knew he might be holding slightly better than a million dollars in his hand, with twice that amount still on the ground. Three point three million so far discovered, with the possibility of finding more. But that assumed it was bona fide.

Belachek was suddenly aware that Alex and Dimitrei were now hunkered down beside him. Their images reflected off the mirror-like finish of the brick he held, and in their eyes he detected a mix of awe and avarice.

"We're rich!" Dimitrei blurted. His tone was giddy. Before Belachek could stop him, he reached for one of the other bricks.

Instinctively, Belachek tackled Alex, slamming him to the ground and shielding him with his body. He was too seasoned a professional to assume the next brick was safe to pick up. His instincts proved correct.

Something sprang laterally from adjacent foliage, pivoting around in a blinding blur of motion. Dimitrei dropped the gold and let out a shrill howl of pain as the thing slammed into his side. Belachek saw it was a wooden plank studded with small pointed dowels, several of which were firmly embedded in Dimitrei's hip.

"You fool!" Belachek chastised. He knew all element of surprise was probably lost now. Jumping to his feet, he yanked the plank free, noting that several of the dowels had come loose and were still lodged in the man's flesh. Already a heavy stain of blood was spreading out from the puncture wounds.

Dimitrei tried to get to his feet, but immediately fell back down, writhing in agony. Belachek could see he would be useless in a fight.

Grabbing Alex by the wrist, Belachek pulled him low. "Stay down and follow me!" he ordered. "We've got to rush that bunker. Chances are they already know we're here."

"What about Dimitrei?" Alex asked in confusion.

"Leave him! We'll come back for him later."

Belachek began low crawling swiftly, hearing the heavy breathing of his protégé right behind him. More gold bricks lay in his path, but he ignored them. Avoiding them completely, he looked behind him to make sure Alex was doing the same. He had to stay focused, keeping vigilant for more trip wires, but strange as it seemed, he did not encounter a single one. The falls were much closer now, letting out a soft pervading rumble, and he wondered if it might have drowned out Dimitrei's cry of pain.

The possibility of this was immediately dismissed when a piercing scream suddenly cut through the forest off to his right, overlaying the sound of tumbling water. Inwardly he cursed, knowing full well one of the men in the adjacent team had also fallen victim to the enticement of gold. *Damn fools!*

A staccato burst from a light assault weapon immediately ensued, and the realization that the plan had completely unraveled hit home. Abruptly, a much heavier machine gun barked back in reply, and he knew the defenders of this place were now fully alerted to their presence.

Hurriedly, Belacheck pulled out his GPS and got a bearing on the bunker he had to neutralize, seeing he was within 8 meters of it. The sound of the firefight had now escalated, with more distant firearms coming alive. A full-fledged battle was now underway.

Belachek checked his watch, aware that time was running out. Only fifteen more minutes remained for his unit to take out these bunkers.

DOLPHIN RIDERS

Yanking the pin from one of the two smoke grenades he carried, he held down the spoon and looked back over his shoulder, expecting to see Alex hunkered down behind him. But Alex had disappeared.

At that moment, the heavy machine gun emplacement from the nearby bunker opened up, sending a torrent of rounds skimming just above his head. Had he been standing, he would have been killed instantly. The barrage was deafening, and foliage all around him disintegrated as the slugs tore into the jungle. The gunner was raking the forest, swinging the weapon back and forth haphazardly.

Still clutching the smoke grenade, Belachek hugged the ground. Caught in the grip of indecision, he considered backtracking to locate Alex. *Damn him!* he raged inwardly. Though he was no novice to the unpredictability that often accompanied firefights, he had never faced chaos to the degree he was now experiencing.

Belachek's ears perked at the sound of another scream, nearly drowned out by the jackhammer roar of the heavy weapon. It had come from the woods directly behind him. A second later the big gun cut out.

Groping the ground where he had dropped the pin to the smoke grenade, Belachek retrieved it, reinserting it back in the device. Quickly, he low crawled back the way he had come. Four meters back he found Alex. The lad lay unmoving with his face to the ground. The bricks of gold they had last encountered were next to him. A pool of blood was slowly gathering under him.

Belachek froze, staring in horror. *No, not this!* he mourned. The thing he had dreaded most had finally come to pass. Gently, he turned Alex over to see where he had been hit. Blood gushed from a hole in his abdomen.

Withdrawing a packet from a pocket, Belachek sprinkled sulfur powder on the injury before applying a gauze compress to stem the bleeding. Hurriedly, he dressed the wound, wrapping it tight with the compress in place. The firefight escalated as he did this, with the din of small arms and heavy machine guns drumming the air in the distance.

Alex opened his eyes to stare up at him. "You probably think I'm a poor excuse for a soldier?" he uttered weakly.

Belachek ignored the question, checking his watch instead. "The choppers will arrive in another five minutes," he said, barely managing to remain stoic as a flood of emotion filled his guts. "Just hold on and we'll get you out of here."

Alex looked ashen, as though every ounce of blood had drained from his face. "Why do you care about me so much?" he asked.

Belachek could see he was fading fast. "Just hold on," he repeated, knowing there was no more time for questions.

Turning, he looked back in the direction of the bunker just as the heavy machine gun let loose again. The jungle all around him was being sprayed with bullets, wreaking havoc on the thick vegetation and pelting him with tree branches and splintered wood.

Belachek ducked lower, suddenly overcome by a vast emptiness. The realization that he had led a meaningless life came back to haunt him yet again. No, it was worse than meaningless. He had let himself fall into a pit of moral decay. The truth tormented him like an open sore, with all the depraved things he had done throughout his existence coming to bear on his soul. Oh how he longed for escape from it.

Redemption! The word clung to his thoughts like a thorn buried deep in his flesh. If only he could carry out one redemptive deed, then he might be free.

Consumed with self-loathing, he began crawling toward the bunker. He would have only one chance at saving Alex, even if it meant losing his life trying.

-37-

Jake felt his strength rapidly returning as he buckled himself into the harness. The harness connected to an electrically-powered winch system that would take him to the top of the gorge. He had installed it several months earlier for emergencies such as this. It was located at the steepest and highest part of the basin, a near vertical ascent of 320 feet next to the falls.

Zimbola handed him the latest firearm Jake had purchased through the Haitian arms dealer he occasionally used back in Port-au-Prince. It was a gas-operated 12-gauge shotgun with a detachable drum magazine. The magazine currently held 32 shells of double-ought buckshot, but the gun could also fire frag-12 rounds that would explode on impact. Called the "Sledgehammer," the weapon was ideally suited for close quarter combat in dense jungle environments. When fired, it had a near-zero recoil with almost no muzzle climb. It had two firing modes – semi and automatic. Having stainless steel components, it required no cleaning or lubrication.

An idea came to Jake and he looked to Destiny. "I need you to stay on the phone." For emphasis, he glanced toward the intercom off to the right side of the winch. It interfaced directly with all four bunkers.

Destiny nodded in understanding.

"Hit the button!" Jake shouted, the sound of sporadic gunfire from high above now gaining in intensity.

"Wait!" Destiny cried. She reached in and gave him a fierce kiss before pulling away. "Please be careful."

Jake gave her an ironic smile. "Aren't I always?!" Swiveling his head, he looked back at Zimbola. "Hit it!"

Abruptly, the cable went taut and Jake felt himself being whisked rapidly upward. Reaching the top in 30 seconds, he unbuckled himself and ducked down on a small outcropping of limestone, taking quick inventory of his surroundings. The discharge of heavy weapons and small arms fire cracked the air in the distance, but with the sound muffled by heavy vegetation, he knew the source of the gunfire would be much closer than perceived. As if to confirm this, something mimicking an enraged bee buzzed past his head.

Reflexively, Jake hugged the ground as several more rounds zipped by, some of them zinging off the rock and kicking up small plumes of dust. This was immediately followed by a deafening barrage from a much heavier weapon almost on top of him.

Jake glanced to his left, knowing from where the sound emanated. A seemingly impenetrable barrier of trees and underbrush stood less than 30 feet away, and barely visible along the edge of it was a tiny little fortress comprised of sandbags and earth. It was armed with twin .50 caliber machine guns. Someone inside was returning fire at unseen attackers.

Jake jumped to his feet and scrambled for the bunker, leaping into a small rear opening that allowed access. A thin wiry individual manning the gun from a swivel seat glanced back, surprised at this unexpected intrusion. A relieved grin broke out on the man's face at seeing Jake.

"Give me an update!" Jake yelled, his ears still ringing from the discharging weapon.

Jimenez swung his head around to keep vigilance of the woods beyond the gun port. "All the bunkers are being attacked simultaneously."

"Has that been confirmed?" Jake asked, noting that Jimenez was not wearing his headphones. He had made it a priority to install a wire network that allowed all four bunkers to communicate with one another.

Jimenez nodded vigorously. "The attackers seem to know exactly where each bunker is situated."

"How do you know?"

"I heard someone cry out from the woods in front of me. So did Maurice. He believes a raiding party has stumbled into the traps you set. He started taking fire right after that. When he returned fire, all hell broke out."

Jimenez let loose with another barrage, swinging the twins through a thirty-degree arc and shredding more foliage a short distance away.

Jake weighed the implications. Maurice was in Bunker Number 2, two bunkers away. From the sound of the battle, he could tell the attackers were armed with only light assault weapons. Coming by way of land to engage the fortified bunkers, carrying heavier weaponry would have been cumbersome and impractical. They had relied instead on stealth to slip up quietly and take out each of the bunkers. Obviously these people had taken great pains to plan the operation, but unfortunately for them it was not going the way they had envisioned it.

This was a subject Ez had breached several months earlier. She had predicted that a rich man like Cardoza would have the right connections to use satellite reconnaissance as a means of pinpointing the location of all the bunkers, and this would have occurred during a change of guard when the men manning those bunkers were most visible along the rim of the basin.

Those fortifications with their armaments had been completed in the nick of time, for they had been indispensable in opposing Cardoza and his henchmen on his last two attempts to take the cove. The first of these attempts had been clumsy, and he had several more of his valuable assets badly damaged on that occasion. Using two large whirlybirds loaded with a small army of thugs, he had attacked by air, failing miserably in the process. Flying into a storm of withering fire coming from multiple positions, both aircraft had proved to be no match for the twin fifties, which could be elevated by 85 degrees to shoot upward, and it didn't take long to send them buzzing off into the sunset billowing dense trails of smoke. With each gun having a maximum effective range of 2,000 yards and a firing rate of 550 rounds per minute, all four gun emplacements were capable of sending out a total of 73 rounds each second in combination.

Cardoza's last attempt at taking the cove had also proved equally clumsy when he had tried to come in by land in the middle of the night. With most of his men stumbling into an array of hidden traps, the bunkers had hardly been needed to fend off that foray.

But Jake had no illusions about the continued effectiveness of these security measures. While they proved to work against inept thugs, they would be crude and rudimentary at best against more capable troops. He knew a man like Cardoza would not give up easily, and Ez had surmised the drug lord would ultimately hire on professional soldiers to do his dirty work, men who were well trained at avoiding booby traps and taking out concealed gun emplacements. To counter such a possibility, Jake had planted bars of gold in the surrounding forest, some rigged with springboard contraptions armed with spiked dowels. He had anticipated the sight of so much gold would cause encroachers to become sloppy.

Upgrading the cove's security with more sophisticated state-of-the-art measures had been on the planning table for some time now, but Jake had been far too busy with the building of Aquaria to turn a set of Ez-created designs into working prototypes.

DOLPHIN RIDERS

Jake heard something pop a short distance away, and he immediately knew what had caused that sound. This was quickly confirmed when the smell of potassium nitrate began to permeate the air. Within seconds, a heavy green mist billowed forth to engulf the bunker, cutting down visibility.

"Stay alert!" Jake cautioned. "They're using smoke to screen their approach. I want you to hold your fire for the time being." Abruptly, he sprang for the exit.

"What are you doing?" Jimenez asked.

Jake spoke quickly without looking back. "Keeping the fox away from the hen house."

Outside the bunker, the smoke was thick. Jake stayed low, slithering along the ground where the haze was thinnest. The thought that he still hadn't rigged Claymore mines around the bunkers nagged away at him, for this would have been an appropriate time to use them. He had put in an order for a supply of them two months earlier through the same black market arms dealer from whom he had purchased the fifties, making him wonder if the requisition had been filled by now. Nevertheless, he had one other measure in reserve.

Like a blind man, Jake groped his way along the sandbags forming the side of the bunker. The bunker was a simple four-sided fortification without a roof, though it had tree limbs and freshly cut leaves laid atop the bags to camouflage it from above. The overhead cover could easily be pushed aside to fend off an aerial assault using the fifties. But a fragmentation grenade lobbed on top of it could easily take out the gunner. Jake's immediate objective was to keep this from happening.

An odd vision suddenly came to Jake, flashing in his mind's eye like a group of neon signs. Bunkers 2, 3 and 4 were also bathed in smoke, but lurking within the thick haze were men he could clearly see. It was as though he were viewing three screens at once on a closed-circuit television system set up for monitoring security, and at this moment they were in striking distance.

Jake had no time to ponder this strange perception. Without hesitation, he fired off a mental directive to his bond mate. Achilles came back a second later. *Destiny has relayed your message.*

Jake felt the shock waves pass underfoot as the detcord exploded. This was the measure he had in reserve. Detcord was flexible plastic tubing filled with PETN - pentrite. He had installed lengths of it fifteen feet out in front of each bunker in a crude semi-circle, overlaying it with stones and gravel to act as shrapnel when the cord detonated. The end result would be almost as effective as Claymore mines.

Another vision flashed briefly within Jake's thoughts, and he counted four fallen men. Two of them lay sprawled along the perimeter of bunker 2, while bunkers 1 and 3 showed one each.

Jake moved to the corner of the tiny fortress, gaining a position to the right side of the gun port. Craning his head around the side, he stopped and waited, pointing the shotgun out in front of him. Wanting to conserve his ammunition, he had set the weapon on semi-automatic.

A slight breeze had sprung up, and from the feel of it on his face he could tell it was causing the smoke to drift across the front of the bunker from left to right. Sensing rather than hearing movement, he kept his trigger finger poised in readiness.

The thing he had anticipated occurred only seconds later. A dark shadow rose up out of the haze on the opposite side of the gun port. The "Sledgehammer" barely bucked as Jake unleashed a single shot. He was firing at close quarters and the possibility of missing his target was zero. Without hesitation he fired again, keeping his body hunkered behind the corner of the bunker.

The shadow teetered forward, brushing past and toppling over. Jake extended an arm and prodded it cautiously with the barrel of the shotgun. It took him less than a second to grasp the situation, and he realized he had been tricked. It was not the form of a man that lay on the ground but that of a tree branch heavy with leaves.

Knowing he had given his position away, Jake rolled to his right, seeking the protection of a large tree he knew was located ten feet away. Muzzle flashes erupted within the gloom, accompanied by the deafening clatter of a light machine gun. Bullets ripped through his clothing but failed to connect with any flesh. Bolting wildly, he stumbled into the tree trunk, taking refuge behind it. Flashes continued to spark in the haze behind him, and he felt the impact of rounds tearing into the timber that shielded him from the onslaught.

Timing a reply, Jake leaned out from behind the tree the instant his attacker stopped firing, pulling back on the "Sledgehammer" trigger and squeezing off five rounds in rapid succession.

A cry of pain suddenly cleaved the air, and Jake was sure he had scored a hit on the unseen attacker. Hugging the ground, he circled wide looking to flank his adversary. Visibility was quickly improving. Carried off by the breeze, the smoke was beginning to thin.

Within moments Jake came upon a dark splotch marring a small cluster of leaves. Testing it with his fingers, he knew it was blood. Creeping forward, he found another splotch, heavier than the previous one. His foe seemed to be retreating, leaving a growing trail of blood in his wake. Doggedly, Jake continued to follow, the sporadic sound of both heavy and light machine gun fire hanging in the background. In moments he came upon something on the ground before him. It was a Kalashnikov AK-104 assault rifle, a compact, modernized version of the ubiquitous AK-47. Obviously the foe he was hunting had discarded the weapon, too weak to carry it any further.

By now the smoke had cleared completely, and Jake espied movement behind some ferns. Creeping up slowly, he discerned two men in a small clearing, one of them on his knees and cradling the other in his arms. Both men were smeared with blood, with the one doing the holding seemingly unconcerned with the battle raging in the distance. This had to be the adversary he had tracked.

Jake held his position, studying the scene with a critical eye. Another AK-104 lay on the ground near both men, and three of the gold bars he had planted littered the forest floor next to them. And while he saw that the spiked plank had been sprung, he didn't think it had caused the injury of the man being held. Blood trickled from his open mouth, a sure sign of internal hemorrhaging, and the bandage girthing his belly was soaked red. The man holding him looked sad, almost apologetic, and Jake suddenly found himself overcome with emotion. All at once the memory of Tora Bora came flooding back, for he had held a dying Myers in the same manner.

The man Jake had wounded abruptly sagged, coming to rest beside the comrade he had been cradling. Jake scanned the foliage all around him, looking for movement but failed to detect any. Bringing his eyes back to the men, he moved into the clearing and knelt beside them.

Still conscious, his adversary stared up at him as though he had anticipated his arrival. Instead of the hate Jake had expected to see, the man's expression conveyed something altogether different. It was the look of a man resigned to his fate, a man not defeated by Jake but by a life spent walking the wrong path. That was what Jake read in his eyes, eyes set in a face that bespoke of countless battles and vanquished foes. Strangely, Jake had the odd sensation this man was looking to atone for the sins he had committed.

And then Jake noticed something peculiar. The eyes did not match. One was brown and the other blue.

Almost at once, Achilles' presence resonated within his thoughts. *JJ, you must not let this man die.*

Why?

Destiny believes this man will play a key role in the Cove's salvation.

Puzzled by this, Jake did not try to question Destiny's instincts. He decided he would do his best to honor her request.

"You are Jake Javolyn," the man stated languidly. The words were enunciated with thick overtones that suggested a Russian or Ukrainian lineage.

"How do you know my name?" Jake asked.

"There is... no time to explain," Belachek uttered, fighting back the pain of his injuries.

Jake noted the cause. Blood oozed slowly from his right shoulder and the left side of his rib cage. Double-ought buckshot could wreak havoc on the human body at close range, and he suspected the underlying bone in both locations was shattered.

Belachek got control of his pain. "If you agree to save my son, I can stop the carnage."

Jake eyed the other man who lay seemingly dead. "This is your son?"

"Yes."

Jake reached down and placed a finger on the man's neck. Though barely perceptible, he felt a pulse. "This madness must end right now if you want my help," he said. "How do you propose to end it?"

"I am the leader of this madness," Belachek replied weakly. With difficulty he groped for a portable radio attached to his harness.

Jake grabbed his wrist. The radio might actually be a concealed suicide device designed to kill all three of them.

Belachek stared up at him with those mismatched eyes, a silent plea held within them. "Though we may be enemies, we are brothers in war," he said softly. "As one warrior to another, you have my word I will not harm you."

Jake relaxed his grip. "Cardoza hired you, didn't he?"

Belachek's eyes went wide, looking past Javolyn at something behind him. Jake whirled to espy a dark form loom over him, unable to swing the Sledgehammer around in time.

The man sneaking up on him abruptly froze, dropping the knife he had been holding. An expression of disbelief and horror consumed his face as both his hands rose up to clutch the metal shaft embedded deeply in his throat. Gurgling horribly, he stumbled off to one side before falling face-first to the ground, his legs twitching spasmodically. Several blood-encrusted dowels jutted from the man's right hip.

Jake whipped his head back around to stare at the mercenary leader, prepared to fend off an attack. The haft of a ballistic knife was held in the man's hand.

Belachek managed a small smile. "I never liked him."

"You're Spetsnaz!" Jake said. A student of war, he knew Spetsnaz agents were notorious for using these spring-loaded weapons, which launched the blade contained within them like a missile.

Belachek's smile turned to a grimace as another bout of pain engulfed him. "If you please," he gasped. "Lift the radio to my lips. I don't have much strength left."

Jake accommodated the request, depressing the transmit button and holding it down as Belachek issued a set of commands in a language he didn't understand.

If you're still linked to me, Achilles, maybe you can tell me what he's saying, Jake petitioned, knowing all the albinos were multilingual.

He speaks in the Russian tongue, JJ, and is ordering his troops to fall back to the staging area.

You're sure of this?

The umbrage Jake detected in his bond mate swept in on him like a gust of arctic wind. *Does a whale defecate in the sea?* Achilles replied sarcastically.

Smart ass!

Within moments the sound of small arms fire began to die off, though sporadic bursts from the heavier guns continued.

Jake focused his thoughts yet again. *Achilles, have Destiny instruct the bunkers to cease firing.*

It took another minute for the twin fifties in bunkers 2, 3 and 4 to cut out entirely, and Jake knew they had heeded Destiny's request.

Belachek spoke into the radio again, and Achilles translated. *JJ, he's trying to make contact with Reaper and Badger.*

Shortly after recovering from his coma, Jake had been apprised of Badger's fate.

A look of bewilderment contorted the Ukrainian's face when Jake pulled the radio away. "Your friends won't be coming," he said. "Both Hinds have been destroyed."

Belachek had weakened further and his tone reflected it. "If that is true, then why am I hearing a helicopter?"

Jake's ears perked. Though subtle, the sound of rotary blades churning the air hung in the background.

What's happening, Achilles?

Help is on the way, JJ. The chopper you hear is one of ours.

Jake was perplexed. Aside from Fernando, who was still down in the cove, there were only three other members of Tursiops capable of piloting a helicopter, and two of them were currently away on business.

Who's piloting it?

You'll find out soon enough, Achilles replied. *Stay put, they're coming back your way to lend assistance.*

Jake listened as the sound of the whirlybird diminished, perceiving it had landed on the outcropping of limestone abutting Jimenez's bunker. Looking back down, he saw that the mercenary leader was now unconscious.

Another minute passed before leaves parted on one side of the clearing, and Jake saw Zimbola emerge from the underbrush. A petite woman followed on his heels, appearing far younger than her years would suggest.

Jake had known Destiny's mother had been learning to fly a helicopter, taking lessons from Fernando, and was proving herself to be a capable pilot. But as he studied her expression, he was suddenly reminded of a woman he had met only briefly in the past. This was not the Harriet Grahm he had come to know so well over the last several years. Some inner sense he could not explain told him this, something arcane and beyond the scope of scientific explanation. Here was the essence that had led to the building of Aquaria.

The mental presence of Achilles reverberated in Jake's head. *Yes, JJ, Amphitrite is back with us again.*

-38-

In spite of mounting pressures, Jacob felt it necessary to summon Amelia to his office. "For your own safety, you should leave this facility now," he advised.

Amelia saw the troubled look on his weathered face, a countenance that seemed to bear the weight of the world. Obviously something dark was quickly approaching, reminding her of the nightmare she had experienced the night before.

"What troubles you?"

Jacob sighed wearily. "A UN task force is being mobilized to take control of Aquaria. It's going to be far larger than the one you witnessed yesterday."

"How do you know?"

Jacob studied her for one brief moment, looking for signs of deception but only seeing naïve innocence. "Ez," he said, "replay the news broadcast you picked up this morning."

Puzzled, Amelia glanced around the room, searching for the person Jacob had addressed. Her eyes came to rest on the far wall, the place where Jacob seemed to be focused. Completely covering it was a sprawling view of Aquaria's lagoons and containment ponds stretching off to the north, with Navassa Island hanging further out amid cobalt blue waters. The panorama was picturesque and breathtaking, and her initial impression was that it was a photograph taken from the highest point on the facility's central structure. But subtle movement within the scene told her otherwise, for a cable car was slowly traversing the tramway toward the offshore

DOLPHIN RIDERS

platform where a small ship was pulling alongside to berth. It suddenly occurred to her she was watching a real-time video display on a flat screen TV at least 15 feet wide and 10 feet tall.

An expression of stunned amazement crossed her face as the screen changed over to a news bulletin. She was watching herself in high definition, standing on the same promenade deck when she had first arrived at the colony. But the perspective was all wrong. Navassa Island and a sparkling blue sea should have been visible in the background, not the bare white wall that dominated the space behind her.

"This is Amelia Amhurst of IBC News, reporting to you live from Aquaria, the world's first large scale sea colony." The smile she had presented to her audience changed as she spoke, slowly turning glum.

"A little known international corporation called Tursiops Worldwide is the builder of this colony, which is located adjacent to Navassa Island, a tiny Caribbean isle that lies midway between Jamaica and Haiti. In 1998, the island and the waters surrounding it fell under the administrative jurisdiction of the U.S. Fish and Wildlife Service, which declared it a National Wildlife Refuge. Such protection was deemed necessary since the submerged coral shelf adjacent to the island was discovered to be one of the most intact and thriving ecosystems in the Caribbean. The island itself has a distinctive biodiversity, providing a home to various plants and animals found nowhere else in the world, one of them being a rare iguana previously thought to be extinct."

A series of videos flashed across the screen as she said this showing aerial views of the island and stunning underwater scenes. Species of animals and plants endemic to the habitat were also shown, including the rare Navassa Island iguana.

"These are examples of what this area of the world used to look like, a habitat untouched and unspoiled by the ravages of man. But through a lease agreement with Tursiops Worldwide, this locale became the site for constructing what amounts to an enormous floating city. One of the conditions of the lease was that this habitat was to be left unharmed."

Amelia saw herself fill the screen again, and she cringed at the look she had given the camera as she listened to herself speak. It was a look designed to please her superiors. Seeing it now, she felt ashamed. "Unfortunately, that was not in the cards. Reports coming from undisclosed sources had indicated extreme ecological abuses taking place within these waters, compelling this news channel to investigate."

She remembered uttering those exact words, there was no denying it.

The scene immediately shifted, and what followed made her jaw drop. Recordings taken from the helicopter prior to landing had been doctored. The clear, pristine water she had witnessed girthing Navassa was shown to be roiled with a milky white sediment. It intruded its way into the containment ponds and lagoons, extending out to the city's central structure and beyond. Randomly interspersed atop the clouded sea were heavy oil slicks. They appeared ebony black and reflected sunlight like polished anthracite.

"As can be seen in these videos, this once healthy and thriving habitat is systematically being destroyed by oil spills and the dumping of other contaminants into these previously undisturbed waters, churning them up and turning them into what amounts to be a massive cesspool. Aside from this despicable and unsightly pollution, it is highly probable the seafood products Aquaria sells so cheaply on world markets is highly tainted with toxins that makes them unsuitable for human consumption."

The news item continued. "Compounding these abuses, it is rumored that the operation is emitting enormous amounts of nitrous oxide into the atmosphere." As she said this, another scene showed dense vaporous clouds being emitted from the facility's superstructure, drifting high into the sky and dispersing into the atmosphere. "Nitrous oxide is highly destructive to the earth's protective ozone layer," she went on to say. "This gas is three hundred times more powerful than carbon dioxide in causing a greenhouse effect. It is believed the phosphates the colony routinely mines on Navassa Island is the cause of this since phosphates favor the formation of a purer form of nitrous oxide."

Amelia's eyes went wide with horror. That was the claim of the UN envoy, Malikai Allotey, made to look as though she had spoken them herself. And while she was not in these incriminating scenes, her voice had been carefully dubbed in to describe what the camera was showing. Though it sounded like her, she had never uttered the wordage that had accompanied those images nor what she was hearing now.

"As is evident from what we've documented, the people running this colony have little regard for the coral reef habitat that surrounds Navassa Island, putting profits well ahead of any concern for the environment."

Outrage took hold of Amelia as more lies ensued, and she began to tremble from the sheer blatancy of them.

"Using explosives for carrying out their operations, Tursiops is systematically destroying a delicate ecosystem that was once unblemished and unpolluted." As if to prove the statement's accuracy, the scene shifted yet again to display the towering geyser her cameraman had captured.

The scene was replaced by another, this one showing the arrival of a helicopter with a United Nations logo. Dubbed in again was Amelia's voice, though she had never voiced what her ears were hearing.

"Having gotten wind of these atrocities, the World Ecological Affairs Council, a newly formed branch of the United Nations, sent in a fact-finding team to determine if they were true. But unfortunately, the team was met with hostility and sent running for their lives. As is evident from the video, a security force stationed at the facility used flame throwers to drive them from the city."

Amelia was appalled by the sight of flames licking out at members of the UN team as they scrambled for the safety of their helicopter to escape, an event that had been meticulously altered with an overlay of special effects.

Adding insult to injury, another scene came to dominate the screen. It showed images of paratroopers landing on the ship she had seen during her last interview with Jacob. Amelia's disembodied voice followed.

"As if to further antagonize the international community, elements of Aquaria have reputedly hijacked the Southern Star, a containership that ventured within close proximity to the floating city. In reaction to this, the United Nations sent in a military force to take back the vessel. Though unconfirmed, it is speculated that the hijackers sought to take control of the ship's cargo of tungsten, a metal that is used in the manufacture of counterfeit gold bars. Rumors have arisen that Tursiops was able to finance the construction of Aquaria by using gold as a trade barter. If this is true, international vendors supplying equipment and goods to Tursiops may discover they took possession of worthless metal in consummating the deals."

The image of the hijacked freighter was suddenly replaced by one of the United Nations General Assembly showing speakers in heated debates.

Amelia's voice droned on. "As a consequence of Aquaria's transgressions, an emergency meeting of the UN has been called to order to decide ownership of Navassa Island, which has been contested for over two hundred years. The Republic of Haiti has disputed sovereignty of this tiny island since 1801, claiming the United States illegally took possession of it under the Guano Act for the purpose of mining guano, a natural occurring fertilizer. As a result of this meeting, the US has graciously accepted the General Assembly's overwhelming unanimous vote to concede sovereignty of this tiny territory back to its rightful owner, that being Haiti. Subsequent to this action, a UN task force is being mobilized to take control of both the island and the adjoining floating city."

Jacob turned off the TV as an image of Amelia followed to end the news bulletin. He knew that no other fabrications would be forthcoming.

Amelia felt dizzy, her mind reeling with what she had seen. It occurred to her that one particular item had been deleted from the newscast, and that was the alleged indiscretions of Allotey and Alvarez as announced by the Haitian woman called Ez. Jacob had been right. The people she worked for had carefully edited the news clips captured by her cameraman, purposely photo shopping them to flagrantly vilify Aquaria in the worst possible light.

Amelia could not bring herself to look at Jacob. "I want you to know I never said most of the things you heard, nor did I have anything to do with their editing," she said shamefully.

Jacob's reply was soft. "I know."

His tone made her turn to face him, and in his eyes she could find no recrimination. Only kindness lingered there. "What are you going to do?" she found it necessary to ask.

"The same thing any living organism does when its survival is placed in jeopardy."

The statement and all that it implied horrified Amelia. "You can't win. If you fight back, you'll put this facility and all those on it at risk." Strangely, she did not fear for herself as she said this. Even so, she was compelled to dissuade Jacob from doing anything rash.

Jacob stared back with a calm demeanor. "I never said I expected to win."

"People might die, is that what you want?"

Jacob noted the wetness that was quickly gathering in her hazel eyes. Strangely, her show of compassion made him want to reach out to comfort her. "I never want to see anyone die," he said soothingly, "not even those who deserve it."

"Then why resist?"

Jacob produced a gentle smile. "Because to submit would reflect a sense of fear on our part, and we will not cave to intimidation by bullies."

"Are you at least going to evacuate the colonists?"

"The possibility of an attack was discussed with the populace long ago. You must understand that the majority of Aquarians are of Haitian heritage. As former members of an impoverished society, they would rather die than go back to the life they once had. And while I don't normally make it a practice to speak for everyone who lives here, I believe there is not one person among us who would refrain from giving up their life if they thought doing so might save Aquaria."

Amelia merely stared back in admiration of his conviction.

Jacob felt it necessary to add more. "If we do nothing, then we will be subjecting ourselves to the chains of tyranny. Only by resisting will we truly be free, even if it means dying."

As he said this, the words of Plato, one of history's great philosophers, resonated within him to strengthen his resolve: *'The price of apathy towards public affairs is to be ruled by evil men.'* He often used the philosophies of noble men to reinforce his own convictions, and under the present circumstances those words could not have rang truer to life.

-39-

Amelia rode one of the twenty high speed elevators that serviced Aquaria's central structure, taking it down to the facility's main level. She was furious. Her cameraman had been deceitful, purposely lying. Eric Bolder had previously told her he had been unable to transmit the news clips they had recorded to IBC headquarters. "Wireless transmission is not always reliable in remote locations, and this place is definitely off the beaten path," Bolder had explained. "We'll most likely have to hand-deliver the recordings once we finish this assignment."

Something was definitely amiss here, and she was going to get to the bottom of it. Upon leaving Jacob's office, she had gone directly to Bolder's suite, which was across the hall from her own. Failing to find him there, she figured she might locate him on the helipad where the IBC chopper sat. Aside from serving as her cameraman, Bolder was a licensed pilot and had flown them out to the colony.

Making her way to the helipad, she was again amazed by the facility's sprawling immensity. In contrast, she saw very few people along the way, but as she passed them they greeted her with welcoming smiles. Jacob had said there were currently 10,000 residents dwelling within Aquaria, with living space designed to accommodate a population of 100,000 once the floating city was completed. He had made it a point that even with that many people, the colony's efficient use of interior and exterior space would prevent the type of congestion often seen within the world's largest urban centers.

Each face Amelia came upon appeared to radiate the same thing, and that was contentment and joy. Looks of discomfort and irritability typically displayed by milling crowds in the cities back home were entirely absent. If left alone by the international community, these people would never go hungry or cold. Poverty would become a thing of the past. They would never lack for anything because Aquaria would take care of all their needs.

Amelia loved this place, moved all the more by the ubiquitous art that flourished among the city's incredible interior architecture. Oil paintings and holographic projections of it were everywhere, each one different and yet eliciting the same feeling of ecstasy within her. Within this wondrous place her spirit was free.

Reaching the helipad, she came around the side of the aircraft and stopped short. Bolder was leaning over something in the chopper's rear compartment, unaware of her presence. He looked ill, and as if to confirm this, a puddle of vomit lay close to his feet. Held within his hand was a syringe, its needle embedded in his thigh. He was breathing deeply, rapidly, as though he were under great physical duress, and as she watched she could see the distress engulfing him suddenly abate. Within moments, his breathing normalized.

Offended by the sight, she spoke without thinking. "What are you doing?"

Bolder spun as though he were a child caught by his mother raiding the cookie jar.

"You're a druggie!" Amelia accused, shocked by what she was seeing.

"No...no! Bolder stuttered with embarrassment. "You have it all wrong. I have to take this to treat my affliction. I have health issues."

Amelia eyed the syringe suspiciously. "What issues?"

"A few years ago I contracted Hepatitis C. This drug keeps it under control."

Amelia stood mute for several seconds, collecting her thoughts. It was then she realized Bolder had never looked quite right ever since arriving here. Now that she thought about it, he had appeared especially queasy while filming the central structure's interior.

"Okay, I'll accept that," she said, "but why did you tell me you were unable to send the recordings when, in fact, you had already done so?"

Bolder's beseeching demeanor suddenly shifted, becoming petulant. "At the time, something was interfering with the transmission, but I kept trying anyway and finally it got through. What's the problem?"

"Did you know they were aired?"

A look of surprise transcended Bolder's face. "Already! That's fantastic. Maybe there'll be a nice bonus in it for us."

"Did you also know those recordings were intentionally altered to criminalize the people working here?"

Bolder shrugged. "So what. In this business it happens all the time. Things are often taken out of context to add drama to an event. You better learn to accept that if you want to advance your career."

Amelia felt it necessary to scream to get through his obstinate manner. "The company went way beyond the context thing. The recordings were overlaid with special effects. They purposely doctored them to vilify this colony. They showed the surrounding water to be polluted with oil and the UN team being chased away with flame throwers."

"My job is to record events on camera and yours is to provide commentary, nothing more," Bolder grumbled. "What the editors do with it is their business."

"They added commentary I never said," Amelia objected hotly. "They dubbed in words using my voice."

"Cry me a river, Amhurst, you're breaking my heart."

Amelia's jaw dropped in disbelief. "I'm stunned you find a deception of this magnitude to be so morally acceptable."

Bolder smiled mockingly. "Sweetheart, the only thing acceptable to me is my paycheck. I do what they pay me to do, no questions asked."

"Then I guess you'll be earning it. A UN task force is on its way to take control of this city."

"That doesn't surprise me."

"These people are being unfairly persecuted," Amelia decried, totally offended by his callous tone. "The truth needs to come out."

Bolder chuckled. "What truth!? Pardon the pun, but this whole operation smells fishy."

"What are you insinuating?"

"Just look around you, Amhurst. Where do you suppose these people got the financing to build this palatial complex? My guess is that it cost several billion to construct it, not to mention the enormous architectural and engineering fees to design it. Have you noticed that most of the people working here come from Haiti?"

"So?"

Bolder shook his head, still grinning. "Don't you get it? Haiti is one of the poorest nations on earth. No lending institution in their right mind would have been foolish enough to fork over billions to a people who obviously had no collateral."

Amelia riposted quickly. "You heard the interview. Jacob said Aquaria carried no debt burden whatsoever due to its exceptional profitability."

"Precisely my point. They obviously needed seed money to get this operation started, so where did it come from?"

Amelia groped for an answer. "Someone must have believed in their vision enough to risk backing them."

Bolder shook his head again, this time with a sneer. "Wrong! The planners must have been involved in some incredibly lucrative illegal activities to get them started."

"Like what?"

"How about drug running for one." Bolder's smile broadened at seeing the look of horror on her face.

"No way!"

"Oh, yeah," he shot back, nodding annoyingly as he said it. "Four years ago I was on assignment in Port-au-Prince investigating the massive corruption that exists there among Haitian officials, including their limited and inadequate police force. Most of them are easily bribed and on the payroll of drug lords to turn a blind eye to their activities, which makes Haiti an ideal staging area for huge transshipments of cocaine and heroin headed for the US and Western Europe."

When Amelia refused to comment, Bolder tossed out another idea. "Or how about scamming their way into an operation of this size."

"Scam? What do you mean by that?"

"Instead of using money to buy materials and equipment, or for that matter, services, they used gold. Only it was counterfeit."

Amelia's eyes widened. "Then you did see the newscast."

"I don't know what you're talking about."

"The newscast implied the very same thing you just mentioned, speculating that fake gold may have been used to pay for the construction."

For one brief moment, Bolder seemed to be thrown off guard, though he still held that insufferable smile. "I did not see the newscast."

"If that is true, then I have to assume you knew about this allegation before we got here. Could it be that someone at IBC headquarters clued you in on what they were planning to do with the fruits of our labor?"

"You're one loony broad if you believe that."

Amelia cast her gaze in the direction of the freighter still visible in the distance. "That ship is called the Southern Star, and according to the newscast, is carrying a large payload of tungsten. The newscast claimed those skydivers you recorded dropping down on it were a UN strike force sent to take it back from hijackers coming from this city. It inferred the Aquarians needed the metal to make counterfeit gold."

Turning back to face Bolder, she looked him in the eye. "Did you have advance notice that event was going to take place?"

Bolder let out a small laugh, and to Amelia, it sounded a tad forced. "You're crazy, Amhurst!"

"You think so. You seemed to know exactly where to point the camera at the time of the incident."

"You're letting your imagination run wild. I saw the skydivers at the same time you did, so I carried out the job I'm paid to do, and that's to document any event potentially relevant to this investigation. But I can tell you one thing, I can easily believe that ship was hijacked by these people."

"You can?"

"This colony is still under construction, which means they still require massive amounts of material and equipment they can't get from the ocean. I'm talking about items that must be retrofitted to the sea-grown structures to make this facility fully operational. Perhaps they need to fabricate more counterfeit gold to pay for it and that ship carries the very metal that will make it possible."

"You know what I believe, Bolder?"

"Tell me!"

"I believe these colonists are purposely being framed and that you're collaborating with the people setting them up."

"Believe what you want, Amhurst, but we've got a job to do. If a UN task force is on its way, there's going to be plenty of stuff for us to document, not to mention the hefty bonuses we'll be getting."

Amelia was growing tired of the patronizing grin plastered on his face. "The people here are not going to give this place up without a fight. Perhaps it's time you left."

Bolder's grin faded to a squinty-eyed scowl. "It sounds like you wouldn't be coming with me if I did."

This time it was Amelia's turn to smile. "Your astute perception is to be congratulated. I'm through working for slimeballs. I'll not abet them again."

-40-

Victor Belachek found himself running. A debilitating pain consumed him, slowly gnawing away at his remaining strength to make the effort seem like he was plodding through a muddy swamp. Nevertheless, he kept pushing himself forward, desperately wanting to escape the familiar though unshakable presence chasing after him. Afraid he might stumble, he risked a peak over his shoulder to glimpse his pursuer, only to see himself. Try as he might, he could not get away.

But then something odd happened. The ground under his feet suddenly firmed, and he felt himself moving faster. Glimpsing back, he saw himself begin to recede.

"He's coming around," he heard a faraway voice say.

All at once the pain lifted as though a deeply rooted spike had been plucked from his body, and the pleasing scent of jasmine drifted in on him. Disoriented and confused, he opened his eyes to find himself immersed in water, kept afloat by...

Belachek started, thrashing about wildly as he realized he was surrounded by several finned creatures.

Hands gripped both his arms, clamping down with shocking power to restrain him. That same voice rang out again, this time up close. "Easy there, fella!" it said. But the voice did not belong to the one immobilizing him.

Javolyn stood above him, perched on the stern platform of a large boat. "I think you can pull him from the water, Zimby."

An arm thick with muscle reached down to grasp him just above the elbow and heft him effortlessly from the water. The arm belonged to a hulking black giant standing next to Javolyn.

"Lie down!" Javolyn ordered as the giant deposited him on the platform. "You're still healing. Give it a few more minutes and you should be good as new."

Dazedly, Belachek stared up at him searchingly, trying to recall how he had gotten here. It took only a moment before images of the battle descended on him, and with that remembrance he reached up to explore the massive wounds that should have killed him. He was stunned to find no shattered bone or torn flesh.

"It's touch and go on this one," Belachek heard someone else mutter. This time it was a woman's voice. Her tone was weary, as though a great strain were imposed on her.

Still lying on his back, Belachek rolled his head to one side to observe two women in the water. They were administering Alex, who was being buoyed up by those same finned creatures. It was then he realized he was looking at several white dolphins, the largest one nearly the size of an orca.

"Some people are not receptive to psychokinetic healing," the same voice uttered.

Psychokinetic. He knew what the word implied. The KGB had performed countless experiments on the subject, and as a young man, he had been one of their guinea pigs.

Belachek saw it was the older of the two who had spoken, though both appeared young and could have passed for sisters.

"You must save him!" Belachek groaned, starting to rise. "He is my only son."

Javolyn pushed him back down. "They're doing everything they can."

A flood of emotion rushed in to take hold of Belachek, spilling onto his tongue. "I have to make things right," he cried, closing his eyes tightly to hold back an eruption of tears. "I was a terrible father. He was two when I deserted him. After his mother was killed in a car crash, I left him at an orphanage. I could not bear the responsibility of having to raise a child by myself. I…"

Belachek caught himself, suddenly aware that he had never bared his soul to anyone. The fact that he was doing it now, and no less to strangers, was totally alien to him. Nevertheless, this newfound experience felt cleansing, as though great gouts of puss were being purged from his body.

They must have done something to me, he thought, *something I cannot explain.*

"Grab hold of the hand before you and let go of your feelings," the older woman urged. "It will help us help your son."

Belachek somehow sensed what she was asking of him, and unashamedly he opened his eyes to release a gush of tears. But the hand he expected to hold was not human, though it had what resembled five digits with an opposable thumb. The hand was large and dwarfed his own as he reached out without fear to clutch it. It belonged to the largest dolphin, which had extended an arm from under a pectoral fin. He noticed the creature had its snout pushed up against Alex, as did the other dolphins.

An anxious moment passed before the older woman let out a deep sigh. "It's working!" she suddenly cried, her tone reflecting the depth of emotion gripping Belachek. "His pulse grows stronger."

"Will he live?" Belachek asked.

"Yes," the woman replied. "Your son will live."

-41-

"Your children?" Belachek asked as he rested in a foldup beach chair Hector had set out for him on the Angel's bow. Though he was recovering rapidly, he needed fresh air, and the sights and pleasing aromas wafting within the cove both fascinated and refreshed him. Intrigued, he watched the playful antics of two young children riding smaller versions of the strange white dolphins that had assisted in healing his injuries. At the moment they were racing each other across the cove's limpid waters, goading each other on and bantering back and forth with gleeful shouts of wild abandon.

"Yes," Jake said, "but sometimes they can be a handful."

"You are a lucky man, Jake Javolyn. You have balance in your life, two beautiful children and a kind, compassionate wife. You are surrounded by people who love you."

Jake said nothing, somewhat taken back by Belachek's open display of wistfulness.

Belachek inhaled deeply, enjoying the sweet smell of jasmine and wild flowers before letting out a prolonged sigh. "I am indebted to you."

"Yes you are," Jake replied. "And now I'm going to request payment."

"What do you wish of me?"

"Cardoza has been a thorn in our side for a long time. We need you to show us the way into his lair, to point out his weaknesses."

Belachek sat quietly, lifting his head to admire the tiered sides of the chasm. "Do you seek revenge?"

"No, not revenge. This man is a threat to my family and must be destroyed. He leaves me no choice but to go after him on his own turf. If I don't do that, sooner or later he's going to succeed with his nefarious schemes. Will you help us?"

Belachek held back an answer, turning to study Jake with those mismatched eyes. "Yes, I'll help you," he finally said. "Get me some paper and a pencil."

-42-

Driven by an unquenchable desire to gain more riches, Senator Brent Van Heflin had made hasty arrangements to go on an overseas trip shortly after his meeting with Truman Hearthwatch. Using the same private charter service he always flew, he boarded the luxurious Lear Jet 35 at 10 a.m. two days later at Dulles International Airport.

At $6,500 an hour, the service was going to be exceptionally expensive. Time spent in the air for round trip passage plus the standby time while the plane sat on the tarmac awaiting his return could easily exceed $150,000 in his estimation. Nevertheless, it was not going to cost him one dime of his own money, and this brought a smile to his jowl-draped face. The trip would be fully paid for at taxpayers' expense, falling under the guise of a fact-finding mission.

As Chairman of the Senate's Science and Technology Committee, Van Heflin had a legitimate claim to undertaking the mission. He had arranged for an impromptu meeting with the Haitian Minister of Agriculture to discuss why stockpiles of crop seeds generously donated by the Plagiarius Corporation were being destroyed by peasant farmers. But he already knew the why? The meeting was scheduled to take place in Port-au-Prince the following day, and the thought of having to land in the slum-ridden and earthquake ravaged city repulsed him. But today he would take care of a more pressing matter in the coastal town of Tiburon. And while he knew this trip would not garner much scrutiny from the press, it was actually a cover to carry out business of a personal nature.

Tiburon. The senator mulled the word, rolling it silently off his tongue. Pronounced *Tee-byoo-ron,* it meant 'shark' in Spanish. He thought it a befitting name for the place, particularly since it epitomized the powerful landowner who resided on its outskirts. Located near the western tip of the country's southern peninsula, the town was one of the oldest, and for that matter, one of the least despoiled in Haiti.

Looking out the window adjacent to his seat, Van Heflin viewed the panorama below him as the Lear began its descent. With the exception of partial defoliation and erosion marring rugged terrain farther inland, the landscape in this region exhibited a subtle, almost idyllic beauty. Along the coast, thin strips of white sandy beaches edged by thick clusters of palm trees contrasted sharply with the steeply rising hills of greenery abutting them. The beauty turned spectacular as the plane dropped over the *Bay of Anse-Milieu* at the entrance to the town and aligned with the private runway on a neatly laid out and sprawling plot of land paralleling the shore.

Though he had seen the place once before, he could not suppress the ardor gripping him as he gawked in awe for the second time around. Zipping by beneath him were lush, well-tended gardens of varying color that gave way to an imposing castle-like fortress of turreted walls. The structure was massive. Originally built by the Spaniards, with adjuncts and auxiliary features added later on by the French, the fortification sat majestically overlooking the deep-water bay. Surrounding it was a 50-foot-wide moat of slate gray water, giving the structure a distinctive medieval aura.

During his prior visit, its landlord had made it a point to tell him what he had stocked the moat with, but Van Heflin had seen the fins cleaving its surface and the sizeable bodies carrying those fins, making him shudder involuntarily. He had learned that they were tiger sharks, and he had counted at least two dozen of them patrolling the encircling canal, with not one of them less than twelve feet in length in his estimation. He had also learned that the moat was constantly recharged with fresh seawater pulled up from the bay by a buried intake pipeline and pumping system that kept the marine carnivores healthy. A filter system in combination with another buried pipeline discharged oxygen depleted water back into the sea. As the Lear swept past, he saw that the drawbridge spanning the moat was in the down position, with the portcullis behind it fully exposed and open.

Where the fortress faced the sea, the land dropped steeply from the edge of the moat, falling to a shoreline littered with outcroppings of gray rock. From there a long pier, perhaps 300 feet in length, extended out into the bay. A paved road connected the pier to the fortification, winding its way up the slope through a series of meandering turns.

Another sight caught his eyes, one he truly coveted. Sitting at anchor amid the bay's indigo and teal blue waters just offshore of the stronghold was an enormous luxury yacht nearly the size of a cruise ship. The place was indeed a paradise. Such amenities he'd like for himself once he left politics, but right now he dared not flaunt such wealth for fear of what it could do to his senatorial image.

In moments the jet settled down on the runway, and the senator unbuckled himself as it taxied to a stop. Hefting his considerable bulk from the leather seat, he arose and smiled lasciviously at the attractive stewardess as she unlatched the cabin door and lowered the steps for him to exit. On the in-bound flight she had performed to his satisfaction in the small but plush sleeping quarters situated at the rear of the plane, and he discovered he was already looking forward to another bout with her on the return trip.

Sweat beaded quickly on his brow as he exposed himself to the hot, muggy climate, so shockingly different from the air-conditioned confines of the aircraft. Eager to escape the stifling heat, anger abruptly welled up in him at seeing no one there to meet him. He hated to sweat. Impatiently, he checked his watch. Fuming in silence, he wondered why there was no one here to pick him up. His pilot had radioed ahead, giving an accurate ETA. As he waited for a vehicle to arrive, perspiration quickly dampened his clothing, and he wondered if he should go back inside the Lear until someone showed.

The senator stared in the direction of an enormous hangar set at the end of the tarmac farthest away from the fortress. Several men were engaged in unloading a truck, and a forklift could be seen moving toward the hanger. It rumbled softly, carrying a pallet full of crates as it disappeared beyond the hanger doors. Idly he watched as it reappeared and headed back toward the truck to pick up another pallet.

A car suddenly appeared at the opposite end of the runway, coming from the direction of the fortress. It was a late model SUV, all white to reflect the heat, and as soon as it pulled alongside him, Van Heflin impatiently opened the front passenger door and sat down heavily on the cool seat, now fully bathed in his own sweat.

"What took you so long?" the senator grumbled.

The swarthy individual in the driver's seat appeared uncomfortable. "Why have you come a week early?" he asked nervously, glancing in the rear view mirror to look back at the fortress. "Cardoza was not expecting you so soon. He is in a terrible mood."

The senator studied him appraisingly. The driver was one of Cardoza's lackeys, the same individual who had picked him up the last time he had paid a visit to this place, a person of little significance within the drug king's organization, but a useful one nevertheless. Van Heflin had felt it prudent to recruit him as a paid informant during his prior trip. He made it a policy to keep tabs on all his associates, and the practice sometimes yielded invaluable information.

"What's bothering him?" the senator demanded.

DOLPHIN RIDERS

The driver's worrisome expression suddenly dissolved, replaced by a sly, toothy grin with one of his incisors missing. "My boy keeps asking me for a pony, but unfortunately I cannot afford to buy him one," he said.

Van Heflin held back his annoyance and reached into a pocket. "Rico, did anyone ever tell you that avarice is sinful?" Taking three crisp $100 bills from his wallet, he handed them to the driver. It felt strange for him to do this, for he was usually the one on the receiving end of deals involving graft.

Rico eyed the wallet wolfishly, seeing it was stuffed with bills. "Ponies are expensive here in Haiti," he declared gruffly.

Reluctantly, the senator withdrew two additional hundred dollar denominations from the billfold, handing them over.

"And, of course, a saddle will be needed if my boy is to ride the pony."

The senator gritted his teeth, pulling out another $300 and shoving it roughly into Rico's extended hand.

Seemingly satisfied, Rico pocketed the money quickly, continuing to let the car sit at idle. "One of Cardoza's ships has been hijacked," he finally offered.

"Tell me something I don't already know," Van Heflin growled petulantly. "The ship was taken back yesterday."

Rico nodded. "Yes, but the engines are not working and Cardoza has sent another of his ships to tow it back to port."

This was something Van Heflin hadn't known. Mulling this tidbit of information, he asked another question. "What else can you tell me?"

"The doctor and Allotey are here," Rico said, checking his rear view mirror again.

The senator's eyebrows rose up in surprise. He already knew about the doctor, but Allotey was the last person he expected to find meeting Cardoza. "Allotey you say?! Why's he here?"

"I don't know."

"When did the doctor arrive?"

"Yesterday."

"I hear the blight is not working," Van Heflin stated. "Is this true?"

Rico nodded again. "So far, there have been no crop failures, and this only adds to Cardoza's bad mood."

Van Heflin digested this, finding it strange. By all rights, non-hybrid food plants should have no resistance to the exceptionally virulent blight that had been purposely unleashed on Haitian food crops, particularly those indigenous to the country's soil and climate. The blight had been released four months earlier and should have sabotaged crops by now. Something was going on here that didn't make sense.

"Anything else?" Van Heflin asked.

"I must warn you to be very careful around Cardoza today. He is like an enraged beast. A raid he had planned did not go well."

"Where was this raid and what was its objective?"

"He hired Russian mercenaries to take control of some land near Malique."

"Malique? Where is that?"

"It is a small fishing village located between Gonaives and Saint-Marc up north."

Something vague bobbed up in Van Heflin's memory. *What was it?* He wrapped his mind around the thread of it, dredging it from the subconscious depths so that its full context came to the surface. All at once, the conversation he had had with Hearthwatch came flooding back, and with sudden clarity, he remembered. Emmanuel Baptiste, the CEO of Tursiops Worldwide, was from Malique.

"What was so important that he had to send mercenaries?" he asked.

"I hear talk that something very valuable lays hidden there. But it is well guarded. Each time he has tried to take it ended in failure."

The senator kept his face composed, though it was tough suppressing the grin wanting to light his features. Now he was getting somewhere. "You didn't by any chance hear mention of gold in that place, did you?"

Rico's eyes widened with alarm. "Cardoza would feed me to his tiger if he knew I told you."

"So these rumors of gold are not just hearsay," Van Heflin proclaimed smugly.

The driver swiveled his head around to look back at the fortress. "We better go now or Cardoza will become suspicious why we're taking so long." Having said that, he put the SUV in gear and turned it in the direction of Cardoza's lair.

-43-

Senator Brent Van Heflin was not intimidated by Rafael Cardoza's ire, though it pulsed from him in intermittent waves. One moment he'd speak in a level, eloquent voice, then openly display his displeasure at something said in a show of uncontained fury. None of his henchmen dared to look at him when this occurred, knowing full well what could happen, and the three hooligans standing with their backs to one wall kept their eyes averted. In spite of Rico's warning, the senator knew Cardoza would not direct his rage at him, for both he and the notorious drug baron were on the same team, indispensable members of a cabal controlled by the most powerful man on the planet, a man even more ruthless and unforgiving than Cardoza, that being Malcolm Maximus.

Sitting at a sprawling conference table, Van Heflin took pause to study one of the men situated across from him. It was evident Malikai Allotey was clearly cowed by Cardoza's outbursts.

"You and your Chilean cohorts are clumsy and useless," Cardoza accused, glaring at the Libyan with contemptuous, smoldering eyes. "Twice you failed us."

Allotey squirmed. He looked around at the others in a bid for support. His normally prim, hubristic air was completely absent. "Unanticipated circumstances arose that were beyond our control," he protested, almost wailing out the words. "You have your ship back."

The Special Envoy to the UN seemed to wither further under Cardoza's unwavering baleful stare, and he dropped his eyes to the table, refraining from adding more.

Cardoza kept scalding eyes fastened on him for a sustained moment before turning to the senator. "I assume your earlier than expected arrival concerns the blight."

Van Heflin gave a nod, sitting regally with self-importance and feeling immune to Cardoza's belligerence. "Why has this supposedly highly toxic Morior strain failed to work accordingly?"

"If I knew the answer, you would be the first to know."

"But you're in charge of Plagiarius' Caribbean branch," the senator stated bluntly. "Isn't it your business to know?"

Cardoza's eyes immediately flared, and Van Heflin wondered if he had overstepped his bounds. A pulsing silence filled the room, and he became aware of the shocked, open-mouthed stares of the other occupants impinging on him. On his way to the conference table, he had been led down a seemingly endless series of stone steps that eventually terminated in a musty, dimly lit corridor with rows of cast iron doors each side of it. He had surmised it was an ancient dungeon, though he couldn't be sure if any of the cells went unused, for only darkness lay beyond the barred rectangular grills set in the doors. A mildly foul odor permeated the air as he passed, making him crinkle his nose.

The dungeon connected with another chamber, and within its gloomy confines he recognized an assortment of implements he had only seen in history books and museums, their intended functions all too obvious. A rack with rollers, chains and leather straps sat ominously to one side along with other devices, and hanging on the dank walls were various instruments, their very appearance somehow conveying terror. It was a medieval torture chamber, and it adjoined the anteroom room where he now sat.

As Van Heflin pondered these things, he fully understood why Cardoza had selected this room for the meeting instead of the one used during his first visit to this place. It had been purposely used to induce fear in those in attendance. The first meeting had taken place several levels higher within the fortress, making guests feel at ease with the magnificent panoramic views beyond the glass windows.

But down here there were no windows, not the kind that offered vistas that would put a visitor at ease, though there was a glass partition that covered an entire wall directly across from where the senator sat. A chill ran up his spine as a huge shadow drifted slowly past within the murky water on the opposite side of the glass.

Van Heflin's abrupt discomfort did not escape Cardoza's notice, and the drug lord suddenly grinned smugly. "I see my creatures fascinate you," he said, turning to watch as another shadow coasted past, this one even larger than the one that had preceded it.

The senator judiciously diverted the conversation to cool Cardoza's impending wrath. Even that smug smile could not hide the violent flames that burned deeply in his eyes, flames Van Heflin had carelessly ignited by the insult, and he knew the man could lay into him at any moment. "I assume they're all tigers?" he found himself saying.

"Not all," Cardoza grunted. "I've added one more since your last visit."

Van Heflin kept his gaze on the glass, avoiding Cardoza's eyes. "And what would that be?"

Just as he uttered the question, the glass went darker, dwarfed by something on the other side that spanned the partition end to end. As it passed, it blocked out the meager sunlight filtering down through the murky water.

"You just saw her, a female great white two inches shy of twenty-three feet. With great whites, the females tend to grow bigger than the males. This one weighs more than three tons. I call her Scylla. Are you familiar with that name?"

"No."

"The name originates from Greek mythology. Scylla was a beautiful woman turned into a monster with three rows of razor-sharp teeth."

"Where did you get it?"

"Same place as all the others. Sharks often end up in the nets of my fishing vessels, and my crews are instructed to keep the biggest ones alive and deliver them here. They know not to bring me anything smaller than a twelve footer."

"But you seem to prefer tigers. Why is that?"

"Their teeth are the nastiest, much more destructive than a white's.

Even a raking slash with them can tear a man open."

As Cardoza said this, something bumped heavily against the partition, startling the senator. An ebony black orb the size of a coffee cup pressed up against the glass, seemingly drawn to the light within the room. The orb appeared to fixate briefly on Van Heflin before drawing back, and the massive body to which it was attached turned to face the glass head on. A gaping mouth edged with serrated triangular teeth tested its surface."

"I believe Scylla regards you as a potential meal, senator," Cardoza declared, his eyes suddenly cold and foreboding as he elicited an ominous grin.

Van Heflin pivoted in his chair, attempting to mask the shudder that swept through him. He was especially fearful of sharks and generally avoided swimming in the ocean. The thought of predatory sharks lurking in the moat made him feel uneasy, but that white monster absolutely terrified him. Only the glass partition was keeping it from entering the room, and he wondered if it was actually capable of withstanding a charge from the 3-ton beast.

Cardoza was about to add something else, enjoying the trepidation he had instilled in the senator, but the door to the room suddenly flew open and another of his lackeys scurried in.

"What is it?" Cardoza yelled, scowling fiercely at being denied his moment to torment.

The man turned ashen, nervously handing him a phone. "You have a call, sir."

Cardoza snatched it from his hand and brought it to his ear. The violence etched on his countenance slowly receded as he listened intently, and after a minute he placed the phone back in the lackey's hands. Eager to get away, the lackey quickly left the room.

Seemingly caught up in deep thought, Cardoza brought only peevish eyes to bear back on the senator, the previous rage held within them moments earlier now reduced to a simmer.

"Our agenda has been stepped up," Cardoza said. "The arms shipment is due to arrive here tomorrow."

"When did this happen and why wasn't I informed?" Van Heflin asked, taken back by this sudden change in plans.

"Our Supreme Leader made the decision yesterday." Cardoza studied the senator critically. "Perhaps you would like to discuss it with him face to face?"

Van Heflin's jaw parted in surprise, but before he could voice a question of his own, the door to the chamber opened again, and two men walked in. The first man gave the impression of a bulldozer paving the way for the man behind him. An over-sized navy blue blazer could not hide his heavily muscled shoulders that spanned more than half the width of the 6-foot-wide doorway, and he was forced to duck his head to keep from hitting it on the upper frame. Sporting a close-cropped crew cut of blond hair, he surveyed the room as if issuing a silent challenge to everyone within it. But there was no mistaking that the second man was the leader.

The senator recognized Malcolm Maximus immediately, who he knew never went anywhere without Swenson, his hulking Nordic bodyguard. Maximus stood a head shorter than his counterpart and carried an austere, aristocratic bearing, impeccably dressed in a gray pinstripe suit that was precisely tailored to his medium-size body. His gaze was sharp and stern as he took in those seated. Though he was well into his sixties, he lit the room with an ice cold aura of supreme authority.

Without hesitation, Maximus moved to the customary place of leadership at the head of the table and seated himself, with Swenson taking up an imposing position behind his chair. It was then that Van Heflin understood why Cardoza had not occupied that chair himself.

Maximus made a show of darting his eyes to each of the four faces at the table before singling out Van Heflin. "I'm rather surprised to see you here, senator," he said in that same halting, raspy voice Van Heflin had heard so many times before, mostly over the phone in coded Latin. "I would think you would have more pressing duties stateside."

Van Heflin cleared his throat, suddenly besieged with nervousness. "Things are moving ahead as necessary."

"You think so?" Maximus said. His tone was derogatory, his eyes flaming with scorn. "Then why is it little headway has so far taken place with these annoying colonists?"

"Certainly you've already heard," Van Heflin replied in a flustered voice, desperately trying to produce a placating smile. "My government is abiding by the UN's decision to concede Navassa Island over to Haiti. Once the final paperwork of concession is signed by our President, any lease agreements it has with Tursiops will become null and void. These colonists will have no choice but to vacate the island."

"What if they insist on staying?" Maximus growled. "Have you forgotten that most of these colonists are Haitian? It is almost a certainty the current Haitian government will allow them to remain and continue fostering their operation. As it is, Tursiops has been providing a significant amount of its resources to help in rebuilding Haiti, and those firmly entrenched in the power structure here are showing far more friendliness toward them than we had expected."

"But a military strike force is being mobilized by the UN to evict and incarcerate them," Van Heflin was quick to point out. "Using the media to our advantage, we've effectively stigmatized them into looking like rogue eco-pirates."

"It won't be enough," Maximus snapped. "At most, UN intervention may prove to be a temporary setback to their operations. Unless there is a change in this country's governing administration, the odds of gaining complete control of their enterprise will be uncertain. Over the past year, the CEO of Tursiops, a Haitian national by the name of Emmanuel Baptiste, has made numerous overtures to the Haitian Ministry of Agriculture, providing large shipments of natural fertilizer to peasant farmers free of charge. The fertilizer is mined on Navassa Island and seems to have doubled, if not tripled, crop yields, particularly the maize they grow here."

"Then maybe we should end this problem by having the UN task force destroy Aquaria altogether," the senator exclaimed impulsively. As soon as he said it, he realized it was a foolish option. If any gold was kept in the floating city, it might very well end up in the briny depths.

"Your judgement disappoints me, senator!" Maximus scolded heatedly. "I don't want it destroyed. I want that city. I want that island. I want to take complete control of their entire project, lock, stock and barrel, including those strange white beasts helping to build it. Already I've learned this Baptiste character is currently in negotiations with the Haitian government to construct a massive automobile manufacturing facility that will produce eco-friendly cars at incredibly low cost to be shipped all over the world. Apparently these colonists have designed cars to run strictly on hydrogen, most of which will be supplied by Tursiops. On top of that, these people are seeking approval from the Haitian Ministry to build several power-generating facilities that will also run exclusively on the hydrogen they produce, and Baptiste has offered to supply it free of charge. On a global scale, they're also providing this same expertise to other nations that rely on oil and coal to power their electric plants, converting them to run on hydrogen. Should these things become fully implemented, the standard of living in Haiti is going to rise exponentially with all the jobs that will become available."

Van Heflin grew increasingly edgy at the severity of the lecture being laid upon him, and he risked a fleeting glance at Swenson's towering form standing behind Maximus. The Nordic giant's eyes bore into him like swords.

"We can't let that happen," Maximus went on, his anger suddenly cooling. "That is why we will have no choice but to accelerate our agenda." Turning, he looked over at Cardoza. "Rafael, give these men a brief summary of the plan," he commanded.

Cardoza spoke gravely. "Once the arms are fully distributed to our constituents in the key cities, our paid agitators will incite the population into the widespread rebellion needed for a government takeover."

Maximus narrowed his eyes, setting them on Van Heflin again. "Let me be clear about this, senator, we'll be relying on your congressional influence to keep your government from interfering in this manufactured coup."

"Certainly you'll have my full cooperation. But without crop failures and the ensuing food shortages to incentivize the masses, how are your agitators going to incite the peasants into armed revolt? I hear sixty percent of the population derives their income through employment with the farming co-opts, and so far the blight has failed to work."

Maximus set his gaze on the only member of the group who had so far not spoken. Dr. Herbert Ermstine was completely bald, short, obese and bespectacled. With his dark skin, he could have easily been mistaken for a Haitian, though he was actually born in Nigeria. He had arrived the previous day to attend this meeting, flown in on Plagiarius' private jet. Nearing 70 years of age, he had once served as the Haitian Minister of Foreign Affairs under "Baby Doc" Duvalier. Currently, he was the leading scientist at Chemtectics International, a subsidiary of Plagiarius, performing most of his work in Africa. He was the man Maximus had groomed to head Haiti's government once the coup took place.

"Do you have any theories why the blight failed, doctor?"

Ermstine appeared tired, still getting over the jet lag that continued to plague him. "Yes. It is probable that something in the fertilizer coming from Tursiops makes the crops resistant. But only through extensive testing will we be able to determine exactly what that something is."

"How long would this testing take?" Maximus demanded.

"It could take months."

Maximus nodded, seemingly unconcerned with the doctor's assessment. "This is another reason why the Aquaria project must be stopped as quickly as possible, senator. We have to end those shipments of fertilizer once and for all, otherwise they might start sending it to other parts of the globe, and that would be a major impediment to our plans."

Maximus leaned back in his padded chair and looked at Cardoza. "Rafael, tell the senator how we plan to trigger a revolt."

A demonic grin came to Cardoza's face. "We are going to contaminate farmland with a specially formulated herbicide capable of killing all native food plants."

"Your Morior chemical was supposed to do that," Van Heflin said, knowing that the meaning of the moniker was a Latin word for *'withering away.'* "What makes you think this new compound will prove any better?"

Cardoza continued to smile. "It is ten times more lethal than the

Morior. The Morior's primary component consisted of metalaxyl, a potent fungicide that should have been deadly to food crops grown here when delivered in the high concentrations we used. But this new compound, called *Sterilis*, is different, one you might categorize as a highly toxic defoliant."

"You mean like the Agent Orange defoliant used in Vietnam?" Van Heflin asked.

"It carries some of those dioxin properties, yes, but the chemical makeup has been altered to make it even more destructive than that used in Vietnam. Once deployed, it will only take two days for food crops to die, bringing on the required widespread unemployment and social unrest. Our agitators will worsen the problem further by stirring public emotions into a frenzy."

Van Heflin appeared skeptical. "And how do you propose to disperse it?"

"The same way we dispersed the Morior compound. We will use the same fleet of unmanned drones retrofitted with aerosol sprayers. Just as before, they will be specially programmed to spray targeted tracts of farmland and fly only under the cover of darkness."

Van Heflin thought about the defoliant name. Cardoza had called it *Sterilis*. In Latin it stood for barren or useless, implying it would turn crop fields barren and render them useless, at least for a time. He realized it was a most adequate description.

"But what are the long term effects of this new compound?" he interjected again.

Cardoza shrugged indifferently as if such a consideration were of no significance. "There will be a sustained period where nothing will be able to grow once it gets into the soil, not even our hybrid seeds."

"Do you know how long?" Van Heflin pressed. He needed to know, aware of all the headaches that could come his way in having to deal with the problem later on. Strapped with the task of appropriating funds for the Haiti Watershed Initiative for Natural Environmental Resources, he would be forced to give a show of looking for a solution to a problem that couldn't be fixed.

"Have you thought about the consequences of doing this? You may inadvertently invoke a permanent state of political upheaval in a nation already beleaguered with economic and social instability."

Van Heflin looked to Dr. Ermstine to see how he was reacting to this, but he could see from his expression that he was unperturbed. "Even if we do gain control of the government, it may prove to be short-lived," he found it necessary to add.

"The defoliant will eventually biodegrade," Ermstine offered,

yawning somnolently as soon as he said it. "But it will take at least three years before even our hybrid seeds will be able to take root in the soil."
"This you know for sure?" Van Heflin asked.
"Yes."
"Then without massive international aid, the population may very well be on the doorstep of starvation by then," Van Heflin pointed out. "Are you willing to deal with all the turmoil and strife that will ensue?"

Ermstine let out a slight titter, and the senator became aware of a sardonic smirk on Cardoza's face as well. "It's all part of the agenda," Ermstine stated smugly. "The Haitian population has gotten much too big, and many of them are nothing more than useless eaters. A prolonged famine will be needed to reduce their numbers. The defoliant is also designed to kill off substantial portions of the masses once it gets into the water supply since it is quite deadly to animal life as well as plants. But eventually the hybrid seeds so painstakingly developed by Plagiarius will grow in the toxic soil while crop varieties that have suitably adapted to local conditions over many generations will not, and by then we will have accomplished our goals."

Van Heflin frowned. "Are these the same seeds the farmers have been burning?"

"Yes," Ermstine said, yawning expansively this time, revealing a set of unusually large, ivory white teeth. "Once the defoliant biodegrades below a critical level, these seeds will be able to withstand the toxicity that remains. As a matter of fact, at lower concentrations the defoliant was developed specifically to react in sympathy with the chemical coating the seeds."

"Are you referring to the Omicron Seven compound?"
"Yes."

Van Heflin looked to Cardoza again. "These farmers are obviously onto the threat these seeds pose. Do we know how they learned of this?"

The smile dominating the drug lord's face abruptly died. "My sources believe someone representing Tursiops alerted them." The smile reasserted itself. "But once we destroy their crops, we will spread a rumor that it was caused by the fertilizer provided by the colonists."

Van Heflin produced a smile of his own, nodding in admiration at the utter simplicity of the ploy. It was yet another way to discredit and vilify the Tursiops organization. And using media participation to expand the fabrication, they would twist the knife even deeper into the scandalous wound they had already inflicted against the colony. The entire world would be screaming for Aquaria heads.

The senator knew what Omicron-7 actually contained. Aside from his role as Chairman of the Senate Science and Technology Committee, it was his business to know that it was a concoction of high levels of *mancozeb, thiram and maxim XL*, not to mention a few other nefarious compounds. It was a dangerous mixture of fungicides and herbicides so toxic that it exceeded acceptable levels put out by the EPA, and according to international law, should have been illegal to use.

But Plagiarius had seen opportunity following the earthquake that had hammered Port-au-Prince and its outlying regions in 2010. The earthquake had been catastrophic, destroying nearly 100,000 homes and injuring 30,000 people. It had claimed 1,000 lives, leaving most of the city in rubble and causing an estimated $8 billion in damages. With farmers having insufficient quantities of seeds for planting, Plagiarius had stepped in to provide assistance, benevolently donating over 500 tons of seeds to Haitian farmers at its own expense. But Plagiarius had profited anyway. Money for the seeds had actually been appropriated by Congress through a last minute earmark cleverly and discretely slipped into a bill by Van Heflin, allowing Plagiarius to be paid for its show of generosity nevertheless. The donated seeds, however, were hybrid varieties of maize and various types of vegetables, genetically modified to withstand the toxicity of the chemicals coating them. From all outward signs, the project's aim was to triple food production for the poverty-stricken Haitian people. Rigged by Van Heflin to appear like a humanitarian gesture by a concerned U.S. Congress, the project was actually a pretext to carry out something sinister. It was a test run to determine the destructive effects of the corporation's Morior blight on native crops before releasing it to other parts of the globe. In addition, it was to more fully assess the special immunity of the hybrid plants against the blight, which would essentially destroy all planetary food crops lacking the genetic makeup of the hybrids. Once the world was forced to rely on Plagiarius as a sole source provider of these seeds, the company stood to make untold mega-fortunes by jacking up the price of this essential commodity to stratospheric levels. And by virtue of that, the wealth of every man at the table would increase multiple times more, with Maximus and Cardoza making off with the largest shares by far.

Through extensive lobbying in Washington, Plagiarius held huge prestige as a government contractor. With no less than 35 former Federal employees on its payroll, most of them having previously served as congressional members and high ranking bureaucrats, it was relatively easy for the biotech giant to get what it wanted. This was further ensured by virtue of a Supreme Court judge currently sitting on the bench who had once represented Plagiarius as a defense lawyer over various lawsuits involving pollution. And recent passage of the latest Agricultural Appropriations Bill by congress had a provision that effectively stripped

Federal courts of the authority to halt the planting of genetically modified seeds even if they posed a health risk. The provision was a rider written by Plagiarius lawyers and covertly inserted in the bill by none other than Van Heflin at the last minute, by-passing the usual review by Agriculture and Judiciary Committees. In essence, it made Plagiarius immune to law suits involving health issues.

In spite of the way Plagiarius would promote the use of its patented seed products, and in spite of their ability to withstand the blight, the hybrids had several shortcomings with which the senator was intimately familiar. They needed more water to grow, and fresh water was scarce in Haiti. They also required more fertilizer. And while they would provide twice the normal yield of most non-hybrids following their planting, the yields would plummet dismally after the first generation, since seeds from the resulting crops had little potency. This was a plus for Plagiarius because it would cause farmers to rely strictly on the company for a never ending supply of seeds.

Use of the seeds even without the blight presented a dangerous problem. When planted near or alongside indigenous food crops with open-pollination, the resulting plants would invariably hybridize, ultimately diluting the gene pool of plants that had adapted to the local environment.

"The wisdom of your scheme is to be congratulated," Van Heflin said, looking at Cardoza with as much admiration as he could muster. "Blaming crop failures on the Tursiops fertilizer is a brilliant stroke of genius."

Pausing momentarily, he could see the praise had the desired effect, for Cardoza seemed to puff up like a peacock. "When do you plan on releasing the defoliant?"

"Tomorrow at midnight," Cardoza said. "We have already stockpiled over six hundred canisters of Sterilis, storing them within the hanger you saw at the end of my runway. The last batch is scheduled to arrive later tonight along with the first of our arms shipment."

Van Heflin nodded, a genuine smile coming to his face. In spite of a few setbacks to their agenda, the staged deceptions and manipulations had so far worked to their advantage with surprising success. They were on the verge of accomplishing great things, and his hunger to enrich himself further suddenly gathered strength to gnaw away at him like a ravenous beast. With the UN now having voted unanimously in favor of ceding Navassa Island back to Haiti, it was imperative he breach the rumor of gold with utmost delicacy, knowing the greed of the men surrounding him surpassed his own.

"Perhaps now's the time to discuss another matter which has come to my attention." The senator stopped speaking to let the statement hang in the air. He sensed all eyes locked on him, waiting for him to continue.

Maximus broke the silence. "Which is?"

"It concerns the financing of Aquaria. To build such an immense facility must have cost billions, yet I am unable to uncover any sources of financing for its construction."

"I've found the same dead end," Maximus concurred.

Van Heflin pressed on, having gone too far now to turn back. "I've heard rumors about how they've been able to obtain the extensive amounts of equipment and materials going into the facility."

"Get to the point!" Maximus grumbled, checking the time on his Emperador Temple wristwatch. Studded with over 1,200 diamonds it was the world's most expensive watch.

The senator espied the timepiece with envy. "I hear they've bartered with gold."

Van Heflin set his gaze on Maximus as he said this, seeing only the impassive stare of a seasoned poker player. In Cardoza, however, he detected something analogous to a fidget, ever so slight.

"Now assuming the rumor is true, where do you suppose these poor, economically depressed Haitians got it? Based on an estimate of the facility's sheer size and scope, a minimum of twelve thousand tons of high grade gold would have been needed to build it."

A cynical smile broke out on Maximus' face. "So this is the reason for your early arrival," he rasped. "You smell gold and you want some of it."

The senator looked around the table. Allotey was practically drooling over the thought of so much gold, his eyes alive with avarice. Ermstine ran his tongue along his thick lips as though actually tasting the precious metal. Cardoza, however, stared back at him with murder in his eyes.

Van Heflin was not to be deterred. He wanted his rightful share. "These people must have it stored someplace," he said. "The question is, where?"

Maximus sat up straighter in his chair, a regal king presiding over his court. "If this gold does exist, I'm sure we'll find out where soon enough," he stated, seemingly eager to end this trivial matter.

"The floating city or the nearby island are the most likely places where it's stored," the senator persisted. "If it's discovered by UN troops once the facility is taken, there's no telling how much of it will disappear."

Van Heflin looked sharply at Allotey as he said this. The Libyan appeared indignant. "It's important we make sure that doesn't happen," he added.

Maximus eyed him curiously. "What do you suggest?"

"I think it would be prudent that at least two of us be there to inspect the facility immediately after it's secured."

Van Heflin knew the only ones among them that would have a valid reason for being at Aquaria following UN intervention were Allotey and himself, for certainly it would appear highly suspect if Ermstine, Cardoza or Maximus showed up. Ermstine had to keep a rather low profile until the coup had actually taken place, and that would be after Tursiops was ousted from the colony. Maximus and Cardoza, on the other hand, had to remain in the shadows. But he, himself, could easily come up with an excuse for being there. As head of the senatorial Science and Technology Committee, he would pull the necessary strings to be on hand to tour the facility once it was in UN hands, feigning an interest in the innovative technology Aquaria used. Of course he'd have to get the antidote Hearthwatch had told him about in order to counter the debilitating effects of the strange art he would surely be exposed to once he ventured into the floating city.

Maximus sneered, then laughed. "You know very well that would be you and Malikai." He riveted the senator with a searing look. "Let me be perfectly clear about what I told you before. You'll be needed stateside to use every ounce of influence you can exert in keeping your government from interfering in this coup. Is that understood?"

Van Heflin nodded staidly, having anticipated such a reaction. "You'll have my full support and cooperation," he replied.

Maximus turned to Allotey. "I will expect a full accounting of whatever your troops find." He let the statement's underlying threat linger a moment longer before going on. "I will expect you to make sure any caches of gold are fully secured until we can come up with a plan to remove it." Suddenly remembering what a glimpse of the holographic art had done to him, a sour expression came to his face. "And make sure all the troops are injected with the drug before entering the city this time."

Allotey shot a nervous glance to Swenson's hulking form hovering behind Maximus. "Of course," he stammered obsequiously, "but how do we deal with the weapon they used against us? The heat was unbearable. All the men felt like they were on fire. Using the drug would have made no difference."

Maximus thought back to what Allotey had conveyed to him following the incident, and he was now quite sure of the weapon used once he had filled in the missing pieces. Through his vast web of informants, he had learned about the breach into the supposedly secure U.S. DOD computer system. Someone had hacked their way into the ADS 2 file months ago and made off with the weapon specs, and that someone had to have been an employee of Tursiops. And while it was obvious they had advanced the technology another step, he would be fully prepared this time around.

"They hit you with non-lethal microwaves," Maximus commented, "but we'll have measures in place to counter them upon your arrival."

Noting the inquisitive look clinging to Allotey's face, Maximus stopped him before he could pose any more questions. "The details of the invasion plan are still being worked out, so there is no point in discussing it further. All will be provided you just prior to the mission."

The senator broke the silence that descended on the room, now taking full advantage of Maximus' unforeseen presence at this meeting. With him here, it would be safe to bring up one last point. "If gold does exist, and I'm almost certain that it does, there may be one other place where it's stored."

Maximus frowned in annoyance. "Where?"

"Somewhere near Malique." Van Heflin risked a darting glance at Cardoza. The drug lord's eyes were like two burning cauldrons, the flames harbored within them now fully stoked and nearing a flashpoint.

"Never heard of it."

"It's a small fishing village near Gonaives up north. The head of Tursiops is from Malique."

"Once the coup is accomplished, we can investigate such a possibility," Maximus conceded.

Van Heflin could no longer hold back his innate greed. He had gone too far now to stop himself from stepping over the threshold. "I assume we will all get a share of whatever's found," he said.

Maximus grinned without warmth. "Your insatiable hunger for riches never ceases to amaze me, Brent. But as you well know, spoils are divided according to rank and privilege within The Order. I shouldn't have to remind you this policy was established by our forbearers long before you were born."

The senator grimaced inwardly. Though he was not privy to all the components that comprised this shadowy hierarchy, he had learned enough over the years that a loosely knit conglomeration of individuals and groups formed the gears of its machinery, including various foundations, private think tanks, union chiefs, political action committees, and other front groups. But then again, as far as he knew, Maximus was the one that held the ultimate rank and privilege, the Supreme Leader who sat at the top of the pyramid. And Maximus had the power to circumvent the rules, dispersing the booty as he saw fit.

"Besides," Maximus went on in a sudden change of voice, "you're going to be quite busy over the next several years, more so than you've ever been, and it will be crucial your career suffers no scandalous setbacks."

The statement puzzled the senator. Maximus was grinning like a fox, his manner noticeably less rigid. "I'm always busy," Van Heflin muttered defensively, "and I've always managed to stay one step ahead of scandals."

"It will be different this time," Maximus persisted emphatically. "Making a run at the Oval Office will put you in a whole new limelight."

A dead silence immediately descended, and Van Heflin could feel every eye in the room scrutinizing him as though he were a newly discovered life form. Truly stunned, he studied Maximus closely to see if this was some kind of joke, but he knew Maximus never joked.

"The Order has decided to back you as a nominee for the U.S. presidency," Maximus clarified, his demeanor abruptly becoming serious again. "You'll have unlimited funds to support your campaign. With your unblemished senatorial record and a mainstream media fully endorsing your run, you should have no trouble getting elected."

Van Heflin remained speechless, too overcome with excitement to say anything for the moment. This was totally unexpected. The presidency was something he had always wanted, but a thing much like a forbidden fruit. Unless the gods granted it, he dared not reach for it. And Maximus was certainly a god. But then again, he was a Bonesman, and having entered the esteemed though semi-clandestine ranks of the Skull and Bones at Yale years earlier, he realized with striking clarity that he had been bred and groomed to be President all along.

But as the senator thought about it, it suddenly dawned on him there would be a problem, and he voiced his concern. "But how can I run? It's already past the deadline to get on the primary ticket, and the presidential election is only months away."

"Let me worry about that," Maximus affirmed with a dark smile. "For what I have planned, there won't be any election in November. By then, martial law will be in effect and the election will be suspended for at least another six months, which will leave us ample time between now and then to get you on the slate and prepare you for the ensuing debates that are sure to focus on preventing another catastrophe that led to imposition of martial law in the first place."

Maximus held back from offering more, letting the statement hang for several more seconds before going on. "We'll strategize your campaign once the coup here in Haiti is accomplished."

Checking his wristwatch, Maximus rose from his chair and placed his knuckles on the table. "Gentlemen," he rasped, "I will expect each of you to carry out your part so that our objectives can be reached. Failure is not an option." Without another word, he turned and strode briskly for the massive cast iron door that sealed off the room and separated it from the torture chamber. The door was as old as the fortress and creaked on rusty hinges as one of Cardoza's men swung it outward to let him pass. Swenson swept the room with an ominous gaze before following.

As soon as the door closed, Cardoza addressed the others, smiling expansively as he spoke. "Too bad our leader could not stay for the entertainment I have planned."

An alarm immediately sounded in Van Heflin's head. There was something sinister in Cardoza's tone. "What kind of entertainment?" he asked suspiciously.

Cardoza ignored the question. "If you gentlemen will follow me," he said, rising and heading unceremoniously for the door.

Begrudgingly, the senator arose, making sure to trail behind the other men in the procession, including Cardoza's hooligans who showed no enthusiasm as they trudged along. Except for Ermstine, everyone appeared glum. As they ambled through the dungeon, he noticed a door to one of the holding cells had been left wide open. He found this odd since it had been closed on his way down here. Slowing his pace, he became aware of the horrible stink hanging in the air. When he had passed this way before, only a mild odor had accosted him, but with the cell's door now fully open, the immediate area reeked. Repulsed but curious, he stopped and peered into the cell's dark interior. Though it was impossible to tell, it appeared to be unoccupied, but he knew someone had been defecating within its confines, and recently at that.

Eager to get away from the stench, he quickened his step to catch up with the others. It was a long walk as they retraced their way along the same dimly lit corridors and stone steps as before. Eventually they left the main keep and came to an outer courtyard within the fortress. It was open to only a sliver of sky, surrounded by massive ramparts, battlements and turreted towers looming overhead, and was the first area visitors encountered after entering the stronghold through the gatehouse.

Once again, Van Heflin found himself marveling over the layout of the fortification, so seemingly impregnable to attack. Recessed into an inner wall of the main keep was a long cage the size of a ship's cargo container, and within the cage was Cardoza's pet Bengal tiger. The cage was situated on the keep's south side, well back from the gatehouse which lay along the western quarter of the fortress.

At seeing the procession of men, the huge beast rose to its feet and began pacing back and forth, setting fierce yellow eyes on the procession. Through information provided by Rico during his previous visit, the senator knew why the drug lord kept the tiger, and once again he noted the barred gate within the cage that separated the pen into two halves. It was then that he wondered if the entertainment Cardoza had spoken of involved the carnivore. But Cardoza ignored his pet, continuing on and rounding a corner, eventually leading everyone to the gatehouse that gave way to the portcullis overlooking the moat. Even before Van Heflin reached the drawbridge, he heard the pleading wail of a man in great distress.

Van Heflin was startled to see Rico dangling by the wrists. He was attached to a rope that wound through a pulley situated at the end of a thick wooden pole. The pole was slowly being extended horizontally from an opening in the fortress wall 30 feet from the side of the bridge. Rico was completely naked, and the senator saw that his thighs had been slashed, smeared red with copious amounts of blood dribbling down to his ankles and dropping to the gray water filling the moat. Already he could see fins racing back and forth directly below.

Cardoza turned to face his entourage, his eyes singling out Van Heflin. "This man betrayed me, and I will not tolerate betrayal."

Van Heflin watched as the tip of the pole was advanced to the middle of the canal, unaware that his legs were quaking. Rico struggled violently, his eyes opened wide and following the mass of fins skittering wildly along the surface beneath him.

The head of a man poked from the opening in the wall from which the pole extended, looking to Cardoza.

"Lower him slowly," Cardoza shouted. "I do not want my guests to be disappointed." He turned and motioned to someone beyond the group of onlookers. "Bring the prisoner to the edge of the bridge," he commanded.

Van Heflin swung around to observe a man being escorted onto the drawbridge by two of Cardoza's ruffians, one on each side. The senator studied him briefly, guessing he was in his early sixties, though it was hard to tell because of the grime smudging his face. He was wearing tattered clothing, soiled as though he had been forced to lie in filth. This was further confirmed by the offensive odor wafting off him. He appeared forlorn and pathetic as he was led to the middle of the bridge and forced to stand overlooking the water. Not really caring why the man had been led here, Van Heflin brought his eyes back to the main event.

Rico let out a bloodcurdling cry that caused hackles to rise along the senator's neck. Inch by inch, he was lowered, his legs kicking wildly, the water's surface now churned fiercely from the horde of predators massed together and competing savagely for a share of him.

"I have been loyal to you," Rico screamed, blood from his wounded thighs flowing more acutely from his intense exertions. The water was now turned red with it. "Please, Rafael, do not do this," he begged.

Cardoza smiled sadistically. "I have been monitoring you, Rico. You have no compunctions about revealing my affairs to anyone willing to pay even a meager sum to obtain that information." As he said this, he turned to stare at the senator.

Van Heflin looked away, unwilling to meet the drug lord's eyes, suddenly unsure if his own life was in jeopardy. *No, that was not possible,* he told himself. *Maximus needs me. Maximus would have Cardoza's head if anything happened to so vital a member of The Order.* For one indecisive moment, he considered walking away from the horrifying scene, but to his own surprise he could not bring himself to look away, overcome with fascination. He discovered he was awakening to a side of himself he never knew existed.

Cardoza studied the senator in annoyance. This was not quite the reaction he should be seeing. Van Heflin appeared to be enjoying himself, thrilled by the prospect of grisly death. Nevertheless, he hoped the sight would be burned into Van Heflin's memory as a harsh reminder never to meddle in his affairs again. The bug he had planted in the SUV had served its purpose, and Cardoza had heard every word of the conversation between Rico and the senator.

Cardoza turned back to take in Rico's torment. Using the tiger to appease his anger no longer had the same luster it once had, but he suddenly found himself enthralled by this new form of revenge. No one outside his immediate clan of henchmen was supposed to have knowledge of the gold, not even Maximus. He had taken great pains to keep it a secret, even after the raid on the cove had ended in failure. Eager to stay abreast of the mission, he had purposely diverted one of his tuna trawlers, the *San Pedro*, from its duties and had stationed it just off the coast in close proximity to the cove he so desperately wanted, staying in close contact with the ship's captain using an encrypted satellite phone. The ship's crew had stood by an inordinate amount of time awaiting the return of Zinova's choppers, but when no Hinds showed up, the trawler had steamed down the coast where it had chanced upon what was left of the raiding party. Only six men had remained, one of them so badly wounded that he was not expected to live, and their leader, the one with the mismatched eyes, had not been one of them. Upon Cardoza's orders, the *San Pedro* had dispatched a boat ashore to retrieve the survivors. No sooner had the band of pitiful marauders set foot aboard the vessel, a bright object slipped from the clothing of one of them and fell, landing heavily on the foot of a crewman and making him roar with pain. Too late to prevent other crewmen from locking eyes on the cause of the ruckus, the careless mercenary had snatched it up quickly and stowed it with his other gear. It was soon discovered that several of these survivors also had gold bars in their possession, and at hearing this Cardoza had consulted with the ship's captain to devise treachery that entailed killing them. The secrets the cove held belonged to him and no one else, and he was not going to let knowledge of its treasures fall into other hands. But these were dangerous men and catching them off guard would not be easy. They needed to be lulled into a state of complacency before the *San Pedro's* crew could dispatch them. So while the mercenaries were feasting in the ship's galley, the crew had made its move. Unfortunately, he had lost two of his men in the short firefight that had preceded the execution, but at least he had possession of the bars, positive proof that gold actually existed within the cove.

The *San Pedro* had also brought back another prize. Immediately upon casting the raiding party's bloodied remains into the sea, an enormous shark had risen up from the depths to feast upon the carcasses. Cardoza had been told it was another great white even larger than Scylla. At hearing this, he had ordered the crew to drop a net and capture it. The shark was to be another addition to the moat's growing horde of ferocious denizens, making him wonder how receptive Scylla would be to the new occupant once the *San Pedro* arrived back.

Cardoza dropped these thoughts and focused on the scene before him, wanting to savor every aspect of it. Ever so slowly, Rico's feet neared the water, now thrashed into a frothing maelstrom of pandemonium as sharks fought for position directly under him. Rico screamed again, his pleadings exploding from his lips in an incoherent stream of gibberish as he stared down in wide-eyed terror.

Equally immersed in the event, Van Heflin watched with glazed eyes. The sound of something intruded its way into his awareness, and he turned his head to espy Ermstine laughing hysterically. The laughter was infectious, and he quickly joined in, unable to hold back the uncontrollable giddiness that had descended on him.

By now, Rico was bringing his knees to his chest in a vain effort to keep his feet beyond the reach of snapping jaws, every few seconds kicking down furiously to fend off a rising snout. But his actions for survival were futile, and inevitably his lower limbs could no longer be kept from the frenzy. Sharks pressed in bumping and jostling one another, the congestion of massed bodies so tight that it was impossible for any of them to get a clean open-mouthed strike on the dangling prey. Nevertheless, their teeth were slashing and raking those limbs, darkening the water a deep crimson that expanded outward.

Van Heflin continued to stare in rapt fixation, utterly captivated by the scene. He realized Cardoza had not exaggerated. The teeth of a tiger shark were like scalpels, able to flay and eviscerate with little effort. Suspended like a side of beef, Rico wailed in agony as flesh was stripped from his legs as though by a swarm of monstrously sized piranha.

And then something unexpected happened. The shark pack suddenly bolted, moving away quickly under the drawbridge upon which the senator stood. Lifting his gaze, Van Heflin saw the reason for the mass exodus. A fin considerably larger than all the rest cleaved the water, charging down the canal from the opposite direction. He perceived it was Scylla, the leviathan great white that had scrutinized him as a meal. She had sensed the commotion and was coming to claim her share. It was apparent she was the queen of this little kingdom, and sensing her approach her subjects had fled to get out of the way of that enormous maw.

By this time, Rico was waist deep in the moat, wallowing in his own blood and looking dazed, though he was still very much alive. Scylla surged past him before swinging around to make another pass, and Rico's orbs immediately widened yet again when he saw her huge dorsal slicing the surface. Looking up, he locked eyes with Cardoza one last time, managing to spit a thick wad of phlegm up at him that fell well short of its target. His momentary display of bravado dissolved as Scylla rose from the water and turned sideways to snare his torso in her massive jaws.

The pole supporting Rico, though having the diameter of a moderately sized tree trunk, bent under Scylla's three-ton mass as she pulled her meal down, and the rope tied to Rico's wrists vacillated erratically as it strained against the excessive load. Rico let out a final agonized scream as both his arms were torn free of their shoulder sockets, the pole jerking upward by the sudden release of tension, and his detached limbs were flung high as he was swept below the surface.

Van Heflin looked on, mesmerized by the bloodied arms falling back down and quivering to a stop, still tethered snugly at the wrists.

"Drop the rest of him!" Cardoza ordered, looking to his henchman manning the pole.

A rush of tiger sharks immediately swarmed back as Rico's arms were lowered into the murky water, and within seconds the limbs vanished, the rope holding them jerking violently.

The drug lord took a few steps toward the individual he had referred to as 'the prisoner' and smiled cruelly. "Would you like to join Rico, Mr. Osgood?" he asked bluntly. The prisoner said nothing, continuing to stare wide-eyed as the water turned crimson, clearly terrorized by what he had seen.

Cardoza moved closer to the man, keeping his voice low so as not to be overheard by his guests. "I'll give you three more days to reconsider my offer," he stated airily. "In the meantime you can continue to enjoy the delightful accommodations I have provided you. But if you refuse to give me what I want, you can look forward to the same fate as Rico."

Cardoza turned, his eyes sweeping the small throng of spectators to study their reactions to the lurid event, his gaze finally coming to rest on Van Heflin. "Perhaps I'll find better ways to entertain each of you in the future," he said, a broad grin clinging to his face.

Van Heflin maintained his composure, his Adam's apple bobbing only slightly at the implied threat. "I'll look forward to it," he said, managing to return the grin, his mind roving over the possibility of someday superseding Cardoza in the cabal's rigid pecking order. Certainly that would be possible once he occupied the Oval Office.

-44-

Sitting at a table in the Angel's salon, Jake studied the plans Belachek had meticulously sketched, not liking what he was seeing. "If the drawbridge is in the up position, the only way in is over the walls."

"I don't advise that," Belachek said.

"Why not?"

Belachek showed him the circles he had drawn in at evenly spaced intervals along the fortification's perimeter. "There are towers that extend up from the outer walls, six of them. I saw movement in two of those towers during my visit. It is probable Cardoza keeps men in them armed with heavy weaponry to ward off an assault."

"But you're not sure?"

Belachek leaned back in his chair. "It is a reasonable assumption. What defensive measures would you take if you were Cardoza?"

Jake let out a deep sigh and shook his head. "I guess that rules out using the chopper to get in."

"There is another way," Belachek offered, placing a finger on the moat abutting the east side of the fortress. He looked up to give Jake a crafty smile. "You have a problem with sharks?"

"I don't, but they might have a problem with me." Jake held up a forearm to show him the jagged puckered scar caused by a mako attack. "So Cardoza keeps sharks in the moat. That doesn't surprise me."

Belachek brought his mismatched eyes back to the paper. "Cardoza likes showing his pets to guests. I was with Zinova when he met with him. We were led to a room on a lower level where a meeting was held. The room borders the moat, and we could see sharks swimming by, big nasty ones."

"A viewing window like an aquarium?"

Belachek nodded. "If you can get through the glass, that is your way in."

"What's this?" Jake asked, pointing to a structure well away from the stronghold.

"I believe it to be an aircraft hangar since it is at the end of the runway. It is large enough to house at least three commercial jetliners. I saw quite a bit of activity taking place there when we landed. Crates were being unloaded from trucks."

"Any idea what was in those crates?"

"None."

At that moment, Zimbola entered the salon, ducking his head down to avoid catching it on the doorframe. "A call has come in for you, Jay Jay." The Jamaican handed him the encrypted satellite phone they routinely used.

Jake shoved himself out of the chair. "Why don't you make our guest feel at home while I take it up in the pilothouse." He stopped at the door, turning to look back at the mercenary. "Do I have your word you won't give us any trouble, Victor?" He had studied the man closely during the last half hour, assessing his reaction to the three albino creations decorating the salon walls, all of them painted by Achilles, and he could not detect any signs of nausea or illness in the man. In fact, Victor appeared happy and at peace with himself as though a great burden had been lifted from him.

"You don't have to worry about me," Belachek avowed sedately. "I owe my life and that of my son to you."

"I'll accept that for now," Jake said dryly. With that, he strode out the door.

Zimby sat down heavily in the chair Jake had vacated, casting wary eyes on Belachek. He was not as trusting as Jake and needed further assurance. Indicating one of the paintings on the portside wall, he looked Belachek squarely in his mismatched orbs. "Look at the painting and tell me what you see?" he said, his voice deep and demanding.

-45-

Upon reaching the privacy of the Angel's pilothouse, Jake put the phone to his ear. He had expected the caller to be Jacob, but was surprised when he heard Mat's voice.

"I heard you came close to buying it, good buddy."

"Close is a meaningless word unless you're talking horseshoes and hand grenades," Jake replied glibly.

"Zimby tells me you're back at the cove."

"Seems I happened to be in the right place at the right time. Our old pal Cardoza is a persistent bastard. This time he hired mercenaries to take this little sanctuary. From what I've learned, they were part of the same team that was laying for me aboard the Southern Star."

"A coordinated operation?"

"Yeah, does the name Zinova ring a bell?"

"Not really."

"How about the Reaper?"

A moment's hesitation ensued before Mat responded, his tone animated. "You just jogged my memory. Karloff Zinova used to be a Spetsnaz operative. During the Cold War, he was the Soviet's most decorated soldier. The Afghans were the ones that came up with that moniker for him. Following the Soviet collapse, he turned mercenary, offering his services to anyone willing to meet his exorbitant fee."

"Well I guess Cardoza was willing to pay it," Jake replied.

"That guy's becoming a nuisance," Mat grumbled. "So how'd you make out?"

"I got lucky and managed to capture one of his lieutenants, a guy by the name of Victor Belachek, also a former Spetsnaz operative. But he's been very cooperative, giving me the big picture."

"How'd you manage that?"

"It's a strange story, one I'll fill you in on later. But from what I've learned, the Hind we captured was piloted by none other than Zinova. What did you do with him and his crew?"

"Locked them up in the ship's brig."

Silence ensued on Mat's end, and Jake was forced to press him. "So what happened after I left you?"

"Things fell apart, I'm sorry to say."

Jake cut in quickly before Mat could go on. "Is Phillipe okay?"

"Relax, buddy. You should be proud to know he saved my ass. Bashir was badly wounded, but your mother-in-law was able to pick him up in one of our choppers. Last I saw, she was heading toward the Haitian coast rather than back to the colony. Any idea where she went?"

"She came here."

Another bout of silence befell the conversation. "I'm confused," Mat said. There was a sudden edge to his voice. "Isn't Phillipe with you?"

"No."

"I had Phillipe carry Bashir up to the Star's helipad," Mat uttered sharply, his tone consumed with panic. "I specifically ordered him to get on the chopper."

"He's not here." Now it was Jake's turn to evoke panic.

"Oh, shit!" Mat shot back. "That means he's still on the ship."

"You're not on the ship?"

"I had to abandon her. The blue helmet captain accompanying

Allotey, I believe his name was Alvarez. He and his gang were sent to take back the ship, making a HALO on her. Phillipe and I were mostly successful in taking him on, but unfortunately Kalid also got wounded. With a second wave of UN reinforcements dropping down on us, I had no choice but to get Kalid out of there."

"I hope to god Phillipe's still not aboard her," Jake shot back dismally. "Any word from Ez? Surely she would have heard something from Perseus about his whereabouts."

"So far nothing! But the kid's smart. He's still got a cloaker and a Masker, so if he's still on the ship, Alvarez and company may not know he's there."

"This is not good," Jake groaned, "but at least the Star's not going anywhere. Maybe we-"

Mat spoke quickly before Jake could go on. "Another ship arrived to tow her away."

"Great, just great! Do you know which way they're headed?"

"Ez has been tracking them using satellite surveillance. They already made the turn below Haiti's lower peninsula. She thinks they may be headed for the *Bay of Anse-Milieu*. The water's deep enough there to accommodate large container ships like the Star."

Jake was puzzled. As far as he knew, there were no ship repair facilities at that location. "Why does she think that?"

"Because that's where Cardoza's yacht is right now. Ez got a bird's eye view of the vessel and has positively identified her as the *Usurpar*. She's currently sitting at anchor near the town of Tiburon."

"Did you say Tiburon?"

"Yes." Mat paused. "You sound as though you know something."

"That's where Cardoza stays holed up when he comes ashore. There's an old fortress located there that overlooks the bay. If that's the Star's destination, then I'm betting she's carrying something Cardoza wants unloaded right away."

"Any idea what it might be?"

"Not a clue."

"I hate to be the bearer of more bad news, Jake, but it's starting to heat up over here. The UN is mobilizing forces to invade us. Seems someone has gone to great lengths to vilify our operation, using the news media to label us as eco pirates. The media also claimed we hijacked the ship. Makes me believe your conspiracy theory is right on the money."

"I wish I were wrong about that. Ez give you any feedback on Big D?"

"She says there's a one-in-twenty probability at best in bringing it on line without blowing the system. Something to do with the crystal array not being large enough yet."

"If only we had more time to grow them bigger," Jake lamented.

"No sense crying over spilled milk," Mat rejoined.

"Listen, Mat, you're going to have to stay put and do whatever you can to defend the city."

The momentary silence that followed told Jake his longtime friend wasn't happy about this. "Aren't you coming back?"

"Not just yet. I'm going to Tiburon to take care of some business that should have been taken care of long ago, but first I'll need a few things from you."

Mat knew exactly what that meant, and he sighed in resignation. "What do you need?"

"Has Dr. Grahm gotten Johnnie up and running yet? Last I spoke with him, he was troubleshooting the auto-guidance system and hydrodrive power inducer."

"I believe he solved both problems. Why do you ask?"

For the next two minutes, Jake elaborated on the plan he had formulated. "You think you can get those things to me in the next few hours?" he finally asked.

"I'll take care of it right away."

"Don't let me down, buddy."

"When have I ever done that?"

"I suppose never would be an appropriate answer."

"You better keep that in mind." Another pause. "And Jake?"

"What?"

"Don't do anything stupid."

Jake sighed. "Doing something stupid is sometimes the only option we have," he riposted flippantly.

-46-

Standing at a railing along one of Aquaria's outer esplanades, Amelia cast a pensive stare at the translucent indigo sea, feeling very much alone and wondering if her own obstinacy had dashed her hopes of a prolific career. A barrage of conflicting thoughts hammered away at her. Could it be that she was far too naïve and idealistic for this business? Bolder's words came back to haunt her. *'My job is to record events on camera and yours is to provide commentary, nothing more. What the editors do with it is their business.'* The idea that Bolder might actually be right tormented her. Even so, all her previous ambitions to become a top-notch news commentator now seemed insignificant when compared to the aspirations of these colonists. Idly she glanced in the direction where she had last seen the Southern Star, though it had vanished hours earlier, towed over the horizon by another large container ship.

"I wonder what thoughts lay beneath those beautiful tresses."

Startled, Amelia spun around to find herself looking into a bronze, masculine face. A pair of mirthful limpid eyes regarded her, seemingly matching the very color and clarity of the surrounding sea. Separating them was the bridge of a perfectly straight nose perched above a mouth turned upward at the corners in an amused smile, and below that mouth was a square chin shadowed with dark stubble that hadn't seen a razor in several days. A thick crop of unkempt jet black hair fluttered lazily in the mild Caribbean breeze, nearly reaching the man's eyebrows.

Amelia continued to stare slack-jawed, lost in those self-assured, appraising eyes.

"I assume you are the Amelia Amhurst I've heard so much about." Mat held the smile and stuck out a hand.

Dazedly, Amelia accepted it, still unable to pull her eyes from his. "Yes, I'm Amelia."

"Name's Mat, Mat Daniels. How do you like our little kingdom?"

Amelia quickly gathered herself in and returned the smile, suddenly aware of how she must look. "Little is not the word I would use to describe this facility. Enormous would be more appropriate. My head is still spinning over what has been accomplished here." She paused, noticing the jump suit he wore was damp, clinging to a trim, athletic body. "Do you always go for a swim fully clothed?"

Mat widened his grin. "Only when circumstances dictate." He knew he badly needed a shower, shave and change of clothing, but habits he had acquired in the Seals were hard to suppress. Even though his battle aboard the Southern Star had ended hours earlier, he had spent over an hour in one of Aquaria's infirmaries to make sure Kalid was out of danger. Then he made the call to Jake, following through on his requests. The thought that he should go against Jake's wishes and leave for the cove at once nagged away at him, but he knew he had to stay put to do whatever was necessary to defend the colony. To alleviate his growing edginess, he had opted to go back in the water to secure a loose cable holding down one of the OTEC water intakes. He knew he could have delegated the task to one of the dolphins, but he needed to keep himself busy to avoid thinking too much about what was brewing.

"Do you work here?" Amelia asked.

"Not really. I don't consider it work at all. When you love doing something, it's hard to classify it as work. To my way of thinking, play would be a better choice of words."

"Then would it be impolite to ask what you play at?" Amelia felt her pulse quicken. Normally she was unaffected by attractive men, but there was something about this man that made her heart race.

Mat shrugged. "Some say I oversee security around here, but then there are others who might disagree."

"Then you must know what's happening."

Mat sighed in resignation, then laughed as though the matter were of no consequence. "Yes, but we knew this sort of thing was bound to happen sooner or later. When you push for something good in the world, there are some that are going to push back."

"I hope you don't think I had anything to do with those deceitful newscasts."

"Jacob briefed me. Said they were doctored by your editors."

"What are you going to do?"

"What any organism does when threatened. We defend ourselves."

Amelia's jaw dropped. Mat seemed way too complacent in the way he said this. What was about to befall the colony was serious, and he seemed to be taking it lightly.

"Aren't you worried?"

A nonchalant smile flashed briefly across Mat's face. "We still have a few tricks up our sleeve."

"They're going to throw a ton of military might against this place," Amelia reminded him. Mat's utter complacency shocked her. "How can you be so calm in the face of that?"

Mat leaned up against the rail, setting his gaze on the horizon. "When a gun is held to a person's head, he has two choices. He can either whine like a baby and beg for his life, or he can look his foe in the eye and grin. I prefer to grin."

Amelia was about to throw more concerns at him but pulled up short when her cameraman suddenly appeared.

"Just got a call from headquarters, sweetheart, and they want us to get footage of the island," Bolder said, speaking as though Mat were not present.

Amelia stared at him in disbelief. "I told you I'm through. I will not abet such despicable deceivers."

"You're gonna blow a huge bonus, Amhurst, for me as well as yourself. If you don't care about it, that's your business, but don't take money out of my pocket."

"I guess you'll have to deal with it."

Bolder scowled darkly, then reached for her wrist as if to drag her away with him, but Mat stuck out an arm to prevent it from happening. "You heard the lady. She said she's through."

Bolder stared up at him, the whites of his eyes streaked red with veins. He gave the impression of a bull fixated on a matador just before charging. Though he was shorter, he outweighed Mat by at least 70 pounds. He had once cleaned house in a wild melee that had broken out in a Beirut bar a few years back, pummeling seven men senseless and sending four of them to the hospital. Regretfully, he had been drunk at the time and didn't remember much about the brawl. But fully sober as he was now, he was keenly aware of his own brute strength and physical prowess. They didn't call him *the Boulder* for nothing. "I don't know who you are, pal, but if you want trouble, you found it."

Amelia watched as Mat produced that same lighthearted smile. "Now why would I look for trouble in a place like this?" he proclaimed innocently. "Peace and tranquility is more my speed."

"Then I recommend you mind your own business," Bolder growled, not understanding why his superior size failed to intimidate this pipsqueak.

"If you insist." Mat lowered his interceding hand.

Bolder nudged him out of the way with a powerful shoulder and reached for Amelia again, but before he could clamp onto her wrist, his eyes mushroomed wide and he sank to his knees.

"I'm terribly sorry," Mat apologized. "I have this problem with my right foot. I just can't seem to control it."

Bolder rolled onto his back, holding his crotch, his eyes squeezed tight in obvious pain. "You fuck!" he gasped, struggling to suck in air. "You're gonna be sorry for that."

"You're absolutely right," Mat conceded flippantly. "I'm sorry for not using my left foot instead. It packs more kick."

Mat turned to Amelia. "How would you like a tour of Aquaria's lower levels? Jacob tells me you haven't seen them yet."

Amelia looked at him in amazement. "I would love it."

Gallantly, Mat stuck out an elbow. "Then latch on and follow me."

By the time Bolder was able to stand again, both Mat and Amelia were gone.

-47-

Hunkered down in the tight quarters of the Avenging Angel's forward hold, Jake busied himself by putting together the gear he would need for the Tiburon mission.

A familiar voice, soft and mellifluous, interrupted his concentration. "I'm going with you!"

Jake stared back, seeing the same stubbornness he had come to know so well. "No way! Too many unknowns, way too dangerous."

"But you're going to need help," insisted Destiny. "You can't do this by yourself."

Jake continued loading shells into the Sledgehammer's detachable drum magazine. This time he would use frag-12 rounds. "I'll have Fernando and Jimenez with me. Victor has also volunteered to help. They'll be enough to get the job done. Too many players will only complicate the mission."

As soon as he said this, another insistent voice rang indignantly in his brain. *You're forgetting someone, JJ.*

Jake shot a look at Destiny, noticing that she had heard it too. "You're not coming either, Achilles!" he said aloud.

Something akin to a sulk impinged on Jake's awareness, but he ignored it. "Who's going to take care of the twins?" he felt it necessary to add.

"Mother can do that." Destiny was not to be dissuaded. "This is my fight as much as it is yours."

Jake stopped what he was doing, his reply gentle and consolatory. "I don't want you tarnishing your soul with what has to be done. It wouldn't suit you." He let his eyes linger on her a moment longer, then went back to loading cartridges. "And besides, I don't want to find myself in the heat of battle worrying about you. It could make me careless."

At that moment, Destiny's mother crowded into the hold to stand next to her daughter. "We are approaching another nexus, Jay Jay, and from what I'm able to foresee, both Destiny and Achilles must accompany you."

Jake looked up, caught completely by surprise by this unexpected intrusion. For one prolonged moment, he could only stare before a sudden surge of understanding took hold of him. A mother would never intentionally place her offspring in harm's way unless there was a damn good reason. But this was not the Harriet Grahm he had come to know since the demise of Ternier. There was now an added dimension to her, the same psychic aura he had encountered long ago. Though it wasn't visible, he could actually feel it, strangely attuned to its glow. Standing before him was Amphitrite, the same enigmatic personage who had played a crucial role in the past in bringing about the chain of events that had led to the building of Aquaria. At this moment she was invoking a jumble of conflicting thoughts within him. Abruptly, all his doubts, fears and reservations about what he was attempting to undertake loomed in his mind's eye, and he realized a great deal of uncertainty hung in the balance. Complete failure was still possible with or without Destiny's participation. But there was one thing he was certain of, and that was to trust what was being revealed to him, for if he failed to heed Amphitrite's words, the mission would be doomed from the very start.

"I have to know something," Jake said.

Amphitrite stared back, looking solemn. "You want to know why Phillipe elected to remain aboard the Southern Star and if I had anything to do with it."

"Yes."

"No, Jay Jay, I played no part in his decision. I don't know why he decided to remain aboard. All I can tell you is that it felt right at the time."

"Is he still aboard the ship?"

"I don't know."

-48-

The sun was low on the horizon when something bobbed to the ocean surface 40 miles west by southwest from the cove.

Jake shielded his eyes from the sun glare shimmering off the water, then checked his watch. "Right on schedule," he said.

Zimbola held the Angel steady as *Johnnie* came around their starboard side. Nearly the size of a bus, the underwater vehicle had been originally designed by the albinos as an interdiction craft capable of capturing large marine predators. But it served other purposes as well. The craft was incredibly maneuverable and streamlined to reach speeds far greater than even Achilles could achieve. At its heart was a specially grown crystal, a power inducer that drew energy directly from the surrounding salt water environment. Jake had trouble wrapping his mind around its operating principle, something to do with quantum entanglement. The scientific explanation was difficult for even Jacob to understand, a manifestation of the superior albino intellect that tended to hinge more on the metaphysical rather than the physical.

What Jake did know was that *Johnnie* had to first achieve a threshold speed of 7 knots before the crystal was able to draw energy from the sea and provide the necessary power for the craft to move at higher speeds. It was basically an electric motor that gave *Johnnie* the kick start it required to go faster. Once the power inducer was engaged, the electric motor shut down.

"Be seeing you, big guy," Jake said, giving a farewell to his longtime friend.

Zimby scowled. "I should be going with you."

"We already discussed this. I need you to stay with the twins and their grandmother."

Jake left quickly, not wanting to debate the issue any longer, eager to get going. Leaving his children in Zimby's care would ease his mind considerably, for no one was better suited to protect them than the black giant. And he didn't have to worry about Bashir either, though he would have preferred to use him rather than Jimenez on the upcoming mission. Though Amphitrite, Destiny and the dolphins had managed to heal Bashir, he would need more time to fully recover, and it was shortly after Jake had been revived from his own critical injury that they had told him Bashir had already been transferred to the nearby village of Malique to be nursed back to health by Samuel's mother, Louwanda. Bashir would need at least another day to get back on his feet, at which time Kobe would take him back to Aquaria aboard the *Exoco*.

Jake let out a deep sigh. So many things to consider and worry about. All he wanted at this moment was to get aboard *Johnnie* and commence with the mission. With UN forces being mobilized to take control of the colony, time was no longer a luxury.

As he climbed down from the pilothouse, he thought about the name oddly bestowed on the submersible. It was Phillipe who had first begun calling it *'Johnnie'* shortly after its construction two years earlier.

"Why *Johnnie*?" Jake recalled asking the boy at the time. Phillipe had merely shrugged, saying, "I just like the name. It reminds me of a friend I once had back in Port-au-Prince." From then on the name had stuck, with all members of the colony, including the dolphins, using the moniker whenever it came up in conversation.

A sense of apprehension gripped Jake as he thought about Phillipe, wondering if his protégé was currently safe. Hopefully he would find out soon enough as he shouldered his way past the two men stationed along the stern railing, their eyes fixated on the strange looking watercraft as it bumped up lightly against the vessel's swim platform. Almost immediately, a hatch on top of the craft's hull opened with a slight hiss.

"Let me make sure everything's in readiness before you climb aboard," he said, glancing briefly at Jimenez and Victor. With catlike agility he jumped down onto the swim platform and then bounded onto *Johnnie's* hull. As he descended through the hatch, he was shocked to see Franklin Grahm sitting at the controls.

"There was no need for you to come, doctor," Jake said. "This baby should have been programmed to get here all by itself."

Normally carrying a cheerful, upbeat demeanor, enhanced all the more by a thick mane of shaggy white hair reaching to his shoulders, the aging scientist appeared apologetic. "Sorry, Jake, but I just don't trust the auto-guidance. Still seems a bit twitchy if you ask me. I wanted to make sure it got here."

Jake glanced at the control panel with its array of multifunctional displays, which glowed with a colorful mix of vibrant luminosity. "The hydrodrive give you any problems?"

"None whatsoever. Had her up to seventy-nine knots at one point."

Jake noticed the canvas bags tied down firmly in a storage rack to the rear of the cabin. "Mat give you everything I asked for?"

"It's all there. Mind telling me what you need all that explosive for? Mat says you could sink an entire armada with what's in those bags."

"I'm worried it won't be enough."

Franklin nodded stoically when Jake failed to offer more. He could pretty much guess what Jake had in mind. Not wanting to press the issue, he changed the subject. "Is Harriet with you?"

"She's here." Jake refrained from mentioning her transformation, wondering if she had completely lost sight of her actual identity as she once did before. As the Amphitrite of old, she had forgotten who Franklin was, failing to remember he was her husband until she met up with him again after an absence of 22 years. But as far as he could tell, her memory seemed to be intact this time around.

Franklin arose from the control panel seat, seemingly ready to vacate the sub but appearing deep in thought. "Mat told me Phillipe may still be aboard the freighter and that you're going after him," he said.

"That's right."

"He also said you were planning on settling a vendetta with Rafael Cardoza."

"It's not a vendetta."

"Listen, son, I had a lot of time to think about this on the way here." Franklin let the statement hang before going on. "I'd hate to see anything happen to the father of my grandchildren. You sure this is necessary?"

"I have to stop Cardoza once and for all, otherwise he's just going to keep coming after Destiny and the twins. If I do nothing, sooner or later he's going to succeed, ransoming them in exchange for Aquaria's wealth. If that ever happened, I'd never be able to forgive myself." Jake had thought long and hard on what he must do, and he voiced his decision adamantly. "The time has come to bring the fight to Cardoza on his own turf. I doubt he will be expecting that."

Franklin stared, saying nothing for several seconds. "Who's going with you?"

Jake was now cornered with no way out. "I've got a capable force."

"May I ask who?"

"If you must know, Destiny will be coming."

The alarm Jake had anticipated did not materialize on Franklin's face. "I see," the scientist said softly. "I rather expected this."

"You did?"

Franklin nodded. "She's too much like her mother and can be stubborn as a mule at times. Deep down, I knew she wouldn't let you go by yourself."

"As her father, I can understand your concern, but even though she's coming, I intend to keep her well away from the danger. I have two others who will accompany me, one with military training on a par with my own." Jake grew impatient. "Listen, doctor, it's critical I get underway without any further delay."

"I'm coming with you."

"Are you crazy?"

Franklin gestured to Johnnie's control panel. "Someone's got to be on hand to protect this asset and keep it intact."

Jake realized the suggestion wasn't such a bad idea. Franklin's presence might very well be the insurance he needed to keep Destiny from doing anything rash. Nevertheless, he felt it necessary to persuade him otherwise. "Tell that to your wife."

Achilles brushed against his awareness as he said this. *She already knows, JJ.*

Are you telling me she condones it?

She senses he must also come with us.

"Is something wrong, lad?" Franklin asked. "You look lost."

Jake broke from his reverie. "Climb aboard the Angel and say hello," he said.

"Give me your word you won't leave without me?"

Jake sighed as though he were hefting a colossal load. "You have it, doctor."

Franklin began climbing through the hatch, but stopped. "Don't you think it's about time you stopped calling me doctor. After all, we are family."

Jake smiled. He had a great deal of affection for the man. "You're right. I should be calling you dad."

Franklin beamed broadly, then ascended through the hatch.

Jake climbed up after him, poking his head above the outer hull. "Time to get aboard the Tiburon Express," he said. Victor and Jimenez stared back, still trying to make sense of the strange looking craft.

-49-

With his cloaker deactivated, Phillipe crept along a dimly lit corridor within the bowels of the ship, every so often stopping and listening. Illumination was poor, provided by a battery-powered emergency lighting system that was apparently running low on juice. With the Southern Star's engine and main generator disabled, it was eerily quiet. The hum and rumble of machinery that normally accompanied a ship underway was completely absent. Only the occasional creak and groan of steel bulkheads and hull plates cut through the silence as the vessel was towed through the sea.

The thought that he had disobeyed Mat by remaining aboard the ship continued to peck away at him, and he had initially tried to rationalize it by telling himself that Mat would still have needed his help in getting Kalid off the ship. But that had only been a partial explanation for his actions. Upon getting Bashir aboard the chopper, Phillipe had at first meant to climb aboard, but then held up, setting his gaze on Harriet at the controls. Time seemed to stop at that moment, and in that timeless interval she had calmly looked back at him without any hint of urgency in her eyes. In that moment he knew he would not be leaving with her, but somehow it felt right. He could not explain the why of it, he only knew he had to remain with the ship. Stepping back from the whirling blades, he had watched as the main rotor gained momentum, and with Harriet's eyes locked on his, she had given him a slight nod of her head as she pulled up on the collective. And then she was gone.

An inborn need to protect Aquaria burned fervently within Phillipe. He wanted to prove himself, to measure up to the deeds of his father. Stories told by Jay Jay and Mat of their days in the Seals further sparked this need, and to strengthen it, he had taken to heart an inspiring quote by Theodore Roosevelt that compelled him to pursue it with a tenacious hunger. *'Far better is it to dare mighty things, to win glorious triumphs, even though checkered by failure than to rank with those poor spirits who neither enjoy nor suffer much, because they live in a gray twilight that knows not victory nor defeat.'* The words drove him on, adding to his resolve.

A short time earlier, he had made his way to the engine room fully cloaked to observe the ship's engineer and several assistants having a discussion in Spanish as they pondered the inner components of a partially disassembled control panel. Fluent in Spanish, Phillipe had listened.

"I don't get it," the engineer said. "All the circuitry is completely fried."

"I never saw anything like this," one of the assistants had uttered in amazement. "The whole system is shot, and unfortunately we do not have the parts to repair it."

Hearing enough, Phillipe had moved on, revisiting the ship's brig where he and Mat had locked up the Hind's crew, only to find the cell vacant. After that, he had wandered almost aimlessly through the hold of the ship until a series of crates caught his eye. Stamped on the wood of the nearest one was the word *Sterilis*. Curiously he pried the lid open, noticing eight keg-like barrels within the crate.

Does the word hold any significance to you, Perseus? he had asked his bond mate, who was still nearby and keeping pace with the ship.

The word is Latin and translates to barren or useless in English.

Phillipe had frowned at the inanity of it, wondering why cargo would be labeled with a word meaning useless. And even now he found himself continuing to ponder the word.

At hearing the approach of footsteps, Phillipe froze. Urgently, he darted into an adjacent corridor that was completely dark and flattened himself up against a wall, waiting for whoever it was to pass and keeping his weapon at the ready. Wanting to conserve the remaining power in his cloaker, he refrained from turning it on. The sound of voices reached him, and from the strained tones he perceived an argument was taking place.

"I have to get off this ship immediately." The voice was deep and gruff, tinged with a heavy accent that sounded Russian. "I have men out there who require evacuation."

"When we reach our destination," another voice replied petulantly, this one sharp with a thick Spanish overtone.

"Have one of your choppers pick me and my crew up," the first voice demanded hotly.

"That is not possible, I have my orders."

"How much longer before we get there?"

"Not long."

Phillipe held to his concealed position as the men passed, their heated bickering continuing and trailing away as they trooped down the passageway. At that moment he sensed the deck under his feet shift a tad, and abruptly he petitioned his bond mate, requesting an update on their heading.

We appear to be turning into the Bay of Anse-Milieu, Phillipe. I can see an exceptionally large stone structure overlooking the bay.

Phillipe digested this information, feeling the ship begin to lose momentum.

-50-

Zimbola was not happy. He was afraid for Jake and Destiny, fearful of what might happen. Dolefully he had watched *Johnnie* submerge a half-hour earlier, leaving the safety of Harriet and the children in his care. Nevertheless, he knew it was a necessary precaution under the present circumstances. But now he was plagued with anxiety.

Broodingly, he looked to the west, setting his gaze on the sun just as it slid below the horizon. Holding to a course that would take the Avenging Angel to the outskirts of the Bay of Anse-Milieu, he was in no hurry to get there, chugging the North Sea trawler at a steady five knots and saving fuel. With the onset of dusk, his growing edginess suddenly mushroomed to newfound heights, and he craned his head out the larboard door to the pilothouse to scan the sea behind him.

"What are you looking for?" Melody asked, standing next to him. She had grown bored and decided to keep him company.

"A sailor must always be vigilant in the open sea," the black giant said, forcing a broad, toothy grin.

Melody scrutinized his face. "Even when the sea is calm like it is now?"

"Especially when the sea is so gentle. A sailor must always be alert."

For emphasis, he leaned his massive frame out the opposite door to check out their six again. Worried as he was, he did his best to keep the child from picking up on his nervousness. Fifteen minutes earlier he had spotted the distant vessel off his port side as it passed him on a northerly heading. It had been moving fast, an ultra-large luxury yacht the size of a cruise ship with distinctive lines. But then it had made a wide turn, swinging around and hanging two miles back off the Angel's stern. He had recognized the vessel, for he had seen it just before pulling Jake and Fernando from the inflatable raft the dolphins had placed them in, and he remembered the unusual name emblazoned along its stern. *Nunquarn Satis*. But now the rapidly descending dusk was beginning to mask the yacht in a darkening gloom.

"*Omega* lets me know when to be vigilant," Melody said. She glanced lovingly at her bond mate keeping pace with the Angel off its port side. "She's very watchful and can sense the approach of danger."

Zimby stared down at his godchild, giving her a reproachful look. "It is not good practice to rely on others to ensure one's safety. Self-reliance is also important." As he completed the statement, he felt a set of tiny hands latch onto one of his tree-trunk legs, and he glanced down in surprise.

"Gotcha!" Troy Jacob said. "Snuck right up on you and you didn't see me coming."

Melody laughed, looking up at Zimby with an accusing grin. "What were you telling me about vigilance?"

"It is difficult to notice someone so tiny creeping up on me," Zimby said.

"Can I steer?" Troy Jacob asked eagerly, reaching for the lower portion of the helm.

"After you grow another foot," Zimby replied sternly. "You're way too small."

"But I can do it!" TJ insisted.

"You can't see over the windshield. How will you know what's ahead?"

"*Alpha* will tell me. He's out in front of us."

Zimby knew what the boy was saying to be true. Reluctantly he let go of the helm wheel. "Okay, but just for a minute. Hold her steady."

"I want to steer, too," Melody said, not wanting to be left out.

"You'll get your turn," Zimby said, taking the moment to look aft again. Though the sky had darkened further, he was startled to see the silhouette of the shadowing vessel much closer now, less than a mile back.

Zimby turned to TJ. "Do not deviate from our present course," he instructed, knowing Jake had familiarized both children with the Angel's helm, letting each of them steer the vessel every so often. "I'm going aft and will return in a moment."

Quickly, he climbed down from the pilothouse and strode briskly toward the stern, only to be met by Harriet.

"Remain calm," Harriet said. "Do not put up a fight with these people. To do so could be disastrous."

Zimby stared down at her for a prolonged moment. He had seen that same look on her face in the past, and it suddenly dawned on him what was happening now.

"You knew this was coming?" he said.

"Yes."

"So what do I call you, Harriet or Amphitrite?"

When Harriet did not answer, Zimby turned his gaze to the rapidly approaching shadow coming up on their stern, now feeling helpless.

-51-

How are you and Hercules doing, Achilles? Jake asked.

Being imprisoned like this is no great shakes, as you like to say, JJ, but we'll survive. How much longer?

We're entering the bay now. Jake looked over Franklin's shoulder, checking the GPS display on *Johnnie's* control panel. *Get ready to stretch your fins, Johnnie's going to spit you out?*

It's about time.

An air gap within the holding compartment fitted with carbon dioxide scrubbers and fed with a continuing supply of breathable air had sustained the dolphins during the trip.

Franklin eased back on the power, allowing the craft to slow down. With his eyes fixed on the digital velocity indicator, he watched as their speed quickly plummeted. As soon as it dropped below five knots, he flooded the holding compartment, then punched the release that opened Johnnie's retractable maw, and both dolphins bolted from their confinement, happy to be free.

Jake could well understand what it must have been like for them to be cooped up like that for the last two and a half hours, but now they had reached their destination.

Don't forget my status report, Achilles! Jake reminded him.

Nag, nag, nag!

Jake nearly burst out laughing at the reply, and he shot a quick glance at Destiny to catch the smile that came to her face. This was an ongoing source of amusement between them. Achilles had picked up on many of Jake's ways during the last several years, frequently echoing back the same phrases Jake tended to use.

As Jake waited for Achilles report, Franklin worked the hydraulic controls that closed Johnnie's maw and purged water from the compartment. The scientist swiveled his head, looking to Jake for instructions. "What now?"

"We wait!"

As soon as Jake uttered the words, Achilles thoughts reverberated in his skull. *It's just as Ez predicted, JJ. The Southern Star is here with another ship moored next to her called the Northern Comet, most likely her sister ship and the one that towed her. Cardoza's yacht is anchored closer to shore. I also see another vessel. From her profile, she appears to be a tuna trawler. When I get closer, I'll give you her name.*

Any activity? Jake asked.

Yes, a tug is berthed alongside the Star and appears to be taking on cargo.

What about Perseus? Is he here?

When Achilles did not immediately answer, Jake grew uneasy.

I've just made contact with Perseus, JJ, and he tells me Phillipe is safe and has so far gone undetected aboard the Star.

Jake let out a deep sigh of relief before sending out another telepathic thought. *By any chance, does Perseus know the nature of cargo being offloaded?*

Another moment passed before Achilles answered. *Phillipe is currently monitoring the operation. He says crates are being offloaded that contain small drums labeled Sterilis.*

Sterilis?
Yes, it translates to barren or useless in Latin. Jake picked up the satellite phone from the control panel and put in a call to the colony. "Ez, you were right on the mark about the Southern Star's destination, but I need you to find out what *Sterilis* is used for and who manufactures it. Crates of it are being offloaded from the Southern Star at this moment"

"I'll get right on it, JJ. Why do you need to know?"

"Something tells me it's important." Ending the call, he looked to Franklin. "Dad," he said, making sure to place extra emphasis on the moniker, "bring us to the east side of the fortress, as close to shore as possible."

Franklin smiled back appreciatively before setting his gaze on the control panel to engage the electric motor. The craft gathered momentum smoothly, then surged forward with more authority as the hydrodrive kicked in.

Turning, Jake looked back at Belachek and Jimenez. "Are you gentlemen ready to go ashore?"

Both men nodded. Jake locked eyes with the former Spetsnaz operative, searching for signs of last-minute misgivings about switching loyalties, but finding none. No bells went off in his head, and some deep-rooted instinct told him he could rely on this man, at least for the time being.

Two more minutes elapsed before *Johnnie* slowed once again and rose to the surface, upon which Franklin punched the button that opened the hatch.

"Good luck!" Jake said, watching as both men climbed out onto *Johnnie's* hull. Bending, he hefted two waterproof backpacks and shoved them through the hatch, letting each man grab one. Reaching down for other items, he lifted several other bundles and pushed them up into waiting hands, one at a time. Climbing a few more rungs, he rose halfway through the hatch as Belachek pulled a cord on the largest bundle. An audible hiss ensued as the small raft inflated, and both men climbed into it.

Jake glanced around, letting his eyes adjust to the semi-darkness. The shadow of Cardoza's fortress loomed above, overlooking the sea as though it were an evil sentinel. Hanging low and still rising in the night sky was the disk of a gibbous moon. Partially obscured by low slung clouds, it cast a feeble light on the water. A distant flash winked briefly off to the east where no stars were visible, and he felt a sudden rush of air against his face coming from that quarter. Another moment passed before a dull boom reached his ears, and he knew a thunderstorm was headed their way, hopefully a powerful, noisy one.

Bringing his eyes back to the water, Jake saw a fin break the surface in front of the raft. It floated there momentarily as Jimenez tossed out a length of rope attached to the raft's bow. As planned, Hercules would tow the raft the remainder of the distance to shore. In seconds, the two men receded into the darkness, and as he watched, a raindrop dashed against his forehead, heralding the storm's rapid approach. Quickly, he dropped back down into the craft, instructing Franklin to close the hatch and head back in the direction of the Southern Star.

Jake looked at Destiny. "A storm is headed this way," he said. "It may work to our advantage."

"Won't that be a problem for Jimenez and Victor?" she asked. "Cloakers don't work well when they get wet."

"That's true, but a nice hard blow with ear-splitting thunder will make a great distraction."

Jake was well familiar with the electrical storms that could suddenly crop up in these waters. They were loud and violent, but tended to pass swiftly. It would provide another element of cover to carry out this mission.

Abruptly, the familiar essence of his bond mate cut into his thoughts. *I'm able to read the name of the fishing vessel, JJ. It's called the San Pedro. There's activity on deck, and there appears to be a large container being readied for unloading.*

Thanks, buddy. Have Perseus pass the word to Phillipe to evacuate the Star. Let's all rendezvous near her stern.

Jake immediately turned to procure several more backpacks. "I wasn't counting on a fourth vessel," he said, "but hopefully we'll have just enough to go around."

Destiny appeared pensive, and Jake could tell she was having second thoughts about what they were going to do. "I know what you're thinking, but we've got to create as much pandemonium and chaos as possible. We've got to keep Cardoza and his thugs off balance in order to succeed."

"What if they're not all bad?" Destiny said. "What if some of them are like Fernando and Antonio?"

Jake had also given this issue much thought. Both men had once worked for Cardoza, but the employment had been against their will. "That's why we have the hologram projector."

"I hope you're right."

Jake sighed. "So do I."

*   *   *   *

-52-

Phillipe continued to monitor the unloading process as the wind picked up, standing off to one side on the Southern Star's deck with his cloaker activated. Though *Perseus* had passed along Jake's instructions, he was hesitant to leave the ship just yet. Remaining unseen, he had observed members of the UN troops that had taken back the ship assisting in bringing up crates from below. At the moment, most of them had gone back into the ship's hold to retrieve the last of the crates, leaving two blue helmeted men standing at the railing. Both men had taken the opportunity to light up cigarettes.

Phillipe crept closer, listening to their conversation as the men looked down at the tugboat with crates stacked up on the rear deck. With the wind gaining strength, the vessel was rocking more heavily in the growing swells.

A squat, powerfully built individual raised his voice loud enough to be heard above the rising wind, speaking in Spanish. "What's so important about these crates anyway?" he asked his taller companion.

The taller man appeared to cringe, turning around sharply to see if anyone was lurking nearby. The unexpected move caused Phillipe to jump back, but the man appeared to look right through him as though he were a ghost. "Quiet down!" he said irritably, turning back to the shorter man. "Do you want Alvarez to hear?"

"So what if he does?"

"Are you stupid, Poco? This operation is classified. We're under strict orders not to discuss or have any knowledge about this cargo. To do so will be a breach of security."

"Ha!" Poco ridiculed. "When did that ever stop you?"

The taller man did not immediately answer. He looked to his rear again, then turned to face his partner, speaking just loud enough for Phillipe to hear. "I overheard one of the ship's crew talking. He said the crates contain aerosol canisters that are used for crop dusting."

"Then why all the hush-hush?"

"This crewman thinks they're filled with highly toxic herbicides used for killing crops."

Poco stood quiet for a moment, turning his gaze toward the coast. "If they're being taken ashore, then they're probably going to be used here in Haiti. Why would they want to do that?"

The taller man shrugged. "How the hell would I know?"

"Herbicides can be dangerous," Poco said. "They can cause pollution and kill people. And if enough crops are destroyed, people will end up starving."

The other man snickered, swiveling his head to observe a series of lightning flashes illuminating the night sky just off to the east and rapidly advancing. "Since when did you become an environmentalist?"

"I'm not," Poco disavowed. "A bunch of Haitians being poisoned is probably a good idea seeing as how the country is so-"

Poco's discourse was abruptly drowned out by the cannonade boom of thunder, and the first spattering of raindrops came down, driven sideways by the wind. It was immediately followed by a drenching downpour.

Both men turned, looking to escape the ferocious blast of wind and rain, but stopped short. Dumbstruck, they gawked at Phillipe.

Phillipe met their confused, gaping stares, suddenly aware that his cloaker had been compromised. In that instant he made a decision, and that was not to use his weapon. He had already killed one man and had no desire to kill another. Instead, he leaped for the railing, intending to launch himself headfirst over it and dive for the water below. With the onslaught of rain, however, the deck had become wet, and his feet slipped out from under him. Off balance, he crashed headlong into the railing. Recovering quickly, he tried rising, but before he could get his legs under him, something slammed into the nape of his neck with brutal force. Dazedly, he felt strong hands haul him roughly to his feet and drag him along.

Regaining his senses, he found himself bound hand and foot and strapped to a chair. A deeply pockmarked face hovered before him. Captain Alvarez grinned sadistically. "Welcome to hell," he said, running a thumb lightly over the edge of his *corvo*. His grin expanded further when he saw Phillipe's eyes go wide at seeing the blade. "We will have much to discuss once I have finished with some important business," he went on, "especially some of the toys you carry." With his free hand, he picked up a Masker.

Startled, Phillipe shot a glance to his left wrist and realized the device had been removed.

"One of your compatriots also carried one," Alvarez said. He picked up a second Masker and dangled it before him, and Phillipe knew it had been taken from Bashir.

Strapping the second Masker onto his own wrist, Alvarez pressed one of the buttons on the device. Almost instantly his features and clothing appeared to change, bulging and deforming hideously before taking on a new shape. Fully transformed into the image of Malikai Allotey, Alvarez looked down at Phillipe with the same stern expression the UN envoy had exhibited at the colony. "A most ingenious little invention," he lauded smugly. "I must admit that even I was fooled when it was used against me by one of your accomplices."

The two men that had apprehended Phillipe stared at Alvarez's morphed image in amazement. This was their first viewing of one of the device's hidden functions.

Alvarez lifted the tiny cap strapped to his right thigh and slapped down on the plunger that lay beneath it, injecting the potent mix of dextroamphetamine and a non-hallucinogenic LSD derivative into his femoral artery. "I've had some time to play with this," Alvarez went on, "and discovered it can be used to first confuse an enemy before making him severely ill."

Turning his attention to his men, he pressed another tiny button on the gadget. Allotey's eyes immediately flamed, emitting a burst of interlaced light that swirled and danced in upon itself. Both men gawked for one brief moment before clutching their temples and screaming out in agony. Overcome by extreme nausea, they fell to the floor where they vomited copiously, their bodies juddering as though being jolted by a severe electric shock.

Alvarez ignored the convulsing men and focused beyond the convoluting lights. In spite of the drug's potency he felt a trace of disorientation creeping up on him. Fighting it back, he studied Phillipe closely as he let the hologram continue for several more seconds before deactivating the device on his wrist. Allotey's image abruptly faded, leaving the Chilean captain standing in his place. "You seem to be immune to what this device holds," Alvarez muttered reflectively. "Why is that?"

Phillipe gazed back starry-eyed, a contented smile on his face. "Only those who are truly evil become sick when they look at it."

Alvarez stared back in deep thought before his expression turned dubious. "More likely you take an antidote as I did." He shifted his gaze to the fallen soldiers. With the hologram no longer visible, their screams had given way to soft moans. "Idiots!" he scolded contemptuously. "You were briefed on what you saw, yet you did not use the drug to counter it."

Both men rose meekly to their feet, wiping off the vomit soiling their clothing. They were still wobbly, recovering slowly.

Alvarez turned to retrieve something on a chair behind him. Facing Phillipe again, he said, "I would like to know what function this serves?" He was hefting the cloaker, and Phillipe could see it was still wet from the rain.

When Phillipe did not answer, Alvarez set down the cloaker and pulled his *corvo*, his demeanor suddenly dark and ominous. He moved the blade close to Phillipe's face, but stopped short as a blue-helmeted lieutenant entered the room. "Captain!" the junior officer barked crisply, addressing his superior in their native tongue. "Ambassador Allotey requests that you come ashore immediately."

"What does he want?" Alvarez growled irritably.

"He does not say, only that it is important."

Grumbling peevishly, Alvarez re-sheathed his *corvo*, then looked back at Phillipe. "I want you to think about the answer to my last question until I return," he advised stonily, reverting back to English. Turning, he looked at the taller of the two men that had apprehended Phillipe. "Do not take your eyes off him until I get back," he ordered gruffly.

"How much longer are we to stay aboard this ship?" the man asked anxiously, still a little unsteady on his feet.

"Only until the arms shipment goes ashore," Alvarez said. "Once we load it aboard the tug, our job will be finished here." The Chilean captain brought his merciless eyes to bear on Phillipe again. "Then we can get on with other business." Just as he was about to leave the room he pulled up short and reached for the cloaker, folding it up and taking it with him.

Dismally, Phillipe watched him go. The thought that he had chosen to remain aboard the ship plagued him, and he realized it had been a mistake not to obey Mat.

-53-

Riding their bond mates, Jake and Destiny approached the Southern Star's stern, keeping below the churning whitecaps stirred up by the storm. Jake noticed a sudden change in Achilles' switchback motion. The dolphin twitched convulsively under him as though agitated, and he immediately knew something was amiss.

What's wrong, Achilles?

There was a strong emotional edge to Achilles' reply, bordering on a wail within Jake's skull. *Perseus informs me Phillipe has been captured, JJ.*

A vision of a nasty *corvo* abruptly loomed in Jake's thoughts, and he saw the leering face of Alvarez behind it. This was not his imagination at work, this was real. Perseus had seen what was taking place through Phillipe's eyes and had relayed the image to Achilles.

Jake did his best to remain calm. *I assume he's still aboard the Star? Yes, they've got him in a room amidships, one deck down.*

Jake's thoughts went into high gear, and he knew their planned assault had now been compromised. As he mulled this, a revised plan quickly came together in his mind's eye, and he shared the rudiments of it with his bond mate before asking the crucial question. *You think you can*

do it, Achilles?
Achilles' despair suddenly shifted to one of vexation. *Of course I can,* the dolphin replied indignantly. *If Hermes was able to do it, so can I.* He was referring to a feat carried out by Hermes several years earlier, one that had allowed Jake to dispatch Sebastion Ortega and Cardoza's evil nephew, Pedro.
Does Destiny and Hercules know what's required of them?
Yes, JJ.
Satisfied with the answer, Jake's resolve turned to granite as they pulled abreast of the massive ship.

-54-

The full brunt of the storm seemed to stall, hanging directly above the Southern Star as the tugboat cast off and headed for shore. The vessel rocked clumsily in the churning swells with its unwieldy payload of stacked crates and squad of blue helmeted commandos massed together on its rear deck. The men would be needed to unload the cargo once the tug reached the pier that stretched out into the bay. The men were soaked to the bone and miserable, pelted unmercifully by riven rain and heavy spray from waves crashing over the gunwales. They were soldiers, not day laborers, and this was reflected on their faces as they looked up in alarm each time a bolt of lightning cracked overhead with disconcerting closeness.

Two men watched the tug depart, also members of the UN strike force that had taken back the Star. Both had been ordered by Captain Alvarez to remain on deck in spite of the downpour, and as a result, both men were completely drenched.

"Do you notice how Alvarez stations himself with the Russians in the tug's pilothouse while everyone else is made to stand out in the elements?" one of the men remarked. He had to shout to be heard above the thunderous din.

His partner suddenly flinched, ducking down as a jagged bolt of lightning met the sea less than a hundred meters away. The bolt lit up his features, revealing a mottled patch of unsightly skin on one side of his face that resembled a pepperoni pizza, the remnants of a severe burn wound acquired earlier in his military career. "Alvarez has always been a poor leader," the man commented contemptuously. "He likes to see his men suffer while he remains comfortable. He always-"

The shadow of something leaping up from the water directly in front of them made him stop in mid-sentence. He followed the object's

DOLPHIN RIDERS

trajectory as it splashed back into the sea. "Did you see that?" he exclaimed.

The other man nodded. "I think it was a dolphin."

Pizza face looked down at the water again. "If it was, I didn't know dolphins got that big."

Both men recoiled as another lightning bolt sizzled the air, this one missing the tug by less than 10 meters as it struck the water. It was immediately followed by a crackling cascade that ended in a colossal boom. Blinded by the intense lingering flash, they failed to see the shadow rise up from the sea a second time. But this shadow was different, appearing longer than the first. By the time both men regained their vision, it was too late.

On a smooth trajectory impelled by Achilles, Jake soared over the ship's railing, separating himself from his bond mate like the second stage of an Atlas rocket. He had once executed this same maneuver to reach Ortega's low-flying helicopter, with Hermes providing the impetus with his snout positioned precisely under Jake's feet to drive him upward from the water in a gravity-defying leap. At the time, Achilles had been an adolescent, lacking the necessary size and power such a feat required. But now Achilles was fully matured and up to the task.

Jake reached the apex of the aerial assault, coming down feet-first. With perfectly timed accuracy, he slammed the heel of his right foot into the nose of pizza face, knocking the man cold and sending him sprawling. The move cushioned Jake's fall, and he landed lightly on his feet. Caught off guard, the other commando failed to react in time to avoid a jaw-cracking right cross. Stunned, the man staggered backward but did not go down. Surprised at the man's resiliency, Jake followed up on the attack, snapping a vicious front kick to the man's crotch and feeling the scrunch of testicles. This time the man slumped, falling to his knees and holding his groin as Jake drove a knee into his face to finish the job.

Jake looked down at the results of his work. Both men were out cold. Not wanting to take any chances, he gathered their firearms and tossed them over the side. Next, he removed their *corvos,* doing the same. Expertly, he used plastic ties to bind both men hand and foot.

Nice work, JJ! Achilles remarked when he was done. *Now I'll guide you to where they are holding Phillipe.*

Listening to Achilles' instructions, Jake raced between cargo containers to find a door that opened to a short flight of stairs. Though Phillipe had been dazed, he had been conscious enough for Perseus to see through Phillipe's eyes and memorize the route his captors had taken him on. This he had relayed to Achilles.

Just follow the hallway at the bottom of the stairs, JJ, Achilles explained. *At the end of the hall you'll find a room where Phillipe is being guarded by two men.*

Jake sidled up to the door, his USP-9 at the ready. Glancing back down the hallway, he made sure no one followed. A vision of the room's interior suddenly sprang into his mind's eye, and he saw Phillipe's perspective of the two men holding him prisoner. Both men sat in chairs, appearing bored, every so often eyeing the door that accessed the room. From the look of them, these men were professionals. They held their Uzis in readiness, seemingly prepared to fend off a potential assault by other foes sneaking about the ship as their captive had. Phillipe was currently relaying the image to Perseus, who was able to transmit it to Jake through Achilles.

Jake thought quickly. *I'm going to need a distraction, Achilles. Tell Phillipe to insult these men in the most vile terms he can come up with.*

What do you suggest, JJ?

Tell him to say they look and smell like sewer rats, that one Navy Seal is worth a thousand of them in battle. Tell him to spit in their direction.

Jake put his ear to the door. A few seconds passed before Jake heard Phillipe's voice, and he was surprised to hear the strength of venom issuing from the lad's mouth. Phillipe was hurling invectives at the men in their native tongue, a language in which Jake had little fluency.

Is he saying what I suggested, Achilles?

That and more, Achilles shot back. *He's telling them their mothers are whores that continue to work in backwater Chilean slums, though I don't have any inkling what the inference means.*

Another image of the men flashed in Jake's mind, and he could see the insults were having the desired effect. They rose from their chairs, moving to stand over Phillipe, their demeanors pugnacious and growing darker with rage. But now they were facing away from the door.

The perspective gave Jake an unobstructed view of the door, and he could see it had no bolting mechanism or latch with which to prevent entry. Emboldened, he gripped the door knob, turning it slowly and hoping it would not squeak. Phillipe did his part, providing the necessary cover the situation demanded by continuing to taunt his captors, jabbering away in a loud provocative manner.

The image of both men as seen by Phillipe stayed fastened in Jake's thoughts, and he saw the shorter man suddenly unleash a nasty backhand that caught the lad flush on the mouth.

In that instant, a whirlwind of anger welled up from the pit of Jake's stomach and he flung the door open to level his weapon at the commando delivering the blow. "Drop your weapons!" Jake growled.

Both men spun, completely startled by this sudden intrusion, and in

DOLPHIN RIDERS

that fleeting moment of time, Jake could see not the slightest bit of surrender in their expressions. Without hesitation, he squeezed off a shot before they could retaliate. The shorter man's head snapped back as a bullet caught him squarely between the eyes, and before the taller man could raise his Uzi, Jake fired again. His second shot was not as precise, the round striking the man high on his forehead before exiting out the back of his skull. The man keeled over backwards, revealing a splattering of blood and brains on the wall behind him.

Phillipe looked up dazedly as Jake pulled out his K-bar to cut him loose. His lower lip was cut and bleeding.

"Why did you remain aboard this ship?" Jake grumbled peevishly, working quickly to slice through the rope binding Phillipe to the chair. "You could have gotten yourself killed."

Phillipe's eyes refocused. "They're going to use herbicides!" he blurted.

"What are you talking about?"

"They loaded herbicides onto a tug. They're going to poison the land so that crops cannot grow."

Jake cut through the final strand of imprisoning rope, now fully understanding what the word *Sterilis* implied, and he couldn't help but wonder about the odd set of circumstances that had led him here. Abruptly, he cast the coincidence aside, not attempting to analyze it any further.

"Then we have to stop it!" he said, his expression hardening further.

-55-

Franklin sat glumly at Johnnie's multi-functional display panel, keeping tabs on sonar images of the surrounding sea. Just after Destiny and Jake had left the sub, he had leveled Johnnie off at a depth of 20 feet, letting the craft float idly with its homing beacon turned on and sending out periodic pulses that would let the dolphins know his exact position. The thought that his daughter was out there now troubled him to no end, and he tried not to think about the first 22 years of her life he had missed. But now he needed to stay close, to do what he could in keeping her safe and out of harm's way. The fact that she was with Jake only increased his anxiety, for he was well acquainted with how the former Navy Seal dealt with matters such as this. There was no denying that Jake would prefer to look death in the face rather than back away from a dangerous situation, and this was certainly a potentially dangerous situation.

Worriedly, Franklin continued to ponder these things, not immediately recognizing the sudden faltering hum of the sub's generator.

It was only when the lights on the MFD suddenly blinked erratically that he became aware of the problem, and as he broke from his reverie, the hum of the generator died altogether. Abruptly, the sub's interior was plunged into an inky darkness.

Franklin groped in a pocket, pulling out a pen light to scrutinize the controls. "Just what I didn't need!" he said aloud. Reaching over, he lifted a toggle guard and flicked the underlying switch that would turn on the emergency power provided by a bank of batteries. Nothing!

Frustrated, he flicked it back and forth several times. Still nothing! It was then he realized the growing magnitude of the system failure and the ensuing problems it would bring on. Without power, the homing beacon would not function. And without power, the air scrubbers would not work. The last thing he needed was a buildup of carbon dioxide in Johnnie's sealed cabin.

Johnnie was also outfitted with a Delphine Translator which could send and receive acoustical signals, converting *hear-see* water-based dolphin speech to English or English back to the Delphine *speak-see* language. But now lacking the necessary power to operate, the DT would not work. With the help of the albinos during the last few years, Franklin had finally succeeded in perfecting the highly complex computer algorithm he had been developing when he had first met Jake, and it allowed those Aquarians who didn't have a bond mate of their own to converse directly with the dolphins. Unfortunately, Franklin did not have a bond mate, so he could not communicate the problem to the dolphins.

That left him only one course of action. He would have to bring Johnnie to the surface and open the hatch. Packed within his utility belt, he carried a small handheld transducer he often carried with him to summon a pod member, and this one put out a sonar pulse that basically asked for their assistance, to please come now.

Moving to an emergency throw-valve, Franklin pulled down on the handle to direct pressurized air into Johnnie's ballast tanks. A barely audible hiss met his ears, and he sensed the craft begin to rise. It was only as it met the surface that he felt the severity of the storm. Johnnie was being tossed around hard in the wind-driven turbulence.

It suddenly dawned on him why the sub had lost power. The storm was the cause. He was only partly familiar with the quantum principles behind Johnnie's extraordinary design, but he knew that too much electrical energy being discharged into the surrounding water could conceivably disrupt the sub's operating system. This, of course, was only conjecture, a theory that was now being put to the test. But he also knew that if the theory was actually true, which seemed to be the case, there was another side to it that also might prove to be accurate. Once the storm passed, it was possible Johnnie would once again be fully functional.

Franklin steadied himself, gripping the crank wheel that would manually open the hatch cover. With waves crashing over the hull, water spilled into the cabin as the circular lid came up. Thoroughly doused and blinded by the spray, he extended his torso through the hatch opening and retrieved the transducer unit from one of the utility belt pouches. Gripping the handle, he squeezed the trigger. The small transducer immediately ejected from a stubby launch tube to arc out over the water. Tethered to a retrieval string, it disappeared in a cresting whitecap 40 feet away.

Salt water and rain buffeted Franklin's face as he waited with his body halfway out of the hatch opening. It was important he give the transducer sufficient time to send out its message before he pulled in the line and closed the hatch. A lightning bolt suddenly flashed, lighting up the coast like an exploding nova, and he was able to perceive Cardoza's stronghold looming above a rocky shoreline where a pier extended out into the bay, the end of it now less than 70 meters away. It occurred to him that if the wind shifted, it was possible Johnnie could end up being driven into the pier or onto the rocks.

The electrical discharge hung for perhaps a second before flickering out, and a pervading tumultuous darkness reasserted itself once again. Franklin felt terrible. He had become a liability and was now compromising the mission. As he thought about this, something slammed into Johnnie's hull, jarring him to the bone and sending the back of his head into the hatch cover. Abruptly, he slumped forward, his head ringing with the sound of a thousand cathedral bells pealing in concert. Barely conscious, he perceived the chatter of voices through the roar of wind, and he felt himself being lifted as spray pelted him.

-56-

Hercules was the first to hear the sonar pulse echoing through the sea. *Your father beckons us,* Hercules said.

Is he alright? Destiny shot back.

I don't know. He calls with his portable transducer.

Then we must go to him at once, Destiny replied, a sudden bout of uncontrollable anxiety building within her. A vision of what she had seen on the chamber ceiling behind the falls suddenly came back to assail her with cruel, piercing lucidity, and she knew the vision had not been a figment of her imagination, for it had been a glimpse into the future.

I'll inform the others, Hercules said, turning his large body to follow the pulses to their source.

-57-

Jake and Phillipe rode side by side, their bond mates keeping well below the surface to avoid the worst of the storm driven turbulence. Only when their mounts sensed they needed to breathe did they streak upward, leaping high above the waves so their riders could suck in another lungful of life sustaining air. Jake sensed the storm had stalled, its forward thrust slowing to hover directly over the bay. Every so often an electrical discharge would flood the sea with a flickering light, this to be followed by a crackling thunderclap that echoed into the depths.

Not having encountered anymore blue helmets or ship's crew after leaving Phillipe's holding cell, they had made their way back to the same location where Jake had boarded the vessel. Once there, Achilles had bolted from the water, rising up to toss each of them a facemask. Even before he had left the sub, Jake had had enough foresight to bring an extra mask with him for Phillipe.

But now they were running late. Jake had checked his watch just before they had left the Star, and he realized they were behind schedule. In formulating the plan, he had not anticipated having to rescue Phillipe. And to make matters worse, they were now being summoned by Franklin. *What else can go wrong?* he wondered.

Achilles suddenly barged into his thoughts. *Uh, JJ, I hate to tell you this, but Destiny has just climbed aboard Johnnie to find Franklin missing. The hatch was still open, and the launcher to his portable transducer lay on the cabin floor with its tethering line still out. All of Johnnie's systems are dead.*

A wave of fear abruptly coursed through Jake's veins. *Search the surrounding water with your sonar, Achilles. If he's fallen overboard, he can't be far away.*

Destiny says she knows where he is.
Where?
He's being taken to Cardoza's lair.
How does she know that?
She just knows, JJ. Call it a vision.

The thought of Franklin in Cardoza's hands increased Jake's dread. *How much farther before we reach Johnnie, Achilles?*

Three minutes thirty-eight seconds.

There was an element of inconsolable despondency in Achilles' reply, and Jake knew at once there was an additional component of this unexpected news, perhaps something the dolphin had just learned. Achilles began to quiver uncontrollably as they sped along, and a quick glance at Perseus beside him showed a similar change in body language.

Jake's dread immediately escalated into the realm of panic, and he let loose a thought as though hurling a grenade. *Tell Destiny to stay where she is!*

Achilles' was now quaking horribly, and Jake knew what he was going to hear even before the dolphin responded. The reply that came back engulfed him like a floodtide of overwhelming anguish. *She has already left, JJ.*

-58-

Calmly and without fear, Destiny made her way up the slope toward the looming shadow of Cardoza's fortress. The storm still had not passed, now hanging tenaciously over the bay where it met the land and continuing to unleash crashing bursts of lightning and torrential rain with unabated fury. With Hercules fighting his way through a pounding, swirling surf, she had managed to come ashore, leaving her bond mate behind in a state of inconsolable sadness. Hercules had tried to dissuade her from going ashore alone, but she had refused to listen. For reasons she could not rationalize, some vague, adumbrate notion was compelling her onward.

When she had first stepped onto the beach, she had remained hidden behind an outcropping of bedrock. With thunderbolts intermittently exploding the night sky into daylight, she had witnessed ten men enter a van at the foot of the pier. Her heart had cried out when she discerned a white-haired individual put up a struggle before being shoved roughly into a rear seat. The van had then left, and she had watched dolefully as it made its way up through a series of winding curves on the road leading to Cardoza's stronghold. Another twenty or so men had been left behind, crowding the end of the pier where a cluster of floodlights showed them hastily offloading crates from the tug as it rocked precariously alongside the platform. Waves washing over the tug's deck had hampered the operation, and she had seen two of the men swept over the side before being pulled from the water by their comrades.

Destiny had stayed hidden, continuing to observe as the last of the crates were hoisted up and loaded onto the back of a large flatbed truck. With the task completed, the men had climbed wearily aboard the vehicle and departed. But as she watched the direction of its headlights, she had noticed it did not take the same road as the van. Instead, it veered off on another road that seemed to head off farther to the east. Only when it was well away did she venture from her concealed position and make her way directly up the rocky slope, only crossing the road at those places where it snaked back to intersect her path.

Lightning continued to erupt overhead as she ascended higher, seemingly growing fiercer each minute, and she found solace in the violent discharges. To her, it was not a strange notion. While she was still developing in her mother's womb, lightning had been one of the ingredients that had made her into the unique person she had become. Lightning was her ally. Lightning was one of the forces that had forged Amphitrite.

Undaunted, she continued on, her resolution escalating with the storm's growing intensity, and the more savage it became, the stronger she felt. Bolts were now striking the edifice above her, scorching and raking the stone that formed it.

Finally reaching the outer bank of the moat that girthed the fortress, she made her way to the area directly across from the portcullis. Seeing that the drawbridge was in the up position, she moved to the center of the road facing it, making herself clearly visible under the flaring electrical bursts.

Staring up, she saw movement in the observation tower directly above the entrance. Another explosive discharge revealed the head of a man looking down at her. He was speaking feverishly into a walkie-talkie raised to his lips. A rapid succession of several more aerial bursts gave animated snapshots of the man's face breaking out into a leer. And then the drawbridge began to swing down.

Destiny waited calmly as the end of the bridge finally came to rest on her side of the moat. Another moment passed before the portcullis gate lifted to reveal the silhouettes of five men rushing out to meet her, their bodies backlit from lights set back in the entrance.

A subtle smile crossed her face seconds before they reached her. Amid the din of wind riven rain and booming thunder, the sound of rotor blades could be discerned cleaving the air.

-59-

Achilles swam hard through the turbulent surf, allowing Jake to make landfall near the place where Belachek and Jimenez had come ashore. Upon searching the area well up from the wash of whitewater, he found their inflatable raft near a cluster of boulders. As planned, the items he would need had been left within it, one of them being a waterproof backpack which he quickly donned. The remaining item was a tubular object sealed in plastic wrap. Hefting it, he grabbed the strap attached to both ends and slung it over his right shoulder.

Squinting against the heavy downpour, he eyed the imposing mass of the fortress looming above him, his face a mask of determination. "Harm a single hair on her head, Cardoza, and you'll wish you were never born," he vowed aloud.

Doggedly, he began heading up the slope at a brisk trot. Bolts of lightning erupted haphazardly, many of them hitting the stone structure as he strode higher. "Even nature despises you," he found himself saying, his mind suddenly embracing a concept Jacob had expounded on years earlier during a fireside discussion in the cove. Perhaps the Gaia theory was true after all. Perhaps the earth was indeed a living organism, capable of purging itself of malignancies through preemptive initiatives before irreversible damage could be done. Didn't that provide a plausible explanation for the new breed of dolphins coming into existence? Wasn't that the reason for the building of Aquaria?

In spite of these musings, the thought that Destiny was already up there intensified his anguish, and Amphitrite's prophesy only added to his dark mood. "We are approaching another nexus, Jay Jay, and from what I'm able to foresee, both Destiny and Achilles must accompany you."

Almost reaching the plateau upon which the fortress stood, Jake stopped, turning to look back at the sea. Amid the cacophony of driving rain and thunder, he heard the muffled drone of an approaching whirlybird. Grimly, he checked the luminous dials on his wristwatch. *Only a minute late*, he thought. *Not bad considering the magnitude of the storm.*

Jake immediately set his gaze toward the middle of the bay, just catching sight of the aircraft as another bolt of lightning flashed. *Time to activate your transponder, Achilles,* he said.

It's already on, JJ. Let's hope it's still functioning.

Yes, let's hope so.

"Time to pay the piper!" Jake said, springing up the remaining distance to the plateau above.

-60-

With wraithlike stealth, Belachek and Jimenez made their way unseen to the hangar at the east end of Cardoza's private runway. The storm had come on swiftly, and both men were completely drenched from the violent downpour. As they neared the enormous structure, they saw it was ablaze with lights and buzzing with activity.

Just beyond the lights of the hangar, they came upon a huge aircraft sitting on the tarmac, intermittently revealed by intense flashes of lightning. Belachek recognized the type immediately. It was a Chinook CH-47F twin-engine, tandem rotor, heavy lift helicopter. Painted in bold letters on its side was an emblem designating it as the property of the United Nations. It was a military helicopter manufactured by Boeing and primarily used for transporting troops. *So even a faction of the UN is tied in with Cardoza,* Belachek thought bitterly. This did not surprise him at all. In his dealings with Zinova over the years, he had been involved in several clandestine operations in which the Reaper had been commissioned by corrupt factions within the world body. Seeing that the Chinook was currently unguarded, he retrieved something from his backpack, and upon setting a timer, placed it under the belly of the aircraft near the fuel tanks. According to Javolyn, it was a highly potent explosive ten times more powerful than TNT per unit weight, and he knew the former Navy Seal had brought enough of it with him to sink every one of Cardoza's vessels currently in the bay.

Moving to the rear of the facility, Belachek and Jimenez found an unlocked door that opened to a dimly lit stairway. Hastily, they shed their jumpsuits, wringing as much water from the cloth as possible before stuffing them into plastic bags taken from their backpacks. Avoiding conversation, they pulled another item from their packs, donning them rapidly. Jake had instructed them thoroughly on the use of the cloakers while they were aboard Johnnie, and Belachek had been awed by the invisibility they invoked. With their cloakers activated, they ascended seven flights of stairs to find themselves on a steel catwalk that overlooked the hanger's cavernous interior. The view was panoramic, allowing them to observe what was taking place on the floor below.

More than 50 men were scurrying about, pulling canisters the size of scuba bottles from crates situated on pushcarts and installing them into compartments under strange looking aircraft. There was a whole fleet of them, row after row and all identical, each about 6 meters long by Belachek's estimate. Taking a quick count, he tallied 42 in all. Seemingly directing the men loading the aircraft were another 12 men wearing white laboratory smocks, several of them sitting before a bank of computer consoles positioned at the center of the hangar.

Having heard Jake's conversation with someone called Ez while he was still aboard the sub, Belachek looked directly below him to scrutinize the nearest pushcart. Though his orbs were mismatched, he had exceptionally good eyesight. He had been born with brown eyes, but with the intent of enhancing their finest soldiers, the Soviets had used him as a guinea pig while training him to be a Spetsnaz warrior, and one of his eyes had been surgically altered to give him telescopic vision whenever he closed the normal eye. The crate on the pushcart had not yet been opened, and displayed on the lid in small letters was the word *Sterilis*, the same name Jake had mentioned.

Turning, Belachek reached out to touch his invisible partner, holding his voice to a whisper. "Whatever these men are doing, it cannot be good." With a practiced gaze, his telescopic orb fell on a medium-size tanker truck slowly working its way between rows of aircraft. As it came to a stop, a man extended a hose from the truck to refuel the next aircraft in line. Two similar tanker vehicles were doing the same in rows further away. "But I see we have the means to stop it."

Something else grabbed Belachek's attention, and he scrutinized the Hind set off to the far side of the sprawling facility. Zinova had purposely left the helicopter behind as backup for his troops, but at the moment it had no crew. As Belachek studied it, he noticed the airplane tug positioned directly in front of its nose bubble. Two men had just completed connecting the hitch, and one of them waved the tug driver forward. With a slight lurch, the Hind began to move as it was towed toward the hangar doors.

The doors parted as the tug neared them, and it was then that Belachek glimpsed an SUV enter the hangar to intercept the towing vehicle and block its path. The tug came to a halt as nine men filed from the SUV, and Belachek immediately recognized Rafael Cardoza as the first man out. Close on his heels were Zinova and Drakov. The rest of the men were members of Zinova's team.

Curiously, Belachek continued to watch as Cardoza moved quickly to the side of the tug, his face contorted with a dark scowl as he exchanged words with the tug driver. Relying on his telescopic eye, Belachek saw the tug driver nod vigorously as Zinova and his men climbed aboard the Hind. Seconds later the tug began to crawl forward again, working its way through the hangar doors and out into the stormy night with the two men who had connected the hitch following on foot.

Cardoza stood fast for a brief moment, eyeing the Hind's passage before getting back into the SUV and saying something to the driver. In seconds, the car zoomed to the center of the hanger, men leaping out of the way to avoid being run down. As the drug lord exited the vehicle again, Belachek noted a look of extreme displeasure on his face as he confronted one of the white smocked supervisors, apparently the man in charge of the operation. The supervisor appeared to wither as Cardoza threw his arms wide, gesturing wildly before pointing to his watch. Based on the display,

Belachek could only conclude that the operation was running behind schedule. With the reprimand over, Cardoza got back in the SUV, glaring belligerently at the supervisor as the man began issuing heated orders to the other men in white overcoats.

Through the car window, Belachek saw the driver hand something resembling a phone to Cardoza, who raised it to an ear. The drug lord appeared to listen intently before his petulant expression changed over to a sneering grin. Abruptly, he lowered the phone and barked something to the driver, who abruptly gunned the vehicle and sped away. Once again, men were forced to leap clear of the SUV to avoid being hit, and seconds later the vehicle left the building.

Belachek reached out to grasp Jimenez's shoulder. "I'll take the nearest two fuel trucks," he whispered. "You take the truck at the far end of the hanger. Plant your charge on the underside of the tank."

Jimenez seemed to hesitate. "Some of these men may be worth saving," he replied. "We must use the hologram first."

Belachek paused, allowing himself a moment to mull the merit of this. Certainly he was tired of killing, but time was running short. "Okay," he conceded. "Perhaps they are not all bad." He was thinking of how he, himself, had abetted Zinova. Though he had been an accomplice of such a wicked man, he had grown weary of pernicious acts.

Jimenez pulled the PHP from under his cloaker and positioned it further out on the catwalk before activating it. This particular unit was much smaller than the one Jake had used aboard the Hind, an upgraded version of the bazooka-shaped Portable Holographic Projector. It was the size of a cell phone and originally developed to display the dolphin art in a fashion much more dynamic than that depicted in the 2-dimensional paintings. For conscientious reasons, Jake had had the foresight to have Mat pack a few of them aboard Johnnie before Franklin sailed from the colony. And Jake had made sure Jimenez was equipped with one just before sending him on this mission, instructing him to employ it if he thought a situation warranted its use.

Pressing the activation button, Jimenez stepped back, making sure to avert his eyes from the projected image that immediately sprang into view just below the hangar roof. Jimenez was one of those people profoundly affected by these enigmatic artistic creations of the albino mind, and had he taken in the 3-dimensional shimmering vision, he would have been rendered ineffective by its seductive narcotic influence. Instead, he focused his gaze on the people below.

A cry of intense pain suddenly erupted. The cry had come from one of the technicians sitting in front of a computer screen. The man had looked up, distracted by the glowing thing snaking and intertwining above him. He had stared for one brief moment before his eyes widened as though viewing some monstrous form hurling itself at him. Abruptly, he had clutched his temples before falling from the chair and screaming out in agony. Several of his peers followed his gaze just before he collapsed, only to suffer the same reaction. A chorus of shrill screams quickly ensued, and men were jerking violently as though being electrocuted. The display spread rapidly, gathering momentum as more and more men broke from their tasks to look up. A growing number of Cardoza's thugs lay sprawled in their own vomit, screaming and writhing and continuing to regurgitate copious portions of their last meal, while others had collapsed to their knees to clutch their skull.

Jimenez scanned the floor rapidly, looking for different symptoms. He spotted two people staring up at the far end of the facility, rapturously drinking in the scintillating vision. Both of them stood near one of the fuel trucks. Directly below him, he became aware of another man gazing up as though in worship, one of the white frocked technicians. From where he was positioned, he could clearly see that the infection had now spread to all quarters of the facility. With the exception of the unfallen three men, all the others appeared severely stricken with sickness.

Satisfied that there were no others to be saved, Jimenez moved back to his original place on the catwalk, reaching out to touch Belachek's invisible form. "I will guide the two men who stand near the far truck to safety once I plant the charges," he said. "Perhaps you can do the same with the man directly below us once you plant your charges."

"Yes, my friend, I will do as you suggest," Belachek readily agreed. Though he desperately wanted to, he also avoided looking at the hologram, managing to keep his eyes focused on the debilitating chaos taking place below. While formulating the plan, Jake had warned him about gazing directly at it. "Three-dimensional representations of the dolphin art are far more powerful than their two-dimensional depictions," Jake had stated while laying out the plan. "Staring at them will cause basically good people to become far too lethargic to be effective in a fight," he had gone on to emphasize.

Belachek had trouble grasping the concept, for he had never thought of himself as a good person. Nevertheless, he had no desire to test Jake's claim. Shaking off his reverie, he checked his watch. "We must hurry!" he said. "Set your timer for two minutes. That should be enough for us to get these men clear." Quickly, he moved back the way they had come.

* * * *

-61-

Jake remained hidden behind the trunk of a fallen tree as errant electrical discharges spiked all around him, many of them striking Cardoza's fortress. Having just reached the moat three minutes earlier, he had arrived just in time to witness a lone SUV cross over the shark-infested water and enter the stronghold. Too late for him to sneak in behind it, he watched regretably as the drawbridge came up to seal off the portcullis.

How you doing, Achilles? Jake queried, barely making out the sound of rotors above the storm's raging cacophony. The noise of blades chopping the air grew progressively louder, adding to the raucous mix of exploding thunder, blasting wind and pounding rain.

Achilles' reply was swift. *Having to hitch a ride like this is no fun, JJ, I can tell you that. If not for the rain, my skin would be dried out and cracking by now.*

Well you're almost here, so hang tight, Jake said, finally able to discern the chopper bearing rapidly in on his position with a sizable object slung beneath it. Reaching out, he placed the portable holographic projector he had been holding on the tree trunk in front of him and pressed the button, hoping the rain would not impede it. He had set the range function on maximum so that the image would coalesce directly in front of the stone structure's nearest tower. He made sure to look away as the PHP sprang to life, projecting the vision it held to the required height.

Time seemed to hold still as Jake waited uncertainly for something to happen, but the scream suddenly emanating from the closest tower was like chamber music to his ears. The moment passed quickly as the chopper flared and came to a hover directly above the moat, its suspended cargo hanging ten feet above the water.

Jake checked his watch again, noting the time. A horrendous boom suddenly cut through the air, sounding different from the thundering discharges. It caused a dark smile to come to his face as he looked in the direction of the blast. A distant fireball rose up above the citadel's eclipsing bulk, throwing out a coruscation of orange and yellow flames into the roiling night sky. The blast was immediately followed by several more explosions, each one sending up a billowing, swirling ball of hot gas similar to the first.

Jake snatched up the PHP and stuffed it into a waterproof pocket on his utility belt. Pulling down his face mask, he bolted from his concealed position just as the chopper's sling parted to release its ponderous load.

Taking three bounding leaps before hitting the water, he made sure to hold on tight to the gear he carried. A heavy blast of rotor wash accosted him as the chopper veered away, causing him to smile inwardly. Fernando had carried out his portion of the mission precisely as planned, flying from the cove at a prearranged time several hours after Jake's departure aboard the Avenging Angel. But now he was to stand by until needed again.

Achilles reached Jake in less than a second, and a moment later Jake sat anxiously astride his bond mate. With Achilles now under him, the dolphin immediately submerged.

Let's hope those sharks don't give us any trouble, Jake commented, handing Achilles the explosive they would need to breach the stronghold.

I think it's too late for that, JJ. I'm picking up an exceptionally large shape with my biosonar. The profile tells me it's a female great white better than twenty feet. I'm projecting the hear-see image so you'll have an idea just how big she is.

The reflected image that formed in Jake's mind startled him. The shark had to be somewhere close to three tons, an eating machine of sheer aggressiveness.

There's a plus side to this, JJ. The other sharks are keeping their distance from her.

Just plant the charge and use your speed to stay clear of her, Jake ordered. The back side of the charge was coated with a water-resistant adhesive that would readily stick to any submerged surface. Once pushed up against the Plexiglas window Belachek had described, a timer button would be activated that was set to trigger the detonator thirty seconds later. Jake was not worried about the deadly shock wave that would propagate through the water following the blast. Strapped to his bond mate's body was a Pressure Wave Inhibitor that would protect both of them.

I'm afraid that won't be immediately possible, JJ. She's coming directly at us. Hold on tight.

Jake felt Achilles turn sharply and accelerate with a burst of speed. Though the water was dark and murky, a sudden electrical discharge from above sent a flaring burst of light into the depths. A massive set of jaws armed with murderous triangular teeth flashed by, narrowly missing them in that fleeting instant of time, and Jake realized how close they had come to being a meal for the huge carnivore.

She's quick, JJ, almost as fast as me. I'm going to try luring her away from our objective before backtracking.

Do whatever you have to, but just make it quick. We have little time to waste. The thought that both Destiny and Franklin were now in Cardoza's hands tormented him like an auger being driven into his skull, for there was no telling what that sadistic bastard was doing to them at this moment.

Are you able to contact Destiny? Jake asked hopefully as his bond mate moved rapidly with darting evasive action.

Achilles did not immediately respond, and Jake felt the nervous shudder go coursing through the dolphin's body. *Well are you?* Jake demanded impatiently.

Yes, JJ, Achilles quailed, *and her situation is not good.*

-62-

Destiny took in the dispiriting sight with heartbreaking despair. Nevertheless, she knew she had to remain strong. Five of Cardoza's thugs had brought her to a musty chamber deep within the stronghold. They had shoved and prodded her along, all the while leering and laughing and groping her lewdly. She had not resisted, distancing herself from the fear that should have consumed her. Instead, she had locked onto the guidance Esmerelda had given her back in the cave. *"You must cleanse your mind of the fear that shackles it,"* Esmerelda had maintained. *"Have faith. Faith and fear will always be at war, so you must choose one or the other. You must have patience and steadfastness, continuing to believe with all your being until the belief is physically manifested. Once you possess it, all is possible."*

Destiny clung to the words as she looked at her father, reminding herself that she had to remain strong. She would not let herself get compromised again. She would not let herself fall victim to negative thoughts. She would not deceive herself by forgetting who she was. Esmerelda's words continued to empower her. *"Your unconditional love for those around you has made you even stronger. It is a source of great power."*

Franklin turned his head, his eyes widening with shock and fear at seeing Destiny in this place. The fear was not for himself, but for his daughter. The men in the chamber were cruel and sadistic, capable of any heinous act. With his body stretched out on the medieval torture rack, he had no doubts she would be subjected to the same atrocity once they finished with him.

The sound of approaching footsteps echoed dully within the confines of the hallway leading to the chamber, causing heads to swivel in that direction. A brief moment passed before Rafael Cardoza emerged, his expression lighting up in a victorious grin at seeing Destiny. "So this is the dolphin girl," he declared expansively.

Destiny stood still, not saying anything as Cardoza made a show of

DOLPHIN RIDERS

sauntering around her to look her up and down.

"You have caused me many problems over the last several years," he suddenly spat, "you and all those associated with you." Coming back around to look her in the face, he stared implacably. "And yet I find it rather amazing that someone so beautiful would have the means to do that."

Destiny stared back calmly, remaining quiet.

Cardoza turned to gaze thoughtfully at Franklin strung out on the rack. "This man must be very special for you to come here alone like this."

"He is my father," Destiny said, her voice low and dulcet.

Cardoza's eyes lit up with apparent delight. "Your father, you say!" He let out a giddy laugh over his unexpected good fortune, and several of his cohorts joined in. He had expended considerable time and expense in planning the girl's capture, with the effort ending in a complete failure. But now here she was, walking right into his midst. "You are either terribly naïve or incredibly stupid if you thought you could save him by coming here."

"I ask that you release him at once," Destiny said without emotion.

Cardoza studied her as though she were insane. There was not a shred of fear showing on her face. "Do you know what this device is?" he asked, turning to indicate the rack Franklin was immobilized on.

When Destiny did not reply, Cardoza answered for her. "It is called a rack. It was developed in medieval times for interrogating and extracting confessions from prisoners. During that era, it was considered to be the ultimate instrument of torture."

Cardoza scrutinized her closely, looking for the fear to well up in her expression. "It can induce the most excruciating pain imaginable," he went on, carefully choosing his words to invoke the optimum psychological distress.

At seeing no reaction in the girl, he turned his gaze on Franklin again and continued the discourse. "As you can plainly see, your father's ankles are fastened to the lower roller, while his wrists are chained to the other." Reaching out he grabbed the long handle extending from the device, applying just enough pressure to move the ratchet attached to the top roller one additional notch. The ratchet moved with an audible click, and as it did, Franklin gasped out in pain.

The drug lord turned to address Destiny again. "Through a stepwise process, the tension on the chains can be gradually increased by means of the lever and pulleys connected to the rollers. They strain the ropes and chains until the victim's joints are eventually dislocated." Pausing, he studied her again, a depraved leer plastering his face.

Destiny barely managed to keep her features composed, though she wanted to scream out in tearful frustration.

At seeing no fear, Cardoza reached out and grabbed the lever handle again, this time yanking it hard. The ratchet advanced two clicks, causing Franklin to elicit a sharp intake of breath.

Destiny's expression did not waver. "With each cruel act you commit, you seal your own fate even more," she said. "I beseech you to release him at once if you wish to live."

Cardoza's jaw abruptly dropped, amazed by the potency of Destiny's audacity. This show of defiance was utterly alien to him. He was used to getting what he wanted by invoking fear in others. He fed off the fear, drawing strength from it.

All at once, Cardoza stopped gaping and let out a raucous laugh. "Salt water must have addled your brain, girl. It is you who have sealed your fate by coming here. But first I want you to see your father's arms pulled from their sockets. Only then will you comprehend who is in control here."

Gripping the rack lever, Cardoza kept his gaze fixated on Destiny's face. "Listen carefully. One aspect of being stretched too far on the rack is the loud popping noises cartilage, ligaments and bones will make when subjected to such severe stress. And when muscle fibers are stretched excessively, they lose their ability to contract."

Before Cardoza moved the lever, a tremor suddenly rumbled underfoot. Startled, he shot a look to one of his men. "What just happened?" he demanded.

The man mirrored his boss' startled expression, but before he could say anything the floor shook again, this time more forcefully.

A vision invaded Destiny's thoughts with flaring lucidity. Through Hercules' eyes, she glimpsed the rising fireballs, seeing parts of the hangar and what it contained fly high into the air under the scorching light of the blasts. It was understandable that the force of the explosions would be felt within the castle even though the hangar was more than a mile away. The shock waves would travel through the bedrock, which both structures were founded on.

"Pull that lever again, and this structure will be destroyed just as your hanger was," Destiny warned.

Cardoza stared back, not fully comprehending what she was saying, but before he found his tongue, a handheld radio carried by one of his thugs suddenly squawked. The thug winced as he lifted the radio to an ear, nearly deafened by the strength of the caller's panicky tone. *"El hangar se ha ido!"* a disembodied voice cried out in Spanish, loud enough for everyone to hear.

Cardoza grabbed the radio from the thug's hand and spoke angrily into the speaker. "Is this some kind of joke?" he asked in English. From the caller's voice, he knew it was Lamont stationed in the east tower, a man known for an occasional prank on some of the other men. If it was a joke, Lamont would pay dearly for it. "What do you mean the hangar is gone?"

Hearing Cardoza, the caller reverted to English. "No, this is no joke. The hangar has been completely destroyed. I saw it explode. All that remains of it is in flames."

"What about the drones?" Cardoza demanded, a shocked look befalling his features. "Did any get out?"

"I did not see any leave the hangar."

In a fit of rage, Cardoza hurled the radio against the closest stone wall, narrowly missing one of his men, who ducked just in time to avoid being hit in the head. The radio shattered, with pieces flying off in various directions. Spinning around, Cardoza turned venomous eyes on Destiny. "You did this!" he accused in a low, guttural hiss.

As Cardoza spat out the words, another vision suddenly coalesced within Destiny's thoughts. Achilles and JJ were being hounded by a huge shark within the moat, impeding them from reaching their objective. Probing with her mind, she extended mental tendrils into the shark's brain to supplant its hardwired primeval instinct with another urge. It was an old trick she had mastered from a young age, an ability to control the actions of sea creatures. She had utilized it once before to cause a massive school of barracuda to disable a boat in order to keep the men aboard it from attacking Jay Jay. Sensing a change in the shark's disposition, she reengaged her telepathic link with Jake's bond mate. *You're clear to go, Achilles.*

Cardoza continued to glower at her, his rage building like a volcano about to explode. "You did this and now you are going to pay," he repeated, this time screaming out the threat. "We will see how brave you are after I put you in the tiger's cage." Shooting a glance at two of his men, he screamed again. "Bind her!"

Feeling rough hands grab her, Destiny pressed the mental trigger, unleashing the energy her body had gathered in from the storm. Following the birth of the twins she had lost this ability, but now she sensed it was back. Like the *thurentra*, she was capable of storing a charge.

An abrupt flash accompanied by a loud crackling resounded as both men were flung backwards to land unconscious on the floor. The biting smell of ozone hung in the air as Cardoza gaped dumbly at their sprawled forms, trying to make sense of the scene he had just witnessed. With bulging eyes, he swiveled his head to look back at the girl. "I don't know what you are, but you haven't won yet," he uttered in a sibilant whisper. "At least I will have the satisfaction of seeing you watch your father's arms ripped from his body." Turning, he reached for the rack lever again, his face consumed with insane hatred.

"Then you have sealed your own fate," Destiny avowed.

Just as Cardoza's fingers made contact with the lever, a deafening boom rocked the chamber. Dumbfounded, Cardoza dropped his hand, his eyes drawn to the heavy cast iron door leading to the antechamber where his last meeting had taken place. An escalating rumble could be heard gathering strength on the opposite side of the door as a gush of water spewed out from beneath it.

Knowing what the sound heralded, Destiny bolted to the side of the rack, taking advantage of the situation. With Cardoza and his three remaining henchmen staring at the door in confused fixation, she quickly disengaged the ratchet, easing the strain on her father's limbs. In moments she had Franklin free, and helping to support him, she was able to guide him to the hallway leading from the chamber just in the nick of time.

With savage ferocity, the door burst open. Unable to withstand Scylla's three-ton mass driven forward by the force of the water, it was torn from its hinges. Like a battering ram, the door was swept forward by the onrushing torrent, slamming into two of the thugs and killing them outright. Knocked off his feet by the deluge flooding the chamber, Cardoza floundered frantically as Scylla's enormous jaws chomped down on the third henchman. Shaking her head savagely, she tore a huge chunk from his torso.

Moving hastily down the passageway, Destiny and her father barely managed to escape the initial onslaught as water from the moat gushed in. Turning her head, Destiny looked back. Carried along with the flood were other large predators, their jaws snapping as they were driven into the chamber by the powerful surge. Within their midst, she caught sight of Jake clinging tightly to Achilles, his head swiveling in her direction. In seconds he was at her side.

"Climb aboard!" Jake shouted, his voice carrying above the rush of water. Reaching out, he grabbed Franklin by the elbow to pull him in. Destiny followed, and with her father now sandwiched between her and Jake, Achilles began fighting his way back against the flow.

"We're going out the way we came in," Jake bellowed, and as he yelled out the words, Cardoza was suddenly before him, his head just above the water, a rabid snarl on his face. It was then Jake saw him raise an arm to level a snub nose revolver directly at him, but before Cardoza could pull the trigger, the drug lord rose up suddenly, lifted clear of the surge. Clearly stunned, Cardoza looked down to find his half his body within Scylla's massive maw, and as he did so his eyes bulged out in terror.

For a seemingly endless moment, Cardoza continued to stare down in horrified silence before a hideous wail escaped his lips. Abruptly, he dropped the revolver and pushed down hard on the edge of the entrapping jaws, squirming frantically in an effort to free himself. His struggles proved futile as Scylla's mouth snapped shut, her serrated teeth cutting through flesh and bone with little effort. Cleaved in two at the waist, Cardoza let out a final piercing scream as the upper half of his body fell away to disappear in the torrent.

Glad to be rid of his longtime nemesis, Jake was perplexed by Achilles' next move. Instead of swimming against the current, his bond mate had turned to drift with the flow. Jake was about to question the dolphin's motive for doing this, but before he could object, Destiny spoke.

"There's a person trapped down here," she shouted. She had sensed him moments before Scylla's timely arrival.

"Where?" Jake yelled back, his voice almost lost in the deafening rush of whitewater crashing into the hallway's confined quarters.

"In one of the holding cells further back."

Jake looked in the direction she indicated. Only one electric light bulb situated at the far end of the passageway still burned, casting just enough illumination for him to see, and he was able to make out a set of stone steps where the hallway terminated. It was then he noticed the rusted doors strung out at intervals along both sides of the corridor. Achilles let the flow carry them past three of the cells on the right before pivoting around. Now swimming against the current, he kept them abreast of a fourth door on their left.

"He's in there," Destiny yelled.

Straining his eyes, Jake discerned the grim smudged face of an elderly white man plastered up against the door's small grill, his hands clutching the bars, his expression filled with fright.

Reaching for the latch handle on the door, Jake discovered it would not budge. Scrutinizing it further, he found the reason why. "We're going to need a key to open this door," he shouted, gauging how quickly the water level was rising. In another minute, the hallway would be completely flooded. "If we're going to get him out, we need to do it now."

"You know the drill!" Destiny yelled back, the deluge's thunderous roar nearly drowning out her words. "Concentrate!"

She was reminding him about an episode aboard Loomin's boat years earlier. It had been his first encounter with telekinesis. Locked away in a storage locker, he and Destiny, aided by two of the albinos swimming alongside the vessel, had merged their thoughts to move the locker's sliding bolt that imprisoned them. But he knew this was different. The lock was ancient and, in all probability, rusted on the inside. It was doubtful it could be moved without the use of a key.

Achilles' essence shrilled within his brain. *Think positive,* his bond mate reprimanded. *Negativity is not an option here.*

Sorry, Achilles, Jake apologized. *I should know better.* Focusing all his mental energy, he threw his entire will into disengaging the door's locking mechanism, and as he did so, he could feel Destiny's, Franklin's, and Achilles' thoughts intertwining with his own.

Something resounded within the lock, and the door suddenly sprang open, the imprisoned man swinging out with it as he continued to hold onto the bars. With his head just above the rising water, the man was clearly on the edge of panic. By this time, only one foot of overhead clearance remained in the flooded corridor.

"I hope you're good at holding your breath," Jake shouted at the man, who flinched in terror as Achilles reached out to grab him about the waist from below the waterline. From the look in his eyes, Jake could tell the man had spotted the fins racing down the passageway. Frozen with fear the way he was, Jake instinctively knew the man would drown if Achilles dragged him along in this manner.

Thinking quickly, Jake petitioned his bond mate. *This guy's too much of a liability in his present state, Achilles, and carrying four of us against this flow is going to be too much for you.*

But I can do it, Achilles protested indignantly.

I'm not going to risk your life, nor that of Destiny and Franklin, Jake shot back adamantly. *I'm taking this guy out by the same route Destiny took to get down here.*

But more of Cardoza's men will be up there, Achilles pointed out.

Maybe so, but it's the only option I'm willing to take. Now stop arguing and get going! Jake ordered, grabbing hold of the terrified man.

The exchange of thoughts was swift, taking place with an urgency the situation demanded. Reluctantly, Achilles began to move against the surge, leaving Jake behind. Destiny turned to look back at him, her head barely above the water. A concerned expression consumed her face, her lips moving in a silent plea. But Jake could tell she was in agreement with his decision and nodded a reply, as if to say "I'll try to be careful." By now, only an air gap of less than six inches remained, which was closing fast.

"Let go of the door!" Jake shouted in the man's ear.

The man continued to grip the bars with a strength born of terror, too traumatized to heed Jake's command. "Let go or I'm leaving you for the sharks," Jake threatened.

The words seemed to galvanize the man, and with a suddenness Jake had not anticipated, he let go of the bars. Swept back by the powerful surge, Jake kept a tight grip on his charge, having enough presence of mind to inhale sharply just before the air gap closed. With the passageway now completely filled with rapidly moving water, he was carried along its length with a violence that surprised him, twisting and turning out of control like a blind man caught in a sandstorm. Continuing to hold onto the man, he could feel him clawing frantically to get away. The sandpaper hide of one confused predator brushed rudely against him, and had the shoulder strap of his slung gear been less tight, he would have lost it.

Jake was again jostled, this time much harder than before. With unyielding tenaciousness, he managed to hold fast to the man, whose struggles had now abated. Something slammed painfully into his shoulder, jarring him to the bone, and he felt himself tumbled end over end. Throwing out his free hand to fend off the obstruction, he felt a series of ridges sweep by, and kicking hard, he sensed he was moving upward. Several moments elapsed before his head broke the surface. The water was rising, whisking him up the steps he had seen at the end of the hallway. But now he perceived an ebbing of the flow as the water pressure in the moat equalized with that in the fortress. Managing to stabilize himself on one of the steps, he climbed the remaining distance to the floor above, dragging his charge with him.

Jake lifted his facemask, pulling the limp and unmoving man onto a stone landing. Light from somewhere above cast just enough light for him to see. Quickly, he laid the man on his back and went to work, pumping the man's chest before applying mouth to mouth resuscitation. Several seconds passed before the man came around, and with an unexpected suddenness, he sat up and coughed out a small amount of water.

Jake placed a hand over the man's mouth to muffle the sound. "Easy there, fella! Try to be quiet," he admonished in a whisper, "otherwise you'll bring the bad guys down on us."

The man stared back vacantly before Jake's words fully registered in his expression. His short immersion in the tunnel had cleansed some of the grime off his face to reveal at least three days' growth of gray stubble clinging to his cheeks, chin and lips. What remained of his slacks and dress shirt was tattered and filthy.

"I'm going to try and get you out of here. Can you walk?"

The man gave a weak nod and rose slowly with Jake helping him to his feet.

Jake unslung the tubular bundle strapped to his shoulder, removing the watertight plastic wrap covering it to reveal the Sledgehammer with its drum magazine. Lowering it to the granite floor, he pulled his USP-9 submachine pistol from the holster hugging his right thigh and removed the clip, replacing it with another from the waterproof utility belt girthing his waist. Slipping it back into its holster, he placed a hand on the hilt of his K-bar at his calf to make sure it was still there. Satisfied, he picked up the Sledgehammer and set the firing mode on semi, hefting the weapon to make sure it balanced comfortably in his hands.

The man he had rescued monitored his every move with curious though fearful eyes, making Jake wonder how he would hold up against the potential conflict that was about to ensue.

Thinking to check on his bond mate, Jake sent out a mental query. *How you doing, Achilles?*

We're back in the moat, Achilles answered back. *What's your status?*

Getting ready to blast my way outta here, Jake replied, setting a stony gaze on the next flight of steps, a narrow medieval stairwell that spiraled up into the dim light cast from above.

Achilles intruded into his thoughts again. *We'll wait for you.*

Don't wait! Get out of there now.

Sorry, JJ, but Destiny insists on waiting.

Jake sighed in frustration, knowing it was an argument he could not win. Even though Achilles was his bond mate, Destiny held dominion over the actions of every dolphin in the pod. She and not he would ultimately have the final say. No matter what the circumstances, her decision would trump his own when telling Achilles what to do.

As an afterthought, Jake queried Achilles again. *Are you in contact with Hercules and Perseus?*

Yes, JJ, they have planted the charges just as you instructed. They are all set to go off simultaneously in exactly three minutes twenty-two seconds.

Jake needed further verification. *Does that include all of Cardoza's water-based assets?*

All of them, JJ. Even his yacht and tugboat.

What about Johnnie? Jake was thinking about their mode of transportation once this business was finished. There was no way Fernando could fly all of them back to the colony in a single trip. The Bell Ranger was not big enough to do the job. It was not designed to carry sizable loads even after Fernando's exceptionally skilled tweaking of its powertrain. It had barely enough lift to carry Achilles' 1,200 pounds to the moat without overstressing the engine.

The tugboat towed Johnnie out to the Southern Star and left it tethered to the freighter without anyone guarding it. While the Blue Helmets were offloading more cargo, Phillipe managed to untie the ropes and sneak aboard. By that time the storm had passed, and without any electrical discharges to scramble the systems, he was able to start the motor and move away.

Where is he now?

He waits for us near the end of Cardoza's pier.

And Fernando?

Hercules saw him set down on the beach two hundred meters west of the pier. Fernando was fortunate to land when he did.

Jake's gut involuntarily tightened, and he interrupted Achilles before his bond mate could add more. *Did he have mechanical problems?* He sensed Achilles wince under the force of the question. He was intensely aware that the Bell would be needed to retrieve Achilles from the moat.

You should refrain from stressing yourself like this, JJ. No, he did not have a mechanical failure. Right after he landed, Hercules observed another chopper fly out to meet the San Pedro. He believes it was another Hind.

Jake's gut tightened further. This was little consolation. The bad news he had anticipated had now taken on another form, one that was potentially worse. *What was it doing at the San Pedro?*

It lowered lifting cables to that large container I told you about earlier and is bringing it this way as we communicate. Got to submerge, JJ. It just turned on a spotlight and is directing it at the water.

Before Jake could ponder this new turn of events, Achilles burst in on his thoughts yet again. *Consider ourselves lucky, JJ.*

What do you mean lucky?

Had Fernando been summoned to lift us out of here, we would have been caught in the Hind's searchlight.

I can't argue that, Achilles. Keep out of sight, but keep me informed. I've got work to do.

Turning back to the man he had rescued, Jake spoke softly. "I think it's only fair that I know your name if I'm going to get you out of here."

"Mort…you can call me Mort," the man stuttered hoarsely.

"Well, Mort, I need you to stay right behind me, so please don't lag if you're set on living. It's gonna get ugly up there."

Mort nodded, his eyes still wide with trepidation.

With a sudden lust for battle building in his veins, Jake ascended the stairs with the Sledgehammer's muzzle pointed upward.

-63-

Malikai Allotey stared open-mouthed, finding it difficult to accept what he was seeing. Where Cardoza's huge aircraft hangar had stood, flames were licking high into the night sky. Straining his eyes against the glowing inferno, he looked in vain for the Chinook troop transport, but the tandem rotor helicopter was also gone. A few moments earlier, he had overheard alarmed shouts coming from some of Cardoza's men scurrying about in confusion, and he had climbed up into the turret of the stronghold's east tower to confirm the cause of their panic. Turning, he addressed the lanky individual standing next to him.

"How did this happen?" he asked, his tone shrill.

Lamont shrugged laconically. "I don't know."

"Give me your radio!" Allotey screeched, his mind churning over the implications of this unanticipated loss. With his mode of transportation now destroyed, he was temporarily stranded. Even worse, the intricate plan so meticulously crafted had fallen apart, and with it, payment for his services. Like the hangar, the money he was to receive had also gone up in flames.

Lamont extended a reluctant arm to offer the radio, and as he did, Allotey snatched it rudely from his hand. Hitting the transmit button, Allotey screamed into it like a woman. "This is Malikai. Do you hear me, Rafael?"

"I have already told him what happened," Lamont said in a manner that suggested both annoyance and contrition.

Allotey ignored him, screaming more fervently this time. "All the drones have been destroyed. Do you hear what I am telling you, Rafael? Where was your security? Maximus is going to be furious."

As Allotey said this, another man climbed into the tower to join him. Captain Alvarez stared pensively in the direction of the blaze. The storm had now passed, and with no downpour to impede the flames, the fire continued to burn fiercely.

"We have come under attack by saboteurs," Alvarez announced gruffly.

Allotey's hysteria suddenly evaporated, and he turned to study the Chilean captain with startled eyes. "Are you certain of this?"

Alvarez leaned out of the turret and pointed down. "Look below you! The moat is only half full."

Allotey looked down. With the storm's cloud cover now gone, the moon had re-emerged directly overhead to reflect a soft glow off the water girthing the fortress. But now the level had dropped by a good fifteen feet.

"Where did the water go?"

"There is only one place for it to go," Alvarez snapped. "The lower level is no doubt flooded. They must have used explosives to breach the moat wall. Did you not feel the blast? It shook the foundation."

Allotey's flummoxed expression abruptly turned. "Are they in the building?"

"I don't know," Alvarez snapped again. "But the destruction of the hangar may not have been their primary objective. It may have been a diversion."

Allotey tensed. "Deploy the men! Station them at all the potential entry points, including the stairs leading to the lower levels."

"I have already done that," Alvarez growled irritably.

At hearing the approach of footsteps echoing dully, Alvarez drew his *corvo* and shouted out a command. "Identify yourself!"

"It is Dr. Ermstine. Don't shoot!"

A few seconds elapsed before Ermstine crowded his paunchy bulk into the turret, his manner grave. "Is what I am hearing true? Have all the drones been destroyed?"

"I am afraid so," Alvarez grumbled.

Ermstine shot a quick glance at all three men. "Where is Rafael?"

"We do not know," Allotey offered dismally. "He does not answer my calls." He was about to say more, but a distinct slapping sound suddenly caught his ears. *Whap, whap, whap!* Poking his head out of the turret in an effort to locate the source, he immediately jerked back as a large object abruptly shot by, the tip of its main rotor blades seemingly inches away from the tower as it passed. A powerful floodlight on the aircraft was aimed down, illuminating the water in the moat. Slung beneath it, he saw a large rectangular box suspended a few feet above the water.

Puzzled by the sight, Allotey leaned out to risk another look. The box had to be at least 30 feet long and 6 feet wide in his estimation.

Lamont raised his weapon, prepared to unleash a salvo at the receding whirlybird, but Alvarez pushed the muzzle down before it could be leveled. "You fool!" the Chilean captain admonished sharply. "Do you not recognize an ally?"

Allotey looked at Alvarez. "Are you able to contact him?"

Alvarez pulled a handheld radio from his belt, adjusting the frequency before he spoke. "This is Captain Alvarez, do you read me Reaper?"

A strained moment of expectation elapsed as all four men listened hopefully for a response. When one did not come back, Alvarez tried another hailing frequency before repeating himself. The enervating din of chopper blades ebbed quickly as the Hind followed the moat around the side of the fortress, continuing to keep its floodlight trained on the water. The Russian's deep voice erupted from the radio just as Alvarez was about to switch channels again. "This is the Reaper."

"We have come under attack," Alvarez blurted savagely. "You are advised to fire upon any movement you detect beyond the walls of this citadel. As must be obvious to you, Cardoza's hangar to the east has been completely destroyed by infiltrators."

A moment of silence ensued before Zinova responded gruffly. "Let me speak to Cardoza."

"He is currently unreachable," Alvarez replied hotly. "The moat wall has been breached by explosives, and it is possible he may have been caught in the flood when it filled the lower level."

"My contract is with Cardoza, not his underlings, and it does not involve keeping this facility secure."

"Then why are you flying reconnaissance around our perimeter?" Alvarez asked in bewilderment.

"Cardoza requisitioned me to move a shark from his trawler to the moat, which I have now done. Since the task is complete, my services here are now finished."

At hearing this, Allotey's face turned puce. He was beside himself with rage. "I will speak to him," he hissed. "Give me your radio."

Pompously he yelled into the speaker, attempting to take charge of the situation. "This is Malikai Allotey, Special Envoy of the United Nations. As a ranking official within this world conclave, I am empowered to commission the services of military contractors whenever circumstances dictate such a need." Although he knew this was not true, he was desperate enough to advance this absurd prevarication. Adjusting his tone to one of benevolence, he threw in a bonus. "Name your fee and I will consider it."

When the Reaper did not immediately answer, Allotey's patience exploded. "Just name your fee," he shouted shrilly, "and I will see that you get paid."

"Twenty million in Euros, and all of it up front," Zinova's disembodied voice came back.

Allotey's jaw dropped. "That is preposterous," he wailed.

"No more preposterous than the claim you just made about your empowerment," Zinova grunted. "Do you think I am an imbecile? I have dealt with UN emissaries before and know they hold no such power."

The sound of the Hind suddenly grew louder, and Allotey saw that it had returned to hover eerily before him, presenting a broadside view with its floodlight now turned off. He glanced below, noticing that the large box it had previously carried was now absent. The Hind's starboard cabin door was open and he could see several men looking back at him, their weapons aimed in his direction. With slowly widening eyes he stared apprehensively as the chopper pivoted around to face him head on. In the moonlight he could vaguely distinguish someone in the chin bubble idly working the controls. Sitting further back behind a canopy was the pilot, who he presumed to be Zinova. It was then he realized he was looking into a twin set of gun barrels protruding from a pod situated under the chin bubble.

Fearing for his life, Allotey thought quickly. "Alright, alright, I have something better to offer you."

"And what might that be," Zinova said, his tone chaffing and sardonic.

"Gold!" Allotey let the word hang for one extended moment to wet the Reaper's appetite. "I can get you tons of it, far more than twenty million in Euros," he rambled on hurriedly.

"You have it with you?"

"Unfortunately no, but I can tell you where you can find it."

"Where?" As Zinova asked the question, the aircraft's floodlight came back on, its powerful beam blinding him.

Allotey threw a hand up to shield his eyes. "It is stored in the floating city of Aquaria," he squealed.

The Reaper let out a harsh laugh. "What good does that do me?" He laughed again. "You make it sound as though I will be able to just walk in there and help myself."

"That is exactly what I am saying," Allotey pleaded quickly. "At this moment the UN is mobilizing a task force to take over the city. As its ranking representative in the Caribbean, all authority concerning Aquaria's temporary governance will revert to me once the facility is secured. I will have full command in taking inventory of its assets, including the stockpiles of precious metals."

The Hind continued to hover ominously as though the chopper itself were mulling the proposal. Zinova looked on, studying the faces in the castle turret and considering the sincerity of the offer. Allotey and the other men averted their eyes from the floodlight's intense glare to avoid burning their retinas. Aquaria, he knew, was a thriving enterprise, and based on that alone there was no reason not to believe Allotey's claim. If tons of gold actually existed there, then he wanted a share of it. Though he hadn't been able to substantiate it as yet, all his instincts told him he had lost both Hinds on the operation Cardoza had hired him to perform, causing him to severely chastise himself endlessly. He had stupidly let his own airship get hijacked simply because he had drastically underestimated Javolyn, but he wouldn't let that happen again. And though he had tried, he had been unable to contact Badger, making him conclude that the other Hind was also gone.

As the Reaper thought about these things, he pondered these lost assets, knowing he had to replace them as quickly as possible. If word ever got out that he had suffered a failed mission, his reputation was certain to crash and burn. The demand for his services would diminish rapidly, not to mention the fees clients were willing to pay. Men of Spetsnaz caliber were hard to replace, and Hinds even harder. Hinds were incredibly expensive on the black market and he would need a ton of money to pay for them.

"What do you want of me?" Zinova found himself asking.

"I want you to get us out of here," Allotey shrieked.

"I only have room for three more people aboard this bird, and I see four of you."

Allotey shot a glance at Lamont. "Then one of us will stay," he blurted. "Can you pick us up from the topmost battlements?"

Zinova opened his mouth to speak, but a flash of light out of the corner of his eye drew his attention to what lay beyond his port window. With the storm now gone, moonlight shed sufficient light on the ocean to give him an unobstructed view of the bay, and he clearly saw the entire stern of the *Southern Star* rise up a few feet before falling back into a foaming sea. A rapid succession of several more flashes ensued at scattered locations on the water, and Zinova glimpsed the rear section of Cardoza's super yacht, *Usurpar*, get consumed in a flaring fireball. Another explosion enveloped the stern of the *Northern Comet* a split second before another flash erupted amidships of the *San Pedro*. The tugboat that had carried supplies ashore was the last to elicit this dazzling display, with the entire vessel spewing flaming parts in all directions. Within seconds, all the vessels began to flounder and sink, and even at his present distance from the disasters he could see men leaping into the sea to escape the drowning ships.

Zinova's radio suddenly resounded with Allotey's panicky voice again. The tone was pleading. "Do you hear me? We will wait for you on the battlements. I will make you a rich man."

The Reaper brought his eyes back to the men in the turret. Judging from the swath of destruction, he knew the attacking force had to be sizable. This could not possibly be the work of a small force of men. In that moment he made a decision.

"Three of you is all I will take," Zinova grunted. "But if you are lying to me about the gold, my men will drop each of you into the ocean from ten thousand feet." Pulling lightly on the Hind's collective lever, he put a slight amount of additional pitch in the main rotor blades. As the aircraft began to rise, he spoke quickly into the intercom. "We are going to evacuate a party of three on the battlements above," he instructed the crew in the language of his homeland. "Stay alert! This facility has come under attack, so be prepared to fend off infiltrators."

*   *   *   *

-64-

Jake treaded his way lightly on the stone steps, his senses on full alert. With only a half-spiral to go, he stopped and whispered to the man behind him. "Stick to me like glue!" he ordered gently.

Rising up the remaining distance, he poked his head above the landing. Three men, two of them wearing United Nations blue helmets, were just taking up positions to monitor the immediate area, their heads swiveling back and forth nervously. He surmised the man lacking UN garb to be one of Cardoza's goons. Ducking down quickly, he activated his Portable Holographic Projector, sliding it over the lip of the top landing and off to one side so that it would not be directly between him and his adversaries. He was unsure of what to expect, but he nevertheless had to give it a try. Based on what Phillipe had told him just before leaving the Southern Star, the UN troops may have found a way to counter the effects of the dolphin art using drugs. Phillipe had seen the blue helmeted captain lift a small convex cap strapped to his thigh and slap down hard on a tiny nodule the cap had protected. The captain had done this just prior to activating Option 2 on the Masker he had taken from Kalid and had remained unaffected by the hologram while his men had fallen violently ill. The captain had made reference to a drug, berating his men for not taking it. Upon learning of this, Jake had immediately asked Achilles for a visual accounting of the event. Achilles had then conjured images of what Perseus had witnessed through Phillipe's eyes, projecting them into Jake's mind as though Jake were viewing a movie, and he was not surprised to see the pockmarked face of Captain Francisco Alvarez leering back at him. The tiny nodule Phillipe had described was in full view, making him conclude that it was a tiny syringe, and he knew that Alvarez had injected himself with something.

Mat had also alerted Jake to the hologram's possible ineffectiveness against UN troops during his last conversation with him. Mat had related Kalid's description of what had taken place prior to his wounding. Kalid had said that the hologram had at first worked and then it didn't.

With these things weighing heavily on his mind, Jake stood fast, waiting for something to happen. His concerns were partially allayed by a loud howl of pain, and he poked his head up a second time to glimpse a man writhing on the floor, his body jerking like a jackhammer. The man was not one of the UN mercenaries, and he could plainly see that the blue helmets were alternating confused gazes between the stricken man and the hologram, their faces harboring scowls. Strapped to the right thigh of each commando was a small convex cap similar to the one Alvarez had worn. One other conspicuous item Jake had not noticed before was the sheathed *corvo* the mercenaries carried, and he immediately knew these men were members of Alvarez's team.

Taking full advantage of the situation, Jake sprang up and let loose with the Sledgehammer, squeezing off two quick shots. The frag-12 rounds caught their intended targets, exploding on impact and blowing gaping holes through the Kevlar body armor protecting the chest of each commando. Both men went down, killed instantly.

Jake scooped up the PHP and turned it off, avoiding eye contact with the light show as he did so. Pocketing the device, he glanced back at Mort to see how he had reacted to the display. The fear Mort had manifested a moment earlier was now gone, replaced by a faraway look of serenity and contentment.

Turning, Jake noticed the Cardoza goon had stopped twitching and was trying to stand. Taking a few quick steps, Jake unleashed a vicious kick that caught him on the side of the head. The man went down again and lay quiet.

Moving back to Mort, Jake took him by the shoulders and shook him hard. "Stay alert!" he ordered. "Better that you're scared than languid."

With UN troops supposedly immune to the dolphin hologram, he wondered if the PHP was worth using any longer. He had no time to consider culling out possible good guys, for to do so would surely get him killed. In light of the present situation, his only option was to assume every man he came upon deserved what he was going to dish out.

Pulling Mort along with him, Jake rounded a bend and nearly ran into three more blue helmeted commandos, catching them by surprise. At close to point-blank range he fired from the hip. Two of the commandos were thrown back violently as the rounds tore through their body armor and slammed them brutally against a wall. The third man dropped to a knee and nearly got off a shot, but Jake was quicker and fired again. The frag-12 caught him full in the face, disintegrating his head. In a weird knee-jerk reaction, the Uzi he had been holding flew backwards to go clattering across the stone floor.

Jake turned to study Mort again, happy to see the serenity supplanted by fright once again. He knew fear could sometimes be a good thing when a person's life was on the line. Fear got the adrenaline flowing. Fear made an individual fight harder.

Continuing on at a trot, Jake was careful to avoid the smear of brain tissue, blood and shards of bone that littered the floor before him. Mort was not as careful, and his feet nearly slipped out from under him as he followed in Jake's wake. In an effort to keep from falling, he managed to get a hand on Jake's shoulder, holding on for support.

"Watch your step!" Jake chided, holding his voice to a whisper. Clearing the mess, he stopped and removed Mort's hand. If they were going to survive, it was critical his body and limbs remained unimpeded. "You know how to use a firearm, Mort?"

Mort shook his head nervously.

"Well you're about to learn," Jake said, continuing to monitor the passageway before him. Reaching down, he snatched up the Uzi dropped by the commando he had beheaded. Removing the clip, he checked to see if was topped off with bullets. Satisfied, he replaced the clip and chambered a round, making sure the weapon's safety switch was on before he handed it over to Mort.

Mort looked terrified, holding the Uzi as though the metal comprising it was toxic to the touch. "How do I operate it?" he asked timidly.

"It's really simple. Just point it at your target and pull the trigger," Jake instructed soothingly, doing his best to quell Mort's unease. "Just be mindful where you aim it, and above all, don't point it in my direction. Can I count on you, Mort?"

When Mort nodded numbly, Jake put the weapon's safety in firing mode. Though Mort's inexperience with a firearm was a potential liability to both of them, some deep inexplicable instinct told him it was the right thing to do under the present circumstances.

"Just remember to keep your finger off the trigger until you have a target to shoot at," Jake said. "You ready, Mort?"

Mort took a deep breath, letting it out slowly before nodding vigorously. "I'm ready," he finally acknowledged.

Jake turned and resumed moving down the corridor again. Up ahead he saw another ninety-degree bend. "You know where this passageway leads, Mort?" he whispered over his shoulder.

"There's an open courtyard just beyond the turn," Mort answered back, his tone seemingly calmer now.

Jake nodded, reaching for something in his utility belt. He only carried one baseball grenade and hoped it would be enough. Pulling the pin, he held down the spoon, advancing cautiously toward the bend. Hugging the wall, he risked a peek around the inside corner. He was immediately met by a hail of bullets. Withdrawing his head and ducking down low, he released the spoon on the grenade, counting off two seconds before tossing it into the courtyard beyond. Contained by stone walls on each side, the detonation was loud and piercing as it sent out shrapnel in all directions.

Feeling wildly indestructible and lightheaded, Jake sprang out into the open. A few low-watt incandescent lights spaced at intervals along the courtyard's outer perimeter provided just enough illumination for Jake to see, and with reckless abandon he let loose with the Sledgehammer, whipping the muzzle around to take out the first two men he came upon. Both were blue-helmeted commandos, already bloodied and staggering from the grenade. The frag-12 rounds exploded against their Kevlar chest protectors and hurled their bodies backwards as if tugged by some mighty hand from behind. Three other blue helmets were already down, two of them unmoving and seemingly mortally wounded. One of them, however, was trying to rise to his feet, dazed and bleeding profusely from shrapnel that had peppered his neck. Taking no chances, Jake pumped off another round, catching the commando in the side and nearly cutting him in half.

Totally consumed by the warrior's lust for battle, Jake took in the courtyard at a glance, looking for other adversaries. From discussions with Belachek, he knew it wasn't so much a courtyard but an area between the inner and outer defensive walls. Based on Belachek's description, he knew the inner wall was actually the façade of the keep, the main living quarters situated in the center of the stronghold.

Jake tensed at the sound of drumming, a low pitched cadence that grew quickly and echoed out into the open area where he now stood. Looking for the source, his eyes were drawn to an arched entrance on the inner wall side, and he recognized the beat of running footsteps in a tunnel. Bolting headlong from the entrance like horses leaving a starting gate, three of Cardoza's thugs were suddenly before him. Startled by Jake's presence, the lead thug skidded to a halt and attempted to raise his weapon, but before he could do so his accomplices flew into him from behind, knocking him off balance. In rapid succession, all three were flung back as the Sledgehammer's explosive rounds found their mark.

Another sight grabbed Jake's attention, one Belachek had briefed him on. It was the Bengal tiger within a large cage situated within a recessed section of inner wall off to his left. He had once seen a rendering of Cardoza's pet carnivore on the ceiling of the mystical chamber behind the cove's majestic waterfall, but now he was actually seeing it with his own eyes. The beast was pacing back and forth, barring its fangs and roaring ferociously, maddened by the scent of blood and carnage filling the courtyard. Years earlier Destiny had claimed the rendering had originally portrayed Jake being mauled by the tiger, but by the time Jake had viewed it, the rendering had changed to show Walter McPherson as the mauling victim.

The clatter of an Uzi abruptly pulled Jake from this momentary reflection, and he spun around in reaction to the sound. Mort had fired his weapon, and to Jake's amazement he saw another blue helmeted commando stagger back as several rounds collided against his body armor.

DOLPHIN RIDERS

Jake followed up with a round of his own, and the commando was knocked off his feet as though tackled by an NFL linebacker.

Jake looked at Mort with newfound respect, surprised that the man had held up under such stressful duress. If not for Mort's alertness, the Chilean mercenary would have surely got the drop on him. "Nice job, Mort!" Jake praised as he scanned the courtyard again. "Any suggestions which way we go from here?"

Mort pointed toward the courtyard's far end. "That way!"

A familiar sound suddenly impinged on Jake's awareness, escalating quickly from a soft susurration to a discordant din. Glancing up, he glimpsed a spotlight playing back and forth on the ramparts above. The spotlight's beam abruptly steadied, and Jake suddenly found himself caught in its blinding glare.

"Get back!" he shouted, grabbing Mort forcefully by the arm and hauling him roughly out of the light. No sooner had he done that, sparks flew up from the stone pavement as a shower of 7.62 millimeter rounds suddenly rained down. Bullets seemed to be ricocheting everywhere as Jake raced for the entrance on the inner wall side, and in less than two seconds he reached the safety of the nearest passageway. Dragging Mort with him, he moved well back from the entrance.

A storm of rounds continued to carom and hammer the opening, sending splinters of stone and fragmented bullets zinging and humming down the passageway but miraculously missing both men. With them no longer visible to the gunner, the sound of heavy machine guns immediately cut out, upon which Jake ran back to the entrance to risk a peak. For one brief moment the spotlight moved searchingly about the courtyard before infringing on the battlements higher up. Jake watched as the silhouette of the Hind shifted beyond his line of sight, the cacophonous din of its powerful engines and rotor blades fading to a dull whine as the stone battlements reflected the sound away.

Prepared to venture back out into the courtyard again, Jake pulled up short as movement caught his eye. The tiger had gotten free of its cage and was now roaming the courtyard. Jake watched as it moved silently among the dead men, sniffing the sprawled bodies before singling one out. Hunkering down on all fours, it began to feast.

Mort moved up behind Jake to crane his head over Jake's shoulder. "This is not good," he said dismally. "That animal's a killer. How do you suppose it got loose?"

"Some of those rounds must have hit the locking bolt on the cage," Jake offered, "but we can't stay here. Stay behind me and don't make any sudden moves." Mort did not protest or cower in fear as Jake ventured beyond the entrance and crept noiselessly along the inner wall.

Sensing the men, the tiger stopped its gnawing and went rigid. Lifting its head, it locked fierce yellow orbs on Jake, a low throaty growl rumbling forth from behind barred, bloodied teeth.

One of the things Jake had heard about big predatory cats was that you didn't look them directly in the eyes, otherwise you immediately invited attack since the cat would take it as a challenge. But something deep down made Jake do just that, something he could not explain. Keeping his Sledgehammer trained on the beast, Jake moved slowly along the wall with Mort sticking to him like glue. Unless it attacked, he had no reason to kill the beast.

The Bengal remained tense, its head swiveling slowly as it fixated on both men sidling past, the low growl continuing to rumble unabated from its throat, and for one fleeting moment Jake expected it to spring. But the tiger suddenly relaxed, dropping its fierce gaze from Jake and resuming its feeding.

Jake blew out a sigh of relief and picked up the pace, turning only once to look back at the cat, which was now ignoring him and feasting contentedly. Based on Belachek's rough sketch of the place, Jake assumed they were heading toward the portcullis. If they were going to escape this place, the drawbridge needed to be in the down position.

Jake opened up a mental link to his bond mate. *What's your status, Achilles?*

We're still avoiding detection, JJ, the dolphin shot back, *but it's doubtful Franklin can continue holding his breath each time I submerge. His condition is fragile. On the bright side, all of Cardoza's vessels have been sunk.*

Jake projected another thought. *Is the drawbridge still up?*

Unfortunately, yes, JJ. Stuck in this moat, Destiny and I have no way of helping you.

Jake continued following the inner wall, reaching where it turned ninety degrees. Taking a quick peak around the corner, he saw that the area beyond was deserted.

Mort grabbed his shoulder, speaking softly. As though he had heard Jake's interchange with Achilles, he said, "We don't need the drawbridge to get out of here."

Jake's expression turned hopeful. "Another way?"

"Yes, about fifty paces ahead there's a doorway a short distance from the gatehouse. It gives access to a portal that opens to the moat."

You hear that, Achilles?

Yes, JJ. I noticed a wooden hatch cover to the south side of the drawbridge just before Fernando dropped me in the moat.

Hold tight, Achilles, I'm going to make a try for it.

Jake turned to Mort. "I hope you're good at sprinting, Mort, because I need you to run like the wind." Having said that, Jake leapt past the corner and raced diagonally for the opposite wall, running in the direction of the gatehouse. Scanning the corridor before him, he prepared to dodge more bullets. In moments he reached the door Mort had described without taking any fire. Finding this odd, he did a quick mental count. So far he had taken out eleven commandos and four of Cardoza's thugs, with one enormous shark dispatching Cardoza and three more of his goons. Altogether, that added up to nineteen men. Perhaps that accounted for most, if not all, the combatants he would face.

The actual number is twenty-one, Achilles corrected, reading his thoughts again.

You mean there were two others? Jake shot back.

Yes, Destiny says she zapped two more of Cardoza's boys just before we reached her, but they either drowned or became shark chow.

Good to know, Jake replied. *So I take it Destiny's getting back to her old self.*

Seems that way.

We better cut the chatter, Achilles. More bad guys might be lurking about. Even though the exchange had occurred in less time than it took to blink, Jake knew a distraction of this sort was potentially dangerous.

With Mort right behind him, Jake examined the door, judging it to open inwardly. Reaching for the door handle, he pushed. The door appeared to be made of solid oak planks and would not budge. "Move back!" he yelled at Mort, aligning the barrel of the Sledgehammer with the door's locking mechanism and stepping away. Just before squeezing the trigger, he caught movement out of the corner of his eye. An assailant poked his head around the side of the gatehouse wall, bringing a weapon to bear on him. Jake spun and fired before the man could get off a shot. The round went high, barely missing the assailant and sending a shower of stone fragments to explode from the wall above his jutting head. For emphasis, Jake let loose another shot as the man ducked back out of sight, sending more stone shards flying.

Turning, Jake pumped off another shot, this time disintegrating the door handle and blowing a jagged hole through the heavy oaken plank supporting the lock. The impact swung the door inward and Jake hastened the movement by throwing a shoulder against the wood. "Go!" he yelled, looking back at Mort and stepping aside.

As Mort sprang through the opening, Jake pivoted to squeeze off another shot. The frag-12 detonated with a muffled sound, this time meeting flesh and bone as it caught the same assailant full in the face as he foolishly leaned out again from his place of cover. Leaping through the doorway, Jake grabbed the edge of the door and slammed it closed. Someone had forgotten to turn off a single low-watt light bulb that lit the room beyond, and he grabbed the first object he saw. It was a large table with piles of paper littering its top. Sweeping the paper off it, he discovered it was quite heavy. The table was topped with a slab of granite and had a cast iron frame.

"Give me a hand!" Jake yelled, glancing briefly at Mort. Grunting laboriously, both men managed to slide the table up against the door. Lying nearby was a stack of small crates, and without hesitation Jake lifted the topmost one, placing it on the table to block off the hole in the door. In rapid succession he stacked a few more crates on the table, noticing the strain they put on his back in moving them.

"Why was Cardoza holding you prisoner?" Jake grunted, hefting another box.

Mort was breathing hard from the exertion, but managed to speak in gasping, halting sentences. "I was a hostage. He was using me as leverage so as to keep my twin brother working for an associate of his, a man of incredible wealth and affluence. We're scientists. We used to work for the U.S. Department of Energy at Los Alamos. We-"

Mort suddenly stopped moving boxes, laboring for breath.

"Take a rest, Mort," Jake said, moving one last box into place. "You were about to say?"

"We retired from government service five years ago to go into business for ourselves. We lent assistance to Uncle Sam as private contractors. My brother specialized in electronics and computers, I in laser science. After Cardoza kidnapped me he somehow learned about our breakthrough."

"What kind of breakthrough?" Jake prodded encouragingly.

"Percy and I were on the threshold of a new idea that would revolutionize laser weaponry. Up to now the most powerful laser developed only puts out thirty kilowatts of energy. Our design, however, could unleash ten times that amount. At least in theory. Without me, Percy could not possibly construct such a weapon. It was not his area of expertise. But together we could. Cardoza wanted the design. When I refused to give it to him he threatened to kill me."

"An interesting story," Jake said.

"There's more to the story than just that," Mort huffed. "My brother and I managed to compile a mountain of incriminating evidence against Cardoza's associate, a man who heads a cabal conspiring to control the world. The reach of this man is enormous. He has tentacles embedded covertly in all the major governments across the globe. Cardoza is subservient to this man, who they call the *Sublimis*."

Jake frowned with puzzlement. "*Sublimis?*"

"The *Sublimis* is the head of the snake that controls the organization. He is at the top of the pyramid of power. The cabal has existed for generations, with the title being passed down from father to son through the ages, and now they have become more powerful than ever. The *Sublimis* knows we have acquired evidence against him and all his associates, and Cardoza has been assigned the task of retrieving it."

"So have you given it him?"

"No. My brother has it stored in a place they'll never think to look, one you might say is right under their noses."

"That is quite an extraordinary story," Jake muttered, his attention preoccupied with the objects now bracing the door.

Satisfied for the moment, he eyed the room. It was a moderately-sized chamber, obviously used for storage. While stacks of boxes, crates and various other items cluttered the walls, one object grabbed his immediate attention. A long wooden shaft the size of a telephone pole dominated the room's center, and attached to its tip was a pulley. The pole was aligned with the hatch that was supposed to be their way out. The pole sat on rollers in a long guide embedded solidly in the floor. A sturdy T-bar situated at its aft end rose up to the height of a man's waist, and he immediately ascertained its purpose. With a man on each side of the pole pushing against the T-bar, the pole could be slid forward or moved back. From what Jake could see, the pole could be extended through the hatch and out over the moat, making him wonder what it was used for, though it reminded him of a buccaneer's cannon waiting to be fired once its muzzle portal was opened.

"You're looking at Cardoza's latest form of amusement," Mort said, correctly reading Jake's curious expression. "He lowers men from it to feed the sharks. I was to be their next meal."

"Well you don't have to worry about Cardoza anymore. One of his sharks had him for dinner," Jake murmured absently, continuing to study the contraption. Moving to the hatch cover, he saw it was hinged at the top and had a heavy sliding bolt that locked it down. It could be raised by using a ratchet pulley that connected to a chain attached to its lower edge.

Jake slid back the locking bolt and grabbed the chain, but stopped short to survey the room again, curious to know what was stored here. His eyes fell upon a large cluster of wooden boxes stacked up against a side wall, all labelled with the word *AZUCAR*.

Achilles immediately translated, sensing Jake's puzzlement. *The word means sugar in Spanish.*

Jake sent back an assessment. *An army couldn't eat that much sugar in a year.* Reaching for a crowbar that lay on the floor next to one of the stacks, he pried off the cover of the topmost box. Probing around momentarily, a smile overtook his features. "Now look what we've got here," he announced blithely.

Mort moved closer to peer inside the box. "What?"

Jake pulled out a small bricklike object. "TNT!" he mumbled softly. He counted thirty-three similar boxes. "There's probably enough here to blow half this place to dust."

Jake swept the room searchingly again, spotting a crimper sitting atop an adjacent stack several feet away. Knowing what such a tool was used for, he scrutinized the small cardboard box that sat next to it. His smile grew larger when he looked inside the box. "Just what the doctor ordered," he remarked jubilantly, "blasting caps and fuse." Removing a three-foot length of coiled fuse, he inserted one end into a blasting cap and secured it with the crimper. Pushing the cap into the small brick of TNT, he placed the brick back in the box he had taken it from. The box held a total of forty bricks, each brick weighing one pound.

"You never told me your name," Mort said, watching the procedure intently.

Jake removed his K-bar from its sheath and sliced through the cord, shortening its length by a foot. "My friends call me Jay Jay."

"Thanks for saving my hide," Mort said.

Jake glanced up with a sober expression. "I'd hold off on the thanks for the time being if I were you. We're not out of the woods yet." Pulling a tiny butane lighter from a pouch on his utility belt, he flicked it several times to test the flame. On the third flick, the flame caught and held steady. "Do us a favor, Mort, and open the hatch."

Mort placed the Uzi down on the floor next to the hatch and grabbed the vertical section of chain attached to the ratchet pulley. Pulling it down, he forced the hatch cover to swing into the room and pivot toward the ceiling.

Jake moved to the opening and poked his head out, seeing that the drawbridge was still up. Withdrawing his head, he stepped back to light the fuse. "I suggest you make the plunge, Mort," he said calmly.

The fear Mort had previously shown was back with a vengeance, and he stood fast on the lip of the hatch opening, uneager to jump. "What about the sharks?"

"They're going to be the least of your worries if you don't get moving."

"I should tell you I have a problem with heights," Mort stammered nervously as he looked down at the water. With the surface of the moat considerably lower, the drop would be close to thirty feet.

A heavy pounding suddenly reverberated against the door to the chamber. Jake glanced behind him to see the table bracing it move back several inches. Abruptly, he snuffed out the lighter and picked up the Sledgehammer. Firing back to back rounds into the door below the level of the table, he was careful to miss the heavy crates he had placed on top of it. God only knew what was in them, and the last thing he needed was to set off an explosion. The pounding abruptly stopped as the rounds blew open the door's lower portion, and a muffled scream followed.

"Give me your weapon, Mort!" Jake commanded sternly as he strapped the Sledgehammer over a shoulder.

Mort turned, reaching down to retrieve the Uzi where he had left it, glad to step back from the precipice. Jake spoke quickly as Mort rose back up and handed him the weapon. "Sorry, Mort, but out you go." Mort let out a startled cry as Jake gave him a powerful shove, and he fell backwards through the opening, dropping from sight.

Jake spun around as more pounding resumed, and he saw the table begin to inch back again. Based on what was stored in the room, he had to assume they wouldn't dare fire their weapons through the door. Taking full advantage of this, he took careful aim with the Uzi and fired. The clip emptied in seconds, sending a barrage of rounds streaming through the jagged holes in the door's lowest section and invoking additional screams.

A sudden vision flashed before Jake's eyes, and he saw two of Cardoza's goons go down on the opposite side of the door, their shins bloodied. Another goon lay off to one side, his left leg blown off at the knee where a frag-12 had caught him a moment earlier. Four more thugs scurried in quickly to drag the first two men out of the way as four blue helmets moved in to place a heavy steel plate against what remained of the lowest section of door. With the shield in position, they picked up a heavy length of pipe that was being used as a battering ram.

The vision blinked out just as the pounding resumed, and Jake saw the door begin to lurch inward inch by inch with each powerful strike. Tossing the Uzi aside, he grabbed the lighter, flicking it savagely to ignite a flame. Though it sparked, it would not light this time. Stubbornly he kept at it, cursing as he ran his thumb over the roller again and again. Almost ready to give up, a flame suddenly caught on the wicker and held, and without hesitation he applied it to the fuse. Satisfied that the fuse was silently burning, he placed two more boxes in front of it. Seeing that it was now effectively hidden, he turned and dove through the hatch. From his stint in the Seals, he was quite knowledgeable on the use of explosives, and based on the length of fuse he had cut, he knew he had roughly two minutes to get away from the devastating blast that would be forthcoming.

Spinning in midair like a cat, Jake adjusted his body posture to meet the water feet first. On the way down he caught a fleeting image of the drawbridge, suddenly aware that it was coming down. Driven deep by the force of his plunge, he felt Achilles' powerful forelimbs latch onto him. A heavy glare beamed down into the water, giving him a shadowy glimpse of the surrounding murk.

Where are the others? Jake asked Achilles, surprised at not seeing any forms clinging to his back.

Franklin and Mort are a safe distance away where I left them standing in waist-deep water. I discovered a narrow ledge below the surface that juts out from the fortress.

What about Destiny? Jake projected the query like a shotgun blast.

Achilles was suddenly unresponsive, and before Jake could press him again, the surrounding water was abruptly alive with a cascade of small projectiles zipping by like wind-driven hailstones. A muted though familiar buzz reached Jake's ears an instant later, and he immediately knew the cause of the sound. He didn't bother to look up. The image was sharp and distinct in his mind's eye, and he saw the Hind hovering ominously above the moat as though he were viewing it from high up.

Without hesitation, Achilles dove deeper to escape the fusillade, bolting along the canal's rocky bottom at full speed. *Where's Destiny?* Jake demanded as he was pulled along. Already he sensed they were well beyond the glaring light and the firestorm of rounds.

She's with Esmerelda, Achilles finally answered.

You're not making sense, Jake fired back.

You'll understand soon enough, was all Achilles would offer.

-65-

Bringing the Hind to a hover, Zinova played the spotlight over the water looking for the man he had seen leap from the fortress. His gunner had riddled the water in the exact spot where the man had landed, yet he could not detect any sign of blood on the surface. Pivoting the chopper around, he cast the light in the opposite direction. A voice suddenly came over the intercom. "One of our passengers is becoming troublesome," his second in command grumbled in annoyance.

"Which one?" Zinova asked, continuing to scan the water.

"The UN emissary. He demands we leave at once."

Zinova looked down the length of the canal, hungering for at least one kill to appease his rage. His involvement with Cardoza had cost him far too much.

"Perhaps we should toss him into the moat," Drakov appealed.

"Let him be!" Zinova muttered. He would need Allotey to recoup his losses. Continuing to hover, he adjusted the spotlight to illuminate the drawbridge. It was now fully lowered, and under the light he noted seven blue helmeted commandos taking positions along each side of the bridge, their weapons pointed down at the water. As far as he could tell, they also sought the man who had leapt from the fortress.

With a deft touch of the cyclic and a little pressure on the left foot pedal, Zinova faced the Hind away from the drawbridge and moved slowly along the moat, keeping the spotlight aimed down at the water. "Everyone is to stay alert!" he commanded his crew brusquely. "I want these infiltrators dead."

Under the searchlight's intense glare, nothing escaped his scrutiny as he brought the aircraft down the length of the moat along the west side of the castle. Something suddenly caught his attention along the fringe of the beam, and he immediately refocused the light as he brought the aircraft to a hover again. He could have sworn he saw the head of a man duck under the water immediately adjacent to the castle wall.

"Boris, fire your guns in the center of the beam!" he ordered his gunner.

The water was chopped into a frothing maelstrom as Boris opened up with the twin machineguns, some of the rounds catching the stone above the waterline and emitting a shower of sparks.

Boris kept the barrage going for several seconds before letting up on the trigger. "If anyone was down there, I'm sure I got him," Boris replied smugly.

"If you got him, the water should be red with his blood," Zinova growled dubiously.

"Then the sharks will get him," Boris riposted evenly, noting the large fin suddenly coming to the surface along the water's edge.

Zinova continued to hover, deciding which way to go as he eyed the fin. It occurred to him the shark below him might very well be agitated by something in the water. Perhaps it was on the scent of human prey as Boris contended. The fin jutting above the surface suddenly charged ahead, moving in the direction of the drawbridge. Opting to follow it, he began to swing the chopper around. Halfway through the turn, the Hind's windshield rattled as though pelted by a storm of pebbles.

"We're taking fire!" Boris yelled.

From the impacts, Zinova knew they were being assailed by small arms fire. Looking for the source, he spotted duel muzzle flashes at 3 o'clock. Leaning the aircraft over, he adjusted the spotlight to illuminate a cluster of small trees fronting a jumble of large boulders 15 meters beyond the moat's edge, but before he could angle the chopper into firing position, the flashes were gone. Boris, however, was not to be denied. Through his seat, Zinova felt the vibration of the Hind's twin 30s opening up.

Bringing the chopper closer to the target, Zinova eyed the area as Boris let up on the guns. The possibility of taking additional hits did not concern him. He knew the Hind was invulnerable to small arms fire. "I don't see anything," he grumbled in a soft hiss, his eyes playing back and forth over the boulders. Slowly, he brought the Hind around to circumvent the trees and rocks, meticulously searching the ground for signs of assailants.

"There has to be at least two of them down there," Boris stated bluntly. "I distinctly saw two muzzle flashes."

"These infiltrators are like phantoms," Zinova grunted in a tone caustic and guttural. "No sooner do we catch sight of them, they disappear." Frustrated, he brought the Hind to the outer rim of the moat, slowly working the light over the ground.

-66-

Feeling it safe to do so, Destiny rose to the surface on the north side of the drawbridge and glanced behind her. Seconds earlier the Hind had passed overhead, sweeping the water with its powerful spotlight before flaring into a hover. Treading water, she saw the drawbridge begin to come down just as Jake leapt clear of the fortress. Turning, she looked in the opposite direction. Under the moon's pervading glow, she discerned the huge fin knifing the surface and bearing straight at her. Try as she might, she found she was not able to control or influence the creature's behavior in any way. This one was different, certainly not like the animal that had killed Cardoza. Nevertheless, she was not afraid as the great fish bore down on her. The white shark just recently dropped in the moat was enormous, a killing machine nearly thirty feet in length. Yet she sensed a familiar presence wafting from it that seemed to reach into her very thoughts. The presence had substance, and it suddenly resonated with astounding clarity.

This is the same creature that took me long ago, Esmerelda said, *but now my spirit controls it rather than Erzulie.*

You know what we must do, Destiny chimed.

Yes, my child, though it will not be easy. The water may not be deep enough.

All is possible if we believe strongly enough, Destiny reminded her, grabbing hold of the fin and straddling the shark's broad back.

Yes, all is possible, Esmerelda maintained, forcing the creature as deep as the water would allow.

-67-

Jake realized just how close he had come to losing Franklin and Mort, and strangely enough it was the shark that had killed Cardoza that saved them. Using his bio-sonar, Achilles had sensed the approach of the creature as it homed in on the ledge supporting the two men.

You sure it's the same shark? Jake queried as he rode his bond mate's back.

Without a doubt, and apparently she's still hungry, Achilles replied, grasping each man firmly under an armpit as he bolted through the murk. He had snatched them away before the shark reached them, but now the strain of carrying three men while eluding the pursuing beast was taxing even his incredible endurance.

Unfortunately, she's forcing us back where we don't want to be, Achilles added, *and if I don't surface immediately, both Franklin and Mort will drown.*

The fact that the shark was in attack mode perplexed Jake. *Can't Destiny control it like before?*

She says the creature will not respond. Controlling marine creatures does not always work, especially with unpredictable predators like sharks.

How much time do we have? Jake asked, knowing Achilles was like a keen biological clock with an extraordinary sense of time.

Not much, maybe thirty seconds at most. But to make matters worse, Destiny tells me there's commandos on the drawbridge with their weapons aimed at the water. It seems we're effectively hemmed in, I'm afraid, and at this moment I'm out of options. I have to choice but to surface to save Franklin and Mort.

Jake held on tight as Achilles broke the surface and lifted his charges so that their heads were above the water. Both men gasped audibly before inhaling sharply, sucking air into oxygen-deprived lungs. Glancing behind him, Jake espied the Hind further back, its spotlight tenaciously roving the ground along the moat's outer perimeter and moving slowly in his direction. Looking ahead, he saw the commandos spread out along the drawbridge. To make matters worse, he discerned the head of another blue helmet poke out from the portal he and Mort had jumped from.

Grabbing the Sledgehammer strapped to his shoulder, Jake brought the barrel around to bear on the opening above him in one smooth lightning-like motion. The thought that they had run out of luck sprang to the forefront of his mind, and he wondered if things could get any worse than this.

Whatever you do, don't shoot at the commandos on the drawbridge, otherwise you'll risk hitting Destiny, Achilles cautioned.

Unsure what Achilles meant, Jake squeezed the trigger before the man looking down at him could align his own weapon. The possibility of a misfire was allayed as the Sledgehammer abruptly discharged. Built for low recoil, it barely bucked as a frag-12 rocketed from its muzzle to explode against the portal's upper lip. Though the shot missed its intended target, the blue helmet screamed out in pain as shrapnel found its way into unprotected parts of his torso, arms and neck.

Water began kicking up all around Jake as men on the drawbridge began shooting. Jake's next thought was projected like thunder as he sought to escape the enfilade. *Take us under, Achilles!*

Achilles seemed to hesitate, and just as quickly as it started, the enfilade ceased. Jake saw commandos being flung from the drawbridge as a monstrous form barreled into them like a runaway semi. It had leapt up from the water on the opposite side of the bridge with enough momentum to completely traverse the structure. With no guard rails on the bridge to impede it, it plummeted to splash down with crushing force on several of the blue helmets it had sent flying into the water.

Jake stared transfixed for one brief moment, aware that Destiny was astride the huge creature. Glancing behind him, he saw the orientation of the Hind change, the chopper's pilot seemingly cognizant of what had just happened. *Get us out of here, Achilles!* Jake ordered, the thought issuing from his mind like a thunderbolt.

With powerful flicks of his tail, Achilles shot ahead, quickly gathering speed but keeping to the surface this time. He was making for the north side of the drawbridge, attempting to put distance between them and the impending explosion. Riding her strange mount, Destiny was suddenly abreast of Jake. "I'm going to keep the other shark away from you," she yelled. Abruptly she fell back, prepared to protect Achilles' rear as Jake's bond mate sounded, pulling Franklin and Mort along with him.

-68-

Though he was more than a hundred meters away, Zinova had caught sight of the disturbance, seeing additional muzzle flashes coming from the vicinity of the drawbridge. Barely illuminated under the pale glow of a gibbous moon, he had discerned a dark form rise up to snuff out those flashes before falling back into the water. Puzzled, he lowered the Hind's nose, throwing power into the churning rotor blades. Picking up speed rapidly, he followed the moat's outside bank to investigate. Already he could see a few blue-helmeted men floundering feebly in the water.

Hungering for a kill, he scanned the area below, hoping to spot infiltrators. Another flash erupted off his starboard side, this one intense and huge like a star going nova, and had he been looking directly at it he would have been temporarily blinded. Stunned by its sheer magnitude and ferocity, he was jarred violently in his seat as something slammed heavily against the fuselage. This was followed by a fleeting onslaught of lesser impacts against the airframe, and with startling swiftness, the Hind leaned precariously to port, the tip of its main rotor coming dangerously close to the ground. A highly experienced pilot, Zinova reacted quickly, fighting madly to regain control of the aircraft, which was now spinning wildly, blown away from the fortress like a leaf caught in a force-5 hurricane.

Drakov's alarmed voice suddenly blared over the intercom with deafening volume. "We've been hit!"

Furiously working the controls to keep from crashing, Zinova barely managed to arrest the Hind's dizzying spin, slowing the counterclockwise rotation before bringing it to a halt. Still, the chopper continued to lean heavily to port, and he had to compensate by tilting the main rotor to starboard. It was touch and go for several more seconds before he was able to level the sturdy aircraft, and bringing it to a hover, he noticed something didn't feel right.

"Bring us down!" Drakov yelled, his tone uncharacteristically fearful.

Zinova pivoted his head to glance out his port window. A long cylindrical object protruded at an awkward angle from the side of the cabin. Looking to his right, he saw the same thing, though the object didn't extend as far. Without hesitation, he spotted a small patch of ground devoid of vegetation and set the Hind down, facing it toward the fortress. Staring straight ahead, he was astonished to find that he was now several hundred meters from the impregnable stone walls, but even more astonishing were the flames and smoke billowing from the structure. As far as he could tell, a good portion of the structure had been obliterated.

-69-

Having managed to escape the blast, Achilles circumvented the undamaged portion of the fortress, eventually reaching the south side. Discerning a suitable place in the rock levee that defined the moat's outer periphery, he released his charges. Assisted by Jake, Franklin was first to climb up using seams and crevices in the abutted stones as handholds. Mort quickly followed, eager to get beyond the reach of predators.

Ascending to the bank, Jake joined up with both men, cautiously taking in his surroundings. Visibility was obscured. A slight breeze had sprung up carrying tendrils of dense smoke from the explosion. A fire continued to rage in the western sector of the fortress, which now lay in total ruins. Sensing movement off to his right, he pulled the Sledgehammer from his shoulder, prepared to use it.

"Don't shoot!" a voice petitioned breathlessly. Two dark forms abruptly materialized out of the haze as they de-activated their cloakers, and Jake recognized Belachek and Jimenez.

Jake addressed the former Spetsnaz operative. "Any idea where that Hind is?" he asked, taking inventory of the sky above through the pall of smoke.

"We saw it go down somewhere to the west," Belachek said. Both he and Jimenez were breathing heavily, and Jake could tell they had rushed here as fast as their legs would carry them. "We were able to fire upon it to keep my old boss distracted and away from you," Belachek rambled on, "but his Hind may have been damaged by the explosion."

Jake stared back in mild surprise. "How do you know it was Zinova?"

"I saw him come into the hangar before we blew it up. He had seven of his men with him. They left with the third Hind he always keeps in reserve."

"You saw his bird go down?"

"Not actually, but it appeared to be spinning out of control when it disappeared from sight."

Jake let out an imperceptible sigh of relief, suddenly willing to gamble that Belachek's assessment was correct. He had felt the brutal shock wave issuing from the blast, and with the Hind not far behind, he was certain it had to be damaged if not destroyed altogether.

Pulling a small handheld radio from one of the waterproof pouches on his utility belt, he brought it to his lips and spoke softly. "Rogue Dog to Fly Boy, come in!"

Jake had to repeat himself before a reply came back garbled with static. "Fly Boy is at your disposal." An easing of anxiety was apparent in Fernando's voice.

"Achilles awaits you for extraction on the moat's south side," Jake instructed. "I don't know if you noticed it, but be on the alert for another Hind in the immediate vicinity. We think it was damaged and went down, but we can't be sure."

"I'm on my way," Fernando shot back eagerly.

Jake put away the radio, looking down into the moat as a curtain of smoke parted. Moon beams twinkled off a turbulent set of expanding ripples, indicating movement just below the surface. His face remained impassive as he projected a concern to his bond mate. *How's our girl doing, Achilles?*

She's fending that brute off me for the moment. It's a good thing Destiny's shark is bigger than the one chasing me, otherwise I'd be expending far more energy than I am now.

Jake turned to Belachek. "I'd be obliged if you and Jimenez would escort these two gentlemen down to the end of the pier where the submersible is standing by," he said, setting his gaze on Franklin and Mort hovering at his side. "Destiny and I will meet up with you as soon as Achilles is extracted."

Belachek nodded stoically. He seemed to have no problem with Jake calling the shots, but Franklin interceded quickly, laying petitioning eyes on Jake. "I prefer to stay with you, son. I have to know that my daughter is safe."

"No need for that," Jake said. "Once Achilles is pulled from the water, she'll be coming."

Franklin was adamant. "I want to see for myself that she's safe."

Jake was on the verge of objecting, but abruptly caved at seeing the look of resolution on his father-in-law's face. "All right, Dad, he acquiesced."

Belachek stared at Mort quizzically. "Who is this man?" he asked, as if noticing him for the first time.

"His name is Mort, a guy Cardoza had locked away in his underground dungeon before I broke him out," Jake said.

Mort cut in before Jake could say more. "Once we're away from this awful place, I'll explain why I was being held prisoner."

Belachek shrugged nonchalantly, but spoke gregariously. "And I will look forward to hearing about it." Setting his mismatched eyes on Jake again, he posed a question of his own. "Did you get Cardoza?"

Jake smiled soberly, turning to indicate the moat. "Let me just say one of his pets got all choked up over his demise."

Belachek grinned, glad to see the mission had succeeded. Placing a guiding arm over Mort's shoulder, he started to lead Mort away but stopped short. Turning, he looked back at Jake. "Stay safe, my friend," he uttered in an amiable tone. "Let us hope my former boss was killed. A man like that will not accept defeat, and as far as I know, you are the first to defeat him. If he is still alive, he will come after you like a maddened animal after all the problems you have caused him." That said, he disappeared into the night with Mort and Jimenez following.

-70-

Walking around the Hind, Karloff Zinova assessed the damage with a critical eye. Though dents marred the armored sides in various places, both the main and tail rotors had miraculously escaped the rain of stone and debris catapulted by the blast. But these were not the things that concerned him. It was the long cylindrical timber exceeding thirty feet in length that extended from both open doors of the aircraft's main cabin. Lodged at an odd angle, most of it jutted cantilever from the portside door. It was this that had been the cause of the Hind's instability following the explosion, for it had created a significant moment that had made the chopper list heavily to port. By some strange quirk of luck, however, it had not wrought any structural damage to the airframe, though it had killed two of his men and the black man called Ermstine as it swept through the cabin.

"Push harder!" Zinova snarled, ordering three of the five remaining men under his command to rid the timber from the cabin. He had already posted two others as sentries, positioning them 50 meters forward on opposite sides of the Hind to interdict the possibility of a sneak attack by infiltrators, but now he was considering bringing them back.

"It will not move," Drakov groaned in exasperation, straining with all his might against the steel T-bar protruding perpendicular from the bottom of the pole. While it provided a place of leverage for multiple hands to push against, its very existence required that the timber be retracted from the Hind's starboard side since the jutting bar would catch obstacles if they tried moving the short end through the cabin.

Zinova went around to the opposite side of the Hind and positioned himself against the end of the pole's long side farthest from Drakov, prepared to pit his bearlike strength against the unyielding timber, but heaving to no avail he cast wrathful eyes on Allotey and Alvarez standing idly apart from the task. "Both of you pitch in and help," he barked furiously. "Unless we remove this timber, we're not going anywhere."

Alvarez lowered his pack, moving quickly to lend a hand, but Allotey hesitated momentarily, appearing resentful of being ordered about like a lackey. The prospect of hard physical exertion was foreign to him. Mumbling under his breath, he joined in to push against the obstinate object keeping them grounded.

With all eight men grunting hard, the timber lurched forward, moving several inches before stopping, and Zinova could see it was lodged more firmly between supporting stanchions within the cabin.

"We need to use the winch," Drakov gasped. Relaxing his hold on the T-bar, he retrieved a heavy-duty come-along winch and two lengths of ¾ inch nylon rope from one of the Hind's storage compartments. Tying one of the ropes off to the base of the T-bar where it met the timber, he knotted the rope to one of the winch's two hooks. Securing the second rope to the remaining hook, he pulled the rope taut before looping it snugly around the trunk of a nearby tree and tying it off. Designed to handle up to five tons, he began ratcheting the winch. "Let's hope this works," he said hoarsely, dubiously eyeing the rope, which would yield long before the winch reached its maximum capacity. He knew that if the rope snapped, someone would likely get hurt pretty badly. "I'll winch as we push," he stated, leaning his weight up against the T-bar.

Once again the timber lurched as everyone pushed hard, but this time it crept forward as the winch added to the effort. Seconds, then minutes ticked by as the pole continued to inch forward. "Just a little more," Drakov grunted, speaking more to the winch than the men assisting him. In another moment the timber sprang free, the end of it falling from the cabin floor and landing with a heavy thud as it met the ground.

Another sound suddenly caught Zinova's attention, and he motioned everyone to keep quiet. Listening, he realized it was the drone of another chopper. "Everyone in the aircraft!" he bellowed in a deep, guttural growl.

"You'll fly us to the colony?" Allotey asked tensely, wondering if Zinova had changed his mind about taking him to Aquaria.

Zinova stared at the UN emissary, seeing a man filled with fright. "You better be right about the gold," he threatened. "If you are wrong I will kill you."

Allotey paled noticeably, his usual arrogance completely absent. He had no doubt the Reaper meant to carry out the threat should the colony fail to show any gold.

-71-

Jake watched apprehensively as Fernando brought the helicopter to a low hover, submerging the sling into the water. Visibility opened up quickly as a potent blast of rotor wash dispersed smoke from the fire, allowing the moon to reassert its soft pervasive glow over the surrounding landscape. Another moment passed before Achilles' familiar essence reverberated in Jake's head. *I'm ready to go, JJ.*

Not bothering to use the radio, Jake looked up at the chopper's cockpit and twirled a finger in a circular motion. Fernando nodded in understanding before putting pitch into the main rotor, and seconds later the sling went taut, lifting Achilles' twelve-hundred-pound mass slowly from the water. As the whirlybird headed for the ocean carrying its heavy burden, Jake moved to the edge of the canal, reaching down to haul Destiny up the last few feet from the rocky embankment. The surface of the moat rippled heavily below her as the gargantuan shark she had been riding sounded, its huge dorsal fin disappearing from sight.

Embracing his wife in his powerful arms, Jake gave her a passionate kiss. "We better get moving," he finally murmured, begrudgingly releasing her. "Once Fernando dumps Achilles back in the ocean, I want you and your father to fly back to the cove with him. I think it's best you stay with the children and your mother."

"You're going back to Aquaria, aren't you!?" Destiny said.

"I have no choice. I can't leave Mat and Jacob alone to fend off a UN task force."

"There's nothing you can do," Destiny protested wearily.

"Perhaps," Jake concurred, "but I have to try." He turned to glimpse the chopper as it moved farther away, the whir of its blades rapidly diminishing.

Grabbing her hand, he led her and Franklin down the slope leading to the shoreline. Two-thirds of the way down, Destiny stopped short, looking back the way they had come. "This is not over, Jay Jay."

Jake went rigid. A vision of the Hind suddenly emerged in his mind's eye, and a moment later he heard the distinctive drone of its engines escalating swiftly in pitch. "Run!" he urged, the word automatically ensuing from his lips in a throaty wail. Now familiar with the instrumentation these Russian-made whirlybirds were equipped with, he knew Zinova would readily see Fernando's chopper on his radar screen.

Jake immediately sent out a rapid-fire warning to his bond mate, the thought leaping from his mind like a gazelle escaping a lion. *Jump as soon as you clear the beach, Achilles!*

As he ran, Jake glanced over his shoulder to spot the Hind coming on quickly. In a few more seconds it would be in firing range of Fernando, who had not yet reached the ocean. In that fleeting moment he knew he had one option to fall back on, and one option only. Pulling the PHP he had retained from his utility belt, he stopped running and depressed the activation button, holding the device above his head. A momentary delay ensued before a holographic projection of the dolphin art sprang into the night sky, its enigmatic pulsing streaks of multicolored light twisting and interlacing directly in front of the approaching attack helicopter.

Please let this work, Jake pleaded inwardly as the Hind bore down on them.

-72-

As soon as he lifted off, Zinova activated the aircraft's radar system. Throwing maximum pitch into the main rotor, he forced the Hind straight up like a runaway elevator. Checking the system gauges on the instrument console, he saw that all the readings were in the normal range. Confirming this, he could feel no odd vibrations shuddering through the airframe. By some strange quirk of luck, he knew that the Hind's powertrain had miraculously escaped damage.

Fully airborne, he had a bird's eye view of what remained of Cardoza's lair. The westernmost portion had collapsed, leaving a mound of stone and timber rubble that sloped down into the moat and disappeared below the waterline. Flames burned heavily, evoking a billowing curtain of dense smoke that drifted off to the south. And while a section of the drawbridge was still intact, what remained of it lay upside down, deposited more than 50 meters west of the canal alongside the road leading to the fortress. Lying on its side next to it was the large cargo container he had used in moving the shark to the moat. Transporting the shark had been Cardoza's last request of him, a task which he now knew had been all for naught, for he was certain Cardoza had perished, and with the drug lord gone, no payment would be forthcoming.

Gaining a height of 300 meters, he slowed the aircraft's vertical ascent and studied the radar screen. Just as he suspected, a blip showed up. It was flying at low altitude and moving directly away from him on a southern heading.

The voice of his gunner came over the intercom. "Look at your screen!" Boris exclaimed briskly. "He's south of us."

"I see him," Zinova grumbled. Lowering the aircraft nose, he brought the Hind into a steep dive, descending through a pall of smoke to come up behind the unknown intruder. Certainly it had to be part of the force that had attacked the fortress, he surmised. And if he was wrong, what difference did it make.

"Take him out with a missile!" Zinova ordered, catching sight of the whirlybird. It looked to be a relatively small helicopter with something slung beneath it.

"With pleasure," Boris replied, eager for a kill. "I will scatter pieces of him all over the beach." As he armed a missile, a swirl of bright lights suddenly danced before his eyes. Confused, he stared transfixed for less than half a second before being assailed by extreme vertigo. With his brain feeling as though it was going to explode, he ripped off his flight helmet and clutched his skull. The scream that left his lips was abruptly cut off as a sudden rush of vomit rose up from his stomach to spew from his mouth.

Reeling from the onslaught of holographic light, Zinova felt his stomach begin to churn in reaction to the invisible vise crushing his head. Too late to stop it, a gush of bile spurted from his lips to splatter across the control panel. As though from far away, the voice of Alvarez rang out to rise above the other screams echoing in the cabin behind him. "Don't look at it!"

Using all his will, Zinova instinctively closed his eyes, fighting back the illness sweeping over him. He was one of those rare individuals who was able to function in the midst of debilitating dizziness and pain, having once been considered for cosmonaut training by the Soviets. Testing him in a high speed centrifuge, they had had discovered he could withstand a g-force of 20 for better than two minutes without losing consciousness. But that was when he was much younger. This, however, was unlike anything he had ever before experienced, and it took every ounce of his remaining willpower to keep from blacking out. In the midst of his torment, he vaguely perceived the Hind yaw stiffly to starboard, and in that instant he knew he was losing control of the chopper. Having enough presence of mind to keep from crashing, he pushed down hard on one of the foot pedals to counter the dangerous yaw. Sensing the airframe pivot back beneath its main rotor, he knew he had overcompensated when the Hind spun violently in the opposite direction. Risking a peek, he opened his eyes. The display of swirling lights was now gone, the Hind having moved past the source of emission. Nevertheless, the severe nausea still festered, and he let go with another involuntary burst of vomit that drenched the console.

Too sick to continue flying, he knew he had no choice but to set the Hind down. Somehow he was able to change course, just barely managing to avoid plunging the chopper into the ocean looming before him. In his present condition he dared not try landing on the beach, which was strewn haphazardly with large boulders and outcroppings of rock. But he needed to land without having to consider hazardous obstacles. His only option was Cardoza's airstrip a little ways upland. Fighting off the debilitation draining him, he used his iron will to combat it. Again he upchucked, unable to stop the surge of bile and vomit leaping from his throat. Just a little further, he urged himself on, guiding the Hind clumsily past the smoldering ruins of Cardoza's hangar. Desperate to reach the runway that lay before him, he wondered if he would be able to land the Hind before unconsciousness overtook him.

-73-

Amphitrite was not intimidated by Swenson's hulking form as he looked down at her with a cold expressionless stare, knowing the man amounted to nothing more than a physically powerful machine ready to carry out the wishes of its master. The real threat resided in the smaller man, and within his eyes she saw the fiery blaze of a psychotic killer many times more potent than anything she had ever before encountered. Unlike the rabidly malicious but now deceased Colonel Ternier whose ambitions had never been achieved, here was a persona that had reached the absolute apex of power yet still hungered for more. Power from any source, she knew, created an appetite for additional power, but before her sat a megalomaniac who aspired to control the wealth of the entire world. If the devil existed in physical form, this was surely him, she concluded, but she also knew that by no means was he acting alone.

Comfortably ensconced in a cushioned chair in the uppermost cabin of the yacht's superstructure, Maximus put down a cup of tea from which he had been sipping. Tinted acrylic windows bordering the oval room along its perimeter provided a three hundred and sixty-degree unobstructed view of the sea in all directions. Casually, he turned his head to take in the small village nestled along the shoreline three miles distant. A soft halo of pink silvery light crowned the steep hills behind it, imparting a fairytale-like setting to the scene. Studying it briefly, he brought his gaze back to Amphitrite. "What is your relationship to the children?" he asked.

Amphitrite kept her gaze fixed and unwavering as she looked into Maximus' soulless, ruthless eyes, sensing a burning cauldron of impatience lurking just below the surface. Thankfully, Zimbola had trusted her insights enough by not putting up any resistance against the boarding party sent from the *Nunquarn Satis* that had stormed aboard the Angel nine hours earlier. And though he and the rest of them were now prisoners, she sensed none of them had as yet been harmed. For the moment, she would appease the man sitting before her by answering his questions truthfully. Something deep inside her told her this was the appropriate action to take. "I am their grandmother," she willingly admitted.

Maximus stared, finding this hard to believe. The woman looked far too youthful and attractive to be a grandmother, appearing to be in her mid-thirties at most. Either she was one of those rare individuals able to resist the ravages of time, or she had assumed the role of grandmother in name only without having any genetic relationship to the children.

"Their biological grandmother?" Maximus questioned, testing the full context of her assertion.

"Yes."

Deciding to accept her claim, he lifted the cup to his lips again, seeming to smile subtly before putting it back down. "Their grandmother," he uttered with satisfaction. "That is most convenient!"

Leaning forward, he placed his elbows on the table and tented his fingers. "Then I'll have to assume you are also the biological mother of the Dolphin Girl."

"Yes."

He turned his head again to scrutinize the village once more. "You and your people have made great strides over the last several years, obviously accomplishing the impossible. But tell me, how is it that a small contingent of seemingly simple and impoverished Haitians was able to get the funding for such a grand undertaking?"

"I sense fear within you," Amphitrite murmured softly. "The thought of more sea colonies coming on line scares the daylights out of you. You see them as an impediment to your own insidious interests."

Maximus smirked wolfishly. "Not at all. I actually applaud your efforts in succeeding to build such a thriving enterprise. It was a monumental undertaking. Unfortunately, you will soon discover those efforts were all in vain once a UN task force seizes your operation. Control of it, including all its assets, will then fall to me, at least indirectly."

Maximus paused for effect, enjoying the moment before going on. "Building an operation of that scale had to have cost Tursiops at least one hundred billion in U.S. currency, yet I know for a fact not one bank, corporation or other entity on the face of the earth provided the funding to build it, nor would they have risked financing it had you applied for loans. This led me to conclude that your people used something to barter with, and that something had to be gold. Through various sources I have learned this to be true. The question is, where did you get such a huge quantity of it?"

Amphitrite smiled sardonically. "The earth is a marvelous super-organism. You're correct about no one on the face of the earth willing to finance our vision, so *Gaia* herself provided for us what no one else would have been willing to do."

Maximus frowned, puzzled by the word. "*Gaia*? Who is this person?"

"I'm surprised you never heard of her. She is the embodiment of our Mother Earth."

For several seconds Maximus stared at her as though she were insane, then abruptly sneered. "You're telling me the planet provided you with the gold to fund your operation."

"Yes."

A mocking laugh erupted from Maximus' lips. "Did she just hand over tons of it, no questions asked?" His laughter suddenly ceased, changing over to a rabid snarl as he shot another look toward the village. "No doubt you found a gold mine, and it's probable it's located somewhere near Malique."

Amphitrite remained calm, not offering anything.

Maximus suddenly relaxed, seemingly bringing his anger under control for the moment. "How much gold do you currently have and where is it stored?" he asked. Though his tone was raspy, he posed the question casually, as though requesting current weather conditions.

"Enough to build at least five more colonies of equal size," Amphitrite stated without hesitation.

The statement invoked surprise in Maximus' countenance, and he responded with another flare of annoyance. "Do not toy with me, woman. That much gold could not possibly exist outside known reserves currently held in vaults around the world."

Amphitrite kept her gaze direct. "*Gaia* holds far more gold than even you can imagine."

"You'd be surprised at what I can imagine," Maximus grumbled irritably. "But it's a known fact that only one ounce of gold actually exists for every 400 ounces traded on world markets."

"Believe what you want. Nevertheless, *Gaia* has all the resources she needs to heal the wounds men like you inflict upon her."

Maximus studied her closely, looking for signs of insanity. "Let's assume I accept what you're telling me," he finally said. "What I don't get is how your people were able to bring forth such a colossal engineering feat. Where did the know-how and technical skills come from to build machinery capable of harvesting energy directly from the ocean?"

Amphitrite responded quickly, her comportment remaining steady and enigmatic. "What *Gaia* lacks, she simply creates."

Once again, Maximus frowned. "What does that mean?"

"She spawns the intelligence necessary to build such machinery."

Understanding slowly replaced the clouded look dominating Maximus' features. "Those creatures," he blurted. "Those strange white beasts with hands. They are the ones that created Aquaria, aren't they?"

"The only way you could possibly know about them is through those robotic fish you sent into the colony to spy upon us. Using them to plant explosives, your objective was to discredit us in the eyes of the world."

Maximus grinned fiendishly. "Yes, and it worked beautifully." Pausing, he took another sip of tea before resuming the conversation. "I've studied the concept behind ocean thermal energy conversion, trying to make sense how Aquaria makes it work, and based on the information I've obtained, the colony's seven OTEC power plants should not be able to work."

"Maybe I can enlighten you," Amphitrite offered.

Maximus seemed pleased that the woman was willing to cooperate. "For one, the seafloor directly beneath Aquaria maxes out at nine hundred and fifty feet," he pointed out. "At that depth, the ambient water temperature and nitrate concentration are insufficient for harvesting the vast amounts of energy and food the colony is obviously producing. For another, your surface water intakes don't conform to a standard OTEC model. You use seven identical pipes that extend horizontally out to the offshore berthing facility near the island. Why go to the expense of constructing lengthy intakes when it is so much simpler to draw in surface water immediately contiguous with the OTEC plants?"

Amphitrite remained stoic as she shed light on the riddle. "For any OTEC process to work effectively, a minimum temperature differential of forty degrees Fahrenheit must exist between the surface and deeper waters. But by increasing this differential further, greater amounts of energy can be produced. We solved this problem by preheating the surface water at the island's offshore berthing facility. That is why the surface intakes extend so far from the power plants."

"To preheat that much water would require enormous amounts of energy," Maximus said, "maybe even more than what your OTEC generators are capable of producing. Where is that energy coming from?"

"Hydrogen gas."

"If what you're telling me is true, it sounds as though the process would be close to a breakeven wash in energy production." Maximus shook his head doubtfully. "Doesn't seem practical to have the hydrogen Aquaria produces channeled back to the berthing facility to be used for producing more energy."

"The hydrogen does not come from Aquaria," Amphitrite said. "It comes from another source."

"From where, then?"

"From deep under Navassa Island."

Maximus stared as though impressed. "A subterranean vent," he concluded. "How convenient! Obviously your people found a way to put it to good use, just as you have done with the *guano* mined on the island. I hear you supply it to Haitian farmers free of charge to double and triple their crop yields. But it seems something has been added to this miracle fertilizer. Not only is it exceptionally potent, it has an unknown ingredient that makes indigenous crops resistant to chemicals that would normally kill them. Isn't that so?"

Maximus smiled smugly when Amphitrite didn't answer. There would be ample time to learn the fertilizer's secret. At the moment, however, he wanted to stay focused on the mysteries Aquaria harbored. "How is so much algae produced? The water beneath Aquaria lacks the nitrates in sufficient quantity needed to grow algae," he contended. "The water is not deep enough."

"We are able to harvest water from deep down in the Cayman Trench, well beyond thirty-three hundred feet where nitrate concentrations begin to level out."

"But your vertical intakes go straight down," Maximus objected with a dark scowl. "They can only end at the seafloor beneath them."

Amphitrite knew he would never have been able to detect what actually lay down there. Navassa Island was the truncated apex of an enormous undersea mountain that sat on the edge of the Cayman Trench. Cold deep water currents flowing along the edge of the trench coming in contact with warmer water from above continually produced odd thermal effects that would distort sonar rays. Add to that the strange and unpredictable electrical fields and anomalies produced by those marvelous creatures dwelling at that depth and the T-crystals they produced and the end result was 'noisy water' that wreaked havoc on sonar and video equipment.

"An assumption on your part, but a valid one even though the ambient acoustical and electrical interference directly below Aquaria would have prevented you from seeing what lay down there."

"And what would that be?"

"*Thurentras!*"

"What the hell are *thurentras*?"

"*Gaia* has the ability to create life forms necessary to carry out objectives. In this case she created creatures to draw cold, nitrate-laden water up from the depths. The vertical intakes collect the water the *thurentras* harvest from the Cayman Trench and bring it to the colony above."

For several seconds, Maximus remained mute, his face contorting with a flood of mixed emotions before settling on a look of intense avarice. "These creatures you speak of, I assume they sit stationary on the seafloor?"

"Yes."

Maximus took another sip from his cup. "That art your colony produces is…" He paused, seeming to grope for the right words. "I suppose arcane and debilitating would be suitable words to describe it since it induces extreme vertigo in people when they look upon it, yet all your colonists seem immune."

Amphitrite allowed herself a small smile. "For reasons we don't fully understand, only those who are truly evil will become ill when viewing it," she stated, seeing the man's eyes flash briefly.

Maximus quickly regained control of himself. "Your people don't use drugs to keep from getting sick?"

"No."

A fleeting, skeptical look crossed Maximus' face like a dark cloud scudding over a roiling sea. "Which brings us back to my first question," he grumbled. "Where do you mine the gold?"

"There is no need for us to mine it," Amphitrite replied, deciding it was time to be evasive. "As I told you, *Gaia* provided it." Amphitrite gauged his reaction, seeing the dam holding back his growing impatience ready to burst.

"Where is it stored?" Maximus demanded, the question coming out in a sharp hiss. "If you want to see your grandchildren alive again, I suggest you tell me." His cheeks and forehead seemed to swell, darkening further with a network of gray veins that pulsed and ticked erratically, making him appear like a cobra on the verge of striking.

"Not far from here," Amphitrite baited calmly. "If you wish, I can take you there."

Maximus settled back into his chair, once again in charge of his emotions. The woman's capture was appearing far more fruitful than he had anticipated, collaborating what Senator Van Heflin had told him about there being a cache of the precious metals somewhere near Malique. The young man taken from the woman's boat, though weak and apparently convalescing from a serious injury, had further substantiated this upon intense interrogation. Maximus had learned his name was Alex Trekov and that he had been part of a team sent by the Reaper to take control of a cove in the vicinity of Malique. Under questioning, Alex had told him about the gold bars littering the ground in the forest that bordered a deep gorge gouged by a plunging waterfall.

So, Maximus surmised, a humorless grin coming to his face in piecing together the whole picture. *Rafael wanted the gold for himself, so he used Zinova to get it. I thought I noticed ire in his eyes when Van Heflin brought up the subject during the fortress meeting. I shall deal with him at the appropriate time.*

Mulling this, he set a probing gaze on the nearby coastline. Though he had known for some time now about the gold, he had mistakenly assumed it was all stored in Aquaria or the adjacent island.

-74-

Curious to see for himself, Troy Jacob kept his face plastered to the lone circular window within the small but lavishly furnished ship's quarters, though the effort wasn't necessary. Through the eyes of his bond mate, he would have seen the small coastal village anyway. Moving toward the village on a slow but steady course off the ship's starboard side was the Avenging Angel. From *Alpha*, he had learned that the Angel had been towed behind the huge vessel on which he was currently being held. Upon capture, he and his twin sister, accompanied by their grandmother, had been locked in the room. But an hour earlier, his grandmother had been taken away by two burly crewmen, and according to *Alpha*, she, Zimby and Hector had been led back aboard the Angel under the watchful eyes of twelve armed men, one of them a large blonde-haired individual the size of Zimby.

Redirecting his gaze, Teejay spotted the dorsal fins of two other pod members. Turning, he looked at his sister, placing his lips to her ear. "Athena and Natalie are here," he whispered.

Melody nodded. "We've got to find a way off this ship," she whispered back, scrutinizing the locked door to the plush sleeping quarters.

"I wonder what they did with Alex," Teejay mumbled in a hushed tone. "He wasn't with grandma and Zimby when they took them aboard the Angel."

"He's probably locked away in another room," Melody guessed. "He was still a little weak when they took him from the Angel." She started to add more, but the lock to the door suddenly clicked audibly, and a baldheaded, middle aged man poked his head into the room. Scrutinizing the children with kind eyes, he gestured with a finger to his lips. Glancing furtively behind him, he entered the room, pulling a pushcart used for serving meals in with him. A jumble of hardware and electronic parts littered the top of the cart. Shutting the door behind him, he quickly pocketed a key into a white lab coat.

"Who are you?" Melody queried warily.

"Keep your voice down," the man cautioned. "I'm here to help you."

Teejay pointed to an object set on a pivot attached to one of the walls. "We're being watched," he warned. This was something his grandmother had pointed out to him and his sister before she was led away.

The man smiled. "Don't worry, I've disabled the camera. I'm going to get you out of here."

Teejay appeared dubious. "What about the cameras set along the corridor outside?"

"All the cameras along this sector of the ship are inoperable at the moment. In another minute they'll notice the problem," the man said, checking his wristwatch. "But I have a little diversion set to go off five seconds from now. Grab hold of something to brace yourselves."

A sudden dawning alighted in the expression of both children, and they automatically grabbed hold of a nearby bedpost. A heavy tremor suddenly shot through the ship, immediately followed by a cacophony of blaring alarms.

"Hop aboard!" the man urged, lifting up one side of the cloth that draped over all four sides of the pushcart. "We don't have much time."

Sensing the man could be trusted, the twins climbed on the cart, barely able to squeeze into the tight space. "Where are you taking us?" Melody asked as the cloth dropped back down to hide them.

"I know that both of you swim like fish," their liberator explained hurriedly, opening the door and looking both ways to make sure the coast was clear before pushing the cart out into the corridor. "I also know that your dolphins are here," he elucidated further. "There's a small platform near the stern about thirty feet above the water. Do you kids have any fears about jumping?"

Teejay and Melody eyed one another with solemn looks. "We're not afraid," Teejay answered for both of them.

"What about you?" Melody asked. "Will you be coming with us?"

"I'm not a very good swimmer, I'm afraid to say, and I have a problem with heights." The man gasped breathlessly, nearly breaking into a trot as he pushed the cart along.

"But what if they find out you helped us escape?" Melody pressed.

"It's a risk I'm willing to take."

"Why are you doing this?" Teejay asked.

"I'm doing this for myself as much as I'm doing it for you. These are bad people and I'm tired of being afraid of them."

"Then why do you work for them?" Teejay needed to know.

"Because I'm a coward. They extorted my skills, and I was too afraid to refuse."

"You're not a coward!" Melody consoled soothingly, liking their savior even more. "How can you be if you're helping us? Can you tell us your name?"

"You can call me Percy."

"Kinda like Phillipe's bond mate, Perseus, without the *eus*," Teejay said. "In Greek mythology, Perseus was a hero. He saved *Andromeda* from *Cetus*, a gigantic sea monster."

"Quiet down, children!" Percy said brusquely. "We have visitors."

The twins' ears immediately perked at the sound of pounding footsteps resounding through the corridor. "What just happened?" they heard Percy say. "I felt something jar the ship."

"There was an explosion and our surveillance cameras stopped working," a disembodied voice grunted irritably. "Where are you going with that cart?"

"I'm on my way to the moon pool. Thought this serving cart would be useful for carrying spare parts," Percy replied smoothly. "One of the robofish isn't working right. Maximus will have my head if I don't get it fixed right away."

The twins noted three pairs of booted feet just below the cloth concealing them. The muzzle of a rifle barrel suddenly poked under the cloth to lift it higher. "Whatcha got under there?" Just as the cloth began to come up, another heavy jolt rocked the ship, this one more severe than the first. Abruptly, the cloth dropped, followed by a rumble of running feet.

"Be on the lookout for saboteurs," the same voice shouted back as the men bolted down the corridor. "We might be under attack."

Teejay let out a tense sigh. "That was close."

"I anticipated this would happen," Percy said, "so I rigged a second charge to go off."

"You timed it that way?" Melody asked incredulously.

"It was a good approximation," Percy said, moving the cart around a corner and opening a door. "A good scientist strives to be as precise as possible, trying to factor in all the possibilities. Anyway, climb on out, we're here."

Just as Percy had described, the twins found themselves on a small platform that overlooked the sea. Actually a sundeck that jutted out from the hull, it had two reclining lounge chairs set back from a low transom railing. Casting their eyes to the east, the children saw that the Angel had almost reached Malique's small harbor.

Melody glanced down, espying Alpha and Omega in the water below before turning to Percy. "Why don't you come with us? We'll make sure you don't drown."

Percy produced an avuncular smile. "I'm better off here where I can be a thorn to these people. The owner of this vessel is the cause of Aquaria's troubles. He wants to take control of the colony and will go to any lengths to get it." A grimace came to his face as he said this. "He's the most evil man I've ever known and the source of most of the world's problems. He is incredibly rich and powerful, with a vast organization serving him that is capable of orchestrating and manipulating world events to get what he wants. He and his cabal must be stopped."

Though they were children, both twins were far smarter than their years would suggest, and they took in the words with a profound understanding. "What's his name?" Teejay asked.

Percy spit out the answer as though disgorging something foul tasting. "Malcolm Maximus. Now I suggest the two of you get going before they discover you're missing."

Both children gave Percy a fervent hug, then climbed over the railing. "We'll always remember what you did for us," they chorused, giving him a farewell smile. Showing no fear, they launched themselves into perfect swan dives, cleaving the water with fluid grace.

-75-

Zimbola eased off the throttle, bringing the engine to a gentle idle as the Angel glided smoothly against the pier. He watched as Hector jumped off the vessel to tie off the stern. With a weapon trained on him by one of the armed men who had followed him onto the pier, Hector's expression was sullen. Another of the henchmen leapt onto the dock to grab a bow line flung by one of his teammates stationed on the bow. With two captors guarding her, Amphitrite was escorted off the Angel.

Several villagers had come out onto the pier in greeting, but at seeing the ominous band of hard-looking men clad in black and the wicked-looking weapons brandished by them, they made a hasty retreat back to the village.

A basso voice rumbled behind Zimbola, a voice almost as deep as his own. "Get off the boat!"

Zimbola turned with an impudent scowl, wondering if he could take a slug from the Glock 42 aimed at his gut and still take on the man holding it. Presenting a dour gaze behind dark sunglasses, the Nordic giant waved the pistol casually as though reading his thoughts.

"A time will come when you don't have that gun to keep me from crushing your throat," Zimbola threatened brazenly.

The threat seemed to hit a nerve, and Zimbola sensed a flash of anger behind the coal-black lenses that hid Swensen's eyes. The man's momentary pique quickly dissolved, however, falling back into the same icy stare Zimbola had been forced to absorb during the short boat ride.

"Move!" Swensen rumbled again.

Continuing to glare belligerently, Zimbola exited the pilothouse and climbed down the steps, mulling what it would take to rile this man. The Nordic displayed little emotion, acting more like an automaton than a human. The dark, round lenses cloaking the man's eyes seemed to accentuate this perception all the more, and with his crew cut of ash blonde hair and prominently jutting lantern-shaped jaw, he gave Zimbola the impression of a huge insect with mandibles stoically sizing up prey. And though he stood an inch shorter than the Jamaican's imposing height, the width and thickness of his shoulders appeared to match Zimbola's powerful physique.

But it was those infernal glasses that caused Zimbola to scrutinize the man a little more closely. All these captors wore them. They did not look like normal sunglasses. And then he realized it was the small node attached to the bridge connecting the lenses that gave the glasses an odd appearance. Studying the frame further, he noticed something else. It resided on one of the temple extenders that allowed the glasses to hug the man's face. Another small node sat on the left extender directly above the ear. All at once it became apparent to him that the central node was a camera and the ear node a radio transmitter. Someone was monitoring this excursion from a remote location. He could only surmise that person was the owner of the super yacht they had previously been taken aboard, though he had not as yet seen the man.

Just before he disembarked the Angel, Zimbola was handed a large backpack by one of the other men. "Put this on!" the man ordered curtly. The backpack was light and felt empty, and as he strapped it on, Zimby saw that Hector was already wearing a similar one.

Forced to trek along behind Amphitrite and her two escorts, Zimbola purposely slowed his pace, openly displaying an unwillingness to cooperate with these men. Whenever he did this, he was prodded harshly in the buttocks with the muzzle of a short-barreled machine pistol the man directly behind him wielded. Except for Swensen, all the men carried identical weapons. Having been tutored by Jake on various types of firearms, Zimbola recognized the weapons to be F-2000 assault rifles, currently one of the most sophisticated and deadly lightweight combat weapons on the planet.

Reaching the end of the newly renovated pier, Zimbola was marched along the red brick pathway that wound its way through the picturesque village. Malique was unlike the typical ramshackle hamlet found along the Haitian coast, exhibiting well-kept structures in brightly painted colors that dotted a landscape rich in vegetation. Everywhere he looked, a sense of pride permeated the sedate, idyllic atmosphere the village conveyed.

Knowing what lay along one side of the path a little further on, Zimbola stared hopefully ahead, anticipating a certain reaction from the two men walking alongside Amphitrite. But the reaction he expected did not come. Conspicuously positioned next to the path was a moderately sized billboard with a glass surface, and behind the glass was an eye-catching exhibit of the enigmatic albino art.

Zimbola was truly dumbstruck when Amphitrite's escort trudged past without a falter in their step. *How can this be?* he wondered. *These men are evil, and evil people always succumb to the art.* When Amphitrite walked past the exhibit with not a hint of hesitation, he could only conclude that she knew this would happen. *Perhaps some of the others will become ill*, he consoled himself. Forcing himself to remain calm, he prepared to take advantage of such a possibility should it arise.

This spark of hope quickly faded as the rest of the group moved on without any signs of sickness. *I have to trust her instincts*, Zimbola reminded himself. *She was the only one able to defeat Erzulie, the evil witch of the voudun, when no one else could.*

Continuing to move along the path, the group encountered several more exhibits of the dolphin art, each one different while still harboring the same underlying theme of arcane surrealism. When no one fell ill, Zimbola's disappointment changed over to acceptance. With regret, Zimbola eyed the PHP affixed to the top of the exhibit residing at the center of the village as they passed it. *If only it were night*, he thought wistfully, knowing holographic displays of the art were so much more effective than the simple 2-dimensional creations at inducing illness in those with iniquitous tendencies. At night the PHP would have been activated to shed a soothing aura over the village, but daylight tended to attenuate the 3-dimensional projections, making them barely visible under a bright sky.

As he looked around, Zimbola saw no residents roaming the village, aware that they had fled to their homes. What little that remained of Zimbola's faith crumbled further as Amphitrite led the group beyond the brick path's terminus. She was now taking them along the trail that wound its way into the hills. The thought that she was actually leading them to the cove was disconcerting. Plodding onward, he berated himself harshly for his weakening resolve. *I must have faith in her*, he vowed. *I must believe.*

-76-

Maximus sat at the multi-screened console, closely monitoring what the remote cameras were showing. At the moment, the woman was leading his men into the forested hills that rose up beyond the village. As always, he made it a habit to let others carry out his objectives, especially where the possibility of danger existed. And in this case, he had to assume the potential for it was quite high. The excruciating pain and vertigo he had suffered when he tried to take down the Hind was something he never wanted to experience again. Having failed to use the drug specifically developed to combat it, he had been defenseless against the swirling lights that had coalesced before his eyes, a 3-dimensional manifestation of the mysterious art produced by the colony. The memory of it made him twinge. He was certain his brain had been on the verge of exploding during the ordeal, and it had taken him hours to fully recuperate after the event. If something similar to that existed in Malique, he would rather avoid it, uncertain just how effective the drug would be if he came into visual contact with those lights. And while he had made sure his men were injected with it prior to going ashore, he knew such a drug might not work for everyone, particularly since it had only been tested against 2-dimensional representations of the strange art. During testing, holographic representations had not been considered. For these reasons he had decided to stay behind, directing the operation from the safety of his vessel. But now he wondered just how safe he was in view of recent events.

Scowling with pent up fury, he continued to mull over the likely suspects among those still aboard the *Nunquarn Satis* who might have perpetrated those events. It infuriated him to know that portions of the video surveillance system had failed just prior to the blasts that had jarred the ship, particularly the camera that provided real-time viewing of the room where the children were being held. Ruling out the possibility of infiltrators, he was now convinced that one of the crew had tampered with the system. Certain that the culprit had to have a good working knowledge of electronics to pull off such a stunt, he systematically narrowed the field. Although the two explosions set off in the portside storage holds did not cause excessive damage, he deduced these were merely diversions designed to cloak a higher aim. And that aim had succeeded all too well, for now the children were missing. As soon as the disabled cameras had come back on line, Maximus had immediately seen that the children were no longer in the room. A frenzied search of the entire vessel by the ship's crew quickly ensued, only to come up empty so far.

The ship's intercom suddenly buzzed sharply, and Maximus snatched up the phone expecting to hear good news. "We've searched everywhere, sir," a disgruntled voice uttered. "They're nowhere to be found."

"You're absolutely certain of this?" Maximus screamed, now thoroughly enraged. Without the children, his trump card was lost.

A brief moment of silence followed before a nervous reply came back. "I'd stake my life on it, sir."

"You had better be right, otherwise you're going to lose it," Maximus snarled in frustration. "Launch two skiffs and search the sea between us and the shore. Those children are good swimmers, so they might be heading for the village."

Maximus slammed down the phone, continuing to reduce the list of suspects one by one through a process of elimination, finally arriving at one name only. And that name was Percy Osgood. He found this rather strange. Though Osgood was a mechanical genius, he was also a withdrawn and timid sort, certainly not the type of person to put his life on the line. Furthermore, Maximus held something that ensured Osgood's continued cooperation. He had Percy's twin brother, Mortimer, locked away in Rafael's fortress, ransoming him in exchange for Percy's skills. But Mortimer had certain information that could potentially have damaging consequences to Plagiarius if that information ever became public, and Maximus had ordered Rafael to use whatever means necessary to find out where that information was kept and to destroy those files.

Overall, though, Maximus sensed he had the upper hand, and while it didn't make sense that Percy would risk his brother's life by committing sabotage, all the evidence seemed to point his way.

Picking the phone back up, Maximus called another member of his staff. "Bring Percy Osgood to me," he ordered shrilly.

-77-

Riding their bond mates, Teejay and Melody traversed the three miles of open water quickly, only periodically coming to the surface when they needed to breathe. Reaching Malique's main pier in just under twelve minutes, they approached the Avenging Angel with utmost caution, coasting alongside and looking up at her stern.

"I don't think anyone's aboard," Melody whispered to her brother, noting the unusual stillness hanging all about them. It was a calm morning, with a glassy, flat sea abutting the shoreline. Only a few boats were currently tied up alongside the long pier, including the 70 foot *Exoco*, a high-speed hydrofoil used for quickly transporting supplies to and from Aquaria. Both twins knew the vessel had been named after a family of flying fish called *Exocoetidae*. Flying fish had exceptionally large pectoral fins that acted as wings, allowing them to glide above the sea for short distances whenever they leapt from the water to escape predators. With dual hydrofoils jutting out on each side of it, the boat clearly resembled its namesake.

At seeing no one among the few vessels, Melody realized that most of the local fishermen would have already taken advantage of the superb conditions, putting out to sea at sunup. Strangely though, she could see no villagers anywhere in the quaint little hamlet, and the quietude was overpowering.

Straddling Alpha, Teejay risked craning his head to scan the area beyond the village. Almost instantly, he caught sight of several black-clad troopers climbing the steep trail that led up into the hills. Following their progress a moment longer, he saw them disappear into the forest. Hunkering back down, he spoke quietly. "I see them. They're taking the trail that leads to *Gaia*. Looks like Grandma's leading them there just like she said she would."

The escalating drone of an outboard engine made both children turn. A small boat carrying three men was heading in their direction. Further back, another motorboat was running a zigzag course over the sea, the men aboard it swiveling their heads back and forth in search of something. "I think they know we escaped and are looking for us," Melody said calmly. "Got any ideas?"

Teejay scrutinized one of the nearest piles supporting the pier. He could see that the tide was close to full ebb, judging how low the ocean surface had receded from the high water mark. Swinging his gaze seaward, he eyed the closest boat for several seconds before his face broke out in a mischievous grin. "As a matter of fact I do."

-78-

Amphitrite continued to lead the way, taking the path that wound through the hills until it ran abreast of the bowl-shaped chasm. "The thing you seek is down there," she said to her escorts.

The men on each side of her stopped to gawk, with the one on her right pulling off his sunglasses to make sure the apparatus was not deceiving his eyes. Falling away below them was a place of wonder, a breathtaking vista of tinted flora hugging the tiered walls that surrounded a limpid blue-green pool with a mirror-like surface. At the far end of the basin, a gush of whitewater tumbled lazily down, sending up a prismatic mist that separated the sunlight into a rainbow of primary hues. Even at this distance, the multitude of fauna darting among the lush vegetation was evident. Birds and butterflies in a myriad of colors seemed to be everywhere.

In moments, the rest of the men caught up, nudging Zimbola and Hector before them. Swensen looked down, seemingly taking in the magnificent scenery with cold indifference. "She says it is down there," the man who had removed his glasses muttered gruffly, addressing the Nordic leader.

Swensen turned to Amphitrite. "Is there a way down there?"

Amphitrite nodded. "But I advise you to watch your step. The way down can be treacherous in places." Without another word, she led them further on, finding the crude ladder that descended to the uppermost tier.

One of the men suddenly shouted, removing some underbrush a short distance away. "There's a bunker over here, but it appears to be empty."

"Make sure it is," Swensen barked sternly.

Without hesitation, six of the band fanned out to form a skirmish line around the enclosure. A minute of cautious investigation ensued before the same man yelled back from inside the bunker. "It's definitely empty, nothing in here."

Amphitrite held back a smile. Unbeknownst to Jay Jay, she had left instructions with members of the cove's security force just prior to departing the cove on the Angel. Because they deemed her to be a mambo, a high voodoo priestess, they had carried out her wishes without question. The men were to stop manning the bunkers, at least temporarily, and they were to hide the dual fifties and ammunition in the forest, including the headphones that allowed communication between the bunkers.

Satisfied that there was no apparent danger, Swensen turned his gaze back on Amphitrite, the dark glasses giving a chilling edge to his unwavering stare. "Lead us on, woman, but do not forget who holds your grandchildren."

"If anything happens to those children, I swear by *Agwe* that I will send you to hell," Zimbola growled, gritting his teeth and fixating Swensen with a fierce, penetrating stare of his own that promised mayhem. Like the villagers, his belief in Caribbean folk religion derived from African mysticism was unshakeable, and *Agwe* was a spirit that ruled over the sea.

A scowl transcended Swensen's face, with the veins on his bull neck bulging to the surface and ticking like a metronome. This was the first show of anger Amphitrite had seen in the man. "When the time comes, I will give you the chance to back up your meaningless threats," he spat in agitation, his deep voice rumbling like an earthquake.

Once again, Amphitrite refrained from smiling. A while earlier, Athena had communicated with her telepathically, and she knew about the children's escape. Unfortunately, she could not convey that to Zimbola.

-79-

Having filled their lungs with deep inhalations, Melody and Teejay held on tight as their bond mates submerged and darted for the open sea. Covering a distance of a thousand meters, they rose back to the surface south of the village and well away from the nearest boat.

"Over here!" Melody and Teejay taunted, laughing and waving their arms wildly over their heads. Though they knew their pursuers were too far away to hear them, they continued these antics until they were sure they were spotted.

With both boats coming on rapidly, the children submerged again, this time angling back toward the coast. Coming up for air, they saw both boats circling their last position, the men aboard them peering down into the water expectantly.

"Over here!" the twins yelled in unison, resuming their previous antics.

As soon as the boats turned in their direction, Alpha and Omega shot into the depths, the children clinging fast and exhilarated by the pursuit. They were enjoying the game, unconcerned about the danger hanging in the balance. Randomly changing course, they came to the surface again and again, gradually drawing their pursuers further and further south. Gauging that they were now close to the cove's entrance, they separated, veering off in different directions, with Omega cruising along the bottom and taking Melody through the narrow channel that provided a way through the barrier reef. With the tide at full ebb, jagged corals lay inches beneath the surface on both sides.

Getting through the reef, Omega turned north, following the intertwined mass of pulsating tentacles that lay atop the sandy bottom like bundled cables. These were the tentacles that extended thousands of feet deep down into the Cayman Trench, endlessly harvesting the tiny gold grains that rose up from hot fissures in the earth's crust. Had Melody and her mount followed the tentacles to their ultimate source, they would have come upon the two huge pumpkin-shaped *thurentra* residing in the cove.

Forty meters from the channel, Melody was brought to the surface, whereupon she waved her arms wildly again. "Over here!" she shouted at the top of her lungs.

The driver of the nearest boat immediately caught sight of her, and maddened by the elusiveness of his prey, swung the runabout around and gunned the outboard to maximum power, coming straight at her with an enraged look on his face. This time she would not get away.

Caught up in the heat of the moment, the driver failed to notice the barrier reef lurking just below the surface. Plowing on at full speed, his rage abruptly turned to befuddlement as a grating crunch resounded. With razor-sharp coral ripping through the hull, the small watercraft jerked sideways and flipped, hurling all three passengers into the water. Screams filled the air as the boat landed atop two of the men, the bottom of its hull facing the sky. Partially pinned between the port gunwale and jagged calcareous growth, both men wailed pitifully as an expanding ring of crimson bespoke of their injuries. Flung further away, the driver lay wedged amid a dense cluster of staghorn coral, his head and torso above the water. Bleeding profusely from a multitude of lacerations, he stared vacantly in Melody's direction, too confused as yet to comprehend what had just happened.

A measure of sorrow caught up with Melody as she looked upon the stricken men. She hated to see suffering of any kind, even if it was caused by the reckless doings of these men. Sitting calmly astride Omega, she watched as the second boat slowed, the ruffians aboard it taking in the scene before them. Bespectacled with dark sunglasses, the trio showed little concern for their injured companions, focusing ominous gazes on Melody like predators deciding how they would go about capturing her.

The boat was identical to the first, a twenty foot open fishermen with a center console. As it slowed further, the driver shifted his scrutiny to what lay below the surface. Coasting to a crawl, he turned the boat to the south and paralleled the outer edge of the reef, searching for a way through it. As Melody watched, she saw the driver's lips moving as though he were speaking to himself and not to his partners. One of the other men was assisting him, leaning over the port side and peering intently down into the water while the third man kept his gaze locked on Melody.

"There!" yelled the man leaning over the side, gesturing wildly to the steersman. "I see a way in."

The steersman nodded, immediately spotting the opening. Abruptly, he turned the boat, angling it away from the entrance and swinging it around to face the channel head on. He hung there momentarily, glancing back in Melody's direction. "If she tries to escape again, shoot her!" she heard him say, her heart skipping a beat as she noticed the third man lift up a rifle with a scope, aiming it directly at her.

In spite of the sudden fear gripping her, Melody held her position, knowing what was about to happen. Two objects broke from the water with blurring momentum, rising up on opposite sides of the boat and leaping over it. Yelps of surprise knifed the air as all three men were swept from the vessel.

With no one to steer it, the boat moved sluggishly beyond the reach of the men, and Melody caught sight of her brother rising to the surface next to it. With Alpha lending support, he managed to clamber up over the side and get behind the controls. Turning the steering wheel, he let the boat coast forward a few seconds longer before pointing the bow back toward the reef.

"Hey!" one of the floundering men screamed upon spitting out a mouthful of water. "Bring back our boat!"

Throwing the throttle all the way forward, Teejay leapt over the side just as the boat took off with a burst of speed. Rejoining Alpha, he watched in fascination as the hull hit the shelf of coral and jerked upward. A split second later, the outdrive snagged against the leading edge of the stationary obstacle, nearly tearing off the outboard motor. Careening wildly, the boat finally came to a stop, its hull ripped apart.

"We'll get you for this," another of the men shrieked, treading water and shaking his fist at Teejay.

Teejay ignored the threat, submerging with his mount to join his sister moments later. As he rose up next to Melody, Athena and Natalie came to the surface beside him.

"Nice job!" Melody marveled at her brother. Turning her head, she brought a loving gaze to Athena and Natalie. "Congratulations! Those jumps were perfectly timed."

"Shall we?" Teejay remarked, a broad grin clinging to his face as he looked at the others.

"Yes!" effused Melody.

"Then off we go," said Natalie.

Without another word, all six slipped below the surface.

-80-

Maximus was beside himself with rage at seeing what had happened to his men. Riding adolescent albino dolphins, those little brats had made fools of them, purposely luring them farther and farther south until the first boat slammed into a reef. He had watched the whole thing unfold through the remote cameras attached to the sunglasses his men wore. Deciding he could not let this game go on, he had ordered the men in the second boat to kill the girl if she tried to escape again. That was just before he caught a fleeting image of something leaping up to sweep the men into the water. Freeze-framing the blurred image on the video recording, he saw that it was another albino dolphin, this one much larger than the ones the children were riding. Also captured within the frame was the gray tail fluke of another dolphin streaking in the opposite direction. With only one of the men managing to keep from losing his glasses, he had observed the boy climb aboard their boat and send it crashing into the reef. After that, he saw two large dolphins, one albino and one gray, join both siblings and their mounts, only to disappear below the water.

A distressed voice crackled over the radio. "We need assistance, sir. Will help be coming soon to evacuate us?"

Maximus ignored the plea. *Screw them*, he thought bitterly. *Let them suffer for their stupidity.* Should he decide to rescue them, it wouldn't be until later, and the loss of the two boats would be coming out of their pay. Switching channels, he brought his attention back to Swensen. "Status?" he rasped.

"The woman says it's in a cave behind the waterfall, but we already found ten gold bars." Swensen shifted his gaze to show the small stack of gleaming bars sitting on the sandy beach. In the background, Maximus could see the nearness of whitewater tumbling into the gorge.

"Where did you find them?"

"Right where you see them. I don't advise touching them, they could be rigged with a bomb. Perhaps I should use the woman to test them."

"No, use the short captive to move them, but first have the men fall back to a safe position."

Maximus studied the one called Hector closely as Swensen ordered him to move the bars. Hector shrugged, glowering up at the Nordic before advancing on the stack and tossing them aside one by one until all ten formed a disorderly pile.

"Test one of the bars to see if they're real," Maximus instructed as Swensen rejoined the shorter man.

On the screen, a knife suddenly came into view, and with the point of the blade thrusting down sharply into one of the bars, Swensen used his considerable brawn to gouge a small cavity into the metal. Holding the bar up, he gave Maximus a close up perspective of his handiwork. "Seems real enough," Swensen said.

"Good, now have the woman take you and your men into the cave, including the captives, but leave two of the men behind as a rear guard."

Within moments, Maximus saw Amphitrite begin to scale the steep crag to the left of the falls, her two escorts struggling to keep pace with her. Shifting screens, he saw the arms of the lead escort reaching out for handholds among the numerous crevices and fractures, and as they climbed higher he realized the ascent was precarious. With the water so close and spray coming off it, moss clung to the rock in many places, making the going slippery.

Changing back to Swensen's perspective, he watched as the lead man followed the woman still higher. She was climbing with the nimbleness of a gibbon and he was having difficulty keeping up with her. An instant later, he bellowed out in horror as he lost his grip, and Maximus saw the man's head smash into a rock outcropping as he plunged into the tumultuous water below.

"Forget about him!" Maximus ordered impatiently. "Just keep the men moving. Finding the gold is all that matters."

Uncharacteristically, an eerie sense of superstition suddenly gripped Maximus, and he had trouble sweeping it aside. The thought that the rainbow might have been a precursor of calamitous events grew irrationally large in his mind, and he wondered if more were yet to come. Through Swensen's glasses, he had seen it arching over the falls when the woman had led his band to the rim of the gorge. *Was it merely coincidence, he asked himself?* Already he had lost the children, with six of his men currently stranded on the reef, three of them no doubt seriously injured. And now one of his men had died. A vision of the double rainbow he had seen arching over Aquaria and the island behind it abruptly assailed him to increase his growing unease, and it took considerable effort to quell the feeling. Angrily, he reminded himself how much he hated the sight of rainbows.

"Leave him!" Swensen yelled down, stopping the two men left behind on the beach from wading into the water to search for their fallen comrade. "No sense trying to retrieve a dead man."

Both men looked up, nodding in acquiescence.

Following behind Amphitrite's guard, Hector groped his way cautiously along the slippery rock with Zimbola right behind him. Reaching out for another handhold, Hector lost his grip, and had not Zimbola reacted instantly, Hector would have been another casualty. As though he had anticipated what was about to happen, Zimbola leaned forward to snare his longtime friend by the wrist to keep him from falling. Holding on with one hand to the rock, the tips of his banana-size fingers held fast to a crevice as he hauled Hector back up with the other. In moments, both men were again working their way higher along the path Amphitrite had chosen.

Several anxious minutes passed, but no other mishaps occurred. With the remainder of the party finally reaching the gloom behind the falls, the troopers began turning on small flashlights they carried. When Amphitrite casually reached for something along a side wall, her lone remaining escort stopped her, blocking her arm with his weapon.

"It's only a lantern," she said, raising her voice to be heard above the thunder of the falls.

Swensen intervened quickly. "Let her use it!" he commanded gruffly. Several men began to remove their sunglasses to see better in the dim light, but Swensen's curt admonishment stopped them from doing so. "Keep your glasses on!" he growled.

When Amphitrite flicked on the battery-powered lantern, the nearby shadows disappeared to reveal a succession of murals painted along the cave walls. The murals receded into the darkness that lay beyond the glow of the lantern. Playing their lights back and forth, Maximus' henchmen eyed the paintings curiously. Enthralled by the grim scenes the murals depicted, they followed Amphitrite deeper into the subterranean cavern.

Visual representations of Hispaniola's early history were laid bare, showing the arrival of the Spanish conquistadors and the subsequent atrocities they inflicted on the native people.

Holding to the rear of the procession, Swensen's voice boomed out again, echoing like a bass drum in the confined quarters. "Stay alert!" he warned. He could tell the murals were distracting the men.

Several moments later, Amphitrite stopped, seemingly reaching the back of the cave where jumbles of fallen rock blocked further progress. Where she currently stood, the pervading roar of the falls had diminished considerably, now reduced to a gentle susurration.

"I see no gold in here, woman," Swensen accused suspiciously.

"There's a passage behind the rock, but getting through is a tight squeeze," she said. "I doubt it will accommodate a man of your size." She turned her gaze to Zimbola, adding, "The Avenging Angel's captain has never been able to go beyond this point, and you are just as big."

"Show me!" Swensen said.

Continuing to hold the lantern, Amphitrite sidled her petite body around the largest boulder, leaving only a thin glow of light streaming back as she disappeared from sight. "Most of your men should be able to squeeze through," her disembodied voice echoed back.

"Keep thinking about your grandchildren," Swensen reminded her. "You hold their lives in the balance. Any trickery on your part will be the end of them." He shot a berating look to her immediate escort. The man stood fast, staring at the narrow opening with distrust. "Follow her!" he ordered. "Test the opening to see if she is lying."

Holding his weapon out in front of him with one hand, the escort overcame his reluctance and squeezed around the bend. A moment later, his voice came back, strained with exertion. "I think she's telling the truth, sir. I can barely squeeze through."

Turning his gaze on two of the nearest men, Swensen barked out another order. "Both of you will stay behind with me to guard the big one." His jaw clenched as he threw a hard stare at Zimbola. "The rest of you will follow the woman and communicate back what you find. I'm placing you in charge, Ratillo."

"What about him?" Ratillo asked, indicating Hector.

"Take him with you, but two of you go in ahead of him."

"I cannot get through wearing this pack," Hector protested haughtily.

"Take it off then and hand it through to the man in front of you," Swensen spat irritably. "You'll need it to carry gold."

Removing the backpack, Hector pushed it through the opening to the trooper that preceded him. He had never been in this cave, and a feeling bordering on claustrophobia gripped him as he squeezed his fireplug frame into the rocky entrance. Once through, the pack was shoved roughly back into his hands, and he was prodded forward to make room for the other troopers coming through. Looking past the men in front of him, he saw Amphitrite. In spite of their situation, she appeared unusually calm as she stood before a flight of steps carved into the stone. The light from her lantern illuminated a shaft that rose up steeply.

Amphitrite made subtle eye contact with Hector as several more grim-faced troopers crowded in behind him to scrutinize their tight quarters. Though her expression was guarded, he knew her well enough to know that something was going to happen, and very soon.

-81-

Maximus cast livid eyes on the monitoring screens. They had all gone blank, filled with the dull gray graininess of static. Once Swensen and his men had entered the cave, he had lost all contact with them. Obviously something was interfering with the transmission, most likely the cave's rocky interior.

Switching channels, he reverted to the sunglass cameras worn by the two lone sentries left behind on the beach adjacent to the base of the falls. It was as though he were looking through their eyes as images sprang onto two of the screens to replace the gray static. One showed the cascading waterfall while the other revealed a serene scene of the cove waters stretching away to the far end of the gorge.

The ship's intercom came alive, buzzing harshly to intrude into his thoughts. "We have located Percy Osgood, sir. Are you ready to receive him?"

A dark frown immediately consumed his face. "Yes, bring him in here now."

Moments later, Osgood was escorted into the control room accompanied by two members of the ship's security.

"Leave us!" Maximus rasped sternly, throwing a contemptuous gaze at both guards. They were well acquainted with the look. They had failed miserably in their duties by letting the children get away.

Both men turned, withdrawing from the room quickly to escape the withering stare.

Maximus remained seated, tilting his head in a sideways glance to study Osgood. Expecting to see the same fidgety expression Osgood always wore in his presence, he was surprised when he saw something different. The man appeared quite relaxed, with no sign of the usual edginess showing on his face. As a matter of fact, he could swear he detected a smirk residing just below the surface.

Indicating the screens behind him, Maximus frowned darkly and said, "As you can see from the monitors, I have lost contact with all but two of the men I sent ashore. Nine cameras are not working. Why is that?"

Percy stared at the two screens, his eyes coming to rest on the one showing a chasm-like setting. The image was stunning. The place seemed to flourish with life in a spectrum of pulsing colors.

"I'm not sure," Percy muttered distractedly, his mind racing along and trying to formulate another plan of action. He was thinking on his feet, and this latest development was something he might be able to use.

"You said those glasses would be exceptionally reliable when you designed them," Maximus grumbled in annoyance.

Boldly, Percy stepped past Maximus and leaned over the computer keyboard set off to one side. "Give me a sec to troubleshoot the system. Is the rest of the shore party at the same location?"

"No," Maximus said, rapidly losing patience with the scientist. "They're in a cave behind the waterfall you're looking at. Is that causing interference?"

Percy manipulated keys swiftly. "Possibly," he said. A map of the nearby Haitian coast replaced the screen showing the falls, with two flashing dots depicting the relative distance between the *Nunquarn Satis* and the shore party. Pulling up the GPS coordinates of the shore-based dot, he memorized the location, less than 5 miles from his current location. Without Maximus knowing what he was doing, he made a few more adjustments to the system settings before the real-time view of the waterfall once again settled on the screen.

"There you go," Percy said, smiling with satisfaction as three other screens suddenly came alive. "I increased the signal."

Maximus gazed critically at the darkened images fading in and out and overlaid with static. "What about the others?"

"Unfortunately that's the best I can do. Wherever those other men are, the rock surrounding them must be far too dense to allow video transmission. As it is, the three signals we're currently receiving from the cave are very weak."

Shifting his eyes between the three monitors, Maximus could just barely make out an image of the largest captive, who seemed to have an incessant scowl plastered on his face. He was being closely watched by the three men guarding him. Based on the primary screen, one of those men was Swensen.

Maximus pointed to the screen representing his bodyguard. "Will he be able to hear me?"

"He should," Percy replied.

Hitting the transmit button, Maximus said. "Can you hear me, Swensen?"

The image from Swensen's camera abruptly moved, facing away from the captive's scowling face. The response that came back was barely audible. "You're coming in very weak, but I can hear you."

"What happened to the others?"

"They moved deeper into the cave where the gold is located. The passage was too narrow for me to follow, so I sent six of the men ahead with the woman and the short one."

"Are you able to communicate with them?"

"No, but I will keep you informed as soon as they get back."

"Good," Maximus said. "I will expect to hear only good news."

Ending the transmission, he eyed Osgood. Necessity had dictated he avoid breaching the subject of the missing children until the scientist got the remote camera system up and running again.

"Two children in my custody managed to get off this ship with someone's help," Maximus said, keeping his rage at a simmer for the moment to gauge Osgood's reaction.

Osgood remained calm, far more relaxed than he should have been even if he was innocent of abetting the children. This uncharacteristic change in behavior made Maximus feel uncomfortable. Tranquil demeanors rattled him.

"And you think I am the party responsible," Percy said, his tone serene.

"Well are you?" Maximus growled, his wrath abruptly surfacing like a burst of hot gas rising rapidly from the ocean depths.

"Yes, I helped them. I also disabled your video system and planted those explosives."

Maximus gaped, suddenly speechless at the man's forthright audacity. That he would openly admit he had done these things was the last thing he had anticipated.

Overcoming his astonishment, Maximus found his tongue. "Then you have signed your brother's death sentence," he stated, nearly stammering out the words.

Percy chuckled. "No I haven't. Mortimer escaped Cardoza's clutches." With his eyes abruptly coming alive with defiance, he let the statement sink in to further unsettle Maximus' composure before going on. "You probably don't even know that Cardoza is dead. Your plan to unleash *Sterilis* on Haitian farmland has gone up in smoke. All the drones have been destroyed along with much of Cardoza's compound."

Maximus stared dumbly, barely able to speak. "That's impossible!" he croaked. "You're bluffing."

"No I'm not." Osgood threw a confident look at the bank of monitoring screens. "See for yourself. You have access to satellite imagery. Would you like me to pull it up for you?"

Without waiting for an answer, Osgood leaned over the computer keyboard again. With the deftness of a concert pianist, his fingers played swiftly over the keys to bring up an image of the Caribbean on the center screen, which was larger than the others. The display changed quickly, enlarging through a rapid sequence of magnified images that homed in on Haiti's southwestern peninsula.

Maximus was numb as he looked upon the final picture. A good third of Cardoza's fortress lay in ruins. Shifting his eyes, he saw what was left of the hangar one mile to the east. Only rubble and charred portions of aircraft littered the landscape. Out in the bay and along the shore, he discerned masses of floating debris, some of it having already washed up on the beach. But there were no vessels sitting at anchor. Both the Southern Star and Northern Comet were gone, along with Cardoza's luxury yacht, *Usurpar*.

"How did you know about this?" Maximus uttered feebly, still in shock. "You had no access to this room."

Osgood studied the screen, his eyes roving over the detailed imagery as if seeing it for the first time. "Mortimer got word to me."

"But how?" Maximus demanded gruffly, suddenly coming out of his stupor.

"Have you forgotten that I am an electronic whiz? Even your seemingly airtight computer security lock could not prevent communication between me and my brother."

Maximus' voice gained volume, now rasping with outrage. "Someone must have helped your brother escape."

"Yes, someone did, and that man is on his way here. If he was able succeed with Cardoza, I can only imagine what he is capable of doing to you."

Maximus shot a hand to the intercom, slamming his fist down on the button. "Guards!" he shrieked.

Osgood looked upon Maximus with repugnance, slipping a hand into a pocket on his lab coat. "You're finished, Malcolm. I'm going to make sure your insidious schemes never come to fruition. My brother and I have all the evidence we need to expose you and your organization to the world."

"I am the world," Maximus crowed mordantly, rising to his feet. "I control it."

Osgood smiled. "But for how much longer once this information gets out. Mortimer and I know about *The Order* and what it is trying to achieve."

The door behind Maximus suddenly burst open, the same two guards entering the room with their weapons drawn.

"You'll tell me where you keep this information," Maximus hissed.

"Or what? You'll torture me." Osgood laughed, lifting something from the pocket and holding it up.

Maximus stared at the small device, his eyes shifting back to the unbearable smile on Osgood's face. "What is that?"

"Should my thumb come off this button, this ship will be destroyed along with everyone on it. There are enough explosives aboard to do that."

"You would sacrifice yourself to kill me?"

"As the old saying goes, 'the ball is in your court,'" Osgood chortled, noticing that the hard expressions the guards wore had changed over to terror.

A troubled look fell across Maximus' face, and he swallowed noisily as though gulping down a disagreeable morsel of food. Nervously, he eyed the device held in Osgood's hand, wondering if it was truly a detonator. Gambling on a hunch was something foreign to his nature, and in making decisions he had always made it a habit to stack the deck in his favor before betting on the outcome. To gamble on the possibility of a bluff had the potential of getting him killed. He realized he had no choice but to negotiate a deal. "What do you want?"

"Have your pilot fly me to shore." Osgood was referring to the helicopter sitting aboard the ship's landing pad. A second chopper sat in an enclosed hanger abutting the pad.

"How do I know you won't destroy the ship once you're off it?"

"You don't. But I know you still have another hostage aboard, and I prefer to avoid soiling my soul with the blood of an innocent unless you force me to. All I want is a ride to shore. Beyond a mile, the signal from this device won't reach the ship, and the coast is farther away than that."

Maximus studied Osgood closely, failing to understand this sudden change that had come over him. The man carried a casual, carefree air, completely devoid of the one thing he valued most for carrying out his goals, and that was fear.

"Very well," he rasped in feigned resignation, his mind quickly racing ahead with a plan of reprisal. He would accommodate Osgood's wishes for the time being, but once the helicopter was away, he would move the ship further out to sea to ensure it was beyond the range of a potential detonation signal, assuming that the scientist was not bluffing and that he would keep his word about not using it. After Osgood disembarked the aircraft, he'd have the pilot fly into the gorge to pick up two of the mercenaries under Swensen's command and fly them to where Osgood was dropped off. Then they would track him down and bring him back after the device was destroyed.

"I should give you fair warning that any move or perceived trickery on the part of your men to disarm me will be met with the destruction of this ship. Then I shall see you all in hell."

Percy was surprised at the calmness of his own voice. Strangely, he felt not the slightest bit of fear as he faced Maximus and his cohorts. His mind was clear, unhampered by dread or anxiety as it once was in the presence of this man. But he knew the cause. It was the mysterious display of interlacing lights he had been exposed to just before Maximus had lost control of the drone. The feeling it had evoked in him had been euphoric. And even now he could sense its effect lingering within him.

Maximus turned, focusing a stern gaze on the two guards. "Escort him to the landing pad and see that he gets off the ship without any interference. Is that understood?"

After both men nodded apprehensively, Maximus looked back at Osgood, his eyes ablaze with pent up anger. "I'll notify the pilot to take you ashore. Now go! Get off my ship."

-82-

Ratillo glanced around the square chamber wearing a scowl. Under the weakening glow of the lantern held by Amphitrite, his features quite distinctly resembled what his namesake suggested. Strangely, he was fond of the moniker bestowed on him by his fellow comrades in arms.

"I see no gold in here," the *"Rat"* grumbled.

"Look upon the walls," Amphitrite said.

Flashing his small flashlight directly on one of the walls, Rat was nearly blinded by the light reflected back at him. Even the dark glasses he wore failed to suppress the intense yellow radiance. Stepping closer, he ran a hand over the mirror-like surface. It was smooth and polished, and as he explored it further, he saw a caricature of his rodent-like image staring back at him, grotesquely distorted as though he were observing himself in a funhouse mirror. All around him, other members of the six-man squad were doing the same.

Rat brought a bewildered gaze back to Amphitrite. "What is this?"

"The walls of this chamber are made of pure gold," Amphitrite said.

As if to confirm her claim, Rat ran his fingers along the surface again, then looked around the room as though he might have missed something. "What good does this do us?" he complained heatedly, bringing his eyes back to Amphitrite. "There's nothing to carry out with us."

"Maximus asked that I show you where the gold was kept, and I've done that," Amphitrite stated calmly.

With a snarl on his face, Rat moved toward her, drawing an arm across his chest to give her a vicious backhand slap, but stopped short as a cascade of light suddenly poured down from the ceiling above. Startled, he looked up.

A whirlpool of glimmering bands spun counterclockwise, the eddy of luminosity quickly gathering speed and growing brighter, and Rat imagined he was glimpsing a far off galaxy in deep space. Intrigued, he could not tear his eyes away as the whirlpool expanded to reveal individual glowing points, the space between them opening up swiftly to show vast gulfs of nothingness. The illusion was mesmerizing, and he had the sensation he was traveling at many times the velocity of light as he flew into the heart of the swirling mass.

"The pursuit of physical gold is merely an imitation of the true gold," Amphitrite said, remembering the words she had spoken long ago when she had cleansed Chester Hennington of all the rot that had built up inside of him. She sensed these men were diametrically different and beyond help, however, truly nefarious by nature, and it stood to reason their wickedness would at least approximate the man they worked for. But if she couldn't help them, she would do what she could to rid the planet of them.

"There is a great deal of difference between true and false gold," she continued. "It is the longing for real gold that causes man to collect the imitation gold."

"Are you implying the walls of this room are made of fake gold?" Rat grunted, keeping his eyes fixated on the overhead display.

Amphitrite ignored the question, sermonizing further. "Because gold represents the color of light and spiritual inspiration, man has unconsciously pursued this divine light by seeking an imitation of it much the way a small child satisfies itself by playing with toys. In this way man attempts to gratify this craving of the soul by seeking the false gold, ignorant that the true gold lies like a hidden spark deep within his heart, his innermost being."

Rat frowned, continuing to look up. "What are you talking about, woman?"

Amphitrite kept her voice neutral, without emotion. "But I see no hidden spark within your heart, only darkness. Men like you will never know the true gold."

Rat grimaced in annoyance, and for one fleeting moment she thought he would look away from the ongoing light show.

"Do you know where physical gold comes from?" Amphitrite asked him.

Rat stared hypnotically, wondering why this woman would ask such a stupid question. "Gold mines!" he muttered absently.

Amphitrite glanced around, aware that all six of her captors were fully entranced by the sight as a lone star loomed up, its surface sending out a deep violet radiance that only the hottest stars could emit.

"Gold comes from heavy element stars that are far more massive than our sun," she said. "After several million years of generating energy by fusing light elements into heavier ones, these stars eventually run out of fuel. But in the process, so much iron builds up in their core that the star can no longer support its own weight. When this happens, immense gravitational forces collapse the ball of iron in upon itself, causing it to erupt in a cataclysmic explosion called a *supernova*. This eruption provides the necessary heat to fuse iron into gold, scattering it to other parts of the galaxy where it combines with other elements and space dust to form new solar systems."

The men stood transfixed as the star erupted in a blinding flash to send out a rush of matter and lethal radiation in all directions.

As Amphitrite spoke, she moved next to Hector, who also appeared entranced. "Following a *supernova* explosion, a small dense star composed primarily of neutrons is all that remains. These neutron-rich stars are called *pulsars*. They become highly magnetized and rotate at a dizzying rate, releasing incredible amounts of energy."

Amphitrite grabbed hold of Hector, pulling him close and placing a hand over his eyes. Making sure to look away, she said. "But at the center of these *pulsars* is a black hole, capable of sucking in anything that comes near it, including dark matter."

Amphitrite closed her eyes as a gale of swirling wind suddenly cropped up, nearly lifting her and Hector off their feet. Men screamed out in panic, their cries of alarm fading away rapidly as though they were falling into a deep well.

The rush of air died quickly, and sensing that the danger had passed, Amphitrite opened her eyes and glanced around.

Except for herself and Hector, the chamber was empty.

* * * *

-83-

The wails of the advance party carried in the confined quarters before fading altogether, and by the time they reached Swensen's ears, the sound was reduced to an indecipherable whisper. Moving close to the narrow fissure in the rock that prevented him from accompanying the men, he poked his head in. "Did you find anything?" he shouted into the opening.

When no reply came back, he repeated the query, only to be met with an unsettling silence that was overlaid by the pervasive rustle of the falls.

Zimbola sneered. Strange things seemed to happen whenever Amphitrite was involved. "Do not expect your men to return," he badgered mockingly.

Swensen spun, aiming his pistol at Zimbola's face. "I have had enough of you," he spat ominously, the dark glasses giving him the look of the android in *The Terminator* movie. "Maybe I should kill you now."

Zimbola gazed at the firearm with disdain. "That is the only way a man like you will be able to kill me…with a gun."

Maddened with rage, Swensen's finger tightened on the trigger, and if not for the voice of Maximus suddenly coming alive in his ear, he would have fired the weapon. "What is happening?" Maximus demanded.

Turning his back on Zimbola, Swensen spoke quickly as the two mercenaries assisting him kept their assault rifles trained on their captive. "I am not sure. I heard something further back in the cave, but the men do not answer when I call to them."

"Perhaps they're too far back to be heard," Maximus said.

"Maybe," Swensen replied, turning a sour gaze back on the hulking Jamaican, who faced the two men guarding him with a ferocious, challenging demeanor. "Do you have any problem with me terminating the big one? He is becoming a nuisance."

Maximus hesitated only momentarily. "Then get rid of him."

A menacing smile crossed Swensen's face. That was all he needed to hear. With sadistic intent, he pointed the Glock at Zimbola's knee. He would make the big man suffer before he killed him.

At that moment, Amphitrite emerged from the fissure in the rock. "Your weapons will not work in here," she said calmly.

Swensen turned at the sudden intrusion, looking behind her in expectation. When no one else appeared, he bared teeth like a maddened dog. "Where are the others?" he rumbled.

"Your men are gone."

"What do you mean gone?"

"They are no longer with us, they are gone from this earth."

Swensen stared, stunned and confused by the implication. "Do not joke with me, woman. What happened to my men?"

"The darkness took them."

The voice of Maximus blurted in Swensen's ear to further fan the flames of his growing rage. "Kill her! Then have your men find out what happened to the others. If there's gold in there, you'll find it without the woman's assistance."

Though he was still bewildered, Swensen's lips curled up into a malicious grin, anxious to carry out the order. But first he would kill the big one, nice and slow as he had planned.

As he raised the Glock, he heard something hum, the sound quickly gathering strength as though heralding the approach of a swarm of bees from the mouth of the cave. The buzz escalated sharply into a piercing whine, causing Swensen to grimace with pain. Lifting a hand to his ear to block the sound, an intense light many times the brightness of the sun suddenly flared before his eyes. Blinded, he gripped the glasses and tore them from his face, instinctively knowing them to be the cause of his discomfort. Blinking and trying to regain his vision, he vaguely perceived two dull thumps resound in the confined quarters. Something clattered harshly on the cave floor, and an instant later he felt a powerful hand grip the wrist of his gun-toting hand.

Squeezing the trigger several times in reaction, Swensen was surprised when the Glock failed to discharge. But if it would not fire, he would use it as a bludgeon. Bracing himself, he used his massive legs and arms to break away from the man grappling with him, but as he did so the gun was yanked from his hand and sent caroming off a wall.

"I told you I would kill you," Zimbola grunted.

Still blinded, Swensen managed to grab an arm, twisting and turning to counter the impossible steel-like grip imposed on him. He knew the Jamaican would be strong, but he found it inconceivable that a human could exert this much strength. At an early age, he had learned to use his superior size and brawn to bully people, establishing himself as a troublemaker on the streets of Oslo where he had developed a fondness for intimidation. Rarely had he ever come across anyone that could match him in brute strength. Pounding someone into a comatose state was something he greatly enjoyed, and it was this propensity for violence that had led him to the wrong side of the law. Only a merciful judge had kept him from going to prison, giving him the option of serving in the Norwegian army to avoid incarceration, and it was in the military where he had taken up wrestling, eventually winning a spot on Norway's Greco-Roman wrestling team. The darkness within him proved to be an asset, and he had learned how to channel it into an unparalleled string of wins for the team. This ultimately took him to the Olympics where he might have medaled if not for being disqualified in a semi-final match in the super heavyweight division eleven years earlier. Frustrated by an exceptionally skilled opponent and unable to restrain the darkness welling up inside him, he had bitten off a finger of his foe. Deeply embittered by the loss, he had competed in a strong man competition a year later, easily winning the event against fifteen of the world's most powerful men. But since then, he had become even stronger with the help of weekly injections of human growth hormone and anabolic steroids, all provided to him by Maximus, who had recruited him to be his personal bodyguard. Yet the man now opposing him seemed to be every bit as strong, and this shocked him.

Pivoting and using his hips, Swensen maneuvered for advantage using his wrestling skills to throw his opponent off balance. Still very much blinded, only spots danced before his eyes in the limited light. Vision, however, would not be necessary for him to execute a throw. Being slightly shorter than Zimbola, he worked his long gorilla-like arms under Zimbola's to clamp them around his torso in a powerful bear hug. Unfortunately, attempting his favorite move, a belly to belly vertical *suplex*, would be foolhardy since it would require lifting his opponent in a high overhead arch and falling back on his own neck on the rocky floor.

Both men struggled like two massive bull elephants locking tusks, turning and driving each other against the cave walls, each vying to knock the other off his feet. With small boulders and rubble littering the floor at this juncture in the cave, it was only inevitable that one of the men would stumble.

A harsh grunt left Zimbola's lips as his left ankle met one of these obstacles, and with Swensen forcing him back, the huge Jamaican lost his balance, the side of his head colliding harshly against a rocky surface. Swensen was on him in an instant, straddling him in a full mount and raining down a hail of thunderous punches. Dazedly, Zimbola reached up through the storm, managing to force a thumb the size of a cucumber into Swensen's throat. The Nordic immediately gagged, clutching his injured windpipe with both hands and wheezing hoarsely. Lifting a leg, Zimbola hooked it around Swensen's head and swept him away. Rising to his feet, he crouched low and drove a shoulder into Swensen's gut. Swensen expelled a low grunt as the wind was driven from him, but he recovered quickly, reaching out blindly to hook an arm around Zimbola's neck.

Ponderously, both giants grappled, breathing heavily as they pivoted and danced, striving for superior leverage. Swensen tried for a hip throw but nearly tripped over the two guards Zimbola had taken out. Both of them lay unconscious, one atop the other in a fallen heap. Regaining his balance, he caught Zimbola with a stiff forearm that opened up a gash under his left eye. Shaking off the blow, Zimbola countered with an overhand right that landed solidly on Swensen's jaw. With a fist the size of a cannonball, he followed up with a vicious left. The Nordic's face distorted in a grimace of pain as blood splattered from his broken nose. Staggering back, he latched onto Zimbola's wrist to keep from falling down. Again they danced and whirled, tenaciously locked up in battle and alternately slamming each other into walls of rock but still managing to hold their feet. Both men were now gasping for air and drenched in sweat, bleeding profusely from a multitude of contusions and cuts about their face and arms.

Sensing that his opponent's endurance was beginning to flag, Zimbola bulled Swensen around, aligning him with the fallen guards. Timing his move, he shoved him violently away. A stunned look of horror swept over Swensen's face as he was sent flying backwards over the men, the back of his head thudding heavily into a boulder as he landed flat on his back.

Swensen stared up with glazed eyes as Zimbola fell on top of him. "The evil fire that burns within you must be extinguished," Zimbola gasped, his left hand grasping Swensen by the throat. Bunching a fist, he came down hard with his right hand, hammering it into Swensen's face like a piston a half dozen times. With his features turned to a bloody pulp, Swensen somehow found the strength to turn onto his stomach to avoid the pulverizing blows. Straddling his adversary's back, Zimbola gripped Swensen's head in his powerful hands and heaved up, cranking it to one side with all of his remaining strength. A sickening crunch echoed sharply as vertebrae snapped, and Swensen's body jerked spasmodically before going slack.

Zimbola rolled off Swensen's inert body and lay on his back, closing his eyes and fighting for breath. Something touched his face, and he realized Amphitrite was kneeling over him with a hand on his cheek. He knew she was healing his injuries with her miraculous touch.

"Is he dead?" Zimbola asked, continuing to gasp. Never had he encountered a man so strong.

"Yes, and so are the other two."

"I didn't think I hit them that hard," Zimbola said, mildly surprised by her statement.

Hector was suddenly hovering over both of them. "What now?" he asked. "There are two more of them outside the cave."

Amphitrite looked up and smiled. "Something tells me they won't be a problem."

-84-

Percy Osgood sat in the spacious cabin of the EC 135, one of two helicopters stationed aboard the massive super-yacht. The high-end luxury chopper manufactured by Eurocopter was typical of Maximus, who indulged himself in the most expensive and extravagant state-of-the-art equipment found on the market. With its plush interior, the rotary-wing aircraft seemed to focus entirely on the needs of high-net worth individuals.

Percy glanced down as the chopper lifted off the landing pad and sped away. As he had anticipated, the *Nunquarn Satis* was already moving further out to sea to increase its distance from the detonator held in his hand. Allowing himself a small smile, he took his thumb off the device and let out a sigh of relief. To his own amazement his bluff had succeeded beyond his wildest expectations. The device was not a detonator but a sending unit he had quickly assembled to interface with the sunglass communication system he had designed, and having gained access to the ship's main control room, he had been able to reprogram the system right under Maximus' nose.

Slumping back into the comfortable handcrafted leather seat, he wondered where this cunning boldness had come from that had allowed him to rescue the children and escape from Maximus' clutches. He had always thought himself to be a coward, but this newfound courage confounded him. Putting aside this self-appraisal, he checked out the reading on the unit's tiny display screen.

Keying the intercom, he said, "Take us on a heading of 120 degrees."

A moment later, the aircraft banked moderately to starboard to take on the new heading. "You made a big mistake in going against Maximus," the pilot grumbled. "You have signed your own death warrant."

Percy ignored the comment, continuing to monitor the screen. According to the reading, Swensen's team was less than four miles away to the southeast where the land along the coastline rose up steeply. Oddly enough, the location closely matched the coordinates Mortimer had given him. Long ago, both brothers had developed a modified version of the *Khoisan* click language indigenous to some tribes of southern Africa, using their tongues to articulate *'click'* consonants of varied inflections through which they could communicate in a coded conversation of their own, and it was while Percy was hastily putting together the device he held in his hand that he received a message from his brother on a short wave instrument he had turned on. To anyone listening in, it would have sounded like inconsequential noise emitted by one of the many electronic gadgets filling his lab, but to Percy it was like the sound of a concerto symphony. Mortimer was safe and with the man who had rescued him, and soon they would arrive at the prearranged location he had sent him, which was a short distance away. His brother had also given him an ETA.

Using a specially prepared program, Percy had replied back to his brother to apprise him of his plans. Checking his watch, he saw that the estimated time of arrival was less than five minutes away.

As the chopper reached the land, Percy scanned the rugged terrain below him, and it was only moments later that he spotted a cascading waterfall spilling into a gorge. The sight took his breath away. With the sun now directly overhead, the sunlight accentuated a kaleidoscope of vibrant colors carpeting tiered slopes that fell away into a mirror-like lagoon of blue-green water. Near the base of the falls, he spotted two lone figures lingering on a narrow strip of white sand.

"Bring us lower and fly donuts over the gorge below us," Percy instructed the pilot.

"Maximus said I was only to drop you off," the pilot protested.

Percy leaned forward and held up the device. "See this! It's a microwave detonator. All I have to do is take my thumb off the button and the *Nunquarn Satis* is deep-sixed. If you want a ship to fly back to you'll do as I say."

"The ship's too far away for the signal to reach it," the pilot insisted, remembering what Maximus had told him.

"No it's not," Percy lied. "This device has a range of twenty miles."

The pilot let out an incomprehensible curse before doing as directed, and Percy felt the change in inertia as the chopper dipped lower to swing around in a tight counterclockwise bank. Looking out the portside window, he was staring almost straight down as he studied the layout of the elongated amphitheater of dazzling hues. He immediately discerned a narrow doglegged channel that connected the basin of water with the ocean, and as the aircraft swung beyond the escarpment that hid the chasm from the sea, he glimpsed the two skiffs caught up on the reef along with several of the men that had rode in them. Two other men had managed to make their way ashore, appearing stranded on a slender ledge that sat below a sheer wall of rock. Hearing the chopper, they looked up hopefully, no doubt believing Maximus had sent the aircraft to rescue them.

Movement under the water drew Percy's eyes, and he perceived a torpedo-like object better than thirty feet in length slide past the men sitting atop the ledge. At first he thought it was a huge sea creature, but as the chopper looped for another pass, he saw that it had entered the channel that gave way to the lagoon.

"How long am I to keep flying circles?" the pilot suddenly peeved.

"Bring us to the beach near the falls and maintain a hover!" Percy ordered.

The two guards on the beach kept their weapons lowered as the EC 135 descended and came closer to hang stationary at a height of 30 meters above the water. Still wearing the sunglasses, they stared stoically up at the chopper as though expecting its arrival.

Percy aimed the device in his hand, depressing the button and sending out a signal. Both men abruptly reeled, dropping their weapons and raising their hands as though to shield their eyes. Tearing off the sunglasses, they appeared to stagger around blindly.

A satisfied smile came to Percy's face as he took in the scene. The device had worked perfectly, its signal causing an overload in the audio receptors and the tiny light emitting diodes embedded in the sunglass lenses. Wherever the rest of the shore party was, the overload would cause a chain reaction throughout the system, deafening and blinding anyone wearing the glasses.

Something rippled the water close to shore, drawing Percy's attention to the disturbance, and an instant later he espied a man rise to the surface and wade onto the beach. Held within the man's hands was an odd looking firearm, its muzzle trained on the two blinded guards.

One of the guards seemed to regain his vision, and scrambling for his dropped weapon, he plucked it from the sand to fire upon this unanticipated interloper. Too late on the trigger, the guard's body was hurled violently back as the interloper fired first. By this time the second guard reacted, pulling a handgun from a holster, only to be thrown back as a powerful round plowed into his body.

"Drop me off on the beach!" Percy commanded the pilot.

"Are you crazy?" the pilot shot back.

"Do it or so help me I'll destroy the ship," Percy said.

"Okay, okay!"

Percy opened the side door as the chopper dropped low to hover a few feet off the sand. Jumping clear, he looked back to watch the helicopter climb above a towering ridgeline to disappear.

Jake Javolyn came over to him cradling the Sledgehammer in his arms. "You must be Percy, Mort's twin brother," he said. "You look just like him."

Percy gripped Jake's hand, shaking it vigorously. "Thank you for rescuing my brother. I am indebted to you, sir." Looking past Jake, he scanned the water. "Where is he?"

Just as he asked the question, *Johnnie* broke the surface twenty meters from shore, its top hatch popping open. A moment later, Mort climbed out onto the hull and waved to him, a broad smile clinging to his face. Several more objects were suddenly alongside the sub, and Percy heard the laughter of two children. In a flash, Melody and Troy Jacob were whisked to shore by their bond mates.

"Do me a favor and hold this," Jake said to Percy, handing him the Sledgehammer and kneeling down to embrace his children as they rushed into his arms.

"Dadoo!" they screamed, hugging him fiercely.

Jake stood, holding a child in each of his brawny arms. "He saved us, Dadoo," they both chorused in unison, looking at Percy in admiration. "He snuck us off that bad man's ship."

Jake kissed each child tenderly on the forehead before setting them back down in the sand. "I think I am much more indebted to you, sir," he said to Percy, who watched eagerly as Mort was towed to shore by Achilles. Percy handed him back the Sledgehammer and waded out into the water to embrace his twin brother.

The sound of another whirlybird caught Jake's ear, and looking up, he spotted Fernando's chopper coming over the cove's southern rise. A minute later, the Bell Ranger set down on the beach, and Destiny and Franklin climbed from the fuselage. Almost immediately, both children dashed over with gushing exuberance to greet their mother and grandfather, cries of unrestrained joy issuing from their lips.

While on his way back from the *Bay of Anse-Milieu*, Jake had learned of the Avenging Angel's hijacking and the subsequent kidnapping of everyone aboard, including his children, but by the time he had been informed of this through Achilles, the children had already escaped. For reasons he was still trying to fathom, his mother-in-law had purposely instructed the dolphins accompanying her to withhold this information from the remainder of the albino telepathic network until the time was right to do so. Not even Destiny had known about the situation. But upon hearing of it, Jake had immediately gotten word to Fernando not to land in the cove. Rather he was to standby at the Devil's Horn until Jake felt it safe for him to enter the hidden sanctuary.

As the moment wore on, Phillipe, Victor Belachek, and Jimenez climbed from *Johnnie's* hatch to join the party ashore. Jake became aware of movement by the falls, and glancing up, he saw Amphitrite, Zimbola and Hector making their way down from the hidden cave.

Upon reaching the beach, Belachek had a brief word with Percy before approaching Jake with a sober expression. "My son is still aboard that ship."

"Yes, I know," Jake said, expelling a deep sigh. He had learned this from Achilles, who had been apprised of the situation by Alpha and

Omega.

Belachek held his gaze with those strange mismatched orbs of his. "Are you going to help me get him back?"

Jake knew he could not refuse him. If not for Belachek, much of Haiti's farmland would have been contaminated and rendered useless for growing crops, at least for several years to come. But with time growing short and a need to get back to Aquaria, he was suddenly confronted by a storm of indecision.

"Yes, I'll help you," Jake said, placing a hand on Belachek's shoulder. "Come with me."

Intruding upon Mort's reunion with his twin brother, Jake looked to Percy. "One other person is still being held prisoner aboard that ship. Do you know where he's being held?"

-85-

Maximus stared at one of the screens showing the receding Haitian coast, his head reeling from what had befallen him. First it had been the children escaping, followed by the death of Cardoza and the destruction of the drones. To make matters worse, the Osgood brothers had also slipped away beyond his grasp, at least temporarily. Even the prized robo-fish Percy had designed were gone, further adding to his woes. He had thought to use the speedy units to chase down the children in the open sea, but Estrada had informed him they were missing from the yacht's moon pool. A highly loyal employee that Maximus had assigned to be Percy's assistant, Estrada was the only person other than Percy capable of programming and operating the robo-fish. He had planned on using the autonomous units to further discredit the colony by setting off explosions on Navassa's pristine reefs just prior to the UN invasion of Aquaria.

And as if to add insult to injury, another rainbow suddenly materialized above the distant shoreline, arching high over the village of Malique and framing it perfectly. The very sight of it rankled him, and he couldn't help but wonder if it was yet another omen of more bad things to come. Ever since he had witnessed the double rainbow hanging above Aquaria and Navassa Island, his troubles had begun to mount.

A meticulous schemer, Maximus was not used to his carefully laid plans going awry, and lately it seemed as though he had been thwarted and outmaneuvered every step of the way. Mulling this, he remembered his last conversation with Percy Osgood.

"*'Someone must have helped your brother escape.'*

'Yes, someone did, and that man is on his way here. If he was able succeed with Cardoza, I can only imagine what he is capable of doing to you.'"

A mental image of Jake Javolyn suddenly loomed large in his mind, and with it, his utter hatred of the man. It had to be Javolyn, he told himself. The former Navy Seal was the only one he could think of with the training and military knowhow to take on a man like Cardoza and come out on top. Here was the man at the heart of his problems, he and all those who worked for Tursiops.

But then there was the matter of the Osgood brothers. *"Mortimer and I know about The Order and what it is trying to achieve,"* Percy had said. The very thought of it disturbed him to no end, and he knew under no circumstances could he ever let that information get out, for if it did, it could potentially bring down *The Order*, exposing from the shadows all those associated with it. But if it somehow managed to leak out, he would use the full clout of the mainstream media in concert with *fifth column* government officials to dismiss it as just another conspiracy theory concocted by lunatics. With public apathy currently at an all-time high, even hard facts could be turned into nothing more than malicious gossip and scuttlebutt, deflected and quashed by the net of deception purposely emplaced to mold the perceptions and opinions of citizenry. Conspiracy theories were in abundance these days, with many of them actually true, he well knew. Nevertheless, he preferred that information never get out.

Over the centuries, the clandestine organization had continued to become ever more prosperous and omnipotent at the expense of the masses, manipulating world affairs to gratify its insatiable hunger for more and more power and riches. If left to flourish, *The Order* would soon control the entire planet, achieving complete dominance over humanity and establishing the global feudal system it had always sought. It would be a system in which there would only be three classes of people, the super-elite, the elite and the peons, with the peons forced to perform all the work.

The thought of the plan being disrupted evoked a deep sense of outrage in Maximus. Only the highest ranking members within the organization had knowledge of the plan's full context, but bringing them all together for face to face clandestine discussions without arousing the suspicions of government officials not connected with the cabal was not always easy, nor advisable. But closed door sessions of the *Bilderbergs* usually presented an opportunity for this to happen, and he made it a habit to take full advantage of these annual summit meetings of the world's elite. Though the press openly acknowledged such forums, as was typical of these gatherings, the agendas and list of attendees was kept strictly confidential. Security was always airtight, sponsored by a strong military presence within the hosting country, and no one other than attendees would be privy to what was discussed. During these meetings it was generally agreed that only the most affluent deserved to govern, for if left to control its own destiny through moral convictions and unworkable dead-end ideals, the mainstream factions of the human race were just too stupid to do an adequate job of governing themselves. In the end, they would undoubtedly destroy the planet through runaway breeding that would ultimately deplete all of its precious resources. Only men like himself, plutocratic elites who shared pragmatic beliefs, would be able to save it, though as a rule the planning of sinister agendas at such meetings were generally avoided unless circumstances dictated it.

Each year when these forums took place, Maximus would take aside those members of *The Order's* royalty he had ordered to attend and conduct a separate closed door session to chart out new or revised goals or report on objectives already underway, though on the surface these discussions would undoubtedly be perceived to be quite unsavory and repugnant to even the most radical *Bilderberg* factions not connected with *The Order*. Lurking at the heart of these discussions, however, was their primary mission, which ultimately entailed establishing a feudalistic world government in combination with a form of slavery in which the peons would produce all the wealth for the other two classes to enjoy at their leisure. The only socialism that would exist would involve providing just enough of the basic necessities needed to sustain the slaves. But first the world population had to be greatly reduced to a more manageable level, and the ways and means by which they would accomplish it were laid out in detail.

Scowling, Maximus brought his eyes to the other screens, all of which remained blank. Seconds earlier, his link to the shore party had suddenly ended, with the network of screens connected to them flaring brightly in unison with an unbearable audio screech that had temporarily deafened him. And then the system had gone inexplicably dead. But just before it happened, he had seen his helicopter fly into the gorge and come to a hover, observed through the glasses of the two rear guards left outside the cave.

Keying the radio, he hailed his pilot. "Report!?"

The pilot's tone was grave. "A man rose up out of the water and killed the two guards outside the cave. I had no choice but to drop Osgood off and get out of there. I'm now inbound for the ship."

Maximus stiffened as though pierced by a lance stabbing deep into his gut, but he quickly gathered himself. "Do not land!" he ordered. "I need you to pick someone up in Port-au-Prince."

"Who?"

"Shut up and stand by!" Maximus snapped irritably. He needed to think this out a bit more carefully. As he mulled the situation, a revised plan formed rapidly in his mind.

Snatching up his cell phone, he activated a programmed number and placed the device to his ear. Though it rang only three times, to Maximus it seemed to take forever before a familiar voice answered. Talking curtly in coded Latin, Maximus spoke quickly, barking out several instructions before ending the call. Hastily, he called another number, not really expecting anyone to answer since it was possible that person was dead. Even so, he had to make sure. From what he had seen of Cardoza's stronghold, he doubted anyone could have survived the destruction.

He was just about to hang up when someone answered after the sixth ring, but he had trouble hearing the person on the other end due to a pervading drone in the background. Again he gave instructions in coded Latin, receiving some information in return.

Another idea came swiftly to him, and Maximus placed one more coded call, this one to someone that was currently in the floating city of Aquaria. The phone only rang twice before that person answered and a quick exchange ensued. Finally satisfied, Maximus hung up and glimpsed the EC 135 circling his ship.

Knowing that his radio link with the pilot was encrypted, Maximus hailed the pilot again. "You're to pick up Senator Brent Van Heflin. He and another man will be waiting for you. Get them back to this ship without delay."

He knew it was quite fortunate that the senator was currently meeting with the Haitian Minister of Agriculture. It made him easily accessible. It meant he could be delivered to the ship in less than an hour to discuss what he had in mind.

-86-

Mat Daniels stood at a window high up in Aquaria's central tower with Amelia Amhurst at his side. They were in the same room where Jacob had shown Amelia the doctored newscasts. As they looked out to sea, they could see a fleet of ships gathering on the horizon, one of them an aircraft carrier.

Amelia turned, setting a questioning gaze on Jacob, who sat glumly at his desk. "What are you going to do?"

"Nothing at the moment," Jacob said.

"Do you think they're going to send in troops?"

Jacob nodded. "Undoubtedly."

Amelia thought about the strange art scattered all about the colony. Out of curiosity she had asked Mat about it, and he had explained what it did to viewers, though if this were true, she wondered why a bad egg like Bolder had not gotten ill from it.

"Then your art should neutralize them," she said hopefully.

Jacob shook his head dejectedly. Jay Jay had gotten word to him about the antidote UN troops had been using to combat the art. "I don't think so," he muttered dolefully. "They seem to have found a way around our passive line of defense."

"How?"

"I've since learned they inject themselves with a drug that allows them to bear up to the art's debilitating effects. I'm sure that any UN forces breaching this facility will have already taken the necessary precautions to avoid possible sickness."

Amelia's eyes widened with horror. The memory of seeing Bolder inject himself with something came rushing back with frightening clarity. "My god!" she cried. "I saw my cameraman inject himself with a drug he claimed was for controlling Hepatitis C. He had been vomiting just before injecting himself."

Mat wheeled away from the window to look at her. "Are you certain of this?"

"Yes."

"Then I better go see what he's up to," Mat said tersely. Pulling a cell phone from a pocket, he spoke quickly as he strode briskly to the door. "Ez, I need a fix on Eric Bolder."

Amelia watched him go before bringing her gaze back to Jacob. "Are you sure you don't want to evacuate the residents?"

"As a precaution, they have already been sent ashore to the nearby island," replied Jacob.

Amelia stared back in surprise. Earlier on, she hadn't noticed any mass exodus leaving the floating city, and now that she thought about it, she hadn't seen any residents on Aquaria's lower levels when Mat had given her a quick tour only an hour ago. Nevertheless, she wondered how nearly ten thousand people managed to reach the island without a convoy of boats to transport them. "How were you able to move them so quickly?" she uttered in amazement.

"We have a tunnel that connects with an underground facility on Navassa," Jacob said softly.

"Can it accommodate all those people?"

"Yes."

"But will they be safe."

"Safe enough for the time being," Jacob acknowledged. Seeing her concern, he added, "I've already given the people the option to leave Aquaria completely, but no one wants to go back to their old lives. But as we already know, the American administration is willing to abide by the UN ruling to cede Navassa back to Haiti, and since the majority of residents are Haitian nationals, I see no reason why they won't be able to stay. Unfortunately, strings will be pulled to install others to administer the running of this complex, though I can't eliminate the possibility they'll close this place down."

"Do you honestly believe the Haitian government will allow that?"

Jacob did not immediately answer, rising up from his desk to look out a window behind him. He stared briefly in the direction of Navassa Island before turning back to her with an expression of deep reflection on his face.

"During the last several years, Tursiops has put considerable effort into rooting out the corruption that exists within the Haitian government. In doing this, we even used bribery in order to urge some officials to enact policies favorable to its citizenry and the welfare of the nation as a whole. And while some progress was made, it still wasn't enough."

Jacob expelled a tired sigh. "In the end, greed will be the determining factor whether or not this enterprise survives. If greed prevails, then Aquaria is finished."

Amelia opened her mouth to say more, but a disembodied voice she had previously heard broke into the conversation to cut her off.

"Jacob, three submarines have just joined up with the UN armada," Ez interjected smoothly. "One of them fits a Kilo-class profile while the other two appear to be the latest Varshavyanka-class variety."

Jacob shook his head in frustration. He hadn't expected submarines, particularly the kind Ez had identified. These were Russian-built vessels. Such submersibles usually exceeded 4,000 tons and were powered by diesel-electric engines. And while all three were designed for stealth, it did not necessarily mean they carried Russian crews, for he knew the Russians routinely sold military hardware to other countries. The fact that submarines had joined up with the UN task force confronting them now added an ominous edge to what was about to take place.

*   *   *   *

-87-

Mat Daniels found Bolder in Level H, one hundred twenty feet below sea level. He was standing with his back to Mat, aiming his camera through a large window of acrylic Plexiglas that provided a magnificent view of the immediate marine environment. At the moment, a huge school of skipjack could be seen drifting by lazily beyond the glass, seemingly herded by a school of gray dolphins.

Mat moved up behind the shorter man, aware that they were currently the only two people at this location. Sensing someone at his back, Bolder spun.

"I take it the footage you're recording will be photo-shopped just like your other work," Mat said snidely. Looking down, he noticed a medium size duffel bag at Bolder's feet. "What's in the bag?"

"None of your business," Bolder said, regarding Mat with hateful eyes.

Mat stepped closer. "As head of security for this facility, it's my business to know."

Bolder bent to set the camera on the floor next to the duffel bag, rising back up and riveting Mat with a pugnacious gaze and bunching his fists. "You were lucky last time, but this time you're gonna find out what the real *Boulder* is made of."

Mat shrugged, more than happy to accommodate the man's wishes. "Let's get it on then." With his guard lowered, he stuck out his chin, presenting it as an easy target. "Swing for the fences."

"You bet I will."

Bolder lunged, rearing back with his right arm and throwing everything he had into an overhand haymaker.

Mat barely leaned back in time to avoid the attack, feeling the wind from Bolder's knuckles miss his jaw by less than a millimeter. The speed of the move surprised him. He had underestimated this squat, powerfully built man, realizing he had to take him more seriously.

Bolder saw the look on Mat's face and sneered. "That was your first mistake."

"And what might that be?" Mat said, circling to Bolder's left with newfound respect.

"You stupidly assume a man with a build like mine will be slow. I've cleaned out bars filled with guys like you."

"Congratulations!"

Mat studied Bolder's footwork, aware that his opponent moved like a seasoned fighter. Unless he could connect with another groin kick, he doubted he would be able to take the man out with only one well-placed strike like before. Nevertheless, he snapped out his left foot to test the water as Bolder bore in on him again. Though the maneuver was lightning quick, Bolder blocked Mat's foot, slapping it away with the edge of his hand before it reached the area between his legs.

Mat winced. Bolder's hand felt as though it were made of stone.

"Forget about using the same move," Bolder grunted, leering admonishingly. "It'll only work once on a guy like me. I'm a quick learner and faster than you think."

Mat danced swiftly to his right before Bolder could trap him up against the Plexiglas window. "Amelia tells me she saw you inject yourself with a syringe," he said.

"So what of it?"

"That's why you haven't taken ill. The people you work for know about our unique art and found a way around it."

Bolder frowned maliciously, stalking Mat like an angered bull looking to gore a matador. "That's right. And once UN troops storm this place, your operation will be finished. They'll all be inoculated to withstand whatever it is that ridiculous art does to people."

"Did it ever occur to you why Amelia never got sick from it and you did?" Mat asked.

"Don't care."

"Only the wicked become sick."

"Is that so! Sounds like a crock."

Bolder suddenly rushed forward again, unleashing a savage right cross, but Mat correctly anticipated the punch, shifting his body weight left to avoid the strike.

"We've never been able to fully understand why the art works," Mat went on, "but it seems to be a visual stimulus that triggers some kind of neurological mechanism in a person's brain. With wicked people, it brings on a severe case of motion sickness."

Bolder attacked again, throwing a flurry of punches, but Mat moved quickly to avoid the barrage.

"We can do this all day," Mat needled. He noticed that Bolder was beginning to wheeze. "I doubt a paunchy bastard like you can keep this up for another minute without falling down."

"Go to hell!"

"Either you're in poor physical shape or that drug is sapping you," Mat continued to badger. "And once it wears off, you'll be sick as a dog."

In desperation, Bolder came at him again, swinging wildly, but Mat could see he was now moving slower, with his punches lacking the same authority as before.

"Stop jumping around and face me like a man," Bolder gasped.

"I'll make a deal with you. You tell me who you work for and I'll stop moving."

Bolder was fatiguing fast, his mouth open wide to suck in air. "You know...very well who I work for...it's the IBC."

Mat smiled, shaking his head. "Wrong answer! Give me the person's name!"

Bolder ceased his stalking, bending at the waist to brace his hands against his knees. He was gasping hard.

"Pooped already?" Mat taunted. "Maybe I should call down a gurney to have you wheeled back to your chopper so you can fly the hell out of here."

Unexpectedly, Bolder reeled. He sank to one knee and clutched his chest with his left hand.

Mat took a step closer, no longer regarding the man as dangerous. "Looks like you're having a heart attack," Mat said unsympathetically.

Bolder's gasping suddenly stopped. He was holding something in his right hand.

Too late, Mat realized what it was as two tiny objects lodged in his chest. Grimacing in severe pain, he found himself jerking crazily on the floor. The involuntary muscle contractions seemed endless as Bolder rose up to stand over him.

"Suckered you in good," the shorter man said smugly. "That was your second mistake, falling for a ruse like that. Hope you enjoyed being electroshocked." Abruptly, he pulled up on the wire to retract the two dart-like electrodes imbedded in Mat's chest.

The pain immediately subsided, but before Mat could get back on his feet, Bolder gave him a vicious kick that landed square on his chin. That was when darkness flooded his consciousness.

-88-

Percy withdrew another small device from a pocket on his lab coat. Looking to Jake, he said, "I don't know if anyone noticed them missing, but right after I helped your kids escape, I launched two robo-fish Maximus carries aboard his yacht."

Jake stared at the device. The memory of the mechanical fish probing the colony came to mind all at once. "Maximus used those fish to recon Aquaria and set off explosions, didn't he?"

Percy nodded abashedly. "I'm afraid so. I'm the one who designed them."

Jake studied the unit. It had a small screen embedded in it. "You can control them with that thing?"

"Yes. The fish are normally preprogrammed to autonomously carry out assigned tasks, but this little baby can override those functions."

"What do you suggest?" Jake asked, failing to see how the robo-fish could be used to rescue Alex.

Percy grinned. "Diversion! Fish One is carrying explosives. If we take out the vessel's props, the ship will be dead in the water. The crew's attention will be focused on the disturbance. While they're busy checking out the damage, you can get aboard through the moon pool located amidships."

Jake pondered the plan. In sinking all of Cardoza's vessels back in the *Bay of Anse-Milieu,* Hercules and Phillipe had used up the remainder of the highly potent explosives brought along for the mission. And he had to forget about frying the circuitry that operated the engine system of the *Nunquarn Satis*. The sub operated by Abdel was currently too far away to put the T-BEMP it carried to good use.

"What about the hull doors?" Jake pointed out, seeing an obvious impediment to the plan. "If they're closed, we won't have access to the moon pool."

Percy's grin broadened. "Fish Two is outfitted with a remote control that can open the doors. Once the ship stops moving under power, it will activate the doors to swing open. The fish has to be in the immediate vicinity of the doors to do that."

"What about an alarm? Won't the bridge detect the doors opening?"

"Normally, yes, but I deactivated the warning system just before I released the fish. There's only one man aboard the ship who has the know-how to bring the system back online."

"How do you know he hasn't already done that?"

"I changed the password. Without the new one, reactivating it is impossible."

"What are the chances of anyone being in the moon pool once the hull doors open?"

Percy's grin slid away. "The odds of that happening should be quite low. My guess is all the technicians will be down in the engine room where there's a small hull door for sending out a ROV on an umbilical to assess the damage."

To Jake, the plan still seemed highly risky, but then again, taking risks was in his blood. "Where are those fish?"

"One mile offshore and standing by. But we'll need to get within a half mile of them to use this device. Beyond that, they'll be out of range to receive the override."

Jake wheeled, studying the faces all around him before singling out his wife. He could tell she already knew what he was thinking. "This is going to be a five-man mission. Fernando, I'll need you to drive *Johnnie*." He caught Franklin's look of disappointment as he said this. "Sorry, dad, but you've done more than your share already." Turning his head, he looked up at his over-sized friend. "Zimby, I'm going to need you to back me and Victor up once we board the vessel. Percy, you'll stand by with Fernando."

"What about me?" Phillipe interjected.

"And me?" said Jimenez.

"I need both of you to stay here to safeguard the women and children."

Phillipe opened his mouth to say more, but Jake cut him off. "I'll be counting on you to keep them safe," Jake said firmly. "Do you have a problem with that?"

Phillipe would not meet Jake's eyes. He could tell Jake was still peeved at him for having remained aboard the Southern Star. "No," he uttered dejectedly.

Jake placed a hand on Jimenez's shoulder. "Round up the men and get them back in the bunkers pronto. There's no telling what might be headed this way again."

Jimenez nodded, happy to oblige.

Looking to Victor, Jake said, "We better get moving if we're going to get your son back."

-89-

Jake glanced at his watch. A feeling of growing impatience was seeping rapidly into his bones. "How you making out, Percy? Are the fish picking up a signal?" He looked back expectantly as Mort's twin brother continued to manipulate the tiny keyboard on the handheld device.

Percy's face was consumed in deep concentration. "I didn't have a chance to test out this little gizmo," Percy explained absently. "I slapped it together in the heat of the moment, so it's understandable that a few bugs have yet to be worked out."

"We've got to get moving," Jake uttered in exasperation.

Percy's expression suddenly changed as he monitored the small screen, his eyes coming alive like those of a man stumbling upon a new discovery. "I see the problem." He turned to Jake. "But I'll need to work on the fish in a dry environment. I need to open them up."

"How do you propose to do that?" Jake asked, his patience almost at an end.

"Open the chamber and let the dolphins out. If you swallow the fish and dewater the chamber, I can correct the problem."

"How long's that going to take?"

"Two minutes, give me two minutes."

Jake turned to Fernando as Victor and Zimbola looked on, their expressions filled with apprehension. "Do as he says, but make it quick."

Jake queried his bond mate. *You following this, Achilles?*

Yes, JJ, I'll let Hercules know you're going to spit us out.

Fernando opened Johnnie's maw to evacuate the dolphins and pull in the robo-fish, both of which were floating stationary side by side ten feet below the ocean surface. A hiss ensued as water was being expelled under pressure from the interdiction chamber.

Satisfied that the chamber was fully dewatered, Jake opened the access hatch to let Percy crawl through.

"Take a look at this," Fernando said.

Jake brought his eyes to bear on the monitor Fernando indicated. Johnnie's periscope had been raised, and on the viewing screen he saw where it was aimed.

"Magnify the view!" Jake ordered.

"Looks like the same chopper that dropped off Percy," Fernando said.

Jake watched the helicopter land on the *Nunquarn Satis*. The vessel was still moving under power. From his angle of approach, he saw that the yacht was enormous, easily surpassing eight hundred feet in length.

"Are you at full magnification?" asked Jake.

"Afraid so," Fernando replied. He studied the aircraft as the main rotor began to slow. "Aside from the pilot, looks like two others getting off. Too far away to tell who they are, though."

Jake nodded. "Keep pace with them," he said. "Don't want them to get too far ahead of us."

-90-

Maximus eyed the Haitian Minister of Agriculture shrewdly, wondering how much it would cost him to get what he wanted. Bronte Pharah was tall and lean, a relative newcomer to the position he held. Maximus had instructed Van Heflin to bring Pharah with him.

Pressed for time, Maximus got right to the point. "Play ball with me, Mr. Pharah, and you'll be a very rich man."

Pharah shot an indignant look to the senator seated across from him. In clipped, carefully enunciated English, he said, "I thought I was invited here to discuss Haiti's future prospects for agricultural development." He turned a displeased gaze back on Maximus. "If you thought you could bribe me, you are mistaken."

Maximus smiled. So he wants to up the ante by playing hard to get, he thought amusedly. He had dealt with Pharah's kind before. "You confuse bribery with career advancement," Maximus said. "What I am offering you is the administration of Aquaria once Navassa is ceded back to Haiti. You would be placed in charge of its day to day operations."

Pharah's irritated expression softened a bit. "My expertise lies in the field of agronomy. I know nothing about marine aquaculture."

"An in-depth knowledge of marine farming will not be required. I don't know if you are aware of it, but Aquaria is a highly profitable enterprise. As head of its day to day operations, you would share in its profits. You would become a multi-millionaire almost overnight."

A mask of skepticism quickly gathered on Pharah's features. "How do you propose to get me installed as its head? That decision can only be made by Haiti's president. First he would have to appoint me to the post, then the appointment would have to be approved by the prime minister and ratified by the national assembly."

Maximus glanced over at Van Heflin. "Leave that to us. I'm sure the senator here can use his considerable congressional influence to have a clause inserted in the ceding agreement to have you placed in charge. What say you, Mr. Pharah? Does my proposition interest you, or are you set on spending the remainder of your career in a position with little financial reward?"

Pharah appeared uncomfortable. He had a wife and five children to support, not to mention two elderly parents that required constant care. The temptation to take the offer was quite strong, though he had no misconceptions about what he would be giving up if he accepted it. His integrity would be lost. He would be nothing more than a puppet dangling on strings controlled by this man. He was proud of his integrity. It had set him apart from his bureaucratic peers, many of whom were steadily enriching themselves through the usual corruption that was so prevalent among government officials. The majority of that corruption, he knew, involved bribes associated with the drug trade. Haiti offered the perfect environment for transshipping vast amounts of illegal narcotics and cocaine.

"What say you, Mr. Pharah?" Maximus repeated, his raspy voice taking on an overtone of vexation.

"I'm not a person prone to making snap decisions," Pharah said. "I will need time to think this over."

Maximus held back the cloud ready to descend on his face, presenting a feigned grin instead. In speaking with Allotey, he had learned that Dr. Herbert Ermstine had been killed. But even if he were still alive, the planned rebellion he had hoped to incite had been snuffed out with the destruction of the drones. The only way he was going to control Aquaria, at least for the short term, was to install a Haitian national to run it, a man who would be directly under his control. And the first thing he needed from that man was to halt the export of the enriched *guano* fertilizer to Haitian farmers. Once that was accomplished, he'd have the mined guano contaminated with the *Sterilis* compound before resuming exports. At that point, drones would no longer be needed to spread the deadly mixture over Haitian farmland.

"What if I sweeten the offer by throwing in a bonus?" Maximus said.

Pharah hesitated. "I don't know...I-"

"Does two hundred thousand dollars in U.S. currency seem reasonable enough, cash up front?"

Maximus lifted a lid on a box that had been sitting on the table and slid it across so that Pharah could view the contents. He had kept it in reserve for a moment like this. He knew such a sum would be a tempting windfall to any bureaucrat within a third world country like Haiti.

Pharah stared at the money for several seconds, appearing like a starving man hungering for food. With an unexpected abruptness that surprised both Maximus and Van Heflin, he pulled his eyes away and stood up, eyeing both men contemptuously. "I cannot accept this," he said angrily. "I am not for sale."

"What if I told you your family is in great danger," Maximus snarled, no longer able to keep up the pretense of civility. "Would you be willing to take the money if it would keep them safe?"

Pharah's composure unraveled further, turning to shock. As though hit with a sedation dart, he slumped down heavily into his chair, a beaten man.

-91-

The two minutes Percy had said it would take to correct the robo-fish problem turned into twenty, then thirty. Jake knew he had to do something, and do it quickly. But with Maximus' vessel cruising along at close to full power, gaining access to the ship was going to be made extremely difficult if not altogether impossible.

In spite of this, Fernando continued to shadow the vessel, hanging back 1000 meters off its stern. Every so often he would raise the periscope, looking for anything unusual to happen. Finally, something did happen.

"There's another whirlybird approaching the ship," he announced.

Jake stared at the monitor, knowing that Fernando had left it on full magnification. "That's a Hind." He turned to Belachek. "Tell me if I'm wrong, Victor, but that chopper looks like the one Zinova was flying."

Victor studied the screen as the Hind set down on the ship. "I think you are right."

Jake crowded close to the screen. From Johnnie's present position relative to the ship, they had a perfect angle for an unobstructed view of the highest portion of the vessel's superstructure. He saw two men ascending the stairs leading up to the landing pad. The Hind's main rotor continued to spin as four figures emerged from it to meet the two men. It was evident a discussion was taking place as the ship plowed on. The discussion appeared heated at times, but even at full magnification the gathering of men was still too far away for Jake to be certain of this. Several minutes passed before the meeting ended, upon which five of the men climbed aboard the Hind, leaving one man behind. Another moment passed before the Hind lifted from the landing pad to dip low over the water before gaining height and speed as it drew away.

Percy suddenly poked his head from the hatch leading to the interdiction chamber. "Problem solved," he said enthusiastically. Pulling himself from the hatch, he dogged it off. "You can flood the chamber."

Jake kept his eyes glued to the screen as Fernando opened the valves to re-flood the chamber. "Looks like the ship's starting to pick up speed," he said, surprised at how fast it was accelerating. Reaching across the control console, he turned on Johnnie's side scan sonar and checked a digital readout. "She's past forty knots and pulling away fast."

Percy stepped up next to him to observe the gauge. "She can go a lot faster than that, I'm afraid to say."

"How fast?"

"Better than sixty knots."

Jake frowned. "A ship that size," he retorted dubiously. "How is that possible?"

"She's outfitted with a Wartsila-Sulzer turbocharged diesel engine usually fabricated for pushing supertankers. But it was specifically designed to also burn nitro fuel."

The answer stunned Jake. With a degree in mechanical engineering, he knew that nitro fuel was actually a highly combustible combination of methanol and nitromethane, with the nitromethane typically comprising anywhere from ten to forty percent of the mixture. He was well aware that nitro engines could turn better than 50,000 rpm as opposed to ducted-fan aircraft engines, which could only go as high as 25,000.

"What percent nitromethane does it use?" Jake asked, continuing to watch in dismay as the ship pulled farther and farther away.

Percy read the look in Jake's eyes. "Fifty percent. The vessel usually cruises on diesel, but if Maximus decides to switch over to nitro, even the robo-fish are going to have a tough time gaining on her."

"Where on the ship are the nitro tanks located?"

"There's only one tank. It holds one hundred thousand gallons, and it's just forward of the diesel tanks."

Jake glanced over at Victor, seeing the deep concern etched on his countenance. Abruptly he turned to face Percy with a stern gaze. "Did it occur to you we run the risk of setting off the nitro if we blow the screws?"

"I don't think there's any chance of that happening."

"Why not?"

"The entire ship's outer hull consists of six-inch titanium plates. Inward of them, the plates are reinforced with ply-layered composites of titanium, carbon and ceramic mesh capable of stopping a small torpedo. The stern is even more heavily shielded."

Jake's mind raced along in analytical mode. "Even so, maybe it would be safer to try boarding her via helicopter."

Percy's response was emphatic. "Forget it! Maximus has two hidden twenty millimeter cannons aboard her, one near the bow and the other near the stern. Anything coming near the ship that is perceived as a threat will be immediately blown out of the sky."

Jake sighed in frustration. "Then I guess we better proceed with the original plan. How we doing, Fernando?"

"The fish are out and the dolphins back in."

Percy pressed a button on his handheld remote, and through the forward viewing portal Jake saw the duo of robo-fish dart rapidly away.

"The ship's speed just passed sixty knots," Fernando announced.

"Then we have to assume Maximus has switched to the nitro fuel," Percy stated.

"Take us to full throttle," Jake ordered, now wondering if the mechanical fish had the speed to catch up with the ship. A vigilant glance at the instrumentation on Johnnie's control panel told him that his quarry was on a bearing headed directly toward Aquaria. Already the *Nunquarn Satis* was within ten miles of the floating city.

* * * *

-92-

From the bridge of the *USS Carl Sagan*, Captain Alfred Delila kept the spyglasses trained on Aquaria's outer perimeter five miles distant. In his early fifties, he was a tall man with an easy smile, but as he studied the complex, a frown came to his face.

Lowering the glasses, he handed them to Lieutenant Myron Johnson. "Tell me what you see, lieutenant."

Johnson, a youthful black man with the build of a football running back, brought the glasses to his eyes, shifting them several degrees right, then left for a good twenty seconds before turning back to the captain. Appearing puzzled, he said, "No oil slicks or billowing clouds of soot, if that's what you're implying, sir. All I see is a pristine environment."

Captain Delila's face clouded further. "Precisely. We were told these people are despoilers of the marine habitat, but I don't see anything that would suggest that. Unfortunately, we have our orders."

Johnson nodded sagely. "But it doesn't mean we have to like them, captain."

The captain turned his gaze to the carrier's deck. The *Carl Sagan* was the latest addition to the U.S. Navy's fleet, an ultra-modern vessel of electronic wizardry. Directly below him were two AW101 helicopters, each prepared to airlift a squad consisting of sixteen Navy Seals onto the landing pads of Aquaria's central structure. The multi-purpose rotary-wing aircraft were massive, powered by three turbo-shaft engines. They were the result of a joint venture by British and Italian engineers, sold to the UN and recently assigned to the carrier for the impending invasion.

Delila swiveled his head to look further down the ship's runway where four heavily armed F/A Super Hornets were currently standing by. Looking at his watch, he turned back to Johnson. "Your men have been briefed and are ready to go?"

"Yes, sir."

Out of curiosity, Delila asked, "Any of them need the drug?"

"No, sir. We were all tested, and it seems none of us experienced the vertigo the art is supposed to bring on."

This did not come as a surprise to the captain. He had seen examples of the strange art and had experienced a sublime sense of euphoria each time he looked upon one of the enigmatic creations.

Without making it obvious, Delila studied the lieutenant with a critical eye. He had seen the man's file, but seeing him in person proved far more interesting. At twenty-four, Johnson seemed far wiser than his years would suggest. A standout during Seal training, he had all the tools necessary to qualify him as a leader of elite warriors. Johnson was undeniably smart and crisply efficient. And now he would lead the Seal teams into the heart of Aquaria to take control of the floating city. But first he must await the arrival of the UN envoy assigned to the task force, the overall figurehead of the operation. The envoy would be accompanied by a U.S. senator, both of whom were to immediately follow on the heels of Johnson's team once they secured the city. Once the city was secured, the envoy would then assume command of the facility. But even before the mission commenced, a briefing was to take place in which explicit instructions were to be issued by the envoy.

Scanning the sky, Delila looked for the Hind that was supposed to deliver Malikai Allotey, Special Envoy of the United Nations' Council on World Ecological Affairs. He found it odd that Senator Brent Van Heflin, Chairman of the senate's Science and Technology Committee, would be with him. The communique had come in a half hour earlier from command headquarters. Delila was not to proceed with the operation until Allotey and the senator arrived.

Delila hated this assignment. Having his ship turned over to the whims of a non-military bureaucrat representing a conglomeration of foreign nations did not sit well with him. He was aware of the corruption that existed within the UN, and all his instincts told him there was something wrong with the whole affair. He had seen strange things occur during his twenty-eight years in the military, with orders coming down from higher up that didn't make sense, and this operation reeked of it.

Swiveling his head, Delila looked across the water at several other nearby ships comprising the UN's multinational task force, his gaze searching out the profile of a large low-squat vessel floating stationary less than a thousand meters away. Disdainfully he eyed the 4,000-ton Kilo-class submarine. Built by the Russians, it was yet the latest addition to Iran's growing naval fleet. Renowned for being able to resist heavy radio and electronic interference, the diesel-electric submersible was equipped with four 533mm torpedo launchers and ten missile launchers. Purchased at a price of $800 million, it had been named the *Iron Fist* and was currently commanded by Captain Sayyari Habibollah, an officer within the Islamic Revolutionary Guard branch of the Iranian navy and a devout member of Hezbollah, a radical Islamic militant group firmly entrenched within the government of Iran. Habibollah, he well knew, had a long-standing history for being a loose cannon and was notorious for trying to provoke international incidents. Delila had had run-ins with the man while captaining aircraft carriers on two separate occasions in the past, once in the Straits of Hormuz and once in the Gulf of Oman, and each time

Habibollah had made threatening runs at his ship in Ghadir-class submarines, which were far smaller in size than the one he was now commanding. Among other things, rumor had it that Habibollah was one of the instigators during the takeover of the American embassy in Tehran in 1979. Unfortunately, and much to his dislike, they were now on the same team, forced to work together at the whims of unknown, and most likely unsavory parties with holds on the strings of power.

Delila scanned the sea farther to the south, spotting two more vessels with low profiles that appeared identical. He had been thoroughly briefed on their capabilities. These were Varshavyanka-class diesel-electric submarines recently purchased from the Russians by Venezuela. Ostentatiously named *El Martillo* and *El Yunque*, which translated to *The Hammer* and *The Anvil*, they were essentially upgraded versions of the Kilo-class model Iran had purchased, designed for conducting anti-shipping and anti-submarine missions in relatively shallow water. Each Varshavyanka-class vessel could accommodate a crew of fifty-two and was equipped with eighteen torpedoes and eight surface-to-air missiles. They featured stealth technology with extended combat range for striking land, surface and underwater targets. Intelligence reports showed them to have advanced hull architecture, optimal level of control process automation, and low noise emission while cruising underwater. Above all, they required low maintenance and were highly reliable.

With this in mind, Delila mulled a follow-up report he had received about these vessels. A third Varshavyanka-class sub was due to be transferred to Venezuela, bringing the entire cost of all three subs to over $1 billion. Though the Russians had given the Venezuelan government a line of credit totaling $800 million, Delila wondered how the South American country could afford such extravagant and expensive military hardware. In spite of the fact that Venezuela was oil-rich, it currently had an ailing economy primarily due to widespread corruption within its government. A recent report he had read by Transparency International, a non-governmental international organization that monitors and publicizes corporate and political corruption globally, ranked the country among the top twenty most corrupt nations on the planet, alleging that $22.5 billion in Venezuela's public funds had been transferred to foreign accounts, with half that money being unaccounted for by any of its government officials. And now rumor had it that its government was allied closely with Iran, providing indispensable support to Hezbollah in its quest to destabilize American influence in the Western Hemisphere.

Delila pondered this knowledge. Even if the submarine purchases were based entirely on credit, a most unlikely scenario, Venezuela could ill afford that scale of defense spending. A combination of prolonged drought and alleged government inefficiencies had plunged the country into crippling cuts in domestic spending, particularly on hydroelectric power generation, which its citizens desperately needed.

"Captain, we have contact," a radioman behind Delila suddenly blurted. "The UN envoy is inbound and will land in the next three minutes."

Delila scanned the sky, spotting a small speck approaching from the east and growing larger by the second. "Give him clearance to land," ordered Delila, watching the aircraft draw closer.

Lieutenant Johnson spoke up as the distinct lines of the helicopter became apparent. "Sir, don't you find it strange that the envoy would be showing up in a Hind."

Delila gave a subtle nod. "Yes, lieutenant, I find it very strange."

-93-

Maximus studied the two photographs held in his hands, his eyes periodically shifting from one to the other in near metronome cadence. "I'll get you sooner or later," he muttered to himself. Sitting in the vessel's observation room that gave a three hundred and sixty-degree view of the sea, he placed the photos on the table before him to look back at Haiti's rapidly receding coastline.

A soft rap on the door resounded just before it opened, and Alex Trekov was led into the room by two guards. Extending a hand, Maximus motioned him to a chair, taking quick inventory of the youth's condition. From all outward appearances, the young man seemed to have recovered significantly since being brought aboard his vessel.

"Tell me what you know about Karloff Zinova," Maximus said, asking the question in Russian, one of the five languages he was fluent in. From the earlier interrogation with the youth, he had learned that Alex only spoke Russian.

Alex shrugged. "I cannot offer much, only that he used to be a Spetsnaz operative who turned mercenary. I worked for him only a few short months and rarely had direct contact with him. That was left to his two lieutenants."

Maximus thought about the burly bear of a man he had met on the landing pad a short time earlier, the infamous *Reaper* Cardoza had told him about, and if not for Javolyn, the *Reaper* would have sustained an unblemished track record in carrying out clandestine missions. But with Javolyn having bested him, he knew Zinova was now thirsting for revenge. He had seen it in the man's eyes. Retribution, he well knew, was a great motivating force. It drove people relentlessly on, turning them into ravenous beasts who would stop at nothing to get what they wanted. Maximus used people the way a farmer used a blade to shear sheep, and he would make full use of that motivation to capture Javolyn and his wife once and for all. With Cardoza presumed dead, he had struck a deal with Zinova during that short meeting, and at Allotey's urging, promised him a share of any gold found on Aquaria or Navassa. Once the gold was secured, he would then use Zinova to launch a foray into the cove to take possession of the remaining precious metal cache.

"You are obviously a very rich man," Alex said, interrupting Maximus' thoughts. He looked enviously about the room with its exquisitely expensive furnishings. "Perhaps if I worked for you, I might be able to someday enjoy such riches."

Maximus sat back in his chair, eyeing the youth appraisingly before replying. "So you fancy yourself working for me, do you? What skills do you offer?"

The question seemed to throw Alex off balance. "I am a soldier, a mercenary for hire."

A sneer crossed Maximus' features. "And not a very good one," he scoffed. "Was that your first mission?"

Alex looked away, unwilling to admit it was.

"What happened to you back there?" Maximus pressed. "You weren't wounded, yet you seemed to be recovering from an illness."

Alex stood, opening his shirt to reveal pink scar tissue where a fifty caliber round had pierced his abdomen. "I was shot in the stomach."

Maximus stared, scrutinizing the remnant of the wound dubiously. "No one heals that quickly."

"Believe what you want, but I did. I would have died, but they did something to me, something I cannot explain."

"Who?"

"Two women. They were helped by strange looking creatures."

"Was one of those women aboard the vessel we took you from?"

"Yes."

"What about the other? Describe her!"

"She was young and very pretty."

Maximus reached for one of the photos sitting on the table, pushing it forward for Alex to see. "Is this her?"

Alex scrutinized the photo taken by the robo-fish during its surveillance of Aquaria. It showed a girl wearing a face mask as she rode a huge albino dolphin, her ebony hair streaming back. "I think so."

"What about the creatures? Did they look anything like the one she's riding?"

"Yes, they were white. One of them was bigger than the rest, maybe the same one in the picture."

"What about this one? Did they have any unusual anatomical features?"

Maximus pushed another photo across the table. It displayed two white dolphins with prehensile appendages extended from beneath their pectoral fins. Each one held a socket wrench and appeared to be tightening bolts on a submerged structure.

"Yes, they all had hands."

Maximus held the youth's gaze for several seconds. "Either you're lying about being shot or these people have the ability to heal life-threatening injuries rather quickly."

"I am telling you the truth," Alex said.

Maximus rose up from his chair to contemplate what Alex was telling him, suddenly feeling a need to pace the room. But as he did so, he was nearly knocked off his feet by a powerful shock wave that coursed through the ship. Klaxons immediately blared as he caught himself from being thrown to the deck. The normal though barely detectable vibration that told him the ship was underway was now gone, and he felt the vessel rapidly losing its forward momentum.

Maximus got on the intercom to the engine room. "What happened?" he screamed.

"Our drive shafts are gone!" someone from engineering answered in a strident voice.

-94-

Holding onto Percy as he clutched Achilles' dorsal fin, Jake broke the surface of the moon pool amidships of the *Nunquarn Satis*. Letting go, he climbed from the water to take rapid inventory of his surroundings. The chamber above the pool was cavernous, and at the moment was bathed in only limited lighting. Perhaps this was normal for this sector of the ship when no activity was taking place, he surmised, for the immediate area appeared to be devoid of any crew members. Blending in with shadows provided by an overhead gantry, Jake hung still for several more seconds to ensure this was the case. Satisfied that no one was around, he slipped off the Sledgehammer strapped to his shoulder. Calling to his bond mate in that silent mode of communication they used, he had Achilles lift Percy from the water to deposit him on the steel grating walkway bordering the pool. Motioning Percy to his side, he summoned his bond mate again.

Achilles, pass the word to Hercules to bring in Victor and Zimby.

Jake looked down at the moon pool, knowing it was too small to accommodate Johnnie's elongated dimensions. Minutes earlier, Achilles had scanned the opening to confirm this, after which he had poked his head above the moon pool's water to recon the area surrounding it. With Fernando holding Johnnie steady below the ship's hull, Jake and Percy were the first to climb into the craft's interdiction chamber before being purged into the open sea, upon which it had only taken seconds for Achilles to whisk them up into the bowels of the ship. And with Hercules now being called upon, the giant albino had rapped twice on Johnnie's forward viewing port to let Fernando know it was time to flood the chamber again and spit out the two men awaiting to be let out. Since the turnaround time to accomplish this was relatively quick, there was no need to have any of the boarding party outfitted with self-contained breathing apparatus. But with Percy not being a seasoned diver like the others, it had taken considerable coaxing on Jake's part to keep him from panicking.

"Remain calm and remember to expel some air from your lungs as Achilles takes us up, otherwise you'll risk suffering an embolism," Jake had instructed him. "You'll only be submerged for a few seconds."

Jake kept his vigilance on full alert, his eyes constantly roaming the chamber. Even though Percy had ensured him he had permanently disabled the surveillance cameras in the immediate area prior to launching the robo-fish, he had the sensation he was being watched.

The sound of burbling water echoed softly as Hercules breached the moon pool's limpid surface, with Zimby astride the dolphin's back directly behind Victor. With the sea being relatively calm, the rise and fall of water in the pool was minimal.

Gesturing silently, Jake motioned them toward him as they hauled themselves from the water. Both men were heavily armed, with Victor wielding the AK-104 he had used back at the cove, and Zimby clutching a firearm that was once a favorite of Jake's, and that was his trusty MK-23 Stoner, a rapid-fire assault weapon that had been popular among Navy Seals during the Vietnam War. With a drum magazine that held 150 rounds of 5.56mm ammo, the Stoner could unleash overwhelming suppressive firepower at a rate of 850 per minute.

Once the men had regrouped, Jake looked to Percy, holding his voice to a whisper. "Where to now?"

Percy pointed aft where a flight of stairs rose up from the lowest part of the chamber. "This way," he said softly.

Stealthily, the four-man team moved rapidly up the stairs with Jake leading the way. At the top was a grated catwalk that formed a ring above the moon pool. Suspended another ten feet above it was another grated catwalk surrounding the gantry used for lowering equipment into the water below. Jake scrutinized the upper catwalk, which was concentric with the one he stood on. Seeing that part of it along the far side was shrouded in darkness made him feel uneasy. Percy stepped past Jake, making for a nearby computer terminal attached to the railing on brackets.

Jake grabbed him by the arm, speaking quietly. "What are you doing?"

Percy looked past him to Belachek. "I'm going to hack into the ship's surveillance system to confirm if Victor's son is still where they put him."

Jake nodded. "Okay, but be quick about it."

Hovering over the keyboard, Percy's fingers danced over the keys. On the screen above the keyboard, a real-time scene of the room where Alex was being held was suddenly displayed.

"He's not in there!" Percy muttered in disappointment.

"Well see if you can find him," Jake said.

Percy manipulated more keys, bringing up images showing other sectors of the vessel. Most of the scenes were devoid of crew, but a few showed handfuls of black-clothed men carrying automatic weapons, whom Jake surmised to be members of ship's security.

"Bingo!" Percy suddenly uttered, a satisfied smile coming to his face.

The screen showed Alex being led down a hallway, a guard on each side of him.

Victor stared over Percy's shoulder, relief falling across his face. "He seems to be fully recovered."

"You know the best way to get to that part of the ship?" Jake asked Percy.

"Yes. My guess is they're taking him back to the room where he was being held."

"Then show us the way," Jake ordered.

All four men froze as the unmistakable sound of firearm bolts being drawn snicked loudly overhead. "Drop your weapons!" a gruff voice said.

Jake looked up to see a balding, bespectacled man in a white lab coat staring down at him from the upper catwalk's railing. On each side of him were three black-clad, Kevlar-vested troopers with machine pistols aimed down. Rapidly assessing this unexpected predicament, Jake analyzed their chances of survival. Had he been alone, he would not have hesitated to put up a fight, blasting away in spite of the odds and the drop these men had on him. But in that instant of decision, discretion won out, though the urge to swing his weapon upward in a lightning-like fashion and squeeze the trigger was almost overpowering.

The bespectacled individual seemed to read his thoughts. "Don't even think about it," he warned brusquely.

"Do what the man says," Jake said, giving Zimby a covert wink before placing his weapon on the steel grating. For reasons he could not rationalize, he did not feel his team was vulnerable. Not so willing to follow Jake's lead, Victor hesitated.

Jake spoke softly out the side of his mouth. "Easy there, Victor. You'll have to trust me on this."

With great reluctance, Victor put his weapon on the grating.

"A wise decision," the spokesman from above said. Swinging his gaze to Percy, he leered gloatingly. "I'm rather surprised you would attempt something like this, Percy. I figured you had something to do with the ship losing power. Right after the explosion, I scanned the surrounding sea using the hull cameras. That's when I spotted one of the robo-fish you stole. No doubt you sacrificed the other one, using its payload of high-grade explosive to take out the ship's screws. Maximus is going to enjoy getting his hands on you for what you did to his yacht."

Percy stared back, a defiant look on his face. "I should have known you would be lurking about, Estrada. I thought I recognized your sickening odor when I climbed aboard."

Estrada's smirk fell away like lead shot, turning immediately to a scowl. "I'm going to enjoy hearing you scream."

"And I'm going to savor the thought of you being locked behind bars for the remainder of your days," Percy riposted evenly.

"What do you mean by that?"

Now it was Percy's turn to smirk. "Everything Maximus has been planning is going to be revealed to the world. *The Order* is finished."

"That's impossible!"

"No it's not. I was able to hack into the encrypted agenda and long term goals of your nefarious cabal, making files and storing them away in a place where Maximus would never find them. Recorded in those files are hundreds of names along with transactions, dates, and objectives to be achieved, all aimed at enslavement of the masses."

"You won't be around to release those files," Estrada contended.

Percy snickered tauntingly. "No matter what happens to me, the information those files contain are destined to fall into the right hands. You won't be able to stop that from happening. The world is going to find out very shortly about the true nature of Plagiarius and Unus Universitas, including *Omicron-7*, the planned *Morior* blights and the dispersal of *Sterilis.*"

Estrada let out a constrained laugh, the same gloating leer returning to his face. "It won't matter if anyone else has access to that information. How are they going to disseminate it? I don't think you realize *The Order* controls most major media outlets around the world. The information would be immediately suppressed."

Percy's retort was swift. "Do you really think you can stop it from leaking into the social media on the worldwide web? One way or the other, the truth will eventually find its way into the public domain. Trying to contain it will be futile."

Estrada's leer evaporated again. "The mainstream media will dismiss it as nothing more than fabrications made by lunatic conspiracy theorists. The media will counter the leaks with a barrage of deceptions designed to keep the public distracted. They are like sheep. Their apathy makes it easy to lead them down the path of ignorance."

"What about governments?" Percy said. "Do you think they'll be able to ignore these claims?"

"*The Order* controls all the major powers like puppets on a string. It will not be in the interests of governments and world leaders to acknowledge the claims. They'll insist they have no credibility and are unsubstantiated. They'll distance themselves from the rumors, continuing to cultivate the contrived philanthropic and humanitarian goals portrayed by Plagiarius and Unus Universitas. They'll avoid impugning the integrity of government officials and bureaucrats already on the payrolls of these industrial giants. No matter which way you go, you're going to be outmaneuvered and outplayed at every turn in the road. You're-"

Estrada was abruptly distracted as the water in the moon pool suddenly erupted. Jake saw a fountain of spray shoot upward, and in the midst of that fountain were two white objects streaking side by side, one much bigger than its companion. Estrada and the six troopers barely had time to turn and glimpse what Jake was seeing, and by then it was too late.

A cacophony of startled screams rang out as two sets of twin prehensile appendages sprang out from beneath pectoral fins. With the objects reaching the apex of their leap, the smaller set of arms enfolded Estrada and the closest trooper on his left, pulling them from the catwalk. Achilles fell backwards, clutching them firmly to his body. Reflexively, the trooper fired his weapon, but his arm was pinned and a dozen rounds caromed harmlessly off steel fixtures off to one side. In the same instant, Hercules was able to embrace all three men on Estrada's right with his wider span, pulling them down with him as gravity took over. A huge splash flew upward as both albinos met the water and disappeared, bringing the men with them.

Jake reacted quickly, snatching up his Sledgehammer and firing off two shots that toppled the last two troopers from their perch. An instant later, they too, disappeared below the moon pool's surface, the water turned red from their mortal wounds.

"So much for the element of surprise," Jake grumbled.

"It's obvious Maximus knows we're here," Percy said, leaning back over the computer terminal and hitting more keys. "And to make matters worse, Alex is not in the original room where they were keeping him." A succession of images showing various sectors of the ship played rapidly across the monitor. "They're taking him to the helipad!" he suddenly exclaimed, stopping on one that showed Victor's son being escorted up a steep flight of stairs by the same two guards as before.

"Are you sure of that?" Jake blurted.

"Why else would they be taking him up the only way to the chopper?" Percy pulled up another image. Four pairs of eyes scrutinized the screen to observe a helicopter sitting on the helipad. Someone was just climbing into the pilot's seat. "That's the pilot," Percy said. "If you hurry, you might be able to stop him before he takes off." Switching screen images, he saw one of Maximus sitting in the ship's control room, a dark scowl consuming his face. "If I were a gambling man, I'd wager Maximus is getting ready to jump ship."

"Which way to get there?" Jake demanded.

Percy pointed at a closed door at the end of the catwalk. "Follow the corridor on the other side of the door. There's a second door thirty feet away that gives access to a stairwell. Go up ten flights. The helipad is at the top." Pulling up more images on the monitor, he added, "As of this moment the entire way is clear. Now go!"

Jake hesitated, seeing that Percy continued to manipulate the keyboard. "Aren't you coming?"

"No, I can do a lot more good here."

"Okay," Jake shot back, "but stay put. We'll be getting off the ship the same way we came in, so be ready for a quick departure once we return." Abruptly, Jake turned and sped down the catwalk with Victor and Zimby on his heels.

-95-

Indecision gripped Maximus. Estrada had alerted him that the ship was about to be boarded, and he had instructed Estrada to bring the invaders to him as soon as they were captured. But now, Estrada was not answering his pages, and try as he might, he could not pull up any images on the computer screens. For reasons unknown, he was effectively locked out of the ship's surveillance system, and without it he felt like a blind man groping about in darkness. A feeling of fear swept over him, intensified all the more by the ship's current situation. Without its screws, the *Nunquarn Satis* was not going anywhere.

Maximus made a decision and contacted his pilot, who was standing by atop the landing pad. "Is everyone aboard yet?"

"The Russian is," the pilot said, "but Pharah is still not here. You want me to crank 'er up?"

Maximus detected impatience in the reply. It was obvious his pilot was eager to get going. "Yes, we're getting off the ship."

"What's our destination?" the pilot asked.

"The *Kraken*."

Maximus got on the ship's radio, hailing Restoff, the leader of his remaining security. "What's the holdup with Pharah?" he rasped heatedly.

"He got sick and had to use the toilet. I didn't think you'd want him soiling the chopper, but they're bringing him up now. Where are you, sir? All the cameras stopped working."

"I'm in the control room." As an afterthought, Maximus said, "How many men with you?"

"Sixteen, not counting myself. Six others are with Estrada. Another two are with Pharah and two more with the Russian."

"Then you should have no trouble neutralizing the intruders. There are only four of them. I'll expect you to either kill or capture them, but bringing them to me alive is preferred. Is that understood?"

"Yes, sir."

-96-

It wasn't until the third flight of stairs that Jake, Victor and Zimby encountered opposition. The stairwell was positioned amidships of the yacht, providing access to each deck through a set of doors, one located to port and the other to starboard. With Jake leading the way, he was almost to the fourth landing when the portside door burst open. Firing from the hip, he caught the trooper coming through with a frag-12 round to the throat that hurled the man backwards into another Kevlar-vested companion following on his heels. Jake fired again before the second trooper could recover, the shot blowing a gaping hole through his body armor and killing him instantly.

Scrambling as fast as his legs would carry him, Jake was halfway up the sixth flight when he heard the starboard door below him open. Trailing up the rear, Zimby let loose with the Stoner, sending a hail of bullets into three more troopers that cut them down quickly. In the confined space of the stairwell, the sound was deafening, reverberating off the walls like a chainsaw on the verge of exploding.

On the eighth landing, the doors on both sides opened at the same time, and Jake took out another two troopers as Victor unleashed a withering enfilade that caught three more armed adversaries before they could raise their weapons.

Jake stopped momentarily to pluck two *flashbangs* from the web belt of one of the men he had killed. He recognized them as M84 stun grenades, non-lethal explosive devices used to temporarily disorient an enemy's senses. Designed to produce a blinding flash of light and disabling noise without causing permanent injury, they could induce a short bout of blindness and loss of hearing in an adversary. *Flashbangs* were often carried by Navy Seals on covert missions, and Jake had utilized them on more than one occasion in the past.

Jake tossed one of the grenades to Victor. "Might come in handy," he remarked. Noticing a small walkie-talkie also attached to the dead trooper's web belt, he grabbed that too.

Leaping for the ninth flight, Jake's legs began to burn with the rapid ascent, Victor now right beside him. An alarm suddenly went off in his head, the same sense of presentiment he had recently experienced ever since being revived from his near-death state back in the cove.

"Get down!" Jake yelled, shoving Victor harshly to one side and stopping his headlong rush.

Taking the last four steps in a single bound, Jake reached the next landing and pulled the pin on the *flashbang.* Opening the portside door, he tossed it through. In his mind's eye he had clearly seen them coming even before they showed themselves. One of the two troopers approaching the door fired his weapon, but Jake sprang to one side of the doorframe to avoid the lethal volley of rounds that swarmed past.

Jake covered his ears and averted his eyes to avoid the blinding flash and jarring concussion as the grenade detonated. Stepping calmly back into the doorway, he turned the Sledgehammer loose on the troopers as they staggered about, unleashing two shots in quick succession. A third man lay on the floor, still stunned. Scrutinizing the fallen man, Jake saw that he was unarmed and wore a dark business suit.

"Don't shoot!" the man screamed, suddenly regaining his senses, his eyes fluttering open like those of a person waking up from a deep sleep and trying to orient himself to his surroundings. "Don't shoot!" he pleaded again, shielding his face with both hands as though to ward off a bullet.

Jake took in the hallway to make sure it was clear of other troopers before stepping over the man, his weapon at the ready. "Who are you?" he demanded.

"Bronte Pharah," the man cried, "Minister of Agriculture in Haiti." "They were holding me against my will."

Jake pulled Pharah to his feet, somehow certain the man was telling the truth. "Come with me!" he said. "Stay close and don't lag behind."

"But-"

Jake cut him off sharply, his reply curt. "There's no time for explanations. Just keep close if you want to get off this ship alive."

Victor was nowhere to be seen as Jake came back onto the landing with Pharah following. Jake shot a quick glance to Zimby, who was keeping a close watch on the stairs below. "Where's Victor?" he demanded.

Zimby indicated the final flight with jerk of his head. "Up there."

The whine of a turbine suddenly intruded its way into Jake's awareness, its growing pitch telling him there was no more time to lose. Bounding up the final flight of stairs, he headed for the lone door that supposedly gave way to where the sound was coming from. As he flung the door open, he saw that he had emerged out into the open below the helipad. Prudently, he looked to both sides to make sure he wasn't walking into an ambush as the roar of the whirlybird's turbine assaulted his ears. From the sound he knew the aircraft was on the verge of liftoff. Another set of stairs with a railing on each side rose up steeply to the lip of the platform supporting the chopper. Quickly, he ran up the steps, shouldering his way against the downdraft of heavy rotor wash pummeling him. Victor was at the top with his AK-104 aimed at the aircraft.

Taking a rapid assessment of the situation, Jake saw that the side door to the chopper was open. Alex stared back with a guard on each side of him, his expression unreadable. One of the guards held an Uzi submachine pistol to the lad's head as another guard wearing a headset pointed his weapon back at Victor. Sitting in the co-pilot's seat was a man Jake assumed to be Maximus, a set of headphones clamped to his head. An incongruous mix of both rage and smugness filled the man's countenance as he glimpsed Jake arriving on the scene.

Helplessly, Victor watched as the main rotor bit the air to lift the chopper sluggishly off the platform. He didn't dare fire his weapon. Even with well-placed shots that disabled the engine or took out the pilot, he risked ricocheting or fragmenting bullets that could kill his son or rupture the fuel tank, which could turn the aircraft into a raging inferno. He was effectively stalemated.

As the chopper rose higher and began to swing away, Jake saw Maximus' face change as he spoke into his lip mike. It was the look of a man on the brink of delivering a deadly blow to a hated enemy, and once again an inexplicable bout of presentiment took hold of him.

Even before the second guard could discharge his weapon, Jake launched himself sideways to tackle Victor and send both of them rolling along the edge of the helipad. A barrage of rounds caromed fiercely off the steel deck, narrowly missing both men.

The helicopter turned as its pilot moved it out over the water, its side door now facing away and nullifying the guard's opportunity to fire in their direction again. Jake rose to his feet, watching the chopper race away. Turning, he took in Victor's anguish. The man appeared lost and forlorn as he stared fixedly at the object taking his son into the distance.

Jake sympathized with him. Being a father himself, he could well understand what the man was going through at that moment.

-97-

Mat came awake with a start. Recognizing the person shaking him, he realized it was Samuel. "What happened?" he asked groggily.

"You were unconscious," Samuel said.

Aware of a dull pain, Mat raised a hand to his chin and flinched. Gingerly he groped his jaw, wiggling it back and forth to test it for a possible fracture. Though it was swollen and his fingertips came away with a slight smear of blood, he could tell it was not broken.

A remembrance of the fight with Bolder and how he had been suckered came oozing back. Mat stiffened, shooting a quick glance around the immediate area. Bolder was gone. "Where'd the news guy go?"

"Ez says he's in the access tunnel leading to Navassa."

Mat rose to his feet. "Whatever he's up to cannot be good," he said. An ominous feeling welled up in him as he thought about the duffel bag Bolder had carried.

"What's the latest with the UN task force?" Mat asked.

"A helicopter landed on the aircraft carrier. Ez says it's similar to the one Jake and Fernando commandeered. Three large submarines are also out there with the other ships."

"Damn!" Mat said, feeling more helpless than ever. "Any word from Jake?"

"No."

Mat looked beyond the acrylic window that gave a view of the hydrosphere that lay beyond. A swarm of bluefin crowded close to the glass, blocking what he was trying to see. Abruptly, the mass of tuna scattered, driven away by two albinos streaking past. It was as though the dolphins had read his mind and had purposely interceded to disperse the obstruction.

Mat's cell phone rang. "I instructed the dolphins to clear the fish out of the way," Ez said without preamble as soon as he answered. "Gauging his current pace, Bolder will reach the shipping platform in ten minutes."

Mat shot a glance at the window again. From this angle he could see the transparent access tunnel as it disappeared into the watery void beneath the algae lagoons. Though his jaw still throbbed, the cobwebs clinging to his thoughts were beginning to clear. Checking his wristwatch, he was shocked to see he had been comatose for almost forty minutes. "What took you so long in sending help?" Mat accused, speaking bitterly into his cell phone.

"With the exception of Jacob and Amelia," Ez shot back, "everyone has been evacuated to Navassa. I decided to avoid compounding Jacob's responsibilities by alerting him to your predicament, so I contacted Abdel and had him send Samuel."

"Where are you going?" Samuel said as Mat stepped past him.

"I'm going after Bolder."

"I'll help you."

Mat shook his head, still feeling a little woozy. "No. Stand by with Abdel in the sub. It's possible we may need to use the T-BEMP to stop those vessels." The fact that not one but three submarines had joined up with the UN task force was a bad omen. Deep down, Mat knew the T-BEMP option stood little chance. The UN vessels would detect the sub and most likely destroy it long before it got within range of their engines. But at least it was an excuse to keep Samuel out of harm's way for the time being.

Samuel looked grim. "You're the boss."

Mat started to leave, but Samuel reached down and lifted two items off the floor near his feet, handing one of them over. "Ez thought you might need these," he said.

Immediately recognizing his utility belt with spare ammo clips and holstered Heckler and Koch USP-9 submachine pistol similar to Jake's, Mat nodded appreciatively as he strapped it about his waist. That accomplished, he hefted the other item. "What's in the knapsack?" he asked.

"A cloaker and a Masker."

Harnessing the knapsack to his shoulders, Mat broke into a trot, chastising himself as he did so. He had severely underestimated Bolder, and there was no telling what the IBC cameraman had hidden in that duffel bag he carried. But one thing was for sure that he could not refute. Bolder was a dangerous man.

*   *   *   *

-98-

Plagued by a feeling of failure, Jake had no other choice but to vacate the ship. Victor had become pensive, appearing like a lost soul and showing signs of intense remorse. It was apparent a huge chunk had been torn from his heart, and Jake had to keep reminding him to stay alert.

Retracing the way they had come, the walkie-talkie Jake had taken from the dead trooper suddenly buzzed noisily with static. "Raven calling Unit Three, report!"

Jake raised his arm for Victor, Zimby and Pharah to stop. Quickly, he adjusted the volume control to reduce the sound issuing from it.

"Raven calling Unit Three, report!" the voice repeated with a touch more urgency behind it.

Jake listened, wondering if Unit Three was one of the teams he and his accomplices had taken out. The latest batch of troopers he had come across had been in groups of two and three.

The disembodied voice grew angry. "Answer me, Unit Three!" When no response occurred, the same voice issued another command. "Calling all units, has anyone seen Unit Three?"

"This is Unit One. Negative on the query," a different voice replied.

"Unit Five here!" another voice barked out in alarm. "We found Unit Three terminated on Level Four of the mid-ship stairwell."

The radio went silent for several seconds before Raven came back. "Units Two and Four, why aren't you answering?" When no reply ensued, Raven issued another order. "Unit Five, proceed with caution up the stairwell."

"This is Unit Five, we're on our way."

Raven came back again. "What's your location, Unit One?"

"Ninth level, starboard corridor. I just found Unit Four, both shot dead."

"What about the Haitian Minister?"

"He's not here."

"Well find him!" Raven growled. "But first I want you to assist Unit Five. If these raiders are still in the stairwell, you'll be able to trap them between you."

Jake turned. "Hand me your *flashbang*," he whispered to Victor.

With the grenade in his hand, Jake proceeded down the stairs slowly, working his way toward the fifth level. He was about to peek over the railing to see if he could catch a glimpse of the men comprising Unit Five, but suddenly realized this wasn't necessary as another vision flashed in his mind's eye. Painted on one of the walls on each landing were big black letters that indicated the level of the ship. Three men had just passed Level Five and were padding silently up the stairs.

Jake turned again. "Keep your hands on your ears and close your eyes," he whispered to the others, mimicking these actions with his hands and eyes. Pulling the pin, he dropped the grenade over the railing.

Even with his hands clamped firmly over his ears, the concussion jarred him. Rushing down the stairs, Jake found the troopers reeling about in stunned confusion, and it was fairly easy for him to finish them off quickly.

"Get back to the moon pool!" Jake said to the others. "I'll follow you."

Zimbola hung back, not willing to leave Jake behind. "I'm staying with you," the big Jamaican said.

From the adamant look on Zimby's face, Jake knew it would be futile to convince his friend otherwise. Instead, he looked to Victor, who still appeared numb. "We'll get your son back, Victor, but right now I need you to get Minister Pharah to the moon pool. The dolphins will be waiting."

The words seemed to snap Victor out of his fugue. "Come with me," Victor said to Pharah, grabbing him by the arm. Pharah looked frightened as he eyed the stairs above Jake, but he turned and let Victor lead him away.

Jake's radio buzzed again. "Raven, this is Unit One. I believe Unit Five has engaged the raiders, judging from the sound. My ears are still ringing."

"Acknowledged," Raven replied brusquely. "Bring any captives to the engine room. I'll be waiting for you there."

Jake made sure Victor and Pharah had a significant lead before eyeing the three troopers he had cut down, looking hopefully for more flashbangs clipped to their utility belts. At seeing none, he turned to Zimby. "I have an idea," he said. "Let's take up a position behind the portside door."

Zimby nodded and both men made a hasty exit through the door. Quickly, Jake explained what he had in mind.

Having retained the PHP after his encounter with Zinova near Cardoza's stronghold, he pulled it from a pouch on his web belt and held it at the ready. Leaning against the backside of the door, Jake peeked through the narrow panel of glass that provided a view of the Level Five landing. Sending out a mental query, he called to his bond mate. *How you doing, Achilles?*

Standing by below the moon pool, Achilles answered. *For the record, there's a keel hatch near the ship's stern where they sent out a ROV on an umbilical to assess the damage to the propulsion system.*

Thanks for the update, Jake said, keeping a wary eye on the stairs above the landing. At that moment, a booted foot appeared, treading cautiously on the next step down.

Motioning for Zimby to get ready, Jake waited for the opposition to show itself, discovering that Unit One consisted of three men. Withdrawing his face from the glass before the lead trooper glanced in his direction, he knelt low and nodded. Standing to one side of the doorway, Zimby flung the door open. With a flick of the activation button, Jake tossed the PHP onto the landing and ducked back behind the wall. He had no idea whether or not these men had immunized themselves to the effects of the dolphin art, but he had to at least give it a try.

All three troopers reacted at the same time, sending a torrent of Uzi rounds through the open doorway. And just as quickly as the barrage had started, it stopped, and wails of intense agony broke the air. Risking a peek around the doorframe, Jake saw that all three troopers had dropped their weapons and sunk to their knees, each clutching his head as though struck by an invisible demon.

Jake looked over at Zimby and rose to his feet. "Let's go!" he said.

Stepping back out onto the landing, Jake was overcome by that same feeling of ecstasy that always accosted him whenever he looked upon the holographic display. With the stress of mortal combat keeping him hair-trigger tense, he found comfort in the three-dimensional geometry as it pulsated before him, and he had trouble looking away from its soothing glow. Though he could have aimed his Sledgehammer and put all three foes out of their misery, he could not bring himself to do so. He was well aware of the potential danger he brought upon himself by staring at these displays too long. Simply put, they weakened the survival instinct. Suddenly calmed by the kinetic art form dancing before his eyes, he willed himself on past the portable holographic projector, leaving it behind and taking the next flight of stairs down. He would let the PHP remain where it lay and serve out its intended function, and that was to hold the downed troopers at bay.

Only when Jake reached the next landing down did the grip of euphoria and well-being begin to subside, and a quick glance behind him showed Zimby following with a subdued, mesmeric expression clinging to his face. It was as though the Jamaican had just undergone a profound religious experience.

* * * *

-99-

Sitting at the controls of the utility cart, Mat moved swiftly along the tubular access tunnel that would take him to the offshore platform. He had traversed its full length only once before to reach the subterranean complex on Navassa Island, and that had been immediately following its construction when he had traversed it on foot. And though it ran directly under the offshore platform to connect with the island, a smaller diameter manhole rose vertically from it to interface with the platform's lowest level. Each end of the tunnel was blocked by a circular hatch door with a dogging wheel that had to be turned by hand. Another overhead hatch at the top of the manhole allowed access onto the platform. As a rule of safety, users were required to batten down the doors upon entry or exit, but he had discovered that Bolder had left the tunnel's entrance hatch ajar. Unfortunately, the wiring systems and mechanisms for automatically opening and closing the hatches remotely had not yet been completed, which made it impossible for Ez to lock down the hatches at the other end to keep Bolder from getting through. And to make matters worse, no Aquarians were currently on the platform to secure the hatch from the other side. Because of the imminent invasion of the facility by UN troops, the majority of Aquarians had been evacuated to the nearby island via the tunnel hours earlier.

Made of clear acrylic polymer, the tube had an inner diameter of eight feet. Schools of various fish species swarmed just beyond the glass as he stared intently ahead looking to catch up with the man who had knocked him senseless. Two recessed grooves located forty-five degrees below the mid-height of the tunnel on each side and running parallel with it provided slotted guides for the cart's runners.

Just before giving chase, Ez had reminded Mat about the utility cart, which lay stored in a nearby locker next to the tunnel entrance. Because he had never used the cart, he had to rely on Ez for instructions on its operation, which was simple enough. Designed for easy storage, the cart was portable and compact, but could be unfolded for transporting equipment through the tunnel. Weighing slightly less than sixty pounds, Mat had found it easy to insert its runners into the recessed guides of the tunnel and get underway. He saw that there was a problem, however, as he stared at the simple gauges attached to the cart's handlebars. The lone battery providing power to the cart was low on juice. Someone had forgotten to recharge it.

Staring intently ahead, he looked for movement, but all he saw was the circular interior of the tube reduced to a pinpoint in the distance. As he moved on, he saw that the seafloor had risen considerably, with vast clusters of thriving coral reef and fish life coming into view beneath him. Though he had moved along the tunnel at a rate much faster than most world class athletes could run in an all-out sprint, he could see that the cart was beginning to move slower, much slower as the battery expended the remainder of its power. Mat estimated he had traversed almost two miles of the three-mile-long access tunnel as the cart suddenly slowed to a crawl, and realizing it was no longer doing him any good, he hopped off and began running. Taking deep breaths, he felt a continuous rush of air at his back. This told him that the blowers located within the floating city were still active. Movement of fresh, breathable air within the access tunnel had been crucial in allowing nearly ten thousand people to reach the island.

-100-

Upon reaching the moon pool, Jake found it to be vacant. Sending a mental query to Achilles, he asked if Victor, Pharah, and Percy were aboard Johnnie.

Victor and Pharah have returned, Achilles informed him, *but Percy was not with them. I have to assume he's still aboard the ship.*

A bad feeling suddenly took hold of Jake, and he let his bond mate know it. *This is not good. I can't leave without him.*

That's understandable, JJ. Fernando is still standing by.

Jake looked over at Zimbola. "I need you to get aboard the sub."

The Jamaican shook his head adamantly. "You're stuck with me whether you like it or not."

Jake was about to argue this, but the radio he had taken from the downed trooper suddenly squawked. "Raven to Units One and Five, give me an update?"

The reply that immediately followed surprised Jake.

"This is Unit Five." Though muffled in static, the voice sounded strained. "We have neutralized the intruders. We were forced to kill all four of them and have no captives. Unit One is with me but their radio took a bullet and is not working."

A moment of dead silence followed before Raven came back. "You sound funny, Unit Five. Everything okay?" A hint of suspicion was obvious in his tone.

"Took a round in the leg but I'm still able to walk. I also lost a man," Five said.

Jake had trouble believing what he was hearing. He was certain he had killed the three men comprising Unit Five. *How could this be?*

Another short pause ensued before Raven came back, his tone now sounding petulant. "Do you have the Haitian in custody?"

"No."

"Head to the moon pool!" Raven ordered impatiently. "He might be trying to board a sub directly under it. We spotted it with our ROV camera."

"If he's there, Estrada will get him," Five answered.

"Estrada's dead," Raven rebuked testily. "His body floated past the ROV. That's when we sent it amidships and saw the sub."

"What about using one of our torpedoes to destroy it?" Five recommended.

"The torpedo hatches refuse to engage," Raven railed in frustration. "They won't open. The ROV hatch is the only one that works, and the techs were forced to open it manually. Now go!"

"We're on our way," Five said.

Jake turned to Zimby and shrugged. "I don't get it. I could have sworn we took out both units."

"You did."

Jake spun, startled by the voice at his back. Percy emerged from the shadows.

"You almost got yourself killed," Jake admonished sharply, easing up his finger on the Sledgehammer trigger. "I assume that was you on the radio."

"Always had this talent for mimicking voices," Percy offered.

"But for what purpose?" Jake needed to know.

"I had to be sure I disabled the hull torpedoes before we left the ship."

Jake frowned. "You never mentioned this ship had torpedoes."

Percy smiled disarmingly. "I doubt it would have made a difference had I told you. As it is, I was able to shut down most of the systems that would have caused us problems, including their internal communications." His gaze fell on the small radio clipped to Jake's utility belt. "It forced them to use those crude walkie-talkies."

"Any idea where Maximus is headed?" Jake asked.

Percy nodded. "He's on his way to the *Kraken*. He owns it."

"The mega-tanker? How can you be sure?"

"I was able to intercept his last transmission." Moving past Jake, Percy made his way over to the computer terminal he had used before. "If you'll indulge me for one moment, I'd like to show you something."

"Whatever it is, be quick about it," Jake grumbled impatiently. "We've got to get going."

"You might find this important," Percy said airily, his fingers playing rapidly over the keyboard again. "Maximus made sure to have a link installed within the onboard surveillance system. It provides real-time viewing of the *Kraken* whenever she's within thirty miles of this ship." The rear deck of an enormous oil tanker as seen from a camera perched high up abruptly sprang into view on the computer screen. "You're looking at her as I speak, so she must be within range."

Jake stared, his eyes falling on a large helicopter that had just settled on one of the tankers landing pads, its main rotor slowing. The chopper was much too big to be the one Maximus had escaped on. Placing a hand on Percy's shoulder, Jake said, "Does that bird hold some meaning to you?"

Percy's features hardened. "Bounty hunters. Maximus hired them to kidnap my brother."

Jake continued to stare as several armed men raced up onto the pad and into the chopper's main cabin. Several seconds elapsed before two figures were ushered out, their hands shackled firmly behind their backs. Two others emerged from the cabin door, following behind the two being led away.

"Are you able to zoom in?" Jake asked, suddenly growing edgy. There was something oddly familiar in the way one of the captives walked.

Percy went to work on the keys once more, and a second later Jake's fear was confirmed.

Turning his head, Percy read the anger blazing across Jake's face. "Do you know them?"

Jake did not answer. He could feel his bond mate's fury growing in concert with his own. The sensation gathered strength before suddenly fading.

Achilles reined in his mushrooming ire, though it was analogous to holding back a volcanic eruption. The dolphin knew a show of anger would do nothing to help the situation, aware that too much of Jake resonated within him. With considerable effort he got control of his emotions, easing his way into Jake's thoughts again with a profound delicacy.

JJ, I just received word the Hind touched down on an aircraft carrier positioned near Aquaria. Ez saw it land forty minutes ago.

The delay in news evoked a tad of petulance in Jake's reply. *And she thought to inform you of this now?*

No, JJ, we were in range of her underwater broadcasts just before you climbed into the moon pool, but I thought it wise not to lay more bad news on you.

Jake was still annoyed. *Anything else you forgot to tell me?*

You had enough on your plate to deal with, JJ, so I thought it best not to tell you before. Three submarines are also on station with the UN task force. Ez has a bad feeling about their intentions and strongly suggests you get back to Aquaria on the double. She'll fill you in on everything once you arrive.

Jake was suddenly aware of Percy appraising him with a penetrating stare. "I hate to intrude on your thoughts," Percy apologized, "but what's our next move?"

Jake let out a troubled sigh. "I need time to think this out, but right now I suggest we get back on the sub and get away just in case Raven is able to re-engage those torpedoes."

The huge head of Hercules broke the surface of the moon pool as Jake uttered this.

A sudden idea struck Jake, and he explored it further by conferring with his bond mate, taking only milliseconds to get Achilles opinion.

Aquaria's outer breakwater is less than five miles away, his bond mate informed him.

Do you think we can get their cooperation? Jake asked.

They have never refused us, Achilles reminded him.

Jake looked at Percy. "I have an idea," he said, quickly laying out the rudiments of a plan. "Think you can do it?"

Percy's eyes narrowed. "I'll give it my best shot," he said. Abruptly he went back to working keys on the computer terminal.

Jake set his eyes on Zimby. "I want you to get Mr. Pharah back aboard Johnnie and have Fernando hightail it to Malique to drop the two of you off."

Seeing the scowl coming to Zimby's face, Jake cut him off quickly before he could object. "It's important you get him away from all this. You can get back to the cove using one of the company jeeps. I need you there to protect everyone, especially the children."

"What about you?" the black goliath grumbled.

"As soon as Fernando drops you off, he is to get back here pronto. Have him bring back a grappling hook with at least a hundred and fifty feet of rope. I know Kobe has both aboard the *Exoco*, which should still be docked there."

Jake glanced at his watch. "Tell Fernando to squeeze every ounce of speed he can get out of Johnnie. This vessel will likely be at Aquaria's southern perimeter by the time he gets back. Round trip shouldn't take more than an hour."

Zimbola was reluctant to leave, though he knew it would be unwise to question his friend's instincts and judgement in situations like this, knowing his partner was usually right most of the time, and following some minor bickering, finally jumped down into the moon pool to climb aboard Hercules' back. Pharah, however, was not so eager to join him, bearing the expression of a frightened child being led to the dentist's chair, and Jake had to literally shove him into the water to get him to go.

Thankful that both men finally disappeared below the waterline, Jake watched as Percy continued to jab away at the keyboard. Out of the clear blue an image of the remaining robo-fish suddenly flashed like a beacon in the back of his mind, and with it a bolt of raw, inexplicable intuition. Looking over Percy's shoulder, he voiced another question. "All your incriminating files on Maximus are stored in the remaining mechanical fish, aren't they?"

Percy stopped punching keys and turned his head, his expression filled with amazement. "How did you know?"

"Call it a wild guess," Jake muttered distantly as another idea came together within his thoughts. "I have one more request of you, that is, if you're willing to trust me."

Percy's reply came quickly. "Fire away!"

-101-

Bolder reached the vertical manhole that rose up to connect with the offshore platform. Like the tunnel he had just traversed, it also appeared to be made of the same clear acrylic polymer material, giving him a three hundred and sixty-degree view of the undersea environment beneath the platform. Breathing hard and slinging the duffel bag he carried over one shoulder, he climbed the twenty rungs embedded on one side of the manhole. Ascending to the top, he turned the dogging wheel in the middle of the hatch that barred his way. It required little effort to swing it down, and he quickly hauled his bulk upward through the opening. On the other side was a maze of pipes, cables and electrical conduits that branched out in various directions before rising up through a ceiling that appeared to be constructed of the same sea cement Jacob had described during his interview with Amelia.

Taking a moment to study this elaborate but confusing network of interlacing components, he made his way forward. Even before he entered this area, the access tunnel's transparency had given him an excellent view of the seven huge pipes running parallel with it, and he could clearly see that they all connected with the massive substructure in which he now found himself. According to information Maximus had given him during their last phone call, the platform received vast amounts of hydrogen gas ducted into it. Housed within the substructure where chambers that burned the gas in order to raise the temperature of surface waters in Lulu Bay.

Maximus had emphasized how this process was key to increasing the temperature differential between surface and deep waters that drove the OTEC turbines within Aquaria's central structure, making them even more efficient at producing electrical power.

But Maximus suspected another process that also took place on the offshore platform, informing Bolder that the natural fertilizer harvested on the nearby island was likely being supplemented by unknown ingredients prior to being shipped off to Haitian farmers, and it was these ingredients that made their food crops immune to the effects of the Omicron-7 compound.

Setting down the duffel bag and unzipping it, Bolder removed a small object contained within and clicked a tiny switch to the 'on' position before placing it behind a large grouping of ductwork. Satisfied that it was well concealed, he reached for the bag and made his way over to a grated stairway off to one side. Pleased with himself, he climbed the stairs, eventually reaching the top four flights up.

Finding himself in the small warehouse he had seen situated on the platform when he had flown over the complex, he glanced around. Bags of what he assumed to be fertilizer were stacked up on pallets along three walls. Within their midst sat a forklift with its forks lowered and nearly touching another pallet loaded with a low stack of small wooden boxes. He judged them to be about thirteen inches on a side and slightly more than five inches high. Curious as to what the boxes contained, he stepped closer and leaned over to inspect one of the topmost boxes, which had a hinged lid secured by a small hasp-like fastener.

Unsnapping the hasp and lifting the lid, his eyes bulged in astonishment at what lay inside. Within the box lay three gold bricks. Assuming the recessed lettering spelling 24 karats stamped on the highly polished surface of each brick was for real, he was looking at gold in its purest form.

Awestruck, Bolder stared for a few more seconds before trying to heft the box, gripping the wooden handles that jutted from each side and finding that it hardly moved. Gold, he knew, was heavier than lead, far heavier. Shifting his stance, he placed his feet on top of the stacked boxes and re-gripped the handles, throwing his back into the effort and using all his bull-like strength to raise the container from the pallet. His eyes widened, certain the weight was close to four hundred pounds. No wonder there were so few boxes on the pallet, he thought. Too many would have exceeded the lifting capacity of the forklift.

Setting the box back down, his mind abruptly surged into high gear. If his calculations were correct, he might be able to come away with seven boxes of the precious metal, and that would be cutting it close. Aside from what he was to be paid for his part in the mission, this was to be a windfall bonus he had least expected.

Whirling around, Bolder eyed the three large articulated rollup bay doors that provided access to the platform deck. All were in the closed position. Striding quickly to the nearest one, he activated the switch that raised it. A low hum ensued as the jointed panels began to slide upward on their rollers. Bolting back to the gold-bearing pallet, he placed the duffel bag atop the boxes before hopping onto the forklift and turning the starter key. He was familiar with operating forklifts, having operated one during a summer job in his youth when he had loaded trucks at a plant in Michigan that manufactured car batteries. As it rumbled to life, he eased the forks under the pallet, raising it no more than six inches above the floor, intent on keeping the center of gravity low as he moved the load. Looking behind him, he backed the forklift through the bay door and out onto the deck.

-102-

Mat climbed up through the manhole to find the hatch open. Cautiously he poked his head up through the opening, glancing around sharply looking for an ambush. At seeing none, he pulled himself the rest of the way through, taking a moment to reseal the hatch and dog it off.

Puzzled as to what Bolder was up to, his mind continued to rove over several possibilities when his cell phone suddenly vibrated. Pulling it from his pocket, he saw that the incoming call was from Ez.

"Bolder is out in the open on top of the platform," Ez informed him. "I can see him clearly. He used the forklift to move a pallet of the gold we use for bartering out onto the deck."

Mat knew Ez was accessing Aquaria's camera system, which would give her views of the platform from various angles. Some of the cameras were located on the platform while others were mounted high up on Aquaria's central structure. "What's he doing now?"

"He has some kind gadget in his hands. A close up view suggests it to be some kind of remote control."

This puzzled Mat even more, but Ez interrupted his thoughts before he could voice another question.

"The IBC chopper is lifting from the pad. It has no pilot, so it's probable Bolder is controlling it with the remote."

"Where's the chopper headed?" Mat blurted.

"Directly for the platform!" Ez said.

"It's obvious he's looking to get away from here-" Mat's words trailed off as he realized there could be only one reason why Bolder had come this way. "Because he planted a bomb," he added flatly to complete the sentence.

A helpless feeling accosted him as he considered the consequences that would befall the colony if his speculation was true. Even a small detonation would trigger a chain reaction in the hydrogen gas being ducted to the platform. The explosion would be disastrous. Not only would it completely obliterate the platform, it would likely destroy the intake pipes leading to the OTEC generators, at least a portion of them. Without power, the colony's operations would come to a complete halt, and it would take months to repair the damage and get the facility up and running again.

Mat looked around in desperation, his eyes roaming searchingly over the forest of conduits and cables that lay all about him. If there was a bomb hidden among this hodgepodge of components, he had to find and disarm it immediately.

-103-

From the bridge of the *Carl Sagan*, Captain Delila watched the two massive AW101 choppers lift from the carrier to ferry their contingent of Navy Seals in the direction of Aquaria. Moments later, the Russian-built Hind carrying the UN's Special Envoy rose from the deck to follow in their wake. Delila had a bitter taste in his mouth. One look at Malikai Allotey and the hard looking men accompanying him only tended to further confirm his suspicions that something was amiss with this whole operation. And a surreptitious sideways glance at Lieutenant Myron Johnson during their short meeting with Allotey told him the Navy Seal officer felt the same way. It was obvious Johnson did not like the pompously arrogant Allotey or the Chilean commando hovering at his side. What was the Chilean's name? Delila searched his memory, trying to recall it. Ah, yes, now he remembered. It was Alvarez, Captain Francisco Alvarez. His dislike of the man suddenly intensified. He had sensed a suppressed viciousness in Alvarez's manner lurking just below the surface, suggested by the way he had fingered the haft of the sheathed *corvo* slung from his belt. Undoubtedly Alvarez would be merciless and cruel in a fight, and he couldn't help but wonder how many men the man had killed with that blade.

The U.S. senator tagging along with Allotey only tended to increase Delila's growing uneasiness over this whole affair. Paunchy and square-jawed with a thick crop of silver hair far too neatly trimmed to be natural,

Senator Brent Van Heflin seemed especially eager to get a firsthand look at the secrets Aquaria held. Delila had studied him surreptitiously during the meeting and he sensed an inordinate amount of corruption lurking just below the surface of the man, so much so that he could have sworn he had actually smelled it wafting off him as he climbed back aboard the Hind to embark for the floating city.

Delila sighed. Unfortunately, he had his orders, and those orders specifically stated that Allotey was to be in overall charge of the mission, a mission that reeked of conspiracy. Allotey had called for a slight change in the mission, though Lieutenant Johnson's team would land on Aquaria's central structure to secure it as originally planned. The second team, however, led by Ensign Patrick Flynn, was to land on Navassa Island to secure the buildings and the tramway leading to the offshore platform.

In the distance directly above the floating city, movement abruptly caught Delila's attention, and he lifted a pair of spyglasses to his eyes. A small helicopter had taken off and appeared to be headed toward the island. Studying it a moment longer, he lowered the glasses.

For a man his age he had exceptionally good vision, and seconds later he brought his eyes back to something else he had been monitoring. A ship he had noticed earlier was moving steadily closer to the floating city, though ever so slowly. Looking through the glasses again, he assessed the magnified view. A frown came to his face as he studied it. There was something odd about what he was seeing. The vessel appeared to be drifting sideways against the wind. With its starboard side facing him, he saw it was now directly off Aquaria's southern breakwater. Carried by the breeze, clouds of mist swept over her superstructure from behind to partially obscure it, adding to his puzzlement. Continuing to focus the glasses, he began to discern huge shapes bunched together near the vessel's bow and stern. A pod of whales was roiling the sea, hundreds of them breaching and spouting as they disappeared on the opposite side of the ship.

Captain Delila turned to address one of his officers approaching him, a young ensign displaying a befuddled demeanor. "Have you been able to raise that ship, Mr. Jefferson?"

"No, sir, they won't acknowledge our call. Don't you find it odd that they're drifting into the wind?"

Delila shook his head slowly, his lips forming a small humorless grin. "Not at all when you realize a herd of whales is pushing her."

Jefferson stared back at the captain, an implacable though dubious expression suddenly coming to his face. The possibility that his superior might be entering the first stages of senility entered his mind.

At reading the look, Delila handed him the glasses. "See for yourself," he offered, not taking any offense at his ensign's dubiousness.

An abrupt transformation in Jefferson's bearing took place as he focused the lenses, his mouth falling open in astonishment. "Why would whales be pushing her, sir?"

"I don't have the foggiest, Mr. Jefferson."

Delila was about to order him to send up a small drone to get the name of the vessel, but at that moment the ship swung around.

"What name do you read on her stern?" asked the captain.

"Looks like *Nunquarn Satis*," Jefferson replied as he handed back the glasses. "Sounds Latin."

Bringing the glasses back to his eyes, Delila confirmed the name before turning back to his ensign. "Run a check on her, Mr. Jefferson," he ordered. "I'd like to know who owns her."

An odd name, thought Delila as Jefferson walked away. He had studied Latin as an elective when he had attended the Naval Academy. Whoever had named the vessel *Never Enough* had to be one greedy bastard. Dismissing the notion, he redirected the glasses toward the floating city's central structure, noting that Johnson's chopper had already set down on one of its landing pads. Swinging the lenses left, he saw that the other AW101 had now reached the island. As for the small chopper that had taken off from Aquaria moments earlier, he observed it just coming to a hover directly over the offshore platform.

-104-

Mat moved quickly among the network of interconnected components, searching for the bomb. Unfortunately, no cameras had as yet been installed at this level of the substructure, so Ez could not tell him where to look.

"I believe you're getting warm," Ez advised him soothingly.

"What brings you to that conclusion?" Mat said irritably, not understanding how Ez could remain so calm under the current circumstance.

"My sensors have picked up an anomalous signal. The source of it seems to be originating close to your location. Move left twelve feet, I'm tracking your cell."

"I don't see anything," grumbled Mat testily upon following her directions.

"You're almost on top of it."

Mat eyed some ductwork before him, extending his arms and groping around blindly on the side opposite him. His hands immediately fell on something, and carefully he pushed it, finding that it moved.

"I think I found it," Mat said in a hushed, constrained voice. Cautiously he eased the object past the duct where he was able to view it. Resting on its base stood a shiny cylindrical canister about eight inches long with a diameter half that. A light at the top glowed red, blinking on and off in measured pulsating cycles. Next to the light was a tiny toggle switch, and next to that was a small LED timer steadily ticking down. At the moment it showed 5 minutes twenty seconds.

Slowly, painstakingly, Mat pulled the object toward him, keeping it upright and making sure to slide it. He couldn't be sure it was not fitted with a concealed spring-loaded trigger on its base that would set it off once it was lifted from the floor. He knew that most land mines were designed this way.

"Ez, I'm sending you a picture," he said, aiming the tiny camera of his cell at the device. "Give me an assessment. If it's a bomb, it appears to have an arming switch, but I can't be sure I won't detonate it if I flick it in the opposite direction." He could not rule out the possibility of such an event. A deviously minded bomb builder might actually incorporate such a feature into the design. If this were the case, once it was armed it could not be disarmed.

"Has Bolder landed his chopper?" asked Mat hurriedly as he eyed the cylinder nervously, knowing it would not distract Ez from carrying out the assessment. He was well aware that Ez was capable of carrying out hundreds of tasks simultaneously.

"It just set down," answered Ez. "He's moving the gold into it. I'm surprised he's able to lift those boxes by himself. Each weighs slightly less than four hundred pounds."

"How you doing on that assessment?" Mat pressed anxiously.

"I've accessed the worldwide web including the data banks of the CIA, NSA and FBI and find nothing that matches the object, but if it's a bomb made for remote triggering, it's a foregone conclusion that it would be suicide for Bolder to detonate it before he's clear of the platform."

"There's something else you should know," Ez added. To Mat, her tone had changed, now sounding downcast. "Two large helicopters have taken off from the aircraft carrier. One of them has already landed on Helipad Eighteen and has disembarked what I believe to be U.S. Navy Seals. The second one is just beginning to set down on Navassa."

"How do you know they're Seals?" Mat demanded in surprise.

"They wear the Special Warfare insignia, the Trident."

A plan suddenly emerged in the back of Mat's mind, and he made a decision. Slipping the knapsack Samuel had given him from his shoulders, he pulled out the cloaker and donned it quickly, listening to the faint hum it emitted as he turned it on. Staring down at the device at his feet, he took a deep breath, then lifted it.

Mat expelled a sigh of relief, somewhat surprised that he was still alive.

-105-

No sooner had the EC 135 set down on the *Kraken's* more than ample landing pad, Maximus hopped out, striding briskly with head lowered to get away from the whirling blades. In moments he descended the helipad steps, quickly making his way to the ship's bridge. As he entered the cavernous helm, a huge bearded individual with leonine features turned to regard him. Sporting a thick, shaggy mane reaching to his shoulders and dyed a striking russet through periodic applications of henna, had the man been transported back in time and festooned with a horned helmet rather than a captain's cap, he would have perfectly matched the classical image of a seafaring Viking preparing to sack a coastal village. Grim-faced with a ruddy complexion, the man's deep-set, squinty eyes blazed with a fierce intensity that suggested a cruel nature, though this was somewhat offset by an impossibly large bulbous nose that bulged comically from between them, giving him the appearance of a circus clown when he was not frowning. Captain Rufus Finley's demeanor, however, was anything but clownish as he ran his ship with all the tact of an oppressive tyrant.

"What's our position?" Maximus demanded, ostensibly eyeing three rough-looking individuals manning the bridge under Finley's watchful eye. Their sole function was to monitor readouts displayed on an assortment of computer screens dominating several control panels. As Maximus well knew, their presence was merely a safety precaution as the entire ship was fully automated and, in theory, could have been run by one man.

"Right where you want us, thirty-two nautical miles northeast of Navassa Island," Finley said courteously, making an effort to suppress the gruff edge he normally carried in his tone. Malcolm Maximus was the only man he allowed himself to take orders from.

"Good," Maximus rasped. "Continue to hold this position for the time being. If necessary, use your bow and stern thrusters."

Finley nodded. "How much longer before Aquaria is secured?"

"Not long. The task force has already deployed the Seal teams."

"You don't see them as a problem?" Finley asked solemnly.

Uncharacteristically, Maximus let a sly, demonic grin flourish on his face. Normally he refrained from displaying a show of emotion. "They have no idea what awaits them."

Finley stared fixedly, waiting for Maximus to tell him more, though he suspected it had something to do with what the ship carried.

"I assume our additional cargo is in full readiness," said Maximus.

"Yes," answered Finley, continuing to stare expectedly. When Maximus failed to divulge more, he turned his eyes away. Though his curiosity was whetted, he knew not to press. If his boss wanted to provide details, he'd tell him.

Maximus dropped the grin, deciding not to elaborate. Sometimes he was better off keeping certain things to himself. Though Finley was an underling, he was also a confidant, one of the few men he made privy to his primary objectives and how they came together to form the grand scheme. The man was intelligent, pragmatic, and above all else, loyal. Nevertheless, in this case he would keep all details of the plan to himself. All Finley had to do was mind the *Kraken*.

Maximus liked surrounding himself with big, physically intimidating men. If anything, men like Finley were a reflection of his own power, which was far reaching if not altogether omnipotent. The thought made him think of Swensen. As soon as this was over, he would find a replacement. Men like Swensen, he well knew, were easy to find as long as you had the means to pay for their services. With such individuals, the lore of money trumped morals and ethics. They were like big trustworthy lapdogs, willing to carry out any type of act no matter how heinous and ruthless it tended to be.

"What's the latest on the ebola outbreak in Africa?" Maximus asked.

"It's reached pandemic status," said Finley. "Cases are now being reported in Europe and the United States."

Maximus' grin returned. Agents of *The Order* had planted the virus in Guinea three months earlier, and now it was spiraling out of control, reaching Sierra Leone and Liberia in rapid succession before finding its way to other parts of the globe. It was just one more of his ingenious schemes to bring on panic and confusion that would further subjugate people while solving a major planetary problem. Governments throughout the world would have no choice but to enact martial law in trying to contain it, but their efforts would ultimately fail. The virus was a genetically modified and laboratory-grown strain even deadlier than its predecessor. Due to the major medical infrastructure challenges that existed in Western Africa, it was the ideal locale for initiating a pandemic. Reversing the mushrooming population in Africa had been one of *The Order's* primary goals for many years now, but only recently did his pharmaceutical laboratories finally develop a reliable antidote to combat the virus. Prior to that he had dared not tamper with releasing it, though he could not guarantee it would not mutate into something even deadlier where there might be no defense against it at all. But with recent projections showing the population within the African continent would grow by another two billion by the year 2050, he was now willing to take that risk, especially since he stood to make a financial killing on the sale of the vaccine, which he would sell to desperate governments at astronomical rates.

Maximus knew that the mere mention of human population control in any form was considered ruthlessly barbaric and unjust by philanthropic thinkers, a nefarious and unholy undertaking that greatly exceeded the bounds of moral rectitude. Nevertheless, it was something that had to be done if the planet was to remain healthy, and he and his followers would do whatever it took to accomplish the task, resorting to the use of pandemics and eugenics to cleanse the earth of the useless eaters. *As such, were not he and his followers the true caretakers of the world?* Was what they were doing any different than what was done to other species of living organisms to preserve them? Weren't elephant herds periodically culled down to hold their numbers in check, purposely slaughtered in the game and wildlife preserves that abounded in Southern and Eastern Africa to keep them from completely stripping the land of all vegetation? Certainly it could be rationally justified as a merciful and proactive approach to keeping the elephants from slowly starving to death. Deprived of their natural food source, wouldn't they eventually die off if not for these measures? In addition, periodic culling served other purposes. Not only did it prevent other herbivores from going without food, it reduced the number of potential hosts for spreading disease.

This train of thought made him think of his great grandfather with prideful admiration. Even back then scientists recruited by *The Order* had been experimenting with various deadly pathogens as a viable way of holding down population explosions during the industrial revolution, and it had been Marcais Maximus who had his minions unleash the Spanish influenza on the planet in 1918, killing off close to 100 million people across the globe. Having played a hand in instigating World War I, Marcais had timed the release of the virus to coincide with massive troop movements, relying on the close quarters of soldiers and modern transportation systems to hasten its transmission. The mass genocide he created, estimated to be somewhere between three and five percent of the world population at that time, made it one of the deadliest disasters in human history.

"Anything new on the Middle East?" asked Maximus.

"ISIS has executed two more, this time Christian priests. The backlash is just as you wanted. Western powers are starting to react, and the Islamic Revolution in Syria and Iraq is intensifying."

Maximus pondered the acronym, which stood for Islamic State in Iraq and Syria when translated to its English equivalent. *What better time to have diversions like these?* he thought cunningly. Through careful planning and implementation, he and his acolytes had been successful in manipulating geopolitical events so that the fascio-Islamic movement in the Middle East and throughout the world had continued to grow. Radical Islam was a most useful tool. This threat alone had allowed *The Order* to tighten the noose on all free societies through the use of massive government security measures aimed at keeping them safe from terrorism. But there had been a price. With the public embracing these seemingly beneficial measures, they failed to see the true diabolical nature behind the increased security imposed on them, and in the end, freedom had slowly been eroded. Liberty had been sacrificed for survival.

How easy it was to manipulate them, thought Maximus disdainfully. What was that phrase Benjamin Franklin had once said? Ah, yes, now he remembered. *Make yourselves sheep and the wolves will eat you.* The thought made him chuckle to himself. He liked being a wolf. More precisely, the supreme Alpha-wolf. Such status allowed him entitlements few human beings enjoyed. As the *Sublimis*, he lived the most lavish lifestyle imaginable, and the power he commanded knew no bounds. He had been born and bred for the position he held. He had been backed by the vast influence *The Order* wielded and provided the seed money to grow his sprawling financial empire into what it had become, and it was still growing. He had just turned six when his father had revealed to him who he was. He was the heir apparent to the position of *Lofty One*, the person *The Order* called the *Sublimis*. He belonged to a privileged clan, a plutocracy whose ancestors could be traced all the way back to the Pharaohs of Egypt and beyond. Attaining power and wealth had been easy for the clan once they had learned how to manipulate the masses through subterfuge and cunning, and as time went on they had developed it into an art form. The clan had been a major force in shaping world events throughout recorded history, going by various names during different periods, with the Hermetic Order of the Golden Dawn, Knights Templar and Illuminati being three of them. And now they were called *The Order of the Righteous*, but for the sake of brevity, most members simply referred to themselves as *The Order*, including the *Sublimis*. Many of the rich and famous throughout the world, both past and present, had been bred by *The Order*. But maintaining total control had not been easy, and at times had been lost. They would have succeeded in attaining their goal of a one world government 70 years earlier through the rise of the Third Reich, but unfortunately Hitler had been defeated. Nevertheless, they had regrouped, and as the world population grew so had their numbers, with members of *The Order* now carefully planted within the governments of every major power on the planet.

As it now was, *The Order* only needed one more major terrorist attack to be carried out in the U.S. in order to force the use of martial law that would finally put an end to the nation's Constitution once and for all. For starters, the Second Amendment would be immediately abolished and all registered firearms seized to ensure that no resistance by the population occurred. Citizens would be defenseless. It was imperative that political upheaval of this magnitude was necessary if *The Order* was to succeed. Once things settled down, martial law would be lifted to allow the presidential election that had been suspended to finally take place, thereby clearing the way for Van Heflin to occupy the Oval Office. And when that happened, the old American republic everyone remembered would cease to exist. Free speech would become a thing of the past. Severely weakening the foundations of the only remaining superpower on the planet would pave the way for the one world government it so desperately sought.

Though it had been a test run, the Boston bombing had clearly shown how easily a major U.S. city could be locked down. Ratcheting up a police state had to be done delicately, incrementally, in order to determine how far the government could go without the masses rioting in response. Suppression of freedoms had started to gain pronounced traction shortly after the attack on the World Trade Center. Through careful coaxing by embedded members of *The Order*, Bin Laden and his radical Islamist followers had been used and manipulated into carrying out the murder of thousands. Pat downs, body scans and searches of air travelers at airports by TSA officials had immediately followed to ensure public safety. The planning for this, he well knew, had taken years in the making, but it had nevertheless worked beautifully, using the power of big government to target the people. Continue to frighten them with staged security alerts and events, and they gladly submitted to increased security measures. Nazi Germany had carried out similar ploys, only it had terrorized its citizenry at gunpoint to consent to illegal searches and violations of their privacy in order to guarantee no one would oppose it. Knowing such tactics were now only a short step away gave Maximus comfort. He was well aware of the widespread complacency and apathy that currently existed in America, and he was convinced the time was now ripe for change. Draconian change. People had become so ignorant of their rights and powers that they would practically submit to anything the government forced on them.

But he had other schemes afoot throughout the globe. Invoking a controlled chaos worked wonders, and in spite of the recent setbacks he was forced to endure, he knew the time was right to orchestrate events aimed at creating as much international turmoil as possible. As intended, these events would certainly dominate the news media and shift public attention away from another of his primary goals, one of them taking control of Aquaria. But he had to do it in a covert manner, one designed to delude the masses and further mold world opinion. The fact that Percy Osgood had absconded with incriminating evidence on *The Order's* objectives continued to irritate him, and he had to remind himself that it was he who controlled 90 percent of the major news outlets throughout the world. Gaining dominion over the remaining media holdouts was already in the works, and he knew that it wouldn't be much longer before he had total control over all of them, either through corporate hostile takeovers, outright bribery too difficult to refuse, or by planting moles in high ranking positions on editorial staffs. Maximus' grandfather, Marauda Maximus, had given Hitler a valuable lesson on the effectiveness of the media in consolidating power. Control it and you controlled the people, making them so brainwashed with propaganda that they lost their ability to think clearly. Whatever information Percy held would be suppressed and refuted as nothing more than far-flung conspiracies aimed at undermining the honorable reputations of Plagiarius and Unus Universitas.

Pacified by these thoughts, Maximus stepped closer to Finley, locking unwavering eyes on him. "I'll let you in on a little secret," he said. "A sub belonging to Iran has joined the task force. It's under the command of Captain Sayyari Habibollah, a low-ranking member of *The Order* who will be answering directly to me."

Maximus glanced out one of the bridge windows, a wide expanse of Plexiglas that gave an unimpeded view of the ship's rear deck trailing away to a distance of one-half mile. Turning around, he glimpsed the tanker's bow section reaching out over the sea another half mile. With such an enormous vessel he had thought it prudent to position the bridge amidships when the design of the ship was first conceived, otherwise navigating through tight channels would have been made exceptionally difficult. Using its incredibly powerful bow and stern thrusters, the tanker could be made to pivot on its central vertical axis much the way a locomotive could be rotated on a railroad turntable.

Staring beyond the bow, Maximus searched the horizon, unable to discern the pinnacle of Navassa's old lighthouse. Finley had done a good job, he had to admit. The *Kraken* sat just beyond the reach of Aquaria's line of sight sensors. Even if they had thought to place a radar dish atop the lighthouse or the floating city's central structure, they would be unable to detect the world's largest ship.

Maximus gazed behind him again, eyeing the EC 135 sitting on the landing pad as his pilot tied down the main rotor. Below the pad, he saw that Alex was just climbing into the cab of a monorail car used for rapid transit of the ship's vast infrastructure. The two guards with him climbed in behind him, and a moment later the cab shot away, disappearing into a tunnel that would take the trio into the bowels of the vessel. Having been involved in the Kraken's design, he had made sure to have a monorail network incorporated throughout the ship, connecting with the various decks and the key sectors within those decks. At the moment he envisioned the cab descending to the tanker's lowest level.

Shifting his gaze, Maximus fixated his eyes on another whirlybird squatting low and unmanned on a second helipad situated a little further back from the EC 135, this one an ancient Jolly Green Giant that had supposedly seen action during the Vietnam War. He knew the people who flew it, bounty hunters, a husband and wife team he occasionally contracted with to carry out nefarious jobs. According to the husband, the chopper had been won in a high stakes poker game, appropriated from a former CIA operative. The aircraft would have fallen into the hands of advancing North Vietnamese Army regulars as spoils of war if not for the quick thinking of the operative, who had used it as a means of escape during the fall of Saigon in 1975. With barely enough fuel in its tanks, the operative, a seasoned helicopter pilot, had been able to reach the safety of Phnom Penh, Cambodia. Not wanting to part with the sizeable asset the chopper represented, he had arranged its shipment to Manila in the Philippines where it had been used for transporting illicit drugs.

"When did they arrive?" asked Maximus.

"An hour ago," grunted Finley. "That should give them a good head start on the softening process."

"Come with me!" Maximus ordered, spotting the hatch bubble of another monorail cab sitting along a far wall. "Let's see if our young protégé truly wants to join us."

Once Finley settled his large bulk into one of the cushioned seats across from him, Maximus pushed several buttons, sending the cab on its way. Smoothly and soundlessly it moved forward several feet before pivoting to keep its orientation upright as it dropped through an opening in the deck. The sensation of falling was immediate as it plunged downward in the manner of a high-speed elevator, and Maximus studied the green readouts that showed the deck numbers flashing rapidly by as the cab descended lower. Beyond the cab's transparent bubble, blue lights set up in the tunnel walls whisked past at periodic intervals, and in moments the cab slowed, then pivoted another ninety degrees before speeding up again along a level stretch of rail. Seconds later it decelerated quickly, coming to a complete stop as though cushioned by a wall of marshmallows.

As soon as the bubble rose, Maximus's ears perked. Loud screams knifed the air before trailing away. Climbing from the cab, he walked through the sliding door that accessed a dimly lit corridor. This was the area of the ship set up for interrogation.

Maximus glanced up. Suspended from the high ceiling was a 36-inch steel pipe that ran along the length of the passageway. It was held in place at periodic intervals by 2-inch diameter steel rods that hung down on each side to connect with a semi-circular cradle supporting the pipe. When needed, tons of seawater water could be forced through it each second by powerful pumps.

"Which cell?" Maximus asked, frowning at how quiet it had become.

Finley indicated the middle of the corridor. "Third one down."

Maximus nodded in acknowledgement. He should have known it would be that one. Third one was the only cell rigged with the specialized equipment. Electro-shock torture could be highly effective if administered properly, and the twosome he had hired were experts at it.

Entering the room, Maximus took in the scene at a glance. With both guards next to him, Alex stood mute, watching in fascination as a nondescript, heavyset man rested his hand on a throw-switch. Seated side by side and strapped tightly to abutting chairs with wires and clamps attached to their arms and feet, two men appeared exhausted, their faces streaked in sweat as they gasped for air. Probes were attached to the chest and head of each man, feeding physiological information to a nearby computer.

The man at the throw-switch glanced over at a woman monitoring the computer. She had long chestnut hair hanging limply past her shoulders, part of it covering the left side of her face. Maximus knew the hair covered scar tissue overlying a deformed cheekbone that three operations involving the latest breakthroughs in plastic surgery had failed to correct. In their profession, things sometimes went awry no matter how meticulously a kidnapping was planned, and two years earlier the woman had ended up on the short end of an undertaking that had gone terribly wrong. Up until the accident, Dr. Gladius Jester, M.D., had been an attractive woman. Both her and her husband had been interrogation experts with the CIA, but upon retirement had offered their skills to various governments as bounty hunters.

"Heart rates came close to pegging out, but you can increase the voltage," Dr. Jester said, her lips parting to reveal a set of perfectly straight teeth that Maximus knew to be dental implants. She had been monitoring the readouts with a predatory look on her face.

The man turned a nearby knob, prepared to throw the switch again.

"Are our guests cooperating?" Maximus rasped, seemingly catching the man by surprise with his sudden arrival.

Herbert Jester turned. "Good to see you again, Mr. Maximus." He returned his gaze to the two men strapped to the chairs, speaking glibly in the manner of a boy enjoying a day at the amusement park. "Didn't get 'em to crack yet, but I believe we're getting close."

Maximus stopped him before he could close the switch. "I want you to let the lad here do it."

Herbert shot him a puzzling look before sizing Alex up and down. "Fine by me," he said, a touch of disappointment evident in his tone. Unenthusiastically, he stepped aside to make room for Alex. "Make sure to open the switch when she tells you," he instructed Alex halfheartedly, "otherwise you might end up killing them, and that's something we don't want until we get the information we're after."

Alex did not move. Turning, he gazed dumbly at Maximus, confusion clearly showing on his face.

"He doesn't understand a word you're saying," Maximus informed Herbert. "You'll have to speak Russian if you want him to understand."

Herbert nodded, repeating himself as instructed. Russian was his second language, having been stationed at the U.S. embassy in Moscow two decades earlier.

Alex stared at the man, a look of comprehension descending on his features. He moved forward and placed a hand on the switch but hesitated, turning to look back at Maximus once again.

Maximus rasped harshly. "Move away if you're not up for-"

Before he could finish the order, Alex threw the switch. A barely perceptible spark arced as the conducting metals came together.

Screams immediately erupted from the men strapped to the chairs, their bodies juddering convulsively as the current surged.

Maximus studied Alex, noting the sadistic look clinging to his face. Yes, he decided. Already the lad was proving himself to be a foot soldier. *The Order* always has need of followers, men that were unconscionable, ruthless, and willing to carry out orders without question. He would need replacements for all the men he had recently lost, though Alex would need careful honing.

"Stop!" the woman blurted.

Obediently, Alex opened the switch, though he would have preferred to keep it closed. The screams of the captives excited him.

Herbert moved to hover over the nearest captive. "Are you ready to talk, Baptiste?" he said softly.

Sweat poured profusely from Emmanuel Baptiste's forehead and temples. He was gasping hard in an effort to catch his breath.

"Go...to...the devil!" he managed to utter.

Herbert swung his gaze to the second captive, a short pudgy individual. "What about you, Hennington?"

Chester Hennington's eyes rolled in their sockets before steadying. "You're... wasting your time...a thousand deaths is preferable to telling you."

Maximus spoke up. "Why be so stubborn, gentlemen? Aquaria is now under UN control. Whether you divulge the information or not, the troops will eventually discover where you mine the gold. Is it on Navassa?"

Maximus had known about the gold long before Van Heflin had brought up the subject during the meeting in Cardoza's castle, but he had kept that knowledge to himself. He had never considered that some of it might be stockpiled near Malique until the senator had conjectured about it, but with the loss of Swensen and his elite security force in that godforsaken cove, he would now focus his efforts on locating it in the floating city or the nearby island. It had to be there, he reasoned. The grandmother of those brats had been evasive when questioned about where it was mined. He clearly remembered her words. *'Gaia provided it,'* she had told him. Tossing the conundrum aside, he thought about his last minute decision to have Van Heflin accompany Allotey during Aquaria's invasion, wondering if it had been a wise move after all. Almost immediately he chastised himself. No, the decision had been a good one under the present circumstances. With Van Heflin being head of the senate's prestigious Science and Technology Committee, the media would be used to put the senator's participation in a positive light, one that might enhance his image all the more during a run for the presidency. Van Heflin would be portrayed as a staunch champion of the planet, leading the charge to take on any and all abusers of the environment.

Maximus broke from these thoughts, aware that the captives were not cooperating. In a voice that magnified his growing rage, he said, "I ask you again, where is your gold mined?"

It was Baptiste who spoke this time, his tone strained and faltering. "It is only the powerless that can be manipulated and used as cattle by men like you, but we are not powerless." Torture was nothing new to him. Both he and his wife, Lucette, had been tortured unmercifully at the hands of the now dead Colonel Ternier before being saved by Javolyn and the dolphin women, but he knew rescue would not come this time.

Maximus glanced over at Herbert Jester, the pent up rage building within him finally reaching its limit. "Maximum voltage!" he screamed.

"You risk killing them," the woman cautioned.

Maximus ignored the warning, turning to Alex instead. "Fry them!"

Alex grinned, more than happy to comply, but as he threw the switch the lights went out.

Maximus froze as the interrogation cell was plunged into total darkness. Except for the startled breathing of those around him, a deafening silence descended. Even the soft background hum of the generators that normally reverberated at this level of the ship was now gone.

Finley's voice resounded in the pitch blackness. "We seem to have lost power, but the emergency lighting will kick on in a moment."

No sooner did he utter the words, the room was once again bathed in light, though the illumination was much dimmer than before.

"Why have we lost power?" Maximus railed, unable to accept the chain of disrupting events plaguing him.

"I don't know," was all Finley could offer. Puzzled, Finley moved to a wall intercom. In a flustered voice he hailed the bridge, speaking quickly. "This is the captain. We have no power down here. What happened?"

The voice that came back was clearly nervous. "We don't know, sir, the problem is throughout the ship. All the generators have stopped working, and so have the three engines. We're attempting to run a diagnostic to pinpoint the problem, but it seems the entire computer system is locked up."

"That's impossible," Finley snapped. Sweat began to bead on his forehead. The tanker was fully automated. Almost every mechanical system aboard it was controlled by two linked mainframe computers. Without them, the ship would not be able to hold its present position. The enormous vessel would become nothing more than a drifting hulk.

"I wish I could give you better news," replied the bridge. "We're trying to re-boot the system. Without it we cannot locate the problem."

"Keep me informed," growled Finley.

An ominous feeling of total vulnerability began to take hold of Maximus as he listened to the conversation. Surely this on top of everything else could not be happening. And yet it was.

Maximus turned wrathful eyes on Finley as though he were the cause of the system failure. "Get up to the bridge and find the problem!" he scolded as though speaking to a child. "I want this ship back in working order immediately."

Finley's face clouded. He did not like being reprimanded in this manner, especially in front of the others. Holding back a biting retort, he simply nodded. "I'm on my way," he grunted, quickly exiting the cell.

Needing to vent his fury further, Maximus turned a ferocious gaze on the two captives before shifting it to Alex. "I thought I told you to fry them!" he hissed.

Anxious to please his new mentor, Alex closed the switch again, but no spark was visible this time as metal met metal.

Maximus stared in expectation at the men strapped to the chairs but saw no torment in their faces, nor quivering in their bodies.

"There's no power," Herbert pointed out in a near whisper.

"Stay here!" Maximus screamed. "All of you stay here until I get back." Like a madman he tore from the room and made his way to the remaining bubble cab. With his emotions running wild, he pressed the buttons that would take him to the sector of the ship he sought.

-106-

In another sector of the *Kraken* on the lowest deck farther astern, an electronic deadbolt clacked loudly when the lights had gone out. Hearing this, a lone figure suddenly stirred within the holding cell imprisoning him. He knew what the sound implied. With a loss of power, the lock would release.

Even before the emergency lighting kicked on to dispel the enshrouding coal-black darkness, he sprang from the cot to push against the hinged bars entrapping him. If he failed to act quickly, he was certain the lock would re-engage and he would miss his chance to escape. Unable to see, he misjudged his leap, chipping a front tooth as his face slammed up against the bars, but the pleasure of triumph was more than enough to transcend his pain as the cell door swung open.

With his thick eyeglasses askew and nearly dislodged from the collision, he repositioned them on the bridge of his large jutting nose and stepped clear of the cell, all the while running his tongue over the jagged edge where the tooth had broken. Groping about like a blind man, he began feeling his way along a wall just as the lights came back on accompanied by the sound of synchronized clicks.

Looking down the length of the passageway, he realized he had been right about the lock. Only one other prisoner had thought to do as he did, noticing that the man being held three cells further up was also free while eight others gripped the rigid bars confining them. Too late, they pushed and tugged on the bars like frenzied berserkers, but the doors would not budge as all the locks had re-engaged.

At five feet six and one hundred fifty-five pounds, he was not a very big man, but sustained imprisonment and the painful things they had done to him had tempered his resolve to kill again. Ever since they had brought him here they had fed him almost nothing, barely enough to keep him alive, and he was famished. Strangely though, he had this hankering for a handgun, but a fire axe affixed to the wall opposite his cell would do just as well. He had been eyeing that axe ever since they had put him in the cell, probably a week earlier he guessed as he had lost all sense of time during his confinement. Whiling away the hours he had stared fixedly at the axe. Though it had been beyond his reach, it invoked memories of his life back in Ankara when he had chopped up six graduate students with a similar weapon at the university research facility where he had worked before setting off to a nearby mosque. There he had slain eight more people, randomly choosing victims before hacking them to death as they kowtowed in worship with rumps in the air and foreheads touching prayer mats.

Still holding the axe in bloodied hands, he had made his way into a crowded marketplace not far away where he had run amok, indiscriminately killing another ten people, all the while keeping a running body count in his head. After that he had lost all sense of himself, and by the time the authorities caught up with him, it was speculated he had murdered as many as forty-three people, though they could not prove all of his crimes as they had only recovered a total of twenty-four bodies, most of them in pieces. Vaguely he remembered running along a riverbank on a moonless night, every so often coming across a person or two out for an evening stroll. These he had dispatched quickly before hurling their remains in the fast flowing water.

The memories abruptly dissolved as he became aware of himself pulling the axe he had been eyeing from the wall. Ambling up to the lone prisoner who had managed to escape his confinement, he acknowledged the man with an affable smile just before swinging the axe.

Satisfied, Peyami Pehlivan made his way down the corridor, wondering who he might encounter next.

-107-

Bolder climbed into the pilot seat of the IBC News chopper and strapped himself in. Pulling up gently on the collective, he tested the additional load, almost sensing the weight of the gold tugging back tenaciously against the upward thrust of the main rotor. With the chopper refusing to rise, he eased more pitch into the blades, willing the aircraft to break the anchoring grip of gravity, but still the chopper refused to lift. Anxiously he glanced at his watch, immediately seeing he had little time left to clear the platform and get out to a safe distance. With less than a minute left, he knew he would be cutting it close. The thought that he might have overestimated the weight he could carry descended on him with a frightening cruelty, and he knew there was no time left to lighten the load.

With the cold hands of fear gripping him, he applied yet more pitch, and this time he felt the airframe shudder sluggishly as it broke free of the deck. Rising to a height of ten feet above the platform, he gently pivoted the aircraft around, prepared to move it laterally out over the water, but as he did so a figure suddenly materialized on the deck in front of him.

A look of surprise came to Bolder's face as he realized who it was. The man he had knocked cold was staring up at him, waving goodbye with a savage grin stretching from ear to ear.

You stupid bastard, Bolder thought smugly. *You have no idea what's going to happen, do you?* Chuckling to himself, he steered the helicopter clear of the platform, slowly gathering air speed. In seconds he was skirting the island, moving east past the old lighthouse to gain distance from the impending explosion. Looking to his left, he glimpsed the huge helicopter that had set down on the island near the warehouses. The invading force of soldiers appeared like tiny ants as they fanned out among the buildings to secure the island.

Bolder expelled a prolonged sigh of relief. The fear that had galvanized him moments earlier was quickly ebbing, displaced by a deep sense of contentment and accomplishment. With all the gold he had gotten away with, he was going to be a rich man. An *exceptionally* rich man.

Just as he reached seventy knots, he became aware of a sound. Though it was subtle and erratic, it was a sound he should not be hearing. Puzzled, he shot a concerned glance at his instrument gauges. Nothing was showing in the red. The turbine was not overheating and the RPMs were right where they should be.

As the aircraft gathered speed, the unfamiliar sound grew louder. Listening carefully, he was convinced it was not coming from the powertrain but from somewhere lower, further back. Maybe he had caught onto something with one of the skids while taking off. Yeah, that had to be it, he reasoned. Feeling he was at a safe enough distance from the platform, he slowed the chopper to a speed where the passage of wind would allow him to open the door and locate the cause.

With the reduction in air speed, the inexplicable banging lessened. Leaning his body out the door, he turned his head and peered back at the undercarriage. His heart nearly seized in his chest as he saw what had made the sound. Dangling from the pilot-side skid by a short length of rope was the bomb he had left to destroy the platform. Pushed back by the wind, it quivered and jerked on its tether to batter against the skid.

Bolder's scream never cleared his throat as the bomb exploded. The chopper disintegrated, raining charred bits of metal, torn flesh and chunks of molten gold into the waiting sea below.

-108-

Captain Delila scanned the far side of the island through the spyglasses. Straining his eyes, he had been able to identify the logo on the small helicopter. Out of curiosity he had been monitoring it every so often for the last several minutes, following its flight to the offshore platform and then watching it lift off again to make its way past the old lighthouse. But without warning it had flared, consumed in a coruscating fireball of expanding gas.

"Sir, am I seeing things or did that helicopter just explode?"

Delila turned. Ensign Jefferson was gazing past him with a befuddled expression.

"Yes, it was a news chopper representing the Interregional Broadcasting Company," answered Delila grimly. "Too far away to tell if it was shot down, though."

"Strange that you say that, sir."

"Say what, Mr. Jefferson?"

Seeing no more debris falling from the sky, Jefferson settled his eyes on the captain. "That it was an IBC chopper." Clearing his throat, he sought to bring light to the confusion registering on Delila's face. "I was able to confirm ownership of that ship, but I had to really delve," he said, looking in the direction of the *Nunquarn Satis* for emphasis. "Working through a maze of twelve shell companies, the search finally ended at a multinational conglomerate called Unus Universitas. During the search I also discovered that Unus Universitas also owns IBC News."

Delila nodded slowly, his mind trying to make a connection between the ship and the destroyed chopper but unable to come up with one. Thinking about the name of the conglomerate, he quickly worked out the translation. *One World.* He could only guess that whoever had named the ship had also named the conglomerate. It was obvious that person had a fondness for Latin. He glanced in the direction of the mega-yacht. It was much closer now, still being pushed into the wind by a vast herd of whales.

"Nice work, Mr. Jefferson. With any luck, maybe we'll find out what that vessel is doing here."

Jefferson gazed past the captain again, pivoting his head in another direction. "What happened to the subs?"

Delila swept his eyes over the sea. His junior officer was observant, he thought. *Iron Fist* was now gone, and so were the two Varshavyanka-class submarines sent by Venezuela. "I wish I knew," the captain said uneasily. "Unfortunately they are under the direct command of the envoy the UN sent to take charge of this mission."

"Beggin' your pardon, sir, but that man gives me the creeps, and so do the men with him. Shall I have the techs engage the sonar in active mode to track the subs."

Delila gave a slight shake of his head, speaking softly. "No, son. Keep it passive. Active can be quite harmful to sea mammals, and the sea around us seems to be crawling with them."

Being a man of sound environmental convictions, Delila would refrain from using the carrier's low-frequency sonar unless absolutely necessary, knowing the danger it posed to whales and dolphins. Better known as SURTASS LFA in naval circles, or Surveillance Towed Array Sensor System, Low Frequency Active, it could produce as much as 215 decibels of intense sonic wave energy capable of producing emboli, or gas bubbles, in the organ tissue of marine mammals at close range like this. Whereas active sonar sends out a sound pulse to be reflected back from an object to calculate its distance as well as direction relative to the sender, passive sonar only listens to sounds emitted by the object to determine its direction. Thus passive cannot tell a listener how far away the object is.

Jefferson blushed abashedly. He should have known better. He knew about the captain's concern for sea creatures, especially when it involved cetaceans. Delila had once related a story to him. An avid surfer in his youth, the captain had grown up in Southern California where he had learned how to ride the waves. It was during an outing along Manhattan Beach that an exceptionally large shark had taken a bite out of his surfboard. The shark had been quite aggressive, and if not for the intervention of a passing school of dolphins which drove it away, he was certain he would have become the predator's next meal.

"You're right, sir, I wasn't thinking," said Jefferson. "But isn't it a certainty that those subs will be using it?"

Delila shrugged helplessly. "Unfortunately, yes."

-109-

Jacob peered out one of the windows to his tower office, watching the remnants of Bolder's chopper rain down into the sea. Swiveling his head, he brought his gaze to Amelia, who had witnessed the same thing in stunned amazement.

"Someone paid your cameraman to blow up our shipping platform, but apparently the effort backfired on him," remarked Jacob. Moments earlier, Ez had apprised him about what Mat had done.

"But why the platform?" questioned Amelia. "If he was intent on sabotaging something, wouldn't this structure be a better target?"

"It's obvious they wanted this structure completely intact. Their objective was to temporarily stop our power production and to halt further exports of the enhanced *guano* fertilizer we routinely send to Haitian farmers."

Jacob looked away to plop down wearily at his desk, prepared to await the arrival of the invading troops. He had instructed Ez not to put up any resistance, including using the non-lethal multi-beam microwave technology she had previously used to drive away Malikai Allotey and his goons.

The familiar holographic image of Jacob's deceased grandmother suddenly coalesced before him. A smile clung to her broad face. "I have just received what you might call some eye-opening news," she said. "It seems to fit in well with your conspiracy theories."

"Please tell me," Jacob replied.

"As you had already been informed, in destroying Cardoza's compound, Jay Jay rescued a man by the name of Mortimer Osgood. Mortimer had been kidnapped by Cardoza and was being held hostage in order to force his twin brother, Percy, to work for a man called Malcolm Maximus, an industrial magnate of incredible wealth. Aside from that, Mortimer had a cache of overwhelming evidence stored in a hidden electronic file to incriminate Maximus, Cardoza, and a broad list of accomplices involved in a plan designed to dramatically change the world as we know it."

"Where did you get this information?"

Ez's smile broadened. "A bluefin delivered it to me."

Baffled, Jacob's weathered brow crinkled. "A bluefin?"

"Yes, would you like to hear what I've learned?"

Jacob sat transfixed, his curiosity aroused. "Talk away, Ez, and don't hold anything back."

-110-

Having reached his destination in the bubble cab, Maximus climbed out. He was furious. Why the ship's sophisticated computer system would lock up defied reason, but the sector of the ship he was now in remained independent of that system and relied exclusively on a huge battery bank for its power needs that was altogether separate from the tanker's electrical grid, as did the vessel's monorail system. Coming to a bulkhead, he reached for a thick section of U-channel that appeared to brace the wall, swiveling it off to one side on a concealed pivot to reveal a small glass plate recessed behind it. Without hesitation he placed his right thumb against it. The plate had sensors that analyzed the DNA in his skin oil. He and Finley were the only ones it was programmed to allow admittance. A small LED light above the plate suddenly flashed green, and an instant later the bulkhead slid up.

As soon as he stepped through, the bulkhead closed behind him, confining him in a dimly lit space the size of a storage closet where a door barred his way. Bringing an eye to a retinal scanner next to the door, he heard a familiar buzz, and a moment later the door slid aside. Walking through, he stood in a glass booth overlooking an enormous chamber. It was a hidden area of the ship that should have housed crude oil, one the Coast Guard would never discover, even in the unlikely event the *Kraken* was to be boarded. Using the potent influence of high-ranking bureaucrats within the U.S. government, both the *Nunquarn Satis* and the gargantuan oil tanker were essentially made off limits to the long arm of the Coast Guard.

Looking below him, Maximus set his gaze on the huge oblong craft just over 300 feet in length. It was supported on cradles, its hull painted a dull metallic gray. Several men were just climbing aboard, entering through a hatch atop a conning tower situated amidships. This was the third Russian-built Varshavyanka-class submarine purchased by Venezuela. The *Order* had been successful in entrenching *fifth column* elements within the government of the oil-rich South American country, spreading corruption around like a virulent plague among its high-ranking officials, and he had taken full advantage of the economic toll such corruption brought to the nation. Knowing it could ill afford the insane cost of another naval vessel, he had stepped in to broker the purchase by offering the Venezuelan government shipments of pure gold bullion to be used as payment for the sub. His only stipulation was that he would have clandestine use of the vessel and its crew for a period of three months following its delivery. Desperate to increase its military assets, the Venezuelans had agreed, and negotiations with the Russians for the third vessel had quickly ensued. With world currencies being rapidly devalued by irresponsible governments around the globe, the Russians were quick to take the bait, turning the sub over to the Venezuelans in good faith without any cash exchanging hands up front. They would instead accept pure gold bullion in three separate installments at later dates.

The gold, however, was to come from Aquaria. Once Maximus gained possession of it, it would be melted down and recast into bars with cores filled with tungsten. And if the Russians discovered the swindle, the blame could be cast on Tursiops. This would be a plausible explanation for the Russians to accept in light of the IBC's spurious smear campaign that depicted Tursiops to be run by crooks. Hadn't it already been shown that the budding enterprise had financed construction of the floating city by bartering with what amounted to watered down gold? Aquaria's unprovoked attack on the Southern Star had been broadcast worldwide, revealing the sea colony's motivation in capturing the freighter. The sea colony needed the tungsten the ship carried to produce more counterfeit bullion. Certainly the Russians could not hold Venezuela responsible for some of this fake gold falling into their possession. Gold bullion switched hands all the time, often making its way through international exchanges much like paper currency.

Another objective concerning Aquaria's gold entered his musings. The sea colony was flooding the market with huge quantities of it, and that was a good thing. It took the pressure off the Federal Reserve Bank and its counterpart, the European Central Bank, to ease up on their short selling. Working in conjunction with the major bullion banks, they had been routinely dumping some of their physical stores of precious metals and gold-based derivatives in order to keep the price down in the face of widening economic rifts in global economies. Artificially manipulating the gold market was in *The Order's* interest, and with *fifth column* operatives firmly embedded in each of these powerful financial institutions, they were able to do just that. But once investors realized a glut of fake gold was finding its way into international markets, the price per troy ounce would go even lower, much lower. When that happened, agents of *The Order* would move back in to buy up as much of the commodity they could get their hands on by going long on futures contracts, ultimately controlling most of the world supply. In fact, that was another of *The Order's* goals, eventually obtaining and holding onto as much genuine gold as possible. Then it would lower the boom by orchestrating several international calamities in concert to destroy both the dollar and the euro once and for all. As it now was, the Federal Reserve had possession of practically all the gold that had once filled the vaults of Fort Knox, and with the value of major currencies having been dramatically devalued through overly excessive stimulus policies by both the Fed and the ECB designed to lure as many investors as possible back into the stock market, the price of bullion would skyrocket to stratospheric heights once a huge selloff in equities ensued.

A dark smile consumed Maximus' features as he continued to dwell on the carefully crafted plan. Like always, a catastrophic event would be needed to trigger that selloff, one that was rapidly approaching. It would bring down global markets yet again. And in knowing precisely when that event was to be triggered, members of *The Order* stood to siphon off a good portion of the world's wealth by short-selling equities just before it occurred. The economic chaos brought on would force a merging of the largest banks on earth. The Fed and the ECB would consolidate with the World Bank and IMF, forming the most powerful financial institution ever devised by man, with a new currency emerging that would become the predominant medium of exchange. Once this happened, the world would quickly change, for the bank rising from the ashes would become the cornerstone of the global government *The Order* had been seeking. Almost overnight, the UN would be transformed to become that government. Nations that refused to conform would not be issued loans to keep their economies going.

A remembrance of the Southern Star being sunk turned Maximus' smile sour. He had almost forgotten. Huge stockpiles of tungsten had been part of the cargo Cardoza's freighter had carried. He would have to obtain more.

Depressing a button on the console before him, he brought his lips close to a microphone connected to a loudspeaker. "I trust everything is in full readiness, Dante?"

The trailing man climbing the conning tower glanced up in surprise to espy Maximus looking down at him. This was the sub commander, a Venezuelan that had spent the last six months of his life in Kola Bay, Russia, learning how to operate the submarine. Like many of the henchmen Maximus used to carry out his schemes, the man was physically large, almost as big as Finley.

Dante nodded. A dour smile took shape on his swarthy features, conveying to Maximus that he was eager to get on with the mission. Maximus had originally planned to have Dante spearhead the government coup scheduled to take place in Port-au-Prince, but recent setbacks pertaining to a takeover of both Haiti and Aquaria had forced this revised mission on the man.

Maximus nodded back grimly before checking the Emperador Temple strapped to his wrist. It was now time to launch the sub. The bomb Bolder had placed had undoubtedly detonated by now. Once activated, it had sent out a signal that Maximus received just before he had landed on the *Kraken*. The bomb had originally been intended for blowing up another section of pristine reef, footage of the event to be documented by Bolder to further bolster world outrage directed at the colonists. He had wanted Aquaria entirely intact and undamaged, but recent events had necessitated this change in plans. While inbound for the *Kraken*, he had contacted Bolder again, redirecting him where to place the bomb, informing him about the subaqueous access tunnel his mechanical fish had documented on video. With Bronte Pharah currently unavailable and possibly dead back aboard the *Nunquarn Satis*, he had decided to destroy the offshore platform to stop the transshipment of the enhanced *guano* fertilizer to Haitian farmers. Once Aquaria was secured, the platform along with the damaged water intakes could be repaired and brought back on line.

Bringing his lips back to the microphone, Maximus heard the echo of his own voice as it reverberated ominously within the cavernous chamber. "I'm opening the bay doors. Do not fail me!"

Dante nodded again as he climbed through the hatch and dogged it off.

Maximus nudged a switch that opened a valve, and within seconds the lower portion of the chamber began to flood with tons of water pouring in each second. Rapidly the water rose to engulf the sub's hull, upon which the eight enormous berthing clamps holding the vessel in place disengaged as a gargantuan pair of hinged doors swung down to reveal an inky blackness below them.

Satisfied that the sub had successfully launched, Maximus closed the first switch and thumbed another, watching as the bay doors pivoted back up slowly. Once they closed, a set of powerful centrifugal pumps whirred to life to empty the cavernous chamber, quickly driving the water through a 36-inch pipe and back into the sea.

Anxious to get an update from Finley, Maximus contacted the bridge. "Status?" he rasped.

"We were able to re-boot the mainframes," Finley proclaimed proudly. "All power should be restored in a matter of moments."

Keeping his tone stern and intolerant, Maximus asked, "Any idea how the failure occurred?"

"Yes, we were hacked."

Maximus gritted his teeth, knowing only one man had the technical knowhow to get past the supposedly unbreachable firewall that had been incorporated into the ship's mainframes. And he had done it from one of the many computer terminals stationed aboard the *Nunquarn Satis*.

"If we were hacked, then it's possible we're going to be boarded by attackers if we haven't already," Maximus snapped. "Make sure everyone on the bridge is heavily armed," he quickly added before exiting the booth.

Going back the way he had come, he made his way hastily through the two hidden doors before emerging past the bulkhead. Quickly, he moved to another nearby bulkhead to swivel another section of U-channel aside to reveal a hidden glass plate the size of a credit card, placing his thumb against it. This one was programmed to allow only one-person access, that being him. As the panel slid up, he set his eyes on what lay on the other side. A gloating smirk came to his face. Here was his insurance against possible invaders boarding the *Kraken*.

-111-

Phillipe studied Destiny's mother as she sat on the white sand bordering the cove's limpid water. "It doesn't feel right staying here when Jay Jay needs our help," he grumbled peevishly, unable to comprehend how she could appear so calm at a time like this.

Amphitrite did not offer a reply. Though she was aware of his concern, she kept her gaze fixed on the arching hues above the falls. *So beautiful*, she thought. She was seeing one of nature's gifts, serenity and beauty arising out of chaos. There was violence in the water. It tumbled from great height to crash harshly into an awaiting pool to create a jumble of vortexes and eddies. And yet it sent a gentle blanket of mist into the air to disperse the sunlight into bands of color that soothed the soul.

Appearing pensive, Troy Jacob echoed Phillipe's apprehension. "Phillipe's right, grandma. We should go back to Aquaria."

"When the time is right," Amphitrite said softly. Continuing to stare at the rainbow, she suddenly discerned Esmerelda's smiling face within the mist. Jacob's deceased grandmother was nodding in agreement.

"Do you see her?" Amphitrite murmured, turning to look at Destiny sitting at her side.

"Yes," Destiny said.

"See who?" Melody asked. Perplexed, she turned to follow her mother's gaze. Abruptly her jaw dropped in astonishment.

"What are you looking at?" TJ questioned, but by the time he looked to where his sister was staring, the vision had vanished. "I don't see anything."

"It's something only girls can see," Melody teased smugly. "It's a secret that boys aren't supposed to know."

TJ was about to lash back at his sister, but the sound of splashing water diffused the tart retort he had in mind. Turning, he saw Phillipe was swimming out to the Angel.

A budding sense caused Amphitrite to reach into the pouch strapped about her waist. "Children, I have something for each of you," she said, producing a violet crystal in the shape of a small pyramid in each hand. Though she couldn't explain the why of it, she only knew the twins would need these.

Melody stared at the crystal held before her with adoring eyes before gently taking hold of it and cupping it in her hands. "How beautiful," she remarked in an awestruck voice.

"Wow!" TJ exclaimed, reaching for his. "What's it do?"

"It gathers in energy and will sometimes react to your thoughts," Amphitrite said, knowing the children had never seen these smaller versions.

"It looks just like the larger crystals being grown under the island," Melody uttered reverently, noticing that the pyramid was beginning to pulsate and grow brighter. She looked over at the one her brother was holding, seeing it do the same thing.

"Did these also come from the giant *thurentra*?" asked TJ.

"Yes," Amphitrite answered. "Hercules retrieved them the other day. Hold onto them, they're yours to keep."

As the children fondled the crystals, Amphitrite glanced at the two men in the dory at the base of the falls. Zimbola and Hector were busy filling ten gallon cans with fresh water to replenish supplies aboard the Angel. Though there were massive quantities of water available to them in a much purer form back at Aquaria, the black giant claimed it lacked the therapeutic qualities contained within the cove's majestic falls. But she knew his true desire for the water. Zimbola believed the water held magical powers, and by filling the Angel's potable water tank with it, the water would protect his beloved vessel as well as those sailing aboard her.

In moments, Franklin strolled up to the group, giving his wife a look which indicated he needed to talk. Rising from the sand, Amphitrite joined him, and together they ambled well away from the others, neither of them speaking for several minutes as they moved along the sand at the water's edge.

"You know as well as I we can't stay here," Franklin finally said.

Amphitrite glanced in the direction of Mortimer Osgood and Bronte Pharah, two distant figures who sat near one of the cottages set further back from the water. Both men seemed to have taken to one another and were passing the time in conversation over a friendly game of chess. Zimbola had arrived back at the cove with Pharah in tow a half hour earlier.

"What about them?" Amphitrite queried.

"Mortimer wants to join his brother."

"And the children?"

"They can remain back here with-" The din of an engine revving made him turn to locate the source. The inflatable water chute at the Angel's stern had been deployed, and an instant later the waverunner stowed aboard the vessel slid gracefully backward along its sloped surface to hurtle into the water. It sent a series of small waves rippling toward the beach. Sitting aboard Jake's STX-12F Kawasaki was Phillipe.

Franklin raised an eyebrow, blurting out the first question coming to mind. "What's he doing?"

Amphitrite immediately sensed Phillipe's intentions, and like the time before when she had airlifted an injured Bashir from the Southern Star and left Phillipe behind, she would once again avoid trying to stop him from following his own convictions. There was a cause and effect outcome in the balance here, and she had to let it run its course.

"He's taking the initiative," Amphitrite said.

Phillipe turned the Kawasaki around to glance briefly in her direction before gunning the engine and speeding toward the cove's narrow inlet that gave way to the sea, and she saw the small watercraft was fully armed. With its souped up engine, she knew it was capable of covering the forty miles to Aquaria in a little over thirty minutes.

Franklin watched him race away. "He's heading for Aquaria, isn't he?"

Amphitrite turned to face Franklin, sighing deeply. "I'll crank up the chopper."

Franklin looked toward the falls. Even at a distance of several hundred feet, he could see Zimbola was not very pleased at seeing Phillipe leave like this. "I'll let Zimby know we're also leaving," he said. "Destiny and the twins can stay here with him."

Amphitrite held his gaze a moment longer. "No, tell him Destiny will be coming with us."

Franklin stared back thoughtfully before nodding slowly in understanding. "I'll tell him but he's not going to like it."

Twenty minutes later, the twins waved goodbye as Amphitrite guided the Bell Ranger over the western ridgeline of the chasm.

Pouting, Melody turned to her brother and said, "I want to go back to Aquaria."

TJ eyed Zimby placing the filled water cans on the Angel's swim platform. At the moment, the Jamaican giant had his back to them. "If we hurry, he'll never know we're missing."

A mischievous grin broke out on Melody's face, and she waded out into the water to grab hold of her bond mate. TJ did the same, and within seconds they were both fully submerged and heading toward the inlet leading to the sea.

-112-

Zipping over the ocean surface at 120 miles per hour, the Bell Ranger overtook Phillipe 10 miles from Aquaria. Phillipe looked up, continuing to barrel over the sea at full throttle as Amphitrite brought the chopper in low. Franklin opened the side door and leaned out of the co-pilots seat, pointing to the radio mic he held in his hand. Slowing the Kawasaki's rate of travel, Phillipe nodded. Bringing the small watercraft to an idle, he pulled the Motorola radio from a storage compartment and attached it to the bracket on the console. Depressing the transmit button, he spoke irritably, raising his voice to be heard above the roar of the rotor blades.

"Don't try to stop me!"

"We're not, son," Franklin replied. "We're also going to Aquaria. I guess I don't have to remind you it might be dangerous." Pausing, he studied the resolute look on Phillipe's face. "We're going to fly ahead. I'll keep you informed about what's going on."

Phillipe nodded in understanding as Amphitrite dipped the chopper's nose to gather airspeed. In seconds the Bell Ranger gained altitude, rising high into the sky.

-113-

Fifteen minutes behind Phillipe, the *Exoco* skimmed over the calm sea, the hull of the sleek craft riding atop its dual hydrofoils. Melody stared ahead, then turned her gaze to the driver, a pudgy Haitian with a seemingly perpetual grin plastered on his face. Truth be told, Melody could not remember a single time when the man did not smile. It was as though the act of living was a constant delight to him. Kobe was always fun to be around. He was the *Exoco's* skipper, assigned to the task of making regular runs between Aquaria and the Haitian coast. Riding their bond mates, the twins had been fortunate to catch up with him just as he was steering the vessel away from Malique's main pier.

Melody shifted her attention to Bashir sitting reclusively and pensively on a cushioned chair bordering the starboard window. He seemed to be fully recovered from his injuries, though his outward manner suggested he was mired in deep reflection. Like her and her brother, she knew he was yearning to get back to Aquaria. Having been dropped off at Louwanda's home in Malique and placed under the woman's doting care, he had recuperated quickly over the last day and a half. Not one to sit idle, he had offered to assist Kobe on one of his regular runs to Gonaives to drop off bottles of hydrogen gas and bags of fertilizer to several farmers that lived on the outskirts of the coastal city.

Standing on the other side of Kobe, TJ asked for the fifth time in the last ten minutes, "How much longer, Kobe?"

Maintaining his signature smile, Kobe glanced down to read the restlessness showing on the boy's face. "Mon, you gonna be old before your time with so much impatience bubbling within you," his words accentuated heavily with a thick island accent that sounded Jamaican.

Abashed by the gentle chiding, TJ turned his gaze aft to check on the dolphins, which were currently immersed in three separate holding tubs filled with seawater. The tubs had been purposely designed to carry members of their species aboard the high speed hydrofoil. Not wanting to be left behind, Phillipe's bond mate, *Perseus*, had accompanied the twins during their escape from the cove and was now occupying the middle tub. While it would normally take the albinos a little over two hours to make the swim between the sea colony and Malique, the *Exoco* could make the crossing in one-third that time when sea conditions were accommodating as they were today. Hydrogen gas powered the vessel, as it did most of the watercraft owned by Tursiops.

A moment later the *Exoco's* radio came alive. "Angel to *Exoco*, come in *Exoco*!" The caller's voice was deep, gruff and brimming with anxiety.

Kobe reached for the mic and brought it to his lips. "Exoco back at you," he answered happily, glancing at the twins as he spoke. "What you need, my Sasquatch friend?"

"You see two little ones scootin' along on their dolphins?"

Melody stared up at Kobe with pleading eyes, putting her hands together as though in prayer and shaking her head fervently.

Kobe hesitated, holding back a reply, his smile taking on a slight waver. Turning, he looked at TJ, who was doing the same as his sister.

"You copy me, *Exoco*?" Zimbola came back, his tone now booming and filled with alarm.

"*Exoco* copies you, Zimby. Are you referring to that waggish duo, those two gremlins belonging to Jay Jay and Destiny?"

"Yes, Kobe, you see them?"

Kobe shot a sly wink at the twins, then forced a series of staccato crackles and hisses from between puckered lips. He was the colony's resident jester, a born comic known for his imitations of various sounds, especially when it involved emulating radio static. If you wanted laughs, just hang around Kobe and he'd give you an endless supply.

"You're break..hiss.. up, Ang..crackle..can't..ear a word you're...aying."

"Quit foolin' around, Kobe."

"..hissss..radio mus..hiss..ee..mal..unctioning."

Turning off the radio, Kobe regarded the twins suspiciously, still holding that ceaseless smile. "Now be honest with your uncle Kobe, what you imps up to?"

The twins had obviously come up with a whopper in order to get him to abet their little scheme. They had told him their father would appreciate him taking them and the three dolphins to within two miles of Aquaria's outer perimeter and drop them off. Jay Jay would be awaiting them there to escort them to the dolphin sanctuary under Navassa Island. Kobe was well aware that Aquaria was currently under siege by UN forces, having been informed of this hours earlier. For the time being the sea colony was a dangerous place, so once his passengers disembarked, he would head for Gonaives, his original destination before the children had caught up with him.

"They wanted us to stay behind with Zimby in the cove," both twins chorused, "but we want to help them."

"Your parents?"

"Yes," Melody said, speaking for both of them. "Both Mumsie and Dadoo are doing what they can to keep invaders from harming the colonists."

Melody was surprised to see Kobe's smile fade.

"I'm sorry, children, but I can't be responsible for droppin' you into a hornet's nest." Movement on the aft deck suddenly caught his eye, and he saw all three dolphins pull themselves from their holding tubs. Using their prehensile limbs, they walked themselves to the vessel's stern and leapt into the water even though the craft was barreling along at a high rate of speed. As if on cue, the twins bolted after them, moving quickly to the *Exoco's* rear.

"Children, wait!" he shouted in alarm, but seeing what they were going to do, he reached for the throttle and cut the engine. Although he knew the dolphins would likely forego sustaining any serious injury at hitting the water at such breakneck speed, he wasn't so sure about the children. The last thing he needed was the twins getting hurt, and he certainly didn't want Zimbola coming after him if this were to happen.

Both Melody and Troy Jacob looked back at him as the boat slowed quickly, their expressions apologetic. Suddenly aware of the situation, Bashir came out of his deep thoughts and sprang from his seat, only to pull up short when he realized it was already too late to stop them. Waving goodbye, the twins jumped clear of the stern just as the vessel settled its hull back in the water.

"Sorry we lied to you," TJ shouted as he and his sister straddled their bond mates. "Hope you're not mad."

Kobe opened his mouth to yell back, but before he could voice his objections the dolphins sounded with their charges only to leave ripples in their wake. Lifting his eyes, he espied the peak of Aquaria's central structure jutting above the horizon. Floating close to it were two large ships, one of them an enormous flat-top vessel.

-114-

Seated comfortably with three House members occupying the booth, Truman Hearthwatch, Green Technology and Climate Advisor to the President, continued to make his case. "...and so, gentlemen, it's crucial we push this bill through as quickly as possible."

The congressman from Idaho glanced furtively around the sports bar, suddenly feeling uncomfortable. It was early afternoon in the U.S. capitol, and white collar workers and bureaucrats of Washington's working class were beginning to crowd into the popular establishment situated a block from Pennsylvania Avenue. Although he had nothing to hide, conversations such as this were not meant for prying ears. Several people at the closest table, however, seemed to be engrossed on a news bulletin displayed on a 65-inch flat screen TV affixed to a nearby wall. Satisfied that he would not be overheard, he brought his eyes back to Hearthwatch, letting his concerns be known in a soft voice.

"A carbon tax is not going to sit well with voters. They've already voiced their displeasure with the country's state of affairs during the mid-term elections."

"I wholeheartedly agree," said the delegate from Iowa, also keeping his tone low. "Endorsing such a bill will amount to political suicide. My seat will be coming up for re-election, and I'd like to hold onto it."

Unperturbed, the Presidential Advisor brought his roast beef sandwich to his mouth and took a hefty bite, chewing the morsel hungrily before setting his gaze on the congressman from California. "What about you, Harry? What's your stance on this?"

The pudgy-cheeked representative from California's 8th District placed his drink back on the table and dabbed his lips with a napkin. "As long as it will bring jobs to my district, I'm all for it. I assume the government will be willing to fund the green techno startups with the tax money."

Hearthwatch smiled magnanimously. "Of course."

The Idaho rep eyed the California rep suspiciously. "Yeah, and what if those startups go bankrupt the same way several others did after the government bankrolled them? You sure you want to be embroiled in a similar scandal, Harry. It was a well-known fact those companies didn't stand a chance at competing with the Chinese even before those loans were given."

Hearthwatch followed the conversation with a calculating ear. It was going just as he had anticipated, one for and two against, but he had needed this informal meeting to confirm how the opposition would react. *The Order*, however, had ways of making them come around, and in these two cases it would be necessary to resort to blackmail. The wife of the Idaho rep was a cocaine addict whom they had lured into a compromising position using a handsome male stripper. Hearthwatch suppressed an urge to laugh as he thought about it. It had been easy for the male stripper to entice the woman into bed, after which it had only taken three trysts for the Adonis to get her thoroughly hooked on the drug, all of which had been recorded by hidden cameras.

It was just the reverse with the happily married Iowa rep with five children. A powerful tranquilizer had been slipped into his drink at a small, informal gathering of House members to discuss matters of national security. Later, he awoke to find himself in the sack with a prostitute. Once again it had all been recorded.

As for the California congressman, it had only taken a mere $20,000 along with a promise he would receive a sizeable chunk of the government subsidies once the startups got their hands on the funds. This was how things were done in Washington these days in order to bring seemingly opposing sides in agreement.

"The companies looking to take root in my district cannot possibly fail," Harry replied calmly. "They'll be manufacturing solar panels with three times more efficiency than the companies that failed, and with all the available cheap labor swarming across the border from Mexico, they'll be producing them at half the cost of the panels coming from China."

The congressman from Iowa appeared skeptical, raising his voice to be overheard above a growing hubbub. "Those failed companies made similar claims, Harry. No doubt these startups will promise the sun, moon and stars to get the funding they want. Then when things go south, these so called entrepreneurs will walk away with millions in bonuses from the seed money given them just like the others did."

"You're mistaken," objected Harry, his eyes narrowing with pique. "I can guaran-"

"Sorry to interrupt you, Harry," the congressman from Idaho cut in, "but it seems our esteemed colleague here is being discussed on the news." He appeared amused as he first looked at Hearthwatch before staring back at the TV behind Harry.

Hearthwatch swiveled his head to follow the Idaho rep's gaze, glancing briefly at the TV before turning back and shrugging. "That doesn't surprise me," he remarked blithely. "Both the President and the press value my recommendations wholeheartedly. You can never take things lightly when it concerns the environment."

Mildly annoyed at being interrupted, Harry turned his head around briefly to catch a glimpse of Hearthwatch's image before turning back to his companions. "As I was saying..." His annoyance turned to indignation as he realized the other three men were no longer listening. Obviously distracted, they were focused on the mounting buzz that pervaded the place. Patrons all around them were speaking in agitated confusion before a hushed silence descended on the room as though by majority consent. Every person in the bar had their gazes fixed intently on the wide screen TV. An attractive newscaster was talking, her strawberry hair fluttering in the breeze. In the far distance behind her, an aircraft carrier could be seen floating atop a fairly calm sea.

"...and because of these lies and mass deception, I have renounced my affiliation with the Interregional Broadcasting Company. Better known as IBC News to the public, the acronym actually stems from the Latin term *Ineptio Beneticium Conservo*, which means playing the masses for fools to benefit a privileged few. For many years now, the IBC along with other mainstream news channels have been systematically engaged in a conspiracy so widespread, so iniquitous and insidious as to defy comprehension. But their dark secret has finally been unearthed and come to light."

Someone behind Harry spoke loudly. "What's she saying?"

"Shussh!" several people chastened in unison.

"But I-"

"Shut up and let me hear!" another scolded sharply.

"...infiltrated by members of this cabal, which seems to have its tentacles embedded in high positions of authority everywhere these days."

In San Francisco, a communications supervisor at IBC headquarters had to pull the phone away from his ear. An officer of the company was livid, screaming at him. "I don't know what happened, sir, we're trying to locate the problem," he was finally able to reply.

Another barrage of foul language immediately assaulted him, and he nodded vigorously. "Yes...yes...I know, sir, we...we've been trying to cut the transmission, but we're unable....no...we can't just simply pull the plug, the system is not set up that way...no, it's all controlled by computer...yes, I know it's supposed to be unbreachable...but...but...it's not just us, all the other stations are experiencing the same problem. We believe a hacker has found a way in. All the stations are airing the same thing."

Nearly deafened by the yelling issuing from the phone, the supervisor pulled it from his ear again. Exasperated, he finished the call by saying. "All I can tell you is we're working on it."

As Hearthwatch listened in stunned silence, all three congressmen turned to regard him as the woman on the screen launched into a list of names.

"...all of these officials have abetted Plagiarius, including Senator Brent Van Heflin, Chairman of the senate's prestigious Science and Technology Committee, and Truman Hearthwatch, the supposedly esteemed Green Technology and Climate Advisor to the U.S. president, a man who has been cleverly dubbed Earthwatch by the corrupted media. But these men are no such champions of issues seemingly aimed at safeguarding the environment. Beneath these carefully erected personas lay ruthless, diabolical rogues motivated by greed and an insatiable lust for power, them and all those they are aligned with. They are in league with a cabal that pushes for legislation which will impose yet another tax on an already overtaxed American public, a carbon tax to be levied commensurate with the size of carbon footprint a citizen or enterprise projects to the environment. On the surface, it would appear this tax is meant to curb the use of carbon based energy sources responsible for the release of greenhouse gases. But this objective is merely a pretext for tightening the economic noose further, not only on the American people but on other countries of the world as well. Once passed into law, it is meant to become the standard for other nations to follow, ultimately to be enforced by United Nations sanction. And while there is a consensus among most scientists that an unrestrained discharge of greenhouse gases into the atmosphere will eventually lead to drastic climatic change detrimental to mankind, such an assumption has never been proven, though it has been aggressively promoted by this group of plotters who have spent hundreds of millions of dollars in creating a crisis quite literally out of thin air, propagating this hoax with nothing more than fabricated and embellished data."

The woman paused momentarily, a look of utter disgust evident on her face before going on with the commentary. "Plainly put, it is a scam. The individuals behind this scam have much to gain. At the heart of their aggressive promotion is a hidden agenda. These schemers stand to reap billions in profits through brokerage fees based on the trading of carbon credits, which are actually licenses to pollute. If such legislation were to be passed, the very use of electricity would be considered a form of pollution since the great majority of power plants rely on the burning of fossil fuels to generate electricity. As is obvious, factories and industry in general would ultimately be required to obtain these licenses in order to continue manufacturing, and these would be available for a hefty price and subject to an exorbitant brokerage fee. These fees would be passed onto consumers, who would also be subject to carbon taxation, causing the price of goods and services to escalate further. In essence, people would be taxed on the very air they breathe since the act of breathing causes the expulsion of carbon dioxide into the atmosphere. In the end, the wealth of both citizens and governments will be looted by these men. From what has been uncovered, this cabal seeks to bring down the American way of life through a systematic dismantling of the Constitution, the foundation upon which life in the United States is based. Senator Brent Van Heflin is currently being groomed and backed by this cabal to run for the Oval Office as an added measure to ensure this scheme becomes a reality."

As he watched and listened, Hearthwatch began to tremble with pent up rage. "Someone turn that lying bitch off!" he growled aloud, unable to control himself any longer.

"Shuddup!' someone hollered. "I wanna hear this!"

"...coupled with this desire to gain huge profits from the general population of the world is another agenda, one far more insidious and sinister, and that is the promotion of a global government." Amelia's voice rose with emotion. "Wake up people, your future is in jeopardy, dire jeopardy, for you are only a few steps away from total enslavement by this cabal. And while it won't be the type of enslavement you see in movies showing sweat-soaked, downtrodden toilers in loincloths being prodded along by overseers with whips, it will be enslavement nonetheless. With disposable incomes slowly eroded and stretched to the limit, the middleclass will cease to exist. Reliance on government will be their only option if they wish to have a roof over their heads and food on their plates, but it will be a bare minimum. This scenario will be very similar to what coal miners had to endure when they were forced to rely on extended credit given them by the company store for all their needs. With their wages unable to keep up with living expenses, they fell further and further into debt, forced into bondage and forever indebted to the company that sustained them, obliging them to keep working for the rest of their days with no option for retirement. In such a world, the average person will become an indentured servant until they are no longer productive. Only two classes of people will emerge from the economic wreckage that will come from this tax, that being the rich and the poor, with indentured servitude becoming the norm among the lower class so that the rich can live in hedonistic comfort."

On the screen, Amelia Amhurst sighed with contempt. "Behind the scenes in shady back room deals and covert conferences held by conspiring plutocrats and elites, the UN is being methodically prepared to evolve into this global government. The push for this to happen rests on three main pillars, the first of them being the pretext of halting global warming. The other two are even more depraved. A dramatic reduction in the world population is the second of these pillars. These plotters believe this can be accomplished through a twofold process involving artificially manufactured pandemics in third world countries and massive crop failures on a planetary scale. Already they have the mechanisms in place to bring about these calamities, one of them being the ebola crisis currently killing off thousands in North Africa. Several nefarious members of this cabal will be portrayed as saviors of mankind when they bring forth panaceas for remediating these problems, panaceas that have already been developed and are awaiting dispersion to the rest of the world. However, these same individuals will contend that the cost of producing these panaceas will be astronomical, thereby forcing additional financial burdens on already bankrupt governments in order to pay for them. This will trigger a global financial crisis that will set the stage for the third pillar, which will necessitate the creation of a global bank. By instigating these events, these schemers believe the surrendering of national sovereignties to the one world government can be achieved."

Amelia paused again, giving her audience a moment to grasp the full context of this disclosure. "We have learned the name of the man heading this cabal, an incredibly rich industrialist who prefers to remain in the shadows, a man who goes by the name of Malcolm Maximus. His followers refer to him as the *Sublimis*. It is a Latin term that means *Lofty One*. He is the Chairman of Unus Universitas, an immensely diversified conglomerate and the largest corporation on the planet. Within his vast holdings is the Plagiarius Corporation, which lies at the heart of this conspiracy."

As Amelia continued to speak, all three Congressmen eyed the Presidential Advisor as though he were toxic, and more and more patrons were beginning to take notice of his presence, suddenly aware of who was in their midst.

Hearthwatch leaned forward, bringing his voice to a panicked whisper. "Don't believe what you're hearing, it's nothing more than an attempt by the opposition to discredit me and stop passage of the bill."

His companions looked back at the TV, intent on hearing what else was being said.

"...seeing Tursiops Worldwide as a major threat to their global interests. A concerted effort has been underway for some time now by these plotters to vilify Aquaria." The image of Amelia abruptly vanished from the screen to be replaced by a succession of scenes depicting various facets of the floating city, Navassa Island, and the pristine tropical waters surrounding both. "By pulling strings with corrupted officials within the UN and the American government, they have coaxed military action upon its peaceful and environmentally conscientious inhabitants. At this moment, a UN task force is invading the facility to take control of it. I dare not…"

Standing on the bridge wing of the *USS Carl Sagan,* Captain Delila lowered the spy glasses from his face. Though he could have monitored the progress of the mission in high definition on a TV screen situated in the bridge, he preferred to remain outside in the breeze. Though in was hot, the smell of saltwater in the air was invigorating.

"Sorry to bother you, sir," a voice at his back beckoned.

Delila turned. It was the young ensign again. "I think you should see something, sir."

"What is it?"

"If you'll follow me, I'll show you, sir."

Leading the way, the ensign brought him before the HDTV. "It came on of its own accord, sir, almost as though someone found a way into our system, but I believe it's worth noting. I've been recording it, so if you'd like to review the full context of what this woman is saying, it's all there."

Delila stared at the image on the screen, suddenly intrigued by the things being said.

Clearly outraged, Truman Hearthwatch arose from the booth. Feeling like an outcast, he eyed the audience of spectators and raised his voice loudly enough to be heard above the TV. "How dare this woman impugn my good name."

The closest patrons diverted their gazes from the TV to eye him coldly. "Charlatan!" someone shouted.

"Yeah, shut the hell up so we can hear!" another person growled.

Hearthwatch recognized one of his admonishers. It was a high-ranking bureaucrat who worked for the Office of General Accounting. Striding for the door to leave the establishment, he would make sure to do whatever it took to get the man fired.

-115-

Within a half mile of the *Kraken* and ten feet below the surface, Jake emerged from the submersible nicknamed Johnnie and straddled his bond mate. Underwater visibility was exceptional, and with Achilles swimming along at full speed, they closed the distance quickly.

JJ, the ship has launched a submarine from hull doors located amidships, Achilles informed his rider.

How big? questioned Jake, scanning the hydrosphere before him in an effort to spot it.

Big, approximately three hundred feet in length. It's too far away now for you to see, but it appears to be heading for Aquaria. I have already alerted the pod.

It's obvious that ship is being used to carry more than just oil, Jake said. *Are the hull doors still open?*

We'll arrive too late to get into the ship that way if that's what you're thinking. Those doors have just closed.

Then I guess we're stuck with Plan A, Jake replied disappointedly. They would resort to the same method they had used in getting Jake aboard the Southern Star, only this time more rope would be needed to reach the main deck, which was slightly more than 130 feet above the water when the vessel was fully loaded. But they had come prepared. They had with them the required length of rope, and Jake knew where to go once he gained the main deck. Just before they had left the *Satis Nunquarn*, Percy had used the computer in the moon pool chamber to pull up plans of the *Kraken*, and Jake had committed Percy's instructions to memory.

"This is where you'll find them," Percy had said, pointing to a place where the bottom deck was located. He had placed a finger on another area on the main deck. "The ship has a rail system. There's a door here that will take you to a bubble car. It works pretty much like an elevator and operating it is quite simple, but two buttons have to be punched instead of one to let it know where you want to go." He scribbled something on a piece of paper, adding, "Just punch in these numbers and it will automatically take you there."

Jake saw the side of the mega-tanker's hull come into view. The sheer size of it was intimidating. *You sure you'll be able to do this, Achilles?*

Jake felt a sudden surge of indignation emanate from his bond mate. *Why must you always doubt me, JJ? If I said I could do it, I meant it.*

Okay, okay, just asking.

In moments they unraveled the rope in the same manner they had done before, but this time the technique would be slightly different. At the apex of Achilles' leap, the dolphin would hurl the grappling hook the remaining distance to the main deck. Then Jake would have the arduous task of climbing hand over hand much higher than he had done in scaling the side of the Southern Star.

Holding onto his end of the rope, Jake glimpsed Achilles shoot into the depths. With a much greater length of rope, the dolphin was able to go deeper, much deeper than what was executed at the Southern Star, and he descended to the rope's full length before turning and throwing the full power of his extraordinary muscularity into a rapid ascent. Up he rose, accelerating quickly and gathering all the speed he could muster that would set the stage for a spectacular leap. Breaking free of the ocean like a guided missile, he reached a height of ninety feet before the pull of gravity negated his upward flight. In that instant of time, a profound feeling of satisfaction and elation took hold of him as he sensed it was the highest he had ever jumped, but even before he reached the peak of his leap he was whirling the grappling hook in a sling-like fashion on eight feet of rope. Releasing it, he glimpsed it arc higher to go sailing over the ship's railing as he fell back into the sea.

Let's hope it grabs, JJ, he uttered just before hitting the water. Exploding past Jake by gravity-induced momentum, he trailed a plume of cavitated whitewater as he was driven deep.

Jake pulled in the slack and tugged on the rope. A smile came to his face as he felt it go taut.

You never cease to amaze me, my friend.
I told you I could do it, didn't I?
Yes, you did.

Jake surveyed the sea behind him just in time to discern Johnnie coast out of the gloom, the sub's maw beginning to open to release Hercules with a rider straddling his back. To convey to the rider they were set to go, he made a show of yanking forcefully on the rope and pointing upward.

Victor Belachek nodded back in understanding as Hercules handed Jake the plastic-wrapped Sledgehammer, a combat harness, and a rucksack filled with gear. With Achilles lending support, Jake strapped on the additional items, aware that they would add an extra 70 pounds to his own weight once he exited the water. Removing his swim fins, he handed them over to his bond mate.

Fully armed in the same manner when he had invaded Maximus' mega-yacht, Jake pulled himself to the surface, and as he did so, Achilles intruded on his thoughts.

You sure you can make it to the top, JJ? It's a long way up and you're carrying a significant load.

Now who's doubting who, wise ass? Jake shot back, grumbling out the thought as he hauled himself clear of the water.

Bracing his booted feet against the tanker hull, he began pulling himself up hand over hand, the sinew in his chiseled arms rippling like slithering serpents from the strain. This was going to be a new challenge, one he wasn't sure he could overcome as he felt the incessant, unyielding pull of gravity begin to take him to the far reaches of his physical limits. But giving up the effort and quitting was a notion completely foreign to him, and despite the fact that his forearms, biceps and lats began to burn with a leaden fatigue that grew painful, he continued to heave himself higher. Finally reaching the main deck, he slithered over the top railing and lay on his back, gasping for air and giving his aching muscles a chance to recover.

The area of the ship he had chosen to scale had not been randomly selected. Percy had recommended a place where Jake would go unobserved from the *Kraken's* bridge. Though Percy had managed to hack into the ship's computer system and shut down most of the systems, including the camera network, Jake would need large deck fixtures to shield him from vigilant eyes located higher up.

Feeling himself quickly recuperating, Jake removed a device from the rucksack. It was a small electric winch, one of several auxiliary winches normally stored aboard Johnnie. But a power source would be needed to operate it. Looking behind him, he spotted an outlet. It was right where Percy said he would find one. Percy had been thorough, for once he had realized what Jake planned to do, he had performed a final task on the moon pool computer before they had vacated Maximus' yacht, scrolling through the *Kraken's* immense electrical grid to locate a working outlet in the area where Jake would reach the main deck. With Percy having disabled the ship's primary generators, Jake had been skeptical about the plan, but Percy had assured him the auxiliary system would kick in to provide Jake with the power he would need.

Pulling the power cord free of the winch, Jake plugged it into the outlet and tested the device. Immediately, it hummed to life. Satisfied, he turned it off and secured it to the lowest railing with two hooks attached to it. Turning it back on, he began playing out the one-eighth inch braided cable, extending his head out between the rails to observe the end of it eventually drop into the water. Letting out 10 more feet, he turned it off.

Several moments passed before Achilles petitioned him. *Victor is ready, JJ.*

Jake turned the winch back on, retracting the cable. Victor had openly admitted he could not possibly make the climb. Well into his forties and a good fifty pounds heavier than Jake, not to mention the additional gear he carried, he knew he would need help to reach the main deck.

Another minute passed before Victor was crouched beside Jake. "You ready," Jake said, noticing the intense look the Russian commando displayed.

Hissing out the words with gritted teeth and murder in his eyes, he said, "Let's get my son back."

Jake pointed aft, showing Victor the door that led to the bubble car.

* * * *

-116-

Captain Delila continued to watch and listen to what was being broadcast on the Military News Channel, a deep foreboding chill creeping up his spine as he took in all the things the newswoman was saying.

Standing at his side, Ensign Jefferson spoke up. "She's on all the major networks, sir. "It's obvious she's broadcasting from the floating city. You can see our ship behind her in the distance."

"...aside from these despicable acts of treason, these men have used their influence to initiate a UN task force to take control of Aquaria. The man in charge of this task force is Malikai Allotey, Special Envoy to the United Nations' Council on World Ecological Affairs, a newly created branch within this world body that was purposely slapped together within recent days to justify the takeover of the sea colony. Acting as agent for the UN for many years now, Allotey has a long history of heinous indiscretions that have allowed him to walk away with millions of dollars while carrying out missions under the UN banner."

A recent though unflattering photo of Allotey replaced Amelia's animated personage as she spoke. "From the start, men like this have routinely infiltrated the UN to severely corrupt an organization originally established for the betterment of mankind, placed within its ranks by members of the cabal plotting for world enslavement." A line of alphanumeric characters began to march across the bottom of the screen. "What you're seeing below Allotey's image is the coded user name and password for accessing his account in the Deutsche Bank of the Cayman Islands where he has stashed more than seventeen million dollars while carrying out his illicit activities. During Saddam Hussein's regime, he was heavily involved in the oil-for-food scams Iraq's former dictator perpetuated, and while he was in charge of UN troops in the Congo, he extorted sex for food from children and exchanged ammunition for ivory with rebels who slaughtered elephants in the Virunga National Park."

Another photo came to the screen, this one showing a swarthy individual with a heavily pockmarked face. "Assisting him in carrying out most of these malicious crimes is Captain Francisco Alvarez, a professional mercenary hired on by the UN to enforce its agendas. While working with Allotey, he was directly responsible for the massacre of seventy-eight innocent villagers in Rwanda fourteen years ago, and during a peace-keeping mission in Uganda a year later, forty-two people mysteriously disappeared under his watch."

Delila stared in stunned silence as he assimilated these revelations.

"Sir, I knew there was something about that guy that didn't feel right," Ensign Jefferson grumbled softly. He turned to study his captain. "What are you going to do?"

Amelia continued to speak, reading the handheld teleprompter given her by Jacob. "At this moment the inhabitants of Aquaria are not putting up any resistance as they come under attack, but it seems the man leading the invading task force has more in mind than taking control of the facility. He is looking to confiscate Aquaria's wealth before an official tally of its assets can be made."

Delila pulled his gaze from the TV, his features suddenly reflecting anger. "Get on the radio and call back the Seal teams. We're aborting the mission."

A smile of genuine admiration broke out on Jefferson's face, proud of his commanding officer's decision. "I don't think it will do any good to remind you that you risk a court martial for disobeying orders, sir."

-117-

Exiting the bubble car, Jake crept stealthily along the dimly lit corridor. With Victor behind him, he came upon the second of the interrogation cells, which proved to be empty. Jake pulled up short, giving Victor a hand signal to do the same. The layout was just as Percy had described and a stark reminder of the way Colonel Ternier's torture chambers were laid out when he had rescued Emanuel and his wife from the clutches of the psychopathic colonel and his depraved mother years earlier. And now he was doing it again, only this time Chester Hennington and Victor's son, Alex, were to be additional torture victims instead of Lucette.

Jake did not delude himself into thinking otherwise. When Percy had used the term "contractors," he knew exactly what that implied. In the business of political scheming, espionage and subterfuge, men who hired contractors used them primarily for two purposes, and that was to either assassinate people or capture and torture them to extract information. This was verified when Percy had hacked into the *Kraken's* surveillance system to show him where Emmanuel and Chester had been taken.

Jake looked at his wristwatch, aware that time was running short. Though Percy had managed to remotely gain access to the mega-tanker's mainframe computers and shut down most of the ship's power, he said it would be temporary at most. But at least without power, electro-shock torture could not be carried out on his friends.

Abruptly the hall lights dimmed just before going brighter, and the low vibration of generators being re-engaged could be felt underfoot. A male voice coming from the third cell suddenly broke the air. With Jake still mentally linked to his bond mate, Achilles translated the strange sounding words for him. "Power's back on. Go ahead and juice them, boy."

Jake moved quickly, raising the Sledgehammer's muzzle and stepping through the doorway. "I think not," he growled irritably.

Startled by the sudden intrusion, two guards whirled.

"Place your weapons on the floor!" Jake snapped sharply, his Sledgehammer trained squarely on one of them, his trigger finger prepared to fire off a round. From experience, he dared not tell them to drop them, knowing the weapons could potential discharge if the safeties were off. "Do it real slow!"

Knowing they had no chance at coming out of this on top, both guards bent slowly, placing their Uzis on the floor in front of them. Rising back up, they raised their hands in surrender.

Movement from the male contractor caught Jake's eye, and he swiveled the Sledgehammer a few degrees to bear on the threat. "Try it and I'll blow you in half!" he warned.

Without being told, Herbert Jester lowered the small handgun to the floor and put his hands in the air as Jake stepped over to check on his friends strapped to the chairs. Both Emmanuel and Chester peered up at him as though in disbelief.

Jake glanced at the woman, her eyes boring into him like hate-filled drills. "Unstrap 'em, lady, and be quick about it or I might decide to shoot your partner just for kicks!"

Alex, his hand still on the throw switch, turned to regard him with a confused stare. His perplexity immediately dissolved at seeing Victor standing behind Jake.

Belachek appeared stunned. Speaking in their native tongue, he said, "What are you doing, Alex? Did they make you do this?"

A defiant smile emerged on Alex's face. "These men are going to tell us where they mine their gold. You do remember the gold we came upon back near that cove, don't you, Victor?"

Victor took stock of the captives Alex had been preparing to electrocute, then looked back at his son with a horror-stricken expression. "You wanted to torture these men?" he said, unwilling to believe what he was seeing. But deep down he knew what lurked within his son's core nature, though he had refused to acknowledge it. It had been confirmed while Alex was convalescing aboard Jake's boat. Alex had asked that those strange surrealistic oil paintings decorating the cabin walls be placed where he could not see them, claiming they were making him nauseous.

Alex stared back at him with cold, distant eyes. "Why should it matter to you? As I recall, you work for a man who engages in torture all the time."

"I don't anymore," Victor replied ruefully. "My days with Zinova are finished."

"Then join me, Victor. We can both work for the man who owns this vessel. He is rich beyond anything you can imagine. He'll reward us for our services. We will be able to live in luxury for the rest of our lives."

Jake stood off to one side keeping a watchful eye on his adversaries, a feeling of rapidly escalating uneasiness taking hold of him as Achilles translated what was being said. Alex still had his hand resting on the throw switch and the woman only had one of his friends free, that being Chester. Abruptly he spoke up, his tone conveying an unmistakable warning.

"Victor, tell him to move his hand away from that switch."

Alex shot a look at Jake. Though he didn't understand English, he sensed the meaning behind the words, and his fingers tightened on the switch.

"Victor!" Jake said curtly, swinging the Sledgehammer around to bear on Alex.

Alex eyed the remaining captive still strapped securely to the chair. The woman was just starting to remove one of the arm straps. Turning his head back round, he first looked at Jake, then at Victor. "He can go ahead and shoot me, I don't care. If I can't be rich, I don't want to live."

"Alex, I am your father!" Victor blurted."

Alex's face clouded darkly. "My father died a long time ago," he spat back in anger. "He was killed in Afghanistan. Why do you lie to me, Victor?"

Wetness welled up in Victor's eyes. "It's true, Alex. I am not lying."

Alex stared back dumbly for one brief moment before comprehension caught up with him. "You," he snarled venomously, his face screwing up with bitter hatred. "You left me when I was a baby." Drawing in a deep breath, he screamed, "You deserted me."

Tears began to roll down Victor's cheeks. "Yes, I know, Alex, and I can only tell you how sorry I am for doing that." His tone took on a pleading edge. "Can you find it in your heart to ever forgive me?"

Alex's expression turned incredulous. "You must be insane. I can never forgive you!" he railed back with dismissive contempt.

Jake continued to follow the exchange, aware that Emmanuel was now almost free. He felt Victor's anguish, an inconsolable yearning for the love of a son who was predisposed to hating him forever. Nothing was going to change that. He sensed it like smoldering coal in a nearby oven, only the oven was Alex, a person with a dark foreboding nature. No wonder Amphitrite and Destiny had such a hard time healing and reviving him. The boy had little to no good residing deep within him.

Jake risked a brief glance at the former Spetsnaz operative while still keeping close vigilance of Maximus' henchmen. He dared not take his eyes off them for more than a second. From the look on Victor's face, he could see the man was crushed. Nevertheless, time was running out and he had to get back to the colony, with or without Alex.

Thinking it prudent to take charge of the situation, Jake spoke up before any more hurtful words could be uttered.

"Are you able to walk, Emmanuel?"

"I think so," Emmanuel gasped, rising slowly out of the chair.

"How about you, Chester?"

"I'll be okay," Chester acknowledged weakly. "Just give me a minute to catch my breath."

Jake took a few steps forward, pointing his weapon at the two guards. "Back away!" he ordered.

As the guards backed up, he used his left foot to slide the two Uzis across the floor toward his friends. "Emmanuel, Chester, pick up their weapons and stand by the door. Warn me if you hear or see anyone coming down the hall." Looking at the male contractor, he issued another command, motioning with the Sledgehammer. "You. Slide your pistol over to me."

Warily, Jake followed the contractor's movements as he bent to slide the weapon toward him with his hand. "With your foot," he hissed.

Straightening back up, the contractor did as instructed, and Jake trapped the handgun under his heel as it slid across the floor.

"Now take a seat!" Jake ordered him, indicating the chair on the left. His gaze swung to the woman. "You too, lady, in the other chair!"

Both contractors glanced at each other and hesitated, their eyes widening in fear.

"Do it!" Jake growled ominously. "I advise you not to try my patience. I'm sure you know the weapon I'm holding can blow you to mush."

Begrudgingly, they complied, and as they settled unwillingly into the chairs, Jake motioned the guards forward. "Strap 'em down!" he said. "Nice and tight and be quick about it."

Aware that Alex had removed his hand from the switch, Jake pulled a roll of duct tape from his utility belt. Satisfied that both contractors were sufficiently constrained, he barked another order at the guards. "Now, both of you sit in their laps." Motioning with the Sledgehammer, he added, "You in his lap and you in hers."

Daunted by Jake's stony gaze and the way his finger hovered menacingly over the Sledgehammer trigger, each guard did as ordered. The woman's face blanched as the heavier of the two guards settled himself onto her lap, and she let out a husky gasp.

"Okay, Victor, I need you to bind them," Jake said, tossing him the roll of duct tape. "For your own safety, I recommend you ask your son to step away from that switch."

Victor looked at him like a man in a stupor, avoiding his son's withering glare. He had barely reacted in time to snare the roll Jake had tossed him, and he nearly stumbled as though intoxicated as he moved forward to carry out the task.

There was no need for Victor to ask Alex to do as Jake requested. Alex had already edged toward the door. Frowning with contempt, the lad watched as Victor bound the wrists and ankles of the guards to the same body parts of the person they sat upon. As his father completed the task, Alex suddenly bolted past Emmanuel and Chester and raced down the corridor in the direction opposite where Jake and Victor had disembarked the bubble car.

Victor turned to see him vanish, his expression helpless and forlorn.

"What do you want to do, Victor?" Jake asked softly, feeling the man's grief as though it were his own. "It's your call."

Victor let out a deep, downcast sigh. "I will not hold you up any longer, my friend. You have already done more than a man in my position can expect. I bid you and your friends good fortune in getting back to Aquaria."

"Come with us."

Victor shook his head dolefully. "No, I have unfinished business here."

Jake opened his mouth to persuade him otherwise, but a premonition of lurking danger suddenly accosted him.

As if to affirm this, Emmanuel spoke up with a hushed warning. "Jay Jay, I hear someone coming!"

The image of something coalesced lucidly in Jake's mind, and for an instant he thought he might be hallucinating. It was coming from the direction in which Alex had run, and he suddenly realized what it was. "Everyone to the bubble car!" he ordered sharply. "Hurry!"

Both Emmanuel and Chester heeded the curt warning, but failed to move as quickly as Jake would have liked. Debilitated from their bout of recent torture, they ambled along sluggishly, panting hard. Jake scooted after them but abruptly pulled up short, realizing Victor was holding back, still within the interrogation cell.

"Victor!" he shouted, turning to look back.

The sound of heavy clomping impinged on Jake's hearing, and movement further down the corridor caught his eye. He became aware of Alex advancing slowly toward him, the expression on the lad's face filled with fright. Directly behind him was a towering figure at least nine feet tall. It was Maximus in a fully armored combat suit. He knew it was Maximus despite the metallic helmet that completely obscured his head and neck. In his mind's eye, he saw the man's face, though it was hidden behind the tinted visor through which the man could see. It was the same face that had stared lividly back at him from the co-pilot's seat when he and Victor had tried to stop the helicopter from taking off from the *Nunquarn Satis*. The suit appeared powerful but bulky, completely encasing Maximus' torso and limbs as well as his head, and from the look of the protective armor, Jake doubted his frag-12 rounds had any chance of penetrating it at all.

"Do not try to run away or I will kill the lad," a raspy voice blared harshly from a loudspeaker built into the suit. In the confines of the corridor, it reverberated ominously.

Jake stared, noticing a nasty looking electronic Gatling gun with six barrels jutting from the suit's left arm, though it was a much smaller version of what military aircraft used. He knew that combat suits like this had been in the development stage by the U.S. military for the last several decades. They were essentially wearable robots with tough, durable shells comprised of a high-strength material designed to resist ballistic impacts originating from machine gun fire and shrapnel from explosive devices. Their biggest flaw, however, was their lack of agility, and this one appeared to be ponderous in the way it moved, telling Jake that the suit was obviously quite heavy, forcing its hydraulic joint actuators to work exceptionally hard to overcome the suit's massive weight.

Stealing a quick glance behind him, Jake saw that Emmanuel and Chester were now out of the corridor, having made it to the bubble car platform. Thinking quickly, he weighed his options, but Victor's voice rang out with strident urgency.

"Don't shoot, I'm coming out." Tossing his weapon from the interrogation cell, Victor stepped from the room with his hands held high in the air.

The robotic head rotated slightly to fixate on Victor before swiveling back to bear on Jake. The amplified voice reverberated again, this time charged with untold menace. "So I am finally meeting the tenacious Mr. Javolyn," Maximus said scornfully, "a man who has foolishly decided to become a thorn in my side. You will tell me what you have done with Bronte Pharah."

Jake decided to act dumb. "Who?"

"I warn you, do not play me for a fool," the *Sublimis* bellowed. "The Haitian Minister of Agriculture. He was being escorted by two of my guards before you disposed of them back on my yacht. Where is he?"

"Oh, that Bronte Pharah," Jake replied flippantly, keeping his mental link with Achilles fully open. "He's in a safe place beyond your control."

"Then perhaps a trade is in order if all of you wish to live," the *Sublimis* boomed back. "But first you will tell me where your cache of gold is stored and where it is mined."

Jake's thoughts raced, searching for a way out of this, but it was evident Maximus had the upper hand at the moment.

Jake let out contemptuous chuckle. "What is it with men like you? You possess staggering wealth and yet you have this obsession with gathering in yet more riches. Don't you think you already have enough?"

This time Maximus laughed, a grating, raspy sound within the narrow hallway. "No, Mr. Javolyn, there will never be enough for men of substance like myself. We are the true caretakers of an already overpopulated world. If left to his own devices, the common man has this proclivity to squander the fruits of his labor by perpetuating a meaningless life. When food and energy are readily available, he floods the earth with overbreeding and runaway consumption of limited resources. The common man is feckless and lacks the intellectual capacity to know what's best for him. Men like me are the chosen ones. As such, we have a duty to take what is produced by the masses to be used for managing the earth in a more responsible manner. Our goal is to prevent humanity's extinction. We seek nothing more than the betterment of mankind through the salvation of the planet."

"Don't you really mean the enslavement of mankind?" Jake spat back in disgust.

"I will not bandy words with you, Mr. Javolyn. Debating this with you is pointless. Our philosophical viewpoints are obviously diametrically opposed. While you see me as utterly ruthless and morally deficient, I see you and those you abet as offensively negligent. Your imagined benevolence is actually a curse that will ultimately be mankind's undoing."

Jake stared back in amazement, his jaw dropping. He couldn't believe what he was hearing. "Undoing you say! I fail to see how you can deem the production of sustainable renewable resources to be mankind's undoing when they are created in total harmony with the earth's environment. We bring forth an unlimited bounty by creating an oasis in what would otherwise be a desert. And we have the potential of creating many more of these oases."

The robotic head appeared to nod in agreement. "Yes, and while that may be true, bringing forth an endless supply of cheap energy and sustenance to billions of people in Third World countries will surely accelerate their already out of control breeding. That is the natural consequence when food and energy are plentiful to humans. The start of the Industrial Revolution bares illuminating testament to this. Once carbon-based fuels were introduced to the masses, their numbers mushroomed dramatically. No, Mr. Javolyn, I can't let that happen. What you are doing is irresponsible. It's far too risky to let your operation continue, for if it did the earth would be swamped with more people than it could sustain. This would result in catastrophic pollution that may be irreversible, not to mention the massive wars between nations that would ultimately ensue. I'm talking extermination of the human race."

Jake let fly another chuckle, this one laced with vitriolic ridicule. "I find that most ironic coming from you. It's you and your kind that instigates wars with the aim of financing opposing sides to increase their indebtedness to you. You continue to grow richer with all the misery you cause."

"Wars are necessary," the *Sublimis* riposted angrily. "They cull down the growing numbers of useless eaters, and once we establish a singular government to control the entire world, national sovereignties will be eliminated along with wars."

"Only after you kill off billions," Jake snarled.

"Yes, and the earth will be better for it. Chaos and anarchy will become things of the past, with only order to follow."

"Isn't it rather hypocritical of you to speak of order when you and your cronies are the cause of much of the havoc and discord that currently exists throughout the world."

Maximus elicited a bored sigh. Magnified by the suit's speaker, it sounded like a prolonged hiss, telling Jake he was growing tired of the conversation. "Enough of your stupidly infantile drivel, Mr. Javolyn. Tell me where the gold is kept and I'll let you and your friends live."

"No, you won't," Jake fired back. "Once you get what you want, you'll eliminate those you consider to be impediments to your insidious schemes. Isn't that right, Maximus? Throughout history men like you have constructed fantasies in which they believed themselves to be gods by self-proclamation. They thought they had all the answers for making the world an orderly place. But by their own actions they caused horrific events that evoked the deaths of millions."

"I need not proclaim myself a god, Mr. Javolyn," Maximus said, his tone taking on one of patronizing superiority and entitlement. "That was decided long ago by my forbearers. My very omnipotence makes me a god. Fate ordains it. Though you have caused me certain inconveniences, in the end I will ultimately prevail and Aquaria will become another of my possessions. But you can save my minions the trouble of searching for the gold by telling me where they can find it."

"You are not a god," Jake declared grimly. "You are a monster. You can't help yourself. Causing misery and strife is what you enjoy most. You are the worst kind of predator, one that is purely evil and demented, surely the devil incarnate himself."

As Jake spoke, he became aware of Victor edging closer to Maximus, whose visored gaze was still fixed firmly on Jake's antagonizing presence. It was evident Maximus felt invincible, certain the suit protecting him was invulnerable and could not be breached. He seemed to show no concern whatsoever for his own safety.

A premonition of disaster and sadness abruptly loomed in Jake's thoughts, and he caught Victor's eye, trying to warn him off with an almost imperceptible shake of his head, masking the gesture with another declaration. "You're wasting your time, Maximus. You want the gold, go find it."

Achilles was suddenly in his mind. *JJ, look above you! The steel pipe you see carries seawater when pumps are activated.*

Jake wasn't sure what Achilles was getting at. *Explain!*

It fills and empties the submarine bay.

How do you know that?

Never mind how, just keep stalling him. The lights will go out in exactly five seconds, but be ready for the intake pumps to initialize. They'll push the water toward Maximus.

A light flickered on in Jake's brain, and he suddenly grasped the full implication of what Achilles was telling him.

How thick is the pipe wall?

Nominal section is one inch.

"I'll give you one last chance to reconsider," Maximus offered irritably.

Jake stared back defiantly. "Go back to hell where you belong!" he growled aloud, stretching out the words slowly.

Risking another glance at Victor, he was answered with a doleful shake of the head that seemed to say, 'I'm sorry, my friend, but this is the only way.'

Peering back at Maximus, Jake's supreme loathing of the man began to build like hot scathing magma below a caldera. Standing before him was another Cardoza, only many times worse. Without giving it any conscious thought, his trigger finger moved idly to the tiny switch that controlled the Sledgehammer's firing mode, shifting it from semi to automatic, and had not Victor's son been standing directly in front of

Maximus, he would have not hesitated to open up with the full fury of the weapon, though he seriously doubted even a barrage of the frag-12 rounds had any chance of getting through the impervious armor encasing him. But there might be another way.

Maximus' armor-clad figure remained transfixed on Jake, the visored helmet regarding him with that same immobile expression of impending doom. The roar that suddenly erupted from the suit's speaker was deafening. "Then prepare to die!"

Victor suddenly sprang, tackling Alex and moving him out of the way. In reaction, Maximus rotated his robotic head to look for the cause of the disruption, and as he did, Jake saw the arm holding the Gatling gun begin to line up on father and son.

Jake swore under his breath. Victor's rashness had removed all options from the table. With only one solution left to keep the twosome from getting killed outright, he pulled back on the Sledgehammer trigger just as the lights went out, aiming high and sending a burst into the armored helmet and upper chest.

An explosion of sparks flared brightly in the ensuing darkness as the enfilade impacted with brutal, jarring savagery. The onslaught was enough to topple Maximus backward on his heavily booted heels and send him crashing to the floor with his left arm flung high. But it was not enough to keep him from letting loose with the Gatling gun.

A thunderous storm of bullets strafed the ceiling directly above him, caroming violently off the steel pipe and sounding like a chain saw gone crazy. Ricochets flew haphazardly, and anticipating this, Jake leaped away to avoid the spray of lethal fragmentation engulfing the hallway. Lasting less than two seconds, the blitzkrieg abruptly ended, and without the coruscated eruption of rounds to provide flickering illumination, the corridor was plunged once again into total darkness. A dead, unsettling silence followed, one so quiet that Jake heard the beat of his own heart.

In moments, backup power kicked in to relight the corridor in a dim afterglow. Creeping cautiously back toward the fallen Maximus, Jake kept the Sledgehammer trained on him as he quickly assessed why the Gatling weapon had stopped firing. Though the barrels remained pointed at the ceiling, the ammunition guide that fed them was bent and ruptured. Apparently the combination of frag-12 rounds and ricochets had been enough to disable the weapon, reminding Jake of a similar event when he had fired a handgun directly into the mini-gun aboard Sebastion Ortega's Bell Ranger years earlier to keep it from destroying the Avenging Angel.

Seeing that Maximus lay unmoving for the moment, Jake risked kneeling beside Victor, who was sprawled atop Alex. A smear of blood crept slowly outward from a hole in Victor's back. Fearing the worst, Jake pulled him gently off his son to cradle his head in his arms. He was immediately struck by a deep sense of déjà vu once again. He had held Myers this way as he lay dying.

Victor stirred, his mismatched eyes fluttering open to stare up at Jake with a near death glaze. Blood trickled from his open mouth. "Thank you..for.. helping me," he managed to say in a faltering whisper.

Jake extended an arm to check on Alex, but immediately saw where one of the ricochets had penetrated the lad's skull. A check of his pulse confirmed he was beyond saving.

Bringing sorrowful eyes back to Victor, he spoke in a gentle voice. "I'm sorry to tell you Alex is gone."

Victor nodded weakly in acknowledgement, then coughed harshly, his lips drenched in blood.

"I'm getting you out of here," Jake said, shifting his body in readiness to lift Victor from the floor.

Victor pushed him away. "Na...*nyet*," he stammered in protest. "Save yourself...I'm finished."

Jake ignored him, preparing to hoist him over his shoulder, but the whir of a joint actuator made him look at the armor-clad figure lying prone on its back. Maximus was trying to rise from the floor, and as he did, the robotic head turned to regard him.

"A valiant move, Mr. Javolyn, but nonetheless a futile one." As Maximus spoke, Jake saw the Gatling gun swivel to bear on his face.

"Your weapon is useless," Jake said smugly.

"But I can still crush you," Maximus retorted, his joint actuators now working hard to roll the massive combat suit over to face the floor. Pushing himself to his knees, he added. "You have no idea what these arms can do to a person."

Not wanting to be trapped against the wall, Jake reached under Victor and heaved him up with a sudden surge of adrenaline, grunting with the effort. Draping him over his left shoulder, he grabbed the Sledgehammer and began moving down the passageway in the direction of the bubble car, but not before Maximus lashed out with his right arm. A starburst of lights erupted behind his eyes as the arcing swipe nicked him on the side of the knee, almost buckling it. Gritting his teeth, he tried to ignore the pain, limping along slowly with Victor's dead weight pushing down to exacerbate the ache.

Stealing a glance behind him, Jake saw Maximus regain his feet and rise to his full height to pound forward, and he felt the floor shake softly underfoot. In his estimation the combat suit had to easily exceed a thousand pounds, with each of its footfalls quaking the deck plates like some monstrous creature out of the dinosaur age. The concept behind its design was rather simple, and speed was not one of its virtues. It was built for defensive protection and brute power, much like a Sherman tank, and if he didn't move any faster, Maximus would catch him before he reached the bubble car.

Jake did not sense any real damage to his knee. The pain brought back memories of his days playing college football. Though a stiff hit to the knee would temporarily sideline him, the ache would ultimately subside, allowing him to get back in the game. But unfortunately he needed more time to shake off the pain, and he was still hobbling along even slower than Maximus' sluggish pace. If he didn't move any faster, those powerful arms would squash him and Victor like bugs against a wall.

Unexpectedly, hands were suddenly lending support, and he realized both Emmanuel and Chester had returned to provide assistance. Pulling up short, Jake hefted Victor from his shoulder awkwardly, placing him into the awaiting arms of his friends. "Get him to the car!" he ordered.

Emmanuel nodded, and with Chester helping, each draped one of Victor's arms behind their neck, sandwiching the wounded man between them and hauling him away with the insteps of his feet dragging along the deck. With his head slumped forward, it was hard to tell if he was still alive.

Jake turned to face the oncoming juggernaut, his leg still hurting and almost collapsing under him. Though Maximus was coming at him like a slow, ponderous bulldozer, he was moving fast enough to overtake the four men before they would have any chance of escaping in the bubble car.

A sound abruptly caught Jake's ear, making him look up. It was a sound he was intimately familiar with, one of rushing water, and it was coming from the pipeline directly overhead. Apparently Ez had succeeded in turning on the pumps. Scrutinizing the pipe's curving surface, he gauged the distance. The bottom of the pipe had to be roughly 5 meters above the deck. *This was a blessing!* The frag-12 rounds the Sledgehammer held were armor-piercing and needed 3 meters to arm themselves once they were fired. But he knew each one was only capable of penetrating one-half inch of steel at most. Multiple strikes, however, just might get through the pipe's inch thick wall and open a sizeable hole.

Bringing the weapon to bear on the underside of the pipe a few meters out in front of him, Jake depressed the trigger, opening up on full automatic as Maximus bore down on him. Bursting flickers of violent incandescence flared hotly as a dozen rounds met steel, and for one fleeting moment he believed the attempt to be a failure. But then a spray of water under tremendous pressure gushed forth from a jagged hole the size of his fist.

Jake sent another 12-round burst into one side of the breach, rending the metal further. The hole changed shape, and aided by the enormous pressure contained within the pipe walls, the steel ruptured outward, no longer able to withstand the severe forces imposed on it. In the span of an instant, a huge oblong tear opened up to send a spate of whitewater gushing into the corridor with a deafening roar as though a dam had burst, and Jake saw it rush toward Maximus with all the pent up fury of a tidal wave charging toward a beach. Lingering a second longer, he watched as the armor-clad figure disappeared under the surge.

The passageway was rapidly filling, and though the flow was moving away from Jake, he was already ankle-deep in water, with the level coming up quickly. Not hesitating any longer, he turned and hastened in the opposite direction. His knee was still smarting, but most of the ache was now gone. In moments he turned a corner to find Emmanuel and Chester awaiting him in the bubble car. Victor's inert body was slumped between them, and he knew it was going to be a tight fit with four men crammed into a space designed to seat two.

Diving through the open door, Jake punched the buttons that would take them back the way he had come. The door immediately hissed shut just as a rush of backwater slammed against it, the water level rapidly climbing sharply to the middle of the window as the car took off, and seconds later they were free of the deluge beginning to engulf them.

As the car rose higher through the decks, Jake fired off a thought to his bond mate. *Get word to Ez to turn off those pumps, Achilles.* The last thing he wanted was the *Kraken's* lower decks filling with so much water that the ship's keel was lowered to the point where it might go aground on the nearby reefs abutting the Windward Passage.

Don't worry yourself, JJ, it's already been taken care of.

Breathing a sigh of relief, Jake came to realize that with the intake pipe now broken, there was no possibility of the submarine returning to the *Kraken's* concealed bay.

-118-

One of the three technicians manning the *Kraken's* bridge lifted his eyes from the computer screen and turned to look at Finley. "The system has gone haywire again," the man declared, his manner clearly frazzled and fraught with exasperation.

"Well fix it, damn you!" Finley yelled. He stood close by, his face smoldering with intense anger.

"We're still being hacked. Someone's got a firm lock on it from the outside, someone who seems to know how to bypass the overrides."

Finley's voice boomed louder. "Then shut it down again and reboot like you did before."

Holland threw up his hands in frustration. "That's what I've been trying to tell you. Whoever's got control won't let us shut it down. They've reset the codes."

Maddened like a tormented bull, Finley was on the verge of reaching out with a huge hand to grab the man by the throat.

Sensing this, Holland spoke up quickly. "But there might be another way."

"How?" Finley grumbled.

"By improvising a wireless shield."

Finley appeared perplexed. He had no idea what Holland was talking about, nor did he care. He just wanted the problem solved. "Do whatever needs to be done, but do it fast," he snarled.

Holland nodded and stepped away from the keyboard, striding briskly to the ship's radar array set up in one corner of the bridge. With the computers being controlled by an outside source, the keyboard terminal was useless to him. He'd have to do this manually by changing the frequency of the pulses emitted by the radar dish and stopping the rotation of the dish so that it faced in only one direction. It was all guesswork, but it was likely the hacking was originating from either the *Nunquarn Satis* or the sea colony, both of which were at the same general location. He prayed his assumption was right, because the last thing he wanted was Finley's wrath befalling him a second time. With hands that squeezed like hydraulic machinery, Finley had grabbed him by the throat once before and his neck had throbbed for a week.

Thinking about the problem at hand, Holland knew wireless hackers used microwave signals to gain access to a computer system, but by aiming the radar dish in the correct direction and jamming those incoming signals with a high enough frequency, he could stop the hacker's attack. Then all he'd have to do was reboot the system and reset the access codes.

Hoping he was right, Holland turned a few knobs and adjusted the digital settings, calling back to McGormack, one of the other techies. "See if she'll reboot now."

"It's working!" McGormack shouted gleefully.

Pleased with himself, Holland glanced over at Finley, using all his will to keep from smirking. Scampering back to the keyboard, he began entering new codes, and two minutes later all the computer monitors came back on line to reveal the status of the various systems. Studying them a minute longer, Holland frowned before setting his gaze on Finley again. "Everything seems to be back to normal except for the intake to the submarine bay."

"What's wrong with it?"

The question was thrown at Holland like a knife. Seeing the same look the *Kraken's* captain had displayed earlier, he swallowed deeply. It was obvious Finley was in no mood to hear about any more problems. "The pipeline is broken and has flooded the interrogation sector. But at least the pumps have shut down," he added, blurting out the words as fast as he could utter them.

Finley's eyes grew large, the statement taking him completely by surprise. The thought that the *Sublimis* along with the two contractors and abductees were down there made his gut tighten. Almost abruptly his features hardened, twisting into another menacing scowl, but before he could cast any blame, the sound of rotor blades slapping the air caught his ear. Rushing to a window facing the ship's bow, he glanced up to espy a helicopter bearing directly at him. Reflexively, he threw an arm up in front of his face and ducked down, the blood in his veins going cold. For one fleeting second he thought it was going to keep coming and crash through the glass, but then it suddenly veered higher to thunder over the bridge.

Spinning around, Finley sprinted across the bridge deck to a sprawling rear window. The chopper had slowed, flaring up sharply in preparation to settle on the ship's helipad that was the size of a football field.

An indecipherable curse sprang from Finley's mouth. Though he had a limited understanding of how the various systems tied into the vessel's mainframe computers, had not Holland tampered with the *Kraken's* radar he might have been alerted of the whirlybird's approach long before it came within earshot, and without clearance to land, he would have promptly blown it out of the sky by engaging one of the ship's concealed 20mm cannons. Whether or not they needed the computers to engage the vessel's weaponry made no difference to him. As far as he was concerned, Holland was to blame. But at seeing the chopper settle down behind the other two aircraft which now effectively shielded it, those being the EC 135 and the contractors' Jolly Green Giant, it was already too late to even think about using those weapons.

Finley continued to stare out the window, searching for signs of the other three men Maximus had brought with him. He remembered seeing the pilot step out to stretch his limbs before tying down the main rotor, but the pilot was nowhere to be seen. The two guards that had flown in with Maximus to escort the boy were also not there. Those guards had not been present in the interrogation room with Alex when he and Maximus had gone down there. Only two of the three guards that normally accompanied the *Kraken* had been in the room. That left three guards somewhere on the ship, making him wonder where they were at the moment.

Finley's apprehension grew as he pondered these things. Moving quickly back to the ship's control console, he lifted a microphone and hit the intercom button that connected with most quarters of the vessel. "Bridge to *Sublimis*, come in *Sublimis*!

When Maximus did not respond, Finley repeated himself, his voice becoming more panicky.

Still no reply.

This time Finley shouted at the top of his lungs. "Answer me, damn it!"

In frustration, Finley threw down the mic and scurried over to a nearby locker. Pulling a key from his pocket, he unlocked the door and pulled out a holstered .357 magnum revolver and hurriedly strapped it on. Because he treated the technicians that normally manned the bridge with the harshness of a tyrannical ogre, he did not trust any of them to carry weapons of any kind around him. And not knowing where the three remaining armed guards were, the task of repelling boarders had now fallen to him.

Reaching for the Heckler and Koch MP5 rifle with scope, he grabbed the fully loaded banana clip next to it and slapped it into place before chambering a round.

Occupied with this, he did not notice the short individual that emerged from a staircase to saunter nonchalantly onto the bridge as though he owned it. Still thoroughly engaged in bringing all the systems back up to speed, none of the other three crew members noticed him either.

Turning, Finley found himself staring down into a pair of maniacal eyes that bulged grotesquely behind a set of thick lenses perched on a nose resembling the beak of a hawk. Too late to react, he barely had time to register the lethal swing of the axe blade arcing toward his skull.

-119-

Destiny scrambled from the Bell Ranger as soon as it touched down, probing her surroundings with a paranormal sense that went way beyond the five normal ones the average person used. Strangely, she did not feel any lurking danger at the moment, though her eyes were automatically drawn to the ship's bridge. Something dark and offensive existed there, sending out pulsations of raw evil that seemed to abrade her soul. The sensation sickened her, nearly making her gag, and if words could describe it, it was as though the air she breathed was rife with the vapors of rotting flesh.

In seconds, Amphitrite and Franklin were beside her as Mortimer sat pensively watching them from the rear portside seat of the chopper, its blades still being spun by an idling engine. Calmly, Amphitrite moved to the portside edge of the landing pad with Destiny and Franklin following.

"Down there!" Amphitrite said, pointing at the four men just emerging from behind a huge curving deck vent to make their way toward the helipad. One of the men was obviously injured, his arms draped over the shoulders of two others as they shuffled along awkwardly bearing his weight. The fourth man followed up their rear, periodically looking behind him and covering their retreat with a firearm at the ready.

With Amphitrite leading the way and Destiny and Franklin following, they dashed to a nearby stairway to rush down the steps. Having already been informed of Victor's condition by Achilles, Destiny knew time was of the essence. Victor was fading fast and they didn't have a moment to lose if they were going to save him.

"Lay him down!" Amphitrite shouted to Emmanuel and Chester as both groups converged at the bottom of the steps.

Victor's face was ashen and he had stopped breathing. Quickly, both women laid hands on him. The thought that they might be too late cast a pall on what they were attempting to do. Destiny pushed down hard on his chest as Amphitrite placed gentle palms on each side of his head.

"Is he still alive?" Emmanuel asked, gasping hard from the strain of carrying the unconscious man.

Totally focused on the task at hand, neither Destiny nor Amphitrite answered.

Jake stood watch as both women went to work, glancing about in all directions as he gripped the Sledgehammer. Knowing he was down to only a few frag-12 rounds at most, he used the moment to remove the drum magazine and pull out a fully loaded spare from the rucksack he carried.

Amphitrite and Destiny remained steadfast and positive in trying to save Victor, but without the albinos channeling their energies into the mortally wounded man through direct contact, the effort was made all the more difficult. Nevertheless, in spite of the distance separating pod members from the event, both women felt the flow of the dolphin energies being telepathically channeled to them and added to their own. And while these energies would certainly amplify their combined healing prowess, the technique would lack the potency the dolphins imparted through direct touch.

Doggedly, both women would not give up, committing themselves entirely to saving the dying man with a trancelike focus for several minutes, unwilling to accept failure.

Victor suddenly stirred with a sharp intake of breath, his chest beginning to heave once again as he sucked in air.

"Get him to the chopper!" Jake yelled. "We got company."

Amphitrite looked up, her features appearing drained. "We need another minute or we still might lose him," she said, her words strained and lacking their normal vigor.

Jake noticed the same drawn look on his wife's face. He had seen this type of thing before and knew she and her mother were donating a significant portion of their own life energies in resuscitating Victor, and without the albinos in attendance and making direct contact with the subject, the effort would invariably leave them in a weakened condition, albeit a temporary one.

"We don't have another minute," Jake warned sharply. He had been struck by another bout of presentiment, and he sensed the approaching danger even before it manifested itself. Somehow Maximus had survived the deluge of water and had managed to make his way up to the main deck, and a quick glance over his shoulder confirmed what he was feeling. Cocooned in his massive robo-suit, Maximus was advancing ponderously in their direction.

Destiny followed Jake's gaze to espy the mechanical monstrosity slowly plodding toward them.

"Now get going!" Jake prompted a second time, taking a few steps toward Maximus and leveling the Sledgehammer. Perhaps he might be able to topple the weighty robo-suit like he had done before.

As Jake stood his ground to confront the oncoming metallic giant, Amphitrite and Destiny managed to get Victor to his feet. In moments they were helping him to climb the stairs, Franklin, Chester and Emmanuel following up the rear.

Jake whipped his head around momentarily to follow their progress, not happy at how slow they were moving. Victor was still far too weak to make the ascent beyond a snail's pace, and none of the others were capable of bearing his weight in a fireman's carriage. Victor was a big man. Complicating the issue was the narrow width of the staircase, which only allowed the group to proceed up the stairs in single file.

Looking back at Maximus, Jake was convinced the only weapon the man currently carried were those powerful mechanical arms, and if he weren't stopped, those arms might be capable of tearing out the staircase supports before the escaping party of six reached the top.

Taking a wide stance and setting the Sledgehammer's firing mode to automatic, Jake waited for Maximus to draw closer. Abruptly, a premonition of additional danger took hold of him, and instinctively he executed a shoulder roll as he dove to one side, coming back to his feet as a storm of bullets pinged and ricocheted, barely missing him. Knowing exactly where the fire was coming from, he opened up with a short 3-round burst to take down one of the guards he had seen aboard Maximus' chopper when it left the *Nunquarn Satis*. Maximus was not the only threat. There were others.

As Maximus bore down on him, Jake stole another quick glance behind him, noticing Victor was nearing the top of the stairway. Without even thinking, Jake instinctively whirled to his left to avoid another volley of automatic fire, the Sledgehammer in his hands seeming to have a mind of its own as it came to bear on another target just as his finger tightened on the trigger for the second time. A scream cut the air, and he saw a second guard crumple to the deck.

With the metal giant almost on top of him, Jake opened fire again, aiming for the helmet as he did before. Seemingly anticipating the blistering enfilade, Maximus leaned into the gale of exploding rounds. This time he did not go down, still advancing like a towering colossus.

Jake held his ground doggedly, refusing to yield and continuing to hammer the robo-suit when something unexpectedly happened. Maximus crashed face forward onto the deck. Seeing the cause, he immediately let up on the trigger to stare slack-jawed.

What are you waiting for, JJ? Achilles chided. *Now get going before he re-gains his feet.*

Had Jake not seen it with his own eyes, he would have not believed it. His bond mate had somehow managed to reach the main deck and, using his prehensile appendages, had hauled his body across the steel surface to come up on Maximus from behind to execute a near perfect shoestring tackle.

You should have clued me, Jake admonished.

Achilles released his hold on the robo-suit ankles and began scurrying back the way he had come. *Had I done so, I risked distracting your clairvoyance.*

Jake mentally sighed. *Wait for me. I'll catch up with you as soon as the others are clear of this ship.*

Turning, Jake tore up the staircase just as Maximus began lumbering to his feet. Almost to the top, the steps beneath his feet suddenly wobbled violently, and a quick glance below him showed Maximus tearing out the supporting stanchions, metal ripping like tissue paper under the onslaught of the suit's powerful arms.

Gripping the railing, Jake managed to keep his balance and bolt up the last remaining steps before the staircase swung forward, held precariously by its topmost connections which were on the verge of pulling free. An instant later, the entire stairway completely dislodged to fall away and crash onto the main deck below.

Taking a moment to look back down, Jake espied the visored helmet locked on him, cognizant of the monstrous evil that lurked behind the impassive shell. Behind that shell he envisioned the intense hatred Maximus wore.

The suit's speaker suddenly boomed stridently with giddy, harsh laughter. "Where are you going to run, Mr. Javolyn? Once your colony falls into my hands, there won't be a place on this planet you can hide."

Jake ignored the chaffing comment and stared in the direction of the Bell Ranger. Though the chopper was designed to carry five people, it was capable of carrying a much heavier load due to the modifications Fernando had made to the engine. And now it was about to lift off with seven people crammed aboard, or so he assumed until Destiny turned back in his direction.

Destiny was pointing at the ancient Jolly Green Giant as she ran toward him, and Jake felt an alarm go off in his head accompanied by a curt warning from Achilles at the exact moment she pointed.

On your left, JJ!

Jake dropped to one knee just in time to avoid a stream of bullets that seemed to part his hair. Catching sight of muzzle flashes coming from the fuselage doorway of the old Marine Corp whirlybird, he returned fire, sending a small burst of well-placed rounds into the darkened interior. And then the Sledgehammer went dead in his hands.

Realizing the drum magazine was now empty, he tossed the weapon aside and pulled the USP-9 submachine pistol from his thigh holster in one smooth motion, chambering a round as he did so. Tuning out the whine of the Bell Ranger's turbine growing to a raucous shriek, he sprang sideways, executing a shoulder roll so as not to present a stationary target. Surprised that no further fire followed him, he eyed the doorway of the ancient chopper, prepared to unleash another sally, though one of lesser magnitude. But when a figure suddenly reeled drunkenly from the interior to tumble down the steps, he knew the Sledgehammer had done its job.

Jake rose to his feet as the assailant lay sprawled on the deck, fragmentation from one of the Sledgehammer rounds apparently having sliced open a huge gash in the man's neck. Blood pumped in heavy spurts from a torn carotid artery, and as the man lay dying, Jake recognized him to be the second guard that had fired upon him and Victor from Maximus' chopper.

The pungent smell of aviation fuel suddenly filled Jake's nostrils, and he became aware of a gathering puddle. Expanding rapidly, it spread outward to surround the guard's prostrate body, and he could only deduce that shrapnel from one of the Sledgehammer's exploding rounds had ruptured the Green Giant's fuel tank.

Reaching Jake's side, Destiny embraced him fiercely as a blast of rotor wash buffeted them gently. Somewhat confused, Jake wondered why Amphitrite was leaving her daughter behind.

"I'm coming with you," Destiny said quickly.

Jake was about to reply when the downdraft from the heli-blades abruptly intensified, and he looked up to see Amphitrite guide the small whirlybird directly overhead.

"Grab hold!" Destiny urged, reaching for one of the skids.

Suddenly Jake understood. Though the helipad spanned the full width of the *Kraken's* main deck, it rose 25 feet higher. At this moment they were 155 feet above the water, and had they attempted a dive from that height, they risked potential injury, especially Jake. With a rucksack strapped to his back and the weaponry he carried, he was all the more vulnerable since those items would likely be torn from his body when he met the sea, though he could have easily tossed them over the side to let the dolphins retrieve them.

Nodding, Jake was about to holster his USP-9 but stopped, sending a thought to his bond mate. *Achilles, let Destiny and Amphitrite know what I'm about to do.*

Jake watched as Amphitrite moved the Bell Ranger farther away, still holding a hover. Destiny left his side and followed. Satisfied that everyone was at a safe distance, he aimed the submachine pistol at the nearby EC 135 and opened fire. Only when it burst into flames did he let up on the trigger. Shifting the weapon, he squeezed the trigger again. Sparks erupted as rounds struck the growing pool of aviation fuel that continued to spill from the other chopper. Almost immediately a flash point was reached and the fuel ignited. He was going to make sure Maximus had no air transport off the ship, at least for the time being.

Taking a few steps, Jake calmly bent to retrieve the expended Sledgehammer and strap it over a shoulder. Breaking into a trot to escape the growing conflagration he caught up with his wife. Reaching for the skid opposite the one Destiny was holding, he gave Amphitrite a thumb's up sign and an instant later felt himself lifted clear of the deck just as the Jolly Green Giant was completely engulfed in flames.

In moments the helo swung out over the sea as the ancient helicopter exploded to eject a swirling fireball into the sky. Jake caught a final glimpse of the robo-suit standing stationary near the portside railing, the jointed head articulating to follow their flight as they descended as though they were on a high speed elevator. Twenty feet above the water he released his grip on the skid a split second after Destiny let go. Plunging beneath the surface, each found their bond mate awaiting them, and a short time later all were aboard Johnnie with Fernando steering the submersible as fast as it could go toward Aquaria.

-120-

Leaving the *Kraken's* galley, Maximus' pilot munched contently on the ham sandwich he had made for himself. Unsure how long his boss planned to stay aboard, he only knew that he was to stand by on the helipad until further notice. Reaching the door that opened to the main deck, the crackling sound of gunfire made him pull up short. Not daring to exit the doorway, he listened to the skirmish for several moments before deciding to take a peek. Realizing the disturbance was coming from the helipad, he felt back to back shockwaves course through the deck under his feet followed by two loud thumps. Abruptly he stiffened at the sight of fireballs rising from where the helicopters sat, and a moment later he glimpsed the Bell Ranger swoop below the ship's port side to escape the flames as two figures clung to its landing skids.

Continuing to stare in disbelief, he was unprepared for the voice that spoke up from behind him. "What is your preference?" it requested, the tone carrying inflections of mockery.

Startled, the pilot turned. A pair of crazed, leering eyes peered at him from behind a set of thick lenses only inches away.

"Huh?" was all the pilot could utter.

"Never mind," Peyami said. "You look like a person that prefers a bullet."

Feeling something jam firmly against his ribs, the pilot glanced down to espy the barrel of a .357 magnum just before it exploded.

-121-

Captain Sayyari Habibollah turned to his sonar expert, keeping his expression stern and holding back the malicious grin yearning to suffuse his features. "Range?" he demanded.

The crewman manning the sonar console continued to monitor the readouts, his earnest gaze never straying from the screen. "Twenty-six hundred meters and closing."

Habibollah stepped forward to stare over the crewman's shoulder, aware that the *Carl Sagan* was not probing the surrounding sea with active sonar. He could only assume its captain was currently using passive mode. *Idiot*, he thought blithely, wondering how the man commanding the carrier had ever advanced to the rank of captain. *Only a fool would drop his guard like this.*

Memories of past encounters with the man danced through Habibollah's thoughts, with his mind coming to bear on one particular incident. Coming upon a herd of whales in the Straits of Hormuz with Habibollah shadowing him, Delila had purposely disengaged his active sonar. And now with hundreds of huge sea mammals swarming close to the sea colony, Habibollah had guessed correctly. Delila was repeating himself.

He's far too predictable, Habibollah mused, only slightly disappointed at how easy this was going to be. *He puts his ship and that of his crew at risk to avoid harming animals that live in the sea. The man is utterly stupid.*

Pivoting his head to glance at the crewman manning the weapons station, Habibollah grunted out a command. "Stand by for launch on my mark." His sub was creeping up on the carrier slowly. At 2,000 meters he'd give the order to fire. Delila was giving him a perfect broadside, and with four torpedoes ripping the carrier's guts out, she was going to go down like a bag of cement.

Finally giving in to his glee, Habibollah let it show. He could not believe his good fortune as of late. Not only was he captaining a Russian-built kilo-class submarine, he had been given the order to take down his longtime nemesis. It was all part and parcel of the plot laid out for him. But these orders had not come from the Ayatollah or the Islamic Revolutionary Guard, though they would have been exuberantly gladdened that a U.S. warship had been destroyed. And while he professed an almost rabid adherence to the teachings of Islam to the men surrounding him, it was all for show, for by nature he was not a religious man. His allegiance resided elsewhere, preferring instead an almost insatiable desire for material gain and the power that accompanied it above all else, and the man promising these things was the only person he was willing to pledge his loyalty. As a young man attending the University of Tehran he along with several others had been recruited by The Order to foment the Iranian masses into overthrowing the Shah's government. In the aftermath of that he had been instrumental in spreading the flames of hatred against the U.S. by organizing and goading a crowd into storming the U.S. embassy in Tehran and taking hostages. The ploy had worked exceedingly well. While on the surface the takeover of the embassy had deceived the world community into believing it was aimed at embarrassing the U.S. government, the actual aim was to heighten international tensions enough to make the public perceive the flow of Middle Eastern crude would be disrupted and create shortages. The oil companies had taken full advantage of the situation, purposely holding back supplies and driving up the price to unheard levels. As a result, members of The Order had profited immensely by going long on futures contracts in advance of the takeover, and overnight he had become a wealthy man.

Habibollah continued to beam at the memory. As more than a foot soldier of *The Order of the Righteous*, his orders had come directly from the *Sublimis* and he was eager to carry them out. Once he fired the torpedoes it would appear that Aquaria had taken aggressive action against a war vessel belonging to the U.S. Navy. The fact that Delila's carrier was also acting as flagship to a UN operation would make the attack even more vicious, further adding to the vilification of the sea colonists.

Without his sonar in active mode, Delila would be alerted he was being probed but he would have no way of knowing the prober's range, though he would be aware of its bearing. He would not know it was coming straight at him, though ever so slowly, and he certainly would be oblivious of its intentions.

Habibollah continued to evaluate the situation, wondering if he should launch the torpedoes at this very moment. No, he decided. Launching at 2,000 meters would be the ideal distance. It would greatly increase his chance of hitting the target. Moreover, it would give Delila insufficient time to evade the subsea missiles homing in on him even if he suddenly decided to be more cautious by reverting back to active sonar mode.

Immediately after Habibollah sank the carrier he was to carry out one additional directive of the *Sublimis*, one far more sinister in nature, one that would allow The Order to make off with a major portion of the world's wealth via the international financial markets. A quick glance at the digital clock overlooking the helm told him the time was drawing close. He knew that an hour earlier agents of The Order had secured vast equity positions on the short side and long positions in precious metals on an unprecedented scale. Members of the cabal were now fully prepared to enrich themselves further. The occurrence would send markets reeling. As far as he knew, this was the cataclysmic event the *Sublimis* had been planning for some time now and one that would plunge the world banking system into paroxysms of chaos. It would force the merging of all the major banks throughout the world and transform the United Nations into the global government The Order had been seeking.

Housed within the *Iron Fist's* missile silo was a warhead carrying enough megatonage to fully destroy a major U.S. city within range of the missile that would deliver it. Miami, as it turned out, lay just within range of the delivery system. Despite all the economic sanctions previously lodged against the Iranian government to keep it from pursuing its nuclear ambitions, and despite a recent pact with the U.S. that supposedly ensured it would give up the effort, the Islamic nation had finally succeeded in producing enough high grade plutonium to manufacture its first atomic bomb in recent months, and it was this bomb that had been assigned to Habibollah's sub, though he had no current orders from Iran's high command to use it. Once launched, members of the remaining U.N. task force would claim the missile originated from Aquaria in retaliation for being attacked.

As the *Iron Fist* continued to creep closer to its intended target, so did the iniquitous smile dominating Habibollah's face grow ever larger.

-122-

Captain Delila pondered the current state of affairs, wondering what was causing the delay. The choppers that had deployed the Seal teams were still not inbound to the carrier at this moment. Though the team leaders, Lieutenant Myron Johnson and Ensign Patrick Flynn, had initially responded to his orders calling them back, he had since lost all contact with both teams and there was still no sign of the ponderous AW101's lifting off, neither from Aquaria's central structure or Navassa Island. He knew the cause that prevented further communication with the teams. Radio signals were being jammed over a wide band of frequencies, telling him the interference was not random but intentional.

As Delila scanned the sky from the carrier's starboard bridge wing, Ensign Jefferson returned at a brisk trot to lay the latest news on him.

"Sir, it seems we're being probed by sonar."

"You sure it's not some of the acoustical anomalies we've already detected in these waters," Delila remarked. With the area brimming with marine mammals, the water below them abounded with the echoes of bio-sonar propagating through the hydrosphere. They had noted other sounds as well, some of them highly unusual and seemingly originating from the sea floor directly below the floating city before the bottom dropped off severely into the abyss to the south. Those sounds tended to distort a clear picture of what lay down there.

"No, sir, it seems to match something we might encounter from a sub, but the sound is garbled by the other noise. It's coming from a source directly in line with Aquaria's central structure and roughly one hundred feet below the surface."

Delila nodded, his mind churning over this latest bit of information. With three Russian-built subs possessing stealth capability prowling the adjacent water, one from Iran and two from Venezuela, he wondered if one of them might be the actual source. Turning back to face the colony, he lifted the binoculars to his eyes to scan the sea in the direction of

Aquaria for the fifth time in as many minutes. "Maybe the captain of one of those subs wants to be sure they don't accidentally run into us," he muttered softly, trying to remind himself that they were all on the same team. In spite of this he continued to shift the spyglasses this way and that, a feeling of rapidly growing vulnerability suddenly plaguing him.

Before Delila could say anything more, Jefferson's phone buzzed. Holding it to his ear he listened momentarily before his manner went rigid. "I'll put you through to him," he uttered quickly, giving the captain a fearful look as he handed the phone over. Words spewed from his lips in a breathless rush. "Sir, we have someone who insists on speaking directly with you. Says it's urgent, that this ship is in jeopardy of being destroyed."

For one fleeting instant Delila's normally laid back composure seemed to unravel, but just as quickly he regained control of himself. Speaking in an uncharacteristically stern and authoritive voice, he addressed the caller. "This is Captain Delila of the USS Carl Sagan. To whom am I speaking?"

The voice emanating from the phone was obviously female and carried a clipped accent distinctive of the Caribbean, but there was no mistaking the urgency in her tone. "My name is of no consequence and we have little time for formalities, captain. I believe your ship is about to be torpedoed by one of the subs in your task force."

"Please identify yourself!" Delila demanded. His entire body went taut as he spun around to search the water for torpedo contrails.

"We'll do what we can to keep this from happening," the caller said quickly, completely ignoring the captain's query, "but I strongly advise you to get your ship underway immediately to take evasive action."

Delila shot a look at Jefferson, bellowing out an order. "Have the helm get us moving now! Hard rudder to forty degrees!"

As Jefferson bolted into the wheelhouse, the caller added one more thing before ending the conversation. "I think I should tell you a fourth submarine of unknown nationality has entered these waters. It arrived on the opposite side of the colony before you recalled your Seal teams, so it is doubtful you would be aware of its presence. It has since deployed a task force of more than one hundred men onto the colony's central structure before dispersing an equal number of men to the nearby island."

Delila's shoulders went rigid as steel as the phone went dead. Pocketing the device, he gripped the railing and leaned over it, his knuckles turning white as he searched frantically for telltale signs of streaking underwater missiles once again. As the ship picked up speed and began to turn in the direction of the colony, he braced himself in expectation of the shattering blasts that would rip the hull apart. If, in fact, torpedoes were inbound, the carrier would at least present a smaller target.

As the bow swung around to line up with Aquaria's central structure towering more than 500 feet above the sea, he began to wonder what the hell was going on here.

-123-

While Lieutenant Myron Johnson was happy about the recall, he was nevertheless disappointed in having to leave the facility so quickly. Since alighting on one of the larger landing pads adjoining Aquaria's central structure, he and his team had not encountered a shred of resistance. As far as he could tell, the facility was deserted, at least the sectors he had so far come upon. But having to leave so soon after entering the vast interior of the complex was a major disappointment. The sights that had so far greeted him were a visual delight. The alien architecture that lay before him enthralled the senses with a seemingly endless wonder of interlacing walkways and terraced decks that wound their way around rising pillars and beneath arching bridges. Serene pools, gently plunging waterfalls and gurgling fountains were interspersed everywhere. Smoothly curving walls, floors and ceilings rose and fell like waves in a rolling sea, much of it suffused by soothing multihued lighting ingeniously placed for maximum effect. Built into the walls in many places were thick panes and bubbles of glass, behind which swam multitudes of exotic fish among brilliant corals and anemones, further enlivening the city's interior with flaming reds and glittering iridescence. But it was the strange art periodically integrated into the whole that punctuated the fantasyland motif, and as he glanced around he could see that his men were equally spellbound by it.

With considerable effort he reminded himself he had been ordered back to the carrier, aware that the pervasive atmosphere which lay all about him was dulling his sharpness and drawing him into a stupor. The last thing he needed was to let his vigilance wander. Managing to harden himself against the alluring imagery, he spoke softly into his lip mic, and using hand signals, directed his men to follow him back the way they had come. Though he would have preferred to explore the place further, it was time to leave. The sound of heavy clomping, however, made him stop dead in his tracks.

Further down the winding walkway a huge figure suddenly loomed, and a short distance behind it, several more like figures came into view.

A mental alarm immediately sounded in the lieutenant's head, and without a moment's hesitation he ordered his men to take cover.

-124-

Staring over the shoulder of the sonar operator, the *Iron Fist's* captain eyed a new blip that suddenly appeared on the screen. It was closing on his stern.

Habibollah extended an arm, pointing at the object. "What is that?"

An expression of intense concentration consumed the operator's countenance as he listened to the echoes coming through his headphones, his eyes roving over the readouts showing on the screen. "A small submarine about thirty meters in length, captain."

Habibollah tracked two larger blips that abruptly materialized on the screen. His face lit up in a sadistic grin as they quickly converged on the smaller blip from opposite sides. With two Venezuelan subs guarding his back, they would engage the threat by destroying it with their own torpedoes.

A frown abruptly transcended Habibollah's features as the screen came alive with several more blips, four of them. They diverged into pairs, streaking across the screen from one corner to intercept the subs protecting his stern. In the blink of an eye, the pulsing dots showing *El Martillo* and *El Yunque* abruptly flared, and from experience Habibollah knew they had been torpedoed.

The sonar operator turned in his seat, exchanging a horrified look with the captain. "The Venezuelan subs are sinking and the carrier has begun moving," he decried in a quavering tone.

Flabbergasted by this sudden turn of events, Habibollah opened his mouth to speak, but before he could issue a new set of orders, a shower of sparks suddenly flew from control panels all around him. Unable to handle the intense electrical surge coursing through them, circuit boards fizzled to fill the air with the acrid smell of scorched plastic and biting ozone. Lights blinked erratically before fading completely, and the susurrating thrum of the sub's power plant could no longer be felt. Except for the labored breathing of crewmen, a hushed quietude descended to immerse the control room in total darkness.

Within moments emergency LED lights began to flutter on and off torpidly, but even these seemed to be on the brink of failure, and Habibollah caught sight of the helmsman's face in the feeble, flickering glow. The man was white as a ghost. In a faltering voice the helmsman broke the stunned silence. "We have no power. We are drifting blindly." He looked hopefully to the captain for guidance. "What can-"

His words were immediately cut off as several explosions rocked the sub on opposite sides of the pressure hull. Losing his balance from the jarring impacts, the helmsman was tumbled to the deck as others, including Habibollah, grabbed hold of anything within reach to steady themselves. Moments later something slammed heavily into the sub's starboard side, tilting the sub precariously to port. A quick glance at the inclinometer told the captain his vessel had listed by more than 40 degrees off an even keel. Several more impacts followed as the sub began to roll back to right itself, but these were less jarring, and to Habibollah it felt as if his vessel was being driven sideways by something colossal and ponderous. Looking all about him he saw crewmembers bracing themselves and holding on in terrified silence.

"What is happening?" someone cried out just as the LED lights failed altogether.

Driven to the threshold of mind-numbing panic, Habibollah's thoughts raced along haphazardly, frantically searching for the cause of their predicament. Somehow he was able to grasp that the *Iron Fist* was being driven to the south where much deeper water existed. That was where the seafloor dropped away precipitously, falling more than 7,600 meters into the Cayman Trench. Though he was engulfed in pitch black darkness, his eyes widened sharply at the thought.

Barely managing to hold onto his sanity by a thread, Habibollah shrieked into the blackness. "Purge all water from the ballast and trim tanks." Hearing his own voice, it sounded uncharacteristically shrill and brittle, as though it had come from the mouth of a stranger. Realizing they had no power, he kept a firmer grip on his tone when he amended the order. "Do it manually."

Hearing movement in the darkness, he knew members of the crew were groping around in search of the throw valves situated against a forward bulkhead. Pipes suddenly hissed as air began to flow, and with it filling the buoyancy tanks the sub would be inexorably lifted toward the surface.

Thinking his vessel was only moments away from rising, Habibollah froze as the pressure hull began to creak and groan, and he knew at once that the sub was sinking.

"The tanks have been breached," a crewman wailed forlornly. "I can hear the air leaking out. We are doomed."

As if in answer, the hull groaned louder, sounding like the moan of a dying leviathan resigned to its fate. With steel being squeezed ever tighter by the growing hydrostatic forces pressing relentlessly against it, the *Iron Fist* slid faster into the yawning abyss awaiting it.

Habibollah gritted his teeth and closed his eyes, anticipating the moment the hull could take no more. His torment seemed to last an eternity before the sub finally imploded, and the last thing he heard was the crunch of his own bones as he was cast into oblivion.

-125-

Percy Osgood stared in amazement at the multiple displays on the huge screen taking up the entire wall high up in Aquaria's central structure. Binary code in the form of zeros and ones continued to flash across one of the displays at a dizzying rate. Data which he had absconded with using the mechanical fish was still being analyzed. If not for the incredible decoding wizardry of the entity called Ez, the *Sublimis'* plan to annihilate a U.S. city would never have been brought to light. This had been something he had not known. Embedded within that data was an immense myriad of interconnected and convoluted schemes of cause and effect aimed at creating an insidious chain reaction of mounting chaos in the world designed to enslave humanity, much of it encrypted in high order algorithms much too complicated for even him to crack. But the artificial intelligence known as Ez was doing it rather easily, and she had been able to uncover the plot to nuke Miami in the nick of time.

Standing behind him, Jacob said, "Your actions saved the lives of millions."

"Yes," Amelia Amhurst concurred admiringly, "and with all the information you've given us, it might even turn out that you saved billions."

Percy nodded ruefully. "Unfortunately it was those same actions that led to the deaths of the men aboard those subs." He had witnessed it all via the marvelous gadgetry several of the dolphins wore. Jacob had called them DBTs, Delphine Biosonar Transmitters. The clarity of the transmissions they had received had been stunning. The gadgets had provided real-time video viewings of exceptional high quality resolution.

"Yes," Jacob commiserated, understanding his bereavement. "But there were no other options available to us. Had we not acted quickly, the missile would have been launched."

"But that sub was completely disabled," Percy responded dismally. "With its electronics fried, it could not possibly have launched that missile."

"We had to be sure," Jacob consoled. "Their weapons station may have survived the attack if the circuitry was shielded, and there wasn't time to determine that."

Percy shrugged laconically, taking a deep breath. Deep down he knew Jacob was right. Changing the subject, he tried to assuage the guilt he felt.

"You'll have to tell me how those transmitters work. Obviously you figured a way to get around the attenuation of telemetry transmission in an underwater environment."

"I'll leave that to Dr. Grahm, he's the one that developed them with the help of the dolphins. I believe you already met him."

Percy nodded, playing over in his mind the recent string of events he had been a party to. At Javolyn's urging he had managed to re-program the torpedo system aboard the *Nunquarn Satis*. With Javolyn giving him further instructions, he had parted company with the former Navy Seal. An albino dolphin named Hermes had swum him to the colony as a multitude of whales began pushing the drifting mega-yacht close to Aquaria's uncompleted section of outer breakwater. With Hermes delivering him to a discrete location along the base of the colony's central structure, he had met up with a large Haitian woman who was there awaiting him. She had introduced herself as Ez, and it didn't take him long to realize she was a holographic manifestation of a sentient, incredibly advanced computer system. Easily evading members of a Seal team that was prowling the facility's lower levels, she had escorted him to an elevator that carried them high up into the central tower. On their way up she had asked him specific questions regarding the *Kraken's* systems layout, projecting 3-dimensional images for him to see to make it easier for him to answer. These had been acquired from information held in the mechanical fish. As they were doing this, he knew she was hacking her way into the mainframe computers that controlled the immense ship. Reaching the room where he now found himself, Ez had introduced him to Jacob and the IBC news reporter, who was just completing a broadcast to major news media stations around the world. Somehow Ez had managed to usurp control of them all, paving the way for Amelia's eye-opening statements read directly from script on a teleprompter. Subsequent to that he had viewed the huge screen dominating one wall, watching intently as a small sub belonging to the colonists crept up on a kilo-class submarine provided to the UN task force by Iran. Having given Ez the code to remotely operate the torpedo system housed aboard Maximus' yacht, she had fired off four torpedoes to accurately intercept and destroy two other kilo-class subs owned by Venezuela before they could lay waste to the Aquarian sub, which was armed with a device that was able to project a tight beam electromagnetic pulse at the sub carrying the nuclear device. As an added measure to ensure that the vessel could not launch its nuclear missile, several albino dolphins had moved upon it to plant explosives on its ballast and trim tanks. To avoid injury from the ensuing lethal pressure waves put out by the explosions, the dolphins had been protected by what Jacob had termed PWIs – Pressure Wave Inhibitors. The albinos, he had learned, had developed such contrivances once the mysterious explosions started occurring on the lush coral reefs that abounded between the floating city and Navassa Island. But it had been twenty leviathans that had provided the final assault on the Iranian sub. Standing by in close proximity, a mix of humpback, gray and blue whales also outfitted with Pressure Wave Inhibitors to avoid injury from the deadly explosions, had used their combined strength to drive the sub toward deeper water where it had fallen away into the Cayman Trench.

But now Percy found himself looking at the screen to observe the latest threat that had arrived to assault the colony. The screen had split to reveal what was currently happening on Navassa Island and Aquaria's lower levels. His face clouded as he took in both scenes. Though he knew the Seal teams had been ordered to scrub the mission and return to the carrier, each had come under attack by unknown assailants.

Jacob stepped closer, reading the confusion Percy's face harbored. "It seems the man responsible for all this has gone to great lengths to make us look like the aggressors once again."

Percy glanced his way briefly before snapping his eyes back to the screen. "What do you mean?" he said, continuing to study the massive robotic forms advancing with impunity into the withering enfilades put out by the Seal teams. The firefights were intense at both locations. Inside the central structure along the lower level, ricocheting rounds were destroying artwork as they tore sizeable chunks from walls, ceilings, pillars and archways. On Navassa, Seals scrambled behind warehouses and heavy machinery to avoid being hit. He could see both units were effectively cut off from escaping to the huge AW101 helicopters that had delivered them. With the lead robots unleashing buzz saw bursts of overpowering counter fire, the Seals were forced to keep retreating, taking refuge behind anything available as they withdrew. Shielded by the huge metallic forms, heavily armed men in all black camos followed behind them, their faces and hands covered by black ski masks and black gloves. It was obvious they were preparing to overwhelm and subdue the Seal teams once the armored monstrosities leading the way overtook them and punched through their positions, but they seemed to be moving far too slowly to make this happen readily.

"Those attackers are supposed to be us putting up resistance against the UN forces," answered Jacob.

Percy appeared glum. "Is there anything you can do to stop them?"

Jacob turned his gaze on Ez, who answered for him. "It seems our primary modes of defense are failing us. Holographic representations of the albino art have no effect on the attackers and the ADS Three appears to be useless as well."

"Please explain?" Jacob asked, his brain already rummaging about on why this was happening. The dolphin art was their preferred line of defense. Though it could be highly debilitating to wicked personas, it was passive in the way it acted and essentially harmless. Through intelligence gathered by Jake, he had learned about the drug UN troops were now using to counter its effect, but the wave of black clad assassins currently storming the Seal teams were obviously not part of the UN task force, so he could only conclude they also had access to the drug. Exhibits of the esoteric art were situated throughout the colony, both in oil paintings and holographic projections, and in those places where there were no displays Ez could project three-dimensional images of it at will as long as a 3-D laser projector was in the immediate area, so avoiding it was impossible. The ADS2 - Active Denial System 2 – which Ez had illicitly appropriated and enhanced and now called ADS Three was their backup line of defense. She had used it to drive away Malikai Allotey and his Chilean commandos when they had tried to impose their presence on Aquaria. And while it could induce intense physical distress on the human anatomy, it inflicted no lasting bodily damage detrimental to a person's health. But why it was not working in this situation he could only wonder.

Ez turned to face Jacob, seemingly reading his thoughts. "Either the core natures of the raiders are uncorrupted, which we can rule out by simple observation, or they have effectively immunized themselves, at least temporarily, against our arcane art with the same drug the UN troops have been using. Since the latter scenario is most probable, that is the one we should assume." She stated this confidently, confirming Jacob's initial deduction.

Ez explained further. "A search of the data held by the mechanical fish shows the drug was developed in Plagiarius laboratories for the sole purpose of invading this facility. As to the ineffectiveness of the ADS Three, my sensors have detected emissions of microwaves that are counter-phased to our own. They nullify and cancel out the ADS microwaves each time I initiate a burst. Those combat suits are the source of those emissions. Apparently the people who designed those suits anticipated the possibility of microwave technology being used against them and installed a system to counter it."

"What about changing the phase of our microwaves?" asked Jacob.

"I've already tried that, but those suits immediately detect the change and alter their emissions to counter our own."

Jacob looked at Ez, shaking his head slowly in frustration. "Don't you find it rather strange that these people already knew about our microwave defense and were prepared to counter it?"

"Not really when you consider that those suits were already retrofitted with microwave generators even before I was able to acquire the ADS technology."

The exasperation pervading Jacob's countenance immediately changed over to puzzlement. "Can you be more specific?"

"I was not the only one to hack into the U.S. Defense Department's computer system to appropriate the original ADS design. Looking at the data uploaded from Percy's fish, it seems a hacker working for Maximus managed to get that same information long before I did. A subsidiary of Unus Universitas specializing in the manufacture of arms and sophisticated weaponry is the developer of those combat suits. They took the ADS design and modified it slightly before incorporating it into the suits as a precautionary measure."

"Why do you say precautionary?"

"As we know, microwaves put out by the ADS system have a frequency of roughly 2.5 gigahertz and can induce intense discomfort on the human body but will generally not damage tissue. But the metal components and circuitry comprising the walls inside those suits become a liability when subjected to those same frequencies. The metal and circuits will quickly heat up, so much so that the suit becomes an oven. The operator inside will be cooked. The result is similar to crumpled aluminum foil being put in a microwave oven. With the newly emerging ADS technology about to revolutionize modern warfare, the developers of the suit were quick to see this flaw and recognized the need for a defensive system to nullify possible microwave attacks being used against it."

"Wouldn't the counter frequency generator in the suit heat up the interior circuitry anyway?" Jacob was quick to point out.

"No, because the generating unit is fitted on the suit's exterior and radiates waves directly away from it."

"Then maybe that in itself will make it vulnerable to damage with concentrated small arms fire," Jacob said hopefully.

"It is shielded by two inches of a carbon-titanium alloy. There is no possibility of the Seals rupturing it with the weapons they carry."

Jacob sighed deeply, wondering if their troubles could get any worse. "Then how do we stop those metallic giants?"

"I'm working on it," was all Ez offered just before she vanished from sight.

Jacob clicked a button on the remote held in his hand, bringing a third picture frame to the screen. This one showed the Hind gunship sitting adjacent to the massive AW101 that had landed one of the Seal teams on Aquaria. Seemingly in conference, eleven men stood out in front of the helicopters with one of the metallic monstrosities guarding them. Almost immediately, Jacob recognized Malikai Allotey and Captain Francisco amid the group.

Percy suddenly spoke up. "Is that who I think it is?"

"Which one?" rejoined Amelia.

Percy pointed. "The fat, paunchy one, that's Senator Brent Van Heflin."

Amelia scrutinized the image briefly before agreeing. "I believe you're right." Turning, she looked at Jacob. "I hope you're recording all this."

Jacob nodded. "Everything you are seeing is being documented."

"Why do you suppose he would come here?" she asked.

To Jacob the answer was simple. "As Chairman of the senate's Science and Technology Committee, he has a legitimate excuse for being here. His presence will be played up by the media to underscore the environmental champion they have so tediously and cunningly built him up to be. At least it will be made to appear that way on the surface. But I'm more apt to believe he wants to make sure he gets a fair share of the bounty."

Amelia stared back in puzzlement. "Bounty?"

Jacob smiled. "Plunder, spoils, booty. His actual reason for being here is to take inventory of our assets and claim his share before any of it disappears at the hands of Allotey and company. My guess is this latest band of raiders are directly under Allotey's control and will make off with anything valuable they can get their hands on once they finish off the Seal teams. With the Seals out of the way they won't have to account for anything missing that was not nailed down. Furthermore, they'll be able to say we were the ones that wiped them out."

The expression on Amelia's face reflected nausea as her eyes fell back on the screen. "How is it that men like that get elected in the first place?" she said.

Jacob's response was concise. "Political ignorance."

"Is that the result of the widespread complacency and apathy you spoke of earlier?"

"It goes much deeper than that, I'm afraid to say," Jacob remarked, his manner becoming eruditic once again. "A rising tide of immorality among the populace may also be responsible."

Surprise showed on Amelia's face. "Are you suggesting that greater numbers of people are becoming wicked?"

Jacob looked back at her with sad eyes. "Not in the strict sense. I refer to the increase in vices that are taking hold of people. Drugs, sloth, greed, essentially anything that makes a person feel good and goes counter to a virtuous nature. A preoccupation with these things does not necessarily make a person wicked, but the general consensus in present day American society seems to have shifted in the way such behavior is becoming more and more acceptable. Vice, or as theologians like to call sin, tends to deaden the intellect. So as more and more people descend into moral depravity, they lose their natural probity. The Old Testament refers to this very thing when God says he will turn them over to a reprobate mind."

Amelia nodded in understanding. "So what you're implying is that a deterioration in personal values causes a person to lose their ability to distinguish between good and evil."

"Yes. Corrupt leaders are mere symptoms of the problems confronting America these days. The real problem resides in the fools that elect them. Their addictions cause them to lose sight of what is actually occurring all around them. They tend to ignore the growing problems and look the other way."

"But we've already exposed these men for what they are. I would think that will wake the public up."

Jacob shook his head dolefully. "Once they regain control of their broadcasting stations they'll say it was all fabricated lies made to cleanse our image."

"But the captain of that carrier called back the invasion force," Amelia argued. "Surely we've accomplished something."

Jacob slumped tiredly into a chair, continuing to monitor the screen and noticing that the band of eleven were now dispersing, with nine of them following behind the person operating the combat suit and making their way inside the facility as two others climbed inside the AW101. "Only if those Seal teams manage to come out of this alive," he remarked in frustration.

-126-

Mat was back in the access tunnel, this time making his way to the island. Though he was not a vindictive person by nature, the fact that he had turned the tables on Bolder gave him satisfaction. But now he had another matter to attend. Having been informed by Ez on the latest developments, he decided he would lend his support to the closest Seal team. After all, weren't they his brothers? From the platform he had counted sixteen of them disembark from the AW101 displaying the UN logo. The fact that U.S. Navy Seals had been assigned to provide the main thrust of the invasion force disturbed him. Obviously someone carried a lot of clout to make this happen, a person with their hands on the strings of governmental power. But Amelia's broadcast must have paid off. At least that was his assumption as to why the Seals had been ordered back to the carrier. And now another force of unknown raiders had come on the scene to attack the Seals and keep them pinned down.

Mat's cell phone came alive as he approached the end of the tunnel. "What is it Ez?"

The voice coming through the phone was abnormally low and filled with static. "I've analyzed the problem. Your best option for taking out the men in those combat suits is the explosives we use for mining the *guano*."

"I can barely hear you, Ez."

"That's because heavy jamming is in progress."

"Where's it coming from?"

"Multiple sources. Those combat suits and the choppers that brought the Seals here."

Mat mulled this momentarily before replying. "Then the chopper pilots must be in league with the new invaders."

"Apparently so."

"How many combat suits have you counted?" Mat asked, continuing to move forward as he spoke.

"Four on the island and four in the city. A band of one hundred and five mercenaries are moving up the rear of each group of four."

"I don't advise using explosives inside the city," Mat said. "You have any other options for neutralizing those combat suits?"

"I'm working on it."

"Tell me what you have in mind," Mat demanded. Growing impatient when she did not immediately answer, he pressed her again. "Ez?!"

-127-

Riding Alpha, Troy Jacob rose up into the vertical tunnel that gave access into the interior of Aquaria. Clinging fast to Omega, Melody was right behind him. In moments they surfaced behind a curtain of thundering water. It was the perfect place to enter the floating city unseen. They were behind the waterfall that dropped into the artificial cove, a shrunken down version of their birthplace back in Haiti. Letting go of their bond mates, they asked them to swim out into the lagoon for a quick reconnaissance. Having accompanied them, Perseus immediately shot off to assist.

Melody's face contorted in a frown as she treaded water beside her brother. "Is that a chainsaw I'm hearing?" This close to the falls she knew something had to be awfully loud to be heard above its pervasive roar. No sooner did she ask the question, the barely audible sound abated.

"I think that's the battle you're hearing," TJ said.

Shortly before their arrival the twins had been alerted by their bond mates about the firefight that was currently taking place above them. With Ez having been notified that the children were on their way via the network of interlinked delphine minds, she had used the facility's array of underwater acoustical speakers to communicate with Alpha and Omega, instructing the young dolphins to bring the twins to the safety of the subterranean cavern underlying Navassa Island. But knowing their parents were on their way to the floating city, the twins had gone against Ez's wishes to keep them out of harm's way.

A short interval passed before the faint din of a chainsaw broke the air again, this time a tad louder than before. It was evident the fighting was getting closer.

Mentally linked to their bond mates, the twins saw what their bond mates were seeing from beyond the curtain of water. Midway up along one side of the chasm they espied figures scrambling near the railing. With their gazes directed inward at their mind's eye, they continued to watch a towering form amble along that same railing as though in pursuit, one of its arms extended out in front of it. An explosion of light seemed to leap forward from the arm, and once again the reverberation of a chainsaw resounded.

Without warning, Ez suddenly appeared in the water between the siblings, startling both of them. "Children!" she reprimanded. "It is too dangerous to be here. Please go at once to the subterranean cavern."

Overcoming his momentary fright, TJ realized they should have expected this. Holographic projectors and speakers had been installed at numerous locations throughout the colony, one of them directly behind the falls. "Is that where mom and dad will be?" he asked.

"No, they are coming here."

"Then we want to be with them," Melody insisted.

The displeased look Ez had given them abruptly fell away at seeing the defiance lodged on their faces. Sighing deeply, she caved in understanding. "All right, then, but at least climb up into the chamber behind the falls," she said, pointing to the rungs embedded in the rock. "I'll let your parents know where to find you."

"What about Alpha and Omega?" both twins queried as one.

"Tell them to go back the way they got in here, but to stay close. Now hurry!" Having said that, Ez's form immediately winked out.

TJ eyed the rungs that rose up behind him, then looked at his sister. "You first."

*   *   *   *

-128-

Moving swiftly, Mat by-passed the primary cavern under Navassa Island, finding it necessary to avoid the throng of Aquarians that had evacuated the floating city. Taking one of the side passageways within the maze of naturally-formed tunnels riddling the subterranean karst, he was able to reach the steel spiral staircase that rose up into one of the large equipment sheds overlooking Lulu Bay. The shed housed heavy earth-moving equipment for mining the huge deposits of *guano* indigenous to the island. These included one Kamatsu 575 super dozer and a 988G Big Cat front end loader, both of which could be operated remotely. The engine of each had been modified to run on compressed hydrogen gas, as were every land-based machine in the colony.

Drenched with sweat and gasping for breath, he raced up the stairs, surprised to find the hinged overhead door already open and two heavily muscled, bare chested Haitian men awaiting his arrival, their torsos and arms gleaming with perspiration in the muggy air. Najac and Kilroy were the colony's supervisors in charge of mining the *guano*. As Mat poked his head above the floor, he was immediately greeted by the staccato din of small arms fire.

As he climbed the rest of the way through the door, Ez's persona suddenly materialized out of thin air, and it dawned on him that the shed was outfitted with a holographic projector and speaker, something he hadn't known. He did know the floating complex had literally thousands of these illusion-producing contrivances situated throughout. They had been necessary components in the facilities construction, primarily installed to instruct the resident Haitian labor force how to wire and retrofit the huge array of electrical and mechanical systems that abounded within the central structure, lagoons and breakwater. Using these projectors gave Ez a multitask omnipresence, allowing her to be in thousands of locations simultaneously while teaching the predominately unskilled laborers how to assemble components through step by step instructions via 3-dimensional diagrams and personal oversight. This had permitted the speed of construction to proceed many times faster than would have normally been expected. Having so many of these projectors on the surface of Navassa, however, was not as necessary, mainly because there were not many structures dotting the terrain.

"We have little time," Ez said, her expression grave as she pointed to four small packets of high explosives sitting on the concrete floor behind the two miners.

Though the packets were smaller than the ones Mat had supplied Jake for the raid on Cardoza's stronghold in Tiburon, the composition of the blasting material they contained was exactly the same, an ingenious mix developed by the dolphins that was many times more powerful than TNT or dynamite.

"I will attempt to take out those iron men with the bulldozer and loader," Ez clarified, "but should the attempt fail, the use of those explosives is our secondary option. In such an event you will need to use your Masker to get close enough to plant the charges on their suits. On the backside of those packets is a heavy adhesive that will allow them to adhere. Each time you plant a charge I suggest you get well clear. Only then will I detonate it remotely."

"Sounds like a plan," Mat muttered uneasily, unable to come up with a better one. "I assume you've already preprogrammed the Masker, but which of those goons out there am I supposed to mimic?"

"The iron men, of course, so try to match their actions. Their hydraulics are poorly designed and unsuitably powered, causing them to move rather slowly."

Eying the small rectangular packets, Mat noticed the radio-activated detonator topping each one and the gooey tar-like adhesive clinging to one side. "You mentioned those things are rigged with radio jammers. Are you sure you'll be able to trigger the detonators?"

"They are set to receive a narrow beamed milli-pulse of exceptionally long wavelengths. By the time the suit's counter-wave system detects them it will be too late. Now hurry!"

"I'll only be able to carry one packet at a time."

Najac spoke up. "I will bring the others to you."

Aware that the firefight was drawing closer due to the escalating sound, Mat shook his head. "No, bullets will be flying every which way out there. Let's hope the heavy machinery works so we don't have to use them."

Removing his backpack, Mat pulled out the Masker and strapped it to his wrist. As he did this, Najac and Kilroy moved to the shed's huge sliding door that allowed entrance for the heavy equipment and shoved it wide open.

Looking through the opening, Mat caught sight of several men in full combat dress as they scurried around the corner of an adjacent structure. One of the men was limping badly, one leg of his fatigue pants covered in blood. The man looked on the verge of collapse, and just as he was about to go stumbling to the ground his companions grabbed hold of him to carry him along.

Mat moved to the door, beckoning frantically and yelling at the top of his lungs. "In here."

One of the men spun, pointing his weapon at Mat and regarding him with suspicious eyes. At that moment a huge metallic humanoid form emerged into the open area between the two structures. Lifting its left arm, it swiveled the Gatling gun protruding from the end of it to track the men it had been pursuing. Picking up the movement, the other uninjured man shouted something to his partners just before pulling them forward to rush headlong into the shed and dive behind the dozer. It was obvious he had no time to consider whether Mat or the men with him were friend or foe.

Seeing what was about to happen, Mat pushed Najac and Kilroy behind the loader just before leaping to where the three soldiers sought cover behind the dozer, which sat sideways to the shed's entrance. No sooner did he do this the unnerving sound of a buzz saw cut the air as a storm of rounds pinged like raging hailstones off the heavy machinery.

"Who are you?" one of the Seals growled as soon as the enfilade ceased. The man's face was painted with green and black camo cream, as were his teammates. Already his partner was attending to the wounded soldier, who grimaced in pain as a tourniquet was cinched tightly around his thigh to staunch the heavy bleeding.

"One of you," Mat said quickly, pulling back a sleeve on his jumpsuit to expose the tattoo on his left forearm. It depicted the Special Warfare insignia worn by Navy Seals, a golden eagle clutching a U.S. Navy anchor, trident, and flintlock pistol in its talons. "At least I used to be," he added, a touch of regret in his tone.

The Seal's eyes widened with surprise and a glint of respect, but he whipped his weapon around lightning fast to confront the Haitian woman suddenly looming over him.

"Who's she?" he asked in a bewildered voice. The woman seemed totally unconcerned for her own safety.

"A friend," Mat said, perceiving the Seal to be the squad leader, whose name he would later learn to be Patrick Flynn.

"Please move back away from the dozer," Ez said hurriedly. "I'm going to pivot it around."

"I suggest we do as she says," Mat urged as Ez's form abruptly winked out, causing all three Seals to stare in wide-eyed disarray. "She's going to do something about that thing out there."

Flynn glanced all about him with disbelieving eyes. "Where'd she go?"

"You'll find out soon enough," Mat said.

With trance-like expressions, all three Seals followed Mat's lead as he kept low and scampered back from the dozer's treads. As soon they were clear, the dozer swung around, its front blade rising slightly to meet the metallic giant head on as it plodded forward to enter the shed.

At seeing this unexpected turn of events, the man in the combat suit opened up with another buzz saw burst to send hundreds of rounds caroming off the blade to no effect. Too late to move out of the way, the huge form was toppled over by the far more massive Kamatsu. Trundling forward, it ground the suit under one of its immense treads.

As Mat watched, the Big Cat front end loader suddenly churned to life and rolled out of the shed to follow the dozer just as another metallic behemoth emerged from the opposite side of the nearby structure. More than a dozen black-clad men swarmed up behind it. With their faces swathed in matching ski masks, they reminded him of marauding *ninjas*.

Mat turned, reading the expression on the squad leader's face and answering the obvious question before the man could raise it.

"Those people attacking you are not part of this colony."

"Then who are they?" Ensign Flynn demanded gruffly.

"That's the sixty-four thousand dollar question I keep asking myself, but if I could guess I'd say they're going to be played up as an Aquarian counterstrike force defending this colony. But don't get yourself in a dither, we still have a few more tricks up our sleeve."

Rising, Mat bolted to snatch up one of the four explosive packets lying nearby. Looking back at Flynn, he blurted, "Don't be alarmed by my sudden transformation. It's going to make me look like one of them, but please pass the word to the rest of your unit not to shoot at any of those mechanical things because they might very well end up killing me." Having uttered the warning, he activated his Masker.

Flynn gawked as Mat's persona morphed, his eyes following the towering giant as it trudged off in the wake of the Big Cat. Though it was justifiably unclear to him what he was witnessing, he spoke quickly into his lip mic, hoping he would get through to the rest of his unit this time, but the static coming through told him he was still being jammed.

Mat could only hope the ploy he had in mind was going to work. From the direction the last metallic behemoth had come from, he doubted the man inside it had seen the Kamatsu crush the first one, so maybe he would think Mat was one of his teammates. Though it was a longshot gamble, it was one he was willing to take, and he realized he was acting in a manner reminiscent of Jake's reckless behavior.

Holding to that thought, Mat made sure to not to proceed too quickly, mimicking the movements of these slow moving monstrosities. Pulling his USP-9 from its holster with his free hand he plodded forward, angling into the midst of the troopers in black.

The attackers appeared to ignore him, but made sure to keep clear of his hulking form so as to avoid being stepped on, seemingly focusing their attention on the Big Cat rumbling forward. Significantly faster than the Kamatsu, it tore directly at the second slow moving monster. At seeing it coming, the monster opened up with its Gatling, shattering the air with its deafening noise. The men accompanying it also opened up, adding to the torrent of rounds clanging into the charging loader, most of them slamming harmlessly into its enormous bucket.

Managing to flank these adversaries, Mat depressed the trigger on his submachine gun, spraying the tightly grouped field of men from left to right and seeing seven of them go down. All too soon, the magazine of his weapon ran out of bullets, but he was prepared for it. Letting go of his USP-9, he reached down to grab a fallen mercenary's Uzi. Squeezing the trigger, he finished off the other five as they glanced around in confusion in an attempt to locate where the fire was coming from. Dropping the weapon he held, he snatched up another Uzi from the hand of a trooper that lay dying.

By this time the loader had rammed into the second combat suit, rolling over it with its huge tires. Coming up behind the Big Cat, the Kamatsu's treads applied the finishing touch, mashing the combat suit into the soil and leaving it in crushed ruins.

Mat rounded the second building, continuing to keep his movements purposely slow as he swiveled his head back and forth looking for more of these giants. Spotting another of them beyond one of the other buildings, he plodded forward to meet it as more than sixty troopers dressed in black trailed in its wake. Following the direction of their pursuit he glimpsed a small detachment of Seals scurry behind a mound of dirt adjoining an open pit where *guano* was being mined. Picking up his pace, he caught up with the combat suit and nonchalantly placed the explosive he had been holding against the suit's rear torso. The man inside seemed not to notice as he unleashed the full fury of his Gatling weapon to strafe the mound.

Drifting away from the pack of marauders, Mat suddenly picked up his pace and sprinted for the Big Cat which was just rounding the building at his rear, aware that several black-clad troopers had turned to stare in his direction. No doubt they were perplexed that one of these giants was able to move so fast. Taking cover behind the massive machine which had come to a halt to protect him, he hoped Ez had noted the placement of the charge. With a heavy assortment of video cameras installed on the outside of buildings and at the top of the old lighthouse overlooking the island, he was certain she would have seen it.

No sooner did these thoughts streak through his brain, a severe shock wave struck the Big Cat, jolting it hard enough to partially lift the machine's gargantuan wheels facing the blast off the ground. The machine bounced heavily as its huge tires landed back on the ground, and leaning his back against one of them, he looked up to espy a mixed assortment of bodies and body parts go sailing end over end overhead before crashing harshly onto the karst edging the bay.

Three juggernauts down and one to go, Mat thought idly. *Number four, show yourself.*

A sudden burst of small arms fire clattered heavily a short distance away. Hugging the backside of the Big Cat, Mat leaned out to take inventory of the damage the blast had incurred. Those of the marauders who had managed to survive the shock wave appeared stunned and incoherent as they tried to rise on wobbly legs, making it easy for the contingent of Seals that had taken refuge behind the mound to systematically cut them down.

Preparing to move out, Mat discerned two figures running toward him, recognizing them to be two of the Seals he had beckoned into the shed. Touching a button on his Masker he reverted to his true form.

"Thought you might need another one of these," Flynn said, handing him an explosive packet. Flynn's partner also held a packet.

Taking hold of the packet, Mat said, "There's one more of those things with about thirty more of those goons still on the loose according to the intel I received."

No sooner did he make the statement his cell phone chirped. "What do you have for me, Ez?"

"The last faction of insurgents is chasing five Navy Seals making for the lighthouse." As if to confirm this latest bit of info, the sound of a chainsaw suddenly broke out in the distance to echo off the rising landscape to the north.

Mat noted a reduction in static coming through the phone this time. "You're coming in a little clearer than before, Ez."

"That is because three jammers have been eliminated," rejoined Ez. "If you want better reception, I suggest the Seals take command of the chopper that brought them here and shut down the jammer aboard it. Only then will they be able to re-establish contact with the carrier. It is evident that the chopper pilots are abetting the insurgents."

Mat pulled the phone from his ear and turned to Flynn. "How many in your squad?" he asked.

"Sixteen including myself." Flynn brought his gaze to the floating city. "An equal number have been dispatched over there."

"The chopper pilots that mobilized your squads are in league with those insurgents," Mat said, staring in the direction of the AW101 sitting downslope of him. "They're jamming your transmissions."

Flynn's eyes suddenly flared as he stared contemplatively at the massive chopper that had transported him and his men to the island, and beneath the camo cream smearing his face Mat saw the man's lantern-like jaw stiffen. By this time the nearby contingent of Seals had been waved over to the Big Cat by Flynn's companion, their expressions filled with befuddlement and questions as they noticed Mat in their midst.

Ensign Flynn immediately began barking orders. "Haskel, Joliard and O'Malley, get down to the chopper and arrest those pilots. They've been jamming our radios, so make sure you shut down their jammer. The rest of you follow me."

Mat watched momentarily as the three Seals tore off in the direction of the chopper before turning to Flynn, who now had only six men under his command.

"This guy's one of us and is here to help," Flynn informed the others. With an expression filled with trust and admiration, he stared thoughtfully back at Mat. "Any ideas?"

Mat brought the phone to his ear again. "What say you, Ez, any ideas as to how we proceed from here?"

"The terrain is too rugged for the dozer and loader to get up there quickly, so you're going to have to do this on your own. But I'll try some holographic distractions that might be enough to keep them occupied."

"Okay, Ez, we're on our way."

Pocketing the cell phone, Mat looked back at Flynn with a somber look on his face, knowing there was only one other place where a holographic projector was located on the island surface. "We'll have to play this one by ear." Having said that, he began trotting in the direction of the old lighthouse.

-129-

Reaching the topmost rung, TJ pulled himself up the rest of the way to follow his sister into the recessed opening resembling the mouth of a cave. Unlike the interior of the real cave located behind the falls tumbling into the cove, which their mother had never allowed them to enter, this one was well lit. As he stood up, astonishment flooded TJ's face.

"I should have known I'd find the two of you here," Phillipe said disapprovingly, his gaze swinging from Melody to TJ. "Why didn't you stay with Zimby?"

"For the same reason you refused to stay," Melody retorted defiantly. "We belong here to help any way we can."

Phillipe's stern expression softened and he let out a prolonged sigh. "You're right, I suppose. But now I have to worry about the two of you when I should be out there doing anything I can to stop this colony from being taken over."

"We can do it together," TJ offered brightly.

Phillipe shook his head. "No, you're both too small and will only get in the way."

"How did you know where to find us?" asked Melody.

"I didn't. When I reached the city, Ez was waiting for me and said there was something important for me to see in here, but she didn't say what. I had no idea it would be the two of you."

"There's fighting going on," TJ informed him. "We heard something that sounds like a chainsaw."

"Yes, I know. Usurpers are storming this place," Phillipe replied in exasperation. Ez had given him a hurried overview of what was currently taking place within the floating city, and it wasn't hard for him to piece together whatever she had left out.

The eyebrows of both children rose up, and they chorused a question in unison. "What are usurpers?" It was a word they had never heard.

"Bad guys trying to take control of this place. They're fighting against Navy Seals."

"Dad used to be a Navy Seal," TJ said, though it was a needless reminder.

"And so was Uncle Mat," Melody added.

Phillipe felt his growing impatience bursting at the seams. "I need you both to stay here. I cannot let you-"

Both twins stared dumbly as Phillipe suddenly grimaced, his hands reaching for something clamped tightly around his throat. Struggling violently, his eyes began to bulge in alarmed surprise as the mulatto skin of his cheeks rapidly took on a blue-tinged shade. It appeared as though he couldn't breathe, and within seconds his body went limp as he lapsed into unconsciousness.

"Phillipe!" the twins cried in unison.

Phillipe crumbled to the floor, and in his place the image of a man with a glowering, pockmarked face abruptly coalesced.

A bout of snickering laughter erupted from Captain Francisco Alvarez as he studied the children, his glower changing over into a malicious grin. "So your father was a Navy Seal," he said, his tone dripping with sarcasm. "Could it be his name is Jake Javolyn?"

Both twins stared back wide-eyed, too frightened to speak.

Alvarez shed the cloaker he wore. Having had time to examine it since departing the Southern Star, he had figured out its purpose. And now he had put it to good use, utilizing it in the same manner Phillipe had used it to skulk about Cardoza's freighter unseen. This had made it rather easy for him to sneak up on the very person that had escaped his custody and apply a chokehold from behind.

The captain could not believe his good fortune as he eyed the children. Eager to locate where the gold was stored, he had left Malikai and company far behind and struck out on his own. Moving along a maze of rising and falling corridors that wound through the facility, he had spotted Phillipe and followed him.

Making a show of pulling his *corvo* slowly from its sheath, Alvarez glanced down at his fallen victim, who lay face down on the floor. Kneeling, he used his free hand to elevate Phillipe's head, placing the blade across his throat. From the look on his face, the twins could see he was enjoying this.

"I will only ask you once where they keep the gold, otherwise your friend will die," Alvarez snarled.

"It's on the island," Melody said, horrified that someone could be so cruel.

"Where on the island?" Alvarez demanded.

"Underground!" TJ blurted. "It's kept underground."

A look of madness consumed the captain's face, and for one fleeting moment it seemed as though he would carry out his threat anyway.

"Where underground?" Alvarez hissed, continuing to present a fierce scowl.

"We can show you if you promise not to hurt him," Melody pleaded with tears spilling from her eyes.

The captain's scowl turned introspective. He had not anticipated this. If what the children were telling him was true, it meant he'd have to find a way of getting to the island without alerting the others. And he had to do this quickly, knowing part of the invading force sent by the *Sublimis* was already on the island and might have located the booty already. If this were to happen, there was no telling how much of it might disappear. As he mulled this, something drew his eye. It was the glint of polished metal.

"Why do you lie?" he accused in a distracted voice as he locked an avarice gaze on a pallet stacked chest high with ingots of solid, gleaming gold. Forgetting about Phillipe he immediately rose to inspect this spectacular find.

Both twins followed his gaze, surprised by the sight. Exchanging looks, a sudden gleaning flooded their expressions, and taking full advantage of the man's preoccupation they scurried over to Phillipe, who was just beginning to stir.

Transfixed by the glistening metal, Alvarez stood mesmerized for several seconds, his mind trying to grasp the full magnitude of the wealth that lay before him. Sheathing his *corvo*, he reached out to grasp one of the topmost ingots. It took a moment before a frown creased his forehead as his hand only met air, and the thought that he might be going mad registered dully in his brain.

"What is this?" he railed, continuing to grope the stack in front of him but finding nothing there.

"It's not real," a voice from behind said.

Alvarez spun, astonished to see Phillipe already recovered and standing with the children behind him. Insane rage gripped him at the thought of being tricked like this, and overcome by it, the double-edged, razor sharp *corvo* was instantly back in his hand. "There's gold here and you will tell me where it is," he stormed apoplectically.

Phillipe shook his head calmly. "No."

Alvarez gave him his most pernicious, intimidating look. "Tell me where it is and I will let you live."

"You're wasting your time," Phillipe said, noticing the Masker taken from him was strapped to the captain's left forearm.

Alvarez considered drawing his Uzi and blasting him but immediately dropped the idea. The *corvo* was his weapon of choice. He wanted to hear his victims scream. Once he finished off this annoyance standing before him, he would have those brats lead him to the treasure.

Phillipe studied the Chilean's face, trying to anticipate his next move. The memory of his encounter with members of the *San Carlo* crew eight years earlier was suddenly in his thoughts. The incident had taken place one night along the waterfront in Port-au-Prince when they had surrounded him. The one called Pedro had also liked using a knife on his victims. He had only been fourteen years old at the time, far too small to defend himself, and if not for the timely arrival of Jay Jay and Zimbola, Pedro would have gutted him like a fish.

Men like Pedro were stone cold killers, unmerciful and sadistic to the core, and Phillipe had no trouble recognizing the same predatory look in the Chilean's expression. Here was another of the same ilk, a man who took immense pleasure in doling out excruciating pain, and he knew at once Alvarez was a monster that had to be stopped. But he was on his own now, for neither Jay Jay nor Zimby would be coming to his rescue this time. By all rights he should have been afraid, but strangely and for reasons he could not explain, he felt an overwhelming calmness sweep over him.

Phillipe slowly drew back into a martial arts stance. "Men like you have no honor," he taunted. "Only a true warrior would throw down the knife and engage me in hand to hand combat."

Alvarez abruptly stopped his advance, scrutinizing Phillipe with a wary frown. He was unaccustomed to dealing with an unarmed adversary who showed no fear, especially when he was wielding his *corvo*. Stunned by the youth's audacity, he decided to take on the challenge. "I don't need this to defeat you," he spat contemptuously, resheathing the blade, "but once I put you down again I will carve you up like a cow in a slaughterhouse." When his threat failed to instill any dread in Phillipe's eyes, the captain's sneer reverted back to a frown once again.

Phillipe waited for Alvarez to come to him. With eight solid years of martial arts training under his belt, he felt he was ready to counter anything the man threw at him.

A silly smirk conveying an utter lack of caution was plastered to the Chilean's face. Obviously overconfident in his fighting skills and completely underestimating Phillipe's, the captain didn't even bother to remove his weapons or the combat belt holding spare ammo clips and other items. The wheel kick he launched was easy to avoid, and Phillipe had no trouble shifting his body clear of the boot intended to smash his face. Alvarez followed up on the maneuver with a spinning back kick using the opposite leg, and again Phillipe sidestepped the attack, keeping just beyond the range of the heel seeking his ribcage.

"I am going to enjoy killing you," Alvarez blustered brashly. Pompously self-assured, he was unprepared for his opponent's counterstrike. Phillipe timed his leap perfectly, delivering a flying knee that caught Alvarez under the chin and staggered him backwards.

Barely able to keep his balance, the captain stared back in shock and awe as he shook off the cobwebs rifling his brain, astounded by the speed of the move. Humiliation quickly caught up with him, and he came back at Phillipe with a vengeance, throwing a series of punches and kicks laced with intense rage. Avoiding the onslaught, Phillipe danced backward, shifting his body and head from side to side or keeping himself just beyond the captain's striking range, all the while looking for a counterstrike. Compared to Jay Jay and Mat, the man before him was not even in the same class as his mentors.

The opening Phillipe sought came quickly. Reversing his retreat, he sprang forward to smash his right elbow into the bridge of Alvarez's nose. With his entire bodyweight behind the blow, the man's forward charge was abruptly halted as he went down on hands and knees. With the speed of a hummingbird, Phillipe slipped to one side to assess the damage, noting the wash of blood spilling copiously from a deep laceration where he had split the cartilage.

Alvarez gasped, wheezing hard and unable to pull in air through a broken nose. With glazed eyes he lifted his head to stare back at Phillipe dazedly, idly raising a hand to his face to inspect the blood smearing his fingers. As his head cleared, insane outrage took hold of him, and he staggered to his feet to fly back at Phillipe like a madman, screaming obscenities in Spanish. Deftly avoiding a shower of ineffectual kicks and punches, Phillipe suddenly ducked under a nasty right cross to lunge forward with a powerful tackle. Catching Alvarez about the waist, he lifted him off his feet and drove him backward with explosive force to slam him into a wall. Knocked senseless, Alvarez lay motionless.

Rising back to his feet, Phillipe stepped clear of his fallen opponent to give him quarter. Alvarez lay there for several seconds, breathing hard and grimacing before raising a hand to fend off another blow. *"No mas, no mas!"* he stammered. *"He terminado."* No more, no more, I'm finished.

"Have you had enough?" Phillipe huffed. "I do not wish to kill you. Perhaps-"

Appearing listless, Alvarez suddenly drew his holstered Uzi and leveled it at Phillipe. Clambering unsteadily back to his feet, a dark, hideous grin came to his bloodied face. "But I wish to kill you," he snarled insanely. Squeezing the trigger, he fired off a volley at close to point blank range, his rabid demeanor turning incredulous as the discharge streamed into a dazzling corona of pulsating violet radiance directly in front of Phillipe.

Astonishment took hold of Phillipe as he realized there was no pain. Nothing was hitting him. He could clearly see flames belching from the Uzi's muzzle from less than four feet away but he was not being struck. In fact, there was not even a sound issuing from the weapon when there should have been. It was as though the brilliant flare of palpitating light separating him from Alvarez was absorbing the enfilade, including the sound.

Phillipe suddenly became aware of a twin standing on each side of him, Teejay to his right and Melody to his left, each extending an arm with something resembling a pyramidal jewel held firmly in their fingers. A flow of radiance spewed forth from each jewel to merge into the aura of violet pulsation that seemed to shield him from the deadly barrage.

The Uzi stopped firing as the last bullet in its clip leapt forth, and the shield of rippling light vanished. Still wearing a look of disbelief, Alvarez threw the firearm aside and drew his *corvo* once again. One way or the other, he was going to kill this adversary. Slashing the air wildly in a whirlwind of motion, he came at Phillipe again.

"I don't know what just happened, but you are going to die anyway," he screamed in a fit of blinding rage.

Aware that each twin had moved clear of the impending showdown, something flickered in the back of Phillipe's brain. Keeping just beyond the blade's lethal swipes, he moved backward.

An ugly leer formed on the Chilean's face as soon as he realized he was backing Phillipe into a place where the tunnel ended and the rush of a pounding waterfall could be heard. Forcing him back further, he suddenly lunged forward to execute an overhead slash. Phillipe was ready for it, however, and he shifted swiftly aside to leave Alvarez hovering slightly off balance at the brink of the drop-off. Turning quickly, the captain was ready to resume the stalk, standing momentarily at the edge of the steep precipice.

"You cannot escape me," he bellowed in frustration. "Sooner or later your head will be rolling-"

Phillipe barely heard him above the thundering water as the Chilean's eyes abruptly went wide. Looking down, Alvarez became cognizant of what amounted to a claw with five digits gripping his right ankle. With mouth agape, he let out a bloodcurdling shriek of unrestrained terror as he was suddenly yanked backward to disappear beyond the tunnel's lip.

Leaning over the edge, Phillipe saw him tumble end over end, the *corvo* held in his hand catching on one of the rungs embedded in the cliff wall a split second before the captain's neck intersected its guillotine edge. With his head lopped off, Alvarez vanished into the churning water far below.

Phillipe brought his gaze to Perseus, who continued to grasp the uppermost rung. Smiling, he sent out a thought to his bond mate. *Thanks for saving my hide, friend, but would you mind retrieving the Masker that bad guy was wearing.*

A thank you is not necessary, Perseus replied wordlessly, *but retrieving your Masker is.* Pushing his streamlined body away from the rung, he released his grip and somersaulted backward to execute a perfect dive into the water.

As both twins joined him, Phillipe couldn't help but ask, "What was that I witnessed?"

"We're not quite sure," Melody offered, holding up her crystal for him to see. "Grandma gave us these. It's a smaller version of the bigger ones being grown under Navassa. She says they gather in energy and might react to our thoughts."

Ez was suddenly standing next to them. "There is still much we have to learn about those crystals," she said, her gaze falling on the one Melody held. "At first I theorized they were only attuned to gathering in energy from seawater, but now it appears they are able to absorb energy in any form like a sponge, including kinetic, heat and even acoustical wave energy."

"That explains why I didn't hear any sound when he fired at me," Phillipe remarked, "but I'm surprised you didn't zap him with microwaves when he pulled his gun."

"That was not possible," replied Ez. "The microwave projectors are only stationed on the outside of this facility to repel undesirables from gaining entry."

"Well it seems they got in anyway," Phillipe contested.

"The infiltrators have several men in combat suits equipped with wave suppressors that nullify our microwave emitters."

"Then how do you propose we stop them?" Phillipe asked.

"For starters I need you to capture the large helicopter that delivered one of the Seal teams. There are no men in combat suits on the landing pad and the two pilots are currently stationed aboard it. Take command of the ship and disable its jamming device. The radio waves it sends out are far more powerful than the ones issuing from those combat suits. We have to reduce the radio interference so those Seals can communicate with one another."

"Why not just zap the pilots with a microwave burst?" Phillipe proposed. "They're outside the facility."

"The microwaves cannot penetrate the aircraft's magnesium skin. I cannot reach them while they sit aboard it, but my sensors indicate that aircraft may also be equipped with a microwave emitter capable of suppressing our own weapon. Also try to locate that and disable it."

Phillipe gave a resolute nod. "And after I capture the chopper and disable both units, then what?"

Ez eyed Melody's crystal again. "We'll cross that bridge once you accomplish the first task, but you might try using those. I have reason to believe the more energy they absorb, the more powerful they become, though it is strictly a theory which I have yet to prove."

A subtle flickering resounded in Phillipe's mind. It was Perseus beckoning him. *I have your Masker,* his bond mate said. *I also found a second one in the captain's utility belt, including three ammo clips for his discarded firearm.*

Phillipe suddenly remembered that Alvarez had also taken the Masker Bashir had worn during their firefight back on the Southern Star. Moving back to the edge of the precipice, he found Perseus clinging once again to the topmost rung, Alvarez's combat belt with holster clamped between the dolphin's jaws. *You'll find the Maskers and ammo clips in the pouches,* Perseus informed him.

Teejay retrieved the discarded Uzi and handed it over to Phillipe, who reloaded the weapon with a fresh ammo clip upon strapping on the belt. Pulling out the Maskers, Phillipe handed one to each child. "I want you to wear these," he instructed them. Turning his gaze back to Ez, he asked, "Can you reprogram them so the twins will look like one of the infiltrators?"

"It's already done."

"It's too loose on my forearm," Melody complained after strapping hers on.

"So's mine," TJ griped.

Phillipe was adamant. "Well you'll have to make do and wear them anyway." Moving away from the falls, he strode briskly to where the cloaker lay. "I want the two of you to stick to me like glue," he ordered the twins as he donned the cloaker.

"How do we do that if we can't see you?" Melody asked.

"I won't activate it unless absolutely necessary," Phillipe assured them, knowing Ez would not be able to track him once he went invisible. Even his infrared thermal emissions would be effectively blocked from Ez's scanning detectors when the cloaker was in active mode. That was why Alvarez had been able to sneak up on him undetected by Ez.

Thinking about what he was going to do, he looked behind him and saw that Ez had vanished from sight.

-130-

Idling up to one of several floating docks jutting out from a white sandy beach at the base of Aquaria's central structure, Kobe and Bashir tied off the *Exoco* and scanned their surroundings cautiously. Looking up, they could still see the upper portion of the massive military chopper resting on one of landing pads two levels above them. Before reaching the dock they had had a better angle in which to study it. Sitting next to it was a smaller whirlybird, but the armaments and weaponry jutting from it made it appear far more ominous.

"I wish I knew where those two mischievous imps went," Kobe muttered, the signature smile that normally pervaded his features completely absent.

With squinted eyes, Bashir surveyed the water behind him to once again take in the enormous yacht floating just beyond the uncompleted portion of the breakwater that was to surround the complex, yet again wondering what it was doing here. It seemed to be drifting without power.

Kobe followed his gaze as they climbed onto the dock and made their way onto the artificial beach. Off to one side of the yacht and farther out to sea he could just make out a speck on the horizon seemingly heading directly for the colony. "Zimby's gonna have me dangling like a mango from one of those trees," he grumbled uneasily, eyeing the nearest citrus grove topping a completed portion of the breakwater well over a mile away.

Kobe swept his eyes along the lee side of the mounded protective barrier lushly populated by various types of fruit-bearing trees and staple crops set in between the various pavilions, hydroponic structures and resident living quarters dotting the breakwater. The sheer size and extent of the facility never ceased to awe him. Once the final modules of the barrier were floated into place, the ring enclosing the sprawling lagoons and containment ponds radiating outward from the central structure would be complete. And after that happened he would no longer be able to bring the *Exoco* inside the enclosure in the same manner as he had done now.

Bashir grabbed Kobe's arm, hastily pulling him along until they were sidling up against one of the columns supporting the esplanade the next level up. "There's armed trooper's up there," he warned, keeping his voice low.

"Did they see us?"

"I don't think so. I saw two of them two levels up. They appeared to be heading for those choppers."

Kobe gave Bashir an anxious stare. Lacking military training or combat experience of any kind, he would need to rely heavily on Bashir's guidance on how to proceed next. The only weapon he carried was the spear gun he normally kept aboard the *Exoco* for occasionally spearing a fish that came alongside the vessel while he was still aboard it. Rarely did he go in the water.

"What should we do?" asked Kobe, dubiously eyeing the webshot held by Bashir. It was the only other item of any significance he usually carried on the vessel. Though it wasn't even a weapon, Bashir thought it might come in handy other than the knives used for cleaning fish, which both of them also carried. Several years earlier, Jay Jay had given Kobe the webshot as a present. In all that time he had never used it.

Wearing a grave expression, Bashir looked all about him. "First we must see if they captured the twins." Indicating a stairway that rose up to the next level, he added, "If we make our way up there, maybe we can find out."

Kobe swallowed hard, glancing out to sea again to espy the Angel getting closer to the unfinished portion of the breakwater. It was either risking going up against armed troopers or dealing with Zimbola. "I'm with you," he said, nodding his head vigorously.

"Let's go!" Bashir prodded, suddenly bolting for the stairs and taking them two at a time. Not used to such physical exertion, Kobe had a hard time keeping up with him.

Reaching the next level, Bashir pulled up short to survey the platform with rapid glances in each direction. Seeing no one lurking about, he bolted for the next flight up, which ended at the foot of the ramp leading to the huge helipad. Risking a peak at the top before exposing himself entirely, he glanced sharply about again.

"Where you get all this energy?" Kobe protested, gasping heavily as he came up behind him. "Lowanda said you still needed rest."

"Quiet or they will hear you!" Bashir cautioned. He now had an unobstructed view of both troopers, who seemed to be lingering at the fuselage door of the larger helicopter and apparently focused on something that lay within.

"Do you see the children?" Kobe whispered hopefully.

"No. Stay here. Those troopers have their backs to us. I think I can sneak up on them."

"Are you crazy?"

Without another word, Bashir bolted from his place of concealment and sprinted up the slightly pitched ramp. The two troopers stood shoulder to shoulder, making it possible to snare both of them simultaneously once he got closer. Bashir knew that Jay Jay had used the webshot with great success during a skirmish with the crew of the *San Carlo* eight years earlier. Once fired, it would launch a 12-ounce projectile from its 37-millimeter bore to unfurl a net capable of entrapping these men without harming them.

As his finger tightened on the trigger, someone suddenly materialized in the doorway of the chopper a split second before springing out in front of the troopers. "Whoa, Bashir!"

Taken completely by surprise, Bashir immediately slowed, lowering the webshot as recognition flooded his countenance. Phillipe stood before him, his arms held out in supplication as a de-activated cloaker draped his body.

"Easy there," Phillipe appealed soothingly.

In an instant, the two troopers standing behind him underwent a transformation, reverting once again to their true identities. Both gazed back at Bashir as Kobe caught up with him, the twins appearing chagrined by their earlier deception.

"I saw you coming from the chopper's cockpit," Phillipe explained curtly, turning to climb back into the chopper. "Give me a hand and help me bind the pilots. I clocked them pretty good but there's no telling how much longer they'll remain in lala land."

As Bashir joined him, Phillipe yelled back to the twins in exasperation. "Will the two of you please turn your Maskers back on."

"Sorry," they chorused as one.

"What am I going to do with you two?" the *Exoco's* captain chided.

Though they once again took on the form of black-clad troopers, both children fidgeted abashedly under Kobe's uncharacteristically stern demeanor.

"When Zimby catches up with Kobe he is going to rearrange my features to make me look like something that swims in the ocean. Are you happy?" Kobe's anger suddenly changed to exude the same jovial humor he normally displayed. "Do you hear me? The next time you see Kobe you will see a tuna with a face that looks like mine."

Both children erupted in laughter, the sound absurdly incongruent with their disguises. Their levity quickly subsided as a familiar though distant noise intruded on their senses. Turning, they espied the approach of a whirlybird, its blades slapping the air in a steadily deepening pitch. In moments the chopper flared to alight behind the Hind.

"It's grandma," Melody shouted to be heard above the blast of rotor wash as the chopper's blades began to wind down. "Maybe we should show ourselves." Looking at her brother she saw he had already done so.

Phillipe poked his head from the troop transport once again to note the cause of the disturbance. Jumping down from the doorway, he swung his head around to take a quick glance down the ramp to see if the noise had drawn the attention of any infiltrators. At seeing no one approaching, he ran to the Bell Ranger as the blades continued to crank at an idle.

"We need to get Victor to the infirmary," Amphitrite said, still sitting at the controls with Franklin next to her.

Phillipe glanced behind her, surprised to see Emmanuel and Chester jammed into the passenger seats along with Mortimer. Held between them was the former Spetnaz soldier, his shirt caked with dried blood. He couldn't help but notice how exceptionally pale and weak Victor appeared.

"None of the medical staff will be up there," Phillipe informed her. "Ez tells me everyone has been evacuated to the island."

"All you need to do is hook him up to life support. Ez will be there to instruct you, then she will do the rest. Use elevator A-12. Ez says the way is clear, but you'll have to hurry. Were you able to shut down the jammer on that troop carrier?" Amphitrite asked as she focused her gaze on the AW101. Before she had landed Ez had told her what Phillipe was attempting to do.

"It's disabled." At seeing Amphitrite was making no move to shut down the engine and exit the chopper, Phillipe asked. "What about you?"

"Mat needs my assistance on the island."

"Let me help you," Phillipe said.

"No, stay with the children."

It suddenly occurred to Phillipe that Victor had been with Jake aboard Johnnie the last time he had seen him. "What happened to Jay Jay?" he demanded.

"He's on his way here. Destiny is with him."

Melody squirmed in front of Phillipe to show her grandmother the crystal she had given her. "These crystals did what you said they would do, grandma," she proclaimed excitedly. "We wanted them to suck up bullets and they did."

Amphitrite elicited a smile. Ez had already informed her of this. "I just had a feeling they would. Now go with Phillipe and use those crystals to protect everyone."

With Mortimer assisting Emmanuel and Chester, the task of removing Victor from the chopper was completed, upon which everyone stepped clear of the Bell Ranger as the main rotor gained momentum to blast them with a rush of wind, and moments later Amphitrite was making a beeline for the island.

As the twins watched her go, they became aware of a multi-hued spectrum gathering in the sky. A rainbow was forming directly over Navassa.

-131-

Clomping along heavily in the armored combat suit, Maximus made his way slowly back to the *Kraken's* bridge. Maddened by the suit's less than satisfactory performance and the latest turn of events, his seething rage immediately turned to bewilderment as he clambered into the ship's cavernous control room. Body parts smeared the floor, and if not for the huge ruddy nose jutting obtrusively from a severed head lying adjacent to a locker, he might have mistakenly assumed Finley was still alive. A bloodied axe lay next to Finley's remains, attesting to the weapon used in the slaying. The door to the locker was wide open, and Maximus saw that several of the firearms Finley normally kept locked up were missing.

Swiveling his visored helmet to take in every part of the room, he stared all about him in search of the murderer. In moments he spotted two more dead men, but each manifested a single gunshot wound to the chest. These he surmised to be the computer technicians that routinely assisted Finley in running the ship. Though Maximus was indirectly responsible for the deaths of millions around the world, rarely did he get a firsthand look at carnage such as this.

Mulling what he was going to do next, Maximus moved toward the ship's control console, the hydraulic joint actuators of the suit whirring noisily with every step he took. The mechanical suit was a major disappointment regardless of its other attributes. It had kept him effectively sealed from the torrent of water inundating the ship's interrogation sector when the pipe had burst, and the built in oxygen supply had sustained him as he fought his way up into the dry levels where he could once again initiate the air intake. But now his Gatling gun was inoperable. Called a SPEFACS for short, the suit was supposed to be the latest generation in military grade Self Powered ExoFrame Armored Combat Suits. Though its designers had told him it was combat ready, adamantly stressing its invincibility against small arms weaponry, they had failed to mention how slowly it moved. Originally, the suits were intended to be used during the planned government takeover in Haiti, but recent setbacks had caused Maximus to use them in taking control of Aquaria instead.

As he neared the console, a panicky voice carried across the room. "Don't shoot! Don't shoot!"

Looking down, Maximus saw a man poke his head from a large cabinet beneath the console. It was Holland, the *Kraken's* Chief Technician.

Watching him withdraw his body from the cramped space, Maximus studied the terrified expression on Holland's face before reaching out to clutch him by a shoulder with the suit's free hand and lifting him from his feet.

"Why did you kill these men?" Maximus snarled through the suit's speaker.

Holland grimaced. The pressure exerted by the pincer-like hand was just short of snapping bones. "I didn't do it!" he screamed.

"Then who did?"

Barely able to speak from the pain, Holland moaned, "You're breaking my shoulder. Release me and I'll tell you."

Needing answers, Maximus set him back on his feet and eased up on the pressure only slightly. "Tell me?" he demanded, the sound projected by the suit's speaker reverberating harshly off the bridge walls.

"It was one of the men in the ship's brig. I saw him clearly before hiding, otherwise I too would be dead."

"How did you know he was from the brig?"

"I saw him when he was brought aboard. He has one of those faces you can't forget, the look of a madman."

"How did he get out?" The possibility that others may have escaped entered Maximus' thoughts, knowing how dangerous these men were. They had been neurologically pre-programmed for carrying out atrocities within the U.S. that were intended to increase gun control and induce politicians to take one step closer to repealing the Second Amendment.

"I'm...not sure," Holland groaned in a frail voice. "I think the locks on the holding cells released when the power went out."

Maximus let up on the pressure a tad more. "Are all the systems working again so the ship can be steered?"

"Yes."

Releasing his hold on the man, Maximus said, "Give me a view of the brig. I need to know how many escaped."

Holland brought a hand to his shoulder, rubbing it tenderly as he turned to a keyboard on the console. Tapping keys quickly, he brought up several real-time images of the holding cells on a wall monitor. The lone corpse littering the floor adjacent to an open cell door immediately caught Maximus' attention. Only one other door situated at the far end of the corridor stood ajar. All the other doors appeared closed, and from behind several of the barred doors the faces of other inmates could be seen staring back with the glazed look of zombies.

"It appears two got out," Holland said.

"Bring up the photos of the men assigned to the open cells."

"As the mug shots appeared on the screen, Holland pointed. "The one on the right is him, Peyami Pehlivan."

Maximus swiveled his helmet again to see if the man was lurking anywhere about. He knew that one was particularly dangerous, and judging from the gunshot wounds that had killed the two technicians, he had to assume Pehlivan was now armed and roaming the ship in search of more victims. Protected by the rigid, impervious suit he had no worries for his own safety. But Holland was another issue. Holland was vulnerable, and he needed Holland to operate the ship.

"Scan the ship and see if you can locate him," the *Sublimis* ordered.

In rapid succession, images of various sectors and hallways of the ship flitted across the screen.

"Back up!" barked Maximus suddenly, his sharp eyes discerning something on the floor where a corridor ended. Reversing the sequence of images, Holland also spotted the oddity, wondering how he had missed it.

"Give me a close-up," said Maximus.

"It seems to be your pilot," Holland offered, studying what the camera revealed. The pilot lay looking up at the ceiling with an expression of surprised horror frozen on his face, the remnants of a sandwich lodged in his mouth. White fragments of splintered bone protruded meekly from a gaping hole in his lower chest where a bullet had savaged his lower ribcage to leave his shirt soaked red with congealing blood.

"Looks like Pehlivan got him too," Holland commented nervously, his gaze sweeping the bridge on the lookout for the madman.

"There's a small galley down the hall," Maximus said, knowing the inmates were fed very little while penned up aboard the ship. Keeping them hungry was a necessary measure. The psychological programmers had been very explicit about this. Hunger would reinforce their desire to kill. "He'll be looking for food."

In moments a view of the galley came up on the screen, and sure enough Pehlivan could be seen standing at a refrigerator, periodically reaching in the open door and ravenously stuffing cold cuts into his mouth.

"What are you going to do?" Holland asked, half expecting the *Sublimis* to make his way down to the galley and end the threat.

Maximus ignored the question. "Do you have head cams?" he queried, knowing Finley had always kept a few handy on the bridge to keep tabs on his technicians.

"Yes."

"Put one on and key it to the same screen."

Puzzled, Holland reached into a cabinet and strapped the device on so that the tiny camera jutted from his forehead. Turning back to the terminal, he manipulated more keys. As he faced Maximus again, the *Sublimis* saw his visored image staring ominously back at him from the monitor, which was now split into two scenes, one showing whatever Holland was looking at and the other continuing to display Pehlivan wolfing down food.

"Good, now engage the drone."

Holland gave him a curious look before doing as ordered. Turning back to the keyboard, his fingers went to work again. A low hum could be heard, and within seconds a nearby section of deck flooring opened up. Something rose from the opening, finally coming to rest with its base locked even with the floor. It resembled the seat of a jet fighter. Directly in front of the seat was a joystick and control console with an assortment of gauges and monitor screen.

Shifting a quizzical gaze from the drone controls back to Maximus, Holland repeated his earlier question. "What are you going to do?"

"It's what you are going to do," Maximus snarled, swiveling his helmet to the open gun locker where a shotgun and Uzi still remained.

Holland followed his gaze.

"Take the shotgun," Maximus grunted. "Go down there and finish him while he's still distracted. The food will make him more docile and less eager to kill."

Holland gulped, a feeling of dread taking hold of him. "I'm not very good with guns," he found it necessary to say, a pleading edge in his tone.

"Do it!" Maximus growled. "I'll be watching from here."

"But-"

Maximus reached out to clutch him by the shoulder again, applying pressure like before. "Deal with him or deal with me, it's your choice."

"Okay!" Holland whimpered.

Behind the suit's tinted visor, Maximus' eyes narrowed as he considered something else. Continuing to keep a tight grip on Holland, he said, "Before you go, I want you to set the ship's autopilot on a course that will take us to the sea colony. Have the ship's dynamic positioning system kick in to hold the ship steady two miles from where the outer breakwater is still unfinished, but I want the bow facing directly at the central structure."

Holland shuddered, nodding rapidly in acquiescence as wetness beaded in both his eyes to trickle down his cheeks. Surely his shoulder was on the verge of breaking.

Maximus released him, watching him move like a wounded animal to the ship's guidance terminal to study a GPS screen and begin entering data. Unlike most ships, the *Kraken* had no steerage wheel at its helm. And while course and speed was run mainly by computer, the helm did have a small joystick, a main throttle for the stern drive, and a smaller set of throttles for both the bow and stern thrusters. This allowed an operator to manually steer or rotate the massive ship once computer guidance was disengaged. And Maximus knew the system's protocol was so simple that even a child could operate it once shown how to make the switch. All it took to do that was to move aside a guard cap and press a button adjacent to the joystick that would shift computer control over to manual.

"I set in the coordinates," Holland finally muttered tiredly as a barely perceptible tremor swept through the vessel. "We're underway."

"Good, now go."

Looking like a whipped puppy, Holland moved reluctantly to the gun locker to retrieve the 12-gauge shotgun and load it with buckshot shells. Turning to glance back at Maximus's armored visage one more time, he shuffled off to carry out the order.

Standing before the monitor, Maximus studied the screen to view Holland move down three flights of stairs and advance along a corridor. The small galley where Pehlivan was gorging himself was not far away, and he estimated it should only take Holland two more minutes to get there.

Feeling it was safe enough to leave his protective cocoon, Maximus touched a switch that opened the suit's chest plate like a clam shell, allowing him to climb out. Striding over to the gun locker, he grabbed the Uzi, inserted a clip, and chambered a round, all the while absorbed in deep thought that made him seethe with rage. He had been apprised of events that were currently taking place on Aquaria and the adjacent island. Just before he arrived at the *Kraken's* bridge he had contacted Dante using an encrypted satellite phone contained within the SPEFACS. Dante had told him he had no word as yet on the unit sent to the main facility, but the attack against the Seal team on Navassa was not going well. The task force sent there had been greatly reduced in numbers by unanticipated tactics that had destroyed three of the four SPEFACS spearheading the assault. But what remained of the task force was currently chasing down Seals headed for the old lighthouse on the southeast side of the island. It also appeared that the Seals may have reestablished communication with each other, as most of the interference caused by the radio jammers had mysteriously abated.

"What about the flagship carrier?" Maximus had demanded anxiously.

"Still afloat last time I looked, which was less than a minute ago, but she's moved from her earlier position," was Dante's response.

Something hadn't sounded right in Dante's tone, and Maximus had correctly pinned it down to evasiveness, for he well knew the carrier should have been destroyed by now. "Didn't Habibollah fire the torpedoes?" he had stormed shrilly.

A prolonged pause had ensued before Dante answered in a subdued voice. "The torpedoes missed their target and the *Iron Fist* has disappeared off my sonar."

"What do you mean disappeared?"

"She's gone. I am unable to pick up any sign of her."

The statement had made Maximus' heart trip violently in his chest. He had purposely revised his carefully planned timetable by stepping it up several months ahead of schedule. Upon leaving the Haitian coast, he had contacted a high ranking constituent within *The Order* and instructed him to have his agents short sell over two trillion dollars in stock market assets and to buy up more than ten million ounces of gold and thirty million ounces of silver. Habibollah's assignment had been the critical element needed to set in motion the cataclysmic event that would increase the cabal's wealth and power tenfold, but only if the nuclear missile were launched. Sinking the *Carl Sagan* and the decimation of Miami could be blamed entirely on the sea colonists.

At hearing such horrific news, Maximus' brain had gone into overdrive looking for alternatives, and he thought about the two Venezuelan subs. "What about *El Martillo* and *El Yunque*?"

Dante had replied in a near whisper. "Destroyed!"

In a panic, Maximus had immediately called back the constituent and commanded him to reverse all the earlier transactions.

The constituent's voice shrieked with hysteria as he responded with a rapid-fire reply. "We'll be ruined if I do that. The market is in freefall and precious metals are going through the roof. Gold has gone up five times in value and is still rising. I beseech you to let the market settle down before we attempt anything."

The news left Maximus only one alternative, and one alternative only if he was to recoup his losses, and that was to take possession of Aquaria's gold supply, including the actual mine. With gold having soared so high in value he might even end up richer than he was before.

Breaking from these disturbing thoughts, Maximus pulled a small case containing a syringe from a pants pocket. Swabbing a forearm with disinfectant, he inserted the hypodermic into a vein. He wasn't about to make the same mistake he had made before. Perhaps he was being overly cautious, he chided himself. It was broad daylight in the sky above Aquaria, and it was doubtful those debilitating holographic displays could be effectively projected amid bright sunlight, but he was not willing to find out without a little protection. He had severely underestimated the people he was up against, and so far they had been incredibly lucky in thwarting him. But that was all about to change. Maybe he was down for the moment, but he wasn't out.

Climbing into the fighter seat, he activated the drone before glancing over at the split screen to check on both men. Absorbed in recent events, he had almost forgotten about them. A puzzling frown came to his face as he realized the galley was now empty. Pehlivan was nowhere to be seen and the view from Holland's head cam was bouncing about in a herky-jerky motion similar to a bobblehead. There was no sound accompanying the video, which made any assessment of the situation even more difficult to figure.

As Maximus stared, the picture suddenly steadied, and he saw the tip of the shotgun in the lower portion of the screen. The lighting in the area was uncommonly dim, but as far as he could tell, Holland was standing in the hallway outside the galley. Perhaps several of the nearby lights had blown out after the ship's power had been restored, Maximus thought idly as he studied the image.

The image abruptly shifted, and he got a fleeting glimpse of what appeared to be a corpse that lay in shadow. With insufficient lighting available to provide clarity, his mind had to work hard to clarify the image more distinctly. It appeared the corpse was shredded beyond recognition by multiple shotgun blasts. The video immediately changed perspective, and he saw at once that Holland was making his way back to the bridge.

Satisfied for the moment, Maximus brought his gaze back to the monitor in front of him and hit the switch that opened twin doors set even with the ship's deck further forward near the bow. Seeing that all systems were in the green, he punched the launch button to allow the drone to leap skyward. A look of pure hatred descended on his features as he remotely guided the unmanned jet fighter toward the floating city at better than Mach 2.

-132-

Having landed the chopper on a flattened portion of ground surrounded by rugged terrain on the east side of the island, Amphitrite and Franklin scrambled up the sloping karst. It took them several minutes of arduous trekking to reach the base of the old lighthouse where the partially concealed entrance to the subterranean cavern was located.

"What are you going to do?" asked Franklin as they finally reached the water's edge deep underground. "You still haven't told me."

"I'm still trying to work it all out, but there's no time to explain. Wait here for me and I'll return shortly," she said just before diving into the water. The sense of impending disaster that had accosted her minutes earlier was now overwhelming, and she knew she had little time left if she was going to avert it. One possibility continued to nag away at her, however. Should her premonition be wrong, Aquaria was finished.

Franklin saw Athena rise up to meet her, and a moment later both disappeared into the depths. Standing there, he felt like an old man in comparison to his wife. For reasons he was unable to fathom, the passage of time had been exceptionally kind to her. Her looks had changed very little since the day she had vanished at sea many years ago. She still looked quite youthful. And though he had no way of proving it, he could only surmise it had something to do with that strange jellyfish. Coming in contact with it had somehow affected her physiology, maybe even altered it in some profound way far beyond his comprehension. Keeping up with her was difficult, for she continued to brim with the same tireless energy that had propelled her into world class athletic competition. Many years earlier she had been an Olympic swimmer, medaling with a bronze despite a serious groin pull that should have kept her from competing at all. She had an unstoppable grit. And while the fire within her still burned with that same fervent intensity, it now glowed with a luminosity more in line with the spiritual rather than the physical.

True to her word, Amphitrite rose back to the surface a few minutes later clutching Athena's dorsal. In her mind's eye she saw two lethal dangers fast approaching, one from the land and one from the sky. As she climbed from the water, Franklin saw she was holding two more of the pyramidal crystals similar to the ones she had given the children. Handing him one, she said, "We've got to hurry."

Franklin studied the crystal momentarily, knowing Hercules had recently retrieved four of them, so these were the last two. Suddenly aware of what she had in mind he said, "How do you know this will attune to my thoughts?"

"It will."

The timber of her voice and the way she had answered him left no doubts in his mind. Her belief was all too clear, and he trusted her instincts implicitly.

Franklin followed her as she made her way back to the surface along the same limestone passageway they had descended a short time earlier. Stepping from the entrance, he found the air to be unusually still and eerily quiet, but the transition from the dimly lit caverns into the bright sunlight made him squint sharply, and he became aware of five men in camos hunkered down behind the base of the old lighthouse. One of the men shifted his gaze and immediately pointed his weapon as he espied Franklin and Amphitrite approaching. A companion next to him seemed to be talking into a lip mic just before saying something to the soldier eyeing them, and for what seemed to be a brief moment of indecision, the man suddenly lowered his firearm.

Amphitrite scooted over to the Seal quickly, knowing that Ez had been able to contact these men. No sooner was she within arm's reach of the closest solider, the man flung out a brawny arm and pulled her in behind him. He watched as Franklin fell in behind her, studying both of them with an intense, inquisitive stare. "You're both lucky you weren't shot," he scolded sharply. "My partner here received a message you were friendlies a second before you arrived. So you're here to help, are you?" His manner abruptly shifted to one of incredulous skepticism at seeing they were completely unarmed. "What in god's name do you expect to do, throw rocks?"

As soon as he said it, the sound of a buzz saw knifed through the stillness, and a shower of concrete chips from higher up on the lighthouse rained down in front of them. Amphitrite saw at once that a piece of the holographic projector that was affixed further up on the lighthouse wall had come down with the concrete hailstorm.

"So much for that part of the plan," Amphitrite muttered amid the cacophony, but she was in no way perturbed.

Franklin also noticed the ruined projector, and he knew at once that Ez would be unable to perform the illusionary magic they had planned on using.

"You shouldn't be here," the Seal rebuked again as soon as the enfilade ceased, setting his gaze on the mechanical monstrosity just beginning to emerge over a nearby rise in the terrain. "I'm not even sure a bazooka will stop that thing."

A devilish grin came to Amphitrite's face. "Watch and learn, sonny, but I don't advise you follow our lead."

Before the Seal realized what she was doing, she stepped out into the open to run forward and stand directly in front of the oncoming metallic giant. Trusting his wife's intuition, Franklin jumped out to face the oncoming monster alongside her.

At seeing a man and woman without any weapons blocking his path, a befuddled frown formed briefly on the face of the man operating the SPEFACS. And then just as quickly, the confusion turned to a sneer as he fired off a heavy burst with the Gatling gun. Even with the protection of the tinted visor shielding his eyes, he was nearly blinded by an explosion of blazing incandescence burning a deep pulsating violet as the barrage streaked out to end the lives standing before him. Thinking the rounds might have set off an explosive carried by these people, he saw no reason to continue firing. The flaring light waned rapidly as soon as the enfilade stopped, and he was stunned to see both people still standing.

Amphitrite felt the crystal in her hand grow a tad larger from the energy it had absorbed. "Stick your tongue at him while we move to our right," she advised her husband. "Draw him in and make him mad. Get him to keep shooting. We have to keep him distracted."

Franklin followed her lead, quickly gathering what she had in mind.

Thoroughly enraged by the display of inflammatory antics goading him on, the SPEFACS operator moved to follow them before turning the Gatling loose again, this time hammering them with a prolonged fusillade. Squinting into the coruscation flaring back at him, he finally stopped the assault, only to be met by the same sight as before.

This is impossible! he shrieked inwardly, letting his emotions take control of him. They were openly mocking him now, gloating and dancing rowdily with infuriating smirks. Again he triggered the Gatling, and once again an eruption of pulsing light bombarded his eyes like a hot violet sun on the verge of going nova, but this time it was flaring with a potency greater than before.

Seething with hatred and frustration as he fixated on the man and woman before him, the operator failed to keep aware of the ground that lay before him. The terrain was studded with jagged limestone and dense thickets of underbrush where he now was. Fissures and sinkholes existed in many places, some of them well camouflaged by thorned cacti and other types of veiling vegetation, and completely distracted, he stumbled into the one Amphitrite had been drawing him toward.

The SPEFACS crashed down hard, jarring the operator inside. He suddenly realized he was stranded in a pit with only the top of the helmet jutting above the edge. Had he not been encased in the suit he would have been torn up by the razor-sharp thorns growing out of the hole. In desperation, he tried using his pincer-tipped arm to free the SPEFACS, managing to clamp the lone pincer on the trunk of a small sapling. The hydraulic arm whined loudly as the suit began to rise from the pit, but then the sapling snapped and the metallic giant fell back, still trapped. With the Gatling gun well below the lip of the depression, the operator could no longer provide cover fire for his comrades trailing behind. Hearing a din of small arms fire abruptly break out behind him, the operator suddenly felt helpless, but refusing to give up, he tried again to extricate the SPEFACS.

The hydraulic actuator screamed like a wild beast gone crazy as the pincer latched onto the base of another sapling. Throwing all the suit's power into the effort, the operator knew he risked blowing the servos, and all at once some of the systems began to fry from the overload, one of them being the radio jammer. Staring through the visor, he saw the small contingent of Seals he had been dogging scramble from behind the lighthouse to run past, and an instant later the sound of the firefight escalated sharply. With their communications now fully restored, the combined Seal unit sent to the island was able to regroup and initiate a coordinated counterattack that outflanked the enemy from two sides, catching them in a withering crossfire, and it wasn't long before the infiltrators were systematically mowed down to a man.

Amphitrite suddenly felt the approach of more danger as Mat charged up to stand close to the SPEFACS trapped in the pit. Held in one hand was a packet of high explosive. Shouting out, she got his attention just before he threw it down into the pit. Running over to him quickly, she said, "Hold off a minute, we need that thing in one piece a little longer."

Mat frowned. "Why?" There was urgency in his tone. The robo-suit had grabbed hold of the trunk of another small tree growing at the edge of the depression. If the threat wasn't ended immediately, it might get free.

"You'll understand in a moment."

-133-

As Maximus guided the drone toward the island, an ugly scowl came to his face. On the screen before him he saw a rainbow had formed directly over the old lighthouse, and as the fighter drew closer, he noticed a second one had coalesced behind it. The sight infuriated him. The last time he had seen such an atmospheric phenomenon he had been thwarted. *Not this time*, he snarled, clenching his teeth.

Bringing the lens setting on the drone's nose camera to full magnification, his face clouded darkly again. Figures were scurrying over the landscape like ants near the lighthouse, but already he could distinguish black clad forms sprawled helter-skelter over the rugged landscape. Farther away, he spotted the *Carl Sagan*, still afloat and seemingly unscathed.

Seething with livid hatred, Maximus contacted Dante via the encrypted radio on the control panel. "Destroy the carrier!" he ordered.

Dante responded in a voice filled with apprehension. "We have already lost three subs, do you want to risk losing a fourth?"

"Do it now or your life won't be worth so much as a drachma!" Maximus snapped, referring to the failed Greek currency.

In no mood for further objections, he ended the transmission, shifting the camera angle to the island's south shore where a cluster of large structures existed. Almost immediately he spotted what appeared to be two destroyed SEFACS smashed into the ground between two partially damaged buildings. More bodies, all black clad, lay scattered around them. Wondering what had caused such annihilation, his eyes came to rest on two pieces of heavy equipment rumbling over the terrain, a huge bulldozer and a payloader almost as big. Further away were parts of a third SPEFACS and several dozen more of his black clad troopers, all of them apparently dead, strewn over a wide swath of the landscape extending almost to the water. He had hoped the news Dante had conveyed to him was in error, but as his eyes took in everything the camera revealed, he knew it was all being confirmed.

And then his eyes fell on something else that made his blood boil all the more. Seeing the offshore platform was still intact told him Bolder had failed to carry out his pre-arranged assignment.

How can this be? he raged inwardly. The idea that every segment of his carefully crafted plan had come apart at the seams defied logic. Hardest to accept were the losses his invasion force had suffered. Using radio jammers to disrupt communication among the Seal units should have taken away any possibility of a coordinated counterattack. More than one hundred of his men had been dispatched to the island along with four SPEFACS that should have been unstoppable. Using superior weaponry and outnumbering the meager Seal team sent there by a factor of more than seven to one, they should have won easily, but his eyes were telling him differently.

Pivoting the camera more, he set his gaze on the floating city. Perhaps his task force sent to there was doing far better, he reasoned irritably. Within the confines of the central structure the Seals would not be able to resort to the same tactics used on the island.

With that thought in mind, Maximus reduced the drone's altitude to make a low pass near the lighthouse. According to Dante, not all his troopers had been decimated, and with the drone coming to their rescue it was now possible the battle for Navassa could be turned around into a decisive victory. Once he distinguished friend from foe, he'd blow those Seals to hell.

As the drone approached the lighthouse at supersonic speed, Maximus immediately spotted the fourth SPEFACS a split second before the unmanned jet flashed over it, and he realized it was trapped in a vegetated fissure with two people perched along its rim.

-134-

The precognizance that gripped Amphitrite was exceptionally strong as she glanced up at the sky to espy the drone swooping in swiftly. Hovering at the edge of the pit, she looked down at the visored helmet, letting out a loud, taunting laugh.

At seeing her, the operator elevated the Gatling arm to fire directly up into her face, and as he triggered the weapon, Amphitrite pulled her head back. Flames shot from the whirling barrels, and a dizzying torrent of rounds streaked straight up into the air. The drone seemed to buck as it flashed by overhead, and a moment later black smoke began to trail behind it as it tore off toward the western end of the island and beyond. The happening was an exact replay of the vision that had invaded her thoughts even before she had landed on the island.

"Now you can dispose of that monster," Amphitrite said, amused by the look on Mat's face.

Mat stared back in awe before tossing the charge down into the pit. Waving his arms wildly, he got the attention of Navy Seals fast approaching. "Everyone back and take cover!" he shouted.

Amphitrite began running toward the lighthouse with Franklin right beside her. Trotting past the Seal who had admonished her, she said, "Follow me!" But the man stood frozen with a dazed look, still astounded by what he had witnessed earlier.

Amphitrite stopped and turned to look back at him. "If you don't want to die, you and your men follow us!" she warned again. "That thing as you call it is going to blow." She knew how god awful powerful those explosives could be. Even the pit containing it would not fully suppress the shock wave, which would fan out in all directions.

Suddenly coming out of his stupor, the Seal turned to the other men and barked an order. "You heard her, move!"

Scrambling into the cave opening, the men followed Amphitrite's lead as she braced herself against a rock wall just before the outside air was shattered. The shock wave tore through the earth, jolting the ground under their feet.

A moment passed before Amphitrite thought it safe to leave the tunnel. Dust wafted all around her as she poked her head outside to look back at the lighthouse. Her worst fear immediately faded as she saw it had weathered the blast, though there was considerable damage further up along its side where it had taken the brunt of the explosion. She well knew that everything depended on the lighthouse standing.

Bringing her eyes to the crystal in her hand, Amphitrite saw it had doubled in size. Tilting her head back, she focused her gaze on the structure's pinnacle towering high above her.

Franklin caught up to her at the same time Mat did. "Have both of you gone crazy standing in the open like that?" Mat scolded. "You're lucky the man inside that mechanical nightmare had such a poor aim. I'm surprised he missed you at such close range."

Franklin smiled. "He didn't."

Mat's brow creased, wondering why Destiny's father would joke like this following such a close call. For confirmation, he swept his eyes over Franklin looking for wounds. "Oh, he missed you all right. Not a scratch."

Franklin showed him the crystal. "When you have one of these, you don't need to worry about being hit." At seeing the perplexity on Mat's face, he quickly clarified the statement. "It attunes to the holder's thoughts. Once you envision it gobbling up lethal energy directed at you, that's exactly what it does. It acts as a shield. For reasons we still don't fully understand, it's able to absorb energy like a sponge."

Mat continued to stare. "Can I see that?"

"Be my guest," Franklin said, handing the crystal over.

Mat turned it over in his fingers as various members of the Seal team congregated around them. "This looks like a smaller version of the ones we're growing for Big D."

"That's exactly what it is," Amphitrite said. Suddenly struck by another premonition, this one more foreboding than the first, she reached out to retrieve the crystal from Mat's hand. "Now if you gentlemen will excuse me, I have one more task to carry out."

Mystified, Mat asked, "Where are you going?"

Amphitrite glanced up toward the tower again before her gaze strayed to the horizon off to the west. Continuing to belch smoke and flames, the drone was still aloft, but now it was turning. "We're not out of the woods yet," she warned as she headed quickly for the door at the base of the lighthouse.

Mat and Franklin exchanged puzzled looks before turning to stare in the direction where she had just gazed. Suddenly realizing what she was up too, both men bolted after her.

Two years earlier the lighthouse had been retrofitted with a high-speed elevator, and before Mat and Franklin caught up with her, Amphitrite was through the elevator doors and on her way to the top.

-135-

Surprise took hold of Maximus as he examined the control console in front of him. The temperature gauge had suddenly risen sharply, indicating the drone engine was beginning to overheat. If he didn't ease back on the power, the turbine driving the aircraft forward at more than twice the speed of sound was in jeopardy of coming apart. The only plausible cause for the problem he could come up with was that the engine had taken a hit, and that thought alone made him scream out in frustration.

Letting up on the throttle, he swung the drone around in a wide turn, the need for retribution now overpowering. The desire to blow something to smithereens was maddening. The huge bulldozer lay directly before him, and as though his hand had a mind of its own, he fired off a missile. A rabid smirk transcended his face as a fireball engulfed the dozer, but with his need for vengeance still unsated, he looked around for another target to destroy.

Something nagged at his subconscious, and suddenly aware of what it was, he quickly manipulated a few buttons on the console, bringing up a video replay of the trapped SPEFACS in one corner of his flight screen. Pausing the picture, he studied it intently before magnifying and sharpening the image. Almost immediately his eyes widened in fury. One of the two people hovering above the robo-suit was the grandmother of those brats that had escaped him. Widening the view, he saw a half dozen Navy Seals nearby.

A cockpit alarm abruptly sounded, jolting him from his smoldering thoughts. Another glance at the temperature gauge reminded him of what these people had done to his prized aircraft. In spite of the power reduction, the temperature had crept further into the red, and he knew at once the unmanned fighter had little remaining life in it. If he was going to act, he had to act fast. Salvaging whatever airspeed he could coax out of the failing aircraft, he piloted it straight for the old lighthouse. Already he was down to 200 knots, with his airspeed continuing to plummet.

As he guided the drone closer to the towering structure, he espied a cluster of people along its base. Sudden movement caught his eye higher up, and he perceived a lone figure emerge on the tower's walk around observation deck on the outside of the tinted windows. Magnifying the view with the drone's nose camera, he saw it was that women again.

The warning alarm abruptly escalated into a piercing wail as Maximus drew forth the final ounces of remaining power from the dying engine, and the jet fighter suddenly surged faster. With his face twisted into a hideous malevolent smile, he simultaneously triggered the guns and all his remaining missiles, vaguely aware that he was screaming out the words, "Die, you bitch!"

-136-

Amphitrite stood fast as the fighter drone raced directly at her. Clutching a T-crystal in each hand, she brought them together and held them out in front of her as she focused her thoughts. Something akin to a spark flared brightly as the gems touched, but she had been prepared for this and had closed her eyes so as not to be blinded. Nevertheless, she saw the event clearly as it unfolded, envisioning a mental image of the drone coming on, its guns suddenly blazing and a cluster of missiles leaping forward. She saw the face behind it all, Maximus' face, a face of pure evil. The sheer magnitude of malevolence racing in on her was the worst she had ever faced, more pernicious than the late Colonel Ternier, more wicked than Erzulie, but like all things of a purely evil nature, she knew it could be stopped, first by capturing and then re-using its own deadly, destructive force to combat it.

Yet there was still the possibility of disaster. T-crystals could be unpredictable. If overwhelmed with more energy than they could absorb, the gems might very well explode, vaporizing her and the lighthouse in the process. Abruptly she dispelled this notion, setting her mind on only the positive, linking her mind with the others, the collective consciousness of the entire pod. It all came down to a battle of wills. Either the light would prevail or the darkness would rule. Standing her ground, Amphitrite felt the crystals swell in her hands as the wave of destruction found its target. There was no sound, nothing to ruffle her skin, but the drone itself was another matter. Far more massive than the combination of missiles and bullets hurled at her, it carried a kinetic energy that could easily disintegrate the lighthouse once it hit.

With her eyes shut tightly, Amphitrite only had to wait an instant longer before it hurtled in upon her.

-137-

Peering through the spy glasses, Captain Delila followed the aircraft as it streaked over Navassa Island leaving a heavy contrail of dark smoke in its wake. Heading directly for the old lighthouse, it appeared to launch missiles a moment before impact. A great flash of light followed, mushrooming out to completely engulf the towering structure. And just as quickly it seemed to shrink back in upon itself, disappearing to a pinpoint before vanishing completely. Frowning in puzzlement, he tried to make sense of what he had just witnessed. It was as though a powerful vacuum had suddenly turned on to suck up a cloud of hot gas before it could expand any further.

"Sir, we have another incoming transmission," Ensign Jefferson informed him, holding out the phone. "Sounds like the same caller as before."

Grabbing the phone, Delila put it to his ear, amazed to see the lighthouse still standing. "Captain Delila speaking."

"That fourth submarine I told you about earlier appears to be turning and heading your way. As a safety precaution it is strongly advised you steer a course of one hundred thirty-five degrees at full speed as the sub's immediate intentions are still unclear, but we'll do whatever is necessary to keep your vessel safe should those intentions be construed as truculent."

Delila looked in the direction indicated. Taking the carrier on such a heading would bring it south of the *Nunquarn Satis,* which appeared to be moving again. From his current vantage point, he had an excellent view of its starboard side and could clearly see a herd of whales now pushing it away from Aquaria.

"I would appreciate it if you'd tell me who you are," replied Delila.

Once again the caller ignored the question. "With our help, the Seal unit sent to the island has defeated the unknown forces the fourth sub had deployed there. You should be able to contact them now. Unfortunately, the other unit sent to Aquaria is still under siege, with their communications still being jammed, but we'll be assisting them shortly."

Delila opened his mouth to say more, but the line suddenly went dead. Turning, he addressed Jefferson. "Instruct the helm to steer a course of one hundred thirty-five degrees at maximum speed." Strangely, he felt he had nothing to worry about.

-138-

Amphitrite opened her eyes. She had felt Maximus' rage just as the drone vanished, and its sheer intensity had startled her. The feel of the T-crystals in her hands was now different, and as she gazed upon them she realized they had changed. Only one remained, but instead of a four-sided pyramid, this one was three-sided. She could only conclude that the two had merged to form a single crystal roughly twice as large. As she studied it, she saw the deep violet glow its predecessors had exhibited had also changed. This one gave off a soothing crimson light.

If only the pod had more of these rare gems, she ruminated in frustration. Almost immediately a new awareness seeped into her thoughts, and she found herself swimming in the depths directly below Aquaria. One of the gargantuan thurentra lay before her, and spewing from its base were hundreds of 4-sided T-crystals gathering on the seafloor.

Something jarred her from her reverie, and she realized Franklin was at her side with Mat standing next to him.

Franklin stared thoughtfully at the crystal in her hand.

Seeing the look on his face, Amphitrite said, "It seems if you hold them together when they are absorbing large amounts of energy, they merge into a single three-sided pyramid."

Mat leaned out over the railing to gape in all directions before bolting to the opposite side of the observation deck. Circling back, his expression was clouded. "Where'd that thing go? I don't see any sign of it."

Franklin nodded at the crystal. "Guessing, I'd say it's in there. Seems to act as a portal in which things disappear."

"Possibly an interdimensional portal," Amphitrite amended. Still linked with the others, she was merely parroting the overall conjecture of the pod mind. They were now aware of the potential.

Glancing toward the floating city, Amphitrite was not seeing the massive central structure surrounded by the vast array of lagoons and containment ponds. Instead, there was an image flashing before her eyes of more than a dozen albinos switchbacking rapidly into the depths. They were diving deep, following behind an enormous sperm whale. The image faded, replaced by something altogether different.

Franklin studied her countenance, noticing the semi-glazed look that seemed to take hold of her as she turned to circle along the observation deck before stopping to take in the view off to the east. Following her, he saw the object drawing her attention. An incredibly large ship was just emerging over the horizon.

"We have little time," Amphitrite suddenly blurted. "We have to get back to the city if we're going to save it."

Turning, she raced for the door that accessed the observation deck. Inside the lighthouse, she scurried past the massive 3-sided pyramidal crystal centered behind the tinted windows. It had been installed there six months earlier. It was an exact duplicate of the one in her hand, only much larger. Radiating a deep crimson, it was beginning to pulse. It was the final component of Big D.

With Franklin and Mat trailing behind her, she bolted down the spiral staircase that wound one flight down to the elevator, aware that the T-crystal in her hand was pulsing in cadence with its much larger cousin.

Amphitrite suddenly pulled up short. Athena and the pod were calling to her in a unified voice again. Franklin noticed the faraway look on her face, and he immediately knew she was once more in conference with those higher delphine minds.

Mat also became aware of her detached mien. "What's wrong?" he asked.

Amphitrite emerged from her momentary stupor. "We have a little mission to undertake before we go back to the city," she stated flatly.

Mat's eyes narrowed suspiciously. "Mission?"

Amphitrite nodded solemnly. "Yes, this will involve an abduction." Keeping a tight grip on the crystal, she could feel the quickening resonation. "Both of you hold onto me. We're going for a little ride."

-139-

The cetacean giant rose to within 100 feet of the surface and opened its massive jaws to expose a mound of T-crystals sitting on its tongue. One by one, a succession of mutated gray dolphins swept into its maw to snatch a crystal in each of its grasping appendages before streaking off in various directions. Hermes had gotten four such crystals at depth and had passed two of them on to Aphrodite, his sister. Interspersed among the grays, a smaller contingent of their albino cousins also shot in to make off with a few of the small 4-sided pyramids, one in each hand jutting obtrusively from under a pectoral fin. Apollo and Artemis had already entered the artificial cove inside Aquaria, as did Coral and Reef, all of them armed with these same crystals. These six albinos were to be the advance guard, the ones whose primary objective was to stop the robo-suit operators before they could kill any Navy Seals within the floating city.

A short distance away, Johnnie materialized out of the gloom to discharge two more albinos, each with a human rider astride its back. In deference, the pack of grays parted to allow them passage, and gracefully, Achilles and Hercules swooped between the sperm whale's open jaws to partake in the proceedings, each grabbing two T-crystals. Both Jake and Destiny reached down and grabbed a dozen more, each stuffing them into a pouch strapped around their waist. But unlike the advance guard, they and their bond mates headed for the open water to the south.

How far? Jake asked Achilles.

Six thousand meters, Achilles answered. *The ship is well clear of Aquaria's outer ring. Shall I tell the whales to stop pushing?*

Yes, but I want them at a safe distance.

And what distance would that be?

Jake thought he detected a little snideness in Achilles reply. *Hell, I don't know. Has Ez run any calculations?*

She has, but it's all based on conjecture, JJ, basically everything we learned in the last hour about these crystals. Ez surmises these latest crystals brought up from depth have slightly different properties than the earlier ones. In theory, there's no safe distance. If the crystals get overwhelmed with more energy than they can handle, all of us, including Aquaria and Navassa, will be vaporized. It seems Big D is somehow linked to them, so a chain reaction is possible.

Just what I needed to hear, more bad news, Jake griped.

You have to remember the power nitro fuel represents. Having remotely taken control of the ship's systems, Ez noted slightly over 80,000 gallons still remained in her tank. *That's a catastrophic explosion no matter how you look at it, especially when you factor in all the explosives carried aboard. You sure you want to take that risk?*

There was something in the way Achilles conveyed the question that made Jake reconsider what was at stake, and he wondered if his bond mate was testing his resolve. Everything they had worked for would be lost, and by their own actions if they failed. No, that wasn't quite right either. It would be the result of his own actions, for he was the one they all looked to for their mutual survival, for Aquaria's survival, and for future generations of the new breed. And though the albinos were light years above him in pure intellect, they all trusted his judgement with an unwavering loyalty even though that judgement might appear grossly reckless on the surface.

What am I doing? Jake questioned himself, blocking the self-assessment from Achilles. As he pondered on it, he realized there was more to what they would be attempting, much more. The causality was mind boggling, for he saw that failure would ultimately ripple its way outward to affect the entire planet. But there was also danger in too much caution, and no matter how he analyzed it, he knew Maximus and his cohorts had to be stopped, otherwise the bright future Tursiops was planning for the Haitian people would turn bleak, just as it would for the mainstream factions of the human race. If Maximus succeeded with his malicious schemes, widespread famines would ensue and huge numbers of mankind would die off, with survivors being sentenced to a life of servitude and misery for the benefit of an elite minority.

Jake needed some kind of reassurance, something to rest his hopes on. If it was solely his own life he was putting at risk, he would not have reflected on the possible consequences of his actions as he was doing now.

Is the pod able to glimpse the future on this one? Jake asked hopefully.

All we see is mist, JJ.

Then I suggest you put this to a vote.

It has already been done and the consensus is unanimous. I believe the term in table stakes poker is called 'all in.'

I should never have taught you that game, Jake grumbled, continuing to hold on tightly as Achilles surged through the hydrosphere.

An odd sensation suddenly nudged its way into Jake's thoughts, causing him to glance over at Destiny riding abreast of him. Behind her facemask he saw she was encouraging him on with a comforting smile stretched across her beautiful face, and within her eyes he was reminded of something he would always remember ever since he had come upon it in a book depicting the works of Robert Vallett, a famous twentieth century French poet, essayist and philosopher. *The human heart can see what is hidden in the eyes, and the heart knows things that the mind cannot begin to understand.*

As he stared into her eyes, all the encumbering chains of doubt fell away, leaving him suddenly electrified with an unstoppable determination. Opening his mind to his bond mate, he let loose the only thought that came to mind, a thought that to a large degree defined who he was.

Let's kick some ass, Achilles!

-140-

Temporary blinded by the intense light that had flashed on the screen, Maximus waited for the dots swimming before his eyes to vanish and his vision to clear. Able to see again, a bitter scowl formed on his face as he stared at the blank screen in front of him, unsure of what he had witnessed just before the drone crashed into the lighthouse. The thought that he had killed the woman only gave him partial satisfaction, and he knew he had much more to do if he was going to put an end to the threat these colonists posed to his grand scheme.

As he climbed from the drone's control seat, a sound behind him made him whirl. Expecting to see Holland, a startled look of shock seared across his face as he stared upon the deranged countenance of Peyami Pehlivan, the 12-gauge shotgun previously wielded by Holland now in his hands.

Pehlivan grinned fiercely as he pointed the shotgun at Maximus. Though his psychotic brain churned with a chilling madness, he had occasional though brief periods of clarity, and a portion of his once brilliant mind had pieced together what they had intended for him. He had overheard conversations of the white-frocked men who had tried to mold his thoughts using painful methods.

"Are you the man responsible for what they did to me?" Pehlivan asked. His tone was mild, almost as though he were inquiring about the weather.

Maximus recovered quickly, looking for a way out of this unanticipated predicament. In a desire to inflict pain on the colonists, he had foolishly let his wariness slip by assuming Holland had killed Pehlivan. How this lunatic had turned the tables on the ship's chief technician he had no idea, but perhaps he could talk his way out of this.

"Of course not," Maximus said, feigning offense. His eyes flicked furtively to the .357 pistol tucked into Pehlivan's waistband before shifting them to the Uzi he had laid on the floorboard of the drone control. It was just beyond his reach. "What they did to you, they also did to me," he went on smoothly. "I hate those people even more than you do and wish to kill them all. Perhaps you can help me. There are more of them aboard this ship." Turning his head, he indicated a door on the starboard side of the bridge. "They're in there."

Pehlivan followed his gaze, and as he did, Maximus sidled ever so slightly for the Uzi. He had previous chambered a round and the safety was off. All he had to do was snatch it up, point it and squeeze the trigger.

Maximus froze as Pehlivan pivoted his head back to regard him again. With his obtrusive hawk-like nose, he appeared like an avian predator sizing up prey.

Speaking quickly, Maximus pointed toward the bow windows, aware that he was a hair away from dying. "If we work together, we can kill a lot more of them. What they did to you, they do to a lot of people in that floating city."

At that moment a barely perceivable shudder reverberated underfoot as the portside bow thrusters kicked in to swing the ship a few degrees to the north, lining it up with Aquaria's central structure. The ship seemed to shiver again, more pronounced this time, and Maximus knew the propellers driving it forward were reversing to slow it down. The *Kraken* was nearing its preprogrammed destination.

Pehlivan's expression hardened, impaling Maximus with cold brooding eyes before turning his head to take in the city. Knowing this might be his only chance for survival, Maximus lunged for the Uzi, snatching it up in one quick adrenaline rushed instant and raking Pehlivan with a fusillade. Rounds stitched the lunatic's chest, staggering him backwards on his heels, but amazingly Pehlivan was able to fire back, and Maximus was spun around and knocked off his feet as a burst of 12-gauge buckshot plowed into his shoulder.

Maximus lay there for several seconds, his breath coming in short, quaking gasps. Somehow he found the strength to stumble to his feet, vaguely aware that his shirt was now sodden with blood. Taking inventory of his wound, he discovered his left arm hung limply and numb, with little feeling in his fingertips. At the moment there was no pain, but he was certain it wouldn't be long before it hit him with a vengeance. Nevertheless, he knew he would live. Setting his gaze on Pehlivan, he saw the man lay unmoving with sightless eyes fixated on the ceiling and half a dozen bullet holes in his torso. A slowly spreading puddle gleaming bright red moved outward from his body as his life juices leaked away.

Satisfied that Pehlivan was dead, Maximum staggered a few steps back to the drone control, his legs nearly buckling under him. Punching in a call to Dante, he needed an update on the mission. According to his calculations, Dante should have destroyed the *Carl Sagan* by now, but when Dante failed to respond, he flew into another rage. "Answer me!" he roared. It suddenly occurred to him he would be unable to reach Dante unless the sub had its communications antenna deployed above the ocean surface, so the sub must currently be on the move and too deep to do that.

Pondering the current situation, Maximus suddenly felt the pain in his left shoulder, a dull throbbing sensation that was quickly escalating. Knowing there was a first aid kit in one of the cabinets that Holland had hid in earlier, he gritted his teeth and reeled his way over to one of them, rummaging around before finding what he was looking for. Quickly, he pulled the syringe from the pack and injected himself with morphine, and in moments he felt the pain begin to subside.

Rising back to his feet, Maximus turned to study the colony in the distance. Almost immediately, a dark, livid scowl enfolded his features as his eyes fell upon the double rainbow he had seen earlier. And now a third one was forming behind those, perfectly framing the other two.

Out of the corner of his eye, he was stunned to see Pehlivan back on his feet, the .357 magnum aimed directly at him. A wavering amused grin hung on Pehlivan's face as he stared back at Maximus. Standing there on unsteady legs, he struggled for breath, and in a halting reedy voice that was barely audible he managed to utter the only words Maximus would ever hear again. "Perhaps... we were always meant...to see the wonders of hell together."

The gun in Pehlivan's hand erupted just before he collapsed, dead before he hit the floor. With the morphine coursing through Maximus' veins, he sensed rather than felt the bullet pierce his chest. Knowing that this time he was truly dying, he staggered on wobbly legs to the helm controls and lifted the guard cap that would allow him to override the autopilot. Awkwardly and with a trembling hand, he punched the button giving him manual control of the ship. With his last remaining strength, he pushed the *Kraken's* throttle all the way forward before his body slumped slowly to the floor.

Dully aware that his life was ebbing away, a feeble smile crossed his face, no longer caring about the task force he had sent to Aquaria, including Van Heflin and Allotey. Having spent most of his life planning and scheming, he had one last card to play. It was his ace in the hole, one he had kept in reserve should his life become forfeit, though he had never imagined it would end like this. With his vision rapidly fading, he groped with tremulous fingers for his Emperador Temple wristwatch and twisted the diamond-studded face. Even to his failing ears he heard the low hum. It was now emitting a powerful microwave that would be picked up by satellite and relayed to a covert base in Venezuela. It would be his final legacy to an ungrateful world. Even before his final breath came, he was happy in the knowledge he would be putting an end to everything the people who had thwarted him had been trying to accomplish.

-141-

That submarine is closing fast, Achilles informed Jake. *As you like to say, they're taking the bait.*

I wouldn't go so far as to say that, Jake qualified. *It seems the commander of that sub is more afraid of Maximus than he is of us, this in spite of what happened to the other three subs in their task force.*

Through the telepathic network the albinos used, Achilles had shared that news with Jake earlier on, also letting him know what Ez had learned a short time ago. Ez had intercepted Maximus' last transmission to the sub commander and had cracked the encryption. The commander's response and tone were enough to convince her of his reticence to actually carry out the order, but now she was certain of his intentions.

Directly in the path of the sub was the *Nunquarn Satis*, and just south of the mega-yacht and below her keel was where the foursome of Jake, Destiny, Achilles and Hercules waited.

Any word on the Kraken? Jake asked anxiously.

Thirty seconds, JJ.

Jake grimaced inwardly, knowing how close this was going to be. And maybe not close at all. Ez had run the calculations. The amount of energy they would need would put them right on the edge, a very precarious edge, most of it based on pure speculation and assumptions. She had felt it only fair to tell them the odds were not favorable, maybe 50 percent at best, but they had no choice but to try anyway, and the only immediate source of that energy was a combination of what the mega-yacht and oncoming sub held within their holds.

Why a man like Maximus would make a suicide run at the colony, he could not imagine…unless…

Achilles burst into his thoughts. *Maximus is dead, JJ.*

How do you know?

Amphitrite saw him die.

One of her visions?

Yes, JJ. I recommend you keep your eyes closed. Ez is going to remotely launch a torpedo at close to point blank range in two more seconds.

Jake became aware of the sub, a huge black shadow suddenly taking on shape as it materialized out of the hydrospheric void. Strangely, he felt at peace. Turning his head, he looked at Destiny sitting astride her mount next to him. She stared back, her eyes seemingly radiating a stream of love in its purest form. Though she held a T-crystal in each hand out in front of her, her gaze never wavered from his face. Even now she was a complete mystery to him, and like a parched man coming upon a water well in the midst of a searing desert, he could not get enough of her, drinking in her profound beauty to savor her sweet enigmatic essence, an essence that seemed to fluctuate somewhere between temporal and spiritual realms. If he was going to die, he wanted her face to be the last thing he would ever see in this world.

Closing his eyes, Jake kept her image firmly entrenched in his mind as he held his own crystals out before him. With Achilles and Hercules bearing four more crystals between them, the foursome was joined by others. More than a hundred crystal-bearing dolphins spread out on each side of them, each separated from its neighbor by 150 meters. In unison they formed a semi-circular phalanx out in front of the oncoming sub, but only the foursome floated directly in its path. If they were all going to die,

Jake could think of no better way to go than being with the woman he loved and his loyal friend, Achilles. He only wished his children were also with him.

A subtle whooshing sound caught his ear heralding the torpedo's launch, and an instant later he sensed a mammoth radiant burst. Involuntarily, Jake's arms were flung wide, nearly wrenched from their sockets as the crystals he held pushed away from one another in the way magnetic poles of similar polarity will repel, but with an unexpected potency and violence. And then just as quickly they flew back together as though they were polar opposites.

Jake was abruptly struck by a massive sensation of vertigo, and he felt himself spinning out of control, no longer feeling Achilles under him. Doggedly he continued to keep a firm grip on the T-crystals, but something had now changed in the way they felt. Risking a peek at his surroundings, he looked for Destiny, but she was no longer next to him.

-142-

Captain Delila stared in disbelief. The huge mega-yacht, *Nunquarn Satis*, had seemed to disappear in a monstrous flash that had first expanded before collapsing in on itself. There had been no sound or shock wave. The fireball had simply contracted to a pinpoint and then vanished, but not before the sea beneath it had risen up sharply in a towering mountain better than 300 feet in height, and for one fleeting moment he thought it would surge forward to swamp the carrier. But amazingly and for reasons beyond his comprehension, the sea abruptly settled to once again reveal the *Kraken* in the distance as it headed straight for the heart of Aquaria.

My god! thought Delila. *The damage will be unimaginable. The oil spill alone will destroy the marine habitat and kill off most of the nearby sea life.*

As he looked upon the impending disaster, his eyes suddenly narrowed with that same puzzlement as before, and he wondered if perhaps his mind was playing tricks on him. Something odd was happening in the distance. Lifting the binoculars to his eyes, he studied the strange phenomenon. Directly ahead of the enormous tanker the air was beginning to shimmer weirdly, growing brighter by the second. Totally bewildered, he continued to watch as a gigantic dome-shaped bubble began to form. It appeared like a great, impossibly huge diaphanous canopy that seemed to enclose the floating city and the island behind it, its closest reach seeming to extend just beyond Aquaria's southern perimeter where the breakwater had yet to be completed.

Continuing to stare through the glasses, Delila noticed that the dome was now glowing with a deep pulsating crimson, and as he puzzled over it, he saw the cause. The apex of the old lighthouse was radiating dazzling ethereal bursts of the same spectral frequency. And now the resonance seemed to be speeding up, making the canopy appear like a mass of dappled molten crimson that obscured all it enclosed.

What am I looking at? he could only wonder.

Just as he completed the thought, *the Kraken's* bow met the dome of light, and a strange, unearthly glow of blinding scintillation seemed to leap forth from its liquid surface as the ship passed into it.

Delila kept the glasses focused until the ship's stern slipped through, and a moment later the pulsating dome dissipated as though it had never existed. A gasp of stark realization escaped the captain's throat.

The *Kraken* was gone.

-143-

The inexplicable force that caused Jake to spin dizzily out of control suddenly abated, and he found himself in a familiar place. A rapid dawning began to impinge on his awareness, and with his base consciousness rekindled, he instinctively grasped the nature of things he was seeing and feeling. He was in the same endless dodecahedron he had been taken to twice before. It was a timeless volume of space so vast that the twelve planes bounding it appeared to extend to infinity where he assumed they intersected. His mind was incredibly lucid and agile, and from experience he knew he was mentally conjoined with all the other albino minds in the super-mind meld they occasionally formed. And if not for this he surmised he would have been unable to grasp the true reality that existed all around him. The laws of physics were different in this place. Time and distance were non-existent here. But what the human brain would normally deem as being impossible in the limited 4-dimensional subspace to which it was naturally attuned, in this place of higher dimensionality anything was possible.

Fully enraptured, Jake felt his inner being reasserting itself, that part of him that was intrinsically pure and uncontaminated by blinding presumption. In this realm, miracles did not exist, for miracles were merely shadows of phenomena that intruded their way into the subspace the lower mind had come to know. In the subspace of human consciousness, miracles transgressed the physical laws of space-time, but in higher dimensions those same laws were superfluous.

DOLPHIN RIDERS

Jake sensed the synchronous joining of spirits all about him, a globular cluster seemingly in orbit about a glowing astral body he knew to be Destiny. She was the lens through which the others were channeling their combined thoughts. Together they forged a singular consciousness that evoked the luminous side of the cosmos, the ethereal, imponderable substance comprising the true essence of hyperspace, the very thing that gave matter pattern and form. And that was unconditional love. It was filling the heavens with sweet harmonious music with infinite keys, resonating between the stars and flowing rampantly everywhere he looked. Fully enlightened by the awesome energy that abounded all around him, it was all so clear to him. Here was an ally offering an unlimited array of vibratory tones. Played correctly, a future of their choosing was not only possible, but probable.

Jake studied the curvature of the ethereal landscape entwining him, and he now understood the power of healing, the positive energy that made all things possible, its purity able to strip away the physical deceptions that trick the unenlightened senses. Awash in the endless range of it, he suddenly became cognizant of an incongruous disturbance within the midst of such harmony. It eclipsed his perception, an inconceivably titanic shadow that seemed to both shrink and elongate as it stretched out along one of the infinite planes, and he knew at once it was the *Kraken*. And then it vanished, swallowed by what he perceived to be the nimbus of a nearby sun.

Jay Jay, the pod mind called out to him, *you are needed elsewhere. Grab hold of the rainbow before it disappears or you will be too late to intervene. Please hurry.*

Jake saw the tail end of the multi-hued thread whipping about erratically like a feather in the wind. It seemed to be beyond his reach. But as he extended an arm to infinity, he was able to take hold of it before it was gone.

All at once, the exhilarating lucidity he had felt seemed to fall away like wings on a cloud, and he found himself earthbound standing waist-deep in a shallow pool with a fountain playing gently over the water. It took a moment to register before he realized where he was. The pool was located in the middle of a winding gallery situated in an upper level of Aquaria. Sensing something in his hand, he realized it was a 3-sided pyramidal T-crystal, and he knew the two crystals he had previously held had fused into one.

Perplexed, Jake sent a mental query to his bond mate. *What just happened, Achilles?*

With focused thoughts, these crystals can also act as portals, JJ, but only those that are three-sided. They can be used for teleportation.

How did you discover that?

We didn't, Ez did. Based on observations she made on the amount of mass conversions and energy these crystals are capable of absorbing, she developed an algorithm that predicted what would happen if a threshold were reached and it proved correct.

Spare me the details. Where's Destiny?

She's with Jacob and the children.

Jake looked all about him, still baffled. The gallery was empty. *But why am I here?*

We put you there. Beware, danger is afoot. We look to you to neutralize it.

Jake moved to a nearby archway. Beyond it was the entrance to the infirmary where he knew Victor had been taken. A vision of what lay inside suddenly came to him, and he saw the reason why he had been summoned. Malikai Allotey hovered threateningly over Victor, who lay in one of the beds used for life support. Next to him stood a portly individual who carried an air of authority about him. Abysmal abhorrence flared in Jake's eyes as he recognized the man. Senator Brent Van Heflin had one of those personas so typical of the leadership pervading Washington these days, the classic embodiment of ultimate corruption, at least from Jake's perspective. Even as a boy growing up he well remembered the man as being at the forefront of politics, and as he assessed the man now he could not help but notice how much the senator's girth had expanded since that time. Standing nearby were four of the fully armed, black-clad invaders Jake had been informed of on his way back to Aquaria aboard Johnnie.

Moving like a phantom, Jake sidled up to the archway, now close enough to hear what was being said. Almost immediately he recognized the smug, contemptuous voice of Allotey, a voice one didn't readily forget.

Allotey raised a hand and slapped Victor harshly across the face. "Do not lie to me!" he screamed. His face was twisted in a rabid snarl. "You will tell me where the wealth of this colony is hidden."

Jake risked a peak around the archway. The black-clad insurgents appeared to have their attention focused entirely on the interrogation and not on their surroundings.

"Go to hell!"

Victor's sharp, biting reply told Jake the Russian was quickly recovering from his wound.

"I can have you killed right now," Allotey spat.

"Then what are you waiting for you fucking piss ant?" Victor bellowed.

At that moment Jake knew he had to do something, and do it fast. It was obvious Victor no longer cared about self-preservation, and from

Allotey's darkening scowl he could tell the Libyan was only a hair-trigger away from ordering one of his henchmen to carry out the threat.

Jake switched the T-crystal to his left hand and quietly slipped the USP-9 from the holster strapped to his right thigh, hoping the rounds it held were still dry enough to fire. He would have preferred his faithful Sledgehammer, but he had left it aboard Johnnie. Assessing the developing situation one more time with a seasoned eye, it appeared that Allotey and the senator carried no weapons. The black-clad troopers accompanying them were another matter, however, and he quickly determined which of them presented the biggest threat. That was the one he would take out first as he charged into the room, but just as he was about to leap forward, a taunting laugh broke the escalating tension.

All six men spun in startled confusion, looking all about for the source of the laughter.

"You men must be blind," a disembodied voice mocked.

"Show yourself!" Allotey challenged, the shadow of fear crossing his face as his eyes continued to dart searchingly about the room.

"As you wish," the unknown speaker said. Abruptly, the manifestation of Ez suddenly appeared.

"You!" Allotey howled, immediately recognizing the Haitian woman who had demeaned him when he had first come to Aquaria. Turning to the troopers, he cried out a shrill order. "Kill her!"

Shocked by the woman's sudden appearance, the trooper's failed to respond, still trying to comprehend how she had seemingly materialized out of thin air right before their eyes.

"I said kill her," Allotey screamed again.

The command registered this time, and all four troopers opened up to assault her body with a withering storm of rounds. Behind Ez, medical equipment and glass components strung out along a curving wall shattered in a deafening cacophony, raining back a hail of splintered shards and debris. The fusillade continued non-stop until all four weapons expended their ammunition.

Completely stunned, Allotey and company could only stare in disbelief as Ez continued to stand before them without injury, her face lit up in a placid smile.

Achilles' voice rang out in Jake's head just before he sprang from hiding to take advantage of the situation. *Not yet, JJ. Ez needs a little more time.*

Time for what? Jake demurred. *Now's my chance to take out those bastards before they reload.*

A slight change in plans, Achilles shot back. *Just be patient a little longer and all will become apparent.*

Grumbling in silence, Jake held his position, wondering what Ez had in mind as he listened to her speak.

"Senator Brent Van Heflin," she declared mockingly. "What a delightful honor to see you here in Aquaria, though it surprises me not the slightest to see you traveling with such sordid company. I would think you would be back in Washington attending to what you do best, pushing along bills designed to bleed the American people and subverting the government."

The jeering diatribe seemed to catch the senator off guard, and for several seconds he stood mute, appearing uncomfortable and chagrined in light of the truth. Gathering himself quickly, he nodded to one of the troopers.

Jake caught the gesture, shooting a glance at the trooper, who slung his spent Uzi over a shoulder and pulled a camcorder from his belt before moving further back. He realized the trooper was preparing to record the exchange that was about to ensue.

Seeing that the trooper was ready, Van Heflin turned his head back to the woman and cleared his throat. "And who might you be?" he asked austerely.

"My identity is of no concern. Think of me as merely one of the residents of this eco-friendly utopia you and your kind have gone to great lengths to defame, with the goal of goading the UN into taking military action against us. But I think it only fair to ask why you have taken the time to break away from your busy, subversive schedule to come here."

Van Heflin's manner abruptly stiffened and his eyes came alive with anger. Unaccustomed to being insulted like this, he retorted in the declamatory mode of voice he typically used when delivering a speech before Congress. "By sanction of the United Nations, this facility has been declared a threat to the planetary environment. Your people have been defiling the local habitat for some time now, and the UN has compiled sufficient evidence to prove it. The massive release of greenhouse gases Aquaria is causing is one such proof, not to mention the toxic pollution it is rapidly spreading to the rest of the Caribbean. As such, I would be grossly negligent in my responsibilities as Science and Technology Chairman not to be here during the takeover of this facility as an earth-saving measure, though I accompany this mission only as a neutral observer to see with my own eyes the atrocities you people have been inflicting on the eco-system and to confirm that your harmful activities are ended once and for all."

Ez laughed sarcastically. "Observer you say. I suppose that function is appropriate, but shouldn't you amend it by being a bit more truthful. Shouldn't you be telling me you're here to observe the sizeable assets this colony holds so you can claim a share?"

The senator subdued the scalding rebuttal before it could escape his mouth, and with an effort, forced a smile. "By debasing an elected representative of the U.S. government with such a fatuous statement, you debase all Americans," he said flatly. "Attacking my integrity by making false allegations is not going to change what is happening here."

Ez riveted him with an all knowing gaze. "Do me a favor, senator, and drop the act. You're here to get a share of the gold, plain and simple, so stop having this farcical speech of yours recorded, which we both know will be carefully edited and then used as a means of covering your ass later on."

Before Van Heflin could reply, Ez turned and looked behind her to indicate a stack of wooden boxes. "But do not waste anymore of your valuable time by questioning this man when some of the booty you seek is right here in this very room. Please help yourself."

Van Heflin frowned. He could have sworn those boxes were not in the room when he had first entered it. Without looking at the cameraman he made another subtle gesture, and Jake saw the trooper lower the camera. Warily, the senator stood fast, not wanting to become the victim of a devious trap.

At seeing his hesitation, Ez moved to the stack and lifted the lid on the topmost box. Reaching in, she pulled out a bar of polished metal. It caught the light, reflecting a lustrous aureate glow that bedazzled the eyes.

"Don't be shy, gentlemen," exhorted Ez pleasantly. "Contained within these boxes is a windfall of gold worth slightly more than a billion dollars at current market value, so please take as much as you can carry away. From what I heard a short while ago, the price of gold is rapidly rising on international markets."

Even before Ez finished speaking she saw the fires of avarice blazing brightly in the senator's eyes. Allotey was practically drooling, evidenced by tiny beads of spittle forming at the corners of his mouth, and the four troopers seemed equally awed. All six were gawking like enraptured children coming upon a pile of neatly wrapped and ribboned presents on Christmas morning. Hesitating only a moment longer they ventured forward, though with obvious caution.

At seeing such auspicious distraction, Jake was ready to dart from hiding but Achilles quickly interceded. *Not yet, JJ.*

At least clue me in on what's next, Jake snapped back in irritation.

Before Achilles replied, the voice of another wailed out loudly. It conveyed distress, quavering nervously with frustration as though the person it belonged to had just undergone a traumatic event. "What is this place?"

From an alcove off to one side a man suddenly emerged, causing Jake's jaw to drop in surprise. The man was Truman Hearthwatch, Green Technology and Climate Advisor to the U.S. president.

Van Heflin gaped wide-eyed. "Truman?"

Hearthwatch turned his head to regard the senator in bewildered silence.

Van Heflin stared for another second before his dumbfounded countenance changed. "I was not informed you would be coming, Truman," he stated bluntly. "How did you get here?"

"I don't know," said the man the media had routinely dubbed as Earthwatch. He seemed visibly shaken and pale. The memory of what he had seen continued to haunt him. Without the feel of gravity to anchor him, he had floated aimlessly in the midst of swirling lights that seemed to go on forever before diminishing to pinpoints. The flashing imagery had made his head throb, bringing on extreme vertigo much the way the Aquarian art had made him ill. But now that the sickness was beginning to subside, he was able to recall the presence of three others, two men and a woman. He had been sitting there, and they seemed to come out of nowhere to lay hands on him just before a burst of crimson light flared. Had it all been a bad dream? Maybe he was still dreaming.

Hearthwatch settled confused eyes on the gold bar held by the woman. "One minute I'm in the White House waiting to see the President, and the next I'm here," he explained feebly. "Where am I?"

Van Heflin eyed him suspiciously, wondering if this was some kind of prank. "Surely you jest."

Hearthwatch's demeanor suddenly hardened like quick-drying cement, and he looked back at the senator with annoyance. "I do not jest," he grumbled testily. "Where am I?"

Allotey glared at him. The idea that Hearthwatch had now seen the gold did not sit well with him, for it was now probable the plunder would be divided further. "Do you actually expect us to believe such a ridiculous story," he ranted in frustration. "Your arrival here is most inappropriate in view of the military action that is currently in progress. Why did you come?"

"I sent him."

Both Van Heflin and Allotey whirled, stunned to see the *Sublimis* saunter into the room behind Hearthwatch. Hearthwatch spun around as well, equally stunned.

Maximus wore a cryptic grin. "One of my scientists recently made a major discovery," he began. "Truman was brought here by a quantum teleporter. Such a device allows instantaneous transport of sentient life forms to any place on the globe." Setting his gaze on Hearthwatch, he explained further. "Once I learned where you were, Truman, agents of mine were able to pluck you from the White House and bring you here." Pausing, he studied the confusion that still lingered on Hearthwatch's face. "If you haven't figured it out by now, you're in Aquaria. I can understand the extreme disorientation and fright you must have experienced, but in the end I think you'll probably agree it was all worthwhile. Other than what I will take for myself, you are to receive the second largest share of the spoils this colony holds."

Allotey appeared dismayed, immediately voicing a protest. "That is not fair. He played no part in this operation. He risked nothing."

Maximus gave him a sharp look. "For all the fine work Truman has done for *The Order*, I think he deserves it. And don't forget the major role he will play in urging Congress to enact the carbon tax. Once that happens, other nations will follow."

Van Heflin was aghast. "What about me? Aren't I just as deserving?"

"Your reward will be the U.S. presidency," rasped Maximus sternly. "I think that will be reward enough. Must I remind you it will cost a great deal of money to finance your campaign, and a significant portion of the assets taken from this facility will be used to pave the way for you."

Van Heflin's innate greed uncoiled like an enraged serpent deep in his gut, and its head rose up sharply to take control of his mouth. "Are you implying I am not to get a share at all?" he quailed ruefully.

Maximus responded without emotion. "That is correct."

The senator cast brooding eyes back to the stack of gold-bearing boxes. "Surely there's more than enough to…" His reply hung unfinished as he noticed the woman was now gone. Glancing about sharply in all directions, he looked to Allotey. "Where did she go?"

The question seemed to startle Allotey, and he scanned the room nervously to echo Van Heflin's concern. Turning, he brought a questioning frown to the nearest trooper. "Did you see the woman leave?"

Wide-eyed, the trooper shook his head fervently as he took in the room at a glance, his hands working quickly as he slapped a fresh clip into his weapon and chambered a round. Other firearms snicked audibly as the other three troopers followed his lead, all of them now on full alert and prepared to engage any surprises.

"Never mind her!" Maximus exclaimed exuberantly. "This facility will soon be under our complete control."

"What about the Seals?" asked Allotey.

"Our invasion force is eradicating them as we speak. Once they are wiped out, Aquaria will be ours to do with as we please."

"What about the international community?" Allotey continued to press. His tone was worried. "How will this operation be reported?"

Maximus grinned cunningly, his voice rising theatrically as though he were a news commentator. "The task force sent by the UN to take control of Aquaria was met with unanticipated stiff resistance by hostile colonists. Using sophisticated weaponry, the colonists were able to sink the invasion fleet, including three kilo-class submarines and the flagship aircraft carrier supporting them. The soldiers representing the UN fared just as poorly, as they were met by a contingent of men in robotic combat suits accompanied by a far superior force of well-armed Aquarians who were able to destroy them."

Dropping the pretension, Maximus resumed a more serious attitude as he explained further. "The defeat will require the UN to marshal another task force, but that will take some time, and by then all the assets of this facility will be removed and in our hands."

Continuing to stifle his vexation, Van Heflin pointed out something Maximus had seemingly overlooked. "But how will this story reconcile the survival of Malikai and myself."

"You recognized the danger and escaped," answered Maximus briskly. His manner suggested he didn't want to waste any more time discussing it. Giving Allotey a harsh, penetrating stare, he added, "Malikai, I'm leaving it up to you to take inventory of all the gold you are able to locate within this city. Use the men in our invasion force as you see fit to have it gathered up and placed aboard the sub that brought them here." Turning, he looked at Hearthwatch. "Truman, you will be responsible for verifying the accuracy of Malikai's inventory. I'll return later to see that these tasks were carried out."

"Where are you going?" Van Heflin asked as Maximus turned to leave.

"I'm making a little visit to the island." With that said, Maximus walked swiftly back the way he had come, disappearing quickly from view.

-144-

The communications supervisor at IBC headquarters cringed at the sound of the ringing phone, uneager to answer it, its shrill, blaring tone seeming to announce the irascible fury of the caller trying to get through to him. Gloomily he picked up the receiver to hold it a good foot away from his ear, knowing what he was in for as he kept his eyes glued to the video screen.

Upon absorbing the initial vitriolic outburst coming through the line, he responded in a contrite voice, nodding repeatedly as if the caller were directly in his face berating him savagely. As the verbal barrage ensued, he attempted to squeeze in a stuttering reply wherever he could. "Yes...yes, I'm well aware of the problem, sir...yes...yes...no, we've been hacked again..." Frustrated, he laid the receiver down on the table until the rants of the company officer on the other end finally began to wane.

Picking up the receiver again, the supervisor said, "We're doing everything we can, sir...no, the built-in firewall is not working. The hacker seems to be highly sophisticated and has found a way around it. I can assure you our technicians are hard at work on the problem, but until they can figure out how the system is being breached, there's nothing we can do to stop these cybernetic intrusions and the rogue transmissions being aired."

The supervisor cringed again as another outburst ripped into his ear. "Yes, I know the video has been broadcast throughout the mainstream media," he was finally able to say. Listening a little more, he agreed with the officer. "Certainly it looks bad for all those portrayed, but I'm sure our damage control team will be able to produce something to downplay it as nothing more than a hoax enacted by actors made to look like the people they played."

After tossing the officer a few more hollow assurances, the supervisor finally shoved the receiver back into its cradle and breathed a sigh of relief. Setting his eyes back on the screen, his brief respite instantly crumbled. To his utter horror the video was being replayed all over again.

-145-

Captain Delila maintained his position on the bridge wing, enjoying the mild breeze and the smell of the sea as he kept his gaze fixed on the floating city in the distance. The tenuous dome of ethereal light that had enshrouded it a short time earlier was now gone, replaced by towering ribbons of multi-hued light. Two full spectrums graced the sky in banded symmetrical splendor, one draped over the other to form a great curving arch that spanned the horizon. The sight of a double rainbow enchanted him. But these were unlike any rainbow he had ever seen. Each band of color was unnaturally vivid, seeming to resonate with points of light that sparkled and flickered as they slide along their respective archways. But now a third rainbow was coalescing directly behind the first two, enveloping them in a display of perfect congruity.

As Delila looked on, Ensign Jefferson joined him. "Sir, ship's sonar shows no sign of the unknown sub."

"What about the *Nunquarn Satis* and *Kraken?*" Delila asked, continuing to behold the spectacular sight. "Any sinking debris detected?"

"None whatsoever, sir. Both ships appear to have vanished completely."

The captain nodded solemnly, still trying to make sense of these strange happenings as he continued to stare at the rainbows.

Jefferson followed his gaze. "Wow, I've never seen anything like that, sir."

"It certainly is an unusual sight," Delila concurred. "Any contact with Lieutenant Johnson?"

"A little. The jamming seems to have eased up a bit, so he's able to send broken transmissions. Seem's he's still under attack."

"And Ensign Flynn's squad?"

"They're getting ready to lift off the island and lend support to Johnson's team." As Jefferson said this, he handed the captain an IPad. "Another of those broadcasts emanating from the colony was picked up minutes earlier. It's all been recorded, sir."

Delila withdrew his eyes from the triple arches and took hold of the IPad, a heavy frown creasing his forehead as the recording began to play out.

-146-

No sooner did Maximus leave the room, Allotey was the first to venture forward to take inventory of the gold, the stacked boxes drawing him like a hyena to carrion. But as he reached for the topmost box, his hands found only air awaiting him.

"What is this?" Allotey screamed. Looking all about him and groping the air wildly, he realized the boxes had vanished.

Okay, you're on, Achilles told Jake.

About time, Jake grumbled back in feigned annoyance as he bolted forward and raised his voice. "Drop your weapons and no one will get hurt," he commanded curtly. If he could avoid killing this time he would do so. And in a situation such as this, prisoners could be very valuable.

All heads snapped around in startled surprise, the troopers reacting instantly to bring their weapons to bear and open fire.

Fully prepared for this, Jake had already focused his thoughts to counter the deluge of rounds impinging on him, and in reaction to these thoughts the T-crystal in his left hand was already pulsating at a high frequency. It flared a blinding crimson as it swallowed up bullets as though they were insubstantial, immediately transmuting the lethal barrage of kinetic energy to another form and sending it into the esoteric abyss of higher dimensionality.

Jake waited for the firearms to deplete their clips. "Hands in the air!" he ordered with a goading grin as he noted expressions of incomprehension on the various faces. Keeping a wary eye on the troopers, he spoke out of the corner of his mouth. "You okay, Victor?"

Victor rose up from the bed to stand next to him. "I will feel a little better once I settle with this piss ant," he said, directing a contemptuous look at the man who had slapped him.

Allotey recovered from his initial shock at seeing something that should have been impossible. "You again!" he snarled disdainfully, immediately recognizing Jake from their previous encounter. "How dare you interfere with a UN official carrying out the directives of the governing world body. Do you realize you can be hung for this?"

Jake chuckled, shaking his head pitifully at Allotey's laughable pomposity. Even now the man's inherent self-righteousness seemed to have no bounds. "Whatever!" he said wearily. "Did anyone ever tell you to audition for Saturday Night Live. I think you have a natural flair for farcical comedy."

Recognition flooded Van Heflin's face as he realized who the man was standing before them. Composing himself quickly, he projected an air of superiority as he jumped in to take control of the situation. In his most authoritative voice, he said, "This is an international matter, Mister Javolyn, so I strongly advise you to put down your weapon. You cannot…"

The senator broke off in open-mouthed silence as three people suddenly winked into existence to stand beside Jake, one of them wielding a firearm also pointed at the troopers.

Jake gave him a wry smile. "You were saying, senator? Or maybe I should start calling you Mr. President."

Still at a loss for words, Van Heflin nearly wet himself as he continued to stare wide-eyed at Amphitrite, Franklin and Mat.

"A little tongue-tied, are we?" said Jake with feigned sympathy. Turning, Jake brought his attention to Hearthwatch. "Perhaps your partner in crime, Mr. Earthwatch here has something to say."

Hearthwatch stared dumbly, his brain suddenly in turmoil as an obscure remembrance came flooding back with a rush. He was now almost certain the threesome standing beside Javolyn were the same ones that had teleported him here. But if they were agents of *The Order* as the *Sublimis* had contended, then why were they siding with Javolyn? And then it hit him. One of them was Mat Daniels. The resemblance of the man he had seen in photos was altogether far too striking for him to be wrong. Still perplexed as to what was going on, he decided to let the conundrum go for the time being, knowing that Maximus would explain it all later.

Gaining control of his senses, Hearthwatch reverted to his old self, and he glowered superciliously at Javolyn. "Maybe at the moment you hold all the trump cards," he spat wrathfully, "but you will soon learn who triumphs in the end. It is we who control the media. It is we who have the means to mold humanity, the majority of which are rather mindless and easily manipulated with deceptions and falsehoods. As I speak, this city is being overrun by paramilitary forces that work for us. The media, however, will play up those same forces as belonging to this colony, and once the Seal teams are eliminated the public will be up in arms screaming for your heads. So do yourselves a favor and hand over your weapons. Admit you're outclassed and outgunned."

Jake let out a deep sigh of disgust. "I hate to burst your bubble, your royal arrogance, but your forces are not faring well. And as for the media which you claim to control, perhaps you should be reminded of what took place a short time earlier and the noose being slowly tightened around your own neck. Ez, please show these deceitful rogues what's being shown on all the mainstream news channels in the U.S. at this moment."

Hearthwatch eyed the newcomers standing next to Jake, wondering who might be Ez. When none of them moved, he glanced around sharply in search of the person, but his expression changed abruptly as his gaze settled on something else.

Jake read the horror-stricken look that came to Hearthwatch's face as five 3-dimensional holograms suddenly took form in the air before him. Swiveling his head, he saw that Van Heflin had the same look, as did Allotey.

Van Heflin felt ill as he watched, realizing all the stations were playing the same exact thing. In desperation he shifted a frenetic gaze on each, identifying the station by the captioned logo it displayed. Nevertheless, he couldn't help but wonder if these broadcasts were truly authentic, and he grasped at this possibility the way a drowning man reaches for a life ring in a tumultuous sea. The thought that the broadcasts might actually be taking place at this very moment tormented him, searing through his mind like a hot poker scorching flesh.

"Oh, they're real all right," Jake affirmed blithely as if reading his mind. "Here in Aquaria we have the means to take control of any news channel we choose, whenever we choose. We're going to flood the worldwide web with this video, exposing all the shenanigans your cabal has been up to. Your days of bamboozling the public are over."

Van Heflin searched for guile in Javolyn's expression. At seeing none, his heart began to pound like a trip hammer suddenly going arrhythmic. If what had transpired moments earlier was being aired for the entire world to see, he knew his political future was in jeopardy, dire jeopardy. Bringing his eyes back to the broadcasts, he realized it was all there, the looks of superiority, surprise and smoldering greed suddenly turned apprehensive and intermixed with dangerous utterances by those involved. The sight of his own image began to haunt him as he scrutinized the way he had acted, but it had been the *Sublimis* himself who had actually admitted their true intentions, further confirmed by the heated discourse Truman had just given. Everything said had been meticulously recorded and was probably still being recorded. It was all there in a plethora of inculpating, irrefutable, mind numbing ugliness.

Hearthwatch was mortified, now fully aware of how the event in the sports bar had come to be. But knowing how various politicians within *The Order's* fifth column ranks had managed to survive one seemingly hopeless scandal after another over long illustrious careers, he took on an air of haughty defiance, no longer caring if his words continued to be recorded. Impaling Javolyn with a savage glare, he vented his fury like super-heated steam escaping a pressure valve. "You won't get away with this," he hissed through clenched teeth. "Once our army gains control of this facility, we'll prevail in the end. You're way out of your depth, Javolyn. I don't think you have a clue as to the countless resources we have at our disposal, nor the vast strength of our influence. World leaders carry out our directives, and many of our member politicians have managed to survive worse than this because of that influence. Once that influence is exerted to its full extent, the tide will swing back in our favor. Your efforts to expose us will ultimately be shown to be fraudulent. After all...," Hearthwatch paused momentarily to check the time on his wristwatch before looking back at Jake with a sly expression, "...how can I possibly be here when less than fifteen minutes ago at least twenty people saw me in the White House. We'll blitz the public with a storm of propaganda designed to further defame your enterprise. We'll demonstrate how you hijacked the media to disseminate a hoax."

"You mean like your buddy here, the senator?" Jake replied flippantly. "I'm not sure the word 'politician' fully captures him, it just seems too inadequate. We need something that better describes him and his kind."

Jake brought a hand to his chin and stroked it as if in deep thought. "Hmmn, now let me see," he said contemplatively as he paced the room slightly. His clouded expression suddenly brightened, and he turned to Mat with sudden vivaciousness. "I've got it! Being that he's actually a charlatan, doesn't *'charlatician'* seem more appropriate?"

Mat shrugged. "You're being far too kind. I think dirt bag is more befitting."

Hearthwatch narrowed his eyes and his voice rose lividly. "Keep making fun of the situation, Javolyn. You won't be smirking once our troops arrive here in numbers."

"That could very well be if you have any troops left once this is over," Jake responded airily. "Ez, give us a fix on the marauders."

Like before, Hearthwatch, Van Heflin and Allotey scanned the room in search of the person called Ez. When that person failed to appear, they noticed something had changed in the holographic displays, these showing what was currently taking place in another sector of the city.

Jake studied the images being shown with a critical eye. "Now pinpoint Zinova and his cohorts," he instructed.

The disembodied voice of Ez answered immediately. "They are at the tail end of the pursuing army." As she said this, one of the displays zoomed in on three figures.

Jake turned his gaze on Belachek. "It's your call, Victor. How should we deal with your old boss?"

Belachek stared at the display, his countenance suddenly mired in deep thought.

-147-

First Lieutenant Myron Johnson had only his instincts to go by in not firing at the portly woman. She had seemed to come out of nowhere right before his eyes. But it was her kindly smile spread benevolently across her broad face that had kept his trigger finger in check as she peered directly at him. Though she bore no resemblance to his own grandmother, the smile she held brought back fond memories.

"Who are you?" he demanded, aware that she carried no weapon.

Just as he completed the question, another deafening roar broke the brief respite of quietude to send a shower of shattered sea cement flying. Had he and three of his men not taken refuge behind the arched pillar, they would have been cut to pieces. With his back up against the pillar, he was astounded by the woman's calm demeanor. She was just beyond the pillar's protection, and she had not even flinched in the face of such destruction.

The woman moved closer, speaking quickly when the enfilade cut out. "If you want to save your men, follow me." Pointing, she indicated a passageway off to her left. "This way."

The lieutenant stood frozen as the woman started walking, his mind churning with indecision. The moment passed quickly as he realized this was his only option. If he didn't get moving, those things would be on top of him and his men. Shooting a look to other members of his team hunkered behind nearby pillars, he waved them to follow. Only half his original contingent of men remained with him, the others becoming separated when the skirmish had raged on, and the thought of losing any of them weighed heavily on him. Radio jamming seemed to be intermittent now, and it was only a minute earlier he had gotten through to the missing men. Miraculously, no casualties had been reported.

The passageway the woman had chosen afforded enough protection to keep them out of a direct line of fire, and as another buzz saw burst broke the air, he was convinced the pursuing monstrosities were now firing blindly.

The lieutenant had a hard time keeping up with their guide, and he began to wonder how such a large woman was able to move so fast. And there was something else going on that he found strange. Her form seemed to wink out, only to reappear further ahead as he ran behind her. This kept recurring over and over again as he and his men followed. There seemed to be no uniformity to the route she had taken. It wound its way snakelike through a forest of arched pillars, rising and falling as though they were traversing a rolling wave. And each time they rounded a bend or ascended a rise, the woman would suddenly vanish before she blinked back into view farther away. At first he thought this to be illusory, created by the soft interior lighting that pervaded the hallway, but then his sharp mind grasped what was really happening. *My god, she's a hologram.* Abruptly he slowed, signaling the men behind him to stop running. Coming to a halt, his eyes roved searchingly over the curved walls and ceiling looking for the projectors that were causing the effect. Was he being led into a trap?

He nearly jumped out of his skin as the woman was suddenly beside him, and in reaction he pointed his firearm but held back on the trigger. As though having read his thoughts, she said, "Search your feelings, lieutenant, I wish you no harm. Though you perceive me to be an illusion I can assure you my sentience is quite real." Her affable smile seemed genuine, and once again he was reminded of his grandmother. Slowly he lowered his weapon as his emotions steadied, and he decided that whoever was evoking the holograms was here to help.

The woman turned to indicate a fork in the passageway a short distance ahead. "You can set up over there to ambush your pursuers. We have something in readiness they will not expect."

Johnson looked to the area she had indicated, sizing it up as the rest of his men crowded alongside to eye the woman in bewilderment. Assessing the situation, he shifted his gaze and squinted. Further away was a huge open area where the lighting was strong. The subdued sound of thunder caught his ears.

Ez caught the look on his face. "You passed this way before," she informed him, "but on a level higher up. If you are still willing to trust me, we have the means to defeat these usurpers, but we will need your help."

The lieutenant frowned. "Those men coming after us are not your people?"

The smile Ez carried turned solemn. "That is what they would like you and the rest of the world to believe. Those men are part of an insidious plan to take control of this city. The task force sent under the UN banner, which you and your men represent, have been pulled into this debacle by the very people who devised this plan. These people hold no fealty to any one nation. Their only allegiance is to the cabal they serve, a shadowy group of conspirators driven by implacable greed and an insatiable lust for power. Apparently their leader considers this city to be a direct threat to his ambitions, a man who believes it will weaken his hold on world affairs. He wants to stop us before we can construct other floating cities capable of harvesting unlimited sources of food and eco-friendly energy at low cost. Contrary to what you've been told, lieutenant, Aquaria poses no threat to the environment."

The Seal leader managed an outwardly calm persona, though he was seething just below the surface. Everything the woman was telling him confirmed his earlier suspicions, and the idea of being used in this manner ignited his anger like gasoline poured on hot coals. "The man placed in charge of the UN task force and the U.S. senator accompanying him. Do you know if they're part of this conspiracy?" he asked.

"We have compiled sufficient evidence of their complicity. Your superior officer, Captain Delila, has already been apprised of what is really going on here, and he has ordered your recall and a suspension of this operation."

Johnson expelled a frustrated sigh. "I managed to receive those orders just prior to our radios being jammed."

"Will you help us?" pressed Ez.

"How do we fight those things?" grumbled Johnson, a pained look coming to his face. "Our weapons can't penetrate their armor and they appear to have more than a hundred well-armed combat troops backing them up. And as you can see, even counting myself, my squad is down to nine men with seven of them somewhere else in this endless maze of corridors you call a city. The only reason we're still alive is probably because those things move so slow and there's plenty of places to hide and take cover, but each time we elude them they still manage to find us. We'd have more men available to fight them if not for that despicable UN clown put in charge of this mission." The supercilious image of Allotey immediately pervaded his thoughts as he said this, and his intense dislike of the man suddenly flared into bitter hatred. It was all too evident that Allotey had purposely sabotaged him. By dividing his original team of thirty-two and sending half of them to the island, it would make it that much easier for Allotey's loathsome collaborators to wipe out both units.

Ez pointed to the small pin he wore on his flak vest. "That is the reason they are able to locate you."

The lieutenant's face clouded as he lifted a hand to the pin. "What this? These were..." He stopped in mid-sentence, his eyes flaring wide.

"UN issue you and your men were ordered to wear," Ez stated bluntly, completing what he was about to say.

Contemptuously, Johnson tore the pin from the vest to glare at the UN logo emblazoned on it. "A damn homing beacon," he grunted angrily. "How did you know?"

"We have sensors in this facility that detected the signals. After that it was only a matter of deductive reasoning."

"I should have known better," Johnson grumbled with self-ridicule. "From the start this whole mission never felt right. I should have trusted my instincts and now half my team may be lost because I didn't oppose that asshole sending them off to the island."

"Do not berate yourself, lieutenant. The unit sent to Navassa has prevailed and is about to join you, and so are the others." Ez looked behind her. "See for yourself."

Johnson followed her gaze. Silhouetted by the bright light at their backs, a band of figures were coming toward him at a stiff trot. His spirits instantly lifted when he saw it was Ensign Flynn at the head of the pack.

The lieutenant suppressed his sudden joy, barely managing to keep a stern face. "You look like shit, Pat!" he said disapprovingly, making a show of eyeing the dust and grime caking Flynn's sweat-soaked fatigues.

Flynn's reply was just as stern. "And you look like you just got your ass kicked, Myron me lad."

The expressions both men wore suddenly changed over to grins of elation, and they embraced heartily. They had gone through Seal training together and were close friends.

The lieutenant swept his gaze over the other men to make a rapid appraisal of numbers, and his grin fell away. "Who did we lose?"

"Blackwell caught one in the leg, but I think he's gonna be alright," Flynn said. "I had O'Malley bring him to one of the infirmaries in this facility to have his wound treated."

The lieutenant frowned. "How would he find it? Navigating this place is confusing as it is."

"A short Latino guy was showing him the way. I think his name was Hector."

Johnson glanced around again. One man he didn't recognize stood more than a full head taller than all the rest, but he ignored him for the moment as two faces were still unaccounted for. "What happened to Joliard and Haskel?"

"They're keeping watch on those turncoat bastards who flew us here. We're going to need them to fly us back to the carrier, and I wanted to make sure they don't skip out on us before we're ready to leave. Seems they were jamming our radio transmissions all along." Flynn saw the look that transposed his friend's features. "You didn't know?"

"We're still being jammed," Johnson remarked. "It's not as bad as before, but I'm still unable to establish clear contact with the *Carl Sagan*."

"Those combat suits are the cause," Ez piped in quickly, "but I suggest you and your men set up for the ambush in there." She indicated the gallery that opened to the left for the second time. "Those things, as you like to call them, will be here shortly. Once they pass, you'll have opportunity to dispatch the troops coming up behind them."

Johnson scrutinized the area again. The entrance had a multi-arched configuration, with six archways forming the opening, beyond which only darkness lay. Out in front of it was a raised circular basin of water twenty feet across with a gurgling fountain at its center. "It looks too obvious," he opined dubiously, though he knew it was wide enough to accommodate a skirmish line for all his men.

Ez smiled disarmingly. "Let me worry about that. I promise you they'll never see you."

As though suddenly remembering, Johnson held up the pin still held in his hand for the men to see. "Everyone get rid of your UN pin," he commanded aloud. "This is how those bastards were able to keep finding us."

Ez stopped him before he could hurl it away. "You and your men will have need of those," she said quickly.

Johnson belayed the throw and stared back at her with a baffled expression. "What do you suggest?"

"Give the pins to the man not of your unit."

Johnson glanced at the giant who had accompanied Flynn's unit before turning to Flynn. "Who is this guy?"

"His name is Zimbola. He's a resident of this city and insists on helping us."

"And I take it you have no objections," the lieutenant shot back.

"No, I'd be crazy to refuse him. He's big enough to take on one of those things all by himself."

Johnson sighed in resignation before turning to the rest of his men and pointing. "You heard the lady, give the big guy your pins and take cover behind those archways and fountain. It's payback time. Let's give those bastards something to think about before we send them off to hell."

-148-

Zinova was beginning to have second thoughts about Allotey's offer as he, Drakov and Boris followed in the wake of the invasion force, and he began to wonder if Allotey had purposely lied to him in order to get his assistance. So far he had seen nothing to indicate the facility contained a large cache of gold, and even if one actually existed among this vast maze of corridors, galleries and passageways winding their way through the floating city's interior, it would likely take many hours of painstaking effort to locate it. Nevertheless, he had felt it prudent to separate himself and his remaining two accomplices from Allotey's company to venture off on his own. Among other things, he did not trust the UN envoy one iota. In spite of this distrust, he was at least thankful for the drug Allotey had recommended he and his men take, but he had only injected himself after seeing Allotey take the drug first. He never wanted to experience the debilitating sickness he had suffered back in Tiburon ever again. It had been triggered by a strange sight that had flashed up at him from the beach, and it was this that had prevented him from firing off a missile on the helicopter he had been pursuing. When it had occurred, his brain had felt as though it had been mashed to jelly, and it had only been a matter of will for him to make an emergency landing without crashing the Hind.

As he walked along, he realized he would never have been able to enter this place without resorting to the drug. Everywhere he looked he saw artistic creations, both two-dimensional and holographic, that were oddly reminiscent of the Tiburon sight that had nearly killed him, but even now he felt himself on the edge of illness. If there were incredible riches to be had, as the little weasel had claimed, he surmised Allotey would try to keep most of it for himself, so it was crucial he keep following the invaders to observe any valuables they might come upon. The U.S. senator was another matter, and one look into the statesman's eyes had told him all he needed to know about the true nature of the man. Surely the senator had to be after the same thing, or why else would he be here.

The Reaper continued to ponder the current state of affairs. Having gotten a close-up look at those combat suits and the Gatling guns they carried, he knew that by comparison the Seal teams stood little chance against them. And in spite of their extreme slowness, they were able to keep the foe they were hunting in complete disarray using their radio jamming capability. Add to that their ability to pinpoint the location of every member of the Seal team further enhanced the inevitability of the outcome. But his patience was beginning to wear thin. This seek and destroy mission was taking far too long for his taste, and he began to consider venturing off in another direction. As it was, the residents of the facility appeared to have vacated the premises, and if any Seals were lurking nearby, the SPEFACS operators would have already detected them and immediately moved to track their electronic scent.

Zinova came to an abrupt halt. Turning, he spoke to the others. "No reason for us to get involved in the fighting. Let's get away from the pack and go off on our own." Using the barrel of the AK-104 Kalashnikov assault rifle he carried, he pointed it at an area off to his right, and just as he did, movement caught his eye. Someone was coming in their direction, but was as yet too far away to determine whether that someone be ally or foe. There was something familiar in the way the person moved, for he kept glancing back over his shoulder to check his six in a stealth-like manner.

"Hold your fire!" Zinova ordered the others as he kept a wary eye on the advancing party. With his weapon aimed and his finger poised gently on the trigger, he was fully prepared to send off a two-tap burst should it become necessary, but the person appeared to be without a firearm.

A stunned expression took hold of Zinova's features before settling into a suspicious stare. "Victor, I gave you up for dead," he spat gruffly. "What happened to you?"

Belachek gazed back soberly. "It's a long story, one I'll fill you in on later, but now is not the time." He looked behind him again before continuing, this time with a conspiratorial smile. "I found gold," he whispered jubilantly.

Zinova put his suspicions on hold for the moment. "Where?"

"Follow me and I'll show you. This facility has tons of it."

"Tons, you say?" The sum flabbergasted Zinova, quelling his immediate need for answers.

Belachek nodded exuberantly. "Yes, and if we hurry we can load the Hind with some of it and fly on out of here before Allotey and his troops even realize what happened."

Zinova's brow immediately bunched, and under the soft light his face almost appeared simian. "How do you know about Allotey?"

"There is no time for explanations, Karloff. I will fill you in on everything once we load the chopper and fly away." Belachek half-turned, beckoning the men to follow. "Come!" he urged.

Against his better judgement, the Reaper followed, the promise of untold riches too much for him to ignore.

-149-

The black-clad marauder kept a wary eye as he followed behind the slowly advancing SPEFACS. With four of these monsters leading the way, he felt safe and protected as they periodically strafed the passageway out in front of them. The damage they wrought was extensive, leaving shattered fixtures and portions of unfathomable artwork littering the floor under a wash of soft illumination of varied tinctures. As far as he could tell, none of the fighting force he was to engage had been hit, but he was certain it was only a matter of time before they were trapped and eradicated. The SPEFACS, he knew, were outfitted with tracking devices, and at this moment the operators were following the signals put out by the homing beacons the Seal units were wearing. Nothing could survive the firepower the SPEFACS were putting out for very long. Their only shortcoming was the sluggish speed at which they moved.

As he looked between two of the ponderous juggernauts he saw the passageway debouched into a cavernous area of intense bright light farther ahead. Abruptly he glanced from right to left. Up to now there had been too many places for an enemy to take refuge behind. A seemingly endless array of archways, foot bridges, and fountains abounded, much of it adorned with paintings and holographic projections of esoteric art forms that gave him a slight sense of vertigo whenever he stared at them too long. Now he fully understood why he and the others had been ordered to inject themselves just before departing the sub. The drug, he had been told, had been purposely designed to counter the debilitating effects the art would cause him, and had he not taken it he suspected he would have become terribly ill. But the area he had come upon did not conform to the rest of the place he had so far seen, and he saw at once that it was completely devoid of the arcane artistic renderings. This sector appeared to be barren, with no evidence of side passages or galleries. For perhaps the last two hundred feet only sterile walls and ceilings of a dull gray texture met his eyes.

Somewhat surprised by the change of scenery, he relaxed his vigilance knowing there was no chance of a flanking surprise attack. Not in this constricted hallway. Something reflected light from the open area directly ahead of him, and as he fixated on it he realized it was the glare of smooth polished metal. The operators of the advancing SPEFACS seemed not to notice, and after they had trudged past, he bent to investigate. But as he stooped down to place a hand on it, the trooper on his right reached for it at the same time and yanked it from his grasp. But he knew at once that it was a gold ingot. And suddenly he was seeing more of them scattered along the floor, a whole lot more. Wanting not to be outmaneuvered by greedier hands, he leapt forward to grab the closest ingot, only to collide headlong into another hooded trooper. Pandemonium seemed to break out all at once as other members of the assault team scrambled up from behind him to get their share, and he was only obtusely aware that all discipline within their ranks was quickly coming apart. Within seconds a full blown melee broke out, and he found himself at odds with another trying to take away his small piece of plunder.

Continuing to focus their attention directly ahead, the SPEFACS operators failed to notice the disintegration of discipline behind them, and they trudged on forward into the well-lit area that lay before them, tenaciously following the tracking signals the Seals were unknowingly emitting. A four-foot parapet lay before them, and tromping heavily to the lip of it, they observed the same cavernous area they had seen before when they had passed along its tiered perimeter at a lower level. There was no mistaking it. The same rush of water descended turbulently from a place near the roof, pounding down harshly into a large pool at the bottom of an amphitheater made to resemble a gorge. But something was different this time around. A cluster of what appeared to be segmented metal columns extended down into the water from an opening in the ceiling made to resemble an azure sky with a bright sun in its midst. The columns were cylindrical and tapered, far thicker at the top than where they met the water. Altogether there were eight of them. At this location the tracking signals were at their strongest, with no other place for their elusive quarry to go or hide except over the side of the short wall. Greatly puzzled, the operators swiveled the robotic heads down to scan the sides of the chasm, fully expecting to glimpse the men they were looking to kill, but it was the leftmost operator hovering at the edge who first noticed more than two dozen identical pins bearing the UN logo laying inconspicuously atop the wall. Shocked by the sight, he yelled into his lip mic, "We've been had." As he belted out the warning, chaos still raged behind him as hooded troopers continued to grapple insanely over the gold.

At that moment all hell broke loose as the unnerving clamor of automatic fire erupted spontaneously to cut down the massed horde of grappling men, and they began dropping like a swarm of flies suddenly sprayed with a lethal dose of exceptionally potent insecticide. Troopers that were not hit straight out glanced around in confusion within the constricted area. Tracers seemed to spring directly from one of the walls.

At hearing the uproar, the leftmost SPEFACS operator turned the robotic suit around to look behind him, unaware that those strange columns set in the water were beginning to move. With unexpected suddenness, all eight seemed to whip and writhe like the tentacles of a great octopus as four other tentacles tipped with huge claw buckets sprang from the opening in the roof and angled their way obliquely toward the combat suits. The movement didn't go unnoticed by the other three SPEFACS operators, and they immediately aligned their Gatling guns to meet the perceived danger. Warned by the others, the leftmost operator turned back to confront the oncoming threats, prepared to unleash a salvo in concert with his peers, but it was then that the other tentacles broke from the water, each supporting an albino dolphin bearing a T-crystal in each of its hand-like appendages. In less than two seconds, a pair of dolphins were positioned slightly ahead and to each side of a claw bucket just as all four Gatling's opened up, and the pounding of the falls was completely drowned out by the horrendous buzz saw roar. Fully shielded by resonating auras of intense violet iridescence, the tentacles remained undamaged as the swarm of rounds were completely absorbed. To Ez, this had been a point of deep concern. Unsure of how much damage the tentacles would be able to withstand against such a devastating barrage, she had decided to have the albinos invoke a shield of protection. As the Gatling's discharged at an enormous rate, the buckets opened like the maws of great serpents, and with amazing precision lunged toward the metallic monsters to close on the rotating barrels. With the guns fully destroyed, the eight albinos were lowered back into the water as the buckets reopened to snatch up all four SPEFACS in powerful jaws. Lifted as though their massive weights were insubstantial, the combat suits were swung out over the water and smashed violently together numerous times, battering and crushing the armored shells as well as the operators inside. Slowly, the tentacles withdrew back into the opening in the roof of the vast chamber as the gunfire from farther away began to die off. And then all was quiet.

Moments later, the holographically created optical illusion Ez had invoked abruptly faded to reveal Navy Seals cautiously emerging from behind the archways and fountain where they had taken cover.

With the air now rife with the smell of cordite and the barrel of his MP5 still smoking, First Lieutenant Myron Johnson called out to his men. "Anyone hit?"

It was Flynn who answered for everyone a few seconds later. "No casualties to report, lieutenant."

Johnson barked an order as his eyes swept over the carnage. "Stay alert, guys! Some of these clowns could be playing possum."

Weapons could be heard snickering as members of his team replaced their spent clips and reloaded before fanning out to tread gingerly among the mass of hooded commando bodies scattered across the floor. "Got one here that's still breathing," one of them shouted. "There's another live one here," someone else called.

Farther back, a body suddenly rose up, but before the marauder could get off a shot he was flung back as a staccato blast from the Stoner held in Zimbola's huge hands ended the threat. Ensign Flynn, who was standing close to the Jamaican giant, eyed him with newfound admiration. "Glad to have you on our team, big guy."

Johnson bellowed a stern warning meant for any survivors among the downed commandos. "Surrender and we will tend your wounds, but any more acts of aggression like the one that clown just pulled and you can expect the same."

The warning appeared to sink in, and within minutes the Seals were attending to five more of the hooded commandos still breathing. Johnson surveyed the death toll, and walking among the bodies he counted 93 fatalities.

Ez was suddenly at his side. "We have an infirmary available to treat the wounded, lieutenant."

"So I've been told," Johnson replied. "You have one of our guys in there now."

Ez displayed a concerned countenance, turning her gaze on the most severely injured. "Those two will not last another hour, but we have the means to save their lives. If you would like, we can stabilize them. Once they are out of danger you can transfer them to your carrier."

Johnson acknowledged the offer with a weary shrug. "I guess I'd be a heartless soul not to accept the invitation, lady, and certainly I owe you for all your help." He noticed her image flicker ever so slightly as he said this. "But please level with me, I have to know. Am I talking to an actual person stationed somewhere else in this facility?"

"You are very observant, lieutenant. It seems one of the holographic projectors at this location was partially damaged during the fighting. We used them to camouflage your place of hiding. Though you are currently interacting with a virtual manifestation of my being, I can assure you I am quite real."

With his curiosity appeased for the moment, Johnson asked, "Do you have a name?"

Ez smiled warmly. "My actually name is Esmerelda but you can call me Ez." Turning her head, she indicated the large individual coming to join them. "Zimby will show your men the way to the infirmary. Motorized gurneys will arrive in moments to transport the wounded, so your men will not have to carry them."

Johnson nodded in appreciation. "In the meantime I have to report to my superior to let him know what's happened here."

"That won't be necessary, lieutenant. Captain Delila observed the whole thing unfold, but you should be able to contact him rather easily now."

Johnson began issuing orders as soon as the gurneys arrived, and his men lifted the seven wounded black-clad commandos unto them.

-150-

Zinova's impatience continued to worsen as he followed Belachek, and he found it necessary to ask, "Where are we going, Victor?"

"We are almost there, Karloff. Just a little farther."

In moments, Belachek led the trio out onto an esplanade near the helipad where the Hind sat. Zinova squinted, suddenly feeling exposed in the harsh glare. Outside in the open air the sunlight was bright, contrasting sharply with the soft lighting that suffused most of Aquaria's interior.

Coming to a halt, Victor pointed. "Here is the gold I promised you," he declared, indicating a motorized flatbed utility cart with a stack of wooden boxes laid atop it. "Slightly more than one hundred million in US greenbacks," he quickly added.

The Reaper held back, eyeing the boxes suspiciously. Was it possible Victor was luring him into a trap?

At seeing Zinova's hesitation, Victor lifted an ingot in the shape of a small elongated bar from one of the topmost boxes. "See for yourself, Karloff," he said earnestly, offering the precious metal to his old boss.

Zinova frowned, searching Victor's face for signs of deception, but overcome by the metal's alluring aureate gloss, he took possession of the ingot, hefting it judiciously to gauge its weight. Handing it to Drakov, he said, "Test it with your knife, Vladimir. It could be fake."

Drakov stepped over to the utility cart, placing the ingot on its flattop bed. Turning to look back at Belachek with an unreadable expression, he drew his knife, and with a powerful overhand strike, plunged the point into the soft metal and wiggled it vigorously to widen the hole. Withdrawing the blade, he inspected what lay beneath the surface. Almost immediately, he beamed with satisfaction. Handing the ingot back to Zinova, he said, "I believe it to be real, at least this one."

The Reaper examined the metal thoughtfully, his keen mind running a rough calculation. He was good with numbers, and he figured slightly more than 2,600 kilograms or 5,800 pounds of pure gold would be worth $100 million at current spot prices on world markets. But that would present a problem. Aside from its armaments, the Hind was only capable of lifting another 1,100 kilograms, and that was also counting the four large men that would be manning it, including himself. Subtract the weight of the crew, and all he could carry was about another 870 kilograms.

"Test a few more from other boxes," Zinova ordered Drakov. Shooting a glance to both Boris and Victor, he added, "Help him. I want to make sure all of these are genuine."

Zinova kept a watchful eye on his surroundings as all three men carried out the order. It was broad daylight out here on the open esplanade, with the sun burning down fiercely, but as far as he could tell the place appeared deserted. Grunting from the exertion, the men assisted one another in removing the topmost boxes to explore the contents of other boxes further down in the stack.

"Vladimir, how many boxes do you count?" asked Zinova, looking to the big burly Russian again.

Drakov walked around the cart, his eyes flitting carefully over the stack. "Fifty-nine in all," he said.

"And what would you estimate each one weighs?"

Drakov took an extra moment to heft a box in an attempt to judge its weight. "About forty-six kilograms," he grunted.

The reply further corroborated what Belachek had said as Zinova worked out the numbers in his head. Discounting roughly two kilograms for the wood comprising each box, the amount of gold added up nicely to approximate the 2,600 kilograms he had originally calculated. Zinova continued to keep a wary eye as each man opened a separate box and randomly selected an ingot for testing before shifting more boxes around, and it soon became evident that every bar sampled was bona fide.

"That's enough," Zinova said, satisfied with the results. Already his mind was entertaining a new thought as he brought his eyes to the massive AW101 sitting forward of the Hind. "Start up the cart, Victor, and move it to the helos."

Victor climbed aboard the cart and activated the electric motor. Humming to life, it began crawling slowly forward with its heavy load toward the ramp leading to the helipad as the other three men followed behind, their vigilance on high alert.

Zinova stared ahead, his gaze locked on the troop carrier. As his angle of perspective changed, two figures came into view, and he immediately recognized the pilots of the AW101 that had flown one of the Seal teams to the floating city. They were still carrying out their assigned duty, which involved standing guard on the air assets provided by the UN. On the way into Aquaria, Allotey had apprised him of the enhanced ADS microwave assault weapon developed by the colonists, but had also assured him that

DOLPHIN RIDERS

both the SPEFACS and troop transports were outfitted with suppressors that neutralized the pain inducing microwaves. With those suppressors turned on, he and the others would continue to remain unharmed.

Surprise caught up with Zinova as an additional sight caught his eye. Sitting on another landing pad farther away was the second AW101. Strangely, though, he saw no sentries guarding it. Nevertheless, the fact that it was here told him the second Seal team sent to the island had obviously been routed. And with more of the black-clad marauders now invading the city, mopping up the remaining Seals would be made that much easier. Unfortunately, that left him with precious little time to load the Hind and make off with the gold. That thought alone continued to nag away at him, and he found it disturbing that he would only be able to fly off with slightly more than a third of what lay on the utility cart.

As the group neared the pilots guarding the troop carrier, Zinova was caught up in a moment of indecision. After all, he had made a deal with Allotey, hadn't he? The last thing he wanted was to burn a bridge that could potentially lead to future work requiring his services, and the United Nations was certainly a wealthy client, as was Malcolm Maximus. And while a little less than $35 million would be more than enough to carry him into a lavish retirement, he was not yet ready to exit the business. He loved the line of work he had spent most of his adult life pursuing, especially the killing. Killing was in his blood, an uncontrollable inclination that could never be fully sated. He lusted for it.

And while $35 million would more than cover the cost of replacing his lost Hinds, maybe even purchase a few more, $100 million would allow him to buy an army three times larger than what he had before.

But now there was another matter to settle, and that was Javolyn. As a warrior, no one had ever bested him until his engagement with Javolyn. It was a defeat that had eaten away at him with mordant corrosiveness, and avenging it had now become an obsession, one by which he was incapable of letting go.

Pulling a small device from a pocket, Zinova aimed it at the Hind. It sent a tiny laser beam to the security lock on the chopper that would allow entry and get the engines cranking remotely. In moments, Victor was driving the utility cart past the two pilots stationed next to the troop carrier, and Zinova saw they only gave him a passing glance of bored curiosity.

With his finger poised precariously on the Kalashnikov trigger, Zinova turned to Drakov and Boris, keeping his voice just loud enough to be heard above the growing whine of the Hind's engines. "Get ready!" he said. "We're taking command of the other helo, and we're going to need those pilots to fly it. We will load the Hind with only nineteen boxes. The rest will go aboard the troop carrier. Vladimir, once the gold is aboard, you will stay with the pilots and instruct them to follow me back to our base in Haiti. Boris will come with me, but Victor will stay with you. Take the headset of one of the pilots to stay in contact with me and set the radio frequency to the one we always use."

Vladimir gave a barely perceptible nod, seemingly having no problem with the plan.

With the Hind's rotors now churning at an idle, Victor hopped off the cart and slid back the fuselage door as both AW101 pilots watched. Distracted for the moment, they became easy hostages for the three Russians.

"Drop your weapons!" the Reaper commanded them, pointing his Kalashnikov threateningly.

Surprise registered briefly on the faces of both pilots before they laid down their firearms and raised their hands.

Motioning with the barrel of his weapon, Zinova indicated the stack of boxes on the cart. "Load those boxes on your helo and be quick about it."

Victor turned, seeing what was currently taking place, his expression stoic as the two AW101 pilots began hauling boxes up the rear ramp and into the cargo hold of the larger helo.

"Nineteen boxes will go aboard the Hind, Victor," Zinova told him. "Boris will help you. The rest will go aboard the other helo."

With Boris assisting in loading the Hind, the two men moved rapidly to carry out the order. With the attack helicopter's rotors continuing to churn the air, they lashed the boxes down securely to tie rings set in the cabin floor. As soon as the task was completed, Boris scrambled forward to man the weapons seat.

Victor hopped out of the cabin and moved over to help with the loading of the troop carrier as Drakov kept his gun trained on the two pilots, who continued to lug boxes into the big chopper's hold, but before he could place a hand on another box, Zinova stopped him.

The Reaper eyed him shrewdly. "You said you found tons of gold."

Victor nodded. "Yes."

Zinova surveyed their immediate surroundings before taking inventory of the next esplanade one level up to make sure no one was watching. On his way into the floating city he had noticed there were a series of these structures that spiraled their way up to ring the central cupola-shaped mountain, with each girthing ring smaller than the one below it. Unable to control his inherent avarice, he said, "We can carry much more." His mind was racing ahead, estimating just how much additional weight the AW101 could fly away with and still make it to a location near Cardoza's destroyed stronghold back in Haiti where he kept a modest supply of aviation fuel stored in 55 gallon drums. Probably ten tons more. While aboard the *Carl Sagan*, he had noticed the troop transports being refueled, but flying such a massive load would cause the large helo to burn a great quantity of fuel. But once both choppers reached his chosen destination and were unloaded, he would provide the AW101 pilots with the necessary fuel to make it back to Aquaria and rejoin Allotey. Being that the troop transport was the property of the UN, it was only fitting that he return it, not to mention the world organization might have need of his services in the future.

"Take the cart and bring back another load," Zinova ordered.

Victor eyed him coldly. "No, Karloff, I cannot do that."

A flummoxed expression crossed Zinova's face before turning dark and malicious. "What do you mean you cannot?"

"I made a deal with these people. One hundred million to buy you off and leave them alone for good, and they agreed."

Zinova stared back in disbelief. "Buy me off!" he repeated. "This place is about to fall into the hands of mercenaries hired on by the United Nations. Either we grab what we can take now, or it will all disappear. The people who built this facility will no longer remain in control."

Victor remained stone-faced. "Those mercenaries are being defeated. Allotey and the American senator have already been captured, and all those abetting them are being killed or taken prisoner."

Zinova's countenance shifted from incredulous to dubious, and his reply showed it. "That's not possible," he countered adamantly.

"Believe what you want, but it's true. I think one hundred million is an incredibly generous offer these people have given you. I suggest we leave now before they change their minds."

Zinova's anger flared, and he raised the barrel of his Kalashnikov, pointing it at Victor's face. "You don't suggest anything. I'll decide how-"

The Reaper suddenly winced hard, the rest of his words seizing in his throat. His weapon fell from his hands to clatter on the deck, and he began slapping violently at the clothing covering his chest. He felt as though he were on fire, but almost as quickly as it had started, the intense pain vanished.

Victor glanced over at Drakov. The burly Russian remained unaffected, positioned just inside the AW101, halfway up its rear loading ramp where he could keep a vigilant eye on the two pilots carrying out the loading task, but Victor could see he was keenly aware of Zinova's sudden distress, having already shifted his weapon to point directly at him.

Victor made no sudden moves as Zinova reached down to retrieve his weapon. From experience, he knew Drakov was a deadly marksman.

"The microwave weapon these people use is no longer being suppressed," Victor said, giving Zinova a grim look. "They are giving you a warning, Karloff. They said they would avoid using it unless you forced them."

Zinova scowled. "How do you know about their weapon?"

"I saw them use it on others," Victor lied.

"That weapon is not supposed to work," Zinova ranted furiously. Turning his head, he glared savagely at the two pilots as they continued to load boxes into cargo netting amidships of the AW101 fuselage. "Turn the wave suppressor back on!" he screamed, his face contorted like a man on the brink of insanity. Both pilots stopped working and looked back at him with confused expressions.

Victor interceded quickly. "I was told it still works, but the people here have found a way around it," he lied again, knowing for a fact that the suppressor had been disabled. He glanced in the direction of the other AW101 sitting on the distant landing pad more than 300 meters away and one level lower. "We should leave now," he urged. "Look over there, Karloff. Navy Seals are already returning to the other troop carrier. That in itself tells you I'm not lying. Allotey and his henchmen have been defeated."

At seeing the Seals, Zinova's eyes flared red with rage. Bringing his gaze to Drakov, he shouted to be heard above the whine of the Hind. "Get them to move faster," he stormed, unhappy at how slowly the pilots were moving boxes.

"There's no time," Victor said. "We have to leave now."

Zinova hesitated, caught in a moment of indecision as he set his gaze on the Seals that were trickling back to the other troop transport before turning back to Belachek. "Did you see Javolyn anywhere in this facility?" The vendetta he wanted to settle was overpowering.

Victor kept a straight face as he lied again. "No. I saw him nowhere."

Zinova studied him carefully before speaking with finality. "I have a matter to settle with him. There will be no bargaining with these people to leave them alone. I didn't make the deal, you did. I will be the one to make deals, not you." As he spoke, he peered behind him to take in the ramp leading to the landing pad and the esplanade further back. At seeing no one, he glanced back at the remaining boxes on the utility cart. Only seven boxes remained. Turning, he stared back at Belachek. "Help the pilots with the rest of the boxes and get aboard their bird, Victor. You and Vladimir will make sure the pilots follow me back to our base in Haiti."

Zinova's manner abruptly shifted, and he eyed Belachek coldly. "When we land, you and I will have much to discuss, particularly what happened on the Malique mission and how you came to be here."

Victor nodded without expression. "You're the boss." Bending, he hefted another box and clambered aboard the AW101, placing the box with the others in the cargo netting. In moments the remaining boxes on the cart joined the others, and standing aside, Victor watched as Drakov belligerently coerced the two pilots forward toward the control seats, motioning with the barrel of his Kalashnikov as an added incentive.

Zinova gave one last glance toward the distant UN helo and the Seals crowding around it. He found it odd that none of them seemed interested in what was taking place on the landing pad upon which he stood. Striding quickly to the Hind, he strapped himself into the pilot seat and donned his flight helmet, his eyes scanning the instrument gauges to make sure no problems existed.

Having remained motionless and invisible within the cargo bay of the troop carrier, Bashir slipped quietly out of the cloaker he had been wearing and brought the webshot to bear, his eyes never leaving the Russian prodding the pilots forward. The man was powerfully built, and he wondered if the netting would be enough to restrain him. With the one called Victor having stepped aside, he squeezed the webshot trigger and felt the harsh recoil as the netting mushroomed out to ensnare its prey from behind. Caught completely by surprise, a startled deep throated bellow erupted from Drakov's mouth as he found himself enveloped in the webbing. In reaction, his finger jerked on the Kalashnikov trigger to discharge a burst of rounds that peppered the port side of the cabin, but in that same instant one of the pilots turned and unleashed a vicious punch that landed squarely on the point of Drakov's jaw. The blow was hard enough to make him lose his grip on the weapon and send him crashing to the deck beneath the webbing. With a knife suddenly in his hand, the pilot placed a knee in the stunned Russian's throat, pressing the tip harshly against his jugular where it broke the skin and forced a slight trickle of blood to emerge.

"Move so much as an inch and you're a dead man," the pilot snarled.

Knowing he had no choice but to heed the warning, Drakov lay still, though his face was frozen in a look of pure hatred. His expression turned even more malignant as he noticed the features of the man above him begin to change. The man was Javolyn.

"You again!" growled Drakov, baring his teeth. His tone was suffused with bitter hatred.

"Yes, me again," replied Jake with a smug sneer. He shot a quick glance at the other pilot to see that the false image had already been shed. Fernando appeared relieved that the deception had succeeded, though most of it had been ad libbed, having only been rudimentarily planned out based on Victor's input. By offering Zinova more gold than the Hind could carry, he knew his old boss would not be able to resist the temptation to use the troop carrier to transport the rest. But at least their main objective had been accomplished, and that was to separate the Reaper from Drakov, knowing these men were far more dangerous than the Chilean commandos they had previously come up against. Initially, Jake had thought it only fair to test Zinova's motives first before turning Ez loose on him, and had the Reaper decided to leave the facility with only what the Hind could fly away with, he would have been more than happy to let him and his two accomplices depart unmolested. Deep down he was growing weary of having to kill in order to protect Aquaria and had decided to give the former Spetsnaz soldier turned mercenary the benefit of the doubt, though he knew Zinova did not possess the same moral fiber as Victor. This he was certain of, having seen him nearly crash the Hind back near Cardoza's destroyed fortress when he had projected the arcane dolphin art at him using the PHP. Unfortunately, by the time he had assessed the full extent of Zinova's greed, Drakov had moved inside the troop carrier's cargo bay where he was beyond the reach of the ADS microwaves. The chopper's magnesium skin prevented that. Had the big Russian been incapacitated at the same time as Zinova, both men could have been neutralized simultaneously, but now the Reaper was at the controls of the Hind.

"Should we follow him?" asked Fernando. "I'm sure I can fly this baby."

"No, I have something better in mind," Jake replied, still holding the point of the K-bar firmly against Drakov's neck. "But first we better bind this sack of shit."

As Jake said this, Victor and Bashir moved in to take over.

-151-

Throttling the warmed up turbines to full power, Zinova lifted off, bringing the helo to a hover to test the load. The chopper responded sluggishly as he manipulated the controls, and he could tell the aircraft was at the very threshold of its lifting capacity. Eying the fuel gauge with a critical assessment, he was convinced he would be able to make it back to his base in Haiti, though he would likely be landing with only fumes left in his fuel tanks. Guiding the Hind out over the water, he pivoted it around to look back at the troop carrier to make sure it was also taking off.

A look of surprise enveloped his face when he saw no motion whatsoever in its main rotor blades. Abruptly he keyed the radio, using the frequency he had told Drakov to use. "What's the holdup, Vladimir?" he asked in a voice ripe with annoyance. When he failed to get a response, he repeated the question, this time more heatedly. "Damn you, Vladimir, answer me!"

Directing an angry stare at the troop carrier, he saw one of its occupants suddenly emerge from the starboard door to look back at him. Stunned by the sight, he immediately paled, the muscles in his neck and shoulders tightening like the string in a fully drawn crossbow.

Jake Javolyn waved up at him in enthusiastic greeting, taunting him further with a jubilant, goading grin accompanied by laughter. Speechless for the moment, Zinova sat frozen at the controls as his hated foe began to trot briskly across the landing pad. Reaching the far end, Javolyn stood at the edge and waved back one more time before launching himself over the side to fall 70 feet to the sea below. Meeting the water feet first, he vanished from view in the midst of a mushrooming splash.

As if suddenly awakening from a bad dream, Zinova turned the Hind and dove for the area where Javolyn had disappeared. Through his headset, Boris was nearly deafened by Zinova's blistering stentorian command. "Kill him!" But having also witnessed the entire scene unfold, he was already swiveling the guns in preparation to unleash a mighty salvo. Depressing the trigger, he watched the water erupt in a storm of whitewater geysers that completely obscured anything within their midst.

Bringing the Hind to a hover, Zinova scanned the water below as Boris stopped firing. Though the surface was still agitated, it was settling quickly, and in moments he was able see what lay below. The water was crystal clear, and anything near the surface could be easily discerned. Continuing to peer down searchingly into those depths, he caught a glimpse of movement. Dolphins were down there, four of them, their forms appearing like ghostly white apparitions rippling leisurely along, and atop those forms he could distinguish human riders, but already they were moving away. Steering the chopper forward, he dropped the gunship still lower to follow.

"Kill them!" Zinova repeated, bellowing vociferously into his lip mic. "Don't let them escape."

Once again, Boris opened up with the guns, exploding the water out in front of them into a foaming maelstrom. Bringing the Hind into another hover, Zinova looked down, waiting for the water to settle. In moments the agitation dispersed back into its former state, a clear shimmering blue with not the slightest sign of red discoloring it. How Boris had missed he could not fathom. Seeing nothing directly under him, he peered further ahead, only to have his temper flare a few more degrees. They were still moving away, no more than 3 or 4 meters below the surface. They seemed to be following a narrow meandering channel that wound its way through a sprawling swath of lagoons, containment ponds, and submerged holding pens.

Dipping the chopper's nose, Zinova coaxed more airspeed out of the turbines, not liking the feel of the controls. Loaded the way it was, the Hind responded all too sluggishly from what he was used to. Continuing his search, he strained his eyes to catch another glimpse of his quarry. This time he came in lower as he shouted to Boris. "Shoot now! You cannot possibly miss."

The water erupted violently, with the guns hammering down in a protracted burst. Pulling back on the cyclic, Zinova flared the chopper and maneuvered into another hover, peering down with the eyes of a rabid dog. He could discern nothing below the surface.

"Look!" Boris sputtered. "Ahead of you."

Zinova glanced up to gaze along the channel ahead of him. Several hundred yards away he spotted dolphins with human riders. Maddened with frustration, he tilted the main rotor, putting more thrust into the blades and tearing off after them. It seemed inconceivable they were able to cover that much distance so quickly.

Boris studied the lay of the meandering channel, aware that farther ahead it angled into a final dogleg that led directly to Aquaria's northern breakwater. "They seem to be moving toward the island," he said hurriedly. "If you fly out ahead of them and cut them off, they won't expect us to be waiting for them."

Normally Zinova did not like taking advice from his gunner, but he had to admit it wasn't a bad idea. Gaining a little altitude, he dipped the Hind's nose forward again, squeezing all the power he could get out of the turbines. Encumbered by the heavy load, they were straining hard. Keeping a close eye on his air speed indicator, he was disappointed at how slowly it was climbing. When it began to peg out at 110 knots, he realized that was all the helo was going to give him weighed down the way it was. Pulling up on the collective, he lifted the Hind above the breakwater, skimming low over a lush orchard and several buildings before dipping back toward the sea. Beyond the shelter of the surrounding breakwater, the water had lost its shimmering tranquility, no longer dampened by containment ponds or buoyancy cells supporting the central structure. Inside the floating mounded structure girthing most of the facility, wave action and undersea surge were largely suppressed, but once outside its calming embrace, the ocean was not as gentle. Out here the wind was in command, and he immediately saw the ruffle of waves marching relentlessly in a westerly direction, making the sea below him appear like an endless washboard stretching off to the horizon. Directly ahead was the offshore platform and the island that lay beyond. Another sight caught the corner of his eye, and he turned his head briefly to assess it. It was the aircraft carrier, the *Carl Sagan*, off to the southeast and better than three miles distant.

Banking the Hind as much as he dared without overstressing the airframe or main rotor, he swung it around to face the elevated mound girthing the facility. Bringing the helo into another hover 300 meters from the breakwater, he waited for his quarry to surface, intermittently monitoring his fuel gauge. Already he could see he was burning fuel at a rapid pace. "Show yourselves, damn you!" he yelled out impatiently. Growing increasingly frustrated when nothing appeared, he pivoted the Hind around clockwise to scan the water in all directions.

"Over there!" Boris shrieked. "Three o'clock."

Zinova whipped his head around. Four dolphin riders had broken the surface to send up a broken curtain of spray, their mounts switchbacking hard. This time he could clearly see that one of them was Javolyn. A woman and two children were with him, no doubt his wife, the notorious Dolphin Girl, and his offspring. Already they had passed the west side of the platform and were heading directly for the island.

With his fuel running low, Zinova instantly knew he would only have one more chance at catching up and killing them, including the strange white beasts they rode. "We've got you now," he howled, his face awash in a deranged grin as he banked the Hind to follow. Closing the distance rapidly, he became giddy with excitement. Strangely, the small group had not yet sounded, still holding to the surface.

At a distance of 200 meters, Zinova saw Javolyn look back over his shoulder with a smile clinging to his face. "Get ready!" Zinova warned his gunner.

As if hearing the command, all four dolphins sounded simultaneously, taking their riders with them and diving deep. A split second too late, Boris turned the guns loose, exploding the water into a seething geysered storm. Keeping the guns trained on the exact spot where their quarry had vanished, he kept up the salvo as the Hind swept past.

Zinova banked hard, no longer caring if he was overstressing the airframe. Bringing the helo into another hover, he scanned the water. Absolutely nothing. No blood and no bodies floated to the surface. The bludgeoning destruction he had turned loose appeared to have been in vain, and already the surface had settled back into a rolling translucent indigo.

With his rage still burning fiercely, the Reaper broke from his hover and veered away, taking on a course that took him over the island and past the old lighthouse, making sure to keep well clear of the *Carl Sagan*. He could not be certain if its captain knew what was really happening, and he certainly didn't want to risk being fired upon. Feeling it now safe to swing the helo around, he took on a heading that would take him to Tiburon, Haiti.

-152-

Captain Delila raised his binoculars again to track the whirlybird. More than two miles away, it had taken on a heading to the northeast before making a wide turn that kept it well clear of the carrier. And now it seemed to be heading in the direction of the Haitian coast. It was only a short time ago that he had caught a fleeting glimpse of it rising up slowly from one of Aquaria's landing pads to hold a stationary hover, but then he had lost sight of it as his angle of observation changed when the immense mound of the floating city's central structure blocked his view. On his orders, the *Carl Sagan* had altered course, taking on a new heading that brought it to Aquaria's northeast side a good three miles from the breakwater where he had been able to spot it again. It had assumed a hover outside the breakwater to face back toward the city. But then it had turned to pick up speed, racing low over the sea toward the offshore platform near Navassa Island where it had flared into another hover. To him, it had seemed to fire down into the water, but if it had actually done so, it had been too distant for him to be certain of this. The chopper, however, appeared to be the Hind that had transported Allotey and Senator Brent Van Heflin to the floating city. The sight didn't surprise him. First Lieutenant Johnson had already alerted him as to what he would see.

"Sir, our radar has detected something that could be a problem," Ensign Jefferson informed him.

Delila turned. Jefferson appeared nervous. "What is it?"

"Hard to tell, sir, but it's traveling at Mach two point one, six hundred feet above the water on a bearing of one hundred forty degrees. It appears to be heading directly toward the floating city."

"A missile?"

"Possibly, sir. It has a very small profile. We were barely able to detect it."

"Get on the radio and see if you can warn those colonists." Delila paused. "And tell Lieutenant Johnson to get his men out of there immediately."

"Yes, sir," said Jefferson as he darted away quickly.

-153-

Having made their way through the undersea tunnel to reach the immense subterranean cavern beneath Navassa Island, Jake, Destiny and the children left their mounts to stand on a ledge where the holographic manifestation of Ez was there to greet them.

"Will Big D be able to absorb the blast?" Jake asked her. His tone conveyed apprehension. Through Achilles he had been informed of the approaching danger immediately after subduing the big Russian aboard the UN troop transport.

"I believe the incoming missile is not meant for Aquaria," declared Ez with a grave expression. She had detected its approach even before the *Carl Sagan* had alerted her to the problem.

"If not for us, then who?"

"Logic suggests it's the same target the Iranian sub wanted to destroy. Maximus needed a catastrophic event to reap immense profits in the stock and commodities markets. Without such an event, he stood to lose most of his wealth."

Jake's jaw dropped. Once again he was reminded of how they had stopped the Rodong rocket launched by Yeslam Raduyev from reaching its intended target eight years earlier. Carrying a nuclear warhead, the rocket's destination had also been Miami. But with Destiny acting as the lens through which the others had channeled their combined mental energies, they had been able to make the rocket disappear into a dimensional void.

Ez explained further. "I've fully analyzed all the data contained in the mechanical fish. It seems Maximus obtained a cruise missile with a nuclear warhead several years ago, which he kept in reserve at a secret location near Valera, Venezuela."

"Why do you say he kept it in reserve?" Jake interjected quickly.

"Because he was a careful planner. It seems he always kept options at his disposal should primary schemes go awry. When *Iron Fist* failed to launch its nuclear weapon, he must have sent a signal relayed by satellite that set the backup plan in motion. He probably did this just before he died."

Jake's thoughts moved along at lightning speed. A cruise missile was an exceptionally dangerous weapon. It had an intermediate range capability of up to 3,000 miles. It could fly low and incredibly fast, and by the time it was picked up on radar, you had little time to react and bring it down, especially if it was preprogrammed to take on an erratic, evasive course prior to reaching its target."

"But how can you be sure the target is Miami? It could be headed anywhere, even Aquaria. Is it coming directly at us?"

"Yes, if you follow a great circle route across the globe connecting Valera with Miami, the arc intersects the heart of Aquaria."

A sudden show of relief fell across Jake's face. "Then activate Big D and swallow it up."

"Just like the *Kraken*, there is a potential risk to do so, but one far greater. The shield may be inadequate to absorb the energy contained in the warhead. The data I've obtained shows it to be a high-yield plutonium device of 1,500 kilotons. If it comes in contact with the shield, it may prematurely detonate. The resulting blast will be far more than the shield can handle."

"But Big D must have grown larger after it swallowed the Kraken," Jake was quick to point out. "Won't it be stronger?"

"Yes it has, and yes it will," replied Ez quickly, "but unfortunately my calculations show it won't be enough." She presented the problem in the simplest terms she could come up with, for time was running out. "We're talking atomics here, not a chemically induced explosion. All sorts of crazy things come into play when you're dealing with atomics."

Jake turned, giving Destiny a hopeful look. "We can stop it just like before, but this time we have the combined hopes of ten thousand people behind us."

Destiny held his gaze, a conflict of emotions beginning to brew within her, and she began to wonder if she had truly changed since meeting Jake. Her own words came back to haunt her when she had confided her feelings to him on this same point just before he had left to investigate the hijacking of the Southern Star when she had told him, 'I don't think I'll be able to do something like that ever again.'

'You have no way of knowing that,' he had replied.

'It's what I feel deep inside,' she had said.

Esmerelda's words back in the cave suddenly resounded in her head. '*You must believe in yourself, my child. Do not lose faith, for you are still the person you have always been.*'

Jake saw the stirrings of doubt growing within her eyes. "You can do it," he encouraged softly.

'*All that you need lies within you,*' Esmerelda had stressed. '*You must never stop believing in yourself.*'

'It is as though the entire world is against us,' she had deplored, overcome with helplessness. Esmerelda had responded by telling her that the aggregate of humanity was not the cause of this, but the power brokers ruled by the puppet master, the person she had since come to know as the

DOLPHIN RIDERS

Sublimis.

'How do we overcome that?' she had asked, but now she had to remind herself that the Sublimis had been defeated. *Or had he?* A nuclear missile was going to kill millions of people.

Draped in a halo of stardust, Esmerelda's smile came back to comfort her, giving her a margin of strength. *'By believing, my child. You must simply believe.'*

'I have been compromised,' she had declared, uncertainty still clinging to her. 'My powers have been corrupted through my own doing. Without them, believing in anything seems futile.'

Esmerelda had shaken her head. *'You deceive yourself, child. Your unconditional love for those around you has made you even stronger. It is a source of great power. It binds all of you together and is the foundation of unblemished faith.'*

Destiny continued to hover at the brink of lost hope. Would everything they had strived for eventually be lost anyway? The task seemed so difficult, maybe impossible.

The image of Esmerelda's confident smile radiated in her mind, and she knew she would never forget her resolute words. *'Have faith. Hope is something not seen. You must have patience and steadfastness, continuing to believe with all your being until the belief is physically manifested. Once you possess it, all is possible.'*

Destiny felt strangely empowered by those words. Yes, all was possible. Why have I let this happen to me? she decried inwardly, suddenly fighting with all her strength against the chains of pessimism, willing them to fall away. Fear was the culprit here. She had allowed it to enter her life, letting it take control of the reality surrounding her, which included everyone she loved. She saw it clearly now.

'You must cleanse your mind of the fear that shackles it,' Esmerelda had reminded her. *'Once you do this, you will realize you are a spiritual being with incredible powers. Only then will you fully understand that you and all those you love are deathless souls having a physical experience. Like those magnificent creatures to whom you are forever linked, you were brought into this world to fulfill a profound purpose. Just believe in yourself and all that you wish for will follow."*

Yes, she had almost forgotten why she had been brought into this world.

She looked down at her children. They stared up at her, their faces revealing their unblemished faith in her.

Turning back to Ez she asked, "How much time do we have?"

Ez spoke urgently. "In exactly one minute thirty-two seconds the missile will pass directly over us."

Destiny knew proximity was crucial for the task at hand. "Alert everyone what we'll need of them. Tell them to link hands and form a line that ends here. I need all of them to focus their thoughts." She knew everyone was in the adjoining subterranean cavern once used as a clandestine base of operations by Yeslam Raduyev. Since then it had been greatly expanded and retrofitted to accommodate the basic needs of the current Aquarian population should an evacuation of the floating city become necessary as recent events had dictated.

Ez nodded, beaming broadly just before winking out.

Destiny knelt close to the edge of the ledge, staring pensively out over the water. All the albinos had now arrived, their perpetually smiling faces elevated above the surface. Behind them was a multitude of mutated grays, including Achilles' mother, Thetis, and her own mother's bond mate, Athena.

Jake turned to see a line of people led by Amphitrite emerge from a large fissure in the rock. They were moving hastily in single file to form a human chain, the trailing hand of each person clasped to the hand of the one immediately to their rear. Behind Amphitrite was Franklin, and behind him was Mat. Kalid was the fourth person in the chain, and following him was Samuel. Trailing closely were a string of other familiar faces.

Grasping Amphitrite's extended hand, Jake looked down. Destiny was gazing up at him, an expression of intense concentration engraved on her features. "Let's do this!" she murmured softly. "Place your hand on my head."

Jake did as asked, noticing that both children had already done so. Almost at once he felt a potent force go rippling through his mind. It was the combined focused thought of thousands of sentient beings, and it was gathering power like that of a rapidly advancing tsunami.

-154-

Captain Delila brought the spy glasses to his eyes as one of the AW101's lifted from the floating city and fluttered into the sky. On his orders, the *Carl Sagan* had moved to a distance of five miles from Aquaria's breakwater, and he wondered if it was safe enough for the time being.

Standing beside him, Jefferson suddenly spoke up, his voice filled with tension. "Sir, if you look to the south you'll see it."

Delila pivoted, looking to where his aide was pointing. A barely visible dot could be seen just above the horizon, but it was growing in size rapidly. He had received a call from that same woman representing the colony only moments earlier, and she had told him the destination of the missile was Miami and not Aquaria. "Do not attempt to destroy it with any of the weaponry your ship carries," she had warned briskly. She had gone on to say that the information she had obtained indicated a direct hit on it would set it off. "It seems whoever constructed the missile has rigged it to trigger the warhead if a counterstrike is used against it. The warhead is a high-yield fifteen hundred kiloton fission bomb with a plutonium core. But do not worry, we believe we have the means to neutralize it."

As he watched the object grow larger, he wondered how she could possibly know that. Wavering at the doorstep of indecision, he considered ignoring the warning. What if she was wrong and the colony was about to be hit? Or what if the target was really Miami as she had alleged? Even though he had already notified the Strategic Air Command in Homestead of the inbound missile, he knew the missile would pass directly over Cuba before it reached Miami, if in fact that was the actual destination. And even if the Cubans managed to shoot it down, there was still the question of a nuclear detonation. The radioactive fallout would be brutal on anything it came in contact with. Either way, if he missed this one and only chance to bring it down and it ended up causing vast destruction, he would never be able to forgive himself. Perhaps he should employ the LaWS anyway. The Laser Weapon System was the latest addition to the carrier's high tech defensive arsenal, capable of directing a 20 megawatt beam directly at the incoming threat. Already the LaWS was locked onto the missile, with the possibility of a miss at zero. All he had to do was give the command to fire and it would be destroyed. But in doing that, he risked triggering a nuclear blast that would vaporize the city and set off a tidal wave that might sink his ship even if the ensuing blast didn't. Nevertheless, he was still tempted to issue the order to fire, but some deep instinct made him refrain from doing just that. Somehow he trusted what the woman was telling him to be true. In spite of this, he grew increasingly nervous as he tracked the rapidly growing dot. Even at this distance he could hear the ruffling susurration that heralded its coming. The air began to tremble, changing over into a quaking rumble as the sound grew, and he knew it was only a matter of seconds before the sonic boom of its passing would stab into his ears. The missile seemed to be heading directly for the floating city, and based on what radar had reported, it would barely miss colliding with the crown of Aquaria's central structure, assuming it was not pre-programmed to gain altitude as it approached.

Jefferson brought a tense gaze to the captain, trying to read the thoughts behind a face seemingly struggling with indecision. Would Delila give the order to fire? The LaWS operator was standing by awaiting the command and the captain was wearing the lip mic. All that was needed was only one word to be uttered.

And then the moment passed. The young ensign immediately noted Delila's change of expression, the captain's eyes going wide with astonishment. In reaction, Jefferson whipped his head around to look for the cause.

The missile had vanished. In wonderment, Jefferson searched the sky, suddenly aware of something else. The sound of its passage was now gone. Totally bewildered, he asked, "Where did it go, sir?"

Delila shook his head slowly, still dazed. No shimmering dome had enveloped the floating city this time. The missile had simply winked out. One moment it was there, then it was not. The weird happenings he had experienced during the last several hours would keep him wondering for the rest of his days. "I don't know, son, I just don't know. See if radar is still picking it up?" But deep down he was certain what the answer would be.

-155-

Making use of the 3-sided pyramidal T-crystals, Jake, Destiny and Amphitrite instantaneously transported themselves along with others to Jacob's office high up in Aquaria's central structure. Jake's first order of business was deciding what to do with the conspirators they had captured, those being Van Heflin, Hearthwatch, and Allotey, including the three mercenaries that had abetted them. Drakov was another matter. All seven had been thoroughly bound hand and foot and were currently being guarded by Zimbola and Bashir in an adjacent room

Mat was the first to voice his concerns. "Turning them over to American authorities, including the Department of Justice, will be a waste of time. Forget about indictments. That would require unbiased parties in positions of authority willing enough to prosecute them, and from what we've seen in the homeland during the last several years, there's no more accountability in government. It seems elected officials and high ranking appointees can do as they please these days, including breaking the law whenever they want." Mat shook his head stubbornly. "No, once the firestorm of conflicting accounts settles down, the American public will go back to sleep and those men will use their influence to shut us down again."

"I fully agree," said Jacob wearily, turning to his cousin, the CEO of Tursiops. "What do you think, Emmanuel?"

Emmanuel adopted a thoughtful expression. "Perhaps we should take a vote," he suggested, looking to other faces around the room.

"What about the UN?" Percy offered. "Surely you can't condemn the entire organization just because of a few bad eggs...." His voice trailed off meekly at seeing the looks his words were eliciting.

Amphitrite jumped to Percy's defense, covering his embarrassment quickly. She was well aware of Percy's contribution to recent events, much of which had been indispensable in saving the colony and other lives as well. "Nice job in imitating Maximus, Mister Osgood. Without your help, the world might never have learned of *The Order* or the men behind it." Having been interrogated by the *Sublimis*, she knew he had captured the man's voice and mannerisms so perfectly that it had even fooled Allotey, Van Heflin, and Hearthwatch. All it had taken was for Percy to wear a Masker, which Ez had preprogrammed using acoustical picture-speak images of the man conveyed to her by Athena using the colony's underwater hydrophones.

Percy looked down, fidgeting self-consciously. "Always did have this talent for mimicking voices," he said softly.

"I think I have a solution that will spare us taking a consensus," Jake interjected, idly hefting the crystal that had brought him and several others to this level of the central structure. He had thought deeply on the matter while bringing the captives to where they were now being held, and he knew Ez had been able to locate Hearthwatch rather easily by hacking her way into the real-time camera surveillance system at the White House. Using deductive reasoning, she had anticipated Hearthwatch rushing off to explain himself to the President once the initial broadcast exposing his involvement with Maximus and *The Order* had taken place, and her reasoning had proved correct. That had made it rather simple to abduct the man, for all that was needed was for Amphitrite to envision that particular room in the White House in order to get there. And although the mechanical fish had contained no collaborating evidence within its memory banks to indicate any Presidential involvement in The Order's insidious schemes, one could never be sure that was not the case. If Van Heflin was to be next in line for the Presidency, it was also possible his predecessor had been bred and groomed for the same position, planted there by Maximus. Either way, Jake knew it would no longer be practical to trust career politicians in high office these days.

With all eyes focused on him, he directed a foxy grin at the sentience running the colony's daily operations, his thoughts hinged on the tiny tracking chip placed on the underside of one of the gold-bearing boxes. Victor had made sure to load that particular box aboard Zinova's chopper. "Ez, we've used these crystals to move between stationary locations, but do you think they'll work taking people from a fixed point to one in motion?"

"Nothing is actually stationary in this three dimensional realm," explained Ez. "Everything is in motion. Every point on or below the planet's surface is constantly moving. The planet rotates while orbiting a white star, and that star revolves around a galaxy moving through space. Yes, based on that, it should certainly work." She suddenly displayed a knowing smile as though reading his mind. "At its present rate of speed, the Hind is fifteen point three two minutes from reaching the southern coast of Haiti's southwestern peninsula."

Jake nodded, bringing his gaze briefly to Victor. "Well, assuming there are no objections, this is what I propose."

-156-

Zinova eyed the fuel gauge apprehensively, his gut in knots. It was now within a hair of empty. As soon as he reached Haiti's southwest peninsula, he had purposely flown the Hind relatively low over the rolling terrain, keeping it no higher than 150 meters. It was a safety precaution in case the turbines should quit. The thought of this happening grated on him, for if the helo lost power, he'd lose his hydraulics, and without hydraulics he would be forced to use his bearlike strength to wrestle with stiff controls in order to auto rotate the chopper down without crashing, and to avoid crashing he'd need a clearing devoid of trees or other obstructions to ensure that. And although he had successfully performed such a maneuver at least a dozen times in the past, he had never felt comfortable doing it.

Staring ahead, the Reaper's spirits lifted a tad as he saw the southern coastline come into view. He had purposely taken the shortest route across the peninsula to reach the southern seashore as quickly as possible. That would give him more opportunity for a safe landing should the turbines run dry, for much of the shoreline consisted of white sandy stretches with only occasional patches of rocky outcroppings to obstruct him. As he neared the coast, some familiar landmarks told him he was just west of Tiburon, and as he swung the Hind onto an easterly heading, he came abreast of the town to follow the beach. It was only a moment later that the ruins of Cardoza's stronghold lay before his eyes, and though the site was disheartening, his spirits began to lift. Perhaps he would reach his destination after all.

Making a slight course adjustment, he risked angling the Hind inland again, lining it up to fly directly over the remnants of the ancient fortress. Barely half of it remained standing, still surrounded by a moat only half filled with water, and where the drawbridge had once spanned the narrow canal, a mound of stone rubble and debris sloped haphazardly down into it.

In the distance beyond, he could discern more destruction. What had been Cardoza's enormous aircraft hangar lay completely destroyed, scattered over a wide swath of charred landscape. But at least he was nearing his destination, which consisted of a small fenced off area in a hollow of ground Cardoza had provided him. It was situated 1,000 meters east of where the hanger used to be. Once he reached it, he would refuel the chopper and begin making plans to fly the gold to the Cayman Islands. There he would have it stored in the vault of the bank he always used, exchanging some of it for cash. And once that was done, he'd begin plotting his revenge on Javolyn and his family.

These thoughts fell away as a strange crimson glow suddenly filled the Hind's interior. It reflected off his instrument panel, flashing briefly before disappearing completely. Almost immediately, the feel of the cyclic stiffened more appreciably in his grip, and an instant later the airframe began to shudder severely, with the rotor blades slapping the air ever more harshly. A quick glance at his altimeter told him he was losing altitude, and though he still had power, it was evident the Hind was struggling to stay aloft.

Something thumped heavily in the cabin behind him, and he turned in his seat to investigate the cause. Abruptly, his eyes went wide. Allotey and the American senator stared back at him with horrified expressions. Adjacent to them was a man he hadn't seen before, and behind them were four others. But unlike Allotey and the two with him, the men to their rear were constrained by wrist ties and shackled to each other, three of them being the same black-clad mercenaries that had been assigned to protect Allotey and the senator. The fourth man, however, was Drakov, his lieutenant.

Stunned by the sight, Zinova's mind staggered under the unreality that lay before him, his flummoxed brain groping feebly for an explanation as to how they had gotten here. All he could do was stare, tottering at the edge of madness as his eyes were drawn to the person he hadn't recognized. The man appeared deathly ill and was obviously nauseous, retching in a series of dry heaves. But then something else caught his gaze that shocked him even more. There were three other people behind the contingent of new passengers, and they were grinning cheerfully as they looked back at him. One of them was a huge black man, a veritable hulking giant. Zinova gave the second man, a dark haired individual only a passing glance as his eyes steadied on the third. The man was Javolyn, his hated foe.

Continuing to stare dumbly, Zinova was suddenly blinded by a vivid eruption of light. Closing his eyes tightly to escape the crimson starburst, he toyed with the possibility that perhaps he was imagining all this. But as his vision cleared, the sheer impact of the mystery returned to torment him further. Except for the one still retching, Allotey and the senator continued to stare back at him in terrified silence, as did the others, but Javolyn and the two that had accompanied him were now gone.

With his mind still reeling, Zinova suddenly realized the whine of the engines had ceased, and turning his head, he now saw the fuel gauge had reached zero. The Hind was falling. In panic, he pulled up on the collective as the terrain rushed up at him. Without hydraulics, it felt as though he were attempting to pry up a huge chunk of lead. In desperation, he searched the ground directly below for a place to land, but all that was available were the ruins of the old stone fortress. With a herculean effort he managed to muscle the cyclic just enough to avoid hitting what remained of a crumbled wall, and coaxing additional pitch into the struggling rotor blades at the last possible second, felt the Hind slow from its dizzying descent. In reaction, he looked all about him, frantically searching for options, but finding none, he realized he would have to ditch the Hind in the only place available that would not cause it to come apart. And that was in the moat.

Yanking up on the collective one last time before impact, he sought to arrest the Hind's plummet further, but as he did, the blades of the main rotor tore off and flew away. The chopper dropped heavily, meeting the water surface in a bone jarring plunge and sending up a towering maelstrom of spray.

Unstrapping himself hurriedly, Zinova's only objective was to evacuate the Hind before it sank. He was keenly aware of the denizens that lived in the canal, and like a panicked animal, wanted to get out of the water as fast as possible. Climbing from his seat, he was nearly bowled over by Boris trying to get out before him. Water sloshed heavily into the cabin and was rising rapidly.

Driving a shoulder into his gunner's stomach, Zinova sent him reeling back. Whirling, he pushed past Allotey and the senator. Both stared dazedly at the water, too petrified to move.

Lunging for the open doorway, Zinova heard Vladimir cry out to him. "Karloff, help me!" Ignoring the plea, he splashed through the doorway, only to find himself nearly pulled back into the cabin. Hands had latched onto his clothing from behind and were tugging him backward. A quick glance over his shoulder showed Allotey and the senator clinging to him with terrified eyes. Lashing out with a balled fist, he slammed it into the nearest face, and though it caused a spurt of blood to spew from Allotey's shattered nose, it was as if the blow had no effect whatsoever. The man held fast, far too frightened to feel any pain.

"Save me!" Allotey shrieked, struggling fiercely to hold on. "I can't swim."

Zinova lashed out again, this time with an elbow that found the side of Allotey's head. Allotey absorbed the blow, grimacing through clenched teeth and still managing to hold on with a superhuman death grip. "I can't swim," he screamed again.

Out of the corner of one eye, Zinova glimpsed movement on the water, and turning his head to inspect it further, spotted a fin cleaving the surface. All of a sudden there were more, many more. They were swarming along the moat and coming straight for the sinking Hind.

Zinova spun, kicking his feet hard to elevate his body higher out of the water, and with all his strength came down with his full weight behind a monstrous blow that landed squarely on Allotey's upturned mouth. The UN dignitary immediately went limp, and Zinova squirmed free, avoiding the senator's outstretched grasping hands. Stroking wildly, he swam for the sloped jumble of stones and rubble that had spilled down into the moat when the explosion had occurred. Reaching out, his fingers found purchase, and he pulled his legs free of the water, half expecting a set of serrated teeth to close on his ankles as he did so. Climbing higher onto the sloped mass, he turned to observe the fate of the others.

Already the water was turning red, fins going every which way, but amazingly Boris had somehow managed to escape the swarm of frenzied sharks and was swimming for his life. Seeking the same area of rocks where Zinova had climbed from the water, he glanced up at his boss with hate-filled eyes. But just before he reached the rocks, a look of consternation crossed his face followed by a horrific cry of distress, and an instant later he was jerked backward. Abruptly he disappeared, the water roiled red with his blood.

Dazedly, Zinova swung his gaze back to the Hind in time to see it slide beneath the surface. The feeding frenzy that had been taking place around it had now ceased. Fins were darting away en masse, leaving in their wake the remaining morsel. The head of a lone figure bobbed just above the water, and Zinova realized it was the senator. A fin far bigger than the others was bearing toward him, coming from the opposite direction in which the other sharks had departed.

Van Heflin let out a bloodcurdling cry as he watched the huge fin knife the water to come straight at him. Words Cardoza had uttered during the meeting were echoing in his head. *I believe Scylla regards you as a potential meal, senator.*

Zinova watched in fascination as the head of the massive great white broke the surface to snatch the senator in its jaws. The senator let out another chilling scream as the jaws clamped down, and a moment later he also disappeared.

Relieved that he had been fortunate enough to survive the onslaught, a dozen thoughts began to race through Zinova's mind as to how he would go about retrieving the sunken gold. Thinking there was no more danger, he was surprised to hear a low rumbling growl behind him. Turning slowly to confront the cause, he found himself looking into a set of fierce amber orbs. The Bengal was only inches away, the stench of its foul breath sickening.

It was then Zinova became cognizant of yet someone else screaming, a scream far more shrill than the ones that had preceded it, and just before the fangs tore into his throat to bore him away into an abode of coal-black darkness, he realized the sound was coming from his open mouth.

-157-

Jake stood with his hands resting leisurely on the railing delimiting the edge of the esplanade halfway up Aquaria's central structure. His gaze was set on what appeared to be a tiny object floating more than a mile beyond the city's eastern breakwater, but he knew distance gave it the illusion of being small. Up close its actual size would be comparable to that of a voluminous hot air balloon capable of carrying aloft several people. It was only minutes earlier that the hydrogen gas contained under its leathery skin had borne it to the ocean surface. During the retrieval of the T-crystals, Hermes had noticed the budding node on one side of the crown of the largest thurentra, and the pod had been in readiness for the moment it broke free. With its destination having already been planned, he knew it was headed for a location closer to Haiti.

Standing next to Jake was Victor, who followed his gaze. "What is that?" he asked.

"You're looking at the start of another floating city."

Victor's countenance immediately clouded. He had no clue as to what the statement implied.

Jake turned to gauge the Russian's reaction. Smiling, he said, "That object carries a seedling. Once it finds a new home on the seafloor, it will eventually mature to turn an otherwise barren sector of ocean into an oasis of life."

His curiosity whetted, Victor studied the thing more carefully. Using his telescopic eye, he magnified the image as though he were only a hundred meters behind it. Further ahead of it he discerned a whale spout, and on each side of the huge cetacean there appeared to be more than a dozen albino dolphin switchbacking along the surface. A cable stretched from the whale to the balloon, and he realized the whale was towing it in an easterly direction.

Jake thought it time to breach another subject. "Victor, have you given any thought as to what you're going to do now?" He felt a strange kinship with this man, one he could not explain. Though they had been combatants during their initial meeting, a great deal had changed since then, and he reminded himself of a similar situation that had occurred eight years earlier with Bashir and Kalid.

Victor answered the question with a slow shake of his head. With sadness still gripping him over the loss of his son, he had not given the matter any thought.

"The colony can use a man like you, Victor. If you'd like, you can come to work for us and live here."

Victor remained quiet. Continuing to stare pensively at the receding balloon, he pondered the invitation. It was then that he realized how much he liked these people. Unlike the meaningless existence he had previously lived, they were committed to a purpose, one that was profoundly altruistic and charitable. Twice they had saved his life, and perhaps that was not such a bad thing after all, for it might give him a chance to redeem himself and atone for his sins.

When he finally replied, his voice was barely above a murmur. "I am unworthy of your enterprise, my friend."

Jake placed a hand on his shoulder. He felt the man's pain. The guilt and shame Victor still carried was almost palpable. "Oh, you're worthy, all right. You've already proven that several times over."

Victor felt himself at a loss for words, and had he tried to respond at that moment, he most assuredly would have broken down then and there, blubbering like a baby. But then the sound of childlike voices broke the air to save him any embarrassment. Turning, he saw Jake's children scurrying ahead of their mother, rushing headlong toward their father in ecstatic greeting. "Dadoo!" they cried in unison.

Jake bent and scooped one up in each of his brawny arms, lifting them easily and giving each a tender kiss on the forehead before setting them back down again. Destiny was right behind them, and she reached up to loop a thin arm around the nape of his neck. With her feet dangling, she gave him a smoldering kiss.

At that moment, a short pudgy Haitian manifesting a jovial grin sauntered out onto the esplanade. At seeing the twins with their parents, his smile wavered fleetingly before re-asserting itself. "So there you little imps are," he said, his mirthful eyes coming to rest on Jake and Destiny in full embrace, their lips locked tightly. "They certainly missed their parents," he said, his signature smile now in full radiance.

Jake and Destiny parted lips to regard him with amused miens, fully aware of how the children had bamboozled Kobe into bringing them here, at least most of the way. But explaining that to Zimby would make no difference. "Better check your six, Kobe," Jake warned.

Looking behind him, Kobe's face immediately blanched. "Gotta be goin'!" he exclaimed, suddenly bolting away quickly and running for an arched doorway further down the esplanade that would take him back inside the city again.

Following on his heels was an imposing figure. "Come back here, Kobe!" Zimbola growled, his features harboring a fierce scowl that would frighten the dead.

Surprised at how fast Kobe could move, Jake suppressed a laugh. Addressing the twins, he said, "You got him in trouble, now you better save him."

TJ and Melody scampered away, adding further to the comical scene. Running after Zimby, they all disappeared through the same doorway Kobe had taken.

As Jake looked on, more of his fellow Aquarians strolled out onto the esplanade to join him, including Jacob and Jacob's cousin, the CEO of Tursiops. Emmanuel appeared uncomfortable with something he wanted to say. "Ez informs me that Zinova's chopper crashed in the moat at Cardoza's stronghold," he announced, managing to overcome the reticence gripping him. It was obvious he had misgivings about what he had consented to.

Jake absorbed this unexpected news with a show of surprise registering on his countenance. "Huh!" was all he could think to mutter before adding, "I wonder what were the odds of that happening?"

The manifestation of Ez was suddenly in their midst. "Thirty thousand six hundred twenty-nine to one," she stated bluntly.

Jake pondered this briefly before eliciting another "huh," though this one sounded much too frivolous by comparison. "Any survivors?"

Ez shook her head. "Other than the mauled body of a dead man near the water, satellite surveillance showed no one roaming the site, though a Bengal tiger was spotted. With all the sharks, it is doubtful any of those men could have survived."

Jake shrugged flippantly. "I guess it could be argued they got their just reward." As soon as he said it, he became aware of Amphitrite and Franklin standing nearby.

"Yes," Amphitrite concurred. "Such is the fate of evildoers when their iniquity becomes so overwhelming it comes back full circle to feed on its host."

Several others nodded in agreement with her sobering words as Chester Hennington, Tursiops' Chief Financial Officer, joined the group to stand next to Emmanuel, and Jake noticed that both men appeared to be fully recovered now from their earlier ordeal at the hands of the bounty hunters hired by Maximus. Jake had since learned they had been abducted in Port-au-Prince following negotiations with Haitian officials concerning the construction of the massive automobile factory on the outskirts of the city. Overpowered by six ruffians apparently working for the bounty hunters, Emmanuel and Chester had been injected with an immobilizing narcotic after being wrestled into a waiting van just outside the government building where the negotiations had taken place. And though they were now safe, he knew precautions would need to be implemented to prevent things like this from happening in the future. But at least the negotiations had been finalized, and it had been sanctioned that Tursiops was to oversee the building and running of the plant, which would produce eco-friendly cars to be exported internationally.

Jacob looked on, quietly taking in what was being said, aware that Mat and Amelia had also come outside to join the gathering. Ez noticed this too, but it was Jake who took the moment to lighten the mood. "I think our hotshot head of security here deserves a round of applause," he proclaimed in a voice loud enough for everyone to hear. "For meritorious conduct, extraordinary valor, and conspicuous bravery..." He was using a phrase spoken by the wizard in the movie The Wizard of Oz when the wizard awarded a badge of courage to the cowardly lion. Quoting it blithely, he ended the laud by saying, "and, I might add, for keeping the offshore platform intact and the fine all around job of ass-kicking he doled out."

Mat immediately recognized the phrase and got into the spirit of the moment by feigning bashfulness and gesticulating with his hands in a futile effort to wave off the enthusiastic chorus of hip, hip, hoorays and clapping that ensued. "Shucks, folks, I'm speechless," he blurted, matching what the lion had said upon receiving the award and emulating the same antics. Projecting an air of chagrin, he turned his back to the crowd. This was a routine both men had often used to evoke laughter from fellow warriors during their days in the Seals, and they had the act down pat.

At seeing Mat's animated waggishness, Amelia burst into riotous, uncontrollable laughter, tears streaming from her eyes.

Ez was next to speak once the cheering trailed off. "And let's not forget Amelia's contribution for her superb commentary. She showed herself to be a true professional during our enlightening newscasts uncovering the insidious and nefarious activities taking place beyond the view of public scrutiny. And if she is not opposed to performing additional newscasts, I have prepared further commentary for her to disseminate to mainstream news channels around the globe."

Another round of lively applause and cheering abruptly resounded, and suddenly self-conscious, Amelia blushed with sincere embarrassment.

Jacob looked all about him to study the faces. A mood of warm, cheerful camaraderie had taken hold of everyone, and he was enjoying the contagion, content to bask in the feel of it. They had come a long way during the last eight years, and though the budding fantasy they had so intensely envisioned and nurtured in its infancy had now been transformed into reality, there was so much more yet to be achieved. The human mind was a wonderful thing, he cogitated. Coupled with other unique intellects that were in some respects much more powerful than those of the people around him, they had fashioned possibilities that could be made real.

Jake's voice rose up again. Holding his T-crystal, he said, "Shield your eyes, everyone. Destiny and I are off to commemorate the planting of the seedling."

Jacob avoided looking directly at him as a blinding burst of crimson light flared, and an instant later, Jake and Destiny were gone.

A feeling of deep-seated pragmatism suddenly invaded Jacob's thoughts, and beset by it, he expelled a resigned sigh. Though they had come out victorious on their recent battles, he was not foolish enough to delude himself into thinking the war was over. Innate wickedness tempered by virulent greed would surely re-assert itself, and another storm would eventually brew. But then again, certain things were meant to happen, and while these things were beyond his understanding and control, they would bring together circumstances that would fuel future battles that might prove even more fierce and exhausting than the ones they had just fought.

With his thoughts drifting, Jacob found himself revisiting past reflections. Revisiting them always bolstered his resolve whenever he found it flagging. Amphitrite had always stressed to him the delicate balance and uncertainty woven into the cosmic structure. There would be choices to be made and actions to be carried out, with any wrong decision leading to disaster. But with their course set and their conviction unshakable, they would continue to act against tyranny, poverty and oppression. They would resolutely strive toward making significant positive changes to a world in desperate need of it. Leaving the beleaguered nation of Haiti to fend for itself was beyond consideration, and to retreat in pursuit of an easier life would be cowardly. Tursiops Worldwide would provide the impetus and corporate structure to attain their goals, one of them being the achievement of a much higher standard of living for the downtrodden masses. But it was the new species of albino dolphin that had initially devised the framework for carrying out this great undertaking, for it was they who had formulated the concept of a sea colony, which had taken root in their minds years earlier when he had thought it prudent to teach them everything he knew about the workings of capitalism, big business, and multi-national corporations.

Jacob smiled to himself as he mused about all the good things a cash-rich corporation could accomplish. Big business could be a powerful tool. Wielded properly, it had clout, able to move heads of state into serving its interests. But here its interests would differ markedly from the mainstream, for the interests of Tursiops would remain purely philanthropic, run by entities incapable of corruption or greed. Tursiops would function in harmony with the ocean environment, incessantly striving for the development and implementation of alternative sources of clean, renewable energy derived from the sea, and producing commodities that could be sold on world markets at exceptionally low prices. Here was Haiti's best hope of escape from its plight of seemingly perpetual poverty. If everything went to plan, the island nation would no longer be suppressed and tortured by recurrent waves of corrupt domestic and international politics that washed away all hope. Innovation would pave the way for change. And though such a grand undertaking would be immensely difficult to achieve, it would not be unworkable.

But Haiti's salvation was not their end goal. No, it would not end there. If Tursiops continued to succeed, it would establish marine-based colonies throughout the planet's seas. By harvesting the oceanic reserves of almost limitless nutrients and previously untapped energy, it would unleash a floodtide of food and commodities that would ultimately enrich every third world country around the globe. Through the production of hydrogen, magnesium, and distilled potable water alone, enormous revenues would be gained to finance the development of new technologies. Henceforth, previous limits on food production resulting from land-based economies would be exceeded to an explosive degree through the implementation of mariculture and ocean farming, not only vastly improving Haiti's standard of living, but all nations of the world. These enterprises would provide unprecedented employment for the poor, sprouting forth an economy of scale never before seen. In its wake, hunger would all but vanish, with new social orders emerging and evolving in total harmony with the planetary ecosystem. A partnership would transpire between man and cetacean that would open the doors to new horizons in scientific research. Spurred on by the albino intellect, the advancement of science and technology would accelerate, with meaningful breakthroughs occurring at a faster rate. In the sea colonies, crime, brutality, and social disorder would give way to intellectual, artistic, philosophical and spiritual pursuits, setting the individual free from the lone struggle for survival that had characterized both old and contemporary societies. In short, a new chapter in social evolution would commence, unrivaled by anything that had come before it.

Contemplating this vision, Jacob hoped Tursiops would be able to provide a positive impact on the global recession that had hit the major economies of the world. In reaction to this, many governments had systematically devalued their paper currencies to counter the growing tide, so much so that their medium of exchange would likely become worthless someday. But Tursiops had something far better to fall back on should this happen. It had its gold. The concept, however, caused him some misgivings, for he remembered what he had taught the albinos years earlier when the first thurentra in the cove began harvesting pure gold and platinum from the Cayman Trench. He had told them no true benefit was derived from the production of such elements, that metals considered to be precious by humanity had been the underlying cause of many wars throughout its history. But as time had gone on, his view on this had changed. Gold did have its benefits. It had provided untold though discrete financial leverage in the building of Aquaria, and in the near future it might continue to provide leverage, for as other economies began to stumble, Tursiops would continue to grow stronger.

A warm glow began to take hold of Jacob as he thought about these things. Through the combined leadership of the company's board of directors, Tursiops would empower Haitians to transform their lives in a single generation. Such thinking tended to heighten his expectations of the future. Sometimes you had to hit rock bottom before you began the arduous climb back up. Here was Haiti's way out of the hole it had become mired in. They just had to be resolute in holding onto their conviction that the dream was possible.

During the last eight years Jacob had learned that anything was possible as long as you believed in it with every fiber of your being. And though it was his grandmother, Esmerelda, who had first tried to make him understand this, it was Amphitrite who had actually made him feel the absolute power underlying it. There would be no try, no meager stab at hoping for the best, for such outlooks were too diluted in ambivalence to have any chance of success. No, the fantasy was made altogether real by stripping away all negative leanings, all doubts. The power of their minds was working in concert, both human and delphine, to forge the path of their choosing, the desired trajectory through time-space. Sentient intelligence would be used to mold the future. He now understood the power of it. The mind was truly an integral part of the cosmos, and somewhere within this seemingly endless chaos and swirling motes, an enigmatic order existed that could be manipulated through conscious, and perhaps even unconscious, thought. Yes, perhaps there was a dimension where physical laws and mysticism eventually merged, intertwining and combining into a simple structure that determined the reality they desired, a place immune to the winds of chance.

Jacob was suddenly pulled from these thoughts as he became aware of a commotion. It was the sound of awestruck gasps coming from those around him, their gazes beholding a spectacular sight. A double rainbow had formed over the Caribbean Sea off to the east to frame the receding thurentra seedling with its escort, but now there were three of them. As he looked on in wonder, he saw something he had never seen before. A fourth rainbow had coalesced to drape over the first three, their redundant arching hues perfectly coinciding. Continuing to gawk, he discerned a seemingly endless series of glowing nodules go hurtling along their respective bands of prismatic color. More vibrant than the arched hue confining their motion, they rose up from one end of the band only to vanish at the opposite end, with nodules of differing color moving in a direction counter to their neighbors. Finding himself totally enraptured by the dazzling display of shifting prismatic light, he was overcome with a profound feeling of euphoria much the way the enigmatic albino art affected him. Unable to pull his eyes from the enchanting sight, he noticed a subtle change that grew more distinct in moments. The face of his long deceased grandmother, Esmerelda, was regarding him with a broad benevolent smile.

Jacob returned the smile with a barely perceptible nod, his mind harboring only one thought.

Thank you for making me a believer.

ABOUT THE AUTHOR

Michael J. Ganas is the award winning author of The Girl Who Rode Dolphins. A licensed engineer and deep sea commercial diver by profession, he has spent most of his career taking on the challenges of civil engineering in underwater environments.

This is his second novel.

Made in the USA
Middletown, DE
09 March 2017